# BLEAK HOUSE

# BLEAK HOUSE

## Charles Dickens

ILLUSTRATED BY EDWARD GOREY

*Arranged for*
*Modern Reading*

THE LITERARY GUILD OF AMERICA, INC.

Garden City, New York

DEDICATED

*As a remembrance of our friendly Union*

TO MY COMPANIONS
IN THE
GUILD OF LITERATURE
AND ART

# CONTENTS

A few months ago, on a public occasion, a Chancery Judge had the kindness to inform me, as one of a company of some hundred and fifty men and women not labouring under any suspicions of lunacy, that the Court of Chancery, though the shining subject of much popular prejudice (at which point I thought the Judge's eye had a cast in my direction), was almost immaculate. There had been, he admitted, a trivial blemish or so in its rate of progress, but this was exaggerated, and had been entirely owing to the "parsimony of the public"; which guilty public, it appeared, had been until lately bent in the most determined manner on by no means enlarging the number of Chancery Judges appointed—I believe by Richard the Second, but any other King will do as well.

This seemed to me too profound a joke to be inserted in the body of this book, or I should have restored it to Conversation Kenge or to Mr. Vholes, with one or other of whom I think it must have originated. In such mouths I might have coupled it with an apt quotation from one of SHAKESPEARE'S Sonnets:

> *My nature is subdued*
> *To what it works in, like the dyer's hand:*
> *Pity me then, and wish I were renew'd!*

But as it is wholesome that the parsimonious public should know what has been doing, and still is doing, in this connexion, I mention here that everything set forth in these pages concerning the Court of Chancery is substantially true, and within the truth. The case of Gridley is in no essential altered from one of actual occurrence, made public by a disinterested person who was professionally acquainted with the whole of the monstrous wrong from beginning to end. At the present moment there is a suit before the Court which was commenced nearly twenty years ago; in which from thirty to forty counsel have been known to appear at one time; in which costs have been incurred to the amount of seventy thousand pounds; which is a *friendly suit*; and which is (I am assured) no nearer to its termination now than when it was begun. There is another well-known suit in Chancery, not yet decided, which was commenced before the close of the last century, and in which more than double the amount of seventy thousand pounds has been swallowed up in costs. If I wanted other authorities for JARNDYCE AND JARNDYCE, I could rain them on these pages, to the shame of—a parsimonious public.

There is only one other point on which I offer a word of remark. The possibility of what is called Spontaneous Combustion has been denied since the death of Mr. Krook; and my good friend Mr. Lewes (quite mistaken, as he soon found, in supposing the thing to have been abandoned by all authorities) published some ingenious letters to me at the time when that event was chronicled, arguing that Spontaneous Combustion could not possibly be. I have no need to observe that I do not wilfully or negligently mislead my readers, and that before I wrote that description I took pains to investigate the subject. There are about thirty cases on record, of which the most famous, that of the Countess Cornelia de Baudi Cesenate, was minutely investigated and described by Giuseppe Bianchini, a prebendary of Verona, otherwise distinguished in letters, who published an account of it at Verona, in 1731, which he afterwards republished at Rome. The appearances beyond all rational doubt observed in that case, are the appearances observed in Mr. Krook's case. The next most famous instance happened at Rheims, six years earlier; and the historian in that case is Le Cat, one of the most renowned surgeons produced by France. The subject was a woman, whose husband was ignorantly convicted of having murdered her; but, on solemn appeal to a higher court, he was acquitted, because it was shown upon the evidence that she had died the death to which this name of Spontaneous Combustion is given. I do not think it necessary to add to these notable facts, and that general reference to the authorities which will be found at page 314, the recorded opinions and experiences of distinguished medical professors, French, English, and Scotch, in more modern days; contenting myself with observing, that I shall not abandon the facts until there shall have been a considerable Spontaneous Combustion of the testimony on which human occurrences are usually received.

In *Bleak House,* I have purposely dwelt upon the romantic side of familiar things. I believe I have never had so many readers as in this book. May we meet again!

LONDON, *August,* 1853.

# CHAPTER 1

*In Chancery*

LONDON. Michaelmas Term lately over, and the Lord Chancellor sitting in Lincoln's Inn Hall. Implacable November weather. As much mud in the streets as if the waters had but newly retired from the face of the earth, and it would not be wonderful to meet a Megalosaurus, forty feet long or so, waddling like an elephantine lizard up Holborn Hill. Smoke lowering down from chimney-pots, making a soft black drizzle, with flakes of soot in it as big as full-grown snowflakes—gone into mourning, one might imagine, for the death of the sun. Dogs, undistinguishable in mire. Horses, scarcely better, splashed to their very blinkers. Foot-passengers jostling one another's umbrellas in a general infection of ill-temper and losing their foothold at street-corners, where tens of thousands of other foot-passengers have been slipping and sliding since the day broke (if this day ever broke), adding new deposits to the crust upon crust of mud.

Fog everywhere. Fog up the river, fog down the river. Fog on the Essex marshes, fog on the Kentish heights. Fog creeping into the cabooses of collier-brigs; fog lying out on the yards and hovering in the rigging of great ships; fog drooping on the gunwales of barges and small boats.

Gas looming through the fog in divers places in the streets, much as the sun may, from the spongy fields, be seen to loom by husbandman and ploughboy. Most of the shops lighted two hours before their time—as the gas seems to know, for it has a haggard and unwilling look.

The raw afternoon is rawest, and the dense fog is densest, and the muddy streets are muddiest, near that leaden-headed old obstruction, appropriate ornament for the threshold of a leaden-headed old corporation, Temple Bar. And hard by Temple Bar, in Lincoln's Inn Hall, at the very heart of the fog, sits the Lord High Chancellor in his High Court of Chancery.

Never can there come fog too thick, never can there come mud and mire too deep, to assort with the groping and floundering condition which this High Court of Chancery, most pestilent of hoary sinners, holds, this day, in the sight of Heaven and earth.

On such an afternoon, if ever, the Lord High Chancellor ought to be sitting here—as here he is—with a foggy glory round his head, softly fenced in with crimson cloth and curtains, addressed by a large advocate with great whiskers, a little voice, and an interminable brief, and outwardly directing his contemplation to the lantern in the roof, where he can see nothing but fog. On such an afternoon, some score of members of the High Court of Chancery bar ought to be—as here they are—mistily engaged in one of the ten thousand stages of an endless cause, tripping one another up on slippery precedents, groping knee-deep in technicalities, running their goat-hair and horse-hair warded heads against walls of words, and making a pretence of equity with serious faces, as players might. On such an afternoon, the various solicitors in the cause, some two or three of whom have inherited it from their fathers, who made a fortune by it, ought to be—as are they not?—ranged in a line in a long matted well (but you might look in vain for Truth at the bottom of it) between the registrar's red table and the silk gowns, with bills, cross-bills, answers, rejoinders, injunctions, affidavits, issues, references to masters, masters' reports, mountains of costly nonsense, piled before them. Well may the court be dim, with wasting candles here and there; well may the fog hang heavy in it, as if it would never get out; well may the stained-glass windows lose their colour, and admit no light of day into the place.

This is the Court of Chancery; which has its decaying houses and its blighted lands in every shire; which has its worn-out lunatic in every madhouse, and its dead in every churchyard; which has its ruined suitor, with his slipshod heels and threadbare dress, borrowing and begging through the round of every man's acquaintance; which gives to monied might the means abundantly of wearying out the right; which so exhausts finances, patience, courage, hope, so overthrows the brain and breaks the heart, that there is not an honourable man among its practitioners who would not give—who does not often give—the warning, "Suffer any wrong that can be done you rather than come here!"

Who happen to be in the Lord Chancellor's Court this murky afternoon besides the Lord Chancellor, the counsel in the cause, two or three counsel who are never in any cause, and the well of solicitors before mentioned? There is the registrar below the Judge, in wig and gown; and there are two or three maces, or petty-bags, or privy purses, or whatever they may be, in legal court suits. These are all yawning; for no crumb of amusement ever falls from Jarndyce and Jarndyce (the cause in hand), which was squeezed dry years upon years ago. Standing on a seat at the side of the hall, the better to peer into the curtained sanctuary, is a little mad old woman in a squeezed bonnet, who is always in court, from its sitting to its rising, and always expecting some incomprehensible judgment to be given in her favour. Some say she really is, or was, a party to a suit; but no one knows for certain, because no one cares. She carries some small litter in a reticule which she calls her documents, principally consisting of paper matches and dry lavender.

Jarndyce and Jarndyce drones on. This scarecrow of a suit has, in course of time, become so complicated that no man alive knows what it means. The parties to it understand it least; but it has been observed that no two Chancery lawyers can talk about it for five minutes without coming to a total disagreement as to all the premises. Innumerable children have been born into the cause; innumerable young people

have married into it; innumerable old people have died out of it. Scores of persons have deliriously found themselves made parties in Jarndyce and Jarndyce without knowing how or why; whole families have inherited legendary hatreds with the suit. There are not three Jarndyces left upon the earth perhaps, since old Tom Jarndyce in despair blew his brains out at a coffee-house in Chancery Lane; but Jarndyce and Jarndyce still drags its dreary length before the Court, perennially hopeless.

Jarndyce and Jarndyce has passed into a joke. That is the only good that has ever come of it. It has been death to many, but it is a joke in the profession. Every master in Chancery has had a reference out of it. Every Chancellor was "in it," for somebody or other, when he was counsel at the bar.

How many people out of the suit Jarndyce and Jarndyce has stretched forth its unwholesome hand to spoil and corrupt, would be a very wide question. From the master, upon whose impaling files reams of dusty warrants in Jarndyce and Jarndyce have grimly writhed into many shapes, down to the copying-clerk in the Six Clerks' Office, who has copied his tens of thousands of Chancery folio-pages under that eternal heading; no man's nature has been made better by it. In trickery, evasion, procrastination, spoliation, botheration, under false pretences of all sorts, there are influences that can never come to good.

Thus, in the midst of the mud and at the heart of the fog, sits the Lord High Chancellor in his High Court of Chancery.

"Mr. Tangle," says the Lord High Chancellor.

"Mlud," says Mr. Tangle. Mr. Tangle knows more of Jarndyce and Jarndyce than anybody. He is famous for it—supposed never to have read anything else since he left school.

"Have you nearly concluded your argument?"

"Mlud, no—variety of points—feel it my duty tsubmit—ludship," is the reply that slides out of Mr. Tangle.

"Several members of the bar are still to be heard, I believe?" says the Chancellor, with a slight smile.

Eighteen of Mr. Tangle's learned friends, each armed with a little summary of eighteen hundred sheets, bob up like eighteen hammers in a pianoforte, make eighteen bows, and drop into their eighteen places of obscurity.

"We will proceed with the hearing on Wednesday fortnight," says the Chancellor. For the question at issue is only a question of costs, a mere bud on the forest tree of the parent suit, and really will come to a settlement one of these days.

# CHAPTER 2

## In Fashion

IT IS but a glimpse of the world of fashion that we want on this same miry afternoon. It is not so unlike the Court of Chancery but that we may pass from the one scene to the other, as the crow flies.

Both the world of fashion and the Court of Chancery are things of precedent and usage; oversleeping Rip Van Winkles, who have played at strange games through a deal of thundery weather; sleeping beauties whom the Knight will wake one day, when all the stopped spits in the kitchen shall begin to turn prodigiously!

It is not a large world. Relatively even to this world of ours, which has its limits too, it is a very little speck. There is much good in it; there are many good and true people in it; it has its appointed place. But the evil of it is that it is a world wrapped up in too much jeweller's cotton and fine wool, and cannot hear the rushing of the larger worlds, and cannot see them as they circle round the sun. It is a deadened world, and its growth is sometimes unhealthy for want of air.

My Lady Dedlock has returned to her house in town for a few days previous to her departure for Paris, where her ladyship intends to stay some weeks, after which her movements are uncertain. The fashionable intelligence says so, for the comfort of the Parisians, and it knows all fashionable things. To know things otherwise were to be unfashionable. My Lady Dedlock has been down at what she calls, in familiar conversation, her "place" in Lincolnshire. The waters are out in Lincolnshire. An arch of the bridge in the park has been sapped and sopped away. The adjacent low-lying ground, for half a mile in breadth, is a stagnant river, with melancholy trees for islands in it, and a surface punctured all over, all day long, with falling rain. The view from my Lady Dedlock's own windows is alternately a lead-coloured view and a view in India ink. The vases on the stone terrace in the foreground catch the rain all day; and the heavy drops fall, drip, drip, drip, upon the broad flagged pavement called, from old time, the Ghost's Walk, all night. My Lady Dedlock (who is childless), looking out in the early twilight from her boudoir at a keeper's lodge and seeing the light of a fire upon the latticed panes and smoke rising from the chimney, and a child, chased by a woman, running out into the rain to meet the shining figure of a wrapped-up man coming through the gate, has been put quite out of temper. My Lady Dedlock says she has been "bored to death."

Therefore my Lady Dedlock has come away from the place in Lincolnshire, and has left it to the rain, and the crows, and the rabbits, and the deer, and the partridges and pheasants. The pictures of the Dedlocks past and gone have seemed to vanish into the damp walls in mere lowness of spirits as the housekeeper has passed along the old rooms shutting up the shutters. And when they will next come forth again, the fashionable intelligence—which, like the fiend, is omniscient of the past and present, but not the future—cannot yet undertake to say.

Sir Leicester Dedlock is only a baronet, but there is no mightier baronet than he. His family is as old as the hills, and infinitely more respectable. He has a general opinion that the world might get on without hills, but would be done up without Dedlocks. He would on the whole admit Nature to be a good idea (a little low, perhaps, when not enclosed with a park-fence), but an idea dependent for its execution on your great county families. He is a gentleman of strict conscience, disdainful of all littleness and meanness, and ready, on the shortest notice, to die any death rather than give occasion for the least impeachment of his integrity. He is an honourable, obstinate, truthful, high-spirited, intensely prejudiced, perfectly unreasonable man.

Sir Leicester is twenty years, full measure, older than my Lady. He will never see sixty-five again, nor perhaps sixty-six, nor yet sixty-seven. He has a twist of the gout now and then, and walks a little stiffly. He is of a worthy presence, with his light-grey hair and whiskers, his fine shirt-frill, his pure-white waistcoat, and his blue coat with bright buttons always buttoned. He is ceremonious, stately, most polite on every occasion to my Lady, and holds her personal attractions in the highest estimation. His gallantry to my Lady, which has never changed since he courted her, is the one little touch of romantic fancy in him.

Indeed, he married her for love. A whisper still goes about that she had not even family; howbeit, Sir Leicester had so much family that perhaps he had enough, and could dispense with any more. But she had beauty, pride, ambition, insolent resolve, and sense enough, to portion out a legion of fine ladies. Wealth and station, added to these, soon floated her upward, and for years now my Lady Dedlock has been at the centre of the fashionable intelligence, and at the top of the fashionable tree.

How Alexander wept when he had no more worlds to conquer everybody knows—or has some reason to know by this time, the matter having been rather frequently mentioned. My Lady Dedlock, having conquered *her* world, fell, not into the melting, but rather into the freezing, mood. An exhausted composure, a worn-out placidity, an equanimity of fatigue not to be ruffled by interest or satisfaction, are the trophies of her victory. She is perfectly well-bred. If she could be translated to Heaven tomorrow, she might be expected to ascend without any rapture.

She has beauty still, and if it be not in its heyday, it is not yet in its autumn. She has a fine face—originally of a character that would be rather called very pretty than handsome, but improved into classicality by the acquired expression of her fashionable state. Her figure is elegant, and has the effect of being tall. Not that she is so, but that "the most is made," as the Honourable Bob Stables has frequently asserted upon oath, "of all her points." The same authority observes that she is perfectly got up; and remarks, in commendation of her hair especially, that she is the best-groomed woman in the whole stud.

With all her perfections on her head, my Lady Dedlock has come up from her place in Lincolnshire (hotly pursued by the fashionable intelligence) to pass a few days at her house in town previous to her departure for Paris. And at her house in town, upon this muddy, murky afternoon, presents himself an old-fashioned old gentleman, attorney-at-law, and eke solicitor of the High Court of Chancery, who has the honour of acting as legal adviser of the Dedlocks, and has many cast-iron boxes in his office with that name outside. Across the hall, and up the stairs, and along the passages, and through the rooms, which are very brilliant in the season and very dismal out of it, the old gentleman is conducted by a Mercury in powder to my Lady's presence.

The old gentleman is rusty to look at, but is reputed to have made good thrift out of aristocratic marriage settlements and aristocratic wills, and to be very rich. He is surrounded by a mysterious halo of family confidences, of which he is known to be the silent depository. There are noble Mausoleums rooted for centuries in retired glades of parks, among the growing timber and the fern, which perhaps hold fewer noble secrets than walk abroad among men shut up in the breast of Mr. Tulkinghorn. He is of what is called the old school—a phrase generally meaning any school that seems never to have been young—and wears knee-breeches tied with ribbons, and gaiters or stockings. One peculiarity of his black clothes, and of his black stockings, be they silk or worsted, is that they never shine. Mute, close, irresponsive to any glancing light, his dress is like himself. He never converses when not professionally consulted. He is found sometimes, speechless but quite at home, at corners of dinner-tables in great country-houses, and near doors of drawing-rooms concerning which the fashionable intelligence is eloquent, where everybody knows him, and where half the Peerage stops to say "How do you do, Mr. Tulkinghorn?"

Sir Leicester Dedlock is with my Lady, and is happy to see Mr. Tulkinghorn. There is an air of prescription about him which is always agreeable to Sir Leicester; he receives it as a kind of tribute. He likes Mr. Tulkinghorn's dress; there is a kind of tribute in that too. It is eminently respectable, and likewise, in a general way, retainer-like. It expresses, as it were, the steward of the legal mysteries, the butler of the legal cellar, of the Dedlocks.

Has Mr. Tulkinghorn any idea of this himself? It may be so, or it may not; but there is this remarkable circumstance to be noted in everything associated with my Lady Dedlock as one of a class—as one of the leaders and representatives of her little world. She supposes herself to be an inscrutable Being, quite out of the reach and ken of ordinary mortals. Yet, every dim little star revolving about her, from her maid to the manager of the Italian Opera, knows her weaknesses, prejudices, follies, haughtinesses, and caprices, and lives upon as accurate a calculation and as nice a measure of her moral nature as her dressmaker takes of her physical proportions. Is a new dress, a new custom, a new singer, a new dancer, a new form of jewellery, a new dwarf or giant, a new chapel, a new anything, to be set up? There are deferential people in a dozen callings, whom my Lady Dedlock suspects of nothing but prostration before her, who can tell you how to manage her as if she were a baby. "If you want to address our people, sir," say Blaze and Sparkle the jewellers—meaning, by "our people," Lady Dedlock and the rest—"you must remember that you are not dealing with the general public; you must hit our people in their weakest place, and their weakest place is such a place." "If you want to get this print upon the tables of my high connexion, sir," says Mr. Sladdery the librarian, "or if you want to secure to this entertainment the patronage of my high connexion, sir, you must leave it, if you please, to me; for I have been accustomed to study the leaders of my high connexion, sir, and I may tell you, without vanity, that I can turn them round my finger"—in which Mr. Sladdery, who is an honest man, does not exaggerate at all.

Therefore, while Mr. Tulkinghorn may not know what is passing in the Dedlock mind at present, it is very possible that he may.

"My lady's cause has been again before the Chancellor, has it, Mr. Tulkinghorn?" says Sir Leicester, giving him his hand.

"Yes. It has been on again today," Mr. Tulkinghorn replies; making one of his quiet bows to my Lady, who is on a sofa near the fire, shading her face with a hand-screen.

"It would be useless to ask," says my Lady, with the dreariness of the place in Lincolnshire still upon her, "whether anything has been done."

"Nothing that *you* would call anything has been done today," replies Mr. Tulkinghorn.

"Nor ever will be," says my Lady.

Sir Leicester has no objection to an interminable Chancery suit. It is a slow, expensive, British, constitutional kind of thing. To be sure, he has not a vital interest in the suit in question, her part in which was the only property my Lady brought him; and he has a shadowy impression that for his name—the name of Dedlock—to be in a cause and not in the title of that cause is a most ridiculous accident. But he regards the Court of Chancery, even if it should involve an occasional delay of justice and a trifling amount of confusion, as a something devised in conjunction with a variety of other somethings, by the perfection of human wisdom, for the eternal settlement (humanly speaking) of everything.

"As a few fresh affidavits have been put upon the file," says Mr. Tulkinghorn, "and as they are short, and as I proceed upon the troublesome principle of begging leave to possess my clients with any new proceedings in a cause"—cautious man Mr. Tulkinghorn, taking no more responsibility than necessary—"and further, as I see you are going to Paris, I have brought them in my pocket."

(Sir Leicester was going to Paris too, by the bye, but the delight of the fashionable intelligence was in his lady.)

Mr. Tulkinghorn takes out his papers, puts on his spectacles, and begins to read by the light of a shaded lamp.

" 'In Chancery. Between John Jarndyce—' "

My Lady interrupts, requesting him to miss as many of the formal horrors as he can. Mr. Tulkinghorn glances over his spectacles, and begins again lower down. My Lady carelessly and scornfully abstracts her attention. Sir Leicester, in a great chair, looks at the fire, and appears to have a stately liking for the legal repetitions and prolixities, as ranging among the national bulwarks. It happens that the fire is hot where my Lady sits, and my Lady, changing her position, sees the papers on the table—looks at them nearer—looks at them nearer still—asks impulsively:

"Who copied that?"

Mr. Tulkinghorn stops short, surprised by my Lady's animation and her unusual tone.

"Is it what you people call law-hand?" she asks, looking full at him in her careless way again, and toying with her screen.

"Not quite. Probably"—Mr. Tulkinghorn examines it as he speaks—"the legal character which it has was acquired after the original hand was formed. Why do you ask?"

"Anything to vary this detestable monotony. Oh, go on, do!"

Mr. Tulkinghorn reads again. The heat is greater, my Lady screens her face. Sir Leicester dozes, starts up suddenly, and cries, "Eh? What do you say?"

"I say I am afraid," says Mr. Tulkinghorn, who had risen hastily, "that Lady Dedlock is ill."

"Faint," my Lady murmurs, with white lips, "only that. Don't speak to me. Ring, and take me to my room!"

Mr. Tulkinghorn retires into another chamber; bells ring, feet shuffle and patter, silence ensues. Mercury at last begs Mr. Tulkinghorn to return.

"Better now," quoth Sir Leicester, motioning the lawyer to sit down and read to him alone. "I have been quite alarmed. I never knew my lady swoon before. But the weather is extremely trying—and she really has been bored to death down at our place in Lincolnshire."

## CHAPTER 3

*A Progress*

I HAVE a great deal of difficulty in beginning to write my portion of these pages, for I know I am not clever. I always knew that. I can remember, when I was a very little girl indeed, I used to say to my doll, when we were alone together, "Now Dolly, I am not clever, you know very well, and you must be patient with me, like a dear!"

And so she used to sit propped up in a great arm-chair, staring at me—or not so much at me, I think, as at nothing—while I busily stitched away, and told her every one of my secrets.

My dear old doll! I was such a shy little thing that I seldom dared to open my lips, and never dared to open my heart, to anybody else. It almost makes me cry to think what a relief it used to be to me when I came home from school of a day, to run upstairs to my room, and say, "O you dear faithful Dolly, I knew you would be expecting me!" and then to sit down on the floor, leaning on the elbow of her great chair, and tell her all I had noticed since we parted. I had always a silent way of noticing what passed before me, and thinking I should like to understand it better. I have not by any means a quick understanding. When I love a person very tenderly indeed, it seems to brighten.

I was brought up, from my earliest remembrance—like some of the princesses in the fairy stories, only I was not charming—by my godmother. At least I only knew her as such. She was a good, good woman! She went to church three times every Sunday, and to morning prayers on Wednesdays and Fridays, and to lectures whenever there were lectures, and never missed. She was handsome, and if she had ever smiled, would have been (I used to think) like an angel—but she never smiled. She was always grave, and strict. She was so very good herself, I thought, that the badness of other people made her frown all her life. I felt so different from her, even making every allowance for the differences between a child and a woman, I felt so poor, so trifling, and so far off that I never could be unrestrained with her—no, could never even love her as I wished. It made me very sorry to consider how good she was, and how unworthy of her I was; and I used ardently to hope that I might have a better heart; and I talked it over very often with the dear old doll. But I never loved my godmother as I ought to have loved her, and as I felt I must have loved her if I had been a better girl. This made me, I dare say, more timid and retiring than I naturally was, and cast me upon Dolly as the only friend with whom I felt at ease. But something happened when I was still quite a little thing that helped it very much.

I had never heard my mama spoken of. I had never heard of my papa either, but I felt more interested about my mama. I had never worn a black frock, that I could recollect. I had never been shown my mama's grave. I had never been told where it was. Yet I had never been taught to pray for any relation but my godmother. I had more than once approached this subject of my thoughts with Mrs. Rachael, our only servant, who took my light away when I was in bed (another very good woman, but austere to me), and she had only said, "Esther, good-night!" and gone away and left me.

Although there were seven girls at the neighbouring school where I was a day boarder, and although they called me little Esther Summerson, I knew none of them at home. All of them were older than I, to be sure (I was the youngest there by a good deal), but there seemed to be some other separation between us besides that, and besides their being far more clever than I was, and knowing much more than I did. One of them, in the first week of my going to the school (I remember it very well), invited me home to a little party, to my great joy. But my godmother wrote a stiff letter declining for me, and I never went. I never went out at all.

It was my birthday. There were holidays at school on other birthdays —none on mine. There were rejoicings at home on other birthdays, as I knew from what I heard the girls relate to one another—there were none on mine. My birthday was the most melancholy day, at home, in the whole year. I have mentioned that my comprehension is quickened when my affection is. My disposition is very affectionate; and perhaps I might still feel such a wound, if such a wound could be received more than once, with the quickness of that birthday.

Dinner was over, and my godmother and I were sitting at the table before the fire. The clock ticked, the fire clicked; not another sound had been heard in the room, or in the house, for I don't know how long. I happened to look timidly up from my stitching, across the table, at my godmother, and I saw in her face, looking gloomily at me, "It would have been far better, little Esther, that you had had no birthday, that you had never been born!"

I broke out crying and sobbing, and I said "O, dear godmother, tell me, pray do tell me, did Mama die on my birthday!"

"No," she returned. "Ask me no more, child!"

"Oh, do pray tell me something of her. Do now, at last, dear godmother, if you please! What did I do to her? How did I lose her? Why am I so different from other children, and why is it my fault, dear godmother? No, no, no, don't go away. Oh, speak to me!"

I was in a kind of fright beyond my grief, and I caught hold of her dress, and was kneeling to her. She had been saying all the while, "Let me go!" But now she stood still. Her darkened face had such power over me that it stopped me in the midst of my vehemence. I put up my trembling little hand to clasp hers, but withdrew it as she looked at me, and laid it on my fluttering heart. She raised me, sat in her chair, and standing me before her, said, slowly, in a cold, low voice—I see her knitted brow, and pointed finger:

"Your mother, Esther, is your disgrace, and you were hers. The time will come—and soon enough—when you will understand this better, and will feel it too, as no one save a woman can. I have forgiven her"—

but her face did not relent—"the wrong she did to me, and I say no more of it, though it was greater than you will ever know—than any one will ever know but I, the sufferer. For yourself, unfortunate girl, orphaned and degraded from the first of these evil anniversaries, pray daily that the sins of others be not visited upon your head, according to what is written. Forget your mother, and leave all other people to forget her who will do her unhappy child that greatest kindness. Now go!"

She checked me, however, as I was about to depart from her—so frozen as I was!—and added this:

"Submission, self-denial, diligent work, are the preparations for a life begun with such a shadow on it. You are different from other children, Esther, because you were not born, like them, in common sinfulness and wrath. You are set apart."

I went up to my room and crept to bed and laid my doll's cheek against mine wet with tears, and holding that solitary friend upon my bosom, cried myself to sleep. Imperfect as my understanding of my sorrow was, I knew that I had brought no joy, at any time, to anybody's heart, and that I was to no one upon earth what Dolly was to me.

Dear, dear, to think how much time we passed alone together afterwards, and how often I repeated to the doll the story of my birthday, and confided to her that I would try, as hard as ever I could, to repair the fault I had been born with (of which I felt guilty and yet innocent), and would strive as I grew up to be industrious, contented, and kindhearted, and to do some good to some one, and win some love to myself if I could. I hope it is not self-indulgent to shed these tears as I think of it. I am very thankful, I am very cheerful, but I cannot quite help their coming to my eyes. There! I have wiped them away now, and can go on again properly.

I felt the distance between my godmother and myself so much more after the birthday, and felt so sensible of filling a place in her house which ought to have been empty, that I found her more difficult of approach—though I was fervently grateful to her in my heart—than ever. I felt in the same way towards my school companions; I felt in the same way towards Mrs. Rachael, who was a widow; and towards her daughter, of whom she was proud, who came to see her once a fortnight. I was very retired and quiet, and tried to be very diligent.

One sunny afternoon, when I had come home from school with my books and portfolio, as I was gliding upstairs to my room as usual, my godmother looked out of the parlour-door and called me back. Sitting with her, I found—which was very unusual indeed—a stranger. A portly, important-looking gentleman, dressed all in black, with a white cravat, large gold watch-seals, a pair of gold eye-glasses, and a large seal-ring upon his little finger.

"This," said my godmother in an undertone, "is the child." Then she said in her naturally stern way of speaking, "This is Esther, sir."

The gentleman put up his eye-glasses and said, "Come here, my dear!" He shook hands with me, and asked me to take off my bonnet—looking at me all the while. When I had complied, he said, "Ah!" and afterwards "Yes!" And then, taking off his eye-glasses and folding them in a red case, and leaning back in his arm-chair, he gave my godmother a nod. My godmother said, "You may go upstairs, Esther!" and I made him my curtsey and left him.

It must have been two years afterwards, and I was almost fourteen, when one dreadful night my godmother and I sat at the fireside. I was reading aloud, and she was listening. I had come down at nine o'clock, as I always did, to read the Bible to her, and was reading, from St. John, how our Saviour stooped down, writing with his finger in the dust, when they brought the sinful woman to him.

" 'So when they continued asking him, he lifted up himself and said unto them, He that is without sin among you, let him first cast a stone at her!' "

I was stopped by my godmother's rising, putting her hand to her head, and crying out, in an awful voice, from quite another part of the book:

" 'Watch ye therefore! lest coming suddenly he find you sleeping. And what I say unto you, I say unto all, Watch!' "

In an instant, while she stood before me repeating these words, she fell down on the floor. I had no need to cry out; her voice had sounded through the house, and been heard in the street.

She was laid upon her bed. For more than a week she lay there, little altered outwardly, with her old handsome resolute frown that I so well knew carved upon her face. Many and many a time, in the day and in the night, with my head upon the pillow by her that my whispers might be plainer to her, I kissed her, thanked her, prayed for her, asked her for her blessing and forgiveness, entreated her to give me the least sign that she knew or heard me. No, no, no. Her face was immovable. To the very last, and even afterwards, her frown remained unsoftened.

On the day after my poor good godmother was buried, the gentleman in black with the white neckcloth reappeared. I was sent for by Mrs. Rachael.

"My name is Kenge," he said. "You may remember it, my child; Kenge and Carboy, Lincoln's Inn." I replied that I remembered to have seen him once before. "Pray be seated—here near me. Don't distress yourself; it's of no use, Mrs. Rachael, I needn't inform you who were acquainted with the late Miss Barbary's affairs that her means die with her; and that this young lady, now her aunt is dead—"

"My aunt, sir!"

"It is really of no use carrying on a deception when no object is to be gained by it," said Mr. Kenge smoothly. "Aunt in fact, though not in law. Don't distress yourself! Mrs. Rachael, our young friend has no doubt heard of—the—a—Jarndyce and Jarndyce."

"Never," said Mrs. Rachael.

"Is it possible," pursued Mr. Kenge, putting up his eye-glasses, "that our young friend never heard of Jarndyce and Jarndyce!"

I shook my head, wondering even what it was.

"Not of Jarndyce and Jarndyce?" said Mr. Kenge, looking over his glasses at me. "Not of one of the greatest Chancery suits known? Not of Jarndyce and Jarndyce—the—a—in itself a monument of Chancery practice. In which (I would say) every difficulty, every contingency, every masterly fiction, every form of procedure known in that Court is represented over and over again? It is a cause that could not exist out of this free and great country. I should say that the aggregate of costs in Jarndyce and Jarndyce, Mrs. Rachael, amounts at the present hour to from *six-ty to seven-ty thousands pounds!*" said Mr. Kenge.

I felt very ignorant, but what could I do? I was so entirely unacquainted with the subject that I understood nothing about it even then.

"And she really never heard of the cause!" said Mr. Kenge. "Surprising!"

"Miss Barbary, sir," returned Mrs. Rachael, "who is now among the Seraphim—" ("I hope so, I am sure," said Mr. Kenge politely.) "wished Esther only to know what would be serviceable to her. And she knows, from any teaching she has had here, nothing more."

"Well!" said Mr. Kenge. "Upon the whole, very proper. Now to the point," addressing me. "Miss Barbary, your sole relation (I am bound to observe that in law you had none), being deceased, and it naturally not being to be expected that Mrs. Rachael—"

"Oh dear no!" said Mrs. Rachael, quickly.

"Quite so," assented Mr. Kenge—"that Mrs. Rachael should charge herself with your maintenance and support (I beg you won't distress yourself), you are in a position to receive the renewal of an offer which I was instructed to make to Miss Barbary some two years ago, and which, though rejected then, was understood to be renewable under the lamentable circumstances that have since occurred. Now if I avow that I represent, in Jarndyce and Jarndyce and otherwise, a highly humane but at the same time singular man, shall I compromise myself by any stretch of my professional caution?" said Mr. Kenge, looking calmly at us both.

He appeared to enjoy beyond everything the sound of his own voice.

I couldn't wonder at that, for it was mellow and full, and gave great importance to every word he uttered. He listened to himself with obvious satisfaction. I was very much impressed by him—even then, before I knew that he formed himself on the model of a great lord who was his client, and that he was generally called Conversation Kenge.

"Mr. Jarndyce," he pursued, "being aware of the—I would say desolate —position of our young friend, offers to place her at a first-rate establishment where her education shall be completed, where her comfort shall be secured, where she shall be eminently qualified to discharge her duty in that station of life unto which it has pleased—shall I say Providence? —to call her."

My heart was filled so full, both by what he said and by his affecting manner of saying it, that I was not able to speak, though I tried.

"Mr. Jarndyce," he went on, "makes no condition, beyond expressing his expectation that our young friend will not at any time remove herself from the establishment in question without his knowledge and concurrence. That she will faithfully apply herself to the acquisition of those accomplishments upon the exercise of which she will be ultimately dependent. That she will tread in the paths of virtue and honour, and —the—a—so forth."

I was still less able to speak than before.

"Now, what does our young friend say?" proceeded Mr. Kenge. "Take time, take time! I pause for her reply. But take time!"

What the destitute subject of such an offer tried to say, I need not repeat. What she did say, I could more easily tell, if it were worth the telling. What she felt, and will feel to her dying hour, I could never relate.

This interview took place at Windsor, where I had passed (as far as I knew) my whole life. On that day week, amply provided with all necessaries, I left it, inside the stage-coach, for Reading.

Mrs. Rachael was too good to feel any emotion at parting, but I was not so good, and wept bitterly. I thought that I ought to have known her better after so many years, and ought to have made myself enough of a favourite with her to make her sorry then. When she gave me one cold parting kiss upon my forehead, like a thaw-drop from the stone porch— it was a very frosty day—I felt so miserable and self-reproachful that I clung to her and told her it was my fault, I knew, that she could say good-bye so easily!

"No, Esther!" she returned. "It is your misfortune!"

The coach was at the little lawn-gate, and thus I left her, with a sorrowful heart. She went in before my boxes were lifted to the coach-roof, and shut the door. My godmother had left Mrs. Rachael all the little property she possessed; and there was to be a sale. A day or two before,

I had wrapped the dear old doll in her own shawl and quietly laid her—I am half ashamed to tell it—in the garden-earth, under the tree that shaded my old window.

When the house was out of sight, I sat forward on the low seat, to look out of the high window, watching the frosty trees, that were like beautiful pieces of spar, and the fields all smooth and white with last night's snow. There was a gentleman in the coach who sat on the opposite seat, and looked very large in a quantity of wrappings; but he sat gazing out of the other window, and took no notice of me.

I thought of my dead godmother; of the night when I read to her; of her frowning so fixedly and sternly in her bed—of the strange place I was going to; of the people I should find there, and what they would be like, and what they would say to me—when a voice in the coach gave me a terrible start.

It said, "What the de-vil are you crying for?"

I was so frightened that I lost my voice, and could only answer in a whisper. "Me, sir?" For of course I knew it must have been the gentleman in the quantity of wrappings, though he was still looking out of his window.

"Yes, you," he said, turning round.

"I didn't know I was crying, sir," I faltered.

"But you are!" said the gentleman. "Look here!" He came quite opposite to me from the other corner of the coach, brushed one of his large furry cuffs across my eyes (but without hurting me), and showed me that it was wet. "And what are you crying for?" said the gentleman. "Don't you want to go there?"

"Where, sir?"

"Where? Why, wherever you are going," said the gentleman.

"I am very glad to go there, sir," I answered.

"Well, then! Look glad!" said the gentleman.

I thought he was very strange; or at least that what I could see of him was very strange, for he was wrapped up to the chin, and his face was almost hidden in a fur cap, with broad fur straps at the side of his head, fastened under his chin; but I was composed again, and not afraid of him. So I told him that I thought I must have been crying because of my godmother's death, and because of Mrs. Rachael's not being sorry to part with me.

"Con-found Mrs. Rachael!" said the gentleman. "Let her fly away in a high wind on a broomstick!"

I began to be really afraid of him now, and looked at him with the greatest astonishment. But I thought that he had pleasant eyes, although he kept on muttering to himself in an angry manner, and calling Mrs. Rachael names. He did not speak to me any more until he got out of the coach a little way short of Reading, when he advised me to be a good girl and to be studious, and shook hands with me. I must say I was relieved by his departure.

When the coach stopped, a very neat lady looked up at the window, and said: "Miss Donny."

"No, ma'am, Esther Summerson."

"That is quite right," said the lady. "Miss Donny."

I now understood that she introduced herself by that name, and begged

Miss Donny's pardon for my mistake, and pointed out my boxes at her request. Under the direction of a very neat maid, they were put outside a very small green carriage; and then Miss Donny, the maid, and I got inside and were driven away.

"Everything is ready for you, Esther," said Miss Donny, "and the scheme of your pursuits has been arranged in exact accordance with the wishes of your guardian, Mr. Jarndyce."

"Of—did you say, ma'am?"

"Of your guardian, Mr. Jarndyce," said Miss Donny.

I was so bewildered that Miss Donny thought the cold had been too severe for me, and lent me her smelling-bottle.

"Do you know my—guardian, Mr. Jarndyce, ma'am?" I asked, after a good deal of hesitation.

"Not personally, Esther," said Miss Donny; "merely through his solicitors, Messrs. Kenge and Carboy, of London. A very superior gentleman, Mr. Kenge. Truly eloquent indeed."

I felt this to be very true, but was too confused to attend to it. Our speedy arrival at our destination, before I had time to recover myself, increased my confusion, and I never shall forget the uncertain and the unreal air of everything at Greenleaf (Miss Donny's house) that afternoon!

But I soon became used to it. I was so adapted to the routine of Greenleaf before long that I seemed to have been there a great while—and almost to have dreamed, rather than really lived, my old life at my godmother's. Nothing could be more precise, exact, and orderly than Greenleaf. There was a time for everything all round the dial of the clock, and everything was done at its appointed moment.

We were twelve boarders, and there were two Miss Donnys, twins. It was understood that I would have to depend, by and by, on my qualifications as a governess, and I was not only instructed in everything that was taught at Greenleaf but was very soon engaged in helping to instruct others. As I began to know more, I taught more, and so in course of time I had plenty to do, which I was very fond of doing, because it made the dear girls fond of me. As last, whenever a new pupil came who was a little downcast and unhappy, she was so sure—indeed I don't know why —to make a friend of me that all new-comers were confided to my care. They said I was so gentle; but I am sure *they* were!

I passed at Greenleaf six happy, quiet years. I never saw in any face there, thank Heaven, on my birthday that it would have been better if I had never been born. When the day came round, it brought me so many tokens of affectionate remembrance that my room was beautiful with them from New Year's Day to Christmas.

In those six years I had never been away, except on visits at holiday time in the neighbourhood. After the first six months or so, I had taken Miss Donny's advice in reference to the propriety of writing to Mr. Kenge to say that I was happy and grateful, and with her approval I had written such a letter. I had received a formal answer acknowledging its receipt and saying, "We note the contents thereof, which shall be duly communicated to our client." After that, I sometimes heard Miss Donny and her sister mention how regularly my accounts were paid, and about twice a year I ventured to write a similar letter. I always received by return of post exactly the same answer in the same round hand, with the signature of Kenge and Carboy in another writing, which I supposed to be Mr. Kenge's.

Six quiet years (I find I am saying it for the second time) I had passed at Greenleaf, seeing in those around me, as it might be in a looking-glass, every stage of my own growth and change there, when one November morning I received this letter. I omit the date.

Old Square, Lincoln's Inn

Madam,

Jarndyce and Jarndyce

Our clt Mr. Jarndyce being abt to rece into his house, under an Order of the Ct of Chy, a Ward of the Ct in this cause, for whom he wishes to secure an elgble compn, directs us to inform you that he will be glad of your serces in the afsd capacity.

We have arrngd for your being forded, carriage free, pr eight o'clock coach from Reading, on Monday morning next, to White Horse Cellar, Picadilly, London, where one of our clks will be in waiting to convey you to our offe as above.

We are, Madam, Your obedt Servts,

Kenge and Carboy

Miss Esther Summerson

Oh, never, never, never shall I forget the emotion this letter caused in the house! It was so tender in them to care so much for me, it was so gracious in that Father who had not forgotten me to have made my orphan way so smooth and easy, and to have inclined so many youthful natures towards me, that I could hardly bear it.

The letter gave me only five days' notice of my removal. When every minute added to the proofs of love and kindness that were given me in those five days; and when at last the morning came, and when they took me through all the rooms that I might see them for the last time, and when they all surrounded me with their parting presents, and clung to me weeping, and cried, "What shall we do when dear, dear Esther's gone!" and when I tried to tell them how I blessed and thanked them every one—what a heart I had!

And when the two Miss Donnys grieved as much to part with me as the least among them; and when the maids said, "Bless you, miss, wherever you go!" and when the ugly lame old gardener, who I thought had hardly noticed me in all those years, came panting after the coach to give me a little nosegay of geraniums, and told me I had been the light of his eyes—what a heart I had then!

But of course I soon considered that I must not take tears where I was going, after all that had been done for me. Therefore, of course, I made myself sob less, and persuaded myself to be quiet by saying very often, "Esther, now you really must! This *will not* do!" I cheered myself up pretty well at last. When I had cooled my eyes with lavender water, it was time to watch for London.

I was quite persuaded that we were there when we were ten miles off; and when we really were there, that we should never get there. However, when we began to jolt upon a stone pavement, and particularly when every other conveyance seemed to be running into us, and we seemed to be running into every other conveyance, I began to believe that we really were approaching the end of our journey. Very soon afterwards we stopped.

A young gentleman addressed me from the pavement, and said, "I am from Kenge and Carboy's, miss, of Lincoln's Inn."

"If you please, sir," said I.

He was very obliging; and as he handed me into a fly, after superintending the removal of my boxes, I asked him whether there was a great fire anywhere. For the streets were so full of dense brown smoke that scarcely anything was to be seen.

"Oh dear no, miss," he said. "This is a London particular." I had never heard of such a thing. "A fog, miss."

"Oh indeed!" said I.

We drove slowly through the dirtiest and darkest streets that ever were seen in the world (I thought), and in such a distracting state of confusion that I wondered how the people kept their senses, until we passed into sudden quietude under an old gateway, and drove on through a silent square until we came to an odd nook in a corner, where there was an entrance up a steep, broad flight of stairs, like an entrance to a church. And there really was a churchyard, outside under some cloisters, for I saw the gravestones from the staircase window. This was Kenge and Carboy's. The young gentleman showed me through an outer office into Mr. Kenge's room—there was no one in it—and politely put an arm-chair for me by the fire. He then called my attention to a little looking-glass hanging from a nail on one side of the chimney-piece.

"In case you should wish to look at yourself, miss, after the journey, as you're going before the Chancellor. Not that it's requisite, I am sure," said the young gentleman civilly.

"Going before the Chancellor?" I said, startled for a moment.

"Only a matter of form, miss," returned the young gentleman. "Mr. Kenge is in Court now. He left his compliments, and would you look over the paper"—which the young gentleman gave me as he spoke. He then stirred the fire, and left me.

Everything was so strange—the stranger from its being night in the day-time, the candles burning with a white flame, and looking raw and cold—that I read the words in the newspaper without knowing what they meant, and found myself reading the same words repeatedly. As it

was of no use going on in that way, I put the paper down, took a peep
at my bonnet in the glass to see if it was neat, and looked at the room,
and at the piles of writings, and at a bookcase full of the most inexpressive-looking books that ever had anything to say for themselves. Then I
went on thinking, thinking, thinking—and the fire went on burning,
burning, burning; and the candles went on flickering and guttering—
for two hours.

At last Mr. Kenge came. *He* was not altered, but he was surprised to
see how altered I was, and appeared quite pleased. "As you are going to
be the companion of the young lady who is now in the Chancellor's
private room, Miss Summerson," he said, "we thought it well that you
should be in attendance also. You will not be discomposed by the Lord
Chancellor, I dare say?"

"No, sir," I said, "I don't think I shall."

So Mr. Kenge gave me his arm, and we went round the corner, under
a colonnade, and in at a side door. And so we came, along a passage,
into a comfortable sort of room where a young lady and a young gentleman were standing near a great loud-roaring fire, talking. They both
looked up when I came in, and I saw in the young lady, with the fire
shining upon her, such a beautiful girl! With such rich golden hair, such
soft blue eyes, and such a bright, innocent, trusting face!

"Miss Ada," said Mr. Kenge, "this is Miss Summerson."

She came to meet me with a smile of welcome and her hand extended,
but seemed to change her mind in a moment, and kissed me. In short,
she had such a natural, captivating, winning manner that in a few minutes we were sitting in the window-seat, talking together, as free and
happy as could be. What a load off my mind! It was so delightful to
know that she could confide in me, and like me! it was so good of her,
and so encouraging to me!

The young gentleman was her distant cousin, she told me, and his
name Richard Carstone. He was a handsome youth, with an ingenuous
face and a most engaging laugh; and after she had called him up to
where we sat, he stood by us talking gaily, like a light-hearted boy. He
was very young; not more than nineteen then, if quite so much, but
nearly two years older than she was. They were both orphans, and had
never met before that day. Our all three coming together for the first
time, in such an unusual place, was a thing to talk about, and we talked
about it.

We conversed in a low tone, because a full-dressed gentleman in a
bag wig frequently came in and out, and when he did so, we could hear
a drawling sound in the distance, which he said was one of the counsel
in our case addressing the Lord Chancellor. Presently we heard a bustle,

and a tread of feet, and Mr. Kenge said that the Court had risen, and his lordship was in the next room.

The gentleman in the bag wig opened the door almost directly, and requested Mr. Kenge to come in. Upon that, we all went into the next room, Mr. Kenge first, with my darling—it is so natural to me now that I can't help writing it—and there, plainly dressed in black, and sitting in an arm-chair at a table near the fire, was his lordship, whose robe, trimmed with beautiful gold-lace, was thrown upon another chair. He gave us a searching look as we entered, but his manner was both courtly and kind. The gentleman in the bag wig laid bundles of papers on his lordship's table, and his lordship silently selected one, and turned over the leaves.

"Miss Clare," said the Lord Chancellor. "Miss Ada Clare?"

Mr. Kenge presented her, and his lordship begged her to sit down near him. That he admired her, and was interested by her, even *I* could see in a moment.

"The Jarndyce in question," said the Lord Chancellor, still turning over leaves, "is Jarndyce of Bleak House?"

"Jarndyce of Bleak House, my lord," said Mr. Kenge.

"A dreary name," said the Lord Chancellor.

"But not a dreary place at present, my lord," said Mr. Kenge.

"And Bleak House," said his lordship, "is in—"

"Hertfordshire, my lord."

"Mr. Jarndyce of Bleak House is not married?" said his lordship.

"He is not, my lord," said Mr. Kenge.

A pause.

"Young Mr. Richard Carstone is present?" said the Lord Chancellor, glancing towards him.

Richard bowed and stepped forward.

"Hum!" said the Lord Chancellor, turning over more leaves.

"Mr. Jarndyce of Bleak House, my lord," Mr. Kenge observed in a low voice, "if I may venture to remind your lordship, provides a suitable companion for Miss Ada Clare. This is the young lady. Miss Summerson."

His lordship acknowledged my curtsey very graciously.

"Miss Summerson is not related to any party in the cause, I think?"

"No, my lord."

Mr. Kenge leant over before it was quite said, and whispered. His lordship, with his eyes upon the papers, listened, nodded twice or thrice, turned over more leaves, and did not look towards me again until we were going away.

Mr. Kenge now retired, and Richard with him, to where I was, near the door, leaving my pet (it is so natural to me that again I can't help it!) sitting near the Lord Chancellor, with whom his lordship spoke a little apart, asking her, as she told me afterwards, whether she had well reflected on the proposed arrangement, and if she thought she would be happy under the roof of Mr. Jarndyce of Bleak House, and why she thought so. Presently he rose courteously and released her, and then he spoke for a minute or two with Richard Carstone.

"Very well!" said his lordship aloud. "I shall make the order. Mr. Jarndyce of Bleak House has chosen, so far as I may judge," and this was when he looked at me, "a very good companion for the young lady, and the arrangement altogether seems the best of which the circumstances admit."

He dismissed us pleasantly, and we all went out, very much obliged to him for being so affable and polite.

When he got under the colonnade, Mr. Kenge remembered that he must go back for a moment, to ask a question, and left us in the fog.

"Well!" said Richard Carstone, "that's over! And where do we go next, Miss Summerson?"

"Don't you know?" I said.

"Not in the least," said he.

"And don't you know, my love?" I asked Ada.

"No!" said she. "Don't you?"

"Not at all!" said I.

We looked at one another, half laughing, when a curious little old woman in a squeezed bonnet, and carrying a reticule, came curtseying and smiling up to us, with an air of great ceremony.

"Oh!" said she. "The wards in Jarndyce! Ve-ry happy, I am sure, to have the honour! It is a good omen for youth, and hope, and beauty when they find themselves in this place and don't know what's to come of it."

"Mad!" whispered Richard, not thinking she could hear him.

"Right! Mad, young gentleman," she returned so quickly that he was quite abashed. "I was a ward myself. I was not mad at that time"—curtseying low, and smiling between every little sentence. "I had youth and hope. I believe, beauty. It matters very little now. Neither of the three served, or saved me. I have the honour to attend Court regularly. With my documents. I expect a judgment. Shortly. On the Day of Judgment. I have discovered that the Sixth Seal mentioned in the Revelations is the Great Seal. It has been open a long time! Pray accept my blessing."

As Ada was a little frightened, I said, to humour the poor old lady, that we were much obliged to her.

"Ye-es!" she said mincingly. "I imagine so. I shall confer estates on both. I expect a judgment. Shortly. On the Day of Judgment. This is a good omen for you. Accept my blessing!"

She stopped at the bottom of the steep, broad flight of stairs; but we looked back as we went up and she was still there, saying, still with a curtsey and a smile between every little sentence, "Youth. And hope. And beauty. And Chancery. Ha! Pray accept my blessing!"

# CHAPTER 4

## Telescopic Philanthropy

WE were to pass the night, Mr. Kenge told us when we arrived in his room, at Mrs. Jellyby's, and then he turned to me and said he took it for granted I knew who Mrs. Jellyby was.

"I really don't, sir," I returned. "Perhaps Mr. Carstone—or Miss Clare—"

But no, they knew nothing whatever about Mrs. Jellyby.

"In-deed! Mrs. Jellyby," said Mr. Kenge, standing with his back to the fire, "is a lady of very remarkable strength of character who devotes herself entirely to the public. She has devoted herself to an extensive variety of public subjects, and is at present devoted to the subject of Africa, with a view to the general cultivation of the coffee-berry—*and* the natives—and the happy settlement on the banks of the African rivers of our superabundant home population. Mr. Jarndyce, who is desirous to aid any work that is considered likely to be a good work, has, I believe, a very high opinion of Mrs. Jellyby."

"And Mr. Jellyby, sir?" suggested Richard.

"Ah! Mr. Jellyby," said Mr. Kenge, "is—a—I don't know that I can describe him to you better than by saying that he is the husband of Mrs. Jellyby."

"A nonentity, sir?" said Richard, with a droll look.

"I don't say that," returned Mr. Kenge, gravely. "I can't say that in-deed, for I know nothing whatever *of* Mr. Jellyby. I never, to my knowl-edge, had the pleasure of seeing Mr. Jellyby. He may be a very superior man, but he is, so to speak, merged—Merged—in the more shining quali-ties of his wife." Mr. Kenge proceeded to tell us that as the road to Bleak House would have been very long, dark, and tedious on such an evening, and as we had been travelling already, Mr. Jarndyce had himself proposed this arrangement. A carriage would be at Mr. Jellyby's to convey us out of town early in the forenoon of tomorrow.

He then rang a little bell, and the young gentleman came in. Addressing him by the name of Guppy, Mr. Kenge inquired whether Miss Summerson's boxes and the rest of the baggage had been "sent round." Mr. Guppy said yes, they had been sent round, and a coach was waiting to take us round too, as soon as we pleased.

"Then it only remains," said Mr. Kenge, shaking hands with us, "for me to express my lively satisfaction in (good-day, Miss Clare!) the arrangement this day concluded, and my (good-bye to you, Miss Summerson!) lively hope that it will conduce to the happiness, the (glad to have had the honour of making your acquaintance, Mr. Carstone!) welfare, the advantage in all points of view, of all concerned! Guppy, see the party safely there."

"Where *is* 'there,' Mr. Guppy?" said Richard, as we went downstairs.

"No distance," said Mr. Guppy—"round in Thavies Inn, you know."

"I can't say I know where it is, for I come from Winchester and am strange in London."

"Only round the corner," said Mr. Guppy. "We just twist up Chancery Lane, and cut along Holborn, and there we are in four minutes' time. This is about a London particular *now,* ain't it, miss?" He seemed quite delighted with it on my account. "Not that it affects you, though, I'm sure," said Mr. Guppy, putting up the steps. "On the contrary, it seems to do you good, miss, judging from your appearance."

I knew he meant well in paying me this compliment, so I laughed at myself for blushing at it when he had shut the door and got upon the box; and we all three laughed, and chatted about our inexperience, and the strangeness of London, until we turned up under an archway to our destination: a narrow street of high houses, like an oblong cistern to hold the fog. There was a confused little crowd of people, principally children, gathered about the house at which we stopped, which had a tarnished brass plate on the door, with the inscription, JELLYBY.

"Don't be frightened!" said Mr. Guppy. "One of the young Jellybys been and got his head through the area railings!"

"Oh poor child," said I, "let me out, if you please!"

"Pray be careful of yourself, miss. The young Jellybys are always up to something," said Mr. Guppy.

I made my way to the poor child, who was one of the dirtiest little unfortunates I ever saw, and found him, very hot and frightened and crying loudly, fixed by the neck between two iron railings while a milkman and a beadle, with the kindest intentions possible, were endeavouring to drag him back by the legs, under a general impression that his skull was compressible by those means. As I found (after pacifying him), that he was a little boy with a naturally large head, I thought that perhaps where his head could go, his body could follow, and mentioned that the best mode of extrication might be to push him forward. This was so favourably received by the milkman and the beadle that he would immediately have been pushed into the area if I had not held his pinafore while Richard and Mr. Guppy ran down through the kitchen, to catch him when he should be released. At last he was happily got down without any accident.

Nobody had appeared belonging to the house except a person in pattens, who had been poking at the child from below with a broom—I don't know with what object, and I don't think she did. I therefore supposed that Mrs. Jellyby was not at home, and was quite surprised when the person appeared in the passage without the pattens, and going up to the back room on the first floor before Ada and me, announced us as "Them two young ladies, Missis Jellyby!" We passed several more children on the way up, whom it was difficult to avoid treading on in the dark; and as we came into Mrs. Jellyby's presence, one of the poor little things fell downstairs—down a whole flight (as it sounded to me)—with a great noise.

Mrs. Jellyby, whose face reflected none of the uneasiness which we could not help showing in our own faces as the dear child's head recorded its passage with a bump on every stair—Richard afterwards said he counted seven, besides one for the landing—received us with perfect equanimity. She was a pretty, very diminutive, plump woman of from forty to fifty, with handsome eyes, though they had a curious habit of seeming to look a long way off. As if—I am quoting Richard again—they could see nothing nearer than Africa!

"I am very glad indeed," said Mrs. Jellyby, in an agreeable voice, "to have the pleasure of receiving you. I have a great respect for Mr. Jarndyce, and no one in whom he is interested can be an object of indifference to me."

We expressed our acknowledgments, and sat down behind the door, where there was a lame invalid of a sofa. Mrs. Jellyby had very good hair, but was too much occupied with her African duties to brush it. The shawl in which she had been loosely muffled dropped on to her chair when she advanced to us, and as she turned to resume her seat, we could not help noticing that her dress didn't nearly meet up the back.

The room, which was strewn with papers and nearly filled by a great writing-table covered with similar litter, was, I must say, not only very untidy, but very dirty. We were obliged to take notice of that with our sense of sight even while with our sense of hearing we followed the poor child who had tumbled downstairs.

But what principally struck us was a jaded, and unhealthy-looking, though by no means plain girl at the writing-table, who sat biting the feather of her pen and staring at us. I suppose nobody ever was in such a state of ink. And from her tumbled hair to her pretty feet, which were disfigured with frayed and broken satin slippers trodden down at heel, she really seemed to have no article of dress upon her, from a pin upwards, that was in its proper condition or its right place.

"You find me, my dears," said Mrs. Jellyby, snuffing the two great office candles in tin candlesticks which made the room taste strongly of hot tallow, "as usual, very busy; but that you will excuse. The African project at present employs my whole time. It involves me in correspondence with public bodies, and with private individuals anxious for the welfare of their species, all over the country. I am happy to say it is advancing. We hope by this time next year to have from a hundred and fifty to two hundred healthy families cultivating coffee and educating the natives of Borrioboola-Gha, on the left bank of the Niger."

I said it must be very gratifying.

"It *is* gratifying," said Mrs. Jellyby. "It involves the devotion of all my energies, such as they are; but that is nothing, so that it succeeds, and I am more confident of success every day. Do you know, Miss Summerson, I almost wonder that *you* never turned your thoughts to Africa."

This application of the subject was really so unexpected to me that I was quite at a loss how to receive it. I hinted that the climate—

"The finest climate in the world!" said Mrs. Jellyby. "With precaution. You may go into Holborn without precaution and be run over. You may go into Holborn with precaution and never be run over. Just so with Africa."

I said, "No doubt."—I meant as to Holborn.

"If you would like," said Mrs. Jellyby, putting a number of papers towards us, "to look over some remarks on that head, and on the general subject, while I finish a letter I am now dictating—to my eldest daughter, who is my amanuensis—"

The girl at the table left off biting her pen and made a return to our recognition which was half bashful and half sulky.

"—I shall then have finished for the present," proceeded Mrs. Jellyby, with a sweet smile, "though my work is never done. Where are you, Caddy?"

" 'Presents her compliments to Mr. Swallow, and begs—' " said Caddy.

"And begs," said Mrs. Jellyby, dictating, "to inform him, in reference to his letter of inquiry on the African project—No, Peepy! Not on any account!"

Peepy (so self-named) was the unfortunate child who had fallen downstairs, who now interrupted the correspondence by presenting himself, with a strip of plaister on his forehead, to exhibit his wounded knees. Mrs. Jellyby merely added, with the serene composure with which she said everything, "Go along, you naughty Peepy!" and fixed her fine eyes on Africa again.

However, as she at once proceeded with her dictation, and as I interrupted nothing by doing it, I ventured quietly to stop poor Peepy as he was going out and to take him up to nurse. He looked very much astonished at it, and at Ada's kissing him, but soon fell fast asleep in my arms, sobbing at longer and longer intervals, until he was quiet.

"Six o'clock!" said Mrs. Jellyby. "And our dinner hour is nominally (for we dine at all hours) five! Caddy, show Miss Clare and Miss Summerson their rooms. You will like to make some change, perhaps? You will excuse me, I know, being so much occupied. Oh, that very bad child! Pray put him down, Miss Summerson!"

I begged permission to retain him, truly saying that he was not at all troublesome, and carried him upstairs and laid him on my bed. Ada and I had two upper rooms, with a door of communication between. They were excessively bare and disorderly.

"You would like some hot water, wouldn't you?" said Miss Jellyby, looking round for a jug with a handle to it, but looking in vain.

"If it is not being troublesome," said we.

"Oh, it's not the trouble," returned Miss Jellyby. "The question is, if there *is* any."

The evening was so very cold, and the rooms had such a marshy smell, that I must confess it was a little miserable, and Ada was half crying. We soon laughed, however, and were busily unpacking when Miss Jellyby came back to say that she was sorry there was no hot water, but they couldn't find the kettle, and the boiler was out of order. We begged her not to mention it, and made all the haste we could to get down to the fire again. But all the little children had come up to the landing outside, to look at the phenomenon of Peepy lying on my bed, and our attention was distracted by the constant apparition of noses and fingers in situations of danger between the hinges of the door. It was impossible to shut the door of either room. Therefore I proposed to the children that they should come in and be very good at my table, and I would tell them the story of Little Red Riding Hood while I dressed—which they did, and were as quiet as mice, including Peepy, who awoke opportunely before the appearance of the wolf.

When we went downstairs we found a mug with "A Present from

Tunbridge Wells" on it lighted up in the staircase window with a
floating wick, and a young woman with a swelled face bound up in a
flannel bandage blowing the fire of the drawing-room (now connected
by an open door with Mrs. Jellyby's room), and choking dreadfully. It
smoked to that degree, in short, that we all sat coughing and crying with
the windows open for half an hour, during which Mrs. Jellyby, with the
same sweetness of temper, directed letters about Africa. Richard told us
that he had washed his hands in a pie-dish, and that they had found the
kettle on his dressing-table.

Soon after seven o'clock we went down to dinner—carefully, by Mrs.
Jellyby's advice, for the stair-carpets, besides being very deficient in stair-
wires, were so torn as to be absolute traps. We had a fine cod-fish, a
piece of roast beef, a dish of cutlets, and a pudding—an excellent dinner
if it had had any cooking to speak of, but it was almost raw. The young
woman with the flannel bandage waited. The person I had seen in
pattens (who I suppose to have been the cook) frequently came and
skirmished with her at the door, and there appeared to be ill-will between them.

All through dinner—which was long, in consequence of such accidents as the dish of potatoes being mislaid in the coal-scuttle, and the
handle of the cork-screw coming off and striking the young woman in the
chin—Mrs. Jellyby preserved the evenness of her disposition. She told
us a great deal that was interesting about Borrioboola-Gha and the
natives, and received so many letters that Richard, who sat by her, saw
four envelopes in the gravy at once. Some of the letters were proceedings of ladies' committees, or resolutions of ladies' meetings, which she
read to us; others were applications from people excited in various ways
about the cultivation of coffee, and natives; others required answers, and
these she sent her eldest daughter from the table three or four times to
write. She was full of business, and undoubtedly was, as she had told us,
devoted to the cause.

I was a little curious to know who a mild bald gentleman in spectacles
was who dropped into a vacant chair after the fish was taken away, and
seemed passively to submit himself to Borrioboola-Gha, but not to be
actively interested in that settlement. As he never spoke a word, he
might have been a native but for his complexion. It was not until we left
the table, and he remained alone with Richard, that the possibility of
his being Mr. Jellyby ever entered my head. But he *was* Mr. Jellyby;
and a loquacious young man called Mr. Quale, with large shining knobs
for temples, who came in the evening, and told Ada he was a philanthropist, also informed her that he called the matrimonial alliance of
Mrs. Jellyby with Mr. Jellyby the union of mind and matter.

This young man, besides having a great deal to say for himself about

Africa, and a project of his for teaching the coffee colonists to teach the natives to turn piano-forte legs and establish an export trade, delighted in drawing Mrs. Jellyby out by saying, "If my memory does not deceive me, Mrs. Jellyby, you once mentioned that you had sent off five thousand circulars from one post-office at one time?" During the whole evening, Mr. Jellyby sat in a corner with his head against the wall, as if he were subject to low spirits. It seemed that he had several times opened his mouth when alone with Richard after dinner, as if he had something on his mind, but had always shut it again, to Richard's extreme confusion, without saying anything.

Mrs. Jellyby, sitting in quite a nest of waste paper, drank coffee all the evening, and dictated at intervals to her eldest daughter. She also held a discussion with Mr. Quale, of which the subject seemed to be— if I understood it—the Brotherhood of Humanity, and gave utterance to some beautiful sentiments. I was not so attentive an auditor as I might have wished to be, however, for Peepy and the other children came flocking about Ada and me in a corner of the drawing-room to ask for another story; so we sat down among them, and told them in whispers Puss in Boots, and I don't know what else, until Mrs. Jellyby, accidentally remembering them, sent them to bed. As Peepy cried for me to take him to bed, I carried him upstairs.

On my return downstairs, I felt that Mrs. Jellyby looked down upon me rather, for being so frivolous. It was nearly midnight before we found an opportunity of going to bed, and even then we left Mrs. Jellyby among her papers drinking coffee, and Miss Jellyby biting the feather of her pen.

"What a strange house!" said Ada, when we got upstairs. "How curious of my cousin Jarndyce to send us here!"

"My love," said I, "it quite confuses me. I want to understand it, and I can't understand it at all."

"What?" asked Ada, with her pretty smile.

"All this, my dear," said I. "It *must* be very good of Mrs. Jellyby to take such pains about a scheme for the benefit of natives—and yet— Peepy and the housekeeping!"

Ada laughed, and put her arm about my neck, as I stood looking at the fire, and told me I was a quiet, dear, good creature, and had won her heart. "You are so thoughtful, Esther," she said, "and yet so cheerful! and you do so much, so unpretendingly! You would make a home out of even this house."

"May I ask you a question?" said I, when we had sat before the fire a little while.

"Five hundred," said Ada.

"Your cousin, Mr. Jarndyce. I owe so much to him. Would you mind describing him to me?"

Shaking her golden hair, Ada turned her eyes upon me with such laughing wonder that I was full of wonder too—partly at her beauty, partly at her surprise.

"Esther!" she cried. "You want a description of my cousin Jarndyce?"

"My dear, I never saw him."

"And *I* never saw him!" returned Ada.

No, she had never seen him. Young as she was when her mama died, she remembered how the tears would come into her eyes when she spoke of him and of the noble generosity of his character, which she had said was to be trusted above all earthly things; and Ada trusted it. Her cousin Jarndyce had written to her a few months ago proposing the arrangement we were now to enter on, and telling her that "in time it might heal some of the wounds made by the miserable Chancery suit." She had replied, gratefully accepting his proposal. Richard had received a similar letter, and had made a similar response. He *had* seen Mr. Jarndyce once, but only once, five years ago, at Winchester school. He had told Ada that he recollected him as "a bluff, rosy fellow." This was the utmost description Ada could give me.

It set me thinking so that when Ada was asleep, I still remained before the fire, wondering and wondering about Bleak House, and wondering and wondering that yesterday morning should seem so long ago. I don't know where my thoughts had wandered when they were recalled by a tap at the door. I opened it softly, and found Miss Jellyby shivering there, with a broken candle in a broken candlestick in one hand, and an egg-cup in the other.

"Good-night!" she said, very sulkily.

"Good-night!" said I.

"May I come in?" she shortly and unexpectedly asked me in the same sulky way.

"Certainly," said I. "Don't wake Miss Clare."

She would not sit down, but stood by the fire, dipping her inky middle finger in the egg-cup, which contained vinegar, and smearing it over the ink-stains on her face, frowning the whole time, and looking very gloomy.

"I wish Africa was dead!" she said, on a sudden. I was going to remonstrate.

"I do!" she said. "Don't talk to me, Miss Summerson. I hate it and detest it. It's a beast!"

I told her she was tired, and I was sorry. I put my hand upon her head, and touched her forehead, and said it was hot now, but would be cool tomorrow. She still stood, pouting and frowning at me, but presently put down her egg-cup, and turned softly towards the bed where Ada lay.

"She is very pretty!" she said, in the same uncivil manner. I assented with a smile.

"An orphan. Ain't she?"

"Yes."

"But knows a quantity, I suppose? Can dance, and play music, and sing? She can talk French, I suppose, and do geography, and globes, and needlework, and everything?"

"No doubt," said I.

"I can't," she returned. "I can't do anything hardly, except write. I'm always writing for Ma. I wonder you two were not ashamed of yourselves to come in this afternoon and see me able to do nothing else. It was like your ill-nature. Yet you think yourselves very fine, I dare say!"

I could see that the poor girl was near crying, and I resumed my chair without speaking, and looked at her (I hope) as mildly as I felt towards her.

"It's disgraceful," she said. "You know it is. The whole house is disgraceful. The children are disgraceful. I'm disgraceful. Pa's miserable, and no wonder! Priscilla drinks—she's always drinking. It was as bad as a public-house, waiting at dinner; you know it was!"

"My dear, I don't know it," said I.

"You do," she said, very shortly. "You shan't say you don't. You do!"

"Oh, my dear!" said I, "if you won't let me speak—"

"You're speaking now. You know you are. Don't tell stories, Miss Summerson."

"My dear," said I, "as long as you won't hear me out—"

"I don't want to hear you out."

"Oh yes, I think you do," said I, "because that would be so very unreasonable. I did not know what you tell me, because the servant did not come near me at dinner; but I don't doubt what you tell me, and I am sorry to hear it."

She was still standing by the bed, and now stooped down (but still with the same discontented face) and kissed Ada. That done, she came softly back and stood by the side of my chair. Her bosom was heaving in a distressful manner that I greatly pitied, but I thought it better not to speak.

"I wish I was dead!" she broke out. "I wish we were all dead. It would be a great deal better for us."

In a moment afterwards, she knelt on the ground at my side, hid her face in my dress, passionately begged my pardon, and wept. I comforted her, and would have raised her, but she cried, No, no, she wanted to stay there!

"You used to teach girls," she said. "If you could only have taught me, I could have learnt from you! I am so very miserable, and I like you so much!"

I could not persuade her to sit by me, or to do anything but move a ragged stool to where she was kneeling, and take that, and still hold my dress in the same manner. By degrees, the poor tired girl fell asleep, and then I contrived to raise her head so that it should rest on my lap, and to cover us both with shawls. The fire went out, and all night long she slumbered thus before the ashy grate. At first I was painfully awake, and vainly tried to lose myself, with my eyes closed, among the scenes of the day. At length, by slow degrees, they became indistinct and mingled. The purblind day was feebly struggling with the fog when I opened my eyes.


# CHAPTER 5

## A Morning Adventure

ALTHOUGH the morning was raw, and although the fog still seemed heavy—I say seemed, for the windows were so encrusted with dirt that they would have made midsummer sunshine dim—I was sufficiently forewarned of the discomfort within doors at that early hour, and sufficiently curious about London, to think it a good idea on the part of Miss Jellyby when she proposed that we should go out for a walk.

"Ma won't be down for ever so long," she said, "and then it's a chance if breakfast's ready for an hour afterwards, they dawdle so. As to Pa, he gets what he can and goes to the office. He never has what you would call a regular breakfast. Priscilla leaves him out the loaf and some milk, when there is any, overnight. Sometimes there isn't any milk, and sometimes the cat drinks it. But I'm afraid you must be tired, Miss Summerson, and perhaps you would rather go to bed."

"I am not at all tired, my dear," said I, "and would much prefer to go out."

"If you're sure you would," returned Miss Jellyby, "I'll get my things on."

Ada said she would go too, and was soon astir. What with the bustle of getting myself ready, and helping Ada, I was soon quite in a glow. We found Miss Jellyby trying to warm herself at the fire in the writing-room. Everything was just as we had left it last night, and was evidently intended to remain so. Crumbs, dust, and waste paper were all over the house.

We met Richard, who was dancing up and down Thavies Inn to warm his feet. He was agreeably surprised to see us stirring so soon, and said he would gladly share our walk. So he took care of Ada, and Miss Jellyby and I went first. Miss Jellyby had relapsed into her sulky manner.

"Where would you wish to go?" she asked.

"Anywhere, my dear," I replied.

"Anywhere's nowhere," said Miss Jellyby, stopping perversely.

"Let us go somewhere, at any rate," said I.

She then walked me on very fast.

"I don't care!" she said. "Now you are my witness, Miss Summerson, I say I don't care—but if he was to come to our house, with his great shining lumpy forehead night after night, till he was as as old as Methuselah, I wouldn't have anything to say to him. Such *Asses* as he and Ma make of themselves!"

"My dear!" I remonstrated. "Your duty as a child—"

"Oh, don't talk of duty as a child, Miss Summerson; where's Ma's duty as a parent? All made over to the public and Africa, I suppose! Then let the public and Africa show duty as a child; it's much more their affair than mine. You are shocked, I dare say! Very well, so am I shocked too; so we are both shocked, and there's an end of it!" She walked me on faster yet. "But for all that, I say again, he may come, and come, and come, and I won't have anything to say to him. I can't bear him. If there's any stuff in the world that I hate and detest, it's the stuff he and Ma talk. I wonder the very paving-stones opposite our house can have the patience to stay there and be a witness of such inconsistencies and contradictions as all that sounding nonsense."

I could not but understand her to refer to Mr. Quale, the young gentleman who had appeared after dinner yesterday. I was saved the disagreeable necessity of pursuing the subject by Richard and Ada coming up at a round pace, laughing, and asking us if we meant to run a race. Thus interrupted, Miss Jellyby became silent, and walked moodily on at my side; while I admired the quantity of people already going to and fro, the number of vehicles passing and repassing, and the extraordinary creatures in rags secretly groping among the swept-out rubbish for pins and other refuse.

"So, Cousin," said the cheerful voice of Richard to Ada, behind me, "we are never to get out of Chancery! We have come by another way to our place of meeting yesterday, and—by the Great Seal, here's the old lady again!"

Truly, there she was, immediately in front of us, curtseying, and smiling, and saying, with her yesterday's air of patronage:

"The wards in Jarndyce! Ve-ry happy, I am sure!"

"You are out early, ma'am," said I as she curtseyed to me.

"Ye-es! I usually walk here early. Before the Court sits. I collect my thoughts here for the business of the day," said the old lady, mincingly. "The business of the day requires a great deal of thought. Chancery justice is so ve-ry difficult to follow."

"Who's this, Miss Summerson?" whispered Miss Jellyby.

The little old lady's hearing was remarkably quick. She answered for herself directly.

"A suitor, my child. At your service. I have the honour to attend Court regularly. With my documents. Have I the pleasure of addressing another of the youthful parties in Jarndyce?" said the old lady.

Richard good-naturedly explained that Miss Jellyby was not connected with the suit.

"Ha!" said the old lady. "She does not expect a judgment? She will still grow old. But not so old. Oh dear no! This is the garden of Lincoln's Inn. I call it my garden. It is quite a bower in the summer-time. Where the birds sing melodiously. I pass the greater part of the long vacation here. In contemplation. You find the long vacation exceedingly long, don't you?" We said yes, as she seemed to expect us to say so. "When the leaves are falling from the trees, and there are no more flowers in bloom to make up into nosegays for the Lord Chancellor's Court," said the old lady, "the vacation is fulfilled, and the Sixth Seal, mentioned in the Revelations, again prevails. Pray come and see my lodging. It will be a good omen for me. Youth, and hope, and beauty, are very seldom there. It is a long long time since I had a visit from either."

She had taken my hand and, leading me and Miss Jellyby away, beckoned Richard and Ada to come too. I did not know how to excuse myself, and looked to Richard for aid. As he was half amused and half curious, and all in doubt how to get rid of the old lady without offence, she continued to lead us away, and he and Ada continued to follow. She lived so close by that we had not time to have done humouring her for a few moments before she was at home. Slipping us out at a little side-gate, the old lady stopped most unexpectedly in a narrow back street, part of some courts and lanes immediately outside the wall of the Inn, and said, "This is my lodging. Pray walk up!"

She had stopped at a shop over which was written, KROOK, RAG AND BOTTLE WAREHOUSE. Also, in long thin letters, KROOK, DEALER IN MARINE STORES; BONES BOUGHT; KITCHEN-STUFF BOUGHT; OLD IRON BOUGHT; WASTE PAPER BOUGHT; LADIES' AND GENTLEMEN'S WARDROBES BOUGHT. Everything seemed to be bought and nothing to be sold there. In the window were quantities of dirty bottles: blacking-bottles, medicine-bottles, ginger-beer and soda-water bottles, pickle-bottles, wine-bottles, ink-bottles. There was a little tottering bench of shabby old volumes outside the door, labelled "Law Books, all at 9d." Some of the inscriptions I have enumerated were written in law-hand, like the papers I had seen in Kenge and Carboy's office, and the letters I had so long received from the firm. Among them was one, in the same writing, having nothing to do with the business of the shop, but announcing that a respectable man aged forty-five wanted engrossing or copying to execute with neatness and dispatch: Address to Nemo, care of Mr. Krook within.

As it was still foggy and dark, and as the shop was blinded besides by the wall of Lincoln's Inn, intercepting the light within a couple of yards, we should not have seen so much but for a lighted lantern that an old man in spectacles and a hairy cap was carrying about in the shop. Turning towards the door, he now caught sight of us. He was short, cadaverous, and withered, with his head sunk sideways between his shoulders, and the breath issuing in visible smoke from his mouth, as if he were on fire within. His throat, chin, and eyebrows were so frosted with white hairs, and so gnarled with veins and puckered skin, that he looked from his breast upward like some old root in a fall of snow.

"Hi hi!" said the old man, coming to the door. "Have you anything to sell?"

We naturally drew back and glanced at our conductress, who had been trying to open the house-door with a key she had taken from her pocket, and to whom Richard now said that, as we had had the pleasure of seeing where she lived, we would leave her, being pressed for time. But she was not to be so easily left. She became so fantastically and pressingly earnest in her entreaties that we would walk up and see her apartment for an instant; and was so bent, in her harmless way, on leading me in, as part of the good omen she desired; that I (whatever the others might do) saw nothing for it but to comply. I suppose we were all more or less curious—at any rate, when the old man added his persuasions to hers, and said, "Ay, ay! Please her! It won't take a minute! Come in, come in! Come in through the shop if t'other door's out of order!" we all went in, stimulated by Richard's laughing encouragement.

"My landlord, Krook," said the little old lady. "He is called among the neighbours the Lord Chancellor. His shop is called the Court of Chancery. He is a very eccentric person. He is very odd. Oh, I assure you he is very odd!" She shook her head a great many times, and tapped her forehead with her finger. "For he is a little—you know!—M—!" said the old lady, with great stateliness. The old man overheard, and laughed.

"It's true enough," he said, going before us with the lantern, "that they call me the Lord Chancellor, and call my shop Chancery. And why do you think they call me the Lord Chancellor, and my shop Chancery?"

"I don't know, I am sure!" said Richard, rather carelessly.

"You see," said the old man, stopping and turning round, "they—Hi! Here's lovely hair! I have got three sacks of ladies' hair below, but none so beautiful and fine as this. What colour, and what texture!"

"That'll do, my good friend!" said Richard, strongly disapproving of his having drawn one of Ada's tresses through his yellow hand. "You can admire as the rest of us do without taking that liberty."

The old man darted at him a sudden look, which even called my attention from Ada, who, startled and blushing, was so remarkably beautiful that she seemed to fix the wandering attention of the little old lady herself. Mr. Krook shrank into his former self as suddenly as he had leaped out of it.

"You see I have so many things here," he resumed, holding up the lantern, "of so many kinds, and all, as the neighbours think, wasting away and going to rack and ruin, that that's why they have given me and my place a christening. And I have so many old parchmentses and papers in my stock. And all's fish that comes to my net. And I can't abear to part with anything I once lay hold of, or to alter anything, or to have any sweeping, nor scouring, nor cleaning, nor repairing going on about me. That's the way I've got the ill name of Chancery. *I* don't mind. I go to see my noble and learned brother pretty well every day, when he sits in the Inn. He don't notice me, but I notice him. There's no great odds betwixt us. We both grub on in a muddle. Hi, Lady Jane!" A large grey cat leaped from some neighbouring shelf on his shoulder, and startled us all. "Hi! show 'em how you scratch. Hi! Tear, my lady!" said her master.

The cat leaped down and ripped at a bundle of rags with her tigerish claws, with a sound that it set my teeth on edge to hear.

"She'd do as much for any one I was to set her on," said the old man. "I deal in cat-skins among other general matters, and hers was offered to me. It's a very fine skin, but I didn't have it stripped off! *That* warn't like Chancery practice though, says you!"

He had by this time led us across the shop, and now opened a door in the back part of it, leading to the house-entry. As he stood with his hand upon the lock, the little old lady graciously observed to him before passing out:

"That will do, Krook. You mean well, but are tiresome. My young friends are pressed for time. I have none to spare myself, having to attend Court very soon. My young friends are the wards in Jarndyce."

"Jarndyce!" said the old man with a start.

"Jarndyce and Jarndyce. The great suit, Krook."

"Hi!" exclaimed the old man in a tone of thoughtful amazement, and with a wider stare than before. "Think of it!"

He seemed so rapt all in a moment, and looked so curiously at us, that Richard said:

"Why, you appear to trouble yourself a good deal about the causes before your noble and learned brother, the other Chancellor!"

"Yes," said the old man abstractedly. "Sure! *Your* name now will be—"

"Richard Carstone."

"Carstone," he repeated, slowly checking off that name upon his forefinger, and each of the others he went on to mention, upon a separate finger. "Yes. There was the name of Barbary, and the name of Clare, and the name of Dedlock too, I think."

"He knows as much of the cause as the real salaried Chancellor!" said Richard, quite astonished, to Ada and me.

"Ay!" said the old man, coming slowly out of his abstraction. "Yes! Tom Jarndyce—you'll excuse me, being related, but he was never known about court by any other name, and was as well known there as—she is now"—nodding slightly at his lodger—"Tom Jarndyce was often in here. He got into a restless habit of strolling about when the cause was on, or expected, talking to the little shopkeepers, and telling 'em to keep out of Chancery, whatever they did. 'For,' says he, 'it's being ground to bits in a slow mill; it's being roasted at a slow fire; it's being stung to death by single bees; it's going mad by grains.' He was as near making away with himself, just where the young lady stands, as near could be."

We listened with horror.

"He come in at the door," said the old man, slowly pointing an imaginary track along the shop, "on the day he did it—the whole neighbourhood had said for months before that he would do it of a certainty sooner or later—he come in at the door that day, and walked along there, and sat himself on a bench that stood there, and asked me to fetch him a pint of wine. 'For,' says he, 'Krook, I am much depressed; my cause is on again, and I think I'm nearer judgment than I ever was.' I persuaded him to go to the tavern over the way there, t'other side my lane, and I followed and looked in at the window, and saw him, comfortable as I thought, in the arm-chair by the fire, and company with him. I hadn't hardly got back here when I heard a shot go echoing and rattling right away into the inn. I ran out—neighbours ran out—twenty of us cried at once, 'Tom Jarndyce!' "

The old man stopped, looked hard at us, looked down into the lantern, blew the light out, and shut the lantern up.

"We were right, I needn't tell the present hearers. Hi! To be sure, how the neighbourhood poured into Court that afternoon while the cause was on! How my noble and learned brother, and all the rest of 'em, grubbed and muddled away as usual, and tried to look as if they hadn't heard a word of the last fact in the case, or as if they had—oh dear me!—nothing at all to do with it, if they had heard of it by any chance!"

Ada's colour had entirely left her, and Richard was scarcely less pale. Nor could I wonder, judging even from my emotions, and I was no party in the suit, that to hearts so untried and fresh it was a shock to come into the inheritance of a protracted misery, attended in the minds of many people with such dreadful recollections. I had another uneasiness, in the application of the painful story to the poor half-witted creature who had brought us there; but, to my surprise, she seemed perfectly unconscious of that, and only led the way upstairs again.

She lived at the top of the house, in a pretty large room, from which she had a glimpse of Lincoln's Inn Hall. This seemed to have been her principal inducement, originally, for taking up her residence there. She could look at it, she said, in the night, especially in the moonshine. Her room was clean, but very, very bare. I noticed the scantiest necessaries in the way of furniture; a few old prints from books, of Chancellors and barristers, wafered against the wall; and some half-dozen reticules and work-bags, "containing documents," as she informed us. There were neither coals nor ashes in the grate, and I saw no articles of clothing anywhere, nor any kind of food. There was a more affecting meaning in her pinched appearance, I thought as I looked round, than I had understood before.

"Extremely honoured, I am sure," said our poor hostess, with the greatest suavity, "by this visit from the wards in Jarndyce. And very much indebted for the omen. I am limited as to situation. In consequence of the necessity of attending on the Chancellor. I have lived here many years. I pass my days in Court, my evenings and my nights here. I find the nights long, for I sleep but little, and think much. That is, of course, unavoidable, being in Chancery. I am sorry I cannot offer chocolate. I expect a judgment shortly, and shall then place my establishment on a superior footing. At present, I don't mind confessing to the wards in Jarndyce (in strict confidence) that I sometimes find it difficult to keep up a genteel appearance. I have felt the cold here. It matters very little. Pray excuse the introduction of such mean topics."

She partly drew aside the curtain of the long low garret-window, and called our attention to a number of bird-cages hanging there, some containing several birds. There were larks, linnets, and goldfinches —I should think at least twenty.

"I began to keep the little creatures," she said, "with an object that the wards will readily comprehend. With the intention of restoring them to liberty. When my judgment should be given. Ye-es! They die in prison, though. Their lives, poor silly things, are so short in comparison with Chancery proceedings that, one by one, the whole collection has died over and over again. I doubt, do you know, whether one of these, though they are all young, will live to be free! Ve-ry mortifying, is it not?" Although she sometimes asked a question, she never seemed to expect a reply, but rambled on as if she were in the habit of doing so when no one but herself was present. "Indeed," she pursued, "I positively doubt sometimes, I do assure you, whether while matters are still unsettled, and the Sixth or Great Seal still prevails, I may not one day be found lying stark and senseless here, as I have found so many birds!"

Richard, answering what he saw in Ada's compassionate eyes, took the opportunity of laying some money, softly and unobserved, on the chimney-piece. We all drew nearer to the cages, feigning to examine the birds.

"I can't allow them to sing much," said the little old lady, "for (you'll think this curious) I find my mind confused by the idea that they are singing while I am following the arguments in Court. And my mind requires to be so very clear, you know! Another time, I'll tell you their names. Not at present. On a day of such good omen, they shall sing as much as they like. In honour of youth"—a smile and curtsey— "hope"—a smile and curtsey—"and beauty"—a smile and curtsey. "There! We'll let in the full light."

The birds began to stir and chirp.

"I cannot admit the air freely," said the little old lady—the room was close and would have been the better for it—"because the cat you saw downstairs—called Lady Jane—is greedy for their lives. She crouches on the parapet outside for hours and hours. I have discovered," whispering mysteriously, "that her natural cruelty is sharpened by a jealous fear of their regaining their liberty. In consequence of the judgment I expect being shortly given. She is sly, and full of malice."

Some neighbouring bells, reminding the poor soul that it was half-past nine, did more for us in the way of bringing our visit to an end than we could easily have done for ourselves. She hurriedly took up her little bag of documents, which she had laid upon the table on coming in, and asked if we were also going into Court. On our answering no, and that we would on no account detain her, she opened the door to attend us downstairs.

"With such an omen, it is even more necessary than usual that I should be there before the Chancellor comes in," said she, "for he might mention my case the first thing. I have a presentiment that he *will* mention it the first thing this morning."

She stopped to tell us in a whisper, as we were going down, that the whole house was filled with strange lumber which her landlord had bought piecemeal, and had no wish to sell, in consequence of being a little—M—. This was on the first floor. But she had made a previous stoppage on the second floor, and had silently pointed at a dark door there.

"The only other lodger," she now whispered, in explanation, "a law-writer. The children in the lanes here say he has sold himself to the Devil. I don't know what he can have done with the money. Hush!"

She appeared to mistrust that the lodger might hear her, even there, and repeating "Hush!" went before us on tiptoe, as though even the sound of her footsteps might reveal to him what she had said. Passing through the shop on our way out, as we had passed through it on our way in, we found the old man storing a quantity of packets of waste paper in a kind of well in the floor. He seemed to be working hard, and had a piece of chalk by him, with which, as he put each separate package or bundle down, he made a crooked mark on the panelling of the wall.

Richard and Ada, and Miss Jellyby, and the little old lady had gone by him, and I was going, when he touched me on the arm and chalked the letter *J* upon the wall—in a very curious manner, beginning with the end of the letter, and shaping it backward. It was a capital letter, not a printed one, but just such a letter as any clerk in Messrs. Kenge and Carboy's office would have made.

"Can you read it?" he asked me with a keen glance.

"Surely," said I. "It's very plain."

"What it is?"

"J."

With another glance at me, and a glance at the door, he rubbed it out and turned an *a* in its place (not a capital letter this time), and said, "What's that?"

I told him. He then rubbed that out, and turned the letter *r*, and asked me the same question. He went on quickly until he had formed in the same curious manner, the word Jarndyce, without leaving two letters on the wall together.

"What does that spell?" he asked me.

When I told him, he laughed. In the same odd way, yet with the same rapidity, he then produced singly, and rubbed out singly, the letters forming the words Bleak House. These, in some astonishment, I also read, and he laughed again.

"Hi!" said the old man, laying aside the chalk, "I have a turn for copying from memory, you see, miss, though I can neither read nor write."

He looked so disagreeable, and his cat looked so wickedly at me, as if I were a blood-relation of the birds upstairs, that I was quite relieved by Richard's appearing at the door and saying:

"Miss Summerson, I hope you are not bargaining for the sale of your hair. Three sacks below are quite enough for Mr. Krook!"

I lost no time in wishing Mr. Krook good morning and joining my friends outside, where we parted with the little old lady, who gave us her blessing with great ceremony, and renewed her assurance of yesterday in reference to her intention of settling estates on Ada and me. Before we finally turned out of those lanes, we looked back and saw Mr. Krook standing at his shop-door, in his spectacles, looking after us, with his cat upon his shoulder.

"Quite an adventure for a morning in London!" said Richard, with a sigh. "Ah, Cousin, Cousin, it's a weary word, this Chancery!"

"It is to me, and has been ever since I can remember," returned Ada. "I am grieved that I should be the enemy—as I suppose I am—of a great number of relations and others; and that they should be my enemies—as I suppose they are; and that we should all be ruining one another, without knowing how or why, and be in constant doubt and discord all our lives. It seems very strange, as there must be right somewhere, that an honest judge in real earnest has not been able to find out through all these years where it is."

"Ah, Cousin!" said Richard. "Strange, indeed! All this wasteful wanton chess-playing *is* very strange. To see that composed Court yesterday jogging on so serenely, and to think of the wretchedness of the pieces on the board, gave me the headache and the heartache both together. My head ached with wondering how it happened, if men were neither fools nor rascals; and my heart ached to think they could possibly be either. But at all events, Ada—I may call you Ada?"

"Of course you may, Cousin Richard."

"At all events, Chancery will work none of its bad influences on *us*. We have happily been brought together, thanks to our good kinsman, and it can't divide us now!"

"Never, I hope, Cousin Richard!" said Ada gently.

In half an hour after our arrival, Mrs. Jellyby appeared, and in the course of an hour the various things necessary for breakfast straggled one by one into the dining-room. I do not doubt that Mrs. Jellyby had gone to bed and got up in the usual manner, but she presented no appearance of having changed her dress. She was greatly occupied during breakfast, for the morning's post brought a heavy correspondence relative to Borrioboola-Gha. The children tumbled about, and notched memoranda of their accidents in their legs, which were perfect little calendars of distress.

At one o'clock an open carriage arrived for us, and a cart for our luggage. Mrs. Jellyby charged us with many remembrances to her good friend Mr. Jarndyce; Caddy left her desk to see us depart, kissed me in the passage, and stood, biting her pen and sobbing, on the steps. Peepy, I am happy to say, was asleep; all the other children got up behind the barouche and fell off, and we saw them with great concern, scattered over the surface of Thavies Inn, as we rolled out of its precincts.

## CHAPTER 6

*Quite at Home*

THE day had brightened very much, and still brightened as we went westward. We went our way through the sunshine and the fresh air, wondering more and more at the extent of the streets, the brilliancy of the shops, the great traffic, and the crowds of people whom the pleasanter weather seemed to have brought out like many-coloured flowers. By and by we began to leave the wonderful city, and to proceed through suburbs, and at last we got into a real country road again, with windmills, rick-yards, milestones, farmers' waggons, scents of old hay, swinging signs, and horse troughs, trees, fields, and hedgerows. It was delightful to see the green landscape before us, and the immense metropolis behind. A waggon with a train of beautiful horses came by us.

Said Richard, "Halloa! what's the matter?" We had stopped, and the waggon had stopped too. "Our postillion is looking after the waggoner," said Richard, "and the waggoner is coming back after us. Good-day, friend!" The waggoner was at our coach-door. "Why, here's an extraordinary thing!" added Richard, looking closely at the man. "He has got your name, Ada, in his hat!"

He had all our names in his hat. Tucked within the band were three small notes: one addressed to Ada, one to Richard, one to me. These the waggoner delivered to each of us respectively, reading the name aloud first. In answer to Richard's inquiry from whom they came, he briefly answered, "Master, sir, if you please," and putting on his hat again, cracked his whip and went away.

"Is that Mr. Jarndyce's waggon?" said Richard, calling to our post-boy. "Yes, sir," he replied. "Going to London."

We opened the notes. Each was a counterpart of the other, and contained these words, in a solid, plain hand.

> I look forward, my dear, to our meeting easily, and without constraint on either side. I therefore have to propose that we meet as old friends, and take the past for granted. It will be a relief to you possibly, and to me certainly, and so my love to you.
>
> JOHN JARNDYCE

I had perhaps less reason to be surprised than either of my companions, having never yet enjoyed an opportunity of thanking one who had been my benefactor and sole earthly dependence through so many years. I had not considered how I could thank him, my gratitude lying too deep in my heart for that; but I now began to consider how I could meet him without thanking him, and felt it would be very difficult indeed.

The notes revived in Richard and Ada a general impression that they both had, without quite knowing how they came by it, that their cousin Jarndyce could never bear acknowledgments for any kindness he performed, and that sooner than receive any, he would resort to the most singular expedients and evasions, or would even run away. Ada dimly remembered to have heard her mother tell, when she was a very little child, that he had once done her an act of uncommon generosity, and that on her going to his house to thank him, he happened to see her through a window coming to the door and immediately escaped by the back gate, and was not heard of for three months. This discourse led to a great deal more on the same theme, and indeed it lasted us all day, and we talked of scarcely anything else.

The short day was spent, and the long night had closed in, before we came to Saint Albans, near to which town Bleak House was, we knew. By that time we were so anxious and nervous that even Richard confessed, as we rattled over the stones of the old street, to feeling an irrational desire to drive back again. As to Ada and me, we trembled from head to foot. When we turned out of the town, round a corner, and Richard told us that the post-boy, who had for a long time sympathized with our heightened expectation, was looking back and nodding, we both stood up in the carriage and gazed round upon the open country and the starlight night, for our destination. There was a light sparkling on the top of a hill before us, and the driver, pointing to it with his whip, and crying, "That's Bleak House!" put his horses into a canter, and took us forward at such a rate, uphill though it was, that the wheels sent the road drift flying about our heads like spray from a water-mill. Presently we lost the light, presently saw it, presently lost it, presently saw it, and turned into an avenue of trees and cantered up towards where it was beaming brightly. It was in a window of what seemed to be an old-fashioned house, with three peaks in the roof in front. A bell was rung as we drew up, and amidst the sound of its deep voice in the still air, and the distant barking of some dogs, and a gush of light from the opened door, and the quickened beating of our own hearts, we alighted in no inconsiderable confusion.

"Ada, my love, Esther, my dear, you are welcome. I rejoice to see you! Rick, if I had a hand to spare at present, I would give it you!"

The gentleman who said these words in a clear bright, hospitable voice had one of his arms round Ada's waist and the other round mine, and kissed us both in a fatherly way, and bore us across the hall into a ruddy little room, all in a glow with a blazing fire. Here he kissed us again and, opening his arms, made us sit down side by side on a sofa near the hearth. I felt that if we had been at all demonstrative, he would have run away in a moment.

"Now, Rick," said he, "I have a hand at liberty! A word in earnest is as good as a speech. I am heartily glad to see you. You are at home. Warm yourself!"

Richard shook him by both hands with an intuitive mixture of respect and frankness, and only saying "You are very kind, sir! We are very much obliged to you!" laid aside his hat and coat, and came up to the fire.

"And how did you like the ride? And how did you like Mrs. Jellyby, my dear?" said Mr. Jarndyce to Ada.

While Ada was speaking to him in reply, I glanced (I need not say with how much interest) at his face. It was a handsome, lively, quick face, full of change and motion, and his hair was a silvered iron-grey. I took him to be nearer sixty than fifty, but he was upright, hearty, and robust. From the moment of his first speaking to us, his voice had connected itself with an association in my mind that I could not define; but now, all at once, a something sudden in his manner, and a pleasant expression in his eyes, recalled the gentleman in the stage-coach, six years ago, on the memorable day of my journey to Reading. I was certain it was he. I never was so frightened in my life as when I made the discovery, for he caught my glance, and appearing to read my thoughts, gave such a look at the door that I thought we had lost him.

However, I am happy to say he remained where he was, and asked me what I thought of Mrs. Jellyby.

"She exerts herself very much for Africa, sir," I said.

"Nobly!" returned Mr. Jarndyce. "But you answer like Ada." Whom I had not heard. "You all think something else, I see."

"We rather thought," said I, glancing at Richard and Ada, who entreated me with their eyes to speak, "that perhaps she was a little unmindful of her home."

"Floored!" cried Mr. Jarndyce. I was rather alarmed again. "Well! I want to know your real thoughts, my dear. I may have sent you there on purpose."

"We thought that perhaps," said I, hesitating, "it is right to begin with the obligations of home, sir; and that, perhaps while those are overlooked and neglected, no other duties can possibly be substituted for them."

"The little Jellybys," said Richard, coming to my relief, "are really—I can't help expressing myself strongly, sir—in a devil of a state."

"She means well," said Mr. Jarndyce, hastily. "The wind's in the east."

"It was in the north, sir, as we came down," observed Richard.

"My dear Rick," said Mr. Jarndyce, poking the fire, "I'll take an oath it's either in the east, or going to be. I am always conscious of an uncomfortable sensation now and then when the wind is blowing in the east."

"Rheumatism, sir?" said Richard.

"I dare say it is, Rick. I believe it is. And so the little Jell—I had my doubts about 'em—are in a—oh Lord, yes, it's easterly!" said Mr. Jarndyce.

He had taken two or three undecided turns up and down while uttering these broken sentences, retaining the poker in one hand and rubbing his hair with the other, with a good-natured vexation, at once so whimsical and so lovable that I am sure we were more delighted with him than we could possibly have expressed in any words. He gave an arm to Ada and an arm to me, and bidding Richard bring a candle, was leading the way out, when he suddenly turned us all back again.

"Those little Jellybys. Couldn't you—didn't you—now, if it had rained sugar-plums, or three-cornered raspberry tarts, or anything of that sort!" said Mr. Jarndyce.

"Oh Cousin—!" Ada hastily began.

"Good, my pretty pet. I like 'Cousin.' Cousin John perhaps is better."

"Then Cousin John!—" Ada laughingly began again.

"Ha, ha! Very good indeed!" said Mr. Jarndyce, with great enjoyment. "Sounds uncommonly natural. Yes, my dear?"

"It did better than that. It rained Esther."

"Ay?" said Mr. Jarndyce. "What did Esther do?"

"Why, Cousin John," said Ada, clasping her hands upon his arm, "Esther was their friend directly. Esther nursed them, coaxed them to sleep, washed and dressed them, told them stories, kept them quiet, bought them keepsakes"—My dear girl! I had only gone out with Peepy, after he was found, and given him a little, tiny horse!—"and, Cousin John, she softened poor Caroline, the eldest one, so much, and was so thoughtful for me and so amiable!—No, no, I won't be contradicted, Esther dear! You know, you know it's true!"

The warm-hearted darling leaned across her cousin John and kissed me, and then, looking up in his face, boldly said, "At all events, Cousin John, I *will* thank you for the companion you have given me." I felt as if she challenged him to run away. But he didn't.

"Where did you say the wind was, Rick?" asked Mr. Jarndyce.

"In the north as we came down, sir."

"You are right. There's no east in it. A mistake of mine. Come, girls, come and see your home!"

It was one of those delightfully irregular houses where you go up and down steps out of one room into another, and where you come upon more rooms when you think you have seen all there are, and where you find still older cottage-rooms in unexpected places, with lattice windows and green growth pressing through them. Mine, which we entered first, was of this kind, with an up-and-down roof that had more corners in it than I ever counted afterwards, and a chimney (there was a wood-fire on the hearth) paved all around with pure-white tiles. Out of this room, you went down two steps into a charming little sitting-room, looking down upon a flower-garden, which room was henceforth to belong to Ada and me. Out of this you went up three steps into Ada's bedroom, which had a fine broad window, commanding a beautiful view, to which there was a hollow window-seat. Out of this room you passed into a little gallery, with which the other best rooms (only two) communicated, and so, by a little staircase of shallow steps, down into the hall. But if instead of going out at Ada's door you came back into my room, and went out at the door by which you had entered and turned up a few crooked steps that branched off from the stairs, you lost yourself in passages with mangles in them, and three-cornered tables. From these, you came on Richard's room, which was part library, part sitting-room, part bedroom. Out of that, you went straight to the plain room where Mr. Jarndyce slept all the year round, with his window open. Out of that, you came into another passage, where there were backstairs, and where you could hear the horses being rubbed down, outside the stable.

The furniture, old-fashioned rather than old, like the house, was as pleasantly irregular. Ada's sleeping-room was all flowers—in chintz and paper, in velvet, in needlework, in the brocade of two stiff courtly chairs, which stood, each attended by a little page of a stool for greater state, on either side of the fire-place. Our sitting-room was green, and had, framed and glazed, upon the wall numbers of surprising and sur-prised birds, staring out of pictures, at the death of Captain Cook, and at the whole process of preparing tea in China, as depicted by Chinese artists. In my room there were oval engravings of the months—ladies hay-making for June, smooth-legged noblemen pointing to village steeples for October. All the movables, from the wardrobes to the chairs and tables, hangings, glasses, even to the pin-cushions and scent-bottles on the dressing-tables, displayed the same quaint variety. They agreed in nothing but their perfect neatness, their display of the whitest linen, and their storing-up, wheresoever the existence of a drawer, small or large, rendered it possible, of quantities of rose-leaves and sweet lavender. Such were our first impressions of Bleak House.

"I am glad you like it," said Mr. Jarndyce, when he had brought us round again to Ada's sitting-room. "It makes no pretensions; but it is a comfortable little place, I hope, and will be more so with such bright young looks in it. You have barely half an hour before dinner. There's no one here but the finest creature upon earth—a child."

"More children, Esther!" said Ada.

"I don't mean literally a child," pursued Mr. Jarndyce—"not a child in years. He is grown-up—he is at least as old as I am—but in simplicity, and freshness, and enthusiasm, and a fine guileless inaptitude for all worldly affairs, he is a perfect child."

We felt that he must be very interesting.

"He knows Mrs. Jellyby," said Mr. Jarndyce. "He is a man of attain-ments and of captivating manners. He has been unfortunate in his affairs, and unfortunate in his pursuits, and unfortunate in his family; but he don't care—he's a child!"

"Did you imply that he has children of his own, sir?" inquired Richard.

"Yes, Rick! Half a dozen. More! Nearer a dozen, I should think. But he has never looked after them. How could he? He wanted somebody to look after *him*. He is a child, you know!" said Mr. Jarndyce. "Harold Skimpole's children have tumbled up somehow or other.—The wind's getting round again, I am afraid. I feel it rather!"

Richard observed that the situation was exposed on a sharp night.

"It *is* exposed," said Mr. Jarndyce. "No doubt that's the cause. Bleak House has an exposed sound."

Our luggage having arrived, and being all at hand, I was dressed in a few minutes, and engaged in putting my worldly goods away, when a maid brought a basket into my room, with two bunches of keys in it, all labelled.

"For you, miss, if you please," said she.

"For me?" said I.

"The housekeeping keys, miss."

I showed my surprise, for she added with some little surprise on her own part, "I was told to bring them as soon as you was alone, miss. Miss Summerson, if I don't deceive myself?"

"Yes," said I. "That is my name."

"The large bunch is the housekeeping, and the little bunch is the cellars, miss. Any time you was pleased to appoint tomorrow morning, I was to show you the presses and things they belong to."

I said I would be ready at half-past six and after she was gone, stood looking at the basket, quite lost in the magnitude of my trust. Ada found me thus, and had such a delightful confidence in me when I showed her the keys and told her about them, that it would have been insensibility and ingratitude not to feel encouraged. I knew, to be sure, that it was the dear girl's kindness; but I liked to be so pleasantly cheated.

When we went downstairs, we were presented to Mr. Skimpole, who was standing before the fire, telling Richard how fond he used to be, in his school-time, of football. He was a little bright creature, with a rather large head but a delicate face, and a sweet voice, and there was a perfect charm in him. All he said was so free from effort and spontaneous, and was said with such a captivating gaiety, that it was fascinating to hear him talk.

I gathered from the conversation that Mr. Skimpole had been educated for the medical profession, and had once lived, in his professional capacity, in the household of a German prince. He told us, however, that as he had always been a mere child in point of weights and measures, and had never known anything about them, he had never been able to prescribe with the requisite accuracy of detail. The prince at last objecting to this, the engagement terminated, and Mr. Skimpole having (as he added with delightful gaiety) "nothing to live upon but love, fell in love, and married, and surrounded himself with rosy cheeks." His good friend Jarndyce and some other of his good friends then helped him, in quicker or slower succession, to several openings in life; but to no purpose, for he must confess to two of the oldest infirmities in the world: one was that he had no idea of time, the other, that he had no idea of money. In consequence of which he never kept an appointment, never could transact any business, and never knew the value of anything! Well! So he had got on in life, and here he was! He was very fond of reading the papers, very fond of making fancy sketches with a pencil, very fond of nature, very fond of art. All he asked of society was to let him live. *That* wasn't much. His wants were few.

All this, and a great deal more, he told us, not only with the utmost brilliancy and enjoyment, but with a certain vivacious candour. He was quite enchanting. If I felt at all confused at that early time, in endeavouring to reconcile anything he said with anything I had thought about the duties and accountabilities of life, I was confused by not exactly understanding why he was free of them. That he *was* free of them, I scarcely doubted; he was so very clear about it himself.

"I covet nothing," said Mr. Skimpole, in the same light way. "Possession is nothing to me. It's only you, the generous creatures, whom I envy," said Mr. Skimpole addressing us, his new friends, in an impersonal manner. "I envy you your power of doing what you do. It is what I should revel in, myself. I don't feel any vulgar gratitude to you. I almost feel as if *you* ought to be grateful to *me* for giving you the opportunity of enjoying the luxury of generosity. I know you like it. For anything I can tell, I may have come into the world expressly for the purpose of increasing your stock of happiness."

Mr. Jarndyce patted him on the head with a smile, as if he had been really a child; and passing a step or two on, and stopping a moment, glanced at the young cousins. His look was thoughtful, but had a benignant expression in it which I often (how often!) saw again. The room in which they were, communicating with that in which he stood, was only lighted by the fire. Ada sat at the piano; Richard stood beside her, bending down. Ada touched the notes so softly, and sang so low, that the wind, sighing away to the distant hills, was as audible as the music. Though Mr. Jarndyce's glance, as he withdrew it, rested for but a moment on me, I felt as if in that moment he confided to me his hope that Ada and Richard might one day enter on a dearer relationship.

After a little while I missed, first Mr. Skimpole, and afterwards Richard; and while I was thinking how could Richard stay away so long and lose so much, the maid who had given me the keys looked in at the door, saying, "If you please, miss, could you spare a minute?"

When I was out in the hall, she said, holding up her hands, "Oh if you please, miss, Mr. Carstone says would you come upstairs to Mr. Skimpole's room. He has been took, miss! Sudden."

I followed her quickly upstairs. She threw open a door, and I went into a chamber where, to my unspeakable surprise, instead of finding Mr. Skimpole stretched upon the bed, I found him standing before the fire smiling at Richard, while Richard, with a face of great embarrassment, looked at a person on the sofa, in a white greatcoat, with smooth hair upon his head and not much of it.

"Miss Summerson," said Richard, hurriedly, "I am glad you are come. You will be able to adivse us. Our friend Mr. Skimpole—don't be alarmed!—is arrested for debt."

"Are you arrested for much, sir?" I inquired of Mr. Skimpole.

"My dear Miss Summerson," said he, shaking his head pleasantly, "I don't know. Some pounds, odd shillings, and half pence, I think, were mentioned."

"It's twenty-four pound, sixteen, and seven pence ha'penny," observed the stranger. "That's wot it is."

"And somehow it sounds," said Mr. Skimpole, "like a small sum?"

"Mr. Skimpole," said Richard to me, "has a delicacy in applying to my cousin Jarndyce, because he has lately—I think, sir, I understood you that you had lately—"

"Oh yes!" returned Mr. Skimpole, smiling. "Though I forgot how much it was, and when it was."

"What do you think will be best, Miss Summerson?" said Richard, aside.

I ventured to inquire, generally, before replying, what would happen if the money were not produced.

"Jail," said the strange man, coolly putting his handkerchief into his hat, which was on the floor at his feet. "Or Coavinses."

"May I ask, sir, what is—"

"Coavinses?" said the strange man. "A 'ouse."

Richard and I looked at one another again. It was a most singular thing that the arrest was our embarrassment, and not Mr. Skimpole's. He observed us with a genial interest; but there seemed, if I may venture on such a contradiction, nothing selfish in it. He had entirely washed his hands of the difficulty, and it had become ours.

"I thought," he suggested, as if good-naturedly to help us out, "that being parties in a Chancery suit concerning (as people say) a large amount of property, Mr. Richard or his beautiful cousin, or both, could sign something, or make over something, or give some sort of undertaking, or pledge, or bond?"

"Not a bit on it," said the strange man.

"Really? Now, my dear Miss Summerson, and my dear Mr. Richard," said Mr. Skimpole, gaily, innocently, and confidingly, "here you see me utterly incapable of helping myself, and entirely in your hands! I only ask to be free. The butterflies are free. Mankind will surely not deny to Harold Skimpole what it concedes to the butterflies!"

"My dear Miss Summerson," said Richard, in a whisper, "I have ten pounds that I received from Mr. Kenge. I must try what that will do."

I possessed fifteen pounds odd shillings, which I had saved from my quarterly allowance during several years. I had always tried to keep some little money by me, that I might not be quite penniless. I told Richard of my having this little store, and having no present need of it; and I asked him delicately to inform Mr. Skimpole, while I should be gone to fetch it, that we would have the pleasure of paying his debt.

When I came back, Mr. Skimpole kissed my hand, and seemed quite touched. Not on his own account (I was again aware of that perplexing and extraordinary contradiction), but on ours. Richard begging me to settle with Coavinses (as Mr. Skimpole now jocularly called him), I counted out the money and received the necessary acknowledgment.

The stranger put the money in his pocket, and shortly said, "Well, then, I'll wish you a good-evening, miss."

As our absence had been long enough already to seem strange down-stairs, I returned at once, and found Ada sitting at work by the fireside talking to her cousin John. Mr. Skimpole presently appeared, and Rich-ard shortly after him. It was late before we separated, for when Ada was going at eleven o'clock, Mr. Skimpole went to the piano and rattled, hilariously, that the best of all ways to lengthen our days was to steal a few hours from Night, my dear! It was past twelve before he took his candle and his radiant face out of the room. Ada and Richard were lingering for a few moments by the fire when Mr. Jarndyce, who had been out of the room, returned.

"Oh dear me, what's this, what's this!" he said, rubbing his head and walking about with his good-humoured vexation. "What's this they tell me? Rick, my boy, Esther, my dear, what have you been doing? Why did you do it? How could you do it? How much apiece was it?—The wind's round again. I feel it all over me!"

We neither of us quite knew what to answer.

"Come, Rick, come! I must settle this before I sleep. How much are you out of pocket? You two made the money up, you know! Why did you? How could you?—Oh, Lord, yes, it's due east—must be!"

"Really, sir," said Richard, "I don't think it would be honourable in me to tell you. Mr. Skimpole relied upon us—"

"Lord bless you, my dear boy! He relies upon everybody!" said Mr. Jarndyce, giving his head a great rub, and stopping short. "And he'll be in the same scrape again next week!" said Mr. Jarndyce, walking again at a great pace, with a candle in his hand that had gone out. "He's always in the same scrape. He was born in the same scrape."

I ventured to take this opportunity of hinting that Mr. Skimpole, being in all such matters quite a child, "and so different from other people—"

"You are right!" said Mr. Jarndyce, brightening. "He is a child—an absolute child. However, Rick, Esther, and you too, Ada, I must have a promise all round that nothing of this sort shall ever be done any more. No advances! Not even sixpences."

We all promised faithfully, Richard, with a merry glance at me, touching his pocket, as if to remind me that there was no danger of *our* transgressing.

"As to Skimpole," said Mr. Jarndyce, "he is in a child's sleep by this time, I suppose; it's time I should take my craftier head to my more worldly pillow. Good-night, my dears. God bless you!"

He peeped in again, with a smiling face, before we had lighted our candles, and said, "Oh! I have been looking at the weathercock. I find it was a false alarm about the wind. It's in the south!" And went away singing to himself.

# CHAPTER 7

~~~~~~~~~~~~~~~~~~~~~~~~~~~~~~~~~~~~~~~~~~~~~~

## *The Ghost's Walk*

IT is still wet weather down at the place in Lincolnshire. The rain is ever falling, drip, drip, drip, by day and night, upon the broad flagged terrace-pavement, The Ghost's Walk. The weather is so very bad, that the liveliest imagination can scarcely apprehend its ever being fine again. Not that there is any superabundant life of imagination on the spot, for Sir Leicester is not here, but is in Paris, with my Lady; and solitude sits brooding upon Chesney Wold.

There may be some motions of fancy among the lower animals at Chesney Wold. The horses in the stables may contemplate some mental pictures of fine weather on occasions, and may be better artists at them than the grooms. So with the dogs in the kennel-buildings across the park, who have their restless fits, and whose doleful voices, when the wind has been very obstinate, have even made it known in the house itself: upstairs, downstairs, and in my lady's chamber. They may hunt the whole country-side while the raindrops are pattering round their inactivity.

It has rained so hard and rained so long, down in Lincolnshire, that Mrs. Rouncewell, the old housekeeper at Chesney Wold, has several times taken off her spectacles and cleaned them, to make certain that the drops were not upon the glasses. She is rather deaf, which nothing will induce her to believe. She is a fine old lady, handsome, stately, wonderfully neat, and has such a back and such a stomacher, that if her stays should turn out when she dies to have been a broad old-fashioned family fire-grate, nobody who knows her would have cause to be surprised. Weather affects Mrs. Rouncewell little. The house is there in all weathers, and the house, as she expresses it, "is what she looks at." She sits in her room and the whole house reposes on her mind. It is shut up now, and lies on the breadth of Mrs. Rouncewell's iron-bound bosom, in a majestic sleep.

The present representative of the Dedlocks is an excellent master. He supposes all his dependents to be utterly bereft of individual characters, intentions, or opinions, and is persuaded that he was born to supersede the necessity of their having any. If he were to make a discovery to the contrary, he would be simply stunned—would never recover himself, most likely, except to gasp and die. But he is an excellent master still, holding it a part of his state to be so. He has a great liking for Mrs. Rouncewell; he says she is a most respectable, creditable woman. He always shakes hands with her when he comes down to Chesney Wold, and when he goes away; and if he were very ill, or if he were knocked down by accident, or run over, or placed in any situation expressive of a Dedlock at a disadvantage, he would say if he could speak, "Leave me, and send Mrs. Rouncewell here!" feeling his dignity, at such a pass, safer with her than with anybody else.

Mrs. Rouncewell has known trouble. She has had two sons, of whom the younger ran wild, and went for a soldier, and never came back. Even to this hour, Mrs. Rouncewell's calm hands lose their composure when she speaks of him, as she says what a likely lad, what a fine lad, what a gay, good-humoured, clever lad he was! Her second son would have been provided for at Chesney Wold, and would have been made steward in due season; but he took, when he was a schoolboy, to constructing steam-engines out of saucepans, and setting birds to draw their own water. This propensity gave Mrs. Rouncewell great uneasiness. But the doomed young rebel (otherwise a mild youth, and very persevering), showing no sign of grace as he got older, but, on the contrary, constructing a model of a power-loom, she was fain, with many tears, to mention his backslidings to the baronet. "Mrs. Rouncewell," said Sir Leicester, "I can never consent to argue, as you know, with any one on any subject. You had better get rid of your boy, you had better get him into some Works. The iron country farther north is, I suppose, the congenial direction for a boy with these tendencies." Farther north he went, and farther north he grew up; and if Sir Leicester Dedlock ever thought of him afterwards, it is certain that he only regarded him as one of a body of some odd thousand conspirators, swarthy and grim, who were in the habit of turning out by torchlight, two or three nights in the week, for unlawful purposes.

Nevertheless Mrs. Rouncewell's son has, in the course of nature and art, grown up, and established himself, and married, and called unto him Mrs. Rouncewell's grandson, who stands leaning against the chimney-piece this very day, in Mrs. Rouncewell's room at Chesney Wold.

"And, again and again, I am glad to see you, Watt!" says Mrs. Rouncewell. "You are a fine young fellow. You are like your poor uncle George.

Ah!" Mrs. Rouncewell's hands unquiet, as usual, on this reference.

"They say I am like my father, Grandmother."

"Like him, also, my dear—but most like your poor uncle George! And your dear father." Mrs. Rouncewell folds her hands again. "He is well?"

"Thriving, Grandmother, in every way."

"He is quite happy?" says she.

"Quite."

"I am thankful! So he has brought you up to follow in his ways? Well, he knows best. There may be a world beyond Chesney Wold that I don't understand. Though I am not young, either. And I have seen a quantity of good company, too!"

"Grandmother," says the young man, changing the subject, "what a very pretty girl that was I found with you just now. You called her Rosa?"

"Yes, child. She is daughter of a widow in the village. Maids are so hard to teach nowadays that I have put her about me young. She's an apt scholar, and will do well. She shows the house already, very pretty. She lives with me at my table here."

"I hope I have not driven her away?"

"She supposes we have family affairs to speak about, I dare say. She is very modest. It is a fine quality in a young woman. And scarcer," says Mrs. Rouncewell, "than it formerly was!"

The young man inclines his head, in acknowledgment of the precepts of experience. Mrs. Rouncewell listens.

"Wheels!" says she. They have long been audible to the younger ears of her companion. "What wheels on such a day as this, for gracious sake?"

After a short interval a tap at the door. "Come in!" A dark-eyed, dark-haired, shy village beauty comes in—so fresh in her rosy and yet delicate bloom that the drops of rain which have beaten on her hair look like the dew upon a flower fresh-gathered.

"What company is this, Rosa?" says Mrs. Rouncewell.

"It's two young men in a gig, ma'am, who want to see the house—and if you please, I told them so!" in reply to a gesture of dissent from the housekeeper. "I told them it was the wrong day, and the wrong hour; but the young man who was driving took off his hat, and begged me to bring this card to you."

"Read it, my dear Watt," says the housekeeper.

"Mr. Guppy" is all the information the card yields.

"Guppy!" repeats Mrs. Rouncewell. "*Mr.* Guppy! Nonsense, I never heard of him!"

"If you please, he told *me* that!" says Rosa. "But he said that he and the other young gentleman came from London only last night by the mail, on business at the magistrates' meeting, ten miles off, this morning; and that as their business was soon over, and they had heard a great deal said of Chesney Wold, they had come through the wet to see it. They are lawyers. He says he is not in Mr. Tulkinghorn's office, but he is sure he may make use of Mr. Tulkinghorn's name, if necessary."

Now Mr. Tulkinghorn is, in a manner, part and parcel of the place and, besides, is supposed to have made Mrs. Rouncewell's will. The old lady relaxes, consents to the admission of the visitors as a favour, and dismisses Rosa. The grandson, however, being smitten by a sudden wish to see the house himself, proposes to join the party. The grandmother accompanies him—though to do him justice, he is exceedingly unwilling to trouble her.

"Much obliged to you, ma'am!" says Mr. Guppy, divesting himself of his wet dreadnought in the hall. "Us London lawyers don't often get an out, and when we do, we like to make the most of it, you know."

The old housekeeper, with a gracious severity of deportment, waves her hand towards the great staircase. Mr. Guppy and his friend follow Rosa, Mrs. Rouncewell and her grandson follow them, a young gardener goes before to open the shutters.

As is usually the case with people who go over houses, Mr. Guppy and his friend are dead-beat before they have well begun. They straggle about in wrong places, look at wrong things, don't care for right things, gape when more rooms are opened, exhibit profound depression of spirits, and are clearly knocked-up. Thus they pass on from room to room, raising the pictured Dedlocks for a few brief minutes as the young gardener admits the light, and reconsigning them to their graves as he shuts it out again. It appears to the afflicted Mr. Guppy and his inconsolable friend, that there is no end to the Dedlocks, whose family greatness seems to consist in their never having done anything to distinguish themselves, for seven hundred years.

Even the long drawing-room of Chesney Wold cannot revive Mr. Guppy's spirits. He is so low that he droops on the threshold, and has hardly strength of mind to enter. But a portrait over the chimney-piece, painted by the fashionable artist of the day, acts upon him like a charm. He recovers in a moment. He stares at it with uncommon interest; he seems to be fixed and fascinated by it.

"Dear me!" says Mr. Guppy. "Who's that?"

"The picture over the fire-place," says Rosa, "is the portrait of the present Lady Dedlock. It is considered a perfect likeness, and the best work of the master."

" 'Blest," says Mr. Guppy, staring in a kind of dismay at his friend, "if I can ever have seen her! Yet I know her! Has the picture been engraved, miss?"

"The picture has never been engraved. Sir Leicester has always refused permission."

"Well!" says Mr. Guppy in a low voice, "I'll be shot if it ain't very curious how well I know that picture! So that's Lady Dedlock, is it! It's unaccountable to me," he says, still staring at the portrait, "how well I know that picture! I'm dashed!" adds Mr. Guppy, looking round, "if I don't think I must have had a dream of that picture, you know!"

As no one present takes any especial interest in Mr. Guppy's dreams, the probability is not pursued. But he still remains so absorbed by the portrait that he stands immovable before it until the young gardener has closed the shutters, when he comes out of the room in a dazed state and follows into the succeeding rooms with a confused stare as if he were looking everywhere for Lady Dedlock again. He sees no more of her. He sees her rooms, which are the last shown, as being very elegant, and he looks out of the windows from which she looked out, not long ago, upon the weather that bored her to death. He has come to the end of the sight, and the fresh village beauty to the end of her description, which is always this:

"The terrace below is much admired. It is called, from an old story in the family, the Ghost's Walk."

"No?" says Mr. Guppy, greedily curious. "What's the story, miss? Is it anything about a picture?"

"I don't know it, sir." Rosa is shyer than ever.

"It is not related to visitors; it is almost forgotten," says the house-keeper, advancing. "It has never been more than a family anecdote."

"You'll excuse my asking again if it has anything to do with a picture, ma'am," observes Mr. Guppy, "because I do assure you that the more I think of that picture, the better I know it, without knowing how I know it!"

The story has nothing to do with a picture; the housekeeper can guar-antee that. Mr. Guppy retires with his friend, and presently is heard to drive away. It is now dusk. Mrs. Rouncewell can trust to the discretion of her two young hearers, and may tell *them* how the terrace came to have that ghostly name. She seats herself in a large chair by the fast-darkening window, and tells them:

"In the wicked days, my dears, of King Charles the First—I mean, of course, in the wicked days of the rebels who leagued themselves against that excellent king—Sir Morbury Dedlock was the owner of Chesney Wold. Whether there was any account of a ghost in the family before those days, I can't say."

"Sir Morbury Dedlock," says Mrs. Rouncewell, "was, I have no occa-sion to say, on the side of the blessed martyr. But it *is* supposed that his lady, who had none of the family blood in her veins, favoured the bad cause. It is said that she had relations among King Charles's enemies, and that she gave them information. When any of the country gentle-men who followed His Majesty's cause met here, it is said that my lady was always nearer to the door of their council-room than they supposed. Do you hear a sound like a footstep passing along the terrace, Watt?"

Rosa draws nearer to the housekeeper.

"I hear the rain-drip on the stones," replies the young man, "and I hear a curious echo—I suppose an echo—which is very like a halting step."

The housekeeper gravely nods and continues:

"Partly on account of this division between them, and partly on other accounts, Sir Morbury and his lady led a troubled life. She was a lady of a haughty temper. They were not well suited to each other in age or character, and they had no children to moderate between them. After her favourite brother, a young gentleman, was killed in the civil wars by Sir Morbury's near kinsman her feeling was so violent that she hated the race into which she had married. When the Dedlocks were about to ride out from Chesney Wold in the King's cause, she is supposed to have more than once stolen down into the stables in the dead of night and lamed their horses; and the story is that once her husband saw her gliding down the stairs and followed her into the stall where his own favourite horse stood. There he seized her by the wrist, and in a struggle or in a fall she was lamed in the hip, and from that hour began to pine away."

The housekeeper has dropped her voice to a little more than a whisper.

"She had been a lady of a handsome figure and a noble carriage. She never complained of the change; she never spoke to any one of being crippled, or of being in pain; but, day by day, she tried to walk upon the terrace, and with the help of the stone balustrade went up and down, up and down, up and down, in sun and shadow, with greater difficulty every day. At last, one afternoon her husband (to whom she had never, on any persuasion, opened her lips since that night), standing at the great south window, saw her drop upon the pavement. He hastened down to raise her, but she repulsed him as he bent over her, and looking at him fixedly and coldly, said, 'I will die here where I have walked. And I will walk here though I am in my grave. I will walk here until the pride of this house is humbled. And when calamity or when disgrace is coming to it, let the Dedlocks listen for my step!'

"There and then she died. And from those days," says Mrs. Rouncewell, "the name has come down—the Ghost's Walk. If the tread is an echo, it is an echo that is only heard after dark, and is often unheard for a long while together. But it comes back, from time to time, and so sure as there is sickness or death in the family, it will be heard then."

"—And disgrace, Grandmother—" says Watt.

"Disgrace never comes to Chesney Wold," returns the housekeeper. Her grandson apologizes with "True. True."

"That is the story. Whatever the sound is, it is a worrying sound," says Mrs. Rouncewell, getting up from her chair, "and what is to be noticed in it, is that it *must be heard*. My lady, who is afraid of nothing, admits that when it is there, it must be heard. You cannot shut it out. So my lady says."

# CHAPTER 8

## Covering a Multitude of Sins

IT was interesting when I dressed before daylight, to peep out of window and, finding all beyond still enshrouded in the indistinctness of last night, to watch how it turned out when the day came on. As the prospect gradually revealed itself, I had a pleasure in discovering the unknown objects that had been around me in my sleep. At first they were faintly discernible in the mist, and above them the later stars still glimmered. Imperceptibly, the dark places in my room all melted away, and the day shone bright upon a cheerful landscape, prominent in which the old Abbey Church, with its massive tower, threw a softer train of shadow on the view than seemed compatible with its rugged character.

Every part of the house was in such order, and every one was so attentive to me, that I had no trouble with my two bunches of keys, though what with trying to remember the contents of each little storeroom drawer and cupboard—and what with making notes on a slate about jams, and pickles, and preserves, and bottles, and glass, and china, and a great many other things; and what with being generally a methodical, old-maidish sort of foolish little person—I was so busy that I could not believe it was breakfast-time when I heard the bell ring. Away I ran, however, and made tea, as I had already been installed into the responsibility of the tea-pot; and then, as they were all rather late, and nobody was down yet, I thought I would take a peep at the garden. I found it quite a delightful place; in front, the pretty avenue and drive by which we had approached, at the back, the flower-garden, with my darling at her window up there, throwing it open to smile out at me. Beyond the flower-garden was a kitchen-garden, and then a paddock, and then a snug little rick-yard, and then a dear little farm yard. As to the House itself—with its three peaks in the roof; its various-shaped windows, some so large, some so small, and all so pretty; its trellis-work against the south front for roses and honeysuckle, and its homely, comfortable, welcoming look—it was, as Ada said when she came out to meet me with her arm through that of its master, worthy of her cousin John—a bold thing to say, though he only pinched her dear cheek for it.

My new duties occupied me for some time, and I was passing through the passages on my return with my basket of keys on my arm when Mr. Jarndyce called me into a small room next his bedchamber, which I found to be in part a little library of books and papers, and in part quite a little museum of his boots and shoes, and hat-boxes.

"Sit down, my dear," said Mr. Jarndyce. "This is the Growlery. When I am out of humour, I come and growl here."

"You must be here very seldom, sir," said I.

"Oh, you don't know me!" he returned. "When I am deceived or disappointed in—the wind, and it's easterly, I take refuge here. The Growlery is the best-used room in the house. You are not aware of half my humours yet. My dear, how you are trembling!"

I could not help it; I tried very hard, but being alone with that benevolent presence, and meeting his kind eyes, and feeling so happy, and so honoured there, and my heart so full—

I kissed his hand. I don't know what I said, or even that I spoke. He was disconcerted, and walked to the window, I almost believed with an intention of jumping out until he turned and I was reassured by seeing in his eyes what he had gone there to hide. He gently patted me on the head, and I sat down.

"There! There!" he said. "That's over. Pooh! Don't be foolish."

"It shall not happen again, sir," I returned, "but at first it is difficult—"

"Nonsense," he said, "it's easy, easy! Why not? I hear of a good little orphan girl without a protector, and I take it into my head to be that protector. She grows up, and more than justifies my good opinion, and I remain her guardian and her friend. What is there in all this? So, so! Now we have cleared off old scores, and I have before me thy pleasant, trusting, trusty face again."

I said to myself, "Esther, my dear, you surprise me! This really is not what I expected of you!" and it had such a good effect that I folded my hands upon my basket and quite recovered myself. Mr. Jarndyce, expressing his approval in his face, began to talk to me as confidentially as if I had been in the habit of conversing with him every morning for I don't know how long; I almost felt as if I had.

"Of course, Esther," he said, "you don't understand this Chancery business?" And of course I shook my head. "I don't know who does," he returned. "The lawyers have twisted it into such a state of bedevilment that the original merits of the case have long disappeared from the face of the earth. It's about a Will, and the trusts under a Will—or it was, once. It's about nothing but Costs, now. We are always appearing, and disappearing, and swearing, and interrogating, and filing, and cross-filing, and arguing, and sealing, and motioning, and referring, and reporting, and revolving about the Lord Chancellor and all his satellites, and equitably waltzing ourselves off to dusty death, about Costs. That's the great question. All the rest, by some extraordinary means, has melted away."

"But it was, sir," said I, "about a Will?"

"Why yes, it was about a Will when it was about anything," he returned. "A certain Jarndyce, in an evil hour, made a great fortune, and made a great Will. In the question how the trusts under that Will are to be administered, the fortune left by the Will is squandered away; the legatees under the Will are reduced to such a miserable condition that they would be sufficiently punished if they had committed an enormous crime in having money left them; and the Will itself is made a dead letter. All through the deplorable cause, everything that everybody in it, except one man, knows already is referred to that only one man who don't know it, to find out—all through the deplorable cause, everybody must have copies, over and over again, of everything that has accumulated about it in the way of cartloads of papers, and must go down the middle and up again, through such an infernal country-dance of costs and fees and nonsense and corruption, as was never dreamed of in the wildest visions of a Witch's Sabbath. Equity sends questions to Law, Law sends questions back to Equity. Law finds it can't do this, Equity finds it can't do that; neither can so much as say it can't do anything without this solicitor instructing and this counsel appearing for A, and that solicitor instructing and that counsel appearing for B, and so on through the whole alphabet, like the history of the Apple-Pie. And thus, through years and years, and lives and lives, everything goes on, constantly beginning over and over again, and nothing ever ends. And we can't get out of the suit on any terms, for we are made parties to it, and *must be* parties to it, whether we like it or not. But it won't do to think of it! When my great-uncle, poor Tom Jarndyce, began to think of it, it was the beginning of the end!"

"The Mr. Jarndyce, sir, whose story I have heard?"

He nodded gravely. "I was his heir, and this was his house, Esther. When I came here, it was bleak indeed. He had left the signs of his misery upon it."

"How changed it must be now!" I said.

"It had been called, before his time, the Peaks. He gave it its present name, and lived here shut up—day and night poring over the wicked heaps of papers in the suit, and hoping against hope to disentangle it from its mystification and bring it to a close. In the meantime, the place became dilapidated, the weeds choked the passage to the rotting door. When I brought what remained of him home here, the brains seemed to me to have been blown out of the house too, it was so shattered and ruined."

He walked a little to and fro, after saying this to himself with a shudder, and then looked at me, and brightened, and came and sat down again with his hands in his pockets.

"I told you this was the Growlery, my dear. Where was I?"

I reminded him, at the hopeful change he had made in Bleak House.

"Bleak House—true. There is, in that city of London there, some property of ours which is much at this day what Bleak House was then—I say property of ours, meaning of the Suit's, but I ought to call it the property of Costs, for Costs is the only power on earth that will ever get anything out of it now, or will ever know it for anything but an eyesore and a heartsore. It is a street of perishing blind houses, with their eyes stoned out; without a pane of glass, without so much as a window-frame. Although Bleak House was not in Chancery, its master was, and it was stamped with the same seal. These are the Great Seal's impressions, my dear, all over England—the children know them! There are things I never talk about, or even think about, excepting in the Growlery here. If you consider it right to mention them to Rick and Ada"—looking seriously at me—"you can. I leave it to your discretion, Esther."

"I hope, sir—" said I.

"I think you had better call me Guardian, my dear."

I felt that I was choking again when he feigned to say this slightly, as if it were a whim instead of a thoughtful tenderness. But I gave the housekeeping keys the least shake in the world as a reminder to myself, and looked at him quietly.

"I hope, Guardian," said I, "that you may not trust too much to my discretion. I am afraid it will be a disappointment to you to know that I am not clever—but it really is the truth, and you would soon find it out if I had not the honesty to confess it."

He did not seem at all disappointed—quite the contrary. He told me, with a smile all over his face, that he knew me very well indeed, and that I was quite clever enough for him.

"I hope I may turn out so," said I, "but I am much afraid of it, Guardian."

"You are clever enough to be the good little woman of our lives here, my dear," he returned playfully, "the little old woman of the child's rhyme:

> " 'Little old woman, and whither so high?'—
> 'To sweep the cobwebs out of the sky.'

You will sweep them so neatly out of *our* sky, in the course of your housekeeping, Esther, that one of these days we shall have to abandon the Growlery, and nail up the door."

This was the beginning of my being called Old Woman, and Little Old Woman, and Cobweb, and Mrs. Shipton, and Mother Hubbard, and Dame Durden, and so many names of that sort that my own name soon became quite lost among them.

"However," said Mr. Jarndyce, "to return to our gossip. Here's Rick, a fine young fellow full of promise. What's to be done with him? Here he is, Esther. He must have a profession; he must make some choice for himself. There will be a world more Wiglomeration about it, I suppose, but it must be done."

"More what, Guardian?" said I.

"More Wiglomeration," said he. "It's the only name I know for the thing. He is a ward in Chancery, my dear. Kenge and Carboy will have something to say about it; Master Somebody will have something to say about it; Counsel will have something to say about it; the Chancellor will have something to say about it; the Satellites will have something to say about it; they will all have to be handsomely fee'd, all round, about it; the whole thing will be vastly ceremonious, wordy, unsatisfactory, and expensive, and I call it, in general, Wiglomeration. How mankind ever came to be afflicted with Wiglomeration, or for whose sins these young people ever fell into a pit of it, I don't know; so it is."

He began to rub his head, and to hint that he felt the wind. But it was a delightful instance of his kindness towards me that whether he rubbed his head, or walked about, or did both, his face was sure to recover its benignant expression as it looked at mine, and he was sure to turn comfortable again.

"Perhaps it would be best, first of all," said I, "to ask Mr. Richard what he inclines to himself."

"Exactly so," he returned. "That's what I mean! You know, just accustom yourself to talk it over, with your tact and in your quiet way, with him and Ada, and see what you all make of it. We are sure to come at the heart of the matter by your means, little woman."

I had not meant this at all; I had meant that he should speak to Richard. But of course I said I would do my best, though I feared (I really felt it necessary to repeat this) that he thought me much more sagacious than I was. At which my guardian only laughed the pleasantest laugh I ever heard.

"Come!" he said, rising and pushing back his chair. "I think we may have done with the Growlery for one day! Only a concluding word. Esther, my dear, do you wish to ask me anything?"

He looked so attentively at me that I looked attentively at him, and felt sure I understood him.

"About myself, sir?" said I.

"Yes."

"Guardian," said I, venturing to put my hand, which was suddenly colder than I could have wished, in his, "nothing! I am quite sure that if there were anything I ought to know, or had any need to know, I should not have to ask you to tell it to me. If my whole reliance and confidence were not placed in you, I must have a hard heart indeed. I have nothing to ask you, nothing in the world."

He drew my hand through his arm, and we went away to look for Ada. From that hour I felt quite easy with him, quite unreserved, quite content to know no more, quite happy.

We lived, at first, rather a busy life at Bleak House, for we had to become acquainted with many residents in and out of the neighbourhood who knew Mr. Jarndyce. It seemed to Ada and me that everybody knew him who wanted to do anything with anybody else's money. It amazed us, when we began to sort his letters, and to answer some of them for him in the Growlery of a morning, to find how the great object of the lives of nearly all his correspondents appeared to be to form themselves into committees for getting in and laying out money. The ladies were as desperate as the gentlemen; indeed, I think they were even more so. They wanted everything. They wanted wearing apparel, they wanted linen rags, they wanted money, they wanted coals, they wanted soup, they wanted interest, they wanted autographs, they wanted flannel, they wanted whatever Mr. Jarndyce had—or had not. Their objects were as various as their demands. They were going to raise new buildings, they were going to pay off debts on old buildings, they were going to give a testimonial to Mrs. Jellyby. They appeared to be always excited about canvassing and electing.

Among the ladies who were most distinguished for this rapacious benevolence (if I may use the expression), was a Mrs. Pardiggle, who seemed, as I judged from the number of her letters to Mr. Jarndyce, to be almost as powerful a correspondent as Mrs. Jellyby herself. We observed that the wind always changed when Mrs. Pardiggle became the subject of conversation. We were therefore curious to see Mrs. Pardiggle, and were glad when she called one day with her five young sons. As only Ada and I were at home, we received her timidly; for she seemed to come in like cold weather, and to make the little Pardiggles blue as they followed.

"These, young ladies," said Mrs. Pardiggle, with great volubility, after the first salutations, "are my five boys."

We had never seen such dissatisfied children. It was not merely that they were weazened and shrivelled—though they were certainly that too —but they looked absolutely ferocious with discontent.

"You have been visiting, I understand," said Mrs. Pardiggle, "at Mrs. Jellyby's?"

We said yes, we had passed one night there.

"Mrs. Jellyby," pursued the lady, always speaking in the same demonstrative, loud, hard tone, "is a benefactor to society, and deserves a helping hand. By this time, young ladies," said Mrs. Pardiggle, "you have found me out, I dare say?"

This was really such a confusing question that Ada looked at me in perfect dismay.

"Found out, I mean," said Mrs. Pardiggle, "the prominent point in my character. I am aware that it is so prominent as to be discoverable immediately. I lay myself open to detection, I know. Well! I freely admit I am a woman of business. I love hard work, I enjoy hard work. I am so accustomed and inured to hard work that I don't know what fatigue is."

We murmured that it was very astonishing, and very gratifying, or something to that effect.

"I do not understand what it is to be tired; you cannot tire me if you try!" said Mrs. Pardiggle. "Miss Summerson, I hope I shall have your assistance in my visiting rounds immediately, and Miss Clare's very soon?"

At first I tried to excuse myself, for the present, on the general ground of having occupations to attend to, which I must not neglect. But as this was an ineffectual protest, I then said, more particularly, that I was not sure of my qualifications. That I was inexperienced in the art of adapting my mind to minds very differently situated, and addressing them from suitable points of view. That I had much to learn myself before I could teach others, and that I could not confide in my good intentions alone. For these reasons, I thought it best to be as useful as I could, and to render what kind services I could, to those immediately about me, and to try to let that circle of duty gradually and naturally expand itself.

"You are wrong, Miss Summerson," said she; "but perhaps you are not equal to hard work, or the excitement of it, and that makes a vast difference. If you would like to see how I go through my work, I am now about—with my young family—to visit a brickmaker in the neighbourhood, and shall be glad to take you with me. Miss Clare also, if she will do me the favour."

Ada and I interchanged looks, and as we were going out in any case, accepted the offer. When we hastily returned from putting on our bonnets, Mrs. Pardiggle took possession of Ada, and I followed with the family.

The brickmaker's house was one of a cluster of wretched hovels in a brick-field, with pigsties close to the broken windows, and miserable little gardens before the doors, growing nothing but stagnant pools. Mrs. Pardiggle, leading the way with a great show of moral determination, conducted us into a cottage at the farthest corner, the ground-floor room of which we nearly filled. Besides ourselves, there were in this damp, offensive room—a woman with a black eye, nursing a poor little gasping baby by the fire; a man, all stained with clay and mud, and looking very dissipated, lying at full length on the ground, smoking a pipe; a powerful young man fastening a collar on a dog; and a bold girl, doing some kind of washing in very dirty water. They all looked up at us as we came in, and the woman seemed to turn her face towards the fire, as if to hide her bruised eye; nobody gave us any welcome.

"Well, my friends," said Mrs. Pardiggle, but her voice had not a friendly sound, I thought; it was much too businesslike and systematic. "How do you do, all of you? I am here again. I told you you couldn't tire me, you know. I am fond of hard work, and am true to my word."

"There an't," growled the man on the floor, whose head rested on his hand as he stared at us, "any more on you to come in, is there?"

"No, my friend," said Mrs. Pardiggle, seating herself on one stool, and knocking down another. "We are all here."

"Because I thought there warn't enough of you, perhaps?" said the man, with his pipe between his lips as he looked round upon us.

"You can't tire me, good people," said Mrs. Pardiggle. "I enjoy hard work, and the harder you make mine, the better I like it."

Mrs. Pardiggle pulled out a good book, as if it were a constable's staff, and took the whole family into custody. I mean into religious custody, of course, but she really did it as if she were an inexorable moral Policeman carrying them all off to a station-house.

Ada and I were very uncomfortable. We both felt intrusive and out of place, and we both thought that Mrs. Pardiggle would have got on infinitely better if she had not had such a mechanical way of taking possession of people. We were much relieved, under these circumstances, when Mrs. Pardiggle left off. The man on the floor then, turning his head round again, said morosely:

"Well! You've done, have you?"

"For today I have, my friend. But I am never fatigued. I shall come to you again, in your regular order," returned Mrs. Pardiggle with demonstrative cheerfulness.

"So long as you goes now," said he, folding his arms and shutting his eyes with an oath, "you may do wot you like!"

Mrs. Pardiggle accordingly rose, and she proceeded to another cottage. She supposed that we were following her; but as soon as the space was left clear, we approached the woman sitting by the fire, to ask if the baby were ill.

She only looked at it as it lay on her lap. We had observed before that when she looked at it she covered her discoloured eye with her hand, as though she wished to separate any association with noise and violence and ill-treatment from the poor little child.

Ada, whose gentle heart was moved by its appearance, bent down to touch its little face. As she did so, I saw what happened and drew her back. The child died.

"Oh Esther!" cried Ada, sinking on her knees beside it. "Look here! Oh Esther, my love, the suffering, quiet, pretty little thing! I am so sorry for it. I am so sorry for the mother. I never saw a sight so pitiful as this before! Oh baby, baby!"

Such compassion, such gentleness, as that with which she bent down weeping, and put her hand upon the mother's, might have softened any mother's heart that ever beat. The woman at first gazed at her in astonishment, and then burst into tears. Presently I took the light burden from her lap; did what I could to make the baby's rest the prettier and gentler, laid it on a shelf, and covered it with my own handkerchief. We tried to comfort the mother, and we whispered to her what Our Saviour said of children. She answered nothing, but sat weeping—weeping very much.

When I turned, I found that the young man had taken out the dog, and was standing at the door looking in upon us, with dry eyes, but quiet. The man had risen. He still smoked his pipe with an air of defiance, but he was silent. An ugly woman, very poorly clothed, hurried in while I was glancing at them, and coming straight up to the mother, said, "Jenny! Jenny!" The mother rose on being so addressed, and fell upon the woman's neck.

She also had upon her face and arms the marks of ill-usage. She had no kind of grace about her but the grace of sympathy; but when she condoled with the woman, and her own tears fell, she wanted no beauty. I say "condoled," but her only words were "Jenny! Jenny!" All the rest was in the tone in which she said them.

I thought it very touching to see these two women, coarse and shabby and beaten, so united; to see what they could be to one another; to see how they felt for one another. I think the best side of such people is almost hidden from us. What the poor are to the poor is little known, except to themselves and God.

We felt it better to withdraw and leave them uninterrupted. We stole out quietly, and without notice from any one except the man. He was leaning against the wall near the door, and finding that there was scarcely room for us to pass, went out before us.

Ada was so full of grief all the way home, and Richard, whom we found at home, was so distressed to see her in tears, that we arranged to return at night, with some little comforts, and repeat our visit at the brickmaker's house. We said as little as we could to Mr. Jarndyce, but the wind changed directly. Richard accompanied us at night to the scene of our morning expedition. On our way there, we had to pass a noisy drinking-house, where a number of men were flocking about the door. Among them, and prominent in some dispute, was the father of the little child.

We left our escort within sight of the brickmaker's dwelling, and proceeded by ourselves. When we came to the door, we found the woman who had brought such consolation with her standing there, looking anxiously out.

"It's you, young ladies, is it?" she said in a whisper. "I'm a-watching for my master. My heart's in my mouth. If he was to catch me away from home, he'd pretty near murder me."

"Do you mean your husband?" said I.

"Yes, miss, my master. Jenny's asleep, quite worn-out. She's scarcely had the child off her lap, poor thing, these seven days and nights, except when I've been able to take it for a minute or two."

As she gave way for us, she went softly in, and put what we had brought near the miserable bed on which the mother slept. No effort had been made to clean the room, but the small waxen form, from which so much solemnity diffused itself, had been composed afresh, and washed, and neatly dressed in some fragments of white linen; and on my handkerchief, which still covered the poor baby, a little bunch of sweet herbs had been laid by the same rough scarred hands, so lightly, so tenderly!

"May Heaven reward you!" we said to her. "You are a good woman."

"Me, young ladies?" she returned with surprise. "Hush! Jenny, Jenny!"

The mother had moaned in her sleep, and moved. The sound of the familiar voice seemed to calm her again. She was quiet once more.

How little I thought, when I raised my handkerchief to look upon the tiny sleeper underneath, and seemed to see a halo shine around the child through Ada's drooping hair as her pity bent her head—how little I thought in whose unquiet bosom that handkerchief would come to lie! I only thought that perhaps the Angel of the child might not be all unconscious of the woman who replaced it with so compassionate a hand, not all unconscious of her presently when we had taken leave, and left her at the door by turns looking and listening in terror for herself, and saying in her old soothing manner, "Jenny, Jenny!"

CHAPTER 9

*Signs and Tokens*

I DON'T know how it is, I seem to be always writing about myself. I mean all the time to write about other people, and I try to think about myself as little as possible. I hope any one who may read what I write will understand that if these pages contain a great deal about me, I can only suppose it must be because I have really something to do with them, and can't be kept out.

My darling and I read together, and worked, and practised, and found so much employment for our time, that the winter days flew by us like bright-winged birds. Generally in the afternoons, and always in the evenings, Richard gave us his company. Although he was one of the most restless creatures in the world, he certainly was very fond of our society.

He was very, very, very fond of Ada. I mean it, and I had better say it at once. I had never seen any young people falling in love before, but I found them out quite soon. I could not say so, of course, or show that I knew anything about it. On the contrary, I was so demure, and used to seem so unconscious, that sometimes I considered within myself whether I was not growing quite deceitful. But there was no help for it. All I had to do was to be quiet, and I was as quiet as a mouse. They were as quiet as mice, too, so far as any words were concerned; but the innocent manner in which they relied more and more upon me was so charming that I had great difficulty in not showing how it interested me.

"Our dear little old woman is such a capital old woman," Richard would say, coming up to meet me in the garden early, with his pleasant laugh and perhaps the least tinge of a blush, "that I can't get on without her. Before I begin my harum-scarum day—galloping up hill and down dale, all the country round, like a highwayman—it does me so much good to come and have a steady walk with our comfortable friend that here I am again!"

"You know, Dame Durden dear," Ada would say at night, with her head upon my shoulder and the firelight shining in her thoughtful eyes, "I don't want to talk when we come upstairs here. Only to sit a little while, thinking, with your dear face for company; and to hear the wind, and remember the poor sailors at sea—"

Ah! Perhaps Richard was going to be a sailor. We had talked it over very often, now, and there was some talk of gratifying the inclination of his childhood for the sea. Mr. Jarndyce had written to a relation of the family, a great Sir Leicester Dedlock, for his interest in Richard's favour, and Sir Leicester had replied in a gracious manner that he would be happy to advance the prospects of the young gentleman if it should ever prove to be within his power, which was not at all probable—and that my Lady sent her compliments to the young gentleman (to whom she perfectly remembered that she was allied by remote consanguinity), and trusted that he would ever do his duty in any honourable profession to which he might devote himself.

"So I apprehend it's pretty clear," said Richard to me, "that I shall have to work my own way. Never mind! Plenty of people have had to do that before now, and have done it. I only wish I had the command of a clipping privateer to begin with, and could carry off the Chancellor and keep him on short allowance until he gave judgment in our cause. He'd find himself growing thin if he didn't look sharp!"

With a buoyancy and hopefulness and a gaiety that hardly ever flagged, Richard had a carelessness in his character that quite perplexed me—principally because he mistook it, in such a very odd way, for prudence. It entered into all his calculations about money, in a singular manner, which I don't think I can better explain than by reverting for a moment to our loan to Mr. Skimpole.

Mr. Jarndyce had ascertained the amount, either from Mr. Skimpole himself or from Coavinses, and had placed the money in my hands with instructions to me to retain my own part of it and hand the rest to Richard. The number of little acts of thoughtless expenditure which Richard justified by the recovery of his ten pounds, and the number of times he talked to me as if he had saved that amount, would form a sum in simple addition.

"My prudent Mother Hubbard," he said to me, "I made ten pounds clear out of Coavinses' business."

"How was that?" said I.

"Why, I got rid of ten pounds which I was quite content to get rid of, and never expected to see any more. Very well! Then I came into possession of ten pounds—"

"The same ten pounds," I hinted.

"That has nothing to do with it!" returned Richard. "I have got ten pounds more than I expected to have, and consequently I can afford to spend it without being particular."

I believe Richard's was as frank and generous a nature as there possibly can be. He was ardent and brave, and, in the midst of all his wild restlessness, was so gentle that I knew him like a brother in a few weeks. His gentleness was natural to him, and would have shown itself abundantly even without Ada's influence; but with it, he became one of the most winning of companions, always so ready to be interested, and always so happy, sanguine, and light-hearted. I am sure that I, sitting with them, and walking with them, and talking with them, and noticing from day to day how they went on falling deeper and deeper in love and saying nothing about it, and each shyly thinking that this love was the greatest of secrets, perhaps not yet suspected even by the other—I am sure that I was scarcely less enchanted than they were.

We were going on in this way, when one morning at breakfast Mr. Jarndyce received a letter, and looking at the superscription said, "From Boythorn? Ay, ay!" and opened and read it with evident pleasure, announcing to us, in a parenthesis, when he was about half-way through, that Boythorn was "coming down" in a visit. Now who was Boythorn? we all thought.

"I went to school with this fellow, Lawrence Boythorn," said Mr. Jarndyce, tapping the letter as he laid it on the table, "more than five-and-forty years ago. He was then the most impetuous boy in the world, and he is now the most impetuous man. He was then the loudest boy in the world, and he is now the loudest man. He was then the heartiest and sturdiest boy in the world, and he is now the heartiest and sturdiest man. He is a tremendous fellow."

"In stature, sir?" asked Richard.

"Pretty well, Rick, in that respect," said Mr. Jarndyce, "being some ten years older than I, and a couple of inches taller, with his head thrown back like an old soldier, his stalwart chest squared, his hands like a clean blacksmith's, and his lungs!—there's no simile for his lungs. Talking, laughing, or snoring, they make the beams of the house shake.

"But it's the inside of the man, the warm heart of the man, the passion of the man, the fresh blood of the man, that I speak of," he pursued. "His language is as sounding as his voice. He is always in extremes, perpetually in the superlative degree. In his condemnation he is all ferocity. You might suppose him to be an Ogre, from what he says, and I believe he has the reputation of one with some people. There! I tell you no more of him beforehand. You must not be surprised to see him take me under his protection, for he has never forgotten that I was a low boy at school, and that our friendship began in his knocking two of my head tyrant's teeth out (he says six) before breakfast."

We looked forward to his arrival with some curiosity. The afternoon wore away, however, and he did not appear. The dinner-hour arrived, and still he did not appear. The dinner was put back an hour, and we were sitting round the fire, with no light but the blaze, when the hall-door suddenly burst open and the hall resounded with these words, uttered with the greatest vehemence and in a stentorian tone:

"We have been misdirected, Jarndyce, by a most abandoned ruffian, who told us to take the turning to the right instead of to the left. He is the most intolerable scoundrel on the face of the earth. His father must have been a most consummate villain, ever to have such a son. I would have had that fellow shot without the least remorse!"

"Did he do it on purpose?" Mr. Jarndyce inquired.

"I have not the slightest doubt that the scoundrel has passed his whole existence in misdirecting travellers!" returned the other. "By my soul, I thought him the worst-looking dog I had ever beheld when he was telling me to take the turning to the right. And yet I stood before that fellow face to face, and didn't knock his brains out! By my soul, Jarndyce, if you had been married, I would have turned back at the garden-gate, and gone away to the remotest summits of the Himalaya Mountains, sooner than I would have presented myself at this unseasonable hour."

"Not quite so far, I hope?" said Mr. Jarndyce.

"By my life and honour, yes!" cried the visitor. "I wouldn't be guilty of the audacious insolence of keeping a lady of the house waiting all this time, for any earthly consideration. I would infinitely rather destroy myself—infinitely rather!"

Talking thus, they went upstairs; and presently we heard him in his bedroom thundering "Ha, ha, ha!" and again "Ha, ha, ha!" until the flattest echo in the neighbourhood seemed to catch the contagion, and to laugh as enjoyingly as he did, or as we did when we heard him laugh.

We all conceived a prepossession in his favour; for there was a sterling quality in this laugh, and in his vigorous healthy voice, and in the very fury of his superlatives, which seemed to go off like blank cannon and hurt nothing. But we were hardly prepared to have it so confirmed by his appearance when Mr. Jarndyce presented him. He was not only a very handsome old gentleman—upright and stalwart as he had been described to us—with a massive grey head, a fine composure of face when silent, and a chin that might have subsided into a double chin but for the vehement emphasis in which it was constantly required to assist; but he was such a true gentleman in his manner, so chivalrously polite, his face was lighted by a smile of so much sweetness and tenderness, and it seemed so plain that he had nothing to hide but showed himself exactly as he was, that really I could not help looking at him with equal pleasure as he sat at dinner, whether he smilingly conversed with Ada and me, or was led by Mr. Jarndyce into some great volley of superlatives, or threw up his head like a bloodhound and gave out that tremendous Ha, ha, ha!

"You have brought your bird with you, I suppose?" said Mr. Jarndyce.

"By heaven, he is the most astonishing bird in Europe!" replied the other. "He *is* the most wonderful creature! I wouldn't take ten thousand guineas for that bird. I have left an annuity for his sole support, in case he should outlive me."

The subject of this laudation was a very little canary, who was so tame that he was brought down by Mr. Boythorn's man on his forefinger, and after taking a gentle flight round the room, alighted on his master's head. To hear Mr. Boythorn presently expressing the most implacable and passionate sentiments with this fragile mite of a creature quietly perched on his forehead was to have a good illustration of his character, I thought.

"By my soul, Jarndyce," he said, very gently holding up a bit of bread to the canary to peck at, "if I were in your place, I would seize every Master in Chancery by the throat tomorrow morning and shake him until his money rolled out of his pockets, and his bones rattled in his skin. I would have a settlement out of somebody, by fair means or by foul. If you would empower me to do it, I would do it for you with the greatest satisfaction!"

"I thank you, Lawrence, but the suit is hardly at such a point at present," returned Mr. Jarndyce, laughing, "that it would be greatly advanced, even by the legal process of shaking the Bench and the whole Bar."

"There never was such an infernal cauldron as that Chancery, on the face of the earth!" said Mr. Boythorn. "Nothing but a mine below it on a busy day in term-time, with all its records, rules, and precedents collected in it, and every functionary belonging to it also, high and low, upward and downward, and the whole blown to atoms with ten thousand hundredweight of gunpowder, would reform it in the least!"

It was impossible not to laugh at the energetic gravity with which he recommended this strong measure of reform. When we laughed, he threw up his head, and shook his broad chest, and again the whole country seemed to echo to his Ha, ha, ha!

"But how do you and your neighbour get on about the disputed right of way?" said Mr. Jarndyce. "You are not free from the toils of the law yourself!"

"The fellow has brought actions against *me* for trespass, and I have brought actions against *him* for trespass," returned Mr. Boythorn. "By heaven, he is the proudest fellow breathing. It is morally impossible that his name can be Sir Leicester. It must be Sir Lucifer."

"Complimentary to our distant relation!" said my guardian laughingly, to Ada and Richard.

"I would beg Miss Clare's pardon and Mr. Carstone's pardon," resumed our visitor, "if I were not reassured by seeing in the fair face of the lady, and the smile of the gentleman, that it is quite unnecessary, and that they keep their distant relation at a comfortable distance."

"Or he keeps us," suggested Richard.

"By my soul," exclaimed Mr. Boythorn, suddenly firing another volley, "that fellow is, and his father was, and his grandfather was, the most stiff-necked, arrogant, imbecile, pigheaded numskull ever, by some inexplicable mistake of Nature, born in any station of life but a walking-stick's! But it's no matter; he should not shut up my path if he were fifty baronets melted into one. The fellow, by his agent, or secretary, or somebody, writes to me, 'Sir Leicester Dedlock, Baronet, presents his compliments to Mr. Lawrence Boythorn, and has to call his attention to the fact that the green pathway by the old parsonage-house; now the property of Mr. Lawrence Boythorn, is Sir Leicester's right of way, being in fact a portion of the park of Chesney Wold; and that Sir Leicester finds it convenient to close up the same.' I write to the fellow, 'Mr. Lawrence Boythorn presents his compliments to Sir Leicester Dedlock, Baronet, and has to call *his* attention to the fact that he totally denies the whole of Sir Leicester Dedlock's positions on every possible subject, and has to add, in reference to closing up the pathway, that he will be glad to see the man who may undertake to do it.' The fellow sends a most abandoned villain with one eye, to construct a gateway. I play upon that execrable scoundrel with a fire-engine until the breath is nearly driven out of his body. The fellow erects a gate in the night. I chop it down and burn it in the morning. He sends his myrmidons to come over the fence, and pass and repass. I catch them in humane man traps, fire split peas at their legs, play upon them with the engine. He brings actions for trespass; I bring actions for trespass. He brings actions for assault and battery; I defend them, and continue to assault and batter. Ha, ha, ha!"

To hear him say all this with unimaginable energy, one might have thought him the angriest of mankind. To see him at the very same time looking at the bird now perched upon his thumb, and softly smoothing its feathers with his forefinger, one might have thought him the gentlest.

"No, no," he said, "no closing up my paths, by any Dedlock! Though I willingly confess"—here he softened in a moment—"that Lady Dedlock is the most accomplished lady in the world, to whom I would do any homage that a plain gentleman, and no baronet with a head seven hundred years thick, may. But, speaking of this trespass—with apologies to Miss Clare and Miss Summerson for the length at which I have pursued so dry a subject—is there nothing for me from your men, Kenge and Carboy?"

"I think not, Esther?" said Mr. Jarndyce.

"Nothing, Guardian."

"Much obliged!" said Mr. Boythorn. "I inquired because, coming from Lincolnshire, I of course have not yet been in town, and I thought some letters might have been sent down here. I dare say they will report progress tomorrow morning."

I saw him so often, in the course of the evening, which passed very pleasantly, contemplate Richard and Ada with an interest and a satisfaction that made his fine face remarkably agreeable that I asked my guardian whether Mr. Boythorn had ever been married.

"No," said he. "No."

"But he meant to be!" said I.

"How did you find that out?" he returned, with a smile.

"Why, Guardian," I explained, "there is something so tender in his manner, after all, and he is so very courtly and gentle to us, and—"

"You are right, little woman," he answered. "He was all but married once. Long ago. And once."

"Did the lady die?"

"No—but she died to him. That time has had its influence on all his later life. Would you suppose him to have a head and a heart full of romance yet?"

"I think, Guardian, I might have supposed so. But it is easy to say that when you have told me so."

"He has never since been what he might have been," said Mr. Jarndyce, "and now you see him in his age with no one near him but his servant and his little yellow friend."

I felt from my guardian's manner that beyond this point I could not pursue the subject without changing the wind. I therefore forbore to ask any further questions. I was interested, but not curious.

With the morning, there came a letter from Messrs. Kenge and Carboy to Mr. Boythorn, informing him that one of their clerks would wait upon him at noon. As it was the day of the week on which I paid the bills, and added up my books, I remained at home while Mr. Jarndyce, Ada, and Richard took advantage of a very fine day to make a little excursion. Mr. Boythorn was to wait for Kenge and Carboy's clerk, and then was to go on foot to meet them on their return.

Well! I was full of business, examining tradesmen's books, adding up columns, paying money, filing receipts, when Mr. Guppy was announced and shown in. I had had some idea that the clerk who was to be sent down might be the young gentleman who had met me at the coach-office, and I was glad to see him, because he was associated with my present happiness.

I scarcely knew him again, he was so uncommonly smart. He had an entirely new suit of glossy clothes on, a shining hat, lilac-kid gloves, a neckerchief of a variety of colours, a large hothouse flower in his button-hole, and a thick gold ring on his little finger. Besides which, he quite scented the dining-room with bear's-grease and other perfumery. He looked at me with an attention that quite confused me when I begged him to take a seat until the servant should return; and as he sat there, crossing and uncrossing his legs in a corner, and I asked him if he had had a pleasant ride, and hoped that Mr. Kenge was well, I never looked at him but I found him looking at me in the same scrutinizing and curious way.

When the request was brought to him that he would go upstairs to Mr. Boythorn's room, I mentioned that he would find lunch prepared for him when he came down. He said with some embarrassment, holding the handle of the door, "Shall I have the honour of finding you here, miss?" I replied yes, I should be there, and he went out with a bow and another look.

I thought him only awkward and shy, for he was evidently much embarrassed, and I fancied that the best thing I could do would be to wait until I saw that he had everything he wanted and then to leave him to himself. The interview with Mr. Boythorn was a long one—and a stormy one too, I should think; for although his room was at some distance, I heard his loud voice rising every now and then like a high wind, and evidently blowing perfect broadsides of denunciation.

At last Mr. Guppy came back, looking something the worse for the conference. "My eye, miss," he said, "he's a Tartar!"

"Pray take some refreshment, sir," said I.

Mr. Guppy sat down at the table and began nervously sharpening a carving-knife on the carving-fork, still looking at me (as I felt quite sure without looking at him), in the same unusual manner. The sharpening lasted so long that at last I felt a kind of obligation on me to raise my eyes. He immediately looked at the dish, and began to carve.

"What will you take yourself, miss? You'll take a morsel of something?"

"No thank you," said I.

"Shan't I give you a piece of anything at all, miss?" said Mr. Guppy, hurriedly drinking off a glass of wine.

"Nothing, thank you," said I. "I have only waited to see that you have everything you want. Is there anything I can order for you?"

"No, I am much obliged to you, miss, I'm sure. I've everything that I can require to make me comfortable—at least I—not comfortable—I'm never that." He drank off two more glasses of wine, one after another. I thought I had better go. "I beg your pardon, miss!" said Mr. Guppy, rising when he saw me rise. "But would you allow me the favour of a minute's private conversation?" Not knowing what to say, I sat down again. "What follows is without prejudice, miss?" said Mr. Guppy.

"I don't understand what you mean," said I, wondering.

"It's one of our law-terms, miss. You won't make any use of it to my detriment, at Kenge and Carboy's, or elsewhere. If our conversation shouldn't lead to anything, it's in total confidence."

"I am at a loss, sir," said I, "to imagine what you can have to communicate in total confidence to me, whom you have never seen but once; but I should be very sorry to do you any injury."

"Thank you, miss. I'm sure of it—that's quite sufficient." All this time Mr. Guppy was either planing his forehead with his handkerchief or tightly rubbing the palm of his left hand with the palm of his right. "If you would excuse my taking another glass of wine, miss, I think it might assist me in getting on without a continual choke that cannot fail to be mutually unpleasant."

He did so, and came back again. I took the opportunity of moving well behind my table.

"You wouldn't allow me to offer you one, would you, miss?" said Mr. Guppy, apparently refreshed.

"Not any," said I.

"Not half a glass?" said Mr. Guppy; "Quarter? No! Then, to proceed. My present salary, Miss Summerson, at Kenge and Carboy's, is two pound a week, and a further rise of five is guaranteed at the expiration of a term not exceeding twelve months from the present date. My mother has a little property, which takes the form of a small life annuity, upon which she lives in an independent though unassuming manner, in the Old Street Road. She is eminently calculated for a mother-in-law. She never interferes, is all for peace, and her disposition easy. My own abode is lodgings at Penton Place, Pentonville. It is lowly, but airy, open at the back, and considered one of the 'ealthiest outlets. Miss Summerson! In the mildest language, I adore you. Would you be so kind as to allow me (as I may say) to file a declaration—to make an offer!"

Mr. Guppy went down on his knees. I was well behind my table, and not much frightened. I said, "Get up from that ridiculous position immediately, sir, or you will oblige me to break my implied promise and ring the bell!"

"Hear me out, miss!" said Mr. Guppy, folding his hands.

"I cannot consent to hear another word, sir," I returned, "unless you get up from the carpet directly, and go and sit down at the table, as you ought to do if you have any sense at all."

He looked piteously, but slowly rose and did so.

"Yet what a mockery it is, miss," he said, with his hand upon his heart, and shaking his head at me in a melancholy manner over the tray, "to be stationed behind food at such a moment. The soul recoils from food at such a moment, miss."

"I beg you to conclude," said I; "you have asked me to hear you out, and I beg you to conclude."

"I will, miss," said Mr. Guppy. "As I love and honour, so likewise I obey. Would that I could make Thee the subject of that vow, before the shrine!"

"That is quite impossible," said I.

"I am aware," said Mr. Guppy, leaning forward over the tray, and regarding me, as I again strangely felt, though my eyes were not directed to him, with his late intent look, "I am aware that in a worldly point of view, according to all appearances, my offer is a poor one. But Miss Summerson! Angel!—No, don't ring—I have been brought up in a sharp school, and am accustomed to a variety of general practice. Though a young man, I have ferreted out evidence, got up cases, and seen lots of life. Blest with your hand, what means might I not find of advancing your interests, and pushing your fortunes! What might I not get to know, nearly concerning you? I know nothing now, certainly, but what *might* I not, if I had your confidence and you set me on?"

I told him that he addressed my interest, or what he supposed to be my interest, quite as unsuccessfully as he addressed my inclination; and he would now understand that I requested him, if he pleased, to go away immediately.

"Cruel miss," said Mr. Guppy, "hear but another word! I think you

must have seen that I was struck with those charms on the day when I put up the steps of the 'ackney-coach. It was a feeble tribute to Thee, but it was well meant. Thy image has ever since been fixed in my breast. I have walked up and down of an evening opposite Jellyby's house, only to look upon the bricks that once contained Thee. If I speak of interest, it is only to recommend myself and my respectful wretchedness. Love was before it, and is before it."

"I should be pained, Mr. Guppy," said I, rising and putting my hand upon the bell-rope, "to do you, or any one who was sincere, the injustice of slighting any honest feeling, however disagreeably expressed. If you have really meant to give me a proof of your good opinion, though ill-timed and misplaced, I feel that I ought to thank you. I hope that you will now go away as if you had never been so exceedingly foolish, and attend to Messrs. Kenge and Carboy's business."

"Half a minute, miss!" cried Mr. Guppy, checking me as I was about to ring. "This has been without prejudice?"

"I will never mention it," said I, "unless you should give me future occasion to do so."

"A quarter of a minute, miss! In case you should think better—at any time, however distant—of anything I have said, Mr. William Guppy, eighty-seven, Penton Place, or if removed, or dead, care of Mrs. Guppy, three hundred and two, Old Street Road, will be sufficient."

I rang the bell, the servant came, and Mr. Guppy, laying his written card upon the table, and making a dejected bow, departed. I sat there for another hour or more, finishing my books and payments, and was so composed and cheerful that I thought I had quite dismissed this unexpected incident. But when I went upstairs to my own room, I surprised myself by beginning to laugh about it, and then surprised myself still more by beginning to cry about it.

CHAPTER 10

*The Law-Writer*

ON the eastern borders of Chancery Lane—that is to say, more particularly in Cook's Court, Cursitor Street—Mr. Snagsby, Law-Stationer, pursues his lawful calling. In the shade of Cook's Court, Mr. Snagsby has dealt in all sorts of blank forms of legal process; in skins and rolls of parchment; in paper—foolscap, brief, draft, brown, white, whitey-brown, and blotting; in stamps; in office quills, pens, ink, Indiarubber, pounce, pins, pencils, sealing-wax, and wafers; in red tape and green ferret; in pocket-books, almanacks, diaries, and law-lists; in penknives, scissors, and other small office-cutlery—in short, in articles too numerous to mention—ever since he was out of his time, and went into partnership with Peffer. On that occasion, Cook's Court was in a manner revolutionized by the new inscription in fresh paint, PEFFER AND SNAGSBY, displacing the time-honoured legend, PEFFER only.

Peffer is never seen in Cook's Court now. He is not expected there, for he has been recumbent this quarter of a century in the churchyard of St. Andrew's, Holborn. In his lifetime, and likewise in the period of Snagsby's "time" of seven long years, there dwelt with Peffer a niece —a short, shrewd niece, something too violently compressed about the waist, and with a sharp nose like a sharp autumn evening inclining to be frosty towards the end. Young Snagsby, having wooed and won its fair subject on his arrival at man's estate, entered into two partnerships at once.

Mr. and Mrs. Snagsby are not only one bone and one flesh, but, to the neighbours' thinking, one voice too. That voice, appearing to proceed from Mrs. Snagsby alone, is heard in Cook's Court very often. Mr. Snagsby is rarely heard. He is a mild, bald, timid man, with a shining head, and a scrubby clump of black hair sticking out at the back. He tends to meekness and obesity. As he stands at his door in Cook's Court, from beneath his feet, as from a shrill ghost unquiet in its grave, there frequently arise complainings and lamentations in the voice already mentioned; and haply, on some occasions when these reach a sharper pitch than usual, Mr. Snagsby mentions to the 'prentices, "I think my little woman is a-giving it to Guster!"

This proper name is the possession, and the only possession, except fifty shillings per annum and a very small box indifferently filled with clothing, of a lean young woman from a workhouse (by some supposed to have been christened Augusta); who "has fits." Guster, really aged three or four and twenty, but looking a round ten years older, goes cheap with this unaccountable drawback of fits; and is so apprehensive of being returned on the hands of her patron saint that except when she is found with her head in the pail, or the sink, or the dinner, or anything else that happens to be near her at the time of her seizure, she is always at work.

Mr. Snagsby refers everything not in the practical mysteries of the business to Mrs. Snagsby. She manages the money, reproaches the taxgatherers, appoints the times and places of devotion on Sundays, licenses Mr. Snagsby's entertainments, and acknowledges no responsibility as to what she thinks fit to provide for dinner. Rumour, always flying, batlike, about Cook's Court, and skimming in and out at everybody's windows, does say that Mrs. Snagsby is jealous and inquisitive, and that Mr. Snagsby is sometimes worried out of house and home, and that if he had the spirit of a mouse he wouldn't stand it.

The day is closing in and the gas is lighted, but is not yet fully effective, for it is not quite dark. Mr. Snagsby, standing at his shop-door looking up at the clouds, sees a crow who is out late skim straight across Chancery Lane and Lincoln's Inn Garden, into Lincoln's Inn Fields. Here, in a large house, formerly a house of state, lives Mr. Tulkinghorn.

It is let off in sets of chambers now, and in those shrunken fragments of its greatness lawyers lie like maggots in nuts. But its roomy staircases, passages, and antechambers still remain; and even its painted ceilings, where Allegory, in Roman helmet and celestial linen, sprawls among balustrades and pillars, flowers, clouds, and big-legged boys. Here, among his many boxes labelled with transcendent names, lives Mr. Tulkinghorn, when not speechlessly at home in country-houses where the great ones of the earth are bored to death. Here he is today, quiet at his table.

As he is to look at, so is his apartment in the dusk of the present afternoon. Rusty, out of date, withdrawing from attention, able to afford it. Here, beneath the painted ceiling, with foreshortened Allegory staring down at his intrusion, Mr. Tulkinghorn has at once his house and office. He keeps no staff; only one middle-aged man, usually a little out at elbows, who sits in a high pew in the hall, and is rarely overburdened with business. Mr. Tulkinghorn is not in a common way. He wants no clerks. He is a great reservoir of confidences, not to be so tapped. His clients want *him*; he is all in all. Drafts that he requires to be drawn are drawn by special-pleaders in the Temple on mysterious instructions; fair copies that he requires to be made are made at the stationers'.

Now! Mr. Tulkinghorn gets up, adjusts his spectacles, puts on his hat, puts a manuscript in his pocket, goes out, tells the middle-aged man, "I shall be back presently." Mr. Tulkinghorn goes as the crow came—not quite so straight, but nearly—to Cook's Court, Cursitor Street. To Snagsby's, Law-Stationer's, Deeds engrossed and copied, Law-Writing executed in all its branches, etc., etc., etc.

It is somewhere about five or six o'clock in the afternoon, and a balmy fragrance of warm tea hovers in Cook's Court. It hovers about Snagsby's door. Mr. Snagsby was about to descend into the subterranean regions to take tea when he looked out of his door just now and saw the crow who was out late. Guster is minding the shop, for the 'prentices take tea in the kitchen, with Mr. and Mrs. Snagsby.

"Master at home?" says Mr. Tulkinghorn.

Master is at home, and Guster will fetch him. Guster disappears, glad to get out of the shop, which she regards with mingled dread and veneration as a storehouse of awful implements of the great torture of the law.

Mr. Snagsby appears, greasy, warm, herbaceous, and chewing. Says, "Bless my soul, sir! Mr. Tulkinghorn!"

"I want half a word with you, Snagsby."

"Certainly, sir! Dear me, sir, why didn't you send your young man round for me? Pray walk into the back shop, sir."

The confined room, strong of parchment-grease, is warehouse, counting-house, and copying-office. Mr. Tulkinghorn sits, facing round, on a stool at the desk.

"Jarndyce and Jarndyce, Snagsby."

"Yes, sir." Mr. Snagsby turns up the gas, and coughs behind his hand. Mr. Snagsby, as a timid man, is accustomed to cough with a variety of expressions, and so to save words.

"You copied some affidavits in that cause for me lately. There was one of them," says Mr. Tulkinghorn, carelessly feeling in the wrong coat-pocket, "the handwriting of which is peculiar, and I rather like. As I happened to be passing, and thought I had it about me, I looked in to ask you—but I haven't got it. No matter, any other time will do—Ah! here it is!—I looked in to ask you who copied this."

"Who copied this, sir?" says Mr. Snagsby, taking it, laying it flat on the desk, and separating all the sheets at once with a twirl and a twist of the left hand peculiar to law-stationers. "We gave this out, sir. I can tell you in a moment who copied it, sir, by referring to my Book."

Mr. Snagsby takes his Book down from the safe, eyes the affidavit aside, and brings his right forefinger travelling down a page of the Book. "Jewby—Packer—Jarndyce."

"Jarndyce! Here we are, sir," says Mr. Snagsby. "To be sure! I might have remembered it. This was given out, sir, to a writer who lodges just over on the opposite side of the lane."

Mr. Tulkinghorn has seen the entry, found it before the law-stationer, read it while the forefinger was coming down the hill.

"*What* do you call him? Nemo?" says Mr. Tulkinghorn.

"Nemo, sir. Here it is. Forty-two folio. Given out on the Wednesday night at eight o'clock; brought in on the Thursday morning at half after nine."

"Nemo!" repeats Mr. Tulkinghorn. "Nemo is Latin for 'No one'."

"It must be English for some one, sir, I think," Mr. Snagsby submits, with his deferential cough. "It is a person's name. Here it is, you see, sir! Forty-two folio."

The tail of Mr. Snagsby's eye becomes conscious of the head of Mrs. Snagsby looking in at the shop-door to know what he means by deserting his tea.

"Our law-writers who live by job-work are a queer lot, and this may not be his name, but it's the name he goes by. I remember now, sir, that he gives it in a written advertisement he sticks up down at the Rule Office, and the King's Bench Office, and so forth. You know the kind of document, sir—wanting employ?"

"Have you given this man work before!" asks Mr. Tulkinghorn.

"Oh dear yes, sir! Work of yours."

"Thinking of more important matters, I forget where you said he lived."

"Across the lane, sir. In fact, he lodges at a rag and bottle shop."

"Can you show me the place as I go back?"

"With the greatest pleasure, sir!"

Mr. Snagsby pulls off his sleeves and his grey coat, pulls on his black coat, takes his hat from its peg. "Oh! here is my little woman!" he says aloud. "My dear, will you be so kind as to tell one of the lads to look after the shop while I step across the lane with Mr. Tulkinghorn? Mrs. Snagsby, sir—I shan't be two minutes, my love!"

Mrs. Snagsby bends to the lawyer, retires behind the counter, peeps at them through the window-blind, goes softly into the back office, refers to the entries in the book still lying open.

"You will find that the place is rough, sir," says Mr. Snagsby, walking deferentially in the road, and leaving the narrow pavement to the lawyer, "and the party is very rough. But they're a wild lot in general, sir. The advantage of this particular man is that he never wants sleep. He'll go at it as long as ever you like."

It is quite dark now, and the gas-lamps have acquired their full effect. Jostling against clerks going to post the day's letters, and against counsel and attorneys going home to dinner, and against plaintiffs and defendants, and against the general crowd—diving through law and equity, and through that kindred mystery, the street mud, which is made of nobody knows what, and collects about us nobody knows whence or how—the lawyer and the law-stationer come to a rag and bottle shop lying in the shadow of the wall of Lincoln's Inn, and kept, as is announced in paint to all whom it may concern, by one Krook.

"This is where he lives, is it?" says the lawyer. "Thank you."

"Are you not going in, sir?"

"No thank you, no, I am going on to the Fields at present. Good-evening. Thank you!" Mr. Snagsby lifts his hat, and returns to his little woman and his tea.

But Mr. Tulkinghorn does not go on to the Fields at present. He goes a short way, turns back, comes again to the shop of Mr. Krook, and enters it straight. It is dim enough, with a blot-headed candle or so in the windows, and an old man and a cat sitting in the back part by a fire. The old man rises and comes forward, with another blot-headed candle in his hand.

"Pray is your lodger within?"

"Male or female, sir?" says Mr. Krook.

"Male. The person who does copying."

"Did you wish to see him, sir?"

"Yes."

"It's what I seldom do myself," says Mr. Krook with a grin. "Shall I call him down? But it's a weak chance if he'd come, sir!"

"I'll go up to him, then," says Mr. Tulkinghorn.

"Second floor, sir. Take the candle. Up there!" Mr. Krook stands at the bottom of the staircase, looking after Mr. Tulkinghorn. "Hi—hi!" he says, when Mr. Tulkinghorn has nearly disappeared. The lawyer looks down over the hand-rail. "You know what they say of my lodger?" whispers Krook, going up a step or two. "They say he has sold himself to the Enemy; but you and I know better—he don't buy. I'll tell you what, though—my lodger is so black-humoured and gloomy that I believe he'd as soon make that bargain as any other. Don't put him out, sir. That's my advice!"

Mr. Tulkinghorn with a nod goes on his way. He comes to the dark door on the second floor. He knocks, receives no answer, opens it, and accidentally extinguishes his candle in doing so.

The air of the room is almost bad enough to have extinguished it if he had not. It is a small room, nearly black with soot, and grease, and dirt. In the rusty skeleton of a grate, a red coke fire burns low. In the corner by the chimney stand a deal table and a broken desk. In another corner, a ragged old portmanteau, on one of the two chairs, serves for cabinet or wardrobe; no larger one is needed, for it collapses like the cheeks of a starved man. The discoloured shutters are drawn together, and through the two gaunt holes pierced in them famine might be staring in.

For on a low bed opposite the fire, a confusion of dirty patchwork, lean-ribbed ticking, and coarse sacking, the lawyer, hesitating just within the doorway, sees a man. He lies there dressed in shirt and trousers, with bare feet. He has a yellow look in the spectral darkness of a candle that has guttered down until the whole length of its wick (still burning) has doubled over, and left a tower of winding-sheet above it. His hair is ragged, mingling with his whiskers and his beard —the latter ragged too, and grown, like the scum around him, in neglect. Foul and filthy as the room is, foul and filthy as the air is, it is not easy to perceive what fumes those are which most oppress the senses in it; but through the general sickliness and faintness, and the odour of stale tobacco, there comes into the lawyer's mouth the bitter, vapid taste of opium.

"Hallo, my friend!" he cries, and strikes his iron candlestick against the door. His friend lies a little turned away, but his eyes are surely open. "Hallo, my friend!" he cries again. "Hallo! Hallo!"

As he rattles on the door, the candle which has drooped so long goes out and leaves him in the dark, with the gaunt eyes in the shutters staring down upon the bed.

## CHAPTER 11

*Our Dear Brother*

A TOUCH on the lawyer's wrinkled hand as he stands in the dark room, irresolute, makes him start and say, "What's that?"

"It's me," returns the old man of the house, whose breath is in his ear. "Can't you wake him?"

"No."

"What have you done with your candle?"

"It's gone out. Here it is."

Krook takes it, goes to the fire, stoops over the red embers, and tries to get a light. The dying ashes have no light to spare, and his endeavours are vain. Muttering that he will go down and bring a lighted candle from the shop, the old man departs. Mr. Tulkinghorn does not await his return in the room, but on the stairs outside. The welcome light soon shines upon the wall as Krook comes slowly up, with his green-eyed cat following at his heels. "Does the man generally sleep like this?" inquires the lawyer, in a low voice. "Hi! I don't know," says Krook, shaking his head and lifting his eyebrows. "I know next to nothing of his habits, except that he keeps himself very close."

Thus whispering, they both go in together. As the light goes in, the great eyes in the shutters, darkening, seem to close. Not so the eyes upon the bed.

"God save us!" exclaims Mr. Tulkinghorn. "He is dead!"

Krook drops the heavy hand he has taken up, so suddenly that the arm swings over the bedside. They look at one another for a moment.

"Send for some doctor! Call for Miss Flite up the stairs, sir. Here's poison by the bed! Call out for Flite, will you?" says Krook.

Mr. Tulkinghorn hurries to the landing and calls "Miss Flite! Flite! Make haste here, whoever you are! Flite!" Krook follows him with his eyes.

"Run, Flite, run! The nearest doctor! Run!" So Mr. Krook addresses a crazy little woman who is his female lodger; who appears and vanishes in a breath; who soon returns, accompanied by a testy medical man—brought from his dinner—with a broad snuffy upper lip and a broad Scotch tongue.

"Ey! Bless the hearts o' ye," says the medical man, looking up at them after a moment's examination. "He's just as dead as Phairy!"

Mr. Tulkinghorn (standing by the old portmanteau) inquires if he has been dead any time.

"Any time, sir?" says the medical man. "It's probable he wull have been dead aboot three hours."

"About that time, I should say," observes a dark young man, on the other side of the bed.

"Air you in the maydickle prayfession yourself, sir?" inquires the first. The dark young man says yes. "Then I'll just tak' my depairture," replies the other, "for I'm nae gude here!" With which remark, he finishes his brief attendance, and returns to finish his dinner.

The dark young surgeon passes the candle across and across the face, and carefully examines the law-writer, who has established his pretensions to his name by becoming indeed No one.

"I knew this person by sight, very well," says he. "He has purchased opium of me for the last year and a half. Was anybody present related to him?"—glancing round upon the three bystanders.

"I was his landlord," grimly answers Krook. "He told me once I was the nearest relation he had."

"He has died," says the surgeon, "of an overdose of opium, there is no doubt. The room is strongly flavoured with it. There is enough here now"—taking an old tea-pot from Mr. Krook—"to kill a dozen people."

"Do you think he did it on purpose?" asks Krook.

"I can't say. I should think it unlikely, as he has been in the habit of taking so much. But nobody can tell. He was very poor, I suppose?"

"I suppose he was. His room—don't look rich," says Krook, who might have changed eyes with his cat as he casts his sharp glance around. "But I have never been in it since he had it, and he was too close to name his circumstances to me."

"Did he owe you any rent?"

"Six weeks."

"He will never pay it!" says the young man, resuming his examination. "It is beyond a doubt that he is indeed as dead as Pharaoh and to judge from his appearance and condition, I should think it a happy release. Yet he must have been a good figure when a youth, and I dare say good-looking. I recollect once thinking there was something in his manner, uncouth as it was, that denoted a fall in life. Was that so?"

Krook replies, "You might as well ask me to describe the ladies whose heads of hair I have got in sacks downstairs. Than that he was my lodger for a year and a half, and lived—or didn't live—by law-writing, I know no more of him."

During this dialogue, Mr. Tulkinghorn has stood aloof by the old portmanteau, with his hands behind him, equally removed, to all appearance, from all kinds of interest. His imperturbable face has been as inexpressive as his rusty clothes. He has shown neither patience nor impatience, nor attention nor abstraction. He has shown nothing but his shell. He now interposes, addressing the young surgeon in his unmoved, professional way.

"I looked in here," he observes, "just before you, with the intention of giving this deceased man, whom I never saw alive, some employment at his trade of copying. I had heard of him from my stationer—Snagsby of Cook's Court. Since no one here knows anything about him, it might be as well to send for Snagsby. Ah!"—to the little crazy woman, who proposes, in frightened dumb-show, to go for the law-stationer—"Suppose you do!"

While she is gone, the surgeon abandons his hopeless investigation, and covers its subject with the patchwork counterpane. Mr. Krook and he interchange a word or two. Mr. Tulkinghorn says nothing, but stands ever near the old portmanteau.

Mr. Snagsby arrives hastily, in his grey coat and his black sleeves.

"Dear me, dear me," he says, "and it has come to this, has it! Bless my soul!"

"Can you give the person of the house any information about this unfortunate creature, Snagsby?" inquires Mr. Tulkinghorn. "He was in arrears with his rent, it seems. And he must be buried, you know."

"Well, sir," says Mr. Snagsby, coughing his apologetic cough behind his hand, "I really don't know what advice I could offer, except sending for the beadle."

"I don't speak of advice, I speak of affording some clue to his connexions, or to where he came from, or to anything concerning him."

"I assure you, sir," says Mr. Snagsby, "that I no more know where he came from than I know—"

"Where he has gone to, perhaps," suggests the surgeon, to help him out.

A pause. Mr. Tulkinghorn looking at the law-stationer. Mr. Krook, with his mouth open, looking for somebody to speak next.

"As to his connexions, sir," says Mr. Snagsby, "if a person was to say to me, 'Snagsby, here's twenty thousand pound down, ready for you in the Bank of England if you'll only name one of 'em,' I couldn't do it, sir! About a year and a half ago, he came into our place one morning after breakfast, and, finding Mrs. Snagsby in our shop, produced a specimen of his handwriting, and gave her to understand that he was in want of copying work to do, and was—not to put too fine a point upon it—hard up! My little woman is not in general partial to strangers, particular when they want anything. But she was rather took by something about this person—whether by his being unshaved, or by his hair being in want of attention, or by what other ladies' reasons, I leave you to judge—and she accepted of the specimen, and likewise of the address. My little woman hasn't a good ear for names, and she considered Nemo equally the same as Nimrod. In consequence of which, she got into a habit of saying to me at meals, 'Mr. Snagsby, you haven't found Nimrod any work yet!' or such-like. And that is the way he gradually fell into job-work at our place; and that is the most I know of him, except that he was a quick hand, and a hand not sparing of night-work."

"Hadn't you better see," says Mr. Tulkinghorn to Krook, "whether he had any papers that may enlighten you? There will be an Inquest, and you will be asked the question. You can read?"

"No, I can't," returns the old man, with a sudden grin.

"Snagsby," says Mr. Tulkinghorn, "look over the room for him. He will get into some trouble or difficulty, otherwise. Being here, I'll wait, if you make haste, and then I can testify on his behalf, if it should ever be necessary, that all was fair and right."

"In the first place, here's an old portmanteau, sir," says Snagsby.

Ah, to be sure, so there is! Mr. Tulkinghorn does not appear to have seen it before, though he is standing so close to it, and though there is very little else, Heaven knows. The marine-store merchant holds the light, and the law-stationer conducts the search. The surgeon leans against the corner of the chimney-piece; Miss Flite peeps and trembles just within the door. The apt old scholar of the old school, with his dull black breeches tied with ribbons at the knees, his large black waist-coat, his long-sleeved black coat, stands in exactly the same place and attitude.

There are some worthless articles of clothing in the old portmanteau; there is a bundle of pawnbrokers' duplicates, those turnpike tickets on the road of Poverty; there is a crumpled paper, smelling of opium, on which are scrawled rough memoranda. There are a few dirty scraps of newspapers, all referring to Coroner's Inquests; there is nothing else. They search the cupboard, and the drawer of the ink-splashed table. There is not a morsel of an old letter, or of any other writing, in either. The young surgeon examines the dress on the law-writer. A knife and some odd halfpence are all he finds. Mr. Snagsby's suggestion is the practical suggestion after all, and the beadle must be called in.

So the little crazy lodger goes for the beadle, and the rest come out of the room. "Don't leave the cat there!" says the surgeon, "that won't do!" Mr. Krook therefore drives her out before him, and she goes furtively downstairs, winding her lithe tail and licking her lips.

"Good-night!" says Mr. Tulkinghorn, and goes home to Allegory and meditation.

By this time the news has got into the court. Groups of its inhab-itants assemble to discuss the thing; and the outposts of the army of observation (principally boys) are pushed forward to Mr. Krook's win-dow, which they closely invest. A policeman has already walked up to the room, and walked down again to the door, where he stands like a tower. People talk across the court out of the window, and bare-headed scouts come hurrying in from Chancery Lane to know what's the matter. In the midst of this sensation, the beadle arrives.

The beadle, though generally understood in the neighbourhood to be a ridiculous institution, is not without a certain popularity for the moment, if it were only as a man who is going to see the body. The sensation is heightened as the tidings spread from mouth to mouth that the beadle is on the ground, and has gone in.

By and by the beadle comes out, once more intensifying the sensa-tion, which has rather languished in the interval. He is understood to be in want of witnesses, for the Inquest tomorrow, who can tell the Coroner and jury anything whatever respecting the deceased. Is immediately referred to innumerable people who can tell nothing whatever. Public loses interest, and undergoes reaction.

And all that night the coffin stands ready by the old portmanteau; and the lonely figure on the bed, whose path in life has lain through five-and-forty years, lies there with no more track behind him, that any one can trace, than a deserted infant.

Next day the court is all alive. The Coroner is to sit in the first-floor room at the Sol's Arms, where the Harmonic Meetings take place twice a week. The Sol's Arms does a brisk stroke of business all the morning.

At the appointed hour arrives the Coroner, who is received with a salute of skittles from the good dry skittle-ground attached to the Sol's Arms. He is conducted by the beadle and the landlord to the Harmonic Meeting Room, where he puts his hat on the piano, and takes a Windsor-chair at the head of a long table formed of several short tables put together. As many of the jury as can crowd together at the table sit there. The rest get among the spittoons and pipes, or lean against the piano.

"Well, gentlemen," the Coroner begins, "you are impanelled here to inquire into the death of a certain man. Evidence will be given before you as to the circumstances attending that death, and you will give your verdict according to the evidence, and not according to anything else. The first thing to be done is to view the body."

So they go out in a loose procession, something after the manner of a straggling funeral, and make their inspection in Mr. Krook's back second floor. The beadle is very careful that two gentlemen should see all that is to be seen. For they are public chroniclers, and he hopes to read in print what "Mooney, the active and intelligent beadle," said and did. On their return, Mr. Tulkinghorn is received with distinction, and seated near the Coroner. The inquiry proceeds. The jury learn how the subject of their inquiry died, and learn no more about him. "A very eminent solicitor is in attendance, gentlemen," says the Coroner, "who, I am informed, was accidentally present when discovery of the death was made; but he could only repeat the evidence you have already heard from the surgeon, the landlord, the lodger, and the law-stationer, and it is not necessary to trouble him. Is anybody in attendance who knows anything more?"

Mrs. Piper pushed forward. Mrs. Piper sworn.

"Anastasia Piper, gentlemen. Married woman. Now, Mrs. Piper, what have you got to say about this?"

Why, Mrs. Piper has not much to tell. Has seen the Plaintive (as she insists on calling the deceased) wexed and worrited by the children. Has seen him hurry away when run and called after as if not partial to children, and never see him speak to neither child nor grown person at any time excepting the boy that sweeps the crossing down the lane over the way round the corner.

Says the Coroner, "Is that boy here?" Says the beadle, "No, sir, he is not here." Says the Coroner, "Go and fetch him then." In the absence of the active and intelligent, the Coroner converses with Mr. Tulkinghorn.

"Oh! Here's the boy, gentlemen!" Here he is, very muddy, very hoarse, very ragged. "Now, boy!"— But stop a minute. Caution. This boy must be put through a few preliminary paces.

Name, Jo. Nothing else that he knows on. Don't know that everybody has two names. Never heerd of sich a think. Don't know that Jo is short for a longer name. Thinks it long enough for *him. He* don't find no fault with it. Spell it? No. *He* can't spell it. No father, no mother, no friends. Never been to school. What's home? Knows a broom's a broom, and knows it's wicked to tell a lie. Don't recollect who told him about the broom, or about the lie, but knows both. Can't exactly say what'll be done to him arter he's dead if he tells a lie to the gentlemen here, but believes it'll be something wery bad to punish him, and serve him right—and so he'll tell the truth.

"This won't do, gentlemen!" says the Coroner, with a melancholy shake of the head.

"Don't you think you can receive his evidence, sir?" asks an attentive juryman.

"Out of the question," says the Coroner. "You have heard the boy. 'Can't exactly say' won't do, you know. We can't take *that,* in a Court of Justice, gentlemen. Put the boy aside."

Boy put aside, to the great edification of the audience.

Now. Is there any other witness? No other witness.

Very well, gentlemen! Here's a man unknown, proved to have been in the habit of taking opium in large quantities for a year and a half, found dead of too much opium. If you think you have any evidence to lead you to the conclusion that he committed suicide, you will come to that conclusion. If you think it is a case of accidental death, you will find a verdict accordingly.

Verdict accordingly. Accidental death. No doubt. Gentlemen, you are discharged. Good-afternoon.

While the Coroner buttons his greatcoat, Mr. Tulkinghorn and he give private audience to the rejected witness in a corner. That graceless creature only knows that the dead man (whom he recognized just now by his yellow face and black hair) was sometimes hooted and pursued about the streets. That the man had often spoken to him, and asked him whether he slept sound at night, and how he bore cold and hunger, and whether he ever wished to die, and similar strange questions. That when the man had no money, he would say in passing, "I am as poor as you today, Jo"; but that when he had any, he had always been glad to give him some.

"He was wery good to me," says the boy, wiping his eyes with his wretched sleeve. "Wen I see him a-layin' so stritched out just now, I wished he could have heerd me tell him so. He wos wery good to me, he wos!"

As he shuffles downstairs, Mr. Snagsby, lying in wait for him, puts a halfcrown in his hand. "If you ever see me coming past your crossing with my little woman—I mean a lady—" says Mr. Snagsby, with his finger on his nose, "don't allude to it!"

Thus gradually the Sol's Arms melts into the shadowy night. There is rest around the lonely figure, now laid in its last earthly habitation; and it is watched by the gaunt eyes in the shutters through some quiet hours of night.

It is anything but a night of rest at Mr. Snagsby's, in Cook's Court, where Guster murders sleep by going, as Mr. Snagsby himself allows, out of one fit into twenty.

Daylight comes, morning comes, noon comes. Then the active and intelligent, who has got into the morning papers as such, comes with his pauper company to Mr. Krook's, and bears off the body of our dear brother here departed, to a hemmed-in churchyard, pestiferous and obscene, whence malignant diseases are communicated to the bodies of our dear brothers and sisters who have not departed. Into a beastly scrap of ground which a Turk would reject as a savage abomination, and a Caffre would shudder at, they bring our dear brother here departed, to receive Christian burial.

With the night comes a slouching figure through the tunnel-court, to the outside of the iron gate. It holds the gate with its hands, and looks in between the bars; stands looking in, for a little while. It then, with an old broom it carries, softly sweeps the step, and makes the archway clean. It does so very busily and trimly, looks in again a little while, and so departs.

# CHAPTER 12

*On the Watch*

Ir has left off raining down in Lincolnshire, at last, and Chesney Wold has taken heart. Mrs. Rouncewell is full of hospitable cares, for Sir Leicester and my Lady are coming home from Paris. The fashionable intelligence has found it out. It has also found out that they will entertain a brilliant and distinguished circle of the *élite* of the *beau monde* (the fashionable intelligence is weak in English, but a giant refreshed in French) at the ancient and hospitable family seat in Lincolnshire.

The clear cold sunshine glances into the brittle woods. It looks in at the windows, and touches the ancestral portraits with bars and patches of brightness. Athwart the picture of my Lady, over the great chimney-piece, it throws a broad bend-sinister of light that strikes down crookedly into the hearth, and seems to rend it.

Through the same cold sunshine my Lady and Sir Leicester, in their travelling chariot, start for home. They canter off out of Paris. Sooth to say, they cannot go away too fast, for even here my Lady Dedlock has been bored to death. Weariness of soul lies before her, as it lies behind.

Sir Leicester is generally in a complacent state, and rarely bored. When he was nothing else to do, he can always contemplate his own greatness. It is a considerable advantage to a man to have so inexhaustible a subject. After reading his letters, he leans back in his corner of the carriage, and generally reviews his importance to society.

"You have an unusual amount of correspondence this morning?" says my Lady, after a long time. "I saw one of Mr. Tulkinghorn's long effusions, I think? Ha!" sighs my Lady. "He is the most tiresome of men!" "He sends—I really beg your pardon—he sends," says Sir Leicester, selecting the letter, and unfolding it, "a message to you. He says, 'I beg my respectful compliments to my lady, who, I hope, has benefited by the change. Will you do me the favour to mention that I have something to tell her on her return in reference to the person who copied the affidavit in the Chancery suit, which so powerfully stimulated her curiosity. I have seen him.'"

My Lady, leaning forward, looks out of her window.

"That's the message," observes Sir Leicester.

"I should like to walk a little," says my Lady, still looking out of her window.

"Walk?" repeats Sir Leicester, in a tone of surprise.

"I should like to walk a little," says my Lady, with unmistakable distinctness. "Please to stop the carriage."

The carriage is stopped, the man alights from the rumble, opens the door, and lets down the steps. My Lady alights so quickly, and walks away so quickly, that Sir Leicester, for all his scrupulous politeness, is unable to assist her, and is left behind. A space of a minute or two has elapsed before he comes up with her. She smiles, takes his arm, lounges with him for a quarter of a mile, is very much bored, and resumes her seat in the carriage. Their courtly politeness to each other at the hotels where they tarry is the theme of general admiration. Though my Lord *is* a little aged for my Lady, says Madame, the hostess of the Golden Ape, and though he might be her amiable father, one can see at a glance that they love each other. It is ravishing! The sea has no appreciation of great men, but knocks them about like the small fry. It is habitually hard upon Sir Leicester. Nevertheless, his dignity gets over it, after stopping to refit, and he goes on with my Lady for Chesney Wold, lying only one night in London on the way to Lincolnshire.

Through the same cold sunlight—colder as the day declines—they drive into the park. The travelling chariot rolls on to the house, where fires gleam warmly through some of the windows.

Mrs. Rouncewell is in attendance, and receives Sir Leicester's customary shake of the hand with a profound curtsey.

"How do you do, Mrs. Rouncewell? I am glad to see you."

"I hope I have the honour of welcoming you in good health, Sir Leicester?"

"In excellent health, Mrs. Rouncewell."

"My lady is looking charmingly well," says Mrs. Rouncewell, with another curtsey.

My Lady signifies, without profuse expenditure of words, that she is as wearily well as she can hope to be. But Rosa is in the distance, behind the housekeeper; and my Lady asks:

"Who is that girl?"

"A young scholar of mine, my lady. Rosa."

"Come here, Rosa!" Lady Dedlock beckons her, with even an appearance of interest. "Why, do you know how pretty you are, child?" she says, touching her shoulder with her two forefingers.

Rosa, very much abashed, says, "No, if you please, my lady!" and glances up, and glances down, and don't know where to look, but looks all the prettier.

"How old are you?"

"Nineteen, my lady."

"Nineteen," repeats my Lady thoughtfully. "Take care they don't spoil you by flattery."

"Yes, my lady."

My Lady taps her dimpled cheek with the same delicate gloved fingers, and goes on to the foot of the oak staircase, where Sir Leicester pauses for her as her knightly escort.

That evening, in the housekeeper's room, Rosa can do nothing but murmur Lady Dedlock's praises. She is so affable, so graceful, so beautiful, so elegant, has such a sweet voice, and such a thrilling touch, that Rosa can feel it yet! Mrs. Rouncewell confirms all this, not without personal pride, reserving only the one point of affability. If my lady would only be "a little more free," not quite so cold and distant, Mrs. Rouncewell thinks she would be more affable.

" 'Tis almost a pity," Mrs. Rouncewell adds, "that my lady has no family. If she had had a daughter now, a grown young lady, to interest her, I think she would have had the only kind of excellence she wants."

"Might not that have made her still more proud, Grandmother?" says Watt, who has been home and come back again.

" 'More' and 'most,' my dear," returns the housekeeper with dignity, "are words it's not my place to use—nor so much as to hear—applied to any drawback on my lady."

"I beg your pardon, Grandmother. But she *is* proud, is she not?"

"If she is, she has reason to be. The Dedlock family have always reason to be."

"Well," says Watt, "it's to be hoped they line out of their prayer-books a certain passage for the common people about pride and vain-glory. Forgive me, Grandmother! Only a joke!"

"Sir Leicester and Lady Dedlock, my dear, are not fit subjects for joking."

"Sir Leicester is no joke by any means," says Watt, "and I humbly ask his pardon. I suppose, Grandmother, that there is no objection to my prolonging my stay at the Dedlock Arms for a day or two?"

"Surely, none in the world, child."

"I am glad of that," says Watt, "because I have an inexpressible desire to extend my knowledge of this beautiful neighbourhood."

He happens to glance at Rosa, who looks down, and is very shy indeed. But according to the old superstition, it should be Rosa's ears that burn, and not her fresh bright cheeks, for my Lady's maid is holding forth about her at this moment.

My Lady's maid is a Frenchwoman of two-and-thirty, from somewhere in the southern country about Avignon and Marseille—a large-eyed brown woman with black hair who would be handsome but for a certain feline mouth, and general uncomfortable tightness of face, rendering the jaws too eager and the skull too prominent. There is something indefinably keen and wan about her anatomy; and she has a watchful way of looking out of the corners of her eyes without turning her head. Besides being accomplished in all the knowledge appertaining to her post, she is almost an Englishwoman in her acquaintance with the language—consequently she is in no want of words to shower upon Rosa for having attracted my Lady's attention and she pours them out with grim ridicule as she sits at dinner.

Ha, ha, ha! She, Hortense, been in my lady's service since five years, and always kept at the distance, and this doll, this puppet, caressed—absolutely caressed—by my lady on the moment of her arriving at the house! Ha, ha, ha! "And do you know how pretty you are, child?"—"No, my lady."—You are right there! "And how old are you, child! And take care they do not spoil you by flattery, child!" Oh how droll! It is the *best* thing altogether.

In short, it is such an admirable thing that Mademoiselle Hortense can't forget it; but at meals for days afterwards, even among her country-women and others attached in like capacity to the troop of visitors, relapses into silent enjoyment of the joke—an enjoyment expressed by an additional tightness of face, thin elongation of compressed lips, and sidewise look.

All the mirrors in the house are brought into action now—many of them after a long blank. They reflect handsome faces, simpering faces, youthful faces, the entire collection of faces that have come to pass a January week or two at Chesney Wold. The place in Lincolnshire is all alive. By day, guns and voices are heard ringing in the woods, horsemen and carriages enliven the park roads, servants and hangers-on pervade the village and the Dedlock Arms. Seen by night, from distant openings in the trees, the row of windows in the long drawing-room, where my Lady's picture hangs over the great chimney-piece, is like a row of jewels set in a black frame. On Sunday, the chill little church is almost warmed by so much gallant company, and the general flavour of the Dedlock dust is quenched in delicate perfumes.

Chesney Wold is quite full. Only one room is empty. It is a turret chamber of the third order of merit, plainly but comfortably furnished, and having an old-fashioned business air. It is Mr. Tulkinghorn's room, and is never bestowed on anybody else, for he may come at any time. He is not come yet. It is his quiet habit to walk across the park from the village, in fine weather—to drop into this room as if he had never been out of it since he was last seen there; to request a servant to inform Sir Leicester that he is arrived, in case he should be wanted; and to appear ten minutes before dinner, in the shadow of the library-door.

Every day before dinner, my Lady looks for him in the dusk of the library, but he is not there. Every day at dinner, my Lady glances down the table for the vacant place that would be waiting to receive him if he had just arrived; but there is no vacant place. Every night, my Lady casually asks her maid:

"Is Mr. Tulkinghorn come?"

Every night the answer is, "No, my lady, not yet."

At length, one afternoon a little before sunset, when the bright groups of figures which have for the last hour or two enlivened the Ghost's Walk are all dispersed, and only Sir Leicester and my Lady remain upon the terrace, Mr. Tulkinghorn appears. He comes towards them at his usual methodical pace, which is never quickened, never slackened. He wears his usual expressionless mask—if it be a mask—and carries family secrets in every limb of his body, and every crease of his dress.

"How do you do, Mr. Tulkinghorn?" says Sir Leicester, giving him his hand.

Mr. Tulkinghorn is quite well. Sir Leicester is quite well. My Lady is quite well. All highly satisfactory. The lawyer, with his hands behind him, walks at Sir Leicester's side along the terrace. My Lady walks upon the other side.

"We expected you before," says Sir Leicester.

"I should have come down sooner but that I have been much engaged with those matters in the several suits between yourself and Boythorn."

"A man of a very ill-regulated mind," observes Sir Leicester, with severity. "An extremely dangerous person in any community."

"He is obstinate," says Mr. Tulkinghorn.

"It is natural to such a man to be so," says Sir Leicester, looking most profoundly obstinate himself. "I am not at all surprised to hear it."

Mr. Tulkinghorn says, "Mr. Boythorn will give us a good deal of trouble."

"It is the character of such a mind, Mr. Tulkinghorn, *to* give trouble. An exceedingly ill-conditioned, levelling person. A person who, fifty years ago, would probably have been tried at the Old Bailey for some demagogue proceeding, and severely punished—if not," adds Sir Leicester, after a moment's pause, "if not hanged, drawn, and quartered. But

night is coming on, and my lady will take cold. My dear, let us go in."

As they turn towards the hall-door, Lady Dedlock addresses Mr. Tulkinghorn for the first time.

"You sent me a message respecting the person whose writing I happened to inquire about. It was like you to remember the circumstance; I had quite forgotten it. Your message reminded me of it again. I can't imagine what association I had with a hand like that, but I surely had some. And did you really take the trouble to find out the writer of that actual thing—what is it!—affidavit?"

"Yes."

"How very odd!"

They passed into a sombre breakfast-room on the ground floor, lighted in the day by two deep windows. It is now twilight. The fire glows brightly on the panelled wall. My Lady lounges in a great chair in the chimney-corner, and Sir Leicester takes another great chair opposite. The lawyer stands before the fire. He looks at my Lady.

"Yes," he says, "I inquired about the man, and found him. And, what is very strange, I found him—dead."

"Oh dear me!" remonstrated Sir Leicester. Not so much shocked by the fact as by the fact of the fact being mentioned.

"I was directed to his lodging—a miserable, poverty-stricken place—and I found him dead."

"You will excuse me, Mr. Tulkinghorn," observes Sir Leicester, "I think the less said—"

"Pray, Sir Leicester, let me hear the story out" (it is my Lady speaking). "It is quite a story for twilight. How very shocking! Dead?"

Mr. Tulkinghorn reasserts it by another inclination of his head.

"Do let me hear the story!" says my Lady.

"Whatever you desire, my dear. But, I must say—"

"No, you mustn't say! Go on, Mr. Tulkinghorn."

Sir Leicester's gallantry concedes the point, though he still feels that to bring this sort of squalor among the upper classes is really—really—

"I was about to say," resumes the lawyer, "that he had unquestionably died of his own act, though whether by his own deliberate intention, or by mischance, can never certainly be known. The Coroner's jury found that he took the poison accidentally."

"And what kind of man," my Lady asks, "was this deplorable creature?"

"Very difficult to say," returns the lawyer, shaking his head. "He had lived so wretchedly, and was so neglected, with his gipsy colour and his wild black hair and beard, that I should have considered him the commonest of the common. The surgeon had a notion that he had once been something better."

"What did they call the wretched being?"

"They called him what he had called himself, but no one knew his name. He was found dead. In fact, I found him."

"Without any clue to anything more?"

"Without any. There was," says the lawyer meditatively, "an old portmanteau, but—there were no papers."

During the utterance of every word of this short dialogue, Lady Dedlock and Mr. Tulkinghorn, without any other alteration in their customary deportment, have looked very steadily at one another—as was natural, perhaps, in the discussion of so unusual a subject. Sir Leicester has looked at the fire. The story being told, he renews his stately protest, saying that as it is quite clear that no association in my Lady's mind can possibly be traceable to this poor wretch, he trusts to hear no more about a subject so far removed from my Lady's station.

"Certainly, a collection of horrors," says my Lady, gathering up her mantles and furs, "but they interest one for the moment! Have the kindness, Mr. Tulkinghorn, to open the door for me."

Mr. Tulkinghorn does so with deference, and holds it open while she passes out. She passes close to him, with her usual fatigued manner and insolent grace. They meet again at dinner—again, next day—again, for many days in succession. Lady Dedlock is always the same exhausted deity, surrounded by worshippers, and terribly liable to be bored to death, even while presiding at her own shrine. Mr. Tulkinghorn is always the same speechless repository of noble confidences: so oddly out of place, and yet so perfectly at home. They appear to take as little note of one another as any two people enclosed within the same walls could.

## CHAPTER 13

*Esther's Narrative*

WE held many consultations about what Richard was to be, first without Mr. Jarndyce, as he had requested, and afterwards with him, but it was a long time before we seemed to make progress. Richard said he was ready for anything. When Mr. Jarndyce doubted whether he might not already be too old to enter the Navy, Richard said he had thought of that, and perhaps he was. When Mr. Jarndyce asked him what he thought of the Army, Richard said he had thought of that too, and it wasn't a bad idea. When Mr. Jarndyce advised him to try and decide within himself whether his old preference for the sea was an ordinary boyish inclination, or a strong impulse, Richard answered, Well, he really *had* tried very often, and he couldn't make out.

"How much of this indecision of character," Mr. Jarndyce said to me, "is chargeable on that incomprehensible heap of uncertainty and procrastination on which he has been thrown from his birth, I don't pretend to say; but that Chancery, among its other sins, is responsible for some of it, I can plainly see. It has engendered or confirmed in him a habit of putting off—and trusting to this, that, and the other chance, without knowing what chance—and dismissing everything as unsettled, uncertain, and confused. The character of much older and steadier people may be even changed by the circumstances surrounding them. It would be too much to expect that a boy's in its formation should be the subject of such influences and escape them."

I felt this to be true, though, if I may venture to mention what I thought besides, I thought it much to be regretted that Richard's education had not counteracted those influences, or directed his character. He had been eight years at a public school, and had learnt, I understood, to make Latin verses of several sorts, in the most admirable manner. But I never heard that it had been anybody's business to find out what his natural bent was, or where his failings lay, or to adapt any kind of knowledge to *him*.

"I haven't the least idea," said Richard, musing, "what I had better be. Except that I am quite sure I don't want to go into the Church, it's a toss-up."

"You have no inclination in Mr. Kenge's way?" suggested Mr. Jarndyce.

"I don't know, sir!" replied Richard.

"Surgeon—" suggested Mr. Jarndyce.

"That's the thing, sir!" cried Richard. I doubt if he had ever once thought of it before. "That's the thing, sir," repeated Richard, with the greatest enthusiasm. "We have got it at last. M.R.C.S.!"

He was not to be laughed out of it, though he laughed *at* it heartily. He said he had chosen his profession, and the more he thought of it, the more he felt that his destiny was clear; the art of healing was the art of all others for him. Mistrusting that he only came to this conclusion because, having never had much chance of finding out for himself what he was fitted for, and having never been guided to the discovery, he was taken by the newest idea, and was glad to get rid of the trouble of consideration, I wondered whether the Latin verses often ended in this, or whether Richard's was a solitary case.

Mr. Jarndyce took great pains to talk with him seriously, and to put it to his good sense not to deceive himself in so important a matter. Richard was a little grave after these interviews, but invariably told Ada and me that it was "all right," and then began to talk about something else.

"By heaven!" cried Mr. Boythorn, who interested himself strongly in the subject, "I rejoice to find a young gentleman of spirit and gallantry devoting himself to that noble profession! The more spirit there is in it, the better for mankind, and the worse for those mercenary taskmasters and low tricksters who delight in putting that illustrious art at a disadvantage in the world. By all that is base and despicable," cried Mr. Boythorn, "the treatment of Surgeons aboard ship is such, that I would submit the legs—both legs—of every member of the Admiralty Board to

a compound fracture and render it a transportable offence in any qualified practitioner to set them if the system were not wholly changed in
eight and forty hours!"

He wound up this vehement declaration by looking round upon us
with a most agreeable smile, and suddenly thundering Ha, ha, ha! over
and over again.

As Richard still continued to say that he was fixed in his choice, after
repeated periods for consideration had been recommended by Mr. Jarndyce and had expired, and he still continued to assure Ada and me, in
the same final manner, that it was "all right," it became advisable to take
Mr. Kenge into council. Mr. Kenge, therefore, came down to dinner one
day, and leaned back in his chair, and turned his eye-glasses over and
over, and spoke in a sonorous voice, and did exactly what I remembered
to have seen him do when I was a little girl.

"Ah!" said Mr. Kenge. "Yes. Well! A very good profession, Mr. Jarndyce, a very good profession."

"The course of study and preparation requires to be diligently pursued," observed my guardian, with a glance at Richard.

"Oh no doubt," said Mr. Kenge. "Diligently. And Mr. Richard
Carstone, who has so meritoriously acquitted himself in the—shall I say
the classic shades?—in which his youth had been passed, will, no doubt,
apply the habits, if not the principles and practice, of versification in that
tongue in which a poet was said (unless I mistake) to be born, not made,
to the more eminently practical field of action on which he enters."

"You may rely upon it," said Richard, in his offhand manner, "that I
shall go at it and do my best."

"Very well, Mr. Jarndyce!" said Mr. Kenge, gently nodding his head.
"Really, when we are assured by Mr. Richard that he means to go at it,
and to do his best, I would submit to you that we have only to inquire
into the best mode of carrying out the object of his ambition. Now with
reference to placing Mr. Richard with some sufficiently eminent practitioner. Is there any one in view at present?"

"No one, Rick, I think?" said my guardian.

"No one, sir," said Richard.

"Quite so!" observed Mr. Kenge. "As to situation, now. Is there any
particular feeling on that head?"

"I should like a little variety," said Richard, "—I mean a good range of
experience."

"Very requisite, no doubt," returned Mr. Kenge. "I think this may be
easily arranged, Mr. Jarndyce? We have only, in the first place, to discover a sufficiently eligible practitioner, and as soon as we make our
want known, our only difficulty will be in the selection of one from a
large number. We have only, in the second place, to observe those little

formalities which are rendered necessary by our time of life, and our being under the guardianship of the Court. It is a coincidence," said Mr. Kenge, "that I have a cousin in the medical profession. He might be deemed eligible by you, and might be disposed to respond to this proposal. I can answer for him as little as for you, but he *might!*"

It was arranged that Mr. Kenge should see his cousin. And as Mr. Jarndyce had before proposed to take us to London for a few weeks, it was settled next day that we should make our visit at once, and combine Richard's business with it.

Mr. Boythorn leaving us within a week, we took up our abode at a cheerful lodging near Oxford Street, over an upholsterer's shop. London was a great wonder to us, and we were out for hours and hours at a time, seeing the sights—which appeared to be less capable of exhaustion than we were. We made the round of the principal theatres, too, with great delight, and saw all the plays that were worth seeing. I mention this because it was at the theatre that I began to be made uncomfortable again by Mr. Guppy.

I was sitting in front of the box one night with Ada, and Richard was in the place he liked best, behind Ada's chair, when, happening to look down into the pit, I saw Mr. Guppy, with his hair flattened down upon his head and woe depicted in his face, looking up at me. I felt all through the performance that he never looked at the actors, but constantly looked at me, and always with a carefully prepared expression of the deepest misery and the profoundest dejection. It quite spoiled my pleasure for that night, because it was so very embarrassing and so very ridiculous. But from that time forth we never went to the play without my seeing Mr. Guppy in the pit, always with his hair straight and flat, his shirt-collar turned down, and a general feebleness about him.

I really cannot express how uneasy this made me. If he would only have brushed up his hair, or turned up his collar, it would have been bad enough; but to know that that absurd figure was always gazing at me, and always in that demonstrative state of despondency, put such a constraint upon me that I did not like to laugh at the play, or to cry at it, or to move or to speak. I seemed able to do nothing naturally.

While we were making this round of gaieties, in which Mr. Guppy so extraordinarily participated, the business which had helped to bring us to town was not neglected. Mr. Kenge's cousin was a Mr. Bayham Badger, who had a good practice at Chelsea, and attended a large public institution besides. He was quite willing to receive Richard into his house, and to superintend his studies; and as it seemed that those could be pursued advantageously under Mr. Badger's roof, and Mr. Badger liked Richard, and as Richard said he liked Mr. Badger "well enough," an agreement was made, the Lord Chancellor's consent was obtained, and it was all settled.

On the day when matters were concluded between Richard and Mr. Badger, we were all under engagement to dine at Mr. Badger's house. We were to be "merely a family party," Mrs. Badger's note said, and we found no lady there but Mrs. Badger herself. She was a lady of about fifty, I should think, youthfully dressed, and of a very fine complexion. If I add that she rouged a little, I do not mean that there was any harm in it.

Mr. Bayham Badger himself was a pink, fresh-faced, crisp-looking gentleman with a weak voice, white teeth, light hair, and surprised eyes —some years younger, I should say, than Mrs. Bayham Badger. He admired her exceedingly, but principally, and to begin with, on the curious ground (as it seemed to us) of her having had three husbands. We had barely taken our seats when he said to Mr. Jarndyce quite triumphantly,

"You would hardly suppose that I am Mrs. Bayham Badger's third!"

"Indeed?" said Mr. Jarndyce.

"Her third!" said Mr. Badger. "Mrs. Bayham Badger has not the appearance, Miss Summerson, of a lady who has had two former husbands?"

I said, "Not at all!"

"And most remarkable men!" said Mr. Badger, in a tone of confidence. "Captain Swosser of the Royal Navy, who was Mrs. Badger's first husband, was a very distinguished officer indeed. The name of Professor Dingo, my immediate predecessor, is one of European reputation."

Dinner was announced, and we went downstairs. It was a very genteel entertainment, very handsomely served. But the Captain and the Professor still ran in Mr. Badger's head, and, as Ada and I had the honour of being under his particular care, we had the full benefit of them.

I observed that evening, as I had observed for some days past, that Ada and Richard were more than ever attached to each other's society, which was but natural, seeing that they were going to be separated so soon. I was therefore not very much surprised, when we got home and Ada and I retired upstairs, to find Ada more silent than usual, though I was not quite prepared for her coming into my arms, and beginning to speak to me with her face hidden.

"My darling Esther!" murmured Ada. "I have a great secret to tell you!"

"What is it, Ada?"

"Oh Esther, you would never guess!"

"Shall I try to guess?" said I.

"Oh no! Don't! Pray don't!" cried Ada, very much startled by the idea of my doing so.

"Now I wonder who it can be about?" said I, pretending to consider.

"It's about," said Ada, in a whisper. "It's about—my cousin Richard!"

"Well, my own!" said I, kissing her bright hair, which was all I could see. "And what about him?"

"Oh Esther, you would never guess! He says—I know it's very foolish, we are both so young—but he says," with a burst of tears, "that he loves me dearly, Esther."

"Does he indeed?" said I. "I never heard of such a thing! Why, my pet of pets, I could have told you that weeks and weeks ago! My darling, what a goose you must take me for! Your cousin Richard has been loving you, as plainly as he could, for I don't know how long!"

"And yet you never said a word about it!" cried Ada, kissing me.

"No, my love," said I. "I waited to be told."

"But now I have told you, you don't think it wrong of me, do you?" returned Ada. I said No, very freely. "And now," said I, "I know the worst of it."

"Oh, that's not quite the worst of it, Esther dear!" cried Ada, holding me tighter, and laying down her face again upon my breast.

"Why, you never mean to say—!" I was beginning in joke.

But Ada, looking up and smiling through her tears, cried, "Yes, I do! You know, you know I do!" and then sobbed out, "With all my heart I do! With all my whole heart, Esther!"

I told her, laughing, why, I had known that too, just as well as I had known the other! And we sat before the fire, and I had all the talking to myself for a little while (though there was not much of it), and Ada was soon quiet and happy.

"Do you think my cousin John knows, dear Dame Durden?" she asked.

"Unless my cousin John is blind, my pet," said I, "I should think my cousin John knows pretty well as much as we know."

"We want to speak to him before Richard goes," said Ada timidly, "and we wanted you to advise us, and tell him so. Perhaps you wouldn't mind Richard's coming in, Dame Durden?"

"Oh! Richard is outside, is he, my dear?" said I.

"I am not quite certain," returned Ada, "but I think he's waiting at the door."

There he was, of course. They brought a chair on either side of me, and put me between them, and really seemed to have fallen in love with me instead of one another, they were so confiding, and so trustful, and so fond of me. They went on in their own wild way for a little while—I never stopped them, I enjoyed it too much myself—and then we gradually fell to considering how young they were, and how there must be a lapse of several years before this early love could come to anything, and how it could come to happiness only if it were real and lasting, and inspired them with a steady resolution to do their duty to each other with constancy, fortitude, and perseverance—each always for the other's sake. Well! Richard said that he would work his fingers to the bone for Ada, and Ada said that she would work her fingers to the bone for Richard, and they called me all sorts of endearing and sensible names, and we sat there, advising and talking, half the night. Finally, before we parted, I gave them my promise to speak to their cousin John tomorrow.

So when tomorrow came, I went to my guardian after breakfast, in the room that was our town-substitute for the Growlery, and told him that I had it in trust to tell him something.

"Well, little woman," said he, shutting up his book, "if you have accepted the trust, there can be no harm in it."

"I hope not, Guardian," said I. "I can guarantee that there is no secrecy in it. For it only happened yesterday."

"Ay? And what is it, Esther?"

"Guardian," said I, "you remember the happy night when first we came down to Bleak House? When Ada was singing in the dark room?

Because—Ada and Richard have fallen in love. And have told each other so."

"Already!" cried my guardian, quite astonished.

"Yes!" said I. "And to tell you the truth, Guardian, I rather expected it."

"The deuce you did!" said he.

He sat considering for a minute or two, with his smile, at once so handsome and so kind, upon his changing face, and then requested me to let them know that he wished to see them. When they came, he encircled Ada with one arm in his fatherly way, and addressed himself to Richard with a cheerful gravity.

"Rick," said Mr. Jarndyce, "I am glad to have won your confidence. I hope to preserve it. When I contemplated these relations between us four which have so brightened my life, and so invested it with new interests and pleasures, I certainly did contemplate, afar off, the possibility of you and your pretty cousin here being in a mind to go through life together. I saw, and do see, many reasons to make it desirable. But that was afar off, Rick, afar off!"

"We look afar off, sir," returned Richard.

"Well!" said Mr. Jarndyce. "That's rational. Now hear me, my dears! I might tell you that you don't know your own minds yet; that a thousand things may happen to divert you from one another; that it is well this chain of flowers you have taken up is very easily broken, or it might become a chain of lead. But I will not do that. Such wisdom will come soon enough, I dare say, if it is to come at all. I will assume that a few years hence you will be in your hearts to one another what you are today. All I say before speaking to you according to that assumption is, if you *do* change don't be ashamed still to confide in me, for there will be nothing monstrous or uncommon in it. I am only your friend and distant kinsman. I have no power over you whatever. But I wish and hope to retain your confidence, if I do nothing to forfeit it."

"I am very sure, sir," returned Richard, "that I speak for Ada too when I say that you have the strongest power over us both—rooted in respect, gratitude, and affection."

"Dear Cousin John," said Ada, on his shoulder, "my father's place can never be empty again. All the love and duty I could ever have rendered to him is transferred to you."

"Come!" said Mr. Jarndyce. "Now for our assumption. Now we lift our eyes up, and look hopefully at the distance! Rick, the world is before you, and it is most probable that as you enter it, so it will receive you. Trust in nothing but in Providence and your own efforts. Constancy in love is a good thing, but it means nothing, and is nothing, without constancy in every kind of effort. If you had the abilities of all the great men, past and present, you could do nothing well without sincerely meaning it, and setting about it. If you entertain the supposition that any real success, in great things or in small, ever was or could be, ever will or can be, wrested from Fortune by fits and starts, leave that wrong idea here, or leave your cousin Ada here."

"I will leave *it* here, sir," replied Richard smiling, "if I brought it here just now (but I hope I did not), and will work my way on to my cousin Ada in the hopeful distance."

"Right!" said Mr. Jarndyce. "If you are not to make her happy, why should you pursue her?"

"I wouldn't make her unhappy—no, not even for her love," retorted Richard, proudly.

"Well said!" cried Mr. Jarndyce. "That's well said! She remains here, in her home with me. Love her, Rick, in your active life no less than in her home when you revisit it, and all will go well. Otherwise, all will go ill. That's the end of my preaching. I think you and Ada had better take a walk."

Ada tenderly embraced him, and Richard heartily shook hands with him, and then the cousins went out of the room—looking back again directly, though, to say that they would wait for me.

The door stood open, and we both followed them with our eyes as they passed down the adjoining room on which the sun was shining, and out at its farther end. Richard with his head bent, and her hand drawn through his arm, was talking to her very earnestly; and she looked up in his face, listening, and seemed to see nothing else. So young, so beautiful, so full of hope and promise, they went on lightly through the sunlight, as their own happy thoughts might then be traversing the years to come, and making them all years of brightness. So they passed away into the shadow, and were gone. It was only a burst of light that had been so radiant. The room darkened as they went out, and the sun was clouded over.

"Am I right, Esther?" said my guardian, when they were gone. "Rick may gain out of this the quality he wants. Wants, at the core of so much that is good!" said Mr. Jarndyce, shaking his head. "I have said nothing to Ada, Esther. She has her friend and counsellor always near." And he laid his hand lovingly upon my head. I could not help showing that I was a little moved, though I did all I could to conceal it. "Tut, tut!" said he. "But we must take care, too, that our little woman's life is not all consumed in care for others."

"Care? My dear guardian, I believe I am the happiest creature in the world!"

"I believe so, too," said he. "But some one may find out what Esther never will—that the little woman is to be held in remembrance above all other people!"

I have omitted to mention in its place that there was some one else at the family dinner party. It was not a lady. It was a gentleman. It was a gentleman of a dark complexion—a young surgeon. He was rather reserved, but I thought him very sensible and agreeable. At least, Ada asked me if I did not, and I said yes.

## CHAPTER 14

*Deportment*

RICHARD left us on the very next evening, to begin his new career, and committed Ada to my charge with great love for her, and great trust in me. It touched me then to reflect, and it touches me now, more nearly, to remember, how they both thought of me, even at that engrossing time. I was a part of all their plans, for the present and the future. I was to write Richard once a week making my faithful report of Ada, who was to write to him every alternate day. I was to be informed, under his own hand, of all his labours and successes, I was to observe how resolute and persevering he would be. I was to be Ada's bridesmaid when they were married, I was to live with them afterwards, I was to keep all the keys of their house.

"And if the suit *should* make us rich, Esther—which it may, you know!" said Richard, to crown all. A shade crossed Ada's face. "My dearest Ada," asked Richard, "why not?"

"It had better declare us poor at once," said Ada.

"Oh! I don't know about that," returned Richard, "but at all events, it won't declare anything at once. It hasn't declared anything in Heaven knows how many years."

"Too true," said Ada.

"Yes, but," urged Richard, answering what her look suggested rather than her words, "the longer it goes on, dear Cousin, the nearer it must be to a settlement one way or other. Now, is not that reasonable?"

"You know best, Richard. But I am afraid if we trust to it, it will make us unhappy."

"But, my Ada, we are not going to trust to it!" cried Richard gaily. "We know it better than to trust to it. We only say that if it *should* make us rich, we have no objection to being rich. The Court is, by solemn settlement of law, our grim old guardian, and we are to suppose that what it gives us (when it give us anything) is our right. It is not necessary to quarrel with our right."

"No," said Ada, "but it may be better to forget all about it."

"Well, well," cried Richard, "then we will forget all about it! We consign the whole thing to oblivion. Dame Durden puts on her approving face, and it's done!"

"Dame Durden's face," said I, "does approve, and she thinks you can't do better."

So Richard said there was an end of it—and immediately began, on no other foundation, to build as many castles in the air as would man the great wall of China. He went away in high spirits. Ada and I, prepared to miss him very much, commenced our quieter career.

On our arrival in London, we had called with Mr. Jarndyce at Mrs. Jellyby's, but had not been so fortunate as to find her at home. It appeared that she had gone somewhere, to a tea-drinking, and had taken Miss Jellyby with her. Besides the tea-drinking, there was to be some considerable speech-making and letter-writing on the general merits of the cultivation of coffee, conjointly with natives, at the settlement of Borrioboola-Gha. All this involved, no doubt, sufficient active exercise of pen and ink to make her daughter's part in the proceedings anything but a holiday.

It being now beyond the time appointed for Mrs. Jellyby's return, we called again. She was in town, but not at home, having gone to Mile End, directly after breakfast, on some Borrioboolan business. I was sitting at the window with my guardian on the following morning, and Ada was busy writing—of course to Richard—when Miss Jellyby was announced, and entered leading Peepy, whom she had made some endeavours to render presentable by wiping the dirt into corners of his face and hands, and making his hair very wet and then violently frizzling it with her fingers. Everything the dear child wore was either too large for him or too small. Most extraordinary specimens of needlework appeared on several parts of his dress, where it had been hastily mended, and I recognized the same hand on Miss Jellyby's. She was, however, unaccountably improved in her appearance, and looked very pretty. Ada and I gave her a cordial welcome, and presented her to Mr. Jarndyce, to whom she said, as she sat down:

"Ma's compliments, and she hopes you'll excuse her, because she's correcting proofs of the plan. She's going to put out five thousand new circulars, and she knows you'll be interested to hear that. I have brought one of them with me. Ma's compliments." With which she presented it sulkily enough.

"Thank you," said my guardian. "I am much obliged to Mrs. Jellyby."

We were busy with Peepy, asking him if he remembered us and so on. Peepy retired behind his elbow at first, but relented at the sight of sponge-cake, and allowed me to take him on my lap, where he sat munching quietly. Mr. Jarndyce then withdrawing into the temporary Growlery, Miss Jellyby opened a conversation with her usual abruptness.

"We are going on just as bad as ever in Thavies Inn," said she. "I have no peace of my life. Talk of Africa! I couldn't be worse off if I was a—what's-his-name—man and a brother!"

I tried to say something soothing.

"Oh, it's of no use, Miss Summerson," exclaimed Miss Jellyby, "though I thank you for the kind intention all the same. I know how I am used, and I am not to be talked over. *You* wouldn't be talked over if you were used so. We really are going on worse than ever. Pa will be a bankrupt before long, and then I hope Ma will be satisfied. There'll be nobody but Ma to thank for it."

We said we hoped Mr. Jellyby's affairs were not in so bad a state as that.

"It's of no use hoping, though it's very kind of you," returned Miss Jellyby, shaking her head. "Pa told me, only yesterday morning (and dreadfully unhappy he is), that he couldn't weather the storm. I should be surprised if he could. When all our tradesmen send into our house any stuff they like, and the servants do what they like with it, and I have no time to improve things if I knew how, and Ma don't care about anything, I should like to make out how Pa *is* to weather the storm. I declare if I was Pa, I'd run away."

"My dear!" said I, "your papa, no doubt, considers his family."

"Oh yes, his family is all very fine, Miss Summerson," replied Miss Jellyby; "but what comfort is his family to him? His family is nothing but bills, dirt, waste, noise, tumbles down stairs, confusion, and wretchedness. His scrambling home, from week's end to week's end, is like one great washing-day—only nothing's washed! I am sure I pity Pa to that degree, and am so angry with Ma, that I can't find words to express myself! However, I am not going to bear it, I am determined. I won't be a slave all my life, and I won't submit to be proposed to by Mr. Quale. A pretty thing, indeed, to marry a Philanthropist. As if I hadn't had enough of *that!*" said poor Miss Jellyby.

I must confess that I could not help feeling rather angry with Mrs. Jellyby myself, seeing and hearing this neglected girl, and knowing how much of bitterly satirical truth there was in what she said.

"If it wasn't that we had been intimate when you stopped at our house," pursued Miss Jellyby, "I should have been ashamed to come here today, for I know what a figure I must seem to you two. But as it is,

I made up my mind to call—especially as I am not likely to see you again, the next time you come to town."

She said this with such great significance that Ada and I glanced at one another, foreseeing something more.

"No!" said Miss Jellyby, shaking her head. "Not at all likely! I know I may trust you two. I am engaged."

"Without their knowledge at home?" said I.

"Why, good gracious me, Miss Summerson," she returned, justifying herself in a fretful but not angry manner, "how can it be otherwise? You know what Ma is—and I needn't make poor Pa more miserable by telling *him*."

"But would it not be adding to his unhappiness, to marry without his knowledge or consent, my dear?" said I.

"No," said Miss Jellyby, softening. "I hope not. I should try to make him happy and comfortable when he came to see me, and Peepy and the others should take it in turns to come and stay with me, and they should have some care taken of them then."

There was a good deal of affection in poor Caddy. She softened more and more while saying this, and cried much over the unwonted little home-picture she had raised in her mind.

"It began in your coming to our house," she said. "I felt I was so awkward that I made up my mind to be improved in that respect, at all events, and to learn to dance. I told Ma I was ashamed of myself, and I must be taught to dance. Ma looked at me in that provoking way of hers as if I wasn't in sight; but I was quite determined to be taught to dance, and so I went to Mr. Turveydrop's Academy in Newman Street."

"And was it there, my dear—" I began.

"Yes, it was there," said Caddy, "and I am engaged to Mr. Turveydrop. There are two Mr. Turveydrops, father and son. My Mr. Turveydrop is the son, of course. I only wish I had been better brought up, and was likely to make him a better wife; for I am very fond of him."

"I am sorry to hear this," said I, "I must confess."

"I don't know why you should be sorry," she retorted, a little anxiously, "but I am engaged to Mr. Turveydrop, whether or no, and he is very fond of me. It's a secret as yet, even on his side, because old Mr. Turveydrop has a share in the connexion, and it might break his heart, or give him some other shock, if he was told of it abruptly. Old Mr. Turveydrop is a very gentlemanly man indeed—very gentlemanly."

"Does his wife know of it?" asked Ada.

"Old Mr. Turveydrop's wife, Miss Clare?" returned Miss Jellyby, opening her eyes. "There's no such person. He is a widower. That's the state of the case. If I ever blame myself, I still think it's Ma's fault. We are to be married whenever we can, and then I shall go to Pa at the office and write to Ma. It won't much agitate Ma, I am only pen and ink to *her*. One great comfort is," said Caddy, with a sob, "that I shall never hear of Africa after I am married. Young Mr. Turveydrop hates it for my sake, and if old Mr. Turveydrop knows there is such a place, it's as much as he does."

"It was he who was very gentlemanly, I think!" said I.

"Very gentlemanly indeed," said Caddy. "He is celebrated, almost everywhere, for his Deportment."

"Does he teach?" asked Ada.

"No, he don't teach anything in particular," replied Caddy. "But his Deportment is beautiful."

Caddy went on to say, with considerable hesitation and reluctance, that there was one thing more she wished us to know, and felt we ought to know, and which she hoped would not offend us. It was that she had improved her acquaintance with Miss Flite, the little crazy old lady, and that she frequently went there early in the morning, and met her lover for a few minutes before breakfast—only for a few minutes. "I go there, at other times," said Caddy, "but Prince does not come then. Young Mr. Turveydrop's name is Prince; I wish it wasn't, because it sounds like a dog, but of course he didn't christen himself. Old Mr. Turveydrop had him christened Prince in remembrance of the Prince Regent. Old Mr. Turveydrop adored the Prince Regent on account of his Deportment. I hope you won't think the worse of me for having made these little appointments at Miss Flite's, where I first went with you, because I like the poor thing for her own sake, and I believe she likes me. If you could see young Mr. Turveydrop, I am sure you would think well of him—at least, I am sure you couldn't possibly think any ill of him. I am going there now, for my lesson. I couldn't ask you to go with me, Miss Summerson, but if you would," said Caddy, who had said all this earnestly and tremblingly, "I should be very glad—very glad."

It happened that we had arranged with my guardian to go to Miss Flite's that day. We had told him of our former visit, and our account had interested him, but something had always happened to prevent our going there again. As I trusted that I might have sufficient influence with Miss Jellyby to prevent her taking any very rash step if I fully accepted the confidence she was so willing to place in me, poor girl, I proposed that she and I and Peepy should go to the Academy, and afterwards meet my guardian and Ada at Miss Flite's—whose name I now learnt for the first time. This was on condition that Miss Jellyby and Peepy should come back with us to dinner. The last article of the agreement being joyfully acceded to by both, we smartened Peepy up a little, with the assistance of a few pins, some soap and water, and a hairbrush, and went out, bending our steps towards Newman Street, which was very near.

I found the academy established in a sufficiently dingy house at the corner of an archway, with busts in all the staircase windows. In the same house there were also established, as I gathered from the plates on the door, a drawing-master, a coal-merchant, and a lithographic artist. On the plate which, in size and situation, took precedence of all the rest, I read MR. TURVEYDROP.

We went upstairs—it had been quite a fine house once, when it was anybody's business to keep it clean and fresh—and into Mr. Turveydrop's great room, which was built out into a mews at the back, and was lighted by a skylight. It was a bare, resounding room, smelling of stables; with cane forms along the walls, and the walls ornamented at regular intervals with painted lyres and little cut-glass branches for candles. Several young-lady pupils, ranging from thirteen or fourteen years of age to two or three and twenty, were assembled, and I was looking among them for their instructor when Caddy, pinching my arm, repeated the ceremony of introduction. "Miss Summerson, Mr. Prince Turveydrop!"

I curtseyed to a little blue-eyed, fair man of youthful appearance, with flaxen hair parted in the middle and curling at the ends all round his head. He had a little fiddle, which we used to call at school a kit, under his left arm, and its little bow in the same hand. His little dancing-shoes were particularly diminutive, and he had a little innocent, feminine manner, which not only appealed to me in an amiable way but made this singular effect upon me: that I received the impression that he was like his mother, and that his mother had not been much considered or well used.

"I am very happy to see Miss Jellyby's friend," he said, bowing low to me. "I began to fear," with timid tenderness, "as it was past the usual time, that Miss Jellyby was not coming."

"I beg you will have the goodness to attribute that to me, who have detained her, and to receive my excuses, sir," said I. "And pray do not allow me to be the cause of any more delay."

With that apology I withdrew to a seat between Peepy and an old lady of a censorious countenance, whose two nieces were in the class. Prince Turveydrop then tinkled the strings of his kit with his fingers, and the young ladies stood up to dance. Just then there appeared, from a side door, old Mr. Turveydrop, in the full lustre of his Deportment.

He was a fat old gentleman with a false complexion, false teeth, false whiskers, and a wig. He had a fur collar, and he had a padded breast to his coat, which only wanted a star or a broad blue ribbon to be complete. He was pinched in, and swelled out, and strapped down, as much as he could possibly bear. He had such a neckcloth on, and his chin and even his ears so sunk into it, that it seemed as though he must inevitably double up if it were cast loose. He had under his arm a hat of great size and weight, shelving downward from the crown to the brim, and in his hand a pair of white gloves, with which he flapped it as he stood poised on one leg, in a high-shouldered, round-elbowed state of elegance not to be surpassed. He had a cane, he had an eye-glass, he had a snuff-box, he had rings, he had wristbands, he had everything but any touch of nature; he was not like youth, he was not like age, he was not like anything in the world but a model of Deportment.

"Father! A visitor. Miss Jellyby's friend, Miss Summerson."

"Distinguished," said Mr. Turveydrop, "by Miss Summerson's presence." As he bowed to me in that tight state, I almost believe I saw creases come into the whites of his eyes.

"My father," said the son, aside to me, with quite an affecting belief in him, "is a celebrated character. My father is greatly admired."

"Go on, Prince! Go on!" said Mr. Turveydrop, waving his gloves condescendingly. "Go on, my son!"

At this command, or by this gracious permission, the lesson went on. Prince Turveydrop sometimes played the kit, dancing; sometimes played the piano, standing; sometimes hummed the tune with what little breath he could spare while he set a pupil right; always conscientiously moved with the least proficient through every step and every part of the figure; and never rested for an instant. His distinguished father did nothing whatever but stand before the fire, a model of Deportment.

"And he never does anything else," said the old lady of the censorious countenance. "Yet would you believe that it's *his* name on the door-plate?"

"His son's name is the same, you know," said I.

"He wouldn't let his son have any name if he could take it from him," returned the old lady.

I felt curious to know more concerning this person. I asked, "Does he give lessons in Deportment, now?"

"Now!" returned the old lady, shortly. "Never did."

After a moment's consideration, I suggested that perhaps fencing had been his accomplishment?

"I don't believe he can fence at all, ma'am," said the old lady.

I looked surprised and inquisitive. The old lady, becoming more and more incensed against the Master of Deportment as she dwelt upon the subject, gave me some particulars of his career. He had married a meek little dancing-mistress, with a tolerable connexion (having never in his life before done anything but deport himself), and had worked her to death, or had, at the best, suffered her to work herself to death, to maintain him in those expenses which were indispensable to his position. At once to exhibit his Deportment to the best models, and to keep the best models constantly before himself, he had found it necessary to frequent all public places of fashionable and lounging resort; to be seen at Brighton and elsewhere at fashionable times; and to lead an idle life in the very best clothes. To enable him to do this, the affectionate little dancing-mistress had toiled and laboured, and would have toiled and laboured to that hour if her strength had lasted so long. For the main-spring of the story was that, in spite of the man's absorbing selfishness, his wife had, to the last, believed in him, and had on her death-bed, in the most moving terms, confided him to their son as one who had an inextinguishable claim upon him. The son, inheriting his mother's be-lief, and having the Deportment always before him, had lived and grown in the same faith, and now, at thirty years of age, worked for his father twelve hours a day, and looked up to him with veneration on the old imaginary pinnacle.

"The airs the fellow gives himself!" said my informant, shaking her head at old Mr. Turveydrop with speechless indignation as he drew on his tight gloves. "He fully believes he is one of the aristocracy! And he is so condescending to the son he so egregiously deludes that you might suppose him the most virtuous of parents. Oh," said the old lady, apostrophizing him with infinite vehemence, "I could bite you!"

I could not help being amused, though I heard the old lady out with feelings of real concern. It was difficult to doubt her, with the father and son before me. My eyes were yet wandering from young Mr. Turveydrop working so hard to old Mr. Turveydrop deporting himself so beautifully when the latter came ambling up to me, and entered into conversation.

He asked me, first of all, whether I conferred a charm and a distinction on London by residing in it. I did not think it necessary to reply that I was perfectly aware I should not do that in any case, but merely told him where I did reside.

"A lady so graceful and accomplished," he said, kissing his right glove, "will look leniently on the deficiencies here. We do our best to polish—polish—polish!" He sat down beside me. "To polish—polish—polish!" he repeated, taking a pinch of snuff and gently fluttering his fingers. "But we are not—if I may say so to one formed to be graceful both by Nature and Art"—with the high-shouldered bow, which it seemed impossible for him to make without lifting up his eyebrows and shutting his eyes—"we are not what we used to be in point of Deportment. We have degenerated. A levelling age is not favourable to Deportment. It develops vulgarity. Perhaps I speak with some little partiality. It may not be for me to say that I have been called, for some years now, Gentleman Turveydrop; or that His Royal Highness the Prince Regent did me the honour to inquire, on my removing my hat as he drove out of the Pavilion at Brighton (that fine building), 'Who is he? Who the devil is he? Why don't I know him? Why hasn't he thirty thousand a year?' But these are little matters of anecdote—the general property, ma'am—still repeated, occasionally, among the upper classes."

"Indeed?" said I.

He replied with the high-shouldered bow. "Where what is left among us of Deportment," he added, "still lingers. England—alas, my country!—has degenerated very much, and is degenerating every day. She has not many gentlemen left. We are few. I see nothing to succeed us but a race of weavers."

"One might hope that the race of gentlemen would be perpetuated here," said I.

"You are very good," he smiled, with the high-shouldered bow again. "You flatter me. But, no—no! I have never been able to imbue my poor boy with that part of his art. Heaven forbid that I should disparage my dear child, but he has—no Deportment."

"He appears to be an excellent master," I observed.

"Understand me, my dear madam, he *is* an excellent master. All that can be acquired, he has acquired. All that can be imparted, he can impart. But there *are* things"—He took another pinch of snuff and made the bow again, as if to add, "this kind of thing, for instance."

I glanced towards the centre of the room, where Miss Jellyby's lover, now engaged with single pupils, was undergoing greater drudgery than ever.

"Your son is indefatigable," said I.

"It is my reward," said Mr. Turveydrop, "to hear you say so. In some respects, he treads in the footsteps of his sainted mother. She was a devoted creature. But Wooman, lovely Wooman," said Mr. Turveydrop, with very disagreeable gallantry, "what a sex you are!"

I rose and joined Miss Jellyby, who was by this time putting on her bonnet. The time allotted to a lesson having fully elapsed, there was a general putting-on of bonnets. When Miss Jellyby and the unfortunate Prince found an opportunity to become betrothed I don't know, but they certainly found none on this occasion to exchange a dozen words.

"My dear," said Mr. Turveydrop benignly to his son, "do you know the hour?"

"No, Father." The son had no watch. The father had a handsome gold one, which he pulled out.

"My son," said he, "it's two o'clock. Recollect your school at Kensington at three."

"That's time enough for me, Father," said Prince. "I can take a morsel of dinner standing, and be off."

"My dear boy," returned his father, "you must be very quick. You will find the cold mutton on the table."

"Thank you, Father. Are *you* off now, Father?"

"Yes, my dear. I suppose," said Mr. Turveydrop, shutting his eyes and lifting up his shoulders, with modest consciousness, "that I must show myself, as usual, about town."

"You had better dine out comfortably somewhere," said his son.

"My dear child, I intend to. I shall take my little meal, I think, at the French house in the Opera Colonnade."

"That's right. Good-bye, Father!" said Prince, shaking hands.

"Good-bye, my son. Bless you!"

Mr. Turveydrop said this in quite a pious manner, and it seemed to do his son good—who, in parting from him, was so pleased with him, so dutiful to him, and so proud of him, that I almost felt as if it were an unkindness to the younger man not to be able to believe implicitly in the elder. The few moments that were occupied by Prince in taking leave of us enhanced my favourable impression of his almost childish character. I felt a liking for him, and a compassion for him, as he put his

little kit in his pocket and went away good-humouredly to his cold
mutton and his school at Kensington, that made me scarcely less irate
with his father than the censorious old lady.

The father opened the room-door for us, and bowed us out in a
manner, I must acknowledge, worthy of his shining original. In the
same style he presently passed us on the other side of the street, on his
way to the aristocratic part of the town, where he was going to show
himself among the few other gentlemen left. For some moments, I was
so lost in reconsidering what I had heard and seen in Newman Street
that I was quite unable to talk to Caddy, or even to fix my attention on
what she said to me—especially when I began to inquire in my mind
whether there were, or ever had been, any other gentlemen, not in the
dancing profession, who lived and founded a reputation entirely on their
Deportment. This became so bewildering, and suggested the possibility of
so many Mr. Turveydrops, that I said, "Esther, you must make up your
mind to abandon this subject altogether, and attend to Caddy." I accordingly did so, and we chatted all the rest of the way to Lincoln's Inn.

Caddy told me that her lover's education had been so neglected that
it was not always easy to read his notes. She said if he were not so
anxious about his spelling, and took less pains to make it clear, he would
do better; but he put so many unnecessary letters into short words that
they sometimes quite lost their English appearance. "He does it with the
best intention," observed Caddy, "but it hasn't the effect he means, poor
fellow!" Caddy then went on to reason, how could he be expected to be
a scholar, when he had passed his whole life in the dancing-school, and
had done nothing but teach and fag, fag and teach, morning, noon, and
night! And what did it matter? She could write letters enough for both,
as she knew to her cost, and it was far better for him to be amiable than
learned. "Besides, it's not as if I was an accomplished girl who had any
right to give herself airs," said Caddy. "I know little enough, I am sure,
thanks to Ma!

"There's another thing I want to tell you, now we are alone," continued Caddy, "which I should not have liked to mention unless you had
seen Prince, Miss Summerson. You know what a house ours is. It's of no
use my trying to learn anything that it would be useful for Prince's
wife to know in *our* house. We live in such a state of muddle that it's
impossible, and I have only been more disheartened whenever I have
tried. So I get a little practice with—who do you think? Poor Miss Flite!
Early in the morning, I help her to tidy her room, and clean her birds;
and I make her cup of coffee for her (of course she taught me), and I
have learnt to make it so well that Prince says it's the very best coffee he
ever tasted, and would quite delight old Mr. Turveydrop, who is very
particular indeed about his coffee. I can make little puddings too, and I

know how to buy neck of mutton, and tea, and sugar, and butter, and a good many housekeeping things. I am not clever at my needle yet," said Caddy, glancing at the repairs on Peepy's frock, "but perhaps I shall improve, and since I have been engaged to Prince, and have been doing all this, I have felt better-tempered, I hope, and more forgiving to Ma. It rather put me out at first this morning to see you and Miss Clare looking so neat and pretty, and to feel ashamed of Peepy, and myself too; but on the whole, I hope I am better-tempered than I was, and more forgiving to Ma."

The poor girl, trying so hard, said it from her heart, and touched mine. "Caddy, my love," I replied, "I begin to have a great affection for you, and I hope we shall become friends." "Oh, do you?" cried Caddy. "How happy that would make me!" "My dear Caddy," said I, "let us be friends from this time, and let us often have a chat about these matters, and try to find the right way through them." Caddy was overjoyed. I said everything I could, in my old-fashioned way, to comfort and encourage her, and I would not have objected to old Mr. Turveydrop that day for any smaller consideration than a settlement on his daughter-in-law.

By this time, we were come to Mr. Krook's, whose private door stood open. There was a bill pasted on the door-post announcing a room to let on the second floor. It reminded Caddy to tell me as we proceeded upstairs that there had been a sudden death there, and an inquest, and that our little friend had been ill of the fright. The door and window of the vacant room being open, we looked in. It was the room with the dark door, to which Miss Flite had secretly directed my attention when I was last in the house. A sad and desolate place it was, a gloomy, sorrowful place, that gave me a strange sensation of mournfulness and even dread.

We had walked slowly while we were talking; and my guardian and Ada were here before us. We found them in Miss Flite's garret. They were looking at the birds while a medical gentleman who was so good as to attend Miss Flite with much solicitude and compassion spoke with her cheerfully by the fire.

"I have finished my professional visit," he said, coming forward. "Miss Flite is much better, and may appear in Court (as her mind is set upon it) tomorrow. She has been greatly missed there, I understand."

Miss Flite received the compliment with complacency, and dropped a general curtsey to us.

"Honoured indeed," said she, "by another visit from the wards in Jarndyce! Ve-ry happy to receive Jarndyce of Bleak House beneath my humble roof! Fitz-Jarndyce my dear"—she had bestowed that name on Caddy, it appeared—"a double welcome!"

"Has she been very ill?" asked Mr. Jarndyce of the gentleman whom we had found in attendance on her. She answered for herself directly, though he had put the question in a whisper.

"Oh, decidedly unwell! Oh, very unwell indeed," she said, confidentially. "Not pain, you know—trouble. Not bodily so much as nervous, nervous! The truth is"—in a subdued voice and trembling—"we have had death here. There was poison in the house. I am very susceptible to such horrid things. It frightened me. Only Mr. Woodcourt knows how much. My physician, Mr. Woodcourt! The wards in Jarndyce—Jarndyce of Bleak House—Fitz-Jarndyce!"

"Miss Flite," said Mr. Woodcourt, in a grave kind of voice as if he were appealing to her while speaking to us, and laying his hand gently on her arm, "Miss Flite describes her illness with her usual accuracy. She was alarmed by an occurrence in the house which might have alarmed a stronger person, and was made ill by the distress and agitation. She brought me here in the first hurry of the discovery, though too late for me to be of any use to the unfortunate man. I have compensated myself for that disappointment by coming here since, and being of some small use to her."

"The kindest physician in the college," whispered Miss Flite to me. "I expect a judgment. On the Day of Judgment. And shall then confer estates."

"She will be as well in a day or two," said Mr. Woodcourt, looking at her with an observant smile, "as she ever will be. In other words, quite well of course. Have you heard of her good fortune?"

"Most extraordinary!" said Miss Flite, smiling brightly. "You never heard of such a thing, my dear! Every Saturday, Conversation Kenge, or Guppy (clerk to Conversation K.), places in my hand a paper of shillings. Shillings. I assure you! Always the same number in the paper. Always one for every day in the week. Now you know, really! So well-timed, is it not? Ye-es! From whence do these papers come, you say? That is the great question. Naturally. Shall I tell you what *I* think? *I* think," said Miss Flite, drawing herself back with a very shrewd look, and shaking her right forefinger in a most significant manner, "that the Lord Chancellor, aware of the length of time during which the Great Seal has been open (for it has been open a long time!), forwards them. Until the judgment I expect is given. Now that's very creditable, you know. To confess in that way that he *is* a little slow for human life. So delicate! Attending Court the other day—I attend it regularly, with my documents—I taxed him with it, and he almost confessed. That is, I smiled at him from my bench, and *he* smiled at me from his bench. But it's great good fortune, is it not?"

I congratulated her (as she addressed herself to me) upon this fortunate addition to her income, and wished her a long continuance of it.

I did not speculate upon the source from which it came. My guardian stood before me, contemplating the birds, and I had no need to look beyond him.

"And what do you call these little fellows, ma'am?" said he in his pleasant voice. "Have they any names?"

"I can answer for Miss Flite that they have," said I, "for she promised to tell us what they were. Ada remembers?"

Ada remembered very well.

"Did I?" said Miss Flite—"Who's that at my door? What are you listening at my door for, Krook?"

The old man of the house, pushing it open before him, appeared there with his fur cap in his hand, and his cat at his heels.

"I warn't listening, Miss Flite," he said. "I was going to give a rap with my knuckles, only you're so quick!"

"Make your cat go down. Drive her away!" the old lady angrily exclaimed.

"Bah, bah!—There ain't no danger, gentlefolks," said Mr. Krook, looking slowly and sharply from one to another until he had looked at all of us. "She'd never offer at the birds when I was here, unless I told her to it."

"You will excuse my landlord," said the old lady with a dignified air. "M, quite M! What do you want, Krook, when I have company?"

"Hi!" said the old man. "You know I am the Chancellor."

"Well?" returned Miss Flite. "What of that?"

"For the Chancellor," said the old man, with a chuckle, "not to be acquainted with a Jarndyce is queer, ain't it, Miss Flite? Mightn't I take the liberty?—Your servant, sir. I know Jarndyce and Jarndyce a'most as well as you do, sir. I knowed old Squire Tom, sir. I never to my knowledge see you afore though, not even in Court. Yet I go there a mortal sight of times in the course of the year."

"I never go there," said Mr. Jarndyce (which he never did on any consideration). "I would sooner go—somewhere else."

"Would you though?" returned Krook, grinning. "You're bearing hard upon my noble and learned brother in your meaning, sir, though perhaps it is but nat'ral in a Jarndyce. The burnt child, sir! What, you're looking at my lodger's birds, Mr. Jarndyce?" The old man had come by little and little into the room, until he now touched my guardian with his elbow, and looked close up into his face with his spectacled eyes. "It's one of her strange ways that she'll never tell the names of these birds if she can help it, though she named 'em all." This was in a whisper. "Shall I run 'em over, Flite?" he asked aloud, winking at us and pointing at her.

"If you like," she answered hurriedly.

The old man, looking up at the cages, after another look at us went through the list.

"Hope, Joy, Youth, Peace, Rest, Life, Dust, Ashes, Waste, Want, Ruin, Despair, Madness, Death, Cunning, Folly, Words, Wigs, Rags, Sheepskin, Plunder, Precedent, Jargon, Gammon, and Spinach. That's the whole collection," said the old man, "all cooped up together by my noble and learned brother."

"This is a bitter wind!" muttered my guardian.

"When my noble and learned brother gives his judgment, they're to be let go free," said Krook, winking at us again. "And then," he added, whispering and grinning, "if that ever was to happen—which it won't— the birds that have never been caged would kill 'em."

"If ever the wind was in the east," said my guardian, pretending to look out of the window for a weathercock, "I think it's there today!"

We found it very difficult to get away from the house. It was not Miss Flite who detained us; she was as reasonable a little creature in consulting the convenience of others as there possibly could be. It was Mr. Krook. He seemed unable to detach himself from Mr. Jarndyce. If he had been linked to him, he could hardly have attended him more closely. He proposed to show us his Court of Chancery, and all the strange medley it contained; during the whole of our inspection (prolonged by himself) he kept close to Mr. Jarndyce, and sometimes detained him, under one pretence or other, until we had passed on, as if he were tormented by an inclination to enter upon some secret subject which he could not make up his mind to approach. I cannot imagine a countenance and manner more singularly expressive of caution and indecision, and a perpetual impulse to do something he could not resolve to venture on, than Mr. Krook's was that day. His watchfulness of my guardian was incessant. He rarely removed his eyes from his face.

At last, having been (always attended by the cat) all over the house, and having seen the whole stock of miscellaneous lumber, which was certainly curious, we came into the back part of the shop. Here, on the head of an empty barrel stood on end, were an ink-bottle, some old stumps of pens, and some dirty playbills, and, against the wall were pasted several large printed alphabets in several plain hands.

"What are you doing here?" asked my guardian.

"Trying to learn myself to read and write," said Krook.

"And how do you get on?"

"Slow. Bad," returned the old man, impatiently. "It's hard at my time of life."

"It would be easier to be taught by some one," said my guardian.

"Ay, but they might teach me wrong!" returned the old man, with a wonderfully suspicious flash of his eye. "I don't know what I may have lost by not being learnd afore. I wouldn't like to lose anything by being learnd wrong now."

"Wrong?" said my guardian, with his good-humoured smile. "Who do you suppose would teach you wrong?"

"I don't know, Mr. Jarndyce of Bleak House!" replied the old man, turning up his spectacles on his forehead. "I don't suppose anybody would—but I'd rather trust my own self than another!"

These answers, and his manner, were strange enough to cause my guardian to inquire of Mr. Woodcourt, as we all walked across Lincoln's Inn together, whether Mr. Krook were really, as his lodger represented him, deranged. The young surgeon replied no, he had seen no reason to think so. He was exceedingly distrustful, as ignorance usually was, and he was always more or less under the influence of raw gin, of which he drank great quantities, but he did not think him mad, as yet.

On our way home, I so conciliated Peepy's affections by buying him a windmill and two flour-sacks that he would sit nowhere at dinner but at my side. Caddy sat upon the other side of me, next to Ada, to whom we imparted the whole history of the engagement as soon as we got back. We made much of Caddy, and Peepy too, and Caddy brightened exceedingly, and my guardian was as merry as we were, and we were all very happy indeed.

I have forgotten to mention—at least I have not mentioned—that Mr. Woodcourt was the same dark young surgeon whom we had met at Miss Flite's. Or that Mr. Jarndyce invited him to dinner that day. Or that he came. Or that when they were all gone, and I said to Ada, "Now, my darling, let us have a little talk about Richard!" Ada laughed and said—

But, I don't think it matters what my darling said. She was always merry.

# CHAPTER 15

*Bell Yard*

WHILE we were in London, Mr. Jarndyce was constantly beset by the crowd of excitable ladies and gentlemen whose proceedings had so much astonished us. Mr. Quale, who presented himself soon after our arrival, was in all such excitements. He seemed to project those two shining knobs of temples of his into everything that went on. All objects were alike to him, but he was always particularly ready for anything in the way of a testimonial to any one. His great power seemed to be his power of indiscriminate admiration. Having first seen him perfectly swallowed up in admiration of Mrs. Jellyby, I had supposed her to be the absorbing object of his devotion. I soon discovered my mistake, and found him to be train-bearer and organ-blower to a whole procession of people.

Mrs. Pardiggle wrote a letter of introduction to my guardian in behalf of her eloquent friend Mr. Gusher. With Mr. Gusher, appeared Mr. Quale again. Mr. Gusher, being a flabby gentleman with a moist surface, and eyes so much too small for his moon of a face that they seemed to have been originally made for somebody else, was not at first sight prepossessing; yet he was scarcely seated before Mr. Quale asked Ada and me, not inaudibly, whether we were not struck by his massive configuration of brow. In short, we heard of a great many missions of various sorts, among this set of people, but it was Mr. Quale's mission to be in ecstasies with everybody else's mission, and that it was the most popular mission of all.

Mr. Jarndyce had fallen into this company in the tenderness of his heart and his earnest desire to do all the good in his power; but that he felt it to be too often an unsatisfactory company—where benevolence took spasmodic forms; where charity was assumed, as a regular uniform, by loud professors and speculators in cheap notoriety, vehement in profession, restless and vain in action, servile in the last degree of meanness to the great, adulatory of one another, and intolerable to those who were anxious quietly to help the weak from falling—he plainly told us.

I mention this because I am coming to Mr. Skimpole again. It seemed to me that his offhand professions of childishness and carelessness were a great relief to my guardian, by contrast with such things. Mr. Skimpole appeared one morning, in his usual agreeable way, and as full of pleasant spirits as ever.

"Boythorn writes me that you and the ladies have promised him a short visit at his bachelor-house in Lincolnshire," observed Mr. Skimpole. "He has invited me, and proposes to frank me down and back again. I suppose it will cost money? Shillings perhaps? Or pounds? Or something of that sort? By the by. Coavinses. You remember our friend Coavinses, Miss Summerson?"

"Oh yes!" said I.

"Coavinses has been arrested by the great Bailiff," said Mr. Skimpole. "His successor is in my house now—in possession, I think he calls it. And he told me, Coavinses had left. Three children. No mother. And that Coavinses' profession. Being unpopular. The rising Coavinses. Were at a considerable disadvantage."

Mr. Jarndyce got up, rubbing his head, and began to walk about.

"I don't like this, Skimpole," he said thoughtfully. "The man was necessary," pursued my guardian. "There was no harm in his trade. He maintained his children. One would like to know more about this."

"Oh, Coavinses?" cried Mr. Skimpole, at length perceiving what he meant. "Nothing easier. A walk to Coavinses' headquarters and you can know what you will."

Mr. Jarndyce nodded to us, who were only waiting for the signal. "Come! We will walk that way, my dears. Why not that way as soon as another!"

We were quickly ready, and went out. Mr. Skimpole went with us. He took us first to Cursitor Street, Chancery Lane, where there was a house with barred windows, which he called Coavinses' Castle. On our going into the entry and ringing a bell, a very hideous boy came out and looked at us over a spiked wicket.

"Who did you want?" said the boy.

"There was a follower, or an officer, or something, here," said Mr. Jarndyce, "who is dead. I want to know his name, if you please?"

"Name of Neckett," said the boy.

"And his address?"

"Bell Yard," said the boy. "Chandler's shop, left-hand side, name of Blinder."

We went back to Lincoln's Inn, where Mr. Skimpole, who had not cared to remain nearer Coavinses, awaited us. Then we all went to Bell Yard, a narrow alley at a very short distance. We soon found the chandler's shop. In it was a good-natured-looking old woman with a dropsy, or an asthma, or perhaps both.

"Neckett's children?" said she, in reply to my inquiry. "Yes, surely, miss. Three pair, if you please. Door right opposite the stairs." And she handed me the key across the counter.

I came out without asking any more questions, and led the way up the dark stairs. We went as quietly as we could; but four of us made some noise on the aged boards, and when we came to the second story, we found we had disturbed a man who was standing there, looking out of his room.

"Is it Gridley that's wanted?" he said, fixing his eyes on me with an angry stare.

"No, sir," said I. "I am going higher up."

Mr. Jarndyce gave him good-day. "Good-day!" he said, abruptly and fiercely. He was a tall, sallow man with a careworn head, a deeply lined face, and prominent eyes. He had a pen in his hand, and in the glimpse I caught of his room in passing, I saw that it was covered with a litter of papers.

Leaving him standing there, we went up to the top room. I tapped at the door, and a little shrill voice inside said, "We are locked in. Mrs. Blinder's got the key!"

I applied the key on hearing this, and opened the door. In a poor room, with a sloping ceiling and containing very little furniture, was a mite of a boy some five or six years old, nursing and hushing a heavy child of eighteen months. There was no fire, though the weather was cold; both children were wrapped in some poor shawls and tippets.

"Who has locked you up here alone?" we naturally asked.

"Charley," said the boy, standing still to gaze at us.

"Is Charley your brother?"

"No. She's my sister Charlotte. Father called her Charley."

"Are there any more of you besides Charley?"

"Me," said the boy, "and Emma," patting the limp bonnet of the child he was nursing. "And Charley."

"Where is Charley now?"

"Out a-washing," said the boy.

We were looking at one another, and at these two children, when there came into the room a very little girl, childish in figure but shrewd and older-looking in the face—pretty-faced too—wearing a womanly sort of bonnet much too large for her, and drying her bare arms on a womanly sort of apron. Her fingers were white and wrinkled with washing, and the soap-suds were yet smoking which she wiped off her arms. She had come running from some place in the neighbourhood, and had made all the haste she could. Consequently, though she was very light, she was out of breath, and could not speak at first.

"Oh, here's Charley!" said the boy.

"Is it possible," whispered my guardian as we put a chair for the little creature, and got her to sit down, "that this child works for the rest? Charley, Charley!" said my guardian. "How old are you?"

"Over thirteen, sir," replied the child.

"Oh! what a great age," said my guardian. "What a great age, Charley! And do you live alone here with these babies, Charley?"

"Yes, sir," returned the child, looking up into his face with perfect confidence, "since Father died."

"And how do you live, Charley?"

"Since Father died, sir, I've gone out to work. I'm out washing today."

"And when did mother die? Poor mother!"

"Mother died just after Emma was born," said the child. "Then Father said I was to be as good a mother to her as I could. And so I tried. And so I worked at home, and did cleaning and nursing and washing for a long time before I began to go out."

"And do you often go out?"

"As often as I can," said Charley, opening her eyes, and smiling, "because of earning sixpences and shillings!"

"And do you always lock the babies up when you go out?"

"To keep 'em safe, sir, don't you see?" said Charley. "Mrs. Blinder comes up now and then, and Mr. Gridley comes up sometimes, and perhaps I can run in sometimes, and they can play you know, and Tom an't afraid of being locked up, are you, Tom?"

"No-o!" said Tom, stoutly.

"He's as good as gold," said the little creature. "And when Emma's tired, he puts her to bed. And when he's tired he goes to bed himself. And when I come home and light the candle, and has a bit of supper, he sits up again and has it with me. Don't you, Tom?"

"Oh yes, Charley!" said Tom. "That I do!"

I stood at the window with Ada, pretending to look at the house-tops, and the blackened stack of chimneys, when I found that Mrs. Blinder, from the shop below, had come in and was talking to my guardian.

"Have many people been kind to the children?" asked Mr. Jarndyce.

"Upon the whole, not so bad, sir," said Mrs. Blinder.

Mr. Jarndyce was turning to speak to us when his attention was attracted by the abrupt entrance into the room of the Mr. Gridley whom we had seen on our way up.

"I don't know what you may be doing here, ladies and gentlemen," he said, as if he resented our presence, "but you'll excuse my coming in. I don't come in to stare about me. Well, Charley! Well, Tom! Well, little one! How is it with us all today?"

He bent over the group, in a caressing way, and clearly was regarded as a friend by the children, though his face retained its stern character, and his manner to us was as rude as it could be. My guardian noticed it, and respected it.

"No one, surely, would come here to stare about him," he said mildly.

"Maybe so, sir, maybe so," returned the other, taking Tom upon his knee and waving him off impatiently. "I don't want to argue with ladies and gentlemen. I have had enough of arguing to last one man his life. Sir," said Gridley, "do you know anything of Courts of Equity?"

"Perhaps I do, to my sorrow."

"To your sorrow?" said the man, pausing in his wrath. "If so, I beg your pardon. Sir," with renewed violence, "I have been dragged for five and twenty years over burning iron, and I have lost the habit of treading upon velvet. Go into the Court of Chancery yonder, and ask what is one of the standing jokes that brighten up their business sometimes, and they will tell you that the best joke they have is the man from Shropshire. I," he said, beating one hand on the other passionately, "am the man from Shropshire."

"I believe I and my family have also had the honour of furnishing some entertainment in the same grave place," said my guardian, composedly. "You may have heard my name—Jarndyce."

"Mr. Jarndyce," said Gridley, with a rough sort of salutation, "you bear your wrongs more quietly than I can bear mine. More than that, I tell you—and I tell this gentleman, and these young ladies, if they are friends of yours—that if I took my wrongs in any other way, I should be driven mad! It is only by resenting them, and by revenging them in my mind, and by angrily demanding the justice I never get, that I am able to keep my wits together. You may tell me that I overexcite myself. I answer that it's in my nature to do it under wrong, and I must do it. There's nothing between doing it and sinking into the smiling state of the poor little mad woman that haunts the Court."

The passion and heat in which he was, and the violent gestures with which he accompanied what he said, were most painful to see.

"Mr. Jarndyce," he said, "consider my case. As true as there is a Heaven above us, this is my case. I am one of two brothers. My father (a farmer) made a will, and left his farm and stock, and so forth, to my mother for her life. After my mother's death, all was to come to me, except a legacy of three hundred pounds that I was then to pay my brother. My mother died. My brother, some time afterwards, claimed his legacy. I, and some of my relations, said that he had had a part of it already, in board and lodging, and some other things. Now mind! That was the question, and nothing else. No one disputed the will; no one disputed anything but whether part of that three hundred pounds had been already paid or not. To settle that question, my brother filing a bill, I was obliged to go into this accursed Chancery; I was forced there, because the law forced me, and would let me go nowhere else. Seventeen people were made defendants to that simple suit! It first came on after two years. It was then stopped for another two years while the Master (may his head rot off!) inquired whether I was my father's son—about which there was no dispute at all with any mortal creature. He then found out that there were not defendants enough— remember, there were only seventeen as yet!—but that we must have another who had been left out, and must begin all over again. The costs at that time—before the thing was begun!—were three times the legacy. My brother would have given up the legacy, and joyful, to escape more costs. My whole estate, left to me in that will of my father's, has gone in costs. The suit, still undecided, has fallen into rack and ruin and despair with everything else—and here I stand, this day! Now, Mr. Jarndyce, in your suit there are thousands and thousands involved where in mine there are hundreds. Is mine less hard to bear, or is it harder to bear, when my whole living was in it, and has been thus shamefully sucked away?

"I have done!" he said, sitting down and wiping his face. "Mr. Jarndyce, I have done! I am violent, I know. I ought to know it. I have been in prison for contempt of Court. I have been in prison for threatening the solicitor. I have been in this trouble, and that trouble, and shall be again. I am the man from Shropshire, and I sometimes go beyond amusing them—though they have found it amusing, too, to see me committed into custody, and brought up in custody, and all that. It would be better for me, they tell me, if I restrained myself. I tell them that if I did restrain myself, I should become inbecile. I was a good-enough-tempered man once, I believe. People in my part of the country say they remember me so; but now I must have this vent under my sense of injury or nothing could hold my wits together. Besides," he added, breaking fiercely out, "I'll shame them. To the last, I'll show myself in that Court to its shame. If I knew when I was going to die, and could be carried there, and had a voice to speak with, I would die there, saying, 'You have brought me here, and sent me from here, many and many a time. Now send me out, feet foremost!' I came to take these babies down to my room for an hour," he said, going to them again, "and let them play about. I didn't mean to say all this, but it don't much signify. You're not afraid of me, Tom, are you?"

"No!" said Tom. "You ain't angry with *me.*"

"You are right, my child. You're going back, Charley? Ay? Come then, little one!" He took the youngest child on his arm, where she was willing enough to be carried. "I shouldn't wonder if we found a gingerbread soldier downstairs. Let's go and look for him!"

He made his former rough salutation, which was not deficient in a certain respect to Mr. Jarndyce, and bowing slightly to us, went downstairs to his room. We kissed Charley, and took her downstairs with us, and stopped outside the house to see her run away to her work.

## CHAPTER 16

### Tom-All-Alone's

MY Lady Dedlock is restless, very restless. The astonished fashionable intelligence hardly knows where to have her. Today she is at Chesney Wold; yesterday she was at her house in town; tomorrow she may be abroad, for anything the fashionable intelligence can with confidence predict. Even Sir Leicester's gallantry has some trouble to keep pace with her. It would have more but that his other faithful ally, for better and for worse—the gout—grips him by both legs.

Sir Leicester receives the gout as a troublesome demon, but still a demon of the patrician order. All the Dedlocks in the direct male line, through a course of time during and beyond which the memory of man goeth not to the contrary, have had the gout. It can be proved, sir. Other men's fathers may have died of the rheumatism, or may have taken base contagion from the tainted blood of the sick vulgar, but the Dedlock family have communicated something exclusive even to the levelling process of dying, by dying of their own family gout. It has come down, through the illustrious line, like the plate, or the pictures, or the place in Lincolnshire. It is among their dignities. Hence Sir Leicester yields up his family legs to the family disorder.

And a goodly show he makes, lying in a flush of crimson and gold in the midst of the great drawing-room, before his favourite picture of my Lady, with broad strips of sunlight shining in through the long line of windows. Outside, the stately oaks, rooted for ages in the green ground which has never known ploughshare, bear witness to his greatness. Inside, his forefathers, looking on him from the walls, bear their testimony to his greatness, too.

My Lady is at present represented, near Sir Leicester, by her portrait. She has flitted away to town, with no intention of remaining there. The house in town is not prepared for her reception. It is muffled and dreary. Only one Mercury in powder gapes disconsolate at the hall-window.

What connexion can there be between the place in Lincolnshire, the house in town, the Mercury in powder, and the whereabout of Jo the outlaw with the broom! Jo sweeps his crossing all day long unconscious of the link, if any link there be. He sums up his mental condition, when asked a question, by replying that he "don't know nothink." He knows that it's hard to keep the mud off the crossing in dirty weather, and harder still to live by doing it. Nobody taught him even that much; he found it out.

Jo lives—that is to say, Jo has not yet died—in a ruinous place, known to the like of him by the name of Tom-all-Alone's. It is a black, dilapidated street avoided by all decent people, where the crazy houses were seized upon when their decay was far advanced by some bold vagrants, who, after establishing their own possession, took to letting them out in lodgings. Now these tumbling tenements contain, by night, a swarm of misery. Twice, lately, there has been a crash and a cloud of dust, like the springing of a mine, in Tom-all-Alone's, and each time a house has fallen. These accidents have made a paragraph in the newspapers, and have filled a bed or two in the nearest hospital. The gaps remain, and there are not unpopular lodgings among the rubbish. As several more houses are nearly ready to go, the next crash in Tom-all-Alone's may be expected to be a good one.

This desirable property is in Chancery, of course. It would be an insult to the discernment of any man with half an eye to tell him so. Whether "Tom" is the popular representative of the original plaintiff or dedendant in Jarndyce and Jarndyce, or whether Tom lived here when the suit had laid the street waste, all alone, until other settlers came to join him—perhaps nobody knows. Certainly Jo don't know.

"For I don't," says Jo, "I don't know nothink."

It must be a strange state to be like Jo! To shuffle through the streets unfamiliar with the shapes, and in utter darkness as to the meaning, of those mysterious symbols so abundant over the shops, and at the corners of streets, and on the doors, and in the windows! To see people read, and to see people write, and to see the postmen deliver letters, and not to have the least idea of all that language—to be, to every scrap of it, stone-blind and dumb! To be hustled, and jostled, and moved on, and really to feel that it would appear to be perfectly true that I have no business, here, or there, or anywhere, and yet to be perplexed by the consideration that I *am* here somehow, too, and everybody overlooked me until I became the creature that I am! Jo's whole material and immaterial life is wonderfully strange, his death the strangest thing of all. Jo comes out of Tom-all-Alone's, meeting the tardy morning, which is always late in getting down there, and munches his dirty bit of bread as he comes along. His way lying through many streets, and the houses not yet being open, he sits down to breakfast on the doorstep of the Society for the Propagation of the Gospel in Foreign Parts, and gives it a brush when he has finished, as an acknowledgment of the accommodation. He admires the size of the edifice, and wonders what it's all about. He has no idea, poor wretch, of the spiritual destitution of a coral reef in the Pacific, or what it costs to look up the precious souls among the coco-nuts and bread-fruit.

He goes to his crossing, and begins to lay it out for the day. The town awakes; the great teetotum is set up for its daily spin and whirl; all that unaccountable reading and writing, which has been suspended for a few hours, recommences. Jo, and the other lower animals, get on in the unintelligible mess as they can. It is market-day. The blinded oxen, overgoaded, overdriven, never guided, run into wrong places and are beaten out, and plunge, red-eyed and foaming, at stone walls, and often sorely hurt the innocent, and often sorely hurt themselves. Very like Jo and his order—very, very like!

The day changes as it wears itself away, and becomes dark and drizzly. Jo fights it out at his crossing, among the mud and wheels, the horses, whips, and umbrellas, and gets but a scanty sum to pay for the unsavoury shelter of Tom-all-Alone's. Twilight comes on; gas begins to start up in the shops; the lamplighter, with his ladder, runs along the margin of the pavement. A wretched evening is beginning to close in.

In his chambers, Mr. Tulkinghorn sits meditating an application to the nearest magistrate tomorrow morning for a warrant. Gridley, a disappointed suitor, has been here today, and has been alarming. We are not to be put in bodily fear, and that ill-conditioned fellow shall be held to bail again. From the ceiling foreshortened Allegory, in the person of one impossible Roman upside down, points with the arm of Samson (out of joint, and an odd one) obtrusively toward the window. Why should Mr. Tulkinghorn, for such a reason, look out of window? And if he did, what would it be to see a woman going by? There are women enough in the world, Mr. Tulkinghorn thinks—too many; they are at the bottom of all that goes wrong in it.

But they are not all like the woman who now leaves him and his house behind, between whose plain dress and her refined manner, there is something exceedingly inconsistent. She should be an upper servant by her attire, yet in her air and step she is a lady. Her face is veiled, and still she sufficiently betrays herself to make more than one of those who pass her look round sharply.

She never turns her head. Lady or servant, she has a purpose in her, and can follow it. She never turns her head until she comes to the crossing where Jo plies with his broom. He crosses with her, and begs. Still she does not turn her head until she has landed on the other side. Then she beckons to him, and says "Come here!" Jo follows her, a pace or two, into a quiet court. "Are you the boy I've read of in the papers?" she asked behind her veil.

"I don't know," says Jo, staring moodily at the veil, "nothink about no papers. I don't know nothink about nothink at all."

"Were you examined at an Inquest?"

"I don't know nothink about no—where I was took by the beadle, do you mean?" says Jo.

"Yes."

"That's me!" says Jo. "You mean about the man? Him as wos dead?"

"Hush! Speak in a whisper! Yes. Did he look, when he was living, so very ill and poor?"

"Oh jist!" says Jo.

"Did he look like—not like *you?*" says the woman with abhorrence.

"Oh not so bad as me," says Jo. "I'm a reg'lar one, *I* am! You didn't know him, did you, my lady?" says Jo, for even he has got at the suspicion of her being a lady.

"I am not a lady. I am a servant."

"You are a jolly servant!" says Jo, without the least idea of saying anything offensive—merely as a tribute of admiration.

"Listen and be silent. Don't talk to me, and stand farther from me! Can you show me all those places that were spoken of in the account I read? The place he wrote for, the place he died at, the place where you were taken to, and the place where he was buried? Do you know the place where he was buried?"

Jo answers with a nod.

"Go before me, and show me all those dreadful places. Stop opposite to each, and don't speak to me unless I speak to you. Don't look back. Do what I want, and I will pay you well."

Jo attends closely while the words are being spoken, pauses to consider their meaning, considers it satisfactory, and nods his ragged head.

"I'm fly," says Jo. "But fen larks, you know. Stow hooking it!"

"What does the horrible creature mean?" exclaims the servant, recoiling from him. "I don't understand you. Go on before! I will give you more money than you ever had in your life."

Jo screws up his mouth into a whistle, takes his broom under his arm, and leads the way, passing deftly with his bare feet over the hard stones and through the mud and mire.

Cook's Court. Jo stops. A pause.

"Who lives here?"

"Him wot give him his writing, and give me half a bull," says Jo in a whisper, without looking over his shoulder.

"Go on to the next."

Krook's house. Jo stops again. A longer pause.

"Who lives here?"

"*He* lived here," Jo answers as before.

After a silence he is asked "In which room?"

"In the back room up there. You can see the window from this corner. Up there! That's where I see him stritched out."

"Go on to the next!"

It is a longer walk to the next; but Jo, relieved of his first suspicions, sticks to the forms imposed upon him, and does not look round. By many devious ways, reeking with offence of many kinds, they come to the little tunnel of a court, and to the gas-lamp (lighted now), and to the iron gate.

"He was put there," says Jo, holding to the bars and looking in.

"Where? Oh, what a scene of horror!"

"There!" says Jo, pointing. "Over yinder. Among them piles of bones, and close to that there kitchin winder! They put him wery nigh the top. They was obliged to stamp upon it to git it in. I could unkiver it for you with my broom if the gate was open. It's always locked. Look at the rat!" cries Jo, excited. "Hi! Look! There he goes! Ho! Into the ground!"

The servant shrinks into a corner—into a corner of that hideous archway, with its deadly stains contaminating her dress, and putting out her two hands and passionately telling him to keep away from her, so remains for some moments. Jo stands staring, and is still staring when she recovers herself.

"Is this place of abomination consecrated ground?"

"I don't know nothink of consequential ground," says Jo, still staring. "Is it blessed?"

"I'm blest if I know," says Jo, staring more than ever; "but I shouldn't think it warn't. Blest?" repeats Jo, something troubled in his mind. "It ain't done it much good if it is. Blest? I should think it was t'othered myself. But I don't know nothink!"

The servant takes as little heed of what he says as she seems to take of what she has said herself. She draws off her glove to get some money from her purse. Jo silently notices how white and small her hand is, and what a jolly servant she must be to wear such sparkling rings.

She drops a piece of money in his hand, shuddering as their hands approach. "Now," she adds, "show me the spot again!"

Jo thrusts the handle of his broom between the bars of the gate, and points it out. At length, looking aside to see if he has made himself intelligible, he finds that he is alone.

His first proceeding is to hold the piece of money to the gas-light and to be overpowered at finding that it is yellow—gold. His next is to give it a one-sided bite at the edge, as a test of its quality. His next, to put it in his mouth for safety, and to sweep the step and passage with great care. His job done, he sets off for Tom-all-Alone's, stopping in the light of innumerable gas-lamps to produce the piece of gold and give it another one-sided bite, as a reassurance of its being genuine.

The Mercury in powder is in no want of society tonight, for my Lady goes to a grand dinner, and three or four balls. Sir Leicester is fidgety, down at Chesney Wold, with no better company than the gout; he complains to Mrs. Rouncewell that the rain makes such a monotonous pattering on the terrace that he can't read the paper.

"Sir Leicester would have done better to try the other side of the house, my dear," says Mrs. Rouncewell to Rosa. "His dressing-room is on my Lady's side. And in all these years I never heard the step upon the Ghost's Walk more distinct than it is tonight!"

## CHAPTER 17

*Esther's Narrative*

RICHARD very often came to see us while we remained in London (though he soon failed in his letter-writing), and with his quick abilities, his good spirits, his good temper, his gaiety and freshness, was always delightful. But though I liked him more and more, the better I knew him, I still felt more and more how much it was to be regretted that he had been educated in no habits of application and concentration. The system which had addressed him exactly as it had addressed hundreds of other boys, all varying in character and capacity, had enabled him to dash through his tasks, always with fair credit, and often with distinction, but in a fitful, dazzling way that had confirmed his reliance on those very qualities in himself which it had been most desirable to direct and train. They were good qualities, without which no high place can be meritoriously won; but, like fire and water, though excellent servants they were very bad masters. If they had been under Richard's direction, they would have been his friends, but Richard being under their direction, they became his enemies.

These were my thoughts about Richard. I thought I often observed, besides, how right my guardian was in what he had said; and that the uncertainties and delays of the Chancery suit had imparted to his nature something of the careless spirit of a gamester who felt that he was part of a great gaming system.

Mr. and Mrs. Bayham Badger coming one afternoon when my guardian was not at home, in the course of conversation I naturally inquired after Richard.

"Why, Mr. Carstone," said Mrs. Badger, "is very well, and is, I assure you, a great acquisition to our society. But I—you won't think me premature if I mention it?"

I said no, as Mrs. Badger's insinuating tone seemed to require such an answer.

"Nor Miss Clare?" said Mrs. Bayham Badger, sweetly.

Ada said no, too, and looked uneasy.

"Why, you see, my dears, I am very much of the opinion, my dears, that he has not chosen his profession advisedly."

Ada looked so very anxious now that I asked Mrs. Badger on what she founded her supposition.

"My dear Miss Summerson," she replied, "on Mr. Carstone's character and conduct. He is of such a very easy disposition that probably he would never think it worth while to mention how he really feels, but he feels languid about the profession. He has not that positive interest in it which makes it his vocation. If he has any decided impression in reference to it, I should say it was that it is a tiresome pursuit. Now this is not promising. Young men like Mr. Allan Woodcourt who take it from a strong interest in all that it can do will find some reward in it through a great deal of work for a very little money, and through years of considerable endurance and disappointment. But I am quite convinced that this would never be the case with Mr. Carstone."

"Does Mr. Badger think so too?" asked Ada timidly.

"Why," said Mr. Badger, "to tell the truth, Miss Clare, this view of the matter had not occurred to me until Mrs. Badger mentioned it. But when Mrs. Badger put it in that light, I naturally gave great consideration to it. The conclusion at which I have arrived is—in short, is Mrs. Badger's conclusion."

We both felt that it was disinterested in them to express the opinion they had communicated to us, and that there was a great probability of its being sound. We agreed to say nothing to Mr. Jarndyce until we had spoken to Richard, and as he was coming next evening, we resolved to have a very serious talk with him.

So after he had been a little while with Ada, I went in and found my darling (as I knew she would be) prepared to consider him thoroughly right in whatever he said.

"And how do you get on, Richard?" said I. I always sat down on the other side of him. He made quite a sister of me.

"Oh, well enough!" said Richard.

"He can't say better than that, Esther, can he?" cried my pet.

"Well enough?" I repeated.

"Yes," said Richard, "well enough. It's rather jog-trotty and humdrum. But it'll do as well as anything else!"

"Oh, my dear Richard!" I remonstrated.

"What's the matter?" said Richard.

"Do as well as anything else!"

"I don't think there's any harm in that, Dame Durden," said Ada, looking so confidingly at me across him, "because if it will do as well as anything else, it will do very well, I hope."

"Oh yes, I hope so," returned Richard, carelessly tossing his hair from his forehead. "After all, it may be only a kind of probation till our suit is—I forgot, though. I am not to mention the suit. Forbidden ground! Oh yes, it's all right enough. Let us talk about something else."

Ada would have done so, willingly, and with a full persuasion that we had brought the question to a most satisfactory state. But I thought it would be useless to stop there, so I began again.

"No, but Richard," said I, "and my dear Ada! Consider how important it is to you both, and what a point of honour it is towards your cousin, that you, Richard, should be quite in earnest without any reservation. I think we had better talk about this, really, Ada. It will be too late very soon."

"Oh yes! We must talk about it!" said Ada. "But I think Richard is right."

"Mr. and Mrs. Badger were here yesterday, Richard," said I, "and they seemed disposed to think that you had no great liking for the profession."

"Did they though?" said Richard. "Oh! Well, that rather alters the case, because I had no idea that they thought so, and I should not have liked to disappoint or inconvenience them. The fact is, I don't care much about it. But oh, it don't matter! It'll do as well as anything else!"

"You hear him, Ada!" said I.

"The fact is," Richard proceeded, half thoughtfully, and half jocosely, "it is not quite in my way. I don't take to it. It's monotonous, and today is too like yesterday, and tomorrow is too like today."

"But I am afraid," said I, "this is an objection to all kinds of application—to life itself, except under some very uncommon circumstances."

"Do you think so?" returned Richard, still considering. "Perhaps! Ha! Why then, you know," he added, suddenly becoming gay again, "we travel outside a circle to what I said just now. It'll do as well as anything else. Oh, it's all right enough! Let us talk about something else."

But even Ada shook her head at this, and looked serious. So I thought it a good opportunity to hint to Richard that if he were sometimes a little careless of himself, I was very sure he never meant to be careless of Ada; and that it was a part of his affectionate consideration for her not to slight the importance of a step that might influence both their lives. This made him almost grave.

"My dear Mother Hubbard," he said, "that's the very thing! I have thought of that, several times, and have been quite angry with myself for meaning to be so much in earnest and—somehow—not exactly being so. I don't know how it is; I seem to want something or other to stand by. Even you have no idea how fond I am of Ada (my darling Cousin, I love you so much!), but I don't settle down to constancy in other things. It's such uphill work, and it takes such a time!" said Richard, with an air of vexation.

"That may be," I suggested, "because you don't like what you have chosen."

"Poor fellow!" said Ada. "I am sure I don't wonder at it!"

"You see, my precious girl," said Richard, passing her golden curls through and through his hand, "I was a little hasty, perhaps; or I misunderstood my own inclinations, perhaps. They don't seem to lie in that direction. I couldn't tell till I tried. Now the question is whether it's worth while to undo all that has been done. It seems like making a great disturbance about nothing particular."

"My dear Richard," said I, "how *can* you say about nothing particular?"

"I don't mean absolutely that," he returned. "I mean that it *may* be nothing particular because I may never want it."

Both Ada and I urged, in reply, not only that it was decidedly worth while to undo what had been done, but that it must be undone. I then asked Richard whether he had thought of any more congenial pursuit.

"There, my dear Mrs. Shipton," said Richard, "you touch me home. Yes, I have. I have been thinking that the law is the boy for me."

"The law!" repeated Ada, as if she were afraid of the name.

"If I went into Kenge's office," said Richard, "and if I were placed under articles to Kenge, I should have my eye on the—hum!—the forbidden ground—and should be able to study it, and master it, and to satisfy myself that it was not neglected, and was being properly conducted. I should be able to look after Ada's interests, and my own interests (the same thing!), and I should peg away at Blackstone and all those fellows with the most tremendous ardour."

I was not by any means so sure of that, and I saw how his hankering after the vague things yet to come of those long-deferred hopes cast a shade on Ada's face. But I thought it best to encourage him in any project of continuous exertion, and only advised him to be quite sure that his mind was made up now.

"My dear Minerva," said Richard, "I am as steady as you are. I made a mistake. I won't do so any more, and I'll become such a lawyer as is not often seen. That is, you know," said Richard, relapsing into doubt, "if it really is worth while, after all, to make such a disturbance about nothing particular!"

This led to our saying again, with a great deal of gravity, all that we had said already, and to our coming to much the same conclusion afterwards. But we so strongly advised Richard to be frank and open with Mr. Jarndyce, without a moment's delay, and his disposition was so opposed to concealment, that he sought him out at once (taking us with him), and made a full avowal.

"Rick," said my guardian, after hearing him attentively, "we can retreat with honour, and we will. But we must be careful—for our cousin's sake, Rick, for our cousin's sake—that we make no more such mistakes. Therefore, in the matter of law, we will have a good trial before we decide. We will look before we leap, and take plenty of time about it."

Richard's energy was of such an impatient and fitful kind that he would have liked nothing better than to have gone to Mr. Kenge's office in that hour, and to have entered into articles with him on the spot. Submitting, however, with a good grace to the caution that we had shown to be so necessary, he contented himself with sitting down in his lightest spirits, and talking as if his one unvarying purpose in life from childhood had been that one which now held possession of him. My guardian was very kind and cordial with him, but rather grave, enough so to cause Ada, when he had departed and we were going upstairs to bed, to say:

"Cousin John, I hope you don't think the worse of Richard?"

"No, my love," said he.

"Because it was very natural that Richard should be mistaken in such a difficult case. It is not uncommon."

"No, no, my love," said he. "Don't look unhappy."

"Oh, I am not unhappy, Cousin John!" said Ada, smiling cheerfully. "But I should be a little so if you thought at all the worse of Richard."

"My dear," said Mr. Jarndyce. "I should think the worse of him only if you were ever in the least unhappy through his means. I should be more disposed to quarrel with myself, even then, than with poor Rick, for I brought you together. But tut, all this is nothing! He has time before him, and the race to run. *I* think the worse of him? Not I, my loving cousin! And not you, I swear!"

"No, indeed, Cousin John," said Ada, "I am sure I could not—I am sure I would not—think any ill of Richard if the whole world did. I could, and I would, think better of him then than at any other time!"

"I think," said my guardian, thoughtfully regarding her, "I think it must be somewhere written that the virtues of the mothers shall, occasionally, be visited on the children, as well as the sins of the fathers. Good-night, my rosebud. Good-night, little woman. Pleasant slumbers! Happy dreams!"

This was the first time I ever saw him follow Ada with his eyes with something of a shadow on their benevolent expression. I well remembered the look with which he had contemplated her and Richard when she was singing in the firelight; but his glance was changed, and even the silent look of confidence in me which now followed it once more was not quite so hopeful and untroubled as it had originally been.

Ada praised Richard more to me that night than ever she had praised him yet. She went to sleep with a little bracelet he had given her clasped upon her arm. I fancied she was dreaming of him when I kissed her cheek, and saw how tranquil and happy she looked.

For I was so little inclined to sleep myself, that night, that I sat up working. I was wakeful and rather low-spirited. I don't know why. At least I don't think I know why. At least, perhaps I do, but I don't think it matters.

At any rate, I made up my mind to be so dreadfully industrious that I would leave myself not a moment's leisure to be low-spirited. If I could have made myself go to sleep, I would have done it directly; but not being able to do that, I took out of my basket some ornamental work for our house.

I soon found myself very busy. But I had left some silk downstairs in a work-table drawer in the temporary Growlery, and coming to a stop for want of it, I took my candle and went softly down to get it. To my great surprise, on going in I found my guardian still there, and sitting looking at the ashes. He was lost in thought, his book lay unheeded by his side, his silvered iron-grey hair was scattered confusedly upon his forehead as though his hand had been wandering among it while his thoughts were elsewhere, and his face looked worn. Almost frightened by coming upon him so unexpectedly, I stood still for a moment; and should have retired without speaking had he not, in again passing his hand abstractedly through his hair, seen me and started.

"Esther! At work so late, my dear?"

"I am working late tonight," said I, "because I couldn't sleep, and wished to tire myself. But dear Guardian, you are late too, and look weary. You have no trouble, I hope, to keep you waking?"

"None, little woman, that *you* would readily understand," said he.

He spoke in a regretful tone so new to me that I inwardly repeated, as if that would help me to his meaning, "that *I* could readily understand!"

"Remain a moment, Esther," said he. "You were in my thoughts."

"I hope I was not the trouble, Guardian?"

He slightly waved his hand, and fell into his usual manner. The change was so remarkable, and he appeared to make it by dint of so much self-command, that I found myself again inwardly repeating, "none that *I* could understand."

"Little woman," said my guardian, "I was thinking—that is, I have been thinking since I have been sitting here—that you ought to know, of your own history, all I know. It is very little."

"Dear Guardian," I replied, "when you spoke to me before on that subject—"

"But since then," he gravely interposed, anticipating what I meant to say, "I have reflected that your having anything to ask me and my having anything to tell you are different considerations. It is perhaps my duty to impart to you the little I know."

"If you think so, Guardian, it is right."

"I think so," he returned, very gently and kindly, and very distinctly. "My dear, I think so now. If any real disadvantage can attach to your position in the mind of any man or woman worth a thought, it is right that you, at least, of all the world should not magnify it to yourself by having vague impressions of its nature."

I sat down, and said, after a little effort to be as calm as I ought to be: "One of my earliest remembrances, Guardian, is of these words: 'Your mother, Esther, is your disgrace, and you were hers. The time will come, and soon enough, when you will understand this better, and will feel it too, as no one save a woman can.'" I had covered my face with my hands in repeating the words; but I took them away now with a better kind of shame, I hope, and told him that to him I owed the blessing that I had from my childhood to that hour never, never felt it. He put up his hand as if to stop me. I well knew that he was never to be thanked, and said no more.

"Nine years, my dear," he said, after thinking for a little while, "have passed since I received a letter from a lady living in seclusion, written with a stern passion and power that rendered it unlike all other letters I have read. It was written to me (as it told me in so many words), perhaps, because it was the writer's idiosyncrasy to put that trust in me, perhaps because it was mine to justify it. It told me of a child, an orphan girl then twelve years old, in some such cruel words as those which live in your remembrance. It told me that the writer had bred her in secrecy from her birth, had blotted out all trace of her existence, and that if the writer were to die before the child became a woman, she would be left entirely friendless, nameless, and unknown. It asked me to consider if I would, in that case, finish what the writer had begun."

I listened in silence, and looked attentively at him.

"Your early recollection, my dear, will supply the gloomy medium through which all this was seen and expressed by the writer, and the distorted religion which clouded her mind with impressions of the need there was for the child to expiate an offence of which she was quite innocent. I felt concerned for the little creature in her darkened life, and replied to the letter."

I took his hand and kissed it.

"It laid the injunction on me that I should never propose to see the writer, who had long been estranged from all intercourse with the world, but who would see a confidential agent if I would appoint one. I accredited Mr. Kenge. The lady said, of her own accord and not of his seeking, that her name was an assumed one. That she was, if there were any ties of blood in such a case, the child's aunt. That more than this she would never, for any human consideration, disclose. My dear, I have told you all."

I held his hand for a little while in mine.

"I saw my ward oftener than she saw me," he added, cheerily making light of it, "and I always knew she was beloved, useful, and happy. She repays me twenty-thousand-fold, and twenty more to that, every hour in every day!"

"And oftener still," said I, "she blesses the guardian who is a father to her!"

At the word "father," I saw his former trouble come into his face. He subdued it as before, and it was gone in an instant; but it had been there, and it had come so swiftly upon my words that I felt as if they had given him a shock. I again inwardly repeated, wondering, none that *I* could readily understand! No, it was true. I did not understand it. Not for many and many a day.

"Take a fatherly good-night, my dear," said he, kissing me on the forehead, "and so to rest. These are late hours for working and thinking. You do that for all of us, all day long, little housekeeper!"

We had a visitor next day. Mr. Allan Woodcourt came. He came to take leave of us; he had settled to do so beforehand. He was going to China, and to India, as a surgeon on board ship. He was to be away a long, long time.

I believe—at least I know—that he was not rich. All his widowed mother could spare had been spent in qualifying him for his profession. It was not lucrative to a young practitioner with very little influence in London; and although he was, night and day, at the service of numbers of poor people, and did wonders of gentleness and skill for them, he gained very little by it in money. He was seven years older than I. Not that I need mention it, for it hardly seems to belong to anything.

I think—I mean he told us—that he had been in practice three or four years, and that if he could have hoped to contend through three or four more, he would not have made the voyage on which he was bound. But he had no fortune or private means, and so he was going away. He had been to see us several times altogther. We thought it a pity he should go away. Because he was distinguished in his art among those who knew it best, and some of the greatest men belonging to it had a high opinion of him.

When he came to bid us good-bye, he brought his mother with him for the first time. She was a pretty old lady, with bright black eyes, but she seemed proud. She came from Wales; and had had, a long time ago, an eminent person for an ancestor of the name of Morgan ap Kerrig —of some place that sounded like Gimlet—who was the most illustrious person that ever was known, and all of whose relations were a sort of Royal Family. He appeared to have passed his life in always getting up into mountains, and fighting somebody; and a Bard whose name sounded like Crumlinwallinwer had sung his praises in a piece which was called, as nearly as I could catch it, Mewlinnwillinwodd.

Mrs. Woodcourt, after expatiating to us on the fame of her great kinsman, said that no doubt wherever her son Allan went, he would remember his pedigree, and would on no account form an alliance below it. She told him that there were many handsome English ladies in India who went out on speculation, and that there were some to be picked up with property; but that neither charms nor wealth would suffice for the descendant from such a line without birth, which must ever be the first consideration. She talked so much about birth that, for a moment, I half fancied, and with pain—but what an idle fancy to suppose that she could think or care what *mine* was!

Mr. Woodcourt seemed a little distressed by her prolixity, but he was too considerate to let her see it, and contrived delicately to bring the conversation round to making his acknowledgments to my guardian for his hospitality, and for the very happy hours—he called them the very happy hours—he had passed with us. The recollection of them, he said, would go with him wherever he went, and would be always treasured. And so we gave him our hands, one after another, and he put his lips to Ada's hand—and to mine; and so he went away upon his long, long voyage!

I was very busy indeed all day, and wrote directions home to the servants, and wrote notes for my guardian, and dusted his books and papers, and jingled my housekeeping keys. I was still busy between the lights, singing and working by the window, when who should come in but Caddy, whom I had no expectation of seeing!

"Why, Caddy my dear," said I, "what beautiful flowers!"

She had such an exquisite little nosegay in her hand.

"Indeed I think so, Esther," replied Caddy. "They are the loveliest I ever saw."

"Prince, my dear?" said I, in a whisper.

"No," answered Caddy, shaking her head, and holding them to me to smell. "Not Prince."

"Well, to be sure, Caddy!" said I. "You must have two lovers!"

"What? Do they look like that sort of thing?" said Caddy.

"Do they look like that sort of thing?" I repeated, pinching her cheek.

Caddy only laughed in return; and telling me that she had come for half an hour, at the expiration of which time Prince would be waiting for her at the corner, sat chatting with me and Ada in the window, every now and then handing me the flowers again, or trying how they looked against my hair. At last, when she was going, she took me into my room and put them in my dress.

"For me?" said I, surprised.

"For you," said Caddy, with a kiss. "They were left behind by Somebody."

"Left behind?"

"At poor Miss Flite's," said Caddy. "Somebody who has been very good to her was hurrying away an hour ago, to join a ship, and left these flowers behind. No, no! Don't take them out. Let the pretty things lie here!" said Caddy, adjusting them with a careful hand, "because I was present myself, and I shouldn't wonder if Somebody left them on purpose!"

"Do they look like that sort of thing?" said Ada, coming laughingly behind me, and clasping me merrily round the waist. "Oh, yes, indeed they do, Dame Durden! They look very, very like that sort of thing! Oh, very like it indeed, my dear!"

CHAPTER 18

*Lady Dedlock*

It was not so easy as it had appeared at first to arrange for Richard's making a trial of Mr. Kenge's office. Richard himself was the chief impediment. As soon as he had it in his power to leave Mr. Badger at any moment, he began to doubt whether he wanted to leave him at all. He didn't know, he said, really. It wasn't a bad profession; he couldn't assert that he disliked it; perhaps he liked it as well as he liked any other—suppose he gave it one more chance! Upon that, he shut himself up for a few weeks with some books and some bones, and seemed to acquire a considerable fund of information with great rapidity. His vacillations between law and medicine lasted so long that midsummer arrived before he finally separated from Mr. Badger and entered on an experimental course of Messrs. Kenge and Carboy. For all his waywardness, he took great credit to himself as being determined to be in earnest "this time." And he was so good-natured throughout, and in such high spirits, and so fond of Ada, that it was very difficult indeed to be otherwise than pleased with him.

"As to Mr. Jarndyce"—who, I may mention, found the wind much given during this period to stick in the east—Richard would say to me, "he is the finest fellow in the world, Esther! I must be particularly careful, if it were only for his satisfaction, to take myself well to task, and have a regular wind-up of this business now."

The idea of his taking himself well to task, with that laughing face and heedless manner, and with a fancy that everything could catch and nothing could hold, was ludicrously anomalous. However, he told us between-whiles that he was doing it to such an extent that he wondered his hair didn't turn grey. His regular wind-up of the business was (as I have said) that he went to Mr. Kenge's about midsummer, to try how he liked it.

All this time he was, in money affairs, what I have described him: generous, profuse, wildly careless, but fully persuaded that he was rather calculating and prudent. I happened to say to Ada in his presence, half jestingly, half seriously, about the time of his going to Mr. Kenge's, that he needed to have Fortunatus's purse, he made so light of money, which he answered in this way:

"My jewel of a dear cousin, you hear this old woman! Why does she say that? Because I gave eight pounds odd (or whatever it was) for a certain neat waistcoat and buttons a few days ago. Now, if I had stayed at Badger's I should have been obliged to spend twelve pounds at a blow for some heart-breaking lecture-fees. So I make four pounds—in a lump—by the transaction!"

It was a question much discussed between him and my guardian what arrangements should be made for his living in London while he experimented on the law; for we had long since gone back to Bleak House, and it was too far off to admit of his coming there oftener than once a week. My guardian told me that if Richard were to settle down at Mr. Kenge's, he would take some apartments or chambers where we, too, could occasionally stay for a few days at a time; "but little woman," he added, rubbing his head very significantly, "he hasn't settled down there yet!" The discussions ended in our hiring for him, by the month, a neat little furnished lodging in a quiet old house near Queen Square. He immediately began to spend all the money he had in buying the oddest little ornaments and luxuries for this lodging; and so often as

154 · BLEAK HOUSE

Ada and I dissuaded him from making any purchase which was particularly unnecessary and expensive, he took credit for what it would have cost, and made out that to spend anything less on something else was to save the difference.

While these affairs were in abeyance, our visit to Mr. Boythorn's was postponed. At length, Richard having taken possession of his lodging, there was nothing to prevent our departure. He could have gone with us at that time of the year, very well; but he was in the full novelty of his new position, and was making most energetic attempts to unravel the mysteries of the fatal suit. Consequently we went without him, and my darling was delighted to praise him for being so busy.

We made a pleasant journey down into Lincolnshire by the coach. It was delightful weather. The green corn waved so beautifully, the larks sang so joyfully, the hedges were so full of wild-flowers, the trees were so thickly out in leaf, the bean-fields, with a light wind blowing over them, filled the air with such a delicious fragrance! Late in the afternoon we came to the market-town where we were to alight from the coach—a dull little town, with a church-spire, and a market-place, and a market-cross, and one intensely sunny street, and a pond with an old horse cooling his legs in it, and a very few men sleepily lying and standing about in narrow little bits of shade.

At the inn, we found Mr. Boythorn on horseback, waiting with an open carriage to take us to his house, which was a few miles off. He was overjoyed to see us, and dismounted with great alacrity.

"By Heaven," said he, after giving us a courteous greeting, "this is a most infamous coach! It is the most flagrant example of an abominable public vehicle that ever encumbered the face of the earth. It is twenty-five minutes after its time, this afternoon. The coachman ought to be put to death! Twenty-six minutes!"—referring to his watch. "With two ladies in the coach, this scoundrel has deliberately delayed his arrival six-and-twenty minutes. Deliberately! It is impossible that it can be accidental!"

While he said this in tones of the greatest indignation, he handed us into the little phaeton with the utmost gentleness, and was all smiles and pleasure.

"I am sorry, ladies," he said, standing bare-headed at the carriage-door, "that I am obliged to conduct you nearly two miles out of the way. But our direct road lies through Sir Leicester Dedlock's park, and in that fellow's property I have sworn never to set foot of mine, or horse's foot of mine, pending the present relations between us, while I breathe the breath of life!" And here, catching my guardian's eye, he broke into one of his tremendous laughs.

"Are the Dedlocks down here, Lawrence?" said my guardian as we drove along and Mr. Boythorn trotted on the green turf by the roadside.

"Sir Arrogant Numskull is here," replied Mr. Boythorn. "Ha ha ha! Sir Arrogant is here, and I am glad to say, has been laid by the heels here. My Lady"—in naming whom he always made a courtly gesture as if particularly to exclude her from any part in the quarrel—"is expected, I believe, daily. I am not in the least surprised that she postpones her appearance as long as possible. Whatever can have induced that transcendent woman to marry that effigy and figure-head of a baronet is one of the most impenetrable mysteries that ever baffled human inquiry. Ha ha ha ha!"

"I suppose," said my guardian, laughing, "*we* may set foot in the park while we are here? The prohibition does not extend to us, does it?"

"I can lay no prohibition on my guests," he said, bending his head to Ada and me, with the smiling politeness which sat so gracefully upon him, "except in the matter of their departure. I am only sorry that I cannot have the happiness of being their escort about Chesney Wold, which is a very fine place! But by the light of this summer day, Jarndyce, if you call upon the owner while you stay with me, you are likely to have a cool reception. He carries himself like an eight-day clock at all times— like one of a race of eight-day clocks in gorgeous cases that never go and never went—Ha ha ha!—but he will have some extra stiffness, I can promise you, for the friends of his friend and neighbour Boythorn!"

"I shall not put him to the proof," said my guardian. "He is as indifferent to the honour of knowing me, I dare say, as I am to the honour of knowing him. The air of the grounds, and perhaps such a view of the house as any other sight-seer might get, are quite enough for me."

"Well!" said Mr. Boythorn, "I am glad of it on the whole. It's in better keeping. I am looked upon about here as a second Ajax defying the lightning. Ha ha ha ha! When I go into our little church on a Sunday, a considerable part of the inconsiderable congregation expect to see me drop scorched and withered on the pavement under the Dedlock displeasure. Ha ha ha ha! I have no doubt he is surprised that I don't. For he is, by Heaven! the most self-satisfied, and the shallowest, and the most coxcombical and utterly brainless ass!"

Our coming to the ridge of a hill we had been ascending enabled our friend to point out Chesney Wold itself to us, and diverted his attention from its master.

It was a picturesque old house, in a fine park richly wooded. Among the trees, and not far from the residence, he pointed out the spire of the little church of which he had spoken. The house seemed scarcely real in its light solidity, and in the serene and peaceful hush that rested on all around it. On everything—house, garden, terrace, green slopes, water, old oaks, fern, moss, woods again, and far away across the openings in the prospect to the distance lying wide before us with a purple bloom upon it—there seemed to be such undisturbed repose.

When we came into the little village, and passed a small inn with the sign of the Dedlock Arms swinging over the road in front, Mr. Boythorn interchanged greetings with a young gentleman sitting on a bench outside the inn-door, some fishing-tackle lying beside him.

"That's the housekeeper's grandson, Mr. Rouncewell by name," said he; "and he is in love with a pretty girl up at the House. Lady Dedlock has taken a fancy to the pretty girl, and is going to keep her about her own fair person—an honour which my young friend himself does not at all appreciate. However, he can't marry just yet, even if his Rosebud were willing, so he is fain to make the best of it. In the meanwhile, he comes here pretty often, for a day or two at a time, to—fish. Ha ha ha ha!"

"Are he and the pretty girl engaged, Mr. Boythorn?" asked Ada.

"Why, my dear Miss Clare," he returned, "I must learn from you on such a point—not you from me."

Ada blushed; and Mr. Boythorn, trotting forward on his comely grey horse, dismounted at his own door and stood ready, with extended arm and uncovered head, to welcome us when we arrived.

He lived in a pretty house, formerly the parsonage-house, with a lawn in front, a bright flower-garden at the side, and a well-stocked orchard and kitchen-garden in the rear, enclosed with a venerable wall that had of itself a ripened ruddy look. But indeed everything about the place wore an aspect of maturity and abundance. The old lime-tree walk was like green cloisters, the very shadows of the cherry-trees and apple-trees were heavy with fruit, the gooseberry-bushes were so laden that their branches arched and rested on the earth, the strawberries and raspberries grew in like profusion, and the peaches basked by the hundred on the wall. There were such heaps of drooping pods, and marrows, and cucumbers, that every foot of ground appeared a vegetable treasury, while the smell of sweet herbs and all kinds of wholesome growth made the whole air a great nosegay. Such stillness and composure reigned within the orderly precincts of the old red wall that even the feathers hung in garlands to scare the birds hardly stirred.

The house, though a little disorderly in comparison with the garden, was a real old house, with settles in the chimney of the brick-floored kitchen, and great beams across the ceilings. On one side of it was the terrible piece of ground in dispute, where Mr. Boythorn maintained a sentry in a smock-frock, day and night, whose duty was supposed to be, in cases of aggression, immediately to ring a large bell hung up there for the purpose, to unchain a great bulldog established in a kennel as his ally, and generally to deal destruction on the enemy. Not content with these precautions, Mr. Boythorn had himself composed and posted there, on painted boards to which his name was attached in large letters, the following solemn warnings: "Beware of the Bulldog. He is most ferocious. Lawrence Boythorn." "Mantraps and spring-guns are set here at all times of the day and night. Lawrence Boythorn." "Take notice. That any person or persons audaciously presuming to trespass on this property will be punished with the utmost severity of private chastisement, and prosecuted with the utmost rigour of the law. Lawrence Boythorn." These he showed us, from the drawing-room window, while his bird was hopping about his head, and he laughed, "Ha ha ha ha! Ha ha ha ha!" to that extent that I really thought he would have hurt himself.

We arrived at his house on a Saturday. On the Sunday morning we all set forth to walk to the little church in the park. Entering the park, almost immediately by the disputed ground, we pursued a pleasant footpath winding among the verdant turf and the beautiful trees until it brought us to the church-porch.

The congregation was extremely small and quite a rustic one, with the exception of a large muster of servants from the House. There were some stately footmen; and there was a perfect picture of an old coachman, who looked as if he were the official representative of all the pomps and vanities that had ever been put into his coach. There was a very pretty show of young women, and above them, the handsome old face and fine responsible portly figure of the housekeeper towered pre-eminent. The pretty girl of whom Mr. Boythorn had told us was close by her. She was so very pretty that I might have known her by her beauty, even if I had not seen how blushingly conscious she was of the eyes of the young fisherman, whom I discovered not far off. One face, and not an agreeable one, though it was handsome, seemed maliciously watchful of this pretty girl, and indeed of every one and everything there. It was a Frenchwoman's.

As the bell was yet ringing and the great people were not yet come, I had leisure to glance over the church, which smelt as earthy as a grave, and to think what a shady, ancient, solemn little church it was. But a stir, a gathering of reverential awe in the rustic faces, and a blandly ferocious assumption on the part of Mr. Boythorn of being resolutely unconscious of somebody's existence, forewarned me that the great people were come, and that the service was going to begin.

"'Enter not into judgment with thy servant, O Lord, for in thy sight—'"

Shall I ever forget the rapid beating at my heart occasioned by the look I met as I stood up! Shall I ever forget the manner in which those handsome proud eyes seemed to spring out of their languor, and to hold mine! It was only a moment before I cast mine down—released again, if

I may say so—on my book; but I knew the beautiful face quite well in that short space of time.

And, very strangely, there was something quickened within me associated with the lonely days at my godmother's; yes, away even to the days when I had stood on tiptoe to dress myself at my little glass. And this, although I had never seen this lady's face before in all my life—I was quite sure of it—absolutely certain.

It was easy to know that the ceremonious, gouty, grey-haired gentleman, the only other occupant of the great pew, was Sir Leicester Dedlock; and that the lady was Lady Dedlock. But why her face should be, in a confused way, like a broken glass to me, in which I saw scraps of old remembrances, and why I should be so fluttered and troubled by having casually met her eyes, I could not think.

I felt it to be an unmeaning weakness in me, and tried to overcome it by attending to the words I heard. Then, very strangely, I seemed to hear them not in the reader's voice, but in the well-remembered voice of my godmother. This made me think, did Lady Dedlock's face accidentally resemble my godmother's? It might be that it did, a little; but the expression was so different, and the stern decision which had worn into my godmother's face, like weather into rocks, was so completely wanting in the face before me, that it could not be that resemblance which had struck me. Neither did I know the loftiness and haughtiness of Lady Dedlock's face, at all, in any one. And yet I—I, little Esther Summerson, the child who lived a life apart, and on whose birthday there was no rejoicing—seemed to arise before my own eyes, evoked out of the past by some power in this fashionable lady, whom I not only entertained no fancy that I had ever seen but whom I perfectly well knew I had never seen until that hour.

It made me tremble so to be thrown into this unaccountable agitation that I was conscious of being distressed even by the observation of the French maid, though I knew she had been looking watchfully here, and there, and everywhere from the moment of her coming into the church. By degrees, though very slowly, I at last overcame my strange emotion. After a long time, I looked towards Lady Dedlock again. It was while they were preparing to sing, before the sermon. She took no heed of me, and the beating of my heart was gone.

The service being concluded, Sir Leicester gave his arm with much taste and gallantry to Lady Dedlock—though he was obliged to walk by the help of a thick stick—and escorted her out of church to the pony carriage in which they had come. The servants then dispersed, and so did the congregation.

The week had gone round to the Saturday following that beating of

my heart in the church; and every day had been so bright and blue that
to ramble in the woods, and to see the light striking down among the
transparent leaves and sparkling in the beautiful interlacings of the
shadows of the trees, while the birds poured out their songs and the air
was drowsy with the hum of insects, had been most delightful. We had
one favourite spot, deep in moss and last year's leaves, where there were
some felled trees from which the bark was all stripped off. Seated among
these, we looked through a green vista supported by thousands of natural
columns, the whitened stems of trees, upon a distant prospect that was
like a glimpse of the better land. Upon the Saturday we sat here, Mr.
Jarndyce, Ada, and I, until we heard thunder muttering in the distance,
and felt the large rain-drops rattle through the leaves.

The weather had been all the week extremely sultry; but the storm
broke so suddenly that before we reached the outskirts of the wood the
thunder and lightning were frequent, and the rain came plunging
through the leaves as if every drop were a great leaden bead. We ran
out of the wood, and up and down the moss-grown steps which crossed
the plantation-fence, and made for a keeper's lodge which was close at
hand. We had often noticed the dark beauty of this lodge standing in a
deep twilight of trees, and how the ivy clustered over it.

The lodge was so dark within, now the sky was overcast, that we only
clearly saw the man who came to the door when we took shelter there
and put two chairs for Ada and me. We sat just within the doorway,
watching the storm. It was grand to see how the wind awoke, and bent
the trees, and drove the rain before it like a cloud of smoke; and to hear
the solemn thunder, and to see the lightning.

"Is it not dangerous to sit in so exposed a place?"

"Oh no, Esther dear!" said Ada quietly.

Ada said it to me, but I had not spoken.

The beating of my heart came back again. I had never heard the voice,
as I had never seen the face, but it affected me in the same strange way.
Again, in a moment, there arose before my mind innumerable pictures
of myself.

Lady Dedlock had taken shelter in the lodge before our arrival there,
and had come out of the gloom within. She stood behind my chair, with
her hand upon it, close to my shoulder.

"I have frightened you?" she said.

No. It was not fright. Why should I be frightened.

"I believe," said Lady Dedlock to my guardian, "I have the pleasure of
speaking to Mr. Jarndyce."

"Your remembrance does me more honour than I had supposed it
would, Lady Dedlock," he returned.

"I recognized you in church on Sunday. I am sorry that any local disputes of Sir Leicester's should render it a matter of some absurd difficulty to show you any attention here."

"I am aware of the circumstances," returned my guardian with a smile, "and am sufficiently obliged."

She had given him her hand, in an indifferent way that seemed habitual to her, and spoke in a correspondingly indifferent manner, though in a very pleasant voice. She was as graceful as she was beautiful, perfectly self-possessed, and had the air, I thought, of being able to attract and interest any one, if she had thought it worth her while. The keeper had brought her a chair, on which she sat in the middle of the porch between us.

"Is the young gentleman disposed of whom you wrote to Sir Leicester about, and whose wishes Sir Leicester was sorry not to have it in his power to advance in any way?" she said, over her shoulder, to my guardian.

"I hope so," said he.

She seemed to respect him, and even wish to conciliate him. There was something very winning in her haughty manner, and it became more familiar as she spoke to him over her shoulder.

"I presume this is your other ward, Miss Clare?"

He presented Ada, in form.

"You will lose the disinterested part of your Don Quixote character," said Lady Dedlock to Mr. Jarndyce, over her shoulder again, "if you only redress the wrongs of beauty like this. But present me," and she turned full upon me, "to this young lady too!"

"Miss Summerson really is my ward," said Mr. Jarndyce. "I am responsible to no Lord Chancellor in her case."

"Has Miss Summerson lost both her parents?" said my Lady.

"Yes."

"She is very fortunate in her guardian."

Lady Dedlock looked at me, and I looked at her, and said I was indeed. All at once she turned from me with a hasty air, almost expressive of displeasure or dislike, and spoke to him again.

"Ages have passed since we were in the habit of meeting, Mr. Jarndyce."

"A long time. At least I thought it was a long time until I saw you last Sunday," he returned.

"What! Even you are a courtier, or think it necessary to become one to me!" she said, with some disdain. "I have achieved that reputation, I suppose."

"You have achieved so much, Lady Dedlock," said my guardian, "that you pay some little penalty, I dare say. But none to me."

"So much!" she repeated, slightly laughing. "Yes!"

With her air of superiority, and power, and fascination, and I know not what, she seemed to regard Ada and me as little more than children. So, as she slightly laughed, and afterwards sat looking at the rain, she was as self-possessed as if she had been alone.

"I think you knew my sister, when we were abroad together, better than you knew me?" she said, looking at him again.

"Yes, we happened to meet oftener," he returned.

"We went our several ways," said Lady Dedlock. "It is to be regretted, I suppose, but it could not be helped."

Lady Dedlock again sat looking at the rain. The storm soon began to pass upon its way. The shower greatly abated, the lightning ceased, the thunder rolled among the distant hills, and the sun began to glisten on the wet leaves. As we sat there, silently, we saw a little pony phaeton coming towards us at a merry pace.

"The messenger is coming back, my lady," said the keeper, "with the carriage."

As it drove up, we saw that there were two people inside. They alighted from it, with some cloaks and wrappers, first the Frenchwoman whom I had seen in church, and secondly the pretty girl, the Frenchwoman with a defiant confidence, the pretty girl confused and hesitating.

"What now?" said Lady Dedlock. "Two!"

"I am your maid, my lady, at the present," said the Frenchwoman. "The message was for the attendant."

"I was afraid you might mean me, my lady," said the pretty girl.

"I did mean you, child," replied her mistress, calmly. "Put that shawl on me."

She slightly stooped her shoulders to receive it, and the pretty girl lightly dropped it in its place. The Frenchwoman stood unnoticed, looking on with her lips very tightly set.

"I am sorry," said Lady Dedlock to Mr. Jarndyce, "that we are not likely to renew our former acquaintance. You will allow me to send the carriage back for your two wards."

But as he would on no account accept this offer, she took a graceful leave of Ada—none of me—and put her hand upon his proffered arm, and got into the carriage.

"Come in, child," she said to the pretty girl, "I shall want you."

The carriage rolled away, and the Frenchwoman, with the wrappers she had brought hanging over her arm, remained standing where she had alighted.

I suppose there is nothing Pride can so little bear with as Pride itself, and that she was punished for her imperious manner. Her retaliation was the most singular I could have imagined. She remained perfectly still until the carriage had turned into the drive, and then, without the least discomposure of countenance, slipped off her shoes, left them on the ground, and walked deliberately in the same direction, through the wettest of the wet grass.

"Is that young woman mad?" said my guardian.

"Oh no, sir!" said the keeper, who, with his wife, was looking after her. "Hortense is not one of that sort. She has as good a headpiece as the best. But she's mortal high and passionate—powerful high and passionate; and what with having notice to leave, and having others put above her, she don't take kindly to it."

"But why should she walk shoeless through all that water?" said my guardian.

"Why indeed, sir, unless it is to cool her down!" said the man.

"Or unless she fancies it's blood," said the woman. "She'd as soon walk through that as anything else, I think, when her own's up!"

We passed not far from the House, a few minutes afterwards. Peaceful as it had looked when we first saw it, it looked even more so now, with a diamond spray glittering all about it, a light wind blowing, the birds no longer hushed but singing strongly, everything refreshed by the late rain. Still, very steadfastly and quietly walking towards it, a peaceful figure too in the landscape, went Mademoiselle Hortense, shoeless, through the wet grass.

## CHAPTER 19

*Moving On*

IT is the long vacation in the regions of Chancery Lane. The good ships Law and Equity, those teak-built, copper-bottomed, iron-fastened, brazen-faced, and not by any means fast-sailing Clippers are laid up in ordinary. The Courts are all shut up, the public offices lie in a hot sleep, Westminster Hall itself is a shady solitude where nightingales might sing.

The Temple, Chancery Lane, Serjeants' Inn, and Lincoln's Inn even unto the Fields, are like tidal harbours at low water. Outer doors of chambers are shut up by the score, messages and parcels are to be left at the porter's lodge by the bushel. There is only one Judge in town. Even he only comes twice a week to sit in chambers.

The Bar of England is scattered over the face of the earth. How England can get on through four long summer months without its Bar—which is its acknowledged refuge in adversity, and its only legitimate triumph in prosperity—is beside the question. The learned gentleman who is always so tremendously indignant at the unprecedented outrage committed on the feelings of his client by the opposite party that he never seems likely to recover it, is doing infinitely better than might be expected in Switzerland. The learned gentleman who does the withering business, and who blights all opponents with his gloomy sarcasm, is as merry as a grig at a French watering-place.

It is the hottest long vacation known for many years. All the young clerks are madly in love, and, according to their various degrees, pine for bliss with the beloved object, at Margate, Ramsgate, or Gravesend. All the middle-aged clerks think their families too large. Temple Bar gets so hot that it is to the adjacent Strand and Fleet Street what a heater is in an urn, and keeps them simmering all night.

In Mr. Krook's court, it is so hot that the people turn their houses inside out, and sit in chairs upon the pavement—Mr. Krook included, who there pursues his studies, with his cat (who never is too hot) by his side.

Over all the legal neighbourhood there hangs, like some great veil of rust or gigantic cobweb, the idleness and pensiveness of the long vacation. Mr. Snagsby, law-stationer of Cook's Court, Cursitor Street, is sensible of the influence, not only in his mind as a sympathetic and con-

templative man, but also in his business. He has more leisure for musing in Staple Inn, and in the Rolls Yard, during the long vacation than at other seasons.

Guster is busy in the little drawing-room, on this present afternoon in the long vacation, when Mr. and Mrs. Snagsby have it in contemplation to receive company. The expected guests are rather select than numerous, being Mr. and Mrs. Chadband, and no more. From Mr. Chadband's being much given to describe himself, both verbally and in writing, as a vessel, he is occasionally mistaken by strangers for a gentleman connected with navigation; but he is, as he expresses it, "in the ministry." Mr. Chadband is attached to no particular denomination, and is considered by his persecutors to have nothing so very remarkable to say on the greatest of subjects as to render his volunteering at all incumbent on his conscience; but he has his followers, and Mrs. Snagsby is of the number.

So Guster, much impressed by regarding herself for the time as the handmaid of Chadband, whom she knows to be endowed with the gift of holding forth for four hours at a stretch, prepares the little drawing-room for tea. All the furniture is shaken and dusted, the portraits of Mr. and Mr. Snagsby are touched up with a wet cloth, the best tea-service is set forth, and there is excellent provision made of dainty new bread, crusty twists, cool fresh butter, thin slices of ham, tongue, and German sausage, and delicate little rows of anchovies nestling in parsley—not to mention new-laid eggs, to be brought up warm in a napkin, and hot buttered toast. For Chadband is rather a consuming vessel—the persecutors say a gorging vessel—and can wield such weapons of the flesh as the knife and fork remarkably well.

Mr. Snagsby, in his best coat, says to Mrs. Snagsby, "At what time did you expect Mr. and Mrs. Chadband, my love?"

"At six," says Mrs. Snagsby.

Mr. Snagsby observes in a mild and casual way, that "it's gone that."

"Perhaps you'd like to begin without them," is Mrs. Snagsby's reproachful remark.

Mr. Snagsby does look as if he would like it very much, but he says, "No, my dear, no. I merely named the time."

"What's time," says Mrs. Snagsby, "to eternity?"

"Very true, my dear," says Mr. Snagsby. "Only when a person lays in victuals for tea, a person does it with a view—perhaps—more to time. And when a time is named for having tea, it's better to come up to it."

"To come up to it!" Mrs. Snagsby repeats with severity. "Up to it! As if Mr. Chadband was a fighter!"

Here Guster, who had been looking out of the bedroom window, comes rustling and scratching down the little staircase like a popular ghost, and falling flushed into the drawing-room, announces that Mr. and Mrs. Chadband have appeared in the court. The bell at the inner door in the passage immediately thereafter tinkling, she is admonished by Mrs. Snagsby not to omit the ceremony of announcement. Much discomposed in her nerves, she so fearfully mutilates that point of state as to announce "Mr. and Mrs. Cheeseming, least which, Imeantersay, whatsername!" and retires conscience-stricken from the presence.

Mr. Chadband is a large yellow man, with a fat smile and a general appearance of having a good deal of train-oil in his system. Mrs. Chadband is a stern, severe-looking, silent woman. Mr. Chadband moves softly and cumbrously, not unlike a bear who has been taught to walk upright. He is very much embarrassed about the arms, as if they were inconvenient to him, and he wanted to grovel; is very much in a per-spiration about the head; and never speaks without first putting up his great hand, as delivering a token to his hearers that he is going to edify them.

"My friends," says Mr. Chadband, "peace be on this house! On the master thereof, on the mistress thereof, on the young maidens, and on the young men! My friends, why do I wish for peace? What is peace? Is it war? No. Is it strife? No. Is it lovely, and gentle, and beautiful, and pleasant, and serene, and joyful? Oh yes! Therefore, my friends, I wish for peace upon you and upon yours."

Mr. Snagsby thinks it expedient on the whole to say "Amen," which is well received.

"Now, my friends," proceeds Mr. Chadband, "since I am upon this theme—"

Guster presents herself. Mrs. Snagsby, in a spectral bass voice, and without removing her eyes from Chadband, says with dread distinctness, "Go away!"

"Now, my friends," says Chadband, "since I am upon this theme, and in my lowly path improving it—"

Guster is heard unaccountably to murmur "one thousing seven hundred and eighty-two." The spectral voice repeats more solemnly, "Go away!"

"Now, my friends," said Mr. Chadband, "we will inquire in a spirit of love—"

Still Guster reiterates "one thousing seven hundred and eighty-two."

Mr. Chadband, pausing with the resignation of a man accustomed to be persecuted, and languidly folding up his chin into his fat smile, says, "Let us hear the maiden! Speak, maiden!"

"One thousing seven hundred and eighty-two, if you please, sir. Which he wish to know what the shilling ware for," says Guster, breath-less.

"For?" returns Mrs. Chadband. "For his fare!"

Guster replied that he "insists on one and eightpence, or on sum-monsizzing the party." Mrs. Snagsby and Mrs. Chadband are proceed-ing to grow shrill in indignation when Mr. Chadband quiets the tumult by lifting up his hand.

"My friends," says he, "I remember a duty unfulfilled yesterday. It is right that I should be chastened in some penalty. I ought not to mur-mur. Rachael, pay the eightpence!"

While Mrs. Snagsby, drawing her breath, looks hard at Mr. Snagsby, as who should say, "You hear this Apostle!" and while Mr. Chadband glows with humility and train-oil, Mrs. Chadband pays the money.

"My friends," says Chadband, "eightpence is not much; it might justly have been one and fourpence; it might justly have been half a crown. Oh let us be joyful, joyful! Oh let us be joyful!"

With which remark, which appears from its sound to be an extract in verse, Mr. Chadband stalks to the table, and before taking a chair, lifts up his admonitory hand.

"My friends," says he, "what is this which we now behold as being spread before us? Refreshment. Do we need refreshment then, my friends? We do. And why do we need refreshment, my friends? Because we are but mortal, because we are but sinful, because we are but of the earth, because we are not of the air. Can we fly, my friends? We cannot. Why can we not fly, my friends?"

Mr. Snagsby, presuming on the success of his last point, ventures to observe in a cheerful and rather knowing tone, "No wings." But is immediately frowned down by Mrs. Snagsby.

"I say, my friends," pursues Mr. Chadband, utterly rejecting and obliterating Mr. Snagsby's suggestion, "why can we not fly? Is it because we are calculated to walk? It is. Could we walk, my friends, without strength? We could not. What should we do without strength, my friends? Our legs would refuse to bear us, our knees would double up, our ankles would turn over, and we should come to the ground. Then from whence, my friends, in a human point of view, do we derive the strength that is necessary to our limbs? Is it," says Chadband, glancing over the table, "from bread in various forms, from butter which is churned from the milk which is yielded untoe us by the cow, from the eggs which are laid by the fowl, from ham, from tongue, from sausage, and from such-like? It is. Then let us partake of the good things which are set before us!"

The persecutors denied that there was any particular gift in Mr. Chadband's piling verbose flights of stairs, one upon another, after this fashion. But this can only be received as a proof of their determination to persecute, since it must be within everybody's experience that the Chadband style of oratory is widely received and much admired.

Mr. Chadband, however, having concluded for the present, sits down at Mr. Snagsby's table, and lays about him prodigiously. The conversion of nutriment of any sort into oil of the quality already mentioned appears to be a process so inseparable from the constitution of this exemplary vessel that in beginning to eat and drink, he may be described as always becoming a kind of considerable Oil Mills. On the present evening of the long vacation, in Cook's Court, Cursitor Street, he does such a powerful stroke of business that the warehouse appears to be quite full when the works cease.

At this period of the entertainment, Guster whispers Mr. Snagsby that he is wanted.

"And being wanted in the—not to put too fine a point upon it—in the shop!" says Mr. Snagsby, rising, "perhaps this good company will excuse me for half a minute."

Mr. Snagsby descends, and finds the two 'prentices intently contemplating a police constable, who holds a ragged boy by the arm.

"Why, bless my heart," says Mr. Snagsby, "what's the matter?"

"This boy," says the constable, "although he's repeatedly told to, won't move on—"

"I'm always a-moving on, sir," cries the boy, wiping away his grimy tears with his arm. "I've always been a-moving and a-moving on, ever since I was born. Where can I possible move to, sir, more nor I do move!"

"He won't move on," says the constable calmly, "although he has been repeatedly cautioned, and therefore I am obliged to take him into custody. He's as obstinate a young gonoph as I know. He *won't* move on."

"Oh my eye! Where can I move to!" cries the boy, beating his bare feet upon the floor of Mr. Snagsby's passage.

"Don't you come none of that or I shall make blessed short work of you!" says the constable. "My instructions are that you are to move on. I have told you so five hundred times."

"But where?" cries the boy.

"Well! Really, Constable, you know," says Mr. Snagsby wistfully, and coughing behind his hand his cough of great perplexity and doubt, "really that does seem a question. Where, you know?"

"My instructions don't go to that," replies the constable. "My instructions are that this boy is to move on."

Do you hear, Jo? It is nothing to you or to any one else that the great lights of the parliamentary sky have failed for some few years, in this business, to set you the example of moving on. The one grand recipe remains for you—the profound philosophical prescription—the be-all and the end-all of your strange existence upon earth. Move on! You are by no means to move off, Jo, for the great lights can't at all agree about that. Move on!

Mr. Snagsby says nothing, but coughs his forlornest cough, expressive of no thoroughfare in any direction. By this time Mr. and Mrs. Chadband and Mrs. Snagsby, hearing the altercation, have appeared upon the stairs. Guster having never left the end of the passage, the whole household are assembled.

"The simple question is, sir," says the constable, "whether you know this boy. He says you do."

Mrs. Snagsby, from her elevation, instantly cries out, "No, he don't!"

"My lit-tle woman!" says Mr. Snagsby. "My love, permit me! I do know something of this lad, and in what I know of him, I can't say that there's any harm—perhaps on the contrary, Constable." To whom the law-stationer relates his Joful and woful experience, suppressing the halfcrown fact.

"Well!" says the constable, "so far, it seems, he had grounds for what he said. When I took him into custody up in Holborn, he said you knew him. Upon that, a young man who was in the crowd said he was acquainted with you, and you were a respectable housekeeper, and if I'd call and make the inquiry, he'd appear. The young man don't seem inclined to keep his word, but—Oh! Here *is* the young man!"

Enter Mr. Guppy, who nods to Mr. Snagsby, and touches his hat with the chivalry of clerkship to the ladies on the stairs.

"I was strolling away from the office just now when I found this row going on," says Mr. Guppy to the law-stationer, "and as your name was mentioned, I thought it was right the thing should be looked into."

"It was very good-natured of you, sir," says Mr. Snagsby, "and I am obliged to you." And Mr. Snagsby again relates his experience, again suppressing the halfcrown fact.

"Now, I know where you live," says the constable, to Jo. "You live down in Tom-all-Alone's. That's a nice innocent place to live in, ain't it?"

"I can't go and live in no nicer place, sir," replies Jo. "They wouldn't have nothink to say to me if I wos to go to a nice innocent place fur to live."

"You are very poor, ain't you?" says the constable.

"Yes, I am indeed, sir, wery poor in gin'ral," replies Jo.

"I leave you to judge now! I shook these two halfcrowns out of him," says the constable, producing them to the company, "in only putting my hand upon him!"

"They're wot's left, Mr. Snagsby," says Jo, "out of a sov'ring as wos give me by a lady in a wale as sed she wos a servant and as come to my crossin one night and asked to be showd this 'ere 'ouse and the 'ouse wot him as you giv the writin to died at, and the berrin-ground wot he's berrid in. She ses to me she ses 'Can you show me all them places?' I ses 'Yes, I can,' I ses. And she ses to me 'Do it' and I dun it and she giv me a sov'ring and hooked it. And I ain't had much of the sov'ring neither," says Jo, with dirty tears, "fur I had to pay five bob down in Tom-all-Alone's afore they'd square it fur to give me change, and then a young man he thieved another five while I was asleep and another boy he thieved ninepence and the landlord he stood drains round with a lot more on it."

"You don't expect anybody to believe this, about the lady and the sovereign, do you?" says the constable.

"I don't know as I do, sir," replies Jo. "I don't expect nothink at all, sir, much, but that's the true hist'ry on it."

"You see what he is!" the constable observes to the audience. "Well, Mr. Snagsby, if I don't lock him up this time, will you engage for his moving on?"

"No!" cries Mrs. Snagsby from the stairs.

"My little woman!" pleads her husband. "Constable, I have no doubt he'll move on. You know you really must do it."

"I'm everyways agreeable, sir," says the hapless Jo.

"Do it, then," observes the constable. "You know what you have got to do. Do it! And recollect you won't get off so easy next time. Catch hold of your money. Now the sooner you're five mile off, the better for all parties."

With this farewell hint, and pointing generally to the setting sun as a likely place to move on to, the constable bids his auditors good-afternoon.

Now Jo's improbable story concerning the lady and the sovereign has awakened more or less the curiosity of all the company. Mr. Guppy, who has an inquiring mind in matters of evidence, and who has been suffering severely from the lassitude of the long vacation, takes that interest in the case that he enters on a regular cross-examination of the witness, which is found so interesting by the ladies that Mrs. Snagsby politely invites him to step upstairs, and drink a cup of tea. Mr. Guppy yielding his assent to this proposal, Jo is requested to follow into the drawing-room doorway, where Mr. Guppy takes him in hand as a witness, patting him into this shape, that shape, and the other shape, like a butterman dealing with so much butter, and worrying him according to the best models. During the progress of this keen encounter, the vessel Chadband, being merely engaged in the oil-trade, gets aground, and waits to be floated off.

"Well," says Mr. Guppy, "either this boy sticks to it like cobbler's-wax, or there is something out of the common here that beats anything that ever came into my way at Kenge and Carboy's."

Mrs. Chadband whispers Mrs. Snagsby, who exclaims, "You don't say so!"

"For years!" replied Mrs. Chadband.

"Has known Kenge and Carboy's office for years," Mrs. Snagsby triumphantly explains to Mr. Guppy. "Mrs. Chadband—this gentleman's wife—Reverend Mr. Chadband."

"Before I married my present husband," says Mrs. Chadband.

"Was you a party in anything, ma'am?" says Mr. Guppy.

Mrs. Chadband shakes her head.

"Perhaps you were acquainted with somebody who was a party in something, ma'am?" says Mr. Guppy.

"Not exactly that, either," replies Mrs. Chadband, humouring the joke with a hard-favoured smile.

"Not exactly that, either!" repeats Mr. Guppy. "Very good. Pray, ma'am, was it a lady of your acquaintance who had some transactions with Kenge and Carboy's office, or was it a gentleman of your acquaintance? Take time, ma'am. We shall come to it presently. Man or woman, ma'am?"

"Neither," says Mrs. Chadband.

"Oh! A child!" says Mr. Guppy, throwing on the admiring Mrs. Snagsby the regular acute professional eye which is thrown on British jurymen. "Now, ma'am, perhaps you'll have the kindness to tell us *what* child."

"You have got it at last, sir," says Mrs. Chadband. "Well, sir, it was before your time, most likely, judging from your appearance. I was left in charge of a child named Esther Summerson, who was put out in life by Messrs. Kenge and Carboy."

"Miss Summerson, ma'am!" cried Mr. Guppy, excited.

"I call her Esther Summerson," says Mrs. Chadband, with austerity. "There was no Miss-ing of the girl in my time. It was Esther. 'Esther, do this! Esther, do that!' And she was made to do it."

"My dear ma'am," returns Mr. Guppy, moving across the small apartment, "the humble individual who now addresses you received that young lady in London when she first came here from the establishment to which you have alluded. Allow me to have the pleasure of taking you by the hand."

Mr. Chadband, at last seeing this opportunity, makes his accustomed signal. Mrs. Snagsby whispers "Hush!"

"My friends," says Chadband, "we have partaken in moderation" (which was certainly not the case so far as he was concerned) "of the comforts which have been provided for us. May this house live upon the fatness of the land; may corn and wine be plentiful therein; may it grow, may it thrive, may it prosper, may it advance, may it proceed, may it press forward! But, my friends, have we partaken of anything else? We have. My friends, of what else have we partaken? Of spiritual profit? Yes. From whence have we derived that spiritual profit? My young friend, stand forth!"

Jo, thus apostrophized, gives a slouch backward, and another slouch forward, and another slouch to each side, and confronts the eloquent Chadband, with evident doubts of his intentions.

"My young friend," says Chadband, "you are to us a pearl, you are to us a diamond, you are to us a gem, you are to us a jewel. And why, my young friend?"

"*I* don't know," replies Jo. "I don't know nothink."

"My young friend," says Chadband, "it is because you know nothing that you are to us a gem and jewel. For what are you, my young friend? Are you a beast of the field? No. A bird of the air? No. A fish of the sea or river? No. You are a human boy, my young friend. A human boy. Oh, glorious to be a human boy! And why glorious, my young friend? Because you are capable of receiving the lessons of wisdom, because you are capable of profiting by this discourse which I now deliver for your good, because you are not a stick, or a stock, or a stone, or a post, or a pillar.

> O running stream of sparkling joy
> To be a soaring human boy!

And do you cool yourself in that stream now, my young friend? No. Why do you not cool yourself in that stream now? Because you are in a state of darkness, because you are in a state of obscurity, because you are in a state of sinfulness, because you are in a state of bondage. My young friend, what *is* bondage? Let us, in a spirit of love, inquire."

At this threatening stage of the discourse, Jo, who seems to have been gradually going out of his mind, smears his right arm over his face and gives a terrible yawn. Mrs. Snagsby indignantly expresses her belief that he is a limb of the Arch-fiend.

"My friends," says Mr. Chadband, "it is right that I should be humbled, it is right that I should be tried, it is right that I should be mortified, it is right that I should be corrected. I stumbled, on Sabbath last, when I thought with pride of my three hours' improving. The account is now favourably balanced; my creditor has accepted a composition. Oh let us be joyful, joyful! Oh let us be joyful!

"My friends," says Chadband, looking round him in conclusion, "I will not proceed with my young friend now. Will you come tomorrow, my young friend, and inquire of this good lady where I am to be found to deliver a discourse untoe you, and will you come like the thirsty swallow upon the next day, and upon the day after that, and upon many pleasant days, to hear discourses?"

Jo, whose immediate object seems to be to get away on any terms, gives a shuffling nod. Mr. Guppy then throws him a penny, and Mrs. Snagsby calls to Guster to see him safely out of the house. But before he goes downstairs, Mr. Snagsby loads him with some broken meats from the table, which he carries away, hugging in his arms.

So, Mr. Chadband retires into private life until he invests a little capital of supper in the oil-trade. Jo moves on down to Blackfriars Bridge, where he finds a baking stony corner wherein to settle to his repast.

And there he sits, munching and gnawing, and looking up at the great Cross on the summit of St. Paul's Cathedral. From the boy's face one might suppose that sacred emblem to be, in his eyes, the crowning confusion of the great, confused city—so golden, so high up, so far out of his reach. There he sits, the sun going down, the river running fast, the crowd flowing by him in two streams—everything moving on to some purpose and to one end—until he is stirred up, and told to "move on" too.

# CHAPTER 20

## *A New Lodger*

THE long vacation saunters on towards term-time, like an idle river very leisurely strolling down a flat country to the sea. Mr. Guppy saunters along with it congenially. He has blunted the blade of his penknife, and broken the point off, by sticking that instrument into his desk in every direction. Not that he bears the desk any ill-will, but he must do something, and it must be something of an unexciting nature, which will lay neither his physical nor his intellectual energies under too heavy contribution. He finds that nothing agrees with him so well as to make little gyrations on one leg of his stool, and stab his desk, and gape.

Kenge and Carboy are out of town, and the articled clerk has taken out a shooting license and gone down to his father's, and Mr. Guppy's two fellow-stipendiaries are away on leave. Mr. Guppy and Mr. Richard Carstone divide the dignity of the office. But Mr. Carstone is for the time being established in Kenge's room, whereat Mr. Guppy chafes. So exceedingly, that he with biting sarcasm informs his mother, in the confidential moments when he sups with her in the Old Street Road, that he is afraid the office is hardly good enough for swells, and that if he had known there was a swell coming, he would have got it painted.

Mr. Guppy suspects everybody who enters on the occupation of a stool in Kenge and Carboy's office of entertaining, as a matter of course, sinister designs upon him. He is clear that every such person wants to depose him. On the strength of these profound views, he in the most ingenious manner takes infinite pains to counterplot, when there is no plot, and plays the deepest games of chess without any adversary.

It is a source of much gratification to Mr. Guppy, therefore, to find the new-comer constantly poring over the papers in Jarndyce and Jarndyce; for he well knows that nothing but confusion and failure can come of that. His satisfaction communicates itself to a third saunterer through the long vacation in Kenge and Carboy's office; to wit, Young Smallweed. Whether Young Smallweed (metaphorically called Small and eke Chick Weed, as it were jocularly to express a fledgling) was ever a boy is much doubted in Lincoln's Inn. He is now something under fifteen, and an old limb of the law. He is a town-made article, of small stature and weazen features, but may be perceived from a considerable distance by means of his very tall hat.

Mr. Guppy has been lolling out of window all the morning. While thus looking out into the shade of Old Square, Lincoln's Inn, surveying the intolerable bricks and mortar, Mr. Guppy becomes conscious of a manly whisker emerging from the cloistered walk below, and turning itself up in the direction of his face. At the same time a low whistle is wafted through the Inn, and a suppressed voice cries, "Hip! Gup-py!"

"Why, you don't mean it?" says Mr. Guppy, aroused. "Small! Here's Jobling! Where have you sprung up from?"

"From the market-gardens down by Deptford. I can't stand it any longer. I must enlist. I say! Just throw out half a crown if you have got one to spare. I want to get some dinner."

"Will you come and dine with me?" says Mr. Guppy throwing out the coin, which Mr. Jobling catches neatly.

"How long should I have to hold out?" says Jobling.

"Not half an hour," returns Mr. Guppy.

"Can you give a fellow anything to read in the meantime?" says Mr. Jobling.

"You shall have the paper," says Mr. Guppy. "But you had better not be seen about here. Sit on our staircase and read. It's a quiet place."

Jobling nods intelligence and acquiescence. The sagacious Smallweed supplies him with the newspaper, and at last fetches Mr. Jobling up.

"Well, and how are you?" says Mr. Guppy, shaking hands with him.

"So, so. How are you?"

During this short colloquy, the active Smallweed, who is of the dinner party, has written in legal characters on a slip of paper, "Return immediately." They betake themselves to a neighbouring dining-house, of the class known among its frequenters by the denomination Slap-Bang.

Into the dining-house Mr. Smallweed leads the way. They know him there, and defer to him. Mr. Guppy consults him in the choice of that day's banquet, saying, "What do *you* take, Chick?" Chick, out of the profundity of his artfulness, preferring "veal and ham and French beans —and don't you forget the stuffing, Polly." Mr. Guppy and Mr. Jobling give the like order. Three pint pots of half-and-half are superadded.

Mr. Jobling is buttoned up closer than mere adornment might require. He has the faded appearance of a gentleman in embarrassed circumstances; even his light whiskers droop with something of a shabby air. His appetite is so vigorous that it suggests spare living for some little time back.

"Now, Small," says Guppy, "what would you recommend about pastry?"

"Marrow puddings," says Mr. Smallweed, instantly.

"Ay, ay!" cries Mr. Jobling, with an arch look. "You're there, are you? Thank you, Mr. Guppy, I don't know but what I *will* take a marrow pudding."

Three marrow puddings produced, to these succeed, by command of Mr. Smallweed, "three Cheshires"; and to those, "three small rums."

"What do you think *now*," says Mr. Guppy, "about enlisting?"

"Why, what I may think after dinner," returns Mr. Jobling, "is one thing, my dear Guppy, and what I may think before dinner is another thing. Still, even after dinner, I ask myself the question, How am I to live? Ill fo manger, you know," says Mr. Jobling, pronouncing that word as if he meant a necessary fixture in an English stable. "Ill fo manger. That's the French saying, and mangering is as necessary to me as it is to a Frenchman. Or more so. If any man had told me," pursues Jobling, "even so lately as when you and I had the frisk down in Lincolnshire, Guppy, and drove over to see that house at Chesney Wold, that I should be as hard up at the present time as I literally find myself, I should have—well, I should have pitched into him," says Mr. Jobling.

"Still, Tony, you were on the wrong side of the post then," remonstrates Mr. Guppy. "You were talking about nothing else in the gig."

"Guppy," says Mr. Jobling, "I will not deny it. I was on the wrong side of the post. But I trusted to things coming round."

That very popular trust in flat things coming round! Not in their being beaten round, or worked round, but in their "coming" round. As though a lunatic should trust in the world's "coming" triangular!

"I had confident expectations that things would come round and be all square," says Mr. Jobling, with some vagueness of expression, and perhaps of meaning, too. "But I was disappointed. They never did. And when it came to creditors making rows at the office, and to people that the office dealt with making complaints about dirty trifles of borrowed money, why, there was an end of that connexion. And of any new professional connexion, too; for if I was to give a reference tomorrow, it would be mentioned, and would sew me up. Then, what's a fellow to do? I have been keeping out of the way, and living cheap, down about the market-gardens; but what's the use of living cheap when you have got no money? You might as well live dear. It's the fashionable way; and fashion and whiskers have been my weaknesses, and I don't care who knows it," says Mr. Jobling. "They are great weaknesses—damme, sir, they are great. Well!" proceeds Mr. Jobling, "what can a fellow do, I ask you, *but* enlist?"

"Jobling," says Mr. Guppy, "myself and our mutual friend Smallweed have had a little conversation on this matter more than once, since you left the Inn, and I have mentioned to our mutual friend Smallweed a plan I have lately thought of proposing. You know Snagsby the stationer?"

"I know there is such a stationer," returns Mr. Jobling. "He was not ours, and I am not acquainted with him."

"He *is* ours, Jobling, and I *am* acquainted with him," Mr. Guppy retorts. "Well, sir! I have lately become better acquainted with him, through some accidental circumstances that have made me a visitor of his in private life. Both Mr. and Mrs. Snagsby are very willing to oblige me; and Snagsby has, in busy times, a good deal of copying work to give out. Now, gentlemen of the jury," says Mr. Guppy "—I mean now, Jobling—you may say this is a poor prospect of a living. Granted. But it's better than nothing, and better than enlistment. You want time. There must be time for these late affairs to blow over. You might live through it on much worse terms than by writing for Snagsby. There are two branches to this subject, Jobling. That is the first. I come to the second. You know Krook, the Chancellor, across the lane. Come, Jobling," says Mr. Guppy, "I think you know Krook, the Chancellor, across the lane?"

"I know him by sight," says Mr. Jobling.

"You know him by sight. Very well. And you know little Flite?"

"Everybody knows her," says Mr. Jobling.

"*Very* well. Now it has been one of my duties of late to pay Flite a certain weekly allowance, deducting from it the amount of her weekly rent, which I have paid (in consequence of instructions I have received) to Krook himself in her presence. This has brought me into communication with Krook, and into a knowledge of his house and his habits. I know he has a room to let. You may live there at a very low charge, under any name you like. He'll ask no questions; and would accept you as a tenant at a word from me. And I tell you another thing, Jobling," says Mr. Guppy, who has suddenly lowered his voice, and become familiar again, "he's an extraordinary old chap—always rummaging among a litter of papers, and grubbing away at teaching himself to read and write—without getting on a bit, as it seems to me. He is a most extraordinary old chap, sir, I don't know but what it might be worth a fellow's while to look him up a bit."

"You don't mean—?" Mr. Jobling begins.

"I mean," returns Mr. Guppy, shrugging his shoulders with becoming modesty, "that *I* can't make him out. I have seen something of the profession, and something of life, Tony, and it's seldom I can't make a man out, more or less. But such an old card as this—so deep, so sly, and secret (though I don't believe he is ever sober)—I never came across. Now, he must be precious old, you know, and he has not a soul about him, and he is reported to be immensely rich. It might pay you to knock up a sort of knowledge of him. I don't see why you shouldn't go in for it, when everything else suits."

Mr. Jobling, Mr. Guppy, and Mr. Smallweed all lean their elbows on the table, and their chins upon their hands, and look at the ceiling. After a time, they all drink, slowly lean back, put their hands in their pockets, and look at one another.

"If I had the energy I once possessed, Tony!" says Mr. Guppy, with a sigh.

Mr. Guppy concludes by resigning the adventure to Tony Jobling, and informing him that during the vacation and while things are slack, his purse, "as far as three or four or even five pound goes," will be at his disposal. "For never shall it be said," Mr. Guppy adds with emphasis, "that William Guppy turned his back upon his friend!—Krook's last lodger died there," observes Mr. Guppy, in an incidental way.

"Did he though!" says Mr. Jobling.

"There was a verdict. Accidental death. You don't mind that?"

"No," says Mr. Jobling, "I don't mind it; but he might as well have died somewhere else. It's devilish odd that he need go and die at *my* place!" Mr. Jobling quite resents this liberty. "There are places enough to die in, I should think!"

However, the compact being virtually made, Mr. Guppy proposes to dispatch the trusty Smallweed to ascertain if Mr. Krook is at home, as in that case they would complete the negotiation without delay. Mr. Jobling approving, Smallweed puts himself under the tall hat and conveys it out of the dining-rooms in the Guppy manner. He soon returns with the intelligence that Mr. Krook is at home, and that he has seen him through the shop-door, sitting in the back premises, sleeping "like one o'clock."

"Then I'll pay," says Mr. Guppy, "and we'll go and see him."

Mr. Guppy and Mr. Jobling repair to the rag and bottle shop, where they find Krook still sleeping like one o'clock; that is to say, breathing stertorously with his chin upon his breast, and quite insensible to any external sounds, or even to gentle shaking. On the table beside him, among the usual lumber, stand an empty gin-bottle and a glass. The unwholesome air is so stained with his liquor that even the green eyes of the cat upon her shelf, as they open and shut and glimmer on the visitors, look drunk.

"Hold up here!" says Mr. Guppy, giving the relaxed figure of the old man another shake. "Mr. Krook! Halloa, sir! Did you ever see such a stupor as he falls into, between drink and sleep?" says Mr. Guppy.

"If this is his regular sleep," returns Jobling, rather alarmed, "it'll last a long time one of these days, I am thinking."

"It's always more like a fit than a nap," says Mr. Guppy, shaking him again. "Halloa, your lordship! Why, he might be robbed fifty times over! Open your eyes!"

After much ado, he opens them, but without appearing to see his visitors, or any other objects.

"He is alive, at any rate," says Mr. Guppy. "How are you, my Lord Chancellor? I have brought a friend of mine, sir, on a little matter of business."

The old man makes an attempt to rise. They help him up, and he staggers against the wall and stares at them.

"How do you do, Mr. Krook?" says Mr. Guppy, in some discomfiture. "How do you do, sir? I hope you are pretty well?"

The old man, in aiming a purposeless blow at Mr. Guppy, or at nothing, feebly swings himself round, and comes with his face against the wall. So he remains for a minute or two, heaped up against it, and then staggers down the shop to the front door. The air, the movement in the court, the lapse of time, or the combination of these things, recovers him. He comes back pretty steadily, adjusting his fur cap on his head, and looking keenly at them.

"Your servant, gentlemen. I've been dozing. Hi! I am hard to wake, odd times." The old man's eye resting on the empty bottle, he takes it up, examines it, and slowly tilts it upside down. "I say!" he cries. "Somebody's been making free here!"

"I assure you we found it so," says Mr. Guppy. "Would you allow me to get it filled for you?"

"Yes, certainly I would!" cries Krook, in high glee. "Certainly I would! Don't mention it! Get it filled next door—Sol's Arms—the Lord Chancellor's fourteenpenny. Bless you, they know *me!*"

He so presses the empty bottle upon Mr. Guppy that that gentleman, with a nod to his friend, accepts the trust and hurries out, and hurries in again with the bottle filled. The old man receives it in his arms like a beloved grandchild, and pats it tenderly.

"But I say," he whispers, with his eyes screwed up, after tasting it, "this ain't the Lord Chancellor's fourteenpenny! This is eighteenpenny!"

"I thought you might like that better," says Mr. Guppy.

"You're a nobleman, sir," returns Krook, with another taste. "You're a baron of the land."

Taking advantage of this auspicious moment, Mr. Guppy presents his friend under the impromptu name of Mr. Weevle, and states the object of their visit. Krook with his bottle under his arm, takes time to survey his proposed lodger, and seems to approve of him. "You'd like to see the room, young man?" he says. "Ah! It's a good room! Been whitewashed. Been cleaned down with soft soap and soda. Hi! It's worth twice the rent, letting alone my company when you want it, and such a cat to keep the mice away."

The old man takes them upstairs, where indeed they do find it cleaner than it used to be, and also containing some old articles of furniture which he has dug up from his inexhaustible stores. The terms are easily concluded—for the Lord Chancellor cannot be hard on Mr. Guppy, associated as he is with Kenge and Carboy, Jarndyce and Jarndyce, and other famous claims on his professional consideration—and it is agreed that Mr. Weevle shall take possession on the morrow. Mr. Weevle and Mr. Guppy then repair to Cook's Court, Cursitor Street, where the personal introduction of the former to Mr. Snagsby is effected, and (more important) the vote and interest of Mrs. Snagsby are secured.

On the morrow, in the dusk of evening, Mr. Weevle modestly appears at Krook's, by no means incommoded with luggage, and establishes himself in his new lodgings; where the two eyes in the shutters stare at him in his sleep, as if they were full of wonder. On the following day Mr. Weevle, who is a handy good-for-nothing kind of young fellow, borrows a needle and thread of Miss Flite, and a hammer of his landlord, and goes to work devising apologies for window curtains, and knocking up apologies for shelves, and hanging up his crockery sundries on a pennyworth of little hooks, like a shipwrecked sailor making the best of it.

But what Mr. Weevle prizes most, of all his few possessions, is a choice collection of copper-plate impressions from that truly national work, The Divinities of Albion, or Galaxy Gallery of British Beauty, representing ladies of title and fashion in every variety of smirk that art, combined with capital, is capable of producing. With these magnificent portraits, unworthily confined in a bandbox during his seclusion among the market-gardens, he decorates his apartment, and the result is very imposing.

He is a quiet lodger, full of handy shifts and devices as before mentioned, able to cook and clean for himself as well as to carpenter, and developing social inclinations after the shades of evening have fallen on the court. At those times when he is not visited by Mr. Guppy, he comes out of his dull room and talks to Krook, or is "very free," as they call it in the court, commendingly, with any one disposed for conversation.

# CHAPTER 21

## The Smallweed Family

In a rather ill-favoured and ill-savoured neighbourhood, though one of its rising grounds bears the name of Mount Pleasant, the elfin Smallweed, christened Bartholomew, and known on the domestic hearth as Bart, passes that limited portion of his time on which the office and its contingencies have no claim. He dwells in a little narrow street, always solitary, shady, and sad, closely bricked in on all sides like a tomb.

There has been only one child in the Smallweed family for several generations. Little old men and women there have been, but no child until Mr. Smallweed's grandmother, now living, became weak in her intellect, and fell (for the first time) into a childish state. With such infantine graces as a total want of observation, memory, understanding, and interest, and an eternal disposition to fall asleep over the fire and into it, Mr. Smallweed's grandmother has undoubtedly brightened the family.

Mr. Smallweed's grandfather is likewise of the party. He is in a helpless condition as to his lower, and nearly so as to his upper, limbs; but his mind is unimpaired. It holds, as well as it ever held, the first four rules of arithmetic, and a certain small collection of the hardest facts. In respect of ideality, reverence, wonder, and other such phrenological attributes, it is no worse off than it used to be. Going out early in life, and marrying late, as his father had done before him, he too begat a lean and anxious-minded son; who, in his turn, going out early in life and marrying late, became the father of Bartholomew and Judith Smallweed, twins.

At the present time, in the dark little parlour certain feet below the level of the street, seated in two black horse-hair porter's chairs, one on each side of the fire-place, the superannuated Mr. and Mrs. Smallweed while away the rosy hours. On the stove are a couple of trivets for the pots and kettles which it is Grandfather Smallweed's usual occupation to watch, and projecting from the chimney-piece between them is a sort of brass gallows for roasting, which he also superintends when it is in action. Under the venerable Mr. Smallweed's seat, and guarded by his spindle legs, is a drawer in his chair, reported to contain property to a fabulous amount. Beside him is a spare cushion, with which he is always provided in order that he may have something to throw at the venerable partner of his respected age whenever she makes an illusion to money—a subject on which he is particularly sensitive.

"And where's Bart?" Grandfather Smallweed inquires of Judy, Bart's twin sister.

"He an't come in yet," says Judy.

"It's his tea-time, isn't it?"

"No."

"How much do you mean to say it wants then?"

"Ten minutes."

"Ho!" says Grandfather Smallweed. "Ten minutes."

Grandmother Smallweed, who has been mumbling and shaking her head at the trivets, hearing figures mentioned, connects them with money, and screeches, like a horrible old parrot without any plumage, "Ten ten-pound notes!"

Grandfather Smallweed immediately throws the cushion at her.

"Drat you, be quiet!" says the good old man.

The effect of this act of jaculation is twofold. It not only doubles up Mrs. Smallweed's head against the side of her porter's chair, and causes her to present, when extricated by her grand-daughter, a highly unbecoming state of cap, but the necessary exertion recoils on Mr. Smallweed himself, whom it throws back into *his* porter's chair like a broken puppet. The excellent old gentleman, being at these times a mere clothes-bag with a black skull-cap on the top of it, does not present a very animated appearance until he has undergone the two operations, at the hands of his grand-daughter, of being shaken up like a great bottle and poked and punched like a great bolster.

Judy the twin is worthy company for these associates. She is so indubitably sister to Mr. Smallweed the younger that the two kneaded into one would hardly make a young person of average proportions. Judy never owned a doll, never heard of Cinderella, never played at any game. It is very doubtful whether Judy knows how to laugh. She has so rarely seen the thing done, that the probabilities are strong the other way.

And her twin brother couldn't wind up a top for his life. He knows no more of Jack the Giant Killer, or of Sinbad the Sailor, than he knows of the people in the stars. He could as soon play at leap-frog, or at cricket, as change into a cricket or a frog himself. But he is so much the better off than his sister that on his narrow world of fact an opening has dawned, into such broader regions as lie within the ken of Mr. Guppy. Hence his admiration and his emulation of that shining enchanter.

Judy, with a gonglike clash and clatter, sets one of the sheet-iron tea-trays on the table, and arranges cups and saucers. The bread she puts on in an iron basket; and the butter (and not much of it) in a small pewter plate. Grandfather Smallweed looks hard after the tea as it is served out, and asks Judy where the girl is.

"Charley, do you mean?" says Judy.

This touches a spring in Grandmother Smallweed, who, chuckling, as usual, at the trivets, cries—"Over the water! Charley over the water, Charley over the water, over the water to Charley," and becomes quite energetic about it. Grandfather looks at the cushion, but has not sufficiently recovered his late exertion.

"Ha!" he says, when there is silence. "She eats a deal. It would be better to allow her for her keep."

Judy, with her brother's wink, shakes her head, and purses up her mouth into No, without saying it.

"No?" returns the old man. "Why not?"

"She'd want sixpence a day, and we can do it for less," says Judy.

Judy calls, as she scrapes the butter on the loaf with every precaution against waste, and cuts it into slices, "You Charley, where are you?" Timidly obedient to the summons, a little girl in a rough apron and a large bonnet, with her hands covered with soap and water and a scrubbing-brush in one of them, appears, and curtseys.

"What work are you about now?" says Judy.

"I'm a-cleaning the upstairs back room, miss," replies Charley.

"Mind you do it thoroughly, and don't loiter. Shirking won't do for me. Go along!" cries Judy, with a stamp upon the ground. "You girls are more trouble than you're worth, by half."

On this severe matron, as she returns to her task of scraping the butter and cutting the bread, falls the shadow of her brother, looking in at the window. For whom, knife and loaf in hand, she opens the street-door.

"Ay, ay, Bart!" says Grandfather Smallweed. "Here you are, hey?"

His grandson takes a chair at the tea-table. The four old faces then hover over tea-cups like a company of ghastly cherubim, Mrs. Smallweed perpetually twitching her head and chattering at the trivets, and Mr. Smallweed requiring to be repeatedly shaken up like a large black draught.

"Now, if everybody has done," says Judy, "I'll have that girl in to her tea. She would never leave off if she took it by herself in the kitchen."

Charley is accordingly introduced and, under a heavy fire of eyes, sits down to her basin and a Druidical ruin of bread and butter, and so disperses the Druidical ruins that Miss Smallweed charges her not to gormandize, which "in you girls," she observes, is disgusting. Charley might find some more difficulty in meeting her views on the general subject of girls but for a knock at the door.

"See who it is, and don't chew when you open it!" cries Judy.

The object of her attentions withdrawing for the purpose, Miss Smallweed takes that opportunity of jumbling the remainder of the bread and butter together, and launching two or three dirty tea-cups into the ebb-tide of the basin of tea, as a hint that she considers the eating and drinking terminated.

"Now! Who is it, and what's wanted?" says the snappish Judy.

It is one "Mr. George," it appears. Without other announcement or ceremony, Mr. George walks in.

"Whew!" says Mr. George. "You are hot here. Always a fire, eh? Well! Perhaps you do right to get used to one." Mr. George makes the latter remark to himself as he nods to Grandfather Smallweed.

"Ho! It's you!" cries the old gentleman. "How de do? How de do?"

"Middling," replies Mr. George, taking a chair. "Your grand-daughter I have had the honour of seeing before—my service to you, miss."

"This is my grandson," says Grandfather Smallweed. "You ha'n't seen him before. He is in the law, and not much at home."

"My service to him, too! He is like his sister. He is devilish like his sister," says Mr. George, laying a great and not altogether complimentary stress on his last adjective.

"And how does the world use you, Mr. George?" Grandfather Smallweed inquires, slowly rubbing his legs.

"Pretty much as usual. Like a football."

He is a swarthy brown man of fifty; well-made, and good-looking, with crisp dark hair, bright eyes, and a broad chest. His sinewy and powerful hands, as sunburnt as his face, have evidently been used to a pretty rough life. What is curious about him is that he sits forward on his chair as if he were, from long habit, allowing space for some dress or accoutrements that he has altogether laid aside. His step too is measured and heavy, and would go well with a weighty clash and jingle of spurs. Altogether, one might guess Mr. George to have been a trooper once upon a time.

A special contrast Mr. George makes to the Smallweed family. Trooper was never yet billeted upon a household more unlike him. It is a broadsword to an oyster-knife. His developed figure, and their stunted forms—his large manner, filling any amount of room, and their little narrow pinched ways, his sounding voice and their sharp spare tones—are in the strongest and the strangest opposition. As he sits in the middle of the grim parlour, leaning a little forward, with his hands upon his thighs and his elbows squared, he looks as though, if he re-mained there long, he would absorb into himself the whole family and the whole four-roomed house, extra little back-kitchen and all.

"Do you rub your legs to rub life into 'em?" he asks of Grandfather Smallweed, after looking round the room.

"Why it's partly a habit, Mr. George, and—yes—it partly helps the circulation," he replies.

"The cir-cu-la-tion!" repeats Mr. George. "Not much of that, I should think."

"Truly I'm old, Mr. George," says Grandfather Smallweed. "But I can carry my years. I'm older than *her*," nodding at his wife, "and see what she is!—You're a brimstone chatterer!"

"Unlucky old soul!" says Mr. George, turning his head in that direc-tion. "Don't scold the old lady. Look at her here, with her poor cap half off her head, and her poor hair all in a muddle. Hold up, ma'am. That's better. There we are! Think of your mother, Mr. Smallweed," says Mr. George, coming back to his seat from assisting her, "if your wife an't enough."

"I suppose you were an excellent son, Mr. George?" the old man hints, with a leer.

The colour of Mr. George's face rather deepens as he replies: "Why, no. I wasn't."

"I am astonished at it."

"So am I. I ought to have been a good son, and I think I meant to have been one. But I wasn't. I was a thundering bad son, that's the long and the short of it. However, the less said about it, the better now. Come! You know the agreement. Always a pipe out of the two months' interest! Here's the new bill, and here's the two months' interest-money, and a devil-and-all of a scrape it is to get it together in my business."

Mr. George sits, with his arms folded, consuming the family and the parlour, while Grandfather Smallweed is assisted by Judy to two black-leather cases out of a locked bureau, in one of which he secures the document he has just received and from the other takes another similar document which he hands to Mr. George, who twists it up for a pipe-light. As the old man inspects through his glasses every up-stroke and down-stroke of both documents before he releases them from their leathern prison, and as he counts the money three times over, and is as tremulously slow of speech and action as it is possible to be, this business is a long time in progress. When it is concluded, and not before, he dis-engages his ravenous eyes and fingers from it, and answers Mr. George's last remark by saying, "Afraid to order the pipe? We are not so mercen-ary as that, sir. Judy, see directly to the pipe and the glass of cold brandy-and-water for Mr. George."

The sportive twins, who have been looking straight before them all this time, except when they have been engrossed by the black-leather cases, retire together, generally disdainful of the visitor, but leaving him to the old man as two young cubs might leave a traveller to the parental bear.

Says Mr. George, "You'll sell me up at last, I suppose, when I am a day in arrear."

"My dear friend!" cries Grandfather Smallweed, "never! Never, my dear friend! But my friend in the city that I got to lend you the money—*he* might!"

"Oh! you can't answer for him?" says Mr. George, finishing the inquiry in his lower key with the words "you lying old rascal!"

"My dear friend, he is not to be depended on. I wouldn't trust him. He will have his bond, my dear friend."

"Devil doubt him," says Mr. George. Charley appearing with a tray, on which are the pipe, a small paper of tobacco, and the brandy-and-water, he asks her, "How do you come here? You haven't got the family face."

"I goes out to work, sir," returns Charley.

The trooper (if trooper he be or have been) takes her bonnet off, with a slight touch for so strong a hand, and pats her on the head. "You give the house almost a wholesome look. It wants a bit of youth as much as it wants fresh air." Then he dismisses her, lights his pipe, and drinks to Mr. Smallweed's friend in the city—the one solitary flight of that esteemed old gentleman's imagination.

"So you think he might be hard upon me, eh?"

"I think he might—I am afraid he would. I have known him do it," says Grandfather Smallweed, "twenty times."

The trooper looks at Mr. Smallweed with grave attention. "I take it," he says, "that I am the only man alive (or dead either) that gets the value of a pipe out of *you?*"

"Well," returns the old man, "it's true that I don't see company, Mr. George, and that I don't treat. I can't afford to it. But as you, in your pleasant way, made your pipe a condition—"

"Why, it's not for the value of it; that's no great thing. It was a fancy to get it out of you. To have something in for my money."

"Ha'n't you no relations, now," asks Grandfather Smallweed, with a twinkle in his eyes, "who would pay off this little principal, or who would lend you a good name or two that I could persuade my friend in the city to make you a further advance upon? Two good names would be sufficient for my friend in the city. Ha'n't you no such relations, Mr. George?"

Mr. George, still composedly smoking, replies, "If I had, I shouldn't trouble them. I have been trouble enough to my belongings in my day. It *may* be a very good sort of penitence in a vagabond who has wasted the best time of his life, to go back then to decent people that he never was a credit to, and live upon them; but it's not my sort. The best kind of amends, then, for having gone away is to keep away, in my opinion."

Grandfather Smallweed has been gradually sliding down in his chair since his last adjustment, and is now a bundle of clothes, with a voice in it calling for Judy. That Houri appearing, shakes him up in the usual manner.

"Ha!" he observes, when he is in trim again. "If you could have traced out the Captain, Mr. George, it would have been the making of you. If when you first came here, in consequence of our advertisements in the newspapers—when I say 'our,' I'm alluding to the advertisements of my friend in the city, and one or two others who embark their capital in the same way—if, at that time, you could have helped us, Mr. George, it would have been the making of you."

"I was willing enough to be 'made,' as you call it," says Mr. George, smoking not quite so placidly as before, for since the entrance of Judy he has been in some measure disturbed by a fascination, not of the admiring kind, which obliges him to look at her; "but on the whole I am glad I wasn't now."

"Why, Mr. George? In the name of—of Brimstone, why?" says Grandfather Smallweed, with a plain appearance of exasperation.

"For two reasons, comrade."

"And what two reasons, Mr. George?"

"In the first place," returns Mr. George, but still looking at Judy as if, she being so old and so like her grandfather, it is indifferent which of the two he addresses, "you gentlemen took me in. You advertised that Mr. Hawdon (Captain Hawdon, if you hold to the saying, 'Once a captain always a captain') was to hear of something to his advantage."

"Well?" returns the old man, shrilly and sharply.

"Well!" says Mr. George, smoking on. "It wouldn't have been much to his advantage to have been clapped into prison by the whole bill and judgment trade of London."

"How do you know that? Some of his rich relations might have paid his debts, or compounded for 'em. Besides, he had taken *us* in. He owed us immense sums, all round. I would sooner have strangled him than had no return. If I sit here thinking of him," snarls the old man, holding up his impotent ten fingers, "I want to strangle him now."

"I don't need to be told," returns the trooper, taking his pipe from his lips for a moment, "that he carried on heavily and went to ruin. I have been at his right hand many a day when he was charging upon ruin full-gallop. I was with him when he was sick and well, rich and poor. I laid this hand upon him after he had run through everything and broken down everything beneath him—when he held a pistol to his head."

"I wish he had let it off," says the benevolent old man, "and blown his head into as many pieces as he owed pounds!"

"That would have been a smash indeed," returns the trooper coolly. "Anyway, he had been young, hopeful, and handsome in the days gone by; and I am glad I never found him when he was neither. That's reason number one."

"I hope number two's as good?" snarls the old man.

"Why, no. It's more of a selfish reason. If I had found him, I must have gone to the other world to look. He was there."

"How do you know he was there?"

"Don't lose your temper as well as your money," says Mr. George, calmly knocking the ashes out of his pipe. "He was drowned long before. I am convinced of it. He went over a ship's side. Whether intentionally or accidentally, I don't know. Prehaps your friend in the city does.—Do you know what that tune is, Mr. Smallweed?" he adds, after breaking off to whistle one, accompanied on the table with the empty pipe.

"Tune!" replies the old man. "No. We never have tunes here."

"That's the Dead March in Saul. They bury soldiers to it, so it's the natural end of the subject. Now, if your pretty grand-daughter—excuse me, miss—will condescend to take care of this pipe for two months, we shall save the cost of one next time. Good-evening, Mr. Smallweed!"

Mr. George, with a parting salutation to the scornful Judy, strides out of the parlour, clashing imaginary sabres as he goes. He makes his way to that curious region lying about the Haymarket and Leicester Square which is a centre of attraction to indifferent foreign hotels and indifferent foreigners, racket-courts, fighting men, swordsmen, foot-guards, old china, gaming-houses, exhibitions, and a large medley of shabbiness and shrinking out of sight. Penetrating to the heart of this region, he arrives, by a court and a long whitewashed passage, at a great brick building composed of bare walls, floors, roof-rafters, and skylights, on the front of which, if it can be said to have any front, is painted GEORGE'S SHOOTING GALLERY, ETC.

Into George's Shooting Gallery, etc., he goes; and in it there are gas-lights (partly turned off now), and two whitened targets for rifle-shooting, and archery accommodation, and fencing appliances, and all necessaries for the British art of boxing. None of these sports or exercises are being pursued in George's Shooting Gallery tonight, which is so devoid of company that a little grotesque man with a large head has it all to himself, and lies asleep upon the floor.

The little man is dressed something like a gunsmith, in a green-baize apron and cap, and his face and hands are dirty with gunpowder and begrimed with the loading of guns. Not far off is the strong, rough, primitive table, with a vice upon it, at which he has been working. He is a little man with a face all crushed together, who appears, from a certain blue and speckled appearance that one of his cheeks presents,

to have been blown up, in the way of business, at some odd time or times.

"Phil!" says the trooper, in a quiet voice.

"All right!" cries Phil, scrambling to his feet.

"Anything been doing?"

"Flat as ever so much swipes," says Phil. "Five dozen rifle and a dozen pistol. As to aim!" Phil gives a howl at the recollection.

"Shut up shop, Phil!"

As Phil moves about to execute this order, it appears that he is lame, though able to move very quickly. On the speckled side of his face he has no eyebrow, and on the other side he has a bushy black one, which want of uniformity gives him a very singular and rather sinister appearance. Everything seems to have happened to his hands that could possibly take place consistently with the retention of all the fingers; for they are notched, and seamed, and crumpled all over. He appears to be very strong, and lifts heavy benches about as if he had no idea what weight was.

"Phil!" says the master, walking towards him without his coat and waistcoat. "You were found in a doorway, weren't you?"

"Gutter," says Phil. "Watchman tumbled over me."

"Then vagabondizing came natural to *you*, from the beginning."

"As nat'ral as possible," says Phil.

"Good-night!"

"Good-night, Guv'ner."

# CHAPTER 22

~~~~~~~~~~~~~~~~~~~~~~~~~~~~~~~~~~~~~~~~~~~~~~~~~~~

*Mr. Bucket*

ALLEGORY looks pretty cool in Lincoln's Inn Fields, though the evening is hot; for both Mr. Tulkinghorn's windows are wide open, and the room is lofty, gusty, and gloomy. Plenty of dust comes in at Mr. Tulkinghorn's windows, and plenty more has generated among his furniture and papers. It lies thick everywhere.

In his lowering magazine of dust, the universal article into which his papers and himself, and all his clients, and all things of earth, animate and inanimate, are resolving, Mr. Tulkinghorn sits at one of the open windows, enjoying a bottle of old port. Though a hard-grained man, close, dry, and silent, he can enjoy old wine with the best. He has a priceless bin of port in some artful cellar under the Fields, which is one of his many secrets. When he dines alone in chambers, as he has dined today, and has his bit of fish and his steak or chicken brought in from the coffee-house, he descends with a candle to the echoing regions below the deserted mansion and, heralded by a remote reverberation of thundering doors, comes gravely back, encircled by an earthy atmosphere, and carrying a bottle from which he pours a radiant nectar two score and ten years old that blushes in the glass to find itself so famous, and fills the whole room with the fragrance of southern grapes.

Mr. Tulkinghorn, sitting in the twilight by the open window, enjoys his wine. As if it whispered to him of its fifty years of silence and seclusion, it shuts him up the closer. More impenetrable than ever, he sits, and drinks, and mellows as it were, in secrecy, pondering at that twilight hour on all the mysteries he knows, associated with darkening woods in the country and vast blank shut-up houses in town—and perhaps sparing a thought or two for himself, and his family history, and his money, and his will—all a mystery to every one.

But Mr. Tulkinghorn is not alone tonight, to ponder at his usual length. Seated at the same table, though with his chair modestly and uncomfortably drawn a little way from it, sits a bald, mild, shining man who coughs respectfully behind his hand when the lawyer bids him fill his glass.

"Now, Snagsby," says Mr. Tulkinghorn, "to go over this odd story again."

"If you please, sir."

"You told me when you were so good as to step round here last night, Snagsby, that you came round without mentioning your intention to your wife. That was prudent, I think, because it's not a matter of such importance that it requires to be mentioned."

"Well, sir," returns Mr. Snagsby, "you see my little woman is—not to put too fine a point upon it—inquisitive. She's inquisitive. Poor little thing, she's liable to spasms, and it's good for her to have her mind employed. In consequence of which she employs it—I should say upon every individual thing she can lay hold of, whether it concerns her or not—especially not. My little woman has a very active mind, sir."

"Therefore you kept your visit to yourself last night?" says Mr. Tulkinghorn. "And tonight, too?"

"Yes, sir, and tonight, too. My little woman is at present in—not to put too fine a point on it—in a pious state, or in what she considers such, and attends the Evening Exertions (which is the name they go by) of a reverend party of the name of Chadband. My little woman being engaged in that way made it easier for me to step round in a quiet manner."

"Will you run over once again what the boy said?" asks Mr. Tulkinghorn, putting his hands into the pockets of his rusty small-clothes and leaning quietly back in his chair.

"With pleasure, sir."

Then, with fidelity, though with some prolixity, the law-stationer repeats Jo's statement made to the assembled guests at his house. On coming to the end of his narrative, he gives a great start, and breaks off with—"Dear me, sir, I wasn't aware there was any other gentleman present!"

Mr. Snagsby is dismayed to see, standing with an attentive face between himself and the lawyer, at a little distance from the table, a person with a hat and stick in his hand who was not there when he himself came in, and has not since entered by the door or by either of the windows. There is a press in the room, but its hinges have not creaked, nor has a step been audible upon the floor. Yet this third person stands there, with his attentive face, and his hat and stick in his hands, and his hands behind him, a composed and quiet listener. He is a stoutly built, steady-looking, sharp-eyed man in black, of about the middle age. Except that he looks at Mr. Snagsby as if he were going to take his portrait, there is nothing remarkable about him at first sight but his ghostly manner of appearing.

"Don't mind this gentleman," says Mr. Tulkinghorn, in his quiet way. "This is only Mr. Bucket."

"Oh indeed, sir?" returns the stationer, expressing by a cough that he is quite in the dark as to who Mr. Bucket may be.

"I wanted him to hear this story," says the lawyer, "because I have half a mind (for a reason) to know more of it, and he is very intelligent in such things. What do you say to this, Bucket?"

"It's very plain, sir. Since our people have moved this boy on, and he's not to be found on his old lay, if Mr. Snagsby don't object to go down with me to Tom-all-Alone's and point him out, we can have him here in less than a couple of hours' time. I can do it without Mr. Snagsby, of course, but this is the shortest way."

"Mr. Bucket is a detective officer, Snagsby," says the lawyer in explanation.

"Is he indeed, sir?" says Mr. Snagsby.

"And if you have no real objection to accompany Mr. Bucket to the place in question," pursues the lawyer, "I shall feel obliged to you if you will do so."

In a moment's hesitation on the part of Mr. Snagsby, Bucket dips down to the bottom of his mind.

"Don't you be afraid of hurting the boy," he says. "You won't do that. It's all right as far as the boy's concerned. We shall only bring him here to ask him a question or so I want to put to him, and he'll be paid for his trouble, and sent away again. It'll be a good job for him. I promise you, as a man, that you shall see the boy sent away all right. Don't you be afraid of hurting him; you an't going to do that."

"Very well, Mr. Tulkinghorn!" cries Mr. Snagsby cheerfully, and reassured, "since that's the case—"

"Yes! And lookee here, Mr. Snagsby," resumes Bucket, taking him aside by the arm, tapping him familiarly on the breast, and speaking in a confidential tone. "You're a man of the world, you know, and a man of business, and a man of sense. That's what *you* are."

"I am sure I am much obliged to you for your good opinion," returns the stationer, with his cough of modesty, "but—"

"That's what *you* are, you know," says Bucket. "Now it an't necessary to say to a man like you, engaged in your business—which is a business of trust and requires a person to be wide awake, and have his senses about him (I had an uncle in your business once)—it an't necessary to say to a man like you that it's the best and wisest way to keep little matters like this quiet. Don't you see? Quiet!"

"Certainly, certainly," returns the other.

"I don't mind telling *you*," says Bucket, with an engaging appearance of frankness, "that as far as I can understand it, there seems to be a doubt whether this dead person wasn't entitled to a little property, and whether this female hasn't been up to some games respecting that property, don't you see? Now, what *you* want," pursues Bucket, "is that every person should have their rights according to justice. That's what *you* want."

"To be sure," returns Mr. Snagsby with a nod.

"On account of which, and at the same time to oblige a—do you call it, in your business, customer or client? I forget how my uncle used to call it."

"Why, I generally say customer myself," replies Mr. Snagsby.

"You're right!" returns Mr. Bucket, shaking hands with him quite affectionately—"On account of which, and at the same time to oblige a real good customer, you mean to go down with me, in confidence, to Tom-all-Alone's, and to keep the whole thing quiet ever afterwards and never mention it to any one. That's about your intentions, if I understand you?"

"You are right, sir. You are right," says Mr. Snagsby.

"Then here's your hat," returns his new friend, quite as intimate with it as if he had made it, "and if you're ready, I am."

They leave Mr. Tulkinghorn, without a ruffle on the surface of his unfathomable depths, drinking his old wine, and go down into the streets.

As they walk along, Mr. Snagsby observes, as a novelty, that however quick their pace may be, his companion still seems in some undefinable manner to lurk and lounge; also, that whenever he is going to turn to the right or left, he pretends to have a fixed purpose in his mind of going straight ahead, and wheels off, sharply, at the very last moment. Now and then, when they pass a police-constable on his beat, Mr. Snagsby notices that both the constable and his guide fall into a deep abstraction as they come towards each other, and appear entirely to overlook each other, and to gaze into space.

When they come at last to Tom-all-Alone's, Mr. Bucket stops for a moment at the corner, and takes a lighted bull's-eye from the constable on duty there, who then accompanies him with his own particular bull's-eye at his waist. Between his two conductors, Mr. Snagsby passes along the middle of a villainous street, undrained, unventilated, deep in black mud and corrupt water—though the roads are dry elsewhere—and reeking with such smells and sights that he, who was lived in London all his life, can scarce believe his senses. Branching from this street and its heaps of ruins are other streets and courts so infamous that Mr. Snagsby sickens in body and mind, and feels as if he were going every moment deeper down into the infernal gulf.

"Draw off a bit here, Mr. Snagsby," says Bucket, as a kind of shabby palanquin is borne towards them, surrounded by a noisy crowd. "Here's the fever coming up the street! Are those the fever-houses, Darby?" Mr. Bucket coolly asks as he turns his bull's-eye on a line of stinking ruins.

Darby replies that "all them are," and further that in all, for months and months, the people "have been down by dozens," and have been carried out, dead and dying "like sheep with the rot." Bucket observing to Mr. Snagsby as they go on again that he looks a little poorly, Mr. Snagsby answers that he feels as if he couldn't breathe the dreadful air.

There is inquiry made, at various houses, for a boy named Jo. As few people are known in Tom-all-Alone's by any Christian sign, there is much reference to Mr. Snagsby whether he means Carrots, or the Colonel, or Gallows, or Young Chisel, or Terrier Tip, or Lanky, or the Brick. Mr. Snagsby describes over and over again. There are conflicting opinions respecting the original of his picture. The Colonel is produced, but it is not at all near the thing. Whenever Mr. Snagsby and his conductors are stationary, the crowd flows round, and from its squalid depths obsequious advice heaves up to Mr. Bucket.

At last there is a lair found out where Toughy, or the Tough Subject, lays him down at night, and it is thought that the Tough Subject may be Jo. Comparison of notes between Mr. Snagsby and the proprietress of the house leads to the establishment of this conclusion. Toughy has gone to the Doctor's to get a bottle of stuff for a sick woman, but will be here anon.

"And who have we got here tonight?" says Mr. Bucket, opening another door and glaring in with his bull's eye. "Two drunken men, eh? And two women? The men are sound enough"—turning back each sleeper's arm from his face to look at him. "Are these your good men, my dears?"

"Yes, sir," returns one of the women. "They are our husbands."

"Brickmakers, eh?"

"Yes, sir."

"What are you doing here? You don't belong to London."

"No, sir. We belong to Hertfordshire, Saint Albans."

"Come up on the tramp?"

"We walked up yesterday. There's no work down with us at present, but we have done no good by coming here, and shall do none, I expect."

"That's not the way to do much good," says Mr. Bucket, turning his head in the direction of the unconscious figures on the ground.

"It an't indeed," replies the woman with a sigh. "Jenny and me knows it full well."

The room, though two or three feet higher than the door, is so low that the head of the tallest of the visitors would touch the blackened ceiling if he stood upright. It is offensive to every sense; even the gross candle burns pale and sickly in the polluted air. There are a couple of benches, and a higher bench by way of table. The men lie asleep where they stumbled down, but the women sit by the candle. Lying in the arms of the woman who has spoken is a very young child.

"Why, what age do you call that little creature?" says Bucket. "It looks as if it was born yesterday." He is not at all rough about it, and as he turns his light gently on the infant, Mr. Snagsby is strangely reminded of another infant, encircled with light, that he has seen in pictures.

"He is not three weeks old yet, sir," says the woman.

"Is he your child?"

"Mine."

The other woman, who was bending over it when they came in, stoops down again and kisses it as it lies asleep.

"You seem as fond of it as if you were the mother yourself," says Mr. Bucket.

"I was the mother of one like it, master, and it died."

"Ah, Jenny, Jenny," says the other woman to her, "better so! Much better to think of dead than alive, Jenny! Much better!"

"Why, you an't such an unnatural woman, I hope," returns Bucket sternly, "as to wish your own child dead?"

"God knows you are right, master," she returns. "I am not. I'd stand between it and death with my own life, if I could."

"Then don't talk in that wrong manner," says Mr. Bucket, mollified again.

"There, there!" says Jenny. "Liz, you're tired and ill. Let me take him."

In doing so, she displaces the mother's dress, but quickly readjusts it over the wounded and bruised bosom where the baby has been lying.

As Mr. Snagsby blows his nose, and coughs his cough of sympathy, a step is heard without. Mr. Bucket throws his light into the doorway, and says to Mr. Snagsby:

"Now, what do you say to Toughy? Will *he* do?"

"That's Jo," says Mr. Snagsby.

Jo stands amazed in the disc of light, like a ragged figure in a magic lantern, trembling to think that he offended against the law in not having moved on far enough. Mr. Snagsby, however, giving him the consolatory assurance, "It's only a job you will be paid for, Jo," he recovers, and on being taken outside by Mr. Bucket for a little private confabulation, tells his tale satisfactorily, though out of breath.

"I have squared it with the lad," says Mr. Bucket, returning, "and it's all right. Now, Mr. Snagsby, we're ready for you."

First, Jo has to complete his errand of good nature by handing over the physic he has been to get, which he delivers with the laconic verbal direction that "it's to be all took d'rectly." Secondly, Mr. Snagsby has to lay upon the table half a crown, his usual panacea for an immense variety of afflictions. Thirdly, Mr. Bucket has to take Jo by the arm a little above the elbow and walk him on before him. These arrangements completed, they give the women good-night, and come out once more into black and foul Tom-all-Alone's.

By the noisome ways through which they descended into that pit, they gradually emerge from it, until they come to the verge, where restoration of the bull's-eyes is made to Darby. Through the clearer and fresher streets, never so clear and fresh to Mr. Snagsby's mind as now, they walk and ride until they come to Mr. Tulkinghorn's gate.

As they ascend the dim stairs (Mr. Tulkinghorn's chambers being on the first floor), Mr. Bucket mentions that he has the key of the outer door in his pocket, and that there is no need to ring. For a man so expert in most things of that kind, Bucket takes time to open the door, and makes some noise too. It may be that he sounds a note of preparation.

Howbeit, they come at last into the hall, where a lamp is burning, and so into Mr. Tulkinghorn's usual room—the room where he drank his old wine tonight. He is not there, but his two old-fashioned candlesticks are, and the room is tolerably light.

Mr. Bucket, still having his professional hold of Jo, makes a little way into this room, when Jo starts and stops.

"What's the matter?" says Bucket in a whisper.

"There she is!" cries Jo.

"Who!"

"The lady!"

A female figure, closely veiled, stands in the middle of the room, where the light falls upon it. It is quite still, and silent. The front of the figure is towards them, but it takes no notice of their entrance, and remains like a statue.

"Now tell me," says Bucket aloud, "how you know that to be the lady."

"I know the wale," replies Jo, staring, "and the bonnet, and the gownd."

"Be quite sure of what you say, Tough," returns Bucket, narrowly observant of him. "Look again."

"I am a-looking as hard as ever I can look," says Jo, with starting eyes, "and that there's the wale, the bonnet, and the gownd."

"What about those rings you told me of?" asks Bucket.

"A-sparkling all over here," says Jo, rubbing the fingers of his left hand on the knuckles of his right.

The figure removes the right-hand glove, and shows the hand.

"Now, what do you say to that?" asks Bucket.

Jo shakes his head. "Not rings a bit like them. Not a hand like that."

"What are you talking of?" says Bucket, evidently pleased though, and well pleased too.

"Hand was a deal whiter, a deal delicater, and a deal smaller," returns Jo.

"Why, you'll tell me I'm my own mother next," says Mr. Bucket. "Do you recollect the lady's voice?"

"I think I does," says Jo.

The figure speaks. "Was it at all like this? I will speak as long as you like if you are not sure. Was it this voice, or at all like this voice?"

Jo looks aghast at Mr. Bucket. "Not a bit!"

"Then what," retorts that worthy, pointing to the figure, "did you say it was the lady for?"

"Cos," says Jo, with a perplexed stare, but without being at all shaken in his certainty, "cos that there's the wale, the bonnet, and the gownd. It is her and it an't her. It an't her hand, nor yet her rings, nor yet her woice. But that there's the wale, the bonnet, and the gownd, and they're wore the same way wot she wore 'em, and it's her height wot she wos, and she giv me a sov'ring and hooked it."

"Well!" says Mr. Bucket, "we haven't got much good out of *you*. However, here's five shillings for you. Take care how you spend it, and don't get yourself into trouble." Bucket stealthily tells the coins from one hand into the other like counters and then puts them, in a little pile, into the boy's hand, and takes him out to the door, leaving Mr. Snagsby, not by any means comfortable under these mysterious circumstances, alone with the veiled figure. But on Mr. Tulkinghorn's coming into the room the veil is raised, and a sufficiently good-looking Frenchwoman is revealed.

"Thank you, Mademoiselle Hortense," says Mr. Tulkinghorn, with his usual equanimity. "I will give you no further trouble about this little wager."

"You will do me the kindness to remember, sir, that I am not at present placed?" said Mademoiselle.

"Certainly, certainly!"

"And to confer upon me the favour of your distinguished recommendation?"

"By all means, Mademoiselle Hortense."

Mademoiselle goes out with an air of native gentility; and Mr. Bucket, to whom it is, on an emergency, as natural to be groom of the ceremonies as it is to be anything else, shows her downstairs, not without gallantry.

"Well, Bucket?" quoth Mr. Tulkinghorn, on his return.

"It's all squared, you see, as I squared it myself, sir. There an't a doubt that it was the other one with this one's dress on. The boy was exact respecting colours and everything. Mr. Snagsby, I promised you as a man that he should be sent away all right. Don't say it wasn't done!"

"You have kept your word, sir," returns the stationer; "and if I can be of no further use, Mr. Tulkinghorn, I think, as my little woman will be getting anxious—"

"Thank you, Snagsby, no further use," says Mr. Tulkinghorn. "I am quite indebted to you for the trouble you have taken already."

"Not at all, sir. I wish you good-night."

"You see, Mr. Snagsby," says Mr. Bucket, accompanying him to the door, and shaking hands with him over and over again, "what I like in you is that you're a man it's of no use pumping; that's what *you* are. When you know you have done a right thing, you put it away, and it's done with and gone, and there's an end of it. That's what *you* do."

"That is certainly what I endeavour to do, sir," returns Mr. Snagsby.

"No, you don't do yourself justice. It an't what you endeavour to do," says Mr. Bucket, shaking hands with him, "it's what you *do*. That's what I estimate in a man in your way of business."

# CHAPTER 23

*Esther's Narrative*

WE came home from Mr. Boythorn's after six pleasant weeks. We were often in the park, and in the woods, and seldom passed the lodge where we had taken shelter without looking in to speak to the keeper's wife; but we saw no more of Lady Dedlock, except at church on Sundays. There was company at Chesney Wold; and although several beautiful faces surrounded her, her face retained the same influence on me as at first. I do not quite know, even now, whether it was painful or pleasurable; whether it drew me towards her, or made me shrink from her. I think I admired her with a kind of fear; and I know that in her presence my thoughts always wandered back, as they had done at first, to that old time of my life. I had a fancy, on more than one of these Sundays, that what this lady so curiously was to me, I was to her—I mean that I disturbed her thoughts as she influenced mine, though in some different way. But when I stole a glance at her, and saw her so composed and distant and unapproachable, I felt this to be a foolish weakness.

One incident that occurred before we quitted Mr. Boythorn's house I had better mention in this place. I was walking in the garden with Ada when I was told that some one wished to see me. Going into the breakfast-room I found it to be the French maid who had cast off her shoes and walked through the wet grass, on the day when it thundered and lightened.

"Mademoiselle," she began, looking fixedly at me with her too-eager eyes, though otherwise presenting an agreeable appearance, and speaking neither with boldness nor servility, "I have taken a great liberty in coming here, but you know how to excuse it, being so amiable, mademoiselle."

"No excuse is necessary," I returned, "if you wish to speak to me."

"That is my desire, mademoiselle. A thousand thanks for the permission. I have your leave to speak. Is it not?" she said, in a quick, natural way.

"Certainly," said I.

"Mademoiselle, you are so amiable! Listen then, if you please. I have left my lady. We could not agree. My lady is so high; so very high. Pardon! Mademoiselle, you are right!" Her quickness anticipated what I might have said presently, but as yet had only thought. "It is not for me to come here to complain of my lady. But I say she is so high, so very high. I will not say a word more. All the world knows that."

"Go on, if you please," said I.

"Assuredly, mademoiselle, I am thankful for your politeness. Mademoiselle, I have an inexpressible desire to find service with a young lady who is good, accomplished, beautiful. You are good, accomplished, and beautiful as an angel. Ah, could I have the honour of being your domestic!"

"I am sorry—" I began.

"Do not dismiss me so soon, mademoiselle!" she said, with an involuntary contraction of her fine black eyebrows. "Let me hope a moment! Mademoiselle, I know this service would be more retired than that which I have quitted. Well, I wish that. I know this service would be less distinguished than that which I have quitted. Well, I wish that. I know that I should win less as to wages here. Good. I am content."

"I assure you," said I, quite embarrassed by the mere idea of having such an attendant, "that I keep no maid—"

"Ah, mademoiselle, but why not? Why not, when you can have one so devoted to you! Who would be enchanted to serve you; who would be so true, so zealous, and so faithful, every day! Mademoiselle, I wish with all my heart to serve you. Do not speak of money at present. Take me as I am. For nothing!"

She was so singularly earnest that I drew back, almost afraid of her. Without appearing to notice it, in her ardour she still pressed herself upon me, speaking in a rapid subdued voice, though always with a certain grace and propriety.

"Mademoiselle, I come from the South country, where we are quick, and where we like and dislike very strong. My lady was too high for me; I was too high for her. It is done—past—finished! Receive me as your domestic and I will serve you well. I will do more for you than you figure to yourself now. Chut! mademoiselle, I will—no matter, I will do my utmost possible, in all things. If you accept my service, you will not repent it, and I will serve you well. You don't know how well!"

There was a lowering energy in her face as she stood looking at me while I explained the impossibility of my engaging her which seemed to bring visibly before me some woman from the streets of Paris in the Reign of Terror. She heard me out without interruption, and then said, with her pretty accent, and in her mildest voice:

"Hey, mademoiselle, I have received my answer! I am sorry of it. But I must go elsewhere, and seek what I have not found here. Will you graciously let me kiss your hand?" She looked at me more intently as she took it, and seemed to take note, with her momentary touch, of every vein in it. "I fear I surprised you, mademoiselle, on the day of the storm?" she said with a parting curtsey. I confessed she had surprised us all. "I took an oath, mademoiselle," she said, smiling, "and I wanted to stamp it on my mind, so that I might keep it faithfully. And I will! Adieu, mademoiselle!"

So ended our conference, which I was very glad to bring to a close. I supposed she went away from the village, for I saw her no more; and nothing else occurred to disturb our tranquil summer pleasures until six weeks were out, and we returned home as I began just now by saying.

At that time, and for a good many weeks after that time, Richard was constant in his visits. Besides coming every Saturday or Sunday, and remaining with us until Monday morning, he sometimes rode out on horseback unexpectedly, and passed the evening with us, and rode back again early next day. He was as vivacious as ever, and told us he was very industrious; but I was not easy in my mind about him. It appeared to me that his industry was all misdirected. I could not find that it led to anything but the formation of delusive hopes in con- nexion with the suit already the pernicious cause of so much sorrow and ruin. He had got at the core of that mystery now, he told us; and noth- ing could be plainer than that the will under which he and Ada were to take I don't know how many thousands of pounds must be finally established, if there were any sense or justice in the Court of Chancery —but oh what a great *if* that sounded in my ears—and that this happy conclusion could not be much longer delayed. He proved this to him- self by all the weary arguments on that side he had read, and every one of them sank him deeper in the infatuation. He had even begun to haunt the Court. He told us how he saw Miss Flite there daily; how they talked together, and how he did her little kindnesses; and how, while he laughed at her, he pitied her from his heart. But he never thought—never, my poor, dear, sanguine Richard—what a fatal link was riveting between his fresh youth and her faded age, between his free hopes and her caged birds, and her hungry garret, and her wandering mind.

Ada loved him too well to mistrust him much in anything he said or did, and my guardian, though he frequently complained of the east wind and read more than usual in the Growlery, preserved a strict silence on the subject. So I thought, one day when I went to London to meet Caddy Jellyby, at her solicitation, I would ask Richard to be in waiting for me at the coach-office, that we might have a little talk together. I found him there when I arrived, and we walked away arm-in-arm.

"Well, Richard," said I, as soon as I could begin to be grave with him, "are you beginning to feel more settled now?"

"Oh yes, my dear!" returned Richard. "I'm all right enough."

"But settled?" said I.

"How do you mean, settled?" returned Richard, with his gay laugh.

"Settled in the law," said I.

"Oh ay," replied Richard, "I'm all right enough."

"You said that before, my dear Richard."

"And you don't think it's an answer, eh? Well! Perhaps it's not. Settled? You mean, do I feel as if I were settling down?"

"Yes."

"Why, no, I can't say I am settling down," said Richard, strongly emphasizing "down," as if that expressed the difficulty, "because one can't settle down while this business remains in such an unsettled state. When I say this business, of course I mean the—forbidden subject."

"Do you think it will ever be in a settled state?" said I.

"Not the least doubt of it," answered Richard.

We walked a little way without speaking; and presently Richard addressed me in his frankest and most feeling manner, thus:

"My dear Esther, I understand you, and I wish to Heaven I were a more constant sort of fellow. I don't mean constant to Ada, for I love her dearly—better and better every day—but constant to myself. If I were a more constant sort of fellow, I should have held on, either to Badger, or to Kenge and Carboy, like grim Death, and should have begun to be steady and systematic by this time, and shouldn't be in debt, and—"

"*Are* you in debt, Richard?"

"Yes," said Richard, "I am a little so, my dear. Also, I have taken rather too much to billiards, and that sort of thing. Now the murder's out; you despise me, Esther, don't you?"

"You know I don't," said I.

"You are kinder to me than I often am to myself," he returned. "My dear Esther, I am a very unfortunate dog not to be more settled, but how *can* I be more settled? If you lived in an unfinished house, you couldn't settle down in it; if you were condemned to leave everything you undertook unfinished, you would find it hard to apply yourself to anything; and yet that's my unhappy case. I was born into this unfinished contention with all its chances and changes, and it began to unsettle me before I knew the difference between a suit at law and a suit of clothes; and it has gone on unsettling me ever since; and here I am now, conscious sometimes that I am but a worthless fellow to love my confiding cousin Ada."

We were in a solitary place, and he put his hands before his eyes and sobbed as he said the words.

"O Richard!" said I, "do not be so moved. You have a noble nature, and Ada's love may make you worthier every day."

"I know, my dear," he replied, pressing my arm, "I know all that. You mustn't mind my being a little soft now, for I have had all this upon my mind for a long time; and have often meant to speak to you, and have sometimes wanted opportunity and sometimes courage. I know what the thought of Ada ought to do for me, but it doesn't do it. I am too unsettled even for that. I love her most devotedly, and yet I do her wrong, in doing myself wrong, every day and hour. But it can't last for ever. We shall come on for a final hearing, and get judgment in our favour, and then you and Ada shall see what I can really be!"

It had given me a pang to hear him sob, and see the tears start out between his fingers; but that was infinitely less affecting to me than the hopeful animation with which he said these words.

"I have looked well into the papers, Esther—I have been deep in them for months"—he continued, recovering his cheerfulness in a moment, "and you may rely upon it that we shall come out triumphant. As to years of delay, there has been no want of them, Heaven knows! and there is the greater probability of our bringing the matter to a speedy close; in fact, it's on the paper now. It will be all right at last, and then you shall see!"

Recalling how he had just now placed Messrs. Kenge and Carboy in the same category with Mr. Badger, I asked him when he intended to be articled in Lincoln's Inn.

"There again! I think not at all, Esther," he returned with an effort. "I fancy I have had enough of it. Having worked at Jarndyce and Jarndyce like a galley-slave, I have slaked my thirst for the law, and satisfied myself that I shouldn't like it. Besides, I find it unsettles me more and more to be so constantly upon the scene of action. So what," continued Richard, confident again by this time, "do I naturally turn my thoughts to?"

"I can't imagine," said I.

"Don't look so serious," returned Richard, "because it's the best thing I can do, my dear Esther, I am certain. It's not as if I wanted a profession for life. These proceedings will come to a termination, and then I am provided for. No. I look upon it as a pursuit which is in its nature more or less unsettled, and therefore suited to my temporary condition—I may say, precisely suited. What is it that I naturally turn my thoughts to?"

I looked at him, and shook my head.

"What," said Richard, in a tone of perfect conviction, "but the Army!"

"The Army?" said I.

"The Army, of course. What I have to do, is, to get a commission, and —there I am, you know!" said Richard.

And then he showed me, proved by elaborate calculations in his pocket-book, that supposing he had contracted, say two hundred pounds of debt in six months, out of the Army; and that he contracted no debt at all within a corresponding period in the Army—as to which he had quite made up his mind—this step must involve a saving of four hundred pounds in a year, or two thousand pounds in five years—which was a considerable sum. And then he spoke so ingenuously and sincerely of the sacrifice he made in withdrawing himself for a time from Ada, and of the earnestness with which he aspired to repay her love, and to ensure her happiness, and to conquer what was amiss in himself, and to acquire the very soul of decision, that he made my heart ache keenly, sorely. For I thought how would this end, how could this end, when so soon and so surely all his manly qualities were touched by the fatal blight that ruined everything it rested on!

I spoke to Richard with all the earnestness I felt, and all the hope I could not quite feel then, and implored him, for Ada's sake, not to put any trust in Chancery. To all I said, Richard readily assented, riding over the Court and everything else in his easy way, and drawing the brightest pictures of the character he was to settle into—alas, when the grievous suit should loose its hold upon him! We had a long talk, but it always came back to that, in substance. At last we came to Soho Square, where Caddy Jellyby had appointed to wait for me, as a quiet place in the neighbourhood of Newman Street. Caddy was in the garden in the centre, and hurried out as soon as I appeared. After a few cheerful words, Richard left us together.

"Prince has a pupil over the way, Esther," said Caddy, "and got the key for us. So if you will walk round and round here with me, we can lock ourselves in, and I can tell you comfortably what I wanted to see your dear good face about."

"Very well, my dear," said I. "Nothing could be better." So Caddy locked the gate, and took my arm, and we began to walk round the garden very cosily.

"You see, Esther," said Caddy, who thoroughly enjoyed a little confidence, "after you spoke to me about its being wrong to marry without Ma's knowledge, or even to keep Ma long in the dark respecting our engagement—though I don't believe Ma cares much for me, I must say—I thought it right to mention your opinions to Prince. In the first place, because I want to profit by everything you tell me, and in the second place, because I have no secrets from Prince."

"I hope he approved, Caddy?"

"Oh, my dear! I assure you he would approve of anything you could say. You have no idea what an opinion he has of you!"

"Indeed!"

"Esther, it's enough to make anybody but me jealous," said Caddy, laughing and shaking her head; "but it only makes me joyful, for you are the first friend I ever had, and the best friend I ever can have, and nobody can respect and love you too much to please me."

"Upon my word, Caddy," said I, "you are in the general conspiracy to keep me in a good humour. Well, my dear?"

"Well! I am going to tell you," replied Caddy, crossing her hands confidentially upon my arm. "So we talked a good deal about it, and so I said to Prince, 'Prince, as Miss Summerson—' "

"I hope you didn't say 'Miss Summerson'?"

"No. I didn't!" cried Caddy, greatly pleased. "I said, 'Esther.' I said to Prince, 'As Esther is decidedly of that opinion, Prince, and has expressed it to me, and always hints it when she writes those kind notes, which you are so fond of hearing me read to you, I am prepared to disclose the truth to Ma whenever you think proper. And I think, Prince,' said I, 'that Esther thinks that I should be in a better, and truer, and more honourable position altogether, if you did the same to your papa.' "

"Yes, my dear," said I, "Esther certainly does think so."

"So I was right, you see!" exclaimed Caddy. "Well! this troubled Prince a good deal—not because he had the least doubt about it, but because he is so considerate of the feelings of old Mr. Turveydrop, and he had his apprehensions that old Mr. Turveydrop might break his heart, or faint away, if he made such an announcement. He feared old Mr. Turveydrop might consider it undutiful, and might receive too great a shock. For old Mr. Turveydrop's Deportment is very beautiful you know, Esther," said Caddy, "and his feelings are extremely sensitive."

"Are they, my dear?"

"Oh, extremely sensitive. Prince says so. Now this has caused my darling child—I didn't mean to use the expression to you, Esther," Caddy apologized, her face suffused with blushes, "but I generally call Prince my darling child."

I laughed, and Caddy laughed and blushed, and went on.

"This has caused him, Esther—"

"Caused whom, my dear?"

"Oh you tiresome thing!" said Caddy, laughing, with her pretty face on fire. "My darling child, if you insist upon it!—This has caused him weeks of uneasiness, and has made him delay, from day to day, in a very anxious manner. At last he said to me, 'Caddy, if Miss Summerson, who is a great favourite with my father, could be prevailed upon to be present when I broke the subject, I think I could do it.' So I promised I would ask you. And I made up my mind, besides," said Caddy, looking at me hopefully, but timidly, "that if you consented, I would ask you afterwards to come with me to Ma. This is what I meant when I said in my note that I had a great favour and a great assistance to beg of you. And if you thought you could grant it, Esther, we should both be very grateful."

"Let me see, Caddy," said I, pretending to consider. "Really I think I could do a greater thing than that, if the need were pressing. I am at your service and the darling child's, my dear, whenever you like."

Caddy was quite transported by this reply of mine, being, I believe, as susceptible to the least kindness or encouragement as any tender heart that ever beat in this world; and after another turn or two round the garden, during which she put on an entirely new pair of gloves, and made herself as resplendent as possible that she might do no avoidable discredit to the Master of Deportment, we went to Newman Street direct.

Prince was teaching, of course. We found him engaged with a not very hopeful pupil. The lesson at last came to an end, and when the little girl had changed her shoes, and had had her white muslin extinguished in shawls, she was taken away. After a few words of preparation, we then went in search of Mr. Turveydrop, whom we found, grouped with his hat and gloves as a Model of Deportment, on the sofa in his private apartment—the only comfortable room in the house.

"Father, Miss Summerson; Miss Jellyby."

"Charmed! Enchanted!" said Mr. Turveydrop, rising with his high-shouldered bow. "Permit me!" handing chairs. "Be seated!" kissing the tips of his left fingers. "Overjoyed!" shutting his eyes and rolling. "My little retreat is made a Paradise." Recomposing himself on the sofa, like the second gentleman in Europe.

"Again you find us, Miss Summerson," said he, "using our little arts to polish, polish! Again the sex stimulates us, and rewards us, by the condescension of its lovely presence. It is much in these times to experience that Deportment is not wholly trodden under foot by mechanics."

I said nothing, which I thought a suitable reply, and he took a pinch of snuff.

"My dear son," said Mr. Turveydrop, "you have four schools this afternoon. I would recommend a hasty sandwich."

"Thank you, Father," returned Prince. "I will be sure to be punctual. My dear father, may I beg you to prepare your mind for what I am going to say!"

"Good heaven!" exclaimed the Model, pale and aghast, as Prince and Caddy, hand in hand, bent down before him. "What is this? Is this lunacy! Or what is this?"

"Father," returned Prince, with great submission, "I love this young lady, and we are engaged."

"Engaged!" cried Mr. Turveydrop, reclining on the sofa and shutting out the sight with his hand. "An arrow launched at my brain, by my own child!"

"We have been engaged for some time, Father," faltered Prince, "and Miss Summerson, hearing of it, advised that we should declare the fact to you, and was so very kind as to attend on the present occasion. Miss Jellyby is a young lady who deeply respects you, Father." Mr. Turveydrop uttered a groan. "No, pray don't! Pray don't, Father," urged his son. "Miss Jellyby is a young lady who deeply respects you, and our first desire is to consider your comfort." Mr. Turveydrop sobbed. "No, pray don't, Father!" cried his son.

"Boy," said Mr. Turveydrop, "it is well that your sainted mother is spared this pang. Strike home, sir, strike home!"

"Pray don't say so, Father," implored Prince, in tears. "It goes to my heart. I do assure you, Father, that our first wish and intention is to consider your comfort. Caroline and I do not forget our duty—what is my duty is Caroline's, as we have often said together—and, with your approval and consent, Father, we will devote ourselves to making your life agreeable."

"Strike home," murmured Mr. Turveydrop. "Strike home!"

But he seemed to listen, I thought, too.

"My dear father," returned Prince, "we well know what little comforts you are accustomed to, and have a right to; and it will always be our study, and our pride, to provide those before anything. If you will bless us with your approval and consent, Father, we shall not think of being married until it is quite agreeable to you; and when we *are* married, we shall always make you—of course—our first consideration. You must ever be the Head and Master here, Father; and we feel how truly unnatural it would be in us if we failed to know it, or if we failed to exert ourselves in every possible way to please you."

Mr. Turveydrop underwent a severe internal struggle, and came upright on the sofa again, a perfect Model of Parental Deportment.

"My son!" said Mr. Turveydrop. "My children! I cannot resist your prayer. Be happy!"

His benignity as he raised his future daughter-in-law and stretched out his hand to his son (who kissed it with affectionate respect and gratitude) was the most confusing sight I ever saw.

"My children," said Mr. Turveydrop, paternally encircling Caddy with his left arm as she sat beside him, and putting his right hand gracefully on his hip. "My son and daughter, your happiness shall be my care. I will watch over you. You shall always live with me"—meaning, of course, I will always live with you—"this house is henceforth as much yours as mine; consider it your home. May you long live to share it with me!"

The power of his Deportment was such that they really were as much overcome with thankfulness as if, instead of quartering himself upon them for the rest of his life, he were making some munificent sacrifice in their favour.

"For myself, my children," said Mr. Turveydrop, "I am falling into the sear and yellow leaf, and it is impossible to say how long the last feeble traces of gentlemanly Deportment may linger in this weaving and spinning age. But so long, I will do my duty to society, and will show myself, as usual, about town. My wants are few and simple. My little apartment here, my few essentials for the toilet, my frugal morning meal, and my little dinner will suffice. I charge your dutiful affection with the supply of these requirements, and I charge myself with all the rest."

They were overpowered afresh by his uncommon generosity.

"My son," said Mr. Turveydrop, "for those little points in which you are deficient—points of Deportment which are born with a man—you may still rely on me. I have been faithful to my post since the days of His Royal Highness the Prince Regent, and I will not desert it now. For yourself, Prince, whose character is different, work, be industrious, earn money, and extend the connexion as much as possible."

"That you may depend I will do, dear Father, with all my heart," replied Prince.

"I have no doubt of it," said Mr. Turveydrop. "Your qualities are not shining, my dear child, but they are steady and useful. And to both of you, my children, I would merely observe, in the spirit of a sainted Wooman on whose path I had the happiness of casting, I believe, *some* ray of light—take care of the establishment, take care of my simple wants, and bless you both!"

Old Mr. Turveydrop then became so very gallant, in honour of the occasion, that I told Caddy we must really go to Thavies Inn at once if we were to go at all that day. So we took our departure, after a very loving farewell between Caddy and her betrothed; and during our walk she was so happy, and so full of old Mr. Turveydrop's praises, that I would not have said a word in his disparagement for any consideration.

The house in Thavies Inn had bills in the windows announcing that it was to let, and it looked dirtier and gloomier and ghastlier than ever. The name of poor Mr. Jellyby had appeared in the list of Bankrupts but a day or two before; he was shut up in the dining-room with two gentlemen, and a heap of blue bags, account-books, and papers, making the most desperate endeavours to understand his affairs. They appeared to me to be quite beyond his comprehension; for when Caddy took me into the dining-room by mistake, and we came upon Mr. Jellyby in his spectacles, forlornly fenced into a corner by the great dining-table and the two gentlemen, he seemed to have given up the whole thing, and to be speechless and insensible.

Going upstairs to Mrs. Jellyby's room, we found that lady in the midst of a voluminous correspondence, opening, reading, and sorting letters, with a great accumulation of torn covers on the floor. She was so preoccupied that at first she did not know me, though she sat looking at me with that curious bright-eyed, far-off look of hers.

"Ah! Miss Summerson!" she said at last. "I was thinking of something so different! I hope you are well. I am happy to see you. Mr. Jarndyce and Miss Clare quite well?"

I hoped in return that Mr. Jellyby was quite well.

"Why, not quite, my dear," said Mrs. Jellyby, in the calmest manner. "He has been unfortunate in his affairs, and is a little out of spirits. Happily for me, I am so much engaged that I have no time to think about it. We have, at the present moment, one hundred and seventy families, Miss Summerson, averaging five persons in each, either gone or going to the left bank of the Niger."

I thought of the one family so near us who were neither gone or going to the left bank of the Niger, and wondered how she could be so placid.

"You have brought Caddy back, I see," observed Mrs. Jellyby, with a glance at her daughter. "It has become quite a novelty to see her here. She has almost deserted her old employment, and in fact obliges me to employ a boy."

"I am sure, Ma—" began Caddy.

"Now you know, Caddy," her mother mildly interposed, "that I *do* employ a boy. What is the use of contradicting?"

"I was not going to contradict, Ma," returned Caddy. "I was only going to say that surely you wouldn't have me be a mere drudge all my life."

"I believe, my dear," said Mrs. Jellyby, still opening her letters, casting her bright eyes smilingly over them, and sorting them as she spoke, "that you have a business example before you in your mother. Besides. A mere drudge? If you had any sympathy with the destinies of the human race, it would raise you high above any such idea. But you have none. I have often told you, Caddy, you have no such sympathy."

"Not if it's Africa, Ma, I have not."

"Of course you have not. Now if I were not happily so much engaged, Miss Summerson," said Mrs. Jellyby, sweetly casting her eyes for a moment on me, "this would distress and disappoint me. But I have so much to think of in connexion with Borrioboola-Gha that there is my remedy, you see."

As Caddy gave me a glance of entreaty, and as Mrs. Jellyby was looking far away into Africa straight through my bonnet and head, I thought it a good opportunity to come to the subject of my visit, and to attract Mrs. Jellyby's attention.

"Perhaps," I began, "you will wonder what has brought me here to interrupt you."

"I am always delighted to see Miss Summerson," said Mrs. Jellyby, pursuing her employment with a placid smile. "Though I wish she was more interested in the Borrioboolan project."

"I have come with Caddy," said I, "because Caddy justly thinks she ought not to have a secret from her mother, and fancies I shall encour-

age and aid her (though I am sure I don't know how), in imparting one."

"Caddy," said Mrs. Jellyby, pausing for a moment in her occupation, and then serenely pursuing it after shaking her head, "you are going to tell me some nonsense."

Caddy untied the strings of her bonnet, took her bonnet off, and crying heartily, said, "Ma, I am engaged."

"Oh, you ridiculous child!" observed Mrs. Jellyby, with an abstracted air, as she looked over the dispatch last opened; "what a goose you are!"

"I am engaged, Ma," sobbed Caddy, "to young Mr. Turveydrop, and old Mr. Turveydrop has given his consent, and I beg and pray you'll give us yours, Ma, because I never could be happy without it. I never,

never could!" sobbed Caddy, quite forgetful of everything but her natural affection.

"You see again, Miss Summerson," observed Mrs. Jellyby, serenely, "what a happiness it is to be so much occupied as I am, and to have this necessity for self-concentration that I have. Here is Caddy engaged to a dancing-master's son—mixed up with people who have no more sympathy with the destinies of the human race than she has herself! This, too, when Mr. Quale, one of the first philanthropists of our time, has mentioned to me that he was really disposed to be interested in her!"

"Ma, I always hated and detested Mr. Quale!" sobbed Caddy.

"Caddy, Caddy," returned Mrs. Jellyby, opening another letter with the greatest complacency. "I have no doubt you did! How could you do otherwise, being totally destitute of the sympathies with which he overflows! Now if my public duties were not a favourite child to me, if I were not occupied with large measures on a vast scale, these petty details might grieve me very much, Miss Summerson. But can I permit the film of a silly proceeding on the part of Caddy (from whom I expect nothing else) to interpose between me and the great African continent? No. No," repeated Mrs. Jellyby, in a calm clear voice, and with an agreeable smile, as she opened more letters and sorted them. "No indeed."

I was so unprepared for the perfect coolness of this reception, though I might have expected it, that I did not know what to say. Caddy seemed equally at a loss. Mrs. Jellyby continued to open and sort letters, and to repeat occasionally, in quite a charming tone of voice and with a smile of perfect composure, "No indeed."

"I hope, Ma," sobbed poor Caddy at last, "you are not angry?"

"Oh Caddy, you really are an absurd girl," returned Mrs. Jellyby, "to ask such questions after what I have said of the preoccupation of my mind."

"And I hope, Ma, you give us your consent, and wish us well?" said Caddy.

"You are a nonsensical child to have done anything of this kind," said Mrs. Jellyby, "and a degenerate child, when you might have devoted yourself to the great public measure. But the step is taken, and I have engaged a boy, and there is no more to be said. Now pray, Caddy," said Mrs. Jellyby—for Caddy was kissing her—"don't delay me in my work, but let me clear off this heavy batch of papers before the afternoon post comes in!"

I thought I could not do better than take my leave. I was detained for a moment by Caddy's saying:

"You won't object to my bringing him to see you, Ma?"

"Oh dear me, Caddy," cried Mrs. Jellyby, who had relapsed into that distant contemplation, "have you begun again? Bring whom?"

"Him, Ma."

"Caddy, Caddy!" said Mrs. Jellyby, quite weary of such little matters. "Then you must bring him some evening which is not a Parent Society night, or a Branch night, or a Ramification night. You must accommodate the visit to the demands upon my time. My dear Miss Summerson, it was very kind of you to come here to help out this silly chit. Goodbye! When I tell you that I have fifty-eight new letters from manufacturing families anxious to understand the details of the Native and Coffee Cultivation question, this morning, I need not apologize for having very little leisure."

I was not surprised by Caddy's being in low spirits when we went downstairs, or by her sobbing afresh on my neck, or by her saying she would far rather have been scolded than treated with such indifference, or by her confiding to me that she was so poor in clothes that how she was ever to be married creditably she didn't know. I gradually cheered her up, by dwelling on the many things she would do for her unfortunate father, and for Peepy, when she had a home of her own; and finally we went downstairs into the damp dark kitchen, where Peepy and his little brothers and sisters were grovelling on the stone floor, and where we had such a game of play with them that to prevent myself from being quite torn to pieces I was obliged to fall back on my fairy-tales.

As I rode quietly home at night after the day's bustle, I thought a good deal of Caddy's engagement, and felt confirmed in my hopes (in spite of the elder Mr. Turveydrop) that she would be the happier and better for it. And if there seemed to be but a slender chance of her and her husband ever finding out what the Model of Deportment really was, why, that was all for the best too, and who would wish them to be wiser? I did not wish them to be any wiser, and indeed was half ashamed of not entirely believing in him myself.

They were so glad to see me when I got home, as they always were, that I could have sat down and cried for joy, if that had not been a method of making myself disagreeable. Everybody in the house, from the lowest to the highest, showed me such a bright face of welcome, and spoke so cheerily, and was so happy to do anything for me, that I suppose there never was such a fortunate little creature in the world. We got into such a chatty state that night, through Ada and my guardian drawing me out to tell them all about Caddy, that I went on prose, prose, prosing, for a length of time. At last I got up to my own room, and then I heard a soft tap at my door. So I said, "Come in!" and there came in a pretty little girl, neatly dressed in mourning, who dropped a curtsey.

"If you please, miss," said the little girl in a soft voice, "I am Charley."

"Why, so you are," said I, stooping down in astonishment, and giving her a kiss. "How glad am I to see you, Charley!"

"If you please, miss," pursued Charley, "I'm your maid. I'm a present to you, with Mr. Jarndyce's love."

I sat down with my hand on Charley's neck, and looked at Charley.

"And oh, miss," says Charley, clapping her hands, with the tears starting down her dimpled cheeks, "Tom's at school, if you please, and learning so good! And little Emma, she's with Mrs. Blinder, miss, a-being took such care of! And Tom, he would have been at school—and Emma, she would have been left with Mrs. Blinder—and me, I should have been here—all a deal sooner, miss, only Mr. Jarndyce thought that Tom and Emma and me had better get a little used to parting first, we was so small. Don't cry, if you please, miss!"

"I can't help it, Charley."

"No, miss, nor I can't help it," says Charley. "And if you please, miss, Mr. Jarndyce's love, and he thinks you'll like to teach me now and then. And if you please, Tom and Emma and me is to see each other once a month. And I'm so happy and so thankful, miss," cried Charley, "and I'll try to be such a good maid!"

"O Charley dear, never forget who did all this!"

"No, miss, I never will. Nor Tom won't. Nor yet Emma. It was all you, miss."

"I have known nothing of it. It was Mr. Jarndyce, Charley."

"Yes, miss, but it was all done for the love of you, and that you might be my mistress. If you please, miss, I am a little present with his love, and it was all done for the love of you. Me and Tom was to be sure to remember it."

Charley dried her eyes, and entered on her functions: going in her matronly little way about and about the room, and folding up everything she could lay her hands upon. Presently, Charley came creeping back to my side, and said:

"Oh, don't cry, if you please, miss."

And I said again, "I can't help it, Charley."

And Charley said again, "No, miss, nor I can't help it." And so, after all, I did cry for joy indeed, and so did she.

# CHAPTER 24

~~~~~~~~~~~~~~~~~~~~~~~~~~~~~~~~~~~~~

*An Appeal Case*

As soon as Richard and I had held the conversation of which I have given an account, Richard communicated the state of his mind to Mr. Jarndyce. I doubt if my guardian were altogether taken by surprise when he received the representation, though it caused him much uneasiness and disappointment. He and Richard were often closeted together, late at night and early in the morning, and passed whole days in London, and had innumerable appointments with Mr. Kenge, and laboured through a quantity of disagreeable business. While they were thus employed, my guardian, though he underwent considerable inconvenience from the state of the wind, was as genial with Ada and me as at any other time, but maintained a steady reserve on these matters. And as our utmost endeavours could only elicit from Richard himself sweeping assurances that everything was going on capitally, and that it really was all right at last, our anxiety was not much relieved by him.

We learnt, however, as time went on, that a new application was made to the Lord Chancellor on Richard's behalf, as an Infant and a Ward, and I don't know what; and that there was a quantity of talking; and that the Lord Chancellor described him, in open court, as a vexatious and capricious infant; and that the matter was adjourned and re-adjourned, and referred, and reported on, and petitioned about, until Richard began to doubt (as he told us) whether, if he entered the Army at all, it would not be as a veteran of seventy or eighty years of age. At last an appointment was made for him to see the Lord Chancellor again in his private room, and there the Lord Chancellor very seriously reproved him for trifling with time, and not knowing his mind, and at last it was settled that his application should be granted. His name was entered at the Horse Guards, as an applicant for an ensign's commission; the purchase-money was deposited at an agent's; and Richard, in his usual characteristic way, plunged into a violent course of military study, and got up at five o'clock every morning to practise the broadsword exercise.

Thus vacation succeeded term, and term succeeded vacation. We sometimes heard of Jarndyce and Jarndyce, as being in the paper or out of the paper, or as being to be mentioned; and it came on, and it went off. Richard, who was now in a Professor's house in London, was able to be with us less frequently than before; my guardian still maintained the same reserve; and so time passed until the commission was obtained, and Richard received directions with it to join a regiment in Ireland.

He arrived post-haste with the intelligence one evening, and had a long conference with my guardian. Upwards of an hour elapsed before my guardian put his head into the room where Ada and I were sitting and said, "Come in, my dears!" We went in, and found Richard, whom we had last seen in high spirits, leaning on the chimney-piece, looking mortified and angry.

"Rick and I, Ada," said Mr. Jarndyce, "are not quite of one mind. Come, come, Rick, put a brighter face upon it!"

"You are very hard with me, sir," said Richard. "The harder, because you have been so considerate to me in all other respects, and have done me kindnesses that I can never acknowledge. I never could have been set right without you, sir."

"Well, well," said Mr. Jarndyce, "I want to set you more right yet. I want to set you more right with yourself."

"I hope you will excuse my saying, sir," returned Richard in a fiery way but yet respectfully, "that I think I am the best judge about myself."

"I hope you will excuse my saying, my dear Rick," observed Mr. Jarndyce with the sweetest cheerfulness and good humour, "that it's quite natural in you to think so, but I don't think so. I must do my duty, Rick, or you could never care for me in cool blood, and I hope you will always care for me, cool and hot."

Ada had turned so pale that he made her sit down in his reading-chair, and sat beside her.

"It's nothing, my dear," he said, "it's nothing. Rick and I have only had a friendly difference, which we must state to you, for you are the theme. Now you are afraid of what's coming."

"I am not indeed, Cousin John," replied Ada, with a smile, "if it is to come from you."

"Thank you, my dear. Do you give me a minute's calm attention, without looking at Rick. And, little woman, do you likewise. My dear girl," putting his hand on hers as it lay on the side of the easy-chair, "you recollect the talk we had, we four, when the little woman told me of a little love-affair?"

"It is not likely that either Richard or I can ever forget your kindness, that day, Cousin John."

"So much the easier what I have to say, and so much the easier for us to agree," returned my guardian, his face irradiated by the gentleness and honour of his heart. "Ada, my bird, you should know that Rick has now chosen his profession for the last time. All that he has of certainty will be expended when he is fully equipped. He has exhausted his resources, and is bound henceforward to the tree he has planted."

"Quite true that I have exhausted my present resources, and I am quite content to know it. But what I have of certainty, sir," said Richard, "is not all I have."

"Rick, Rick!" cried my guardian, with a sudden terror in his manner, and in an altered voice, "for the love of God, don't found a hope or expectation on the family curse! Whatever you do on this side the grave, never give one lingering glance towards the horrible phantom that has haunted us so many years. Better to borrow, better to beg, better to die!"

We were all startled by the fervour of this warning. Richard bit his lip and held his breath, and glanced at me as if he felt, and knew that I felt too, how much he needed it.

"Ada, my dear," said Mr. Jarndyce, recovering his cheerfulness, "these are strong words of advice; but I live in Bleak House, and have seen a sight here. Enough of that. All Richard had, to start him in the race of life, is ventured. I recommend to him and you, for his sake and your own, that he should depart from us with the understanding that there is no sort of contract between you. I must go further. I will be plain with you both. You were to confide freely in me, and I will confide freely in you. I ask you wholly to relinquish, for the present, any tie but your relationship."

"Better to say at once, sir," returned Richard, "that you renounce all confidence in me, and that you advise Ada to do the same."

"Better to say nothing of the sort, Rick, because I don't mean it."

"You think I have begun ill, sir," retorted Richard. "I *have*, I know."

"How I hoped you would begin, and how go on, I told you when we spoke of these things last," said Mr. Jarndyce, in a cordial and encouraging manner. "You have not made that beginning yet; but there is a time for all things, and yours is not gone by—rather, it is just now fully come. Make a clear beginning altogether. You two (very young, my dears) are cousins. As yet, you are nothing more. What more may come must come of being worked out, Rick, and no sooner."

"You are very hard with me, sir," said Richard. "Harder than I could have supposed you would be."

"My dear boy," said Mr. Jarndyce, "I am harder with myself when I do anything that gives you pain. You have your remedy in your own hands. Ada, it is better for him that he should be free, and that there should be no youthful engagement between you. Rick, it is better for her, much better. Come! Each of you will do what is best for the other, if not what is best for yourselves."

"Why is it best, sir?" returned Richard, hastily. "It was not when we opened our hearts to you. You did not say so then."

"I have had experience since. I don't blame you, Rick—but I have had experience since."

"You mean of me, sir."

"Well, yes, of both of you," said Mr. Jarndyce, kindly. "The time is not come for your standing pledged to one another. It is not right, and I must not recognize it. Come, come my young cousins, begin afresh! Bygones shall be bygones, and a new page turned for you to write your lives in."

Richard gave an anxious glance at Ada, but said nothing.

"I have avoided saying one word to either of you, or to Esther," said Mr. Jarndyce, "until now, in order that we might be open as the day, and all on equal terms. I now affectionately advise, I now most earnestly entreat, you two to part as you came here. Leave all else to time, truth, and steadfastness. If you do otherwise, you will do wrong; and you will have made me do wrong, in ever bringing you together."

A long silence succeeded.

"Cousin Richard," said Ada then, raising her blue eyes tenderly to his face, "after what our cousin John has said, I think no choice is left us.

Your mind may be quite at ease about me; for you will leave me here under his care, and will be sure that I can have nothing to wish for—quite sure, if I guide myself by his advice. I—I don't doubt, Cousin Richard," said Ada, a little confused, "that you are very fond of me, and I—I don't think you will fall in love with anybody else. But I should like you to consider well about it, too, as I should like you to be in all things very happy. You may trust in me, Cousin Richard. I am not at all changeable; but I am not unreasonable, and should never blame you. Even cousins may be sorry to part, and in truth I am very, very sorry, Richard, though I know it's for your welfare. I shall always think of you affectionately, and often talk of you with Esther, and—and perhaps you will sometimes think a little of me, Cousin Richard. So now," said Ada, going up to him and giving him her trembling hand, "we are only cousins again, Richard—for the time, perhaps—and I pray for a blessing on my dear cousin wherever he goes!"

It was strange to me that Richard should not be able to forgive my guardian for entertaining the very same opinion of him which he himself had expressed of himself in much stronger terms to me. But it was certainly the case. I observed, with great regret, that from this hour he never was as free and open with Mr. Jarndyce as he had been before. He had every reason given him to be so, but he was not; and, solely on his side, an estrangement began to arise between them.

In the business of preparation and equipment he soon lost himself, and even his grief at parting from Ada, who remained in Hertfordshire while he, Mr. Jarndyce, and I went up to London for a week. He remembered her by fits and starts, even with bursts of tears, and at such times would confide to me the heaviest self-reproaches. But in a few minutes he would recklessly conjure up some undefinable means by which they were both to be made rich and happy for ever, and would become as gay as possible.

It was a busy time, and I trotted about with him all day long, buying a variety of things of which he stood in need. Of the things he would have bought if he had been left to his own ways, I say nothing. He was perfectly confidential with me, and often talked sensibly and feelingly about his faults and his vigorous resolutions.

There used, in that week, to come backward and forward to our lodging, to fence with Richard, a person who had formerly been a cavalry soldier; he was a fine bluff-looking man, of a frank free bearing, with whom Richard had practised for some months. I heard so much about him, not only from Richard but from my guardian too, that I was purposely in the room, with my work, one morning after breakfast when he came.

"Good morning, Mr. George," said my guardian, who happened to be alone with me. "Mr. Carstone will be here directly. Meanwhile, Miss Summerson is very happy to see you, I know. Sit down."

He sat down, a little disconcerted by my presence, I thought, and, without looking at me, drew his heavy sunburnt hand across and across his upper lip.

"You are as punctual as the sun," said Mr. Jarndyce.

"Military time, sir," he replied. "Force of habit. A mere habit in me, sir. I am not at all businesslike."

"Yet you have a large establishment, too, I am told?" said Mr. Jarndyce.

"Not much of a one, sir. I keep a shooting gallery, but not much of a one."

"And what kind of a shot, and what kind of a swordsman, do you make of Mr. Carstone?" said my guardian.

"Pretty good, sir," he replied, folding his arms upon his broad chest, and looking very large. "If Mr. Carstone was to give his full mind to it, he would come out very good."

"But he don't, I suppose?" said my guardian.

"He did at first, sir, but not afterwards. Not his full mind. Perhaps he has something else upon it—some young lady, perhaps." His bright dark eyes glanced at me for the first time.

"He has not me upon his mind, I assure you, Mr. George," said I, laughing, "though you seem to suspect me."

He reddened a little through his brown, and made me a trooper's bow. "No offence, I hope, miss. I am one of the Roughs."

"Not at all," said I. "I take it as a compliment."

If he had not looked at me before, he looked at me now, in three or four quick successive glances. "I beg your pardon, sir," he said to my guardian, with a manly kind of diffidence, "but you did me the honour to mention the young lady's name—"

"Miss Summerson."

"Miss Summerson," he repeated, and looked at me again.

"Do you know the name?" I asked.

"No, miss. To my knowledge, I never heard it. I thought I had seen you somewhere."

"I think not," I returned, raising my head from my work to look at him. "I remember faces very well."

"So do I, miss!" he returned, meeting my look with the fulness of his dark eyes and broad forehead. "Humph! What set me off, now, upon that!"

His being disconcerted by his efforts to remember the association brought my guardian to his relief.

"Have you many pupils, Mr. George?"

"They vary in their number, sir. Mostly, they're but a small lot to live by."

"And what classes of chance people come to practise at your gallery?"

"All sorts, sir. Natives and foreigners. From gentlemen to 'prentices."

"People don't come with grudges, and schemes of finishing their practice with live targets, I hope?" said my guardian, smiling.

"Not much of that, sir, though that *has* happened. Mostly they come for skill—or idleness. Six of one and half a dozen of the other. I beg your pardon," said Mr. George, sitting stiffly upright, "but I believe you're a Chancery suitor, if I have heard correct?"

"I am sorry to say I am."

"I have had one of *your* compatriots in my time, sir."

"A Chancery suitor?" returned my guardian. "How was that?"

"Why, the man was so badgered, and worried, and tortured by being knocked about from post to pillar, and from pillar to post," said Mr. George, "that he got out of sorts. I don't believe he had any idea of taking aim at anybody, but he was in that condition of resentment and violence that he would come and pay for fifty shots and fire away till he was red-hot. One day I said to him when there was nobody by, and he had been talking to me angrily about his wrongs, 'If this practice is a safety-valve, comrade, well and good; but I don't altogether like your being so bent upon it, in your present state of mind, I'd rather you took to something else.' I was on my guard for a blow, he was that passionate, but he received it in very good part, and left off directly. We shook hands, and struck up a sort of friendship."

"What was that man?" asked my guardian, in a new tone of interest.

"Why, he began by being a small Shropshire farmer, before they made a baited bull of him," said Mr. George.

"Was his name Gridley?"

"It was, sir."

Mr. George directed another succession of quick bright glances at me as my guardian and I exchanged a word or two of surprise at the coincidence, and I therefore explained to him how we knew the name.

"I don't know," he said, as he looked at me, "what it is that sets me off again—but—bosh! what's my head running against!" He passed one of his heavy hands over his crisp dark hair, as if to sweep the broken thoughts out of his mind, and sat a little forward, looking in a brown study at the ground.

"I am sorry to learn that the same state of mind has got this Gridley into new troubles, and that he is in hiding," said my guardian.

"So I am told, sir," returned Mr. George, still musing and looking on the ground. "So I am told."

"You don't know where?"

"No, sir," returned the trooper, lifting up his eyes and coming out of his reverie. "I can't say anything about him. He will be worn-out soon, I expect. You may file a strong man's heart away for a good many years, but it will tell all of a sudden at last."

Richard's entrance stopped the conversation. Mr. George rose, made me another of his soldierly bows, wished my guardian a good day, and strode heavily out of the room.

This was the morning of the day appointed for Richard's departure. We had no more purchases to make now; I had completed all his packing early in the afternoon, and our time was disengaged until night, when he was to go to Liverpool for Holyhead. Jarndyce and Jarndyce being again expected to come on that day, Richard proposed to me that we should go down to the Court and hear what passed. As it was his last day, and he was eager to go, and I had never been there, I gave my consent, and we walked down to Westminster, where the Court was then sitting. We beguiled the way with arrangements concerning the letters that Richard was to write to me, and the letters that I was to write to him; and with a great many hopeful projects. My guardian knew where we were going, and therefore was not with us.

When we came to the Court, there was the Lord Chancellor—the same whom I had seen in his private room in Lincoln's Inn—sitting, in great state and gravity, on the bench—with the mace and seals on a red table below him, and an immense flat nosegay, like a little garden, which scented the whole Court. Below the table was a long row of solicitors, with bundles of papers on the matting at their feet; and then there were the gentlemen of the bar in wigs and gowns—some awake and some asleep, and one talking, and nobody paying much attention to what he said. The Lord Chancellor leaned back in his very easy chair, with his elbow on the cushioned arm and his forehead resting on his hand; some of those who were present dozed; some read the newspapers; some walked about, or whispered in groups; all seemed perfectly at their ease, by no means in a hurry, very unconcerned, and extremely comfortable.

To see everything going on so smoothly, and to think of the roughness of the suitors' lives and deaths—to see all that full dress and ceremony, and to think of the waste, and want, and beggared misery it represented; to consider that, while the sickness of hope deferred was raging in so many hearts, this polite show went calmly on from day to day, and year to year, in such good order and composure; to behold the Lord Chancellor, and the whole array of practitioners under him, looking at one another and at the spectators as if nobody had ever heard that all over England the name in which they were assembled was a bitter jest, was held in universal horror, contempt, and indignation, was known for something so flagrant and bad that little short of a miracle could bring any good out of it to any one—this was so curious and self-contradictory to me, who had no experience of it, that it was at first incredible, and I could not comprehend it. There seemed to be no reality in the whole scene except poor little Miss Flite, the madwoman, standing on a bench, and nodding at it.

Miss Flite soon espied us, and came to where we sat. She gave me a gracious welcome to her domain, and indicated, with much gratification and pride, its principal attractions. Mr. Kenge also came to speak to us, and did the honours of the place in much the same way, with the bland modesty of a proprietor. It was not a very good day for a visit, he said, he would have preferred the first day of term; but it was imposing, it was imposing.

When we had been there half an hour or so, the case in progress—if I may use a phrase so ridiculous in such a connexion—seemed to die out of its own vapidity, without coming, or being by anybody expected to come, to any result. The Lord Chancellor then threw down a bundle of papers from his desk to the gentleman below him, and somebody said, "Jarndyce and Jarndyce." Upon this there was a buzz, and a laugh, and a general withdrawal of the bystanders, and a bringing in of great heaps, and piles, and bags and bags full of papers.

I think it came on "for further directions,"—about some bill of costs, to the best of my understanding, which was confused enough. But I counted twenty-three gentlemen in wigs who said they were "in it," and none of them appeared to understand it much better than I. They chatted about it with the Lord Chancellor, and contradicted and explained among themselves, and some of them said it was this way, and some of them said it was that way, and some of them jocosely proposed to read huge volumes of affidavits, and there was more buzzing and laughing, and everybody concerned was in a state of idle entertainment, and nothing could be made of it by anybody. After an hour or so of this, and a good many speeches being begun and cut short, it was "referred back for the present," as Mr. Kenge said, and the papers were bundled up again before the clerks had finished bringing them in.

I glanced at Richard on the termination of these hopeless proceedings, and was shocked to see the worn look of his handsome young face. "It can't last for ever, Dame Durden. Better luck next time!" was all he said.

I had seen Mr. Guppy bringing in papers, and arranging them for Mr. Kenge; and he had seen me and made me a forlorn bow, which rendered me desirous to get out of the Court. Richard had given me his arm and was taking me away when Mr. Guppy came up.

"I beg your pardon, Mr. Carstone," said he in a whisper, "and Miss Summerson's also; but there's a lady here, a friend of mine, who knows her, and wishes to have the pleasure of shaking hands." As he spoke I saw before me, as if she had started into bodily shape from my remembrance, Mrs. Rachael of my godmother's house.

"How do you do, Esther?" said she. "Do you recollect me?"

I gave her my hand, and told her yes, and that she was very little altered.

"I wonder you remember those times, Esther," she returned with her old asperity. "They are changed now. Well! I am glad to see you, and glad you are not too proud to know me."

"Proud, Mrs. Rachael!" I remonstrated.

"I am married, Esther," she returned, coldly correcting me, "and am Mrs. Chadband. Well, I wish you good-day, and I hope you'll do well."

Mr. Guppy, who had been attentive to this short dialogue, heaved a sigh in my ear, and elbowed his own and Mrs. Rachael's way through the confused little crowd of people coming in and going out. Richard and I were making our way through it, and I was yet in the first chill of the late unexpected recognition, when I saw, coming towards us, but not seeing us, no less a person than Mr. George. He made nothing of the people about him as he tramped on, staring over their heads into the body of the Court.

"George!" said Richard, as I called his attention to him.

"You are well met, sir," he returned. "And you, miss. Could you point a person out to me I want? I don't understand these places. There's a little cracked old woman that—"

I put up my finger, for Miss Flite was close by me, having kept beside me all the time, and having called the attention of several of her legal acquaintance to me.

"Hem!" said Mr. George. "You remember, miss, that we passed some conversation on a certain man this morning?—Gridley," in a low whisper behind his hand.

"Yes," said I.

"He is hiding at my place. I couldn't mention it. Hadn't his authority. He is on his last march, miss, and has a whim to see her. He says they can feel for one another, and she has been almost as good as a friend to him here. I came down to look for her; for when I sat by Gridley this afternoon, I seemed to hear the roll of the muffled drums."

"Shall I tell her?" said I.

"Would you be so good?" he returned, with a glance of something like apprehension at Miss Flite. "It's a Providence I met you, miss. I doubt if I should have known how to get on with that lady." And he stood in a martial attitude as I informed little Miss Flite, in her ear, of the purport of his kind errand.

"My angry friend from Shropshire! Almost as celebrated as myself!"

she exclaimed. "Now really! My dear, I will wait upon him with the greatest pleasure."

"He is living concealed at Mr. George's," said I. "Hush! This is Mr. George."

"In—deed!" returned Miss Flite. "Very proud to have the honour! A military man, my dear. You know, a perfect General!" she whispered to me.

Poor Miss Flite deemed it necessary to be so courtly and polite, as a mark of her respect for the Army, and to curtsey so very often, that it was no easy matter to get her out of the Court. When this was at last done, and addressing Mr. George, as "General," she gave him her arm, he was so discomposed, and begged me so respectfully "not to desert him," that I could not make up my mind to do it, especially as Miss Flite was always tractable with me and as she too said, "Fitz-Jarndyce, my dear, you will accompany us, of course." As Richard seemed quite willing, and even anxious, that we should see them safely to their destination, we agreed to do so. And as Mr. George informed us that Gridley's mind had run on Mr. Jarndyce all the afternoon, after hearing of their interview in the morning, I wrote a hasty note in pencil to my guardian to say where we were gone, and why. Mr. George sealed it at a coffee-house, that it might lead to no discovery, and we sent it off by a ticket-porter.

We then took a hackney-coach and drove away to the neighbourhood of Leicester Square. We walked through some narrow courts, for which Mr. George apologized, and soon came to the Shooting Gallery, the door of which was closed. As he pulled a bell-handle which hung by a chain to the door-post, a very respectable old gentleman with grey hair, wearing spectacles, and dressed in a black spencer and gaiters and a broad-brimmed hat, and carrying a large gold-headed cane, addressed him.

"I ask your pardon, my good friend," said he, "but is this George's Shooting Gallery?"

"It is, sir," returned Mr. George, glancing up at the great letters in which that inscription was painted on the whitewashed wall.

"Oh! To be sure!" said the old gentleman, following his eyes. "Thank you. Have you rung the bell?"

"My name is George, sir, and I have rung the bell."

"Oh indeed?" said the old gentleman. "Your name is George? Then I am here as soon as you, you see. You came for me, no doubt?"

"No, sir. You have the advantage of me."

"Oh indeed?" said the old gentleman. "Then it was your young man who came for me. I am a physician, and was requested—five minutes ago—to come and visit a sick man at George's Shooting Gallery."

"The muffled drums," said Mr. George, turning to Richard and me, and gravely shaking his head. "It's quite correct, sir. Will you please to walk in?"

The door being at that moment opened—by a very singular-looking little man in a green-baize cap and apron, whose face, and hands, and dress were blackened all over—we passed along a dreary passage into a large building with bare brick walls, where there were targets, and guns, and swords, and other things of that kind. When we had all arrived here, the physician stopped and, taking off his hat, appeared to vanish by magic, and to leave another and quite a different man in his place.

"Now look 'ee here, George," said the man, turning quickly round upon him, and tapping him on the breast with a large forefinger. "You know me, and I know you. You're a man of the world, and I'm a man of the world. My name's Bucket, as you are aware, and I have got a peace-warrant against Gridley. You have kept him out of the way a long time, and you have been artful in it, and it does you credit."

Mr. George, looking hard at him, bit his lip, and shook his head.

"Now, George," said the other, keeping close to him, "you're a sensible man, and a well-conducted man; that's what *you* are, beyond a doubt. And mind you, I don't talk to you as a common character, because you have served your country, and you know that when duty calls we must obey. Consequently, you're very far from wanting to give trouble. If I required assistance, you'd assist me; that's what *you*'d do. Ladies and gentlemen, you'll excuse anything that may appear to be disagreeable in this, for my name's Inspector Bucket of the Detective, and I have a duty to perform. George, I know where my man is, because I was on the roof last night and saw him through the skylight, and you along with him. He is in there, you know," pointing; "that's where *he* is—on a sofy. Now I must see my man, and I must tell my man to consider himself in custody; but you know me, and you know I don't want to take any uncomfortable measures. You give me your word, as from one man to another, that it's honourable between us two, and I'll accommodate you to the utmost of my power."

"I give it," was the reply. "But it wasn't handsome in you, Mr. Bucket."

"Gammon, George! Not handsome?" said Mr. Bucket. "I don't say it wasn't handsome in you to keep my man so close, do I? Be equally good-tempered to me, old boy! Old William Tell, Old Shaw, the Life Guardsman! Why, he's a model of the whole British Army in himself, ladies and gentlemen. I'd give a fifty-pun' note to be such a figure of a man!"

Mr. George, after a little consideration, proposed to go in first to his comrade (as he called him), taking Miss Flite with him. Mr. Bucket agreeing, they went away to the further end of the gallery, leaving us sitting and standing by a table covered with guns. Mr. Bucket took this opportunity of entering into a little light conversation—asking me if I were afraid of fire-arms, as most young ladies were, asking Richard if he were a good shot. After a time he followed us to the further end of the gallery, and Richard and I were going quietly away when Mr. George came after us. He said that if we had no objection to see his comrade, he would take a visit from us very kindly. The words had hardly passed his lips when the bell was rung, and my guardian appeared, "on the chance," he observed, "of being able to do any little thing for a poor fellow involved in the same misfortune as himself." We all four went back together, and went into the place where Gridley was.

It was a bare room, partitioned off from the gallery with unpainted wood. As the screening was not more than eight or ten feet high, and only enclosed the sides, not the top, the rafters of the high gallery roof were overhead, and the skylight through which Mr. Bucket had looked down. The sun was low—near setting—and its light came redly in above, without descending to the ground. Upon a plain canvas-covered sofa lay the man from Shropshire—dressed much as we had seen him last, but so changed that at first I recognized no likeness in his colourless face to what I recollected.

He had been still writing in his hiding-place, and still dwelling on his grievances, hour after hour. A table and some shelves were covered with manuscript papers, and with worn pens, and a medley of such tokens. Touchingly and awfully drawn together, he and the little madwoman were side by side and, as it were, alone. She sat on a chair holding his hand, and none of us went close to them. His voice had faded, with the old expression of his face, with his strength, with his anger, with his resistance to the wrongs that had at last subdued him. He inclined his head to Richard and me, and spoke to my guardian.

"Mr. Jarndyce, it is very kind of you to come to see me. I am not long to be seen, I think. I am very glad to take your hand, sir. You are a good man, superior to injustice, and God knows I honour you."

They shook hands earnestly, and my guardian said some words of comfort to him.

"It may seem strange to you, sir," returned Gridley, "I should not have liked to see you if this had been the first time of our meeting. But you know I made a fight for it, you know I stood up with my single hand against them all, you know I told them the truth to the last, and told them what they were, and what they had done to me; so I don't mind you seeing me this wreck."

"You have been courageous with them, many and many a time," returned my guardian.

"Sir, I have been"—with a faint smile. "I told you what would come of it when I ceased to be so, and see here! Look at us—look at us!" He drew the hand Miss Flite held through her arm and brought her something nearer to him.

"This ends it. Of all my old associations, of all my old pursuits and hopes, of all the living and the dead world, this one poor soul alone comes natural to me, and I am fit for. There is a tie of many suffering years between us two, and it is the only tie I ever had on earth that Chancery has not broken."

"Accept my blessing, Gridley," said Miss Flite, in tears. "Accept my blessing!"

"I thought, boastfully, that they could never break my heart, Mr. Jarndyce. I was resolved that they should not. I did believe that I could, and would, charge them with being the mockery they were until I died of some bodily disorder. But I am worn out. How long I have been wearing out, I don't know; I seemed to break down in an hour. I hope they may never come to hear of it. I hope everybody here will lead them to believe that I died defying them, consistently and perseveringly, as I did through so many years."

Here Mr. Bucket, who was sitting in a corner, by the door, good-naturedly offered such consolation as he could administer.

"Come, come!" he said from his corner. "Don't go on in that way, Mr. Gridley. You are only a little low. We are all of us a little low sometimes. *I* am. Hold up, hold up! You'll lose your temper with the whole round of 'em, again and again; and I shall take you on a score of warrants yet, if I have luck."

He only shook his head.

"Don't shake your head," said Mr. Bucket. "Nod it, that's what I want to see you do. Why, Lord bless your soul, what times we have had together! Haven't I seen you in the Fleet over and over again, for contempt? Haven't I come into Court twen-ty afternoons for no other purpose than to see you pin the Chancellor like a bulldog? Don't you remember when you first began to threaten the lawyers, and the peace was sworn against you two or three times a week? Ask the little old lady there; she has been always present. Hold up, Mr. Gridley, hold up, sir!"

"What are you going to do about him?" asked George, in a low voice.

"I don't know yet," said Bucket, in the same tone.

"He is very weak," said the trooper, in a low voice.

"Is he?" returned Bucket, anxiously. "I only want to rouse him. I don't like to see an old acquaintance giving in like this. It would cheer him up more than anything if I could make him a little waxy with me. He's welcome to drop into me, right and left, if he likes. I shall never take advantage of it."

The roof rang with a scream from Miss Flite which still rings in my ears.

"Oh no, Gridley!" she cried as he fell heavily and calmly back from before her, "not without my blessing. After so many years!"

The sun was down, the light had gradually stolen from the roof, and the shadow had crept upward. But to me, the shadow of that pair, one living and one dead, fell heavier on Richard's departure than the darkness of the darkest night. And through Richard's farewell words I heard it echoed:

"Of all my old associations, of all my old pursuits and hopes, of all the living and the dead world, this one poor soul alone comes natural to me, and I am fit for. There is a tie of many suffering years between us two, and it is the only tie I ever had on earth that Chancery has not broken!"

# CHAPTER 25

*Mrs. Snagsby Sees It All*

THERE is disquietude in Cook's Court, Cursitor Street. Black suspicion hides in that peaceful region. The mass of Cook's-Courtiers are in their usual state of mind, no better and no worse, but Mr. Snagsby is changed, and his little woman knows it.

For Tom-all-Alone's and Lincoln's Inn Fields persist in harnessing themselves, a pair of ungovernable coursers, to the chariot of Mr. Snagsby's imagination; and Mr. Bucket drives; and the passengers are Jo and Mr. Tulkinghorn; and the complete equipage whirls through the Law-Stationery business at wild speed, all round the clock. Even in the little front kitchen where the family meals are taken, it rattles away at a smoking pace from the dinner-table when Mr. Snagsby pauses in carving the first slice of the leg of mutton baked with potatoes, and stares at the kitchen wall.

Mr. Snagsby cannot make out what it is that he has had to do with. Something is wrong, somewhere; but what something, what may come of it, to whom, when, and from which unthought-of and unheard-of quarter, is the puzzle of his life. His remote impressions of the robes and coronets, the stars and garters, that sparkle through the surface-dust of Mr. Tulkinghorn's chambers—his veneration for the mysteries presided over by that best and closest of his customers, whom all the Inns of Court, all Chancery Lane, and all the legal neighbourhood agree to hold in awe; his remembrance of Detective Mr. Bucket with his confidential manner impossible to be evaded or declined—persuade him that he is a party to some dangerous secret, without knowing what it is. And it is the fearful peculiarity of this condition that at any hour of his daily life, at any opening of the shop-door, at any pull of the bell, at any entrance of a messenger, or any delivery of a letter, the secret may take aim and fire, explode, and blow up—Mr. Bucket only knows whom.

For which reason, whenever a man unknown comes into the shop (as many men unknown do), and says, "Is Mr Snagsby in?" or words to that innocent effect, Mr. Snagsby's heart knocks hard at his guilty breast. The little woman herself is not the least item in his difficulty. To know that he is always keeping a secret from her, that he has, under all circumstances, to conceal and hold fast a tender double tooth, which her sharpness is ever ready to twist out of his head, gives Mr. Snagsby, in her dentistical presence, much of the air of a dog who has a reservation from his master, and will look anywhere rather than meet his eye.

These various signs and tokens, marked by the little woman, are not lost upon her. They impel her to say, "Snagsby has something on his mind!" And thus suspicion gets into Cook's Court, Cursitor Street. From suspicion to jealousy, Mrs. Snagsby finds the road as natural and short as from Cook's Court to Chancery Lane. And thus jealousy gets into Cook's Court, Cursitor Street. Once there, it is very active and nimble in Mrs. Snagsby's breast—prompting her to nocturnal examinations of Mr. Snagsby's pockets; to secret perusals of Mr. Snagsby's letters; to private researches in the Day Book and Ledger, till, cash-box, and iron safe; to watchings at windows, listenings behind doors, and a general putting of this and that together by the wrong end. Mrs. Snagsby is so perpetually on the alert that the house becomes ghostly with creaking boards and rustling garments.

"Who was Nimrod?" Mrs. Snagsby repeatedly inquires of herself. "Who was that lady—that creature? And who is that boy?" Now Nimrod being as dead as the mighty hunter whose name Mrs. Snagsby has appropriated, and the lady being unproducible, she directs her mental eye, for the present, with redoubled vigilance, to the boy. "And who," quoth Mrs. Snagsby, for the thousand and first time, "is that boy? Who is that—!" And there Mrs. Snagsby is seized with an inspiration.

He has no respect for Mr. Chadband. No, to be sure, and he wouldn't have, of course. Naturally he wouldn't, under those contagious circumstances. He was invited and appointed by Mr. Chadband to come back, and be told where he was to go, to be addressed by Mr. Chadband; and he never came! Why did he never come? Because he was told not to come. Who told him not to come? Who? Ha, ha! Mrs. Snagsby sees it all.

But happily (and Mrs. Snagsby tightly shakes her head and tightly smiles) that boy was met by Mr. Chadband yesterday in the streets; and that boy, as affording a subject which Mr. Chadband desires to improve for the spiritual delight of a select congregation, was seized by Mr. Chadband and threatened with being delivered over to the police unless he showed the reverend gentleman where he lived, and unless he entered into, and fulfilled, an undertaking to appear in Cook's Court tomorrow night, and tomorrow night that boy will be here, and tomorrow night Mrs. Snagsby will have her eye upon him and upon some one else.

Mrs. Snagsby sounds no timbrel in anybody's ears, but holds her purpose quietly, and keeps her counsel. Tomorrow comes, the savoury preparations for the oil-trade come, the evening comes. Comes Mr. Snagsby in his black coat; come the Chadbands; come the 'prentices and Guster, to be edified; comes, at last, with his slouching head, and his shuffle backward, and his shuffle forward, and his shuffle to the right, and his shuffle to the left, and his bit of fur cap in his muddy hand, Jo, the very, very tough subject Mr. Chadband is to improve.

Mrs. Snagsby screws a watchful glance on Jo as he is brought into the little drawing-room by Guster. He looks at Mr. Snagsby the moment he comes in. Aha! Why does he look at Mr. Snagsby? Mr. Snagsby looks at him. Why should he do that but that Mrs. Snagsby sees it all? Why else should that look pass between them, why else should Mr. Snagsby be confused, and cough a signal cough behind his hand? It is as clear as crystal that Mr. Snagsby is that boy's father.

"Peace, my friends," says Chadband, rising and wiping the oily exudations from his reverend visage. "Peace be with us! My friends, why with us? Because," with his fat smile, "it cannot be against us, because it must be for us; because it is not hardening, because it is softening; because it does not make war like the hawk, but comes home untoe us like the dove. Therefore, my friends, peace be with us! My human boy, come forward!"

Stretching forth his flabby paw, Mr. Chadband lays the same on Jo's arm, and considers where to station him. Jo, very doubtful of his reverend friend's intentions, and not at all clear but that something practical and painful is going to be done to him, mutters, "You let me alone. I never said nothink to you. You let me alone."

"No, my young friend," says Chadband, smoothly, "I will not let you alone. And why? Because I am a harvest-labourer, because I am a toiler and a moiler, because you are delivered over untoe me, and are become as a precious instrument in my hands. My friends, may I so employ this instrument as to use it toe your advantage, toe your profit, toe your gain, toe your welfare, toe your enrichment! My young friend, sit upon this stool."

Jo, apparently possessed by an impression that the reverend gentleman wants to cut his hair, shields his head with both arms, and is got into the required position with great difficulty and every possible manifestation of reluctance.

When he is at last adjusted like a lay-figure, Mr. Chadband, retiring behind a table, holds up his bear's-paw and says, "My friends!" This is the signal for a general settlement of the audience. The 'prentices giggle internally, and nudge each other. Guster falls into a staring and vacant state. Mrs. Snagsby silently lays trains of gunpowder. Mrs. Chadband composes herself grimly by the fire and warms her knees, finding that sensation favourable to the reception of eloquence.

It happens that Mr. Chadband has a pulpit habit of fixing some member of his congregation with his eye, and flatly arguing his points with that particular person, who is understood to be expected to be moved to an occasional grunt, groan, gasp, or other audible expression of inward working; which expression of inward working, being echoed by some elderly lady in the next pew, and so communicated, like a game of forfeits, through a circle of the more fermentable sinners present, serves the purpose of parliamentary cheering, and gets Mr. Chadband's steam up. From mere force of habit, Mr. Chadband in saying "My friends!" has rested his eye on Mr. Snagsby, and proceeds to make that ill-starred stationer, already sufficiently confused, the immediate recipient of his discourse.

"We have here among us, my friends," says Chadband, "a Gentile and a Heathen, a dweller in the tents of Tom-all-Alone's and a mover-on upon the surface of the earth. We have here among us, my friends, a brother and a boy. Devoid of parents, devoid of relations, devoid of flocks and herds, devoid of gold and silver, and of precious stones. Now, my friends, why do I say he is devoid of these possessions? Why? Why is he?" Mr. Chadband states the question as if he were propounding an entirely new riddle, of much ingenuity and merit, to Mr. Snagsby.

Mr. Snagsby, greatly perplexed by the mysterious look he received just now from his little woman—at about the period when Mr. Chadband mentioned the word "parents"—is tempted into modestly remarking, "I don't know, I'm sure, sir." On which interruption, Mrs. Chadband glares, and Mrs. Snagsby says, "For shame!"

"I hear a voice," says Chadband. "Is it a still small voice, my friends? I fear not, though I fain would hope so. Which says, 'I don't know.' Then I will tell you why. I say this brother, present here among us, is devoid of parents, devoid of relations, devoid of flocks and herds, devoid of gold, of silver, and of precious stones, because he is devoid of the light that shines in upon some of us. What is that light? What is it? I ask you what is that light?"

Mr. Chadband draws back his head and pauses, but Mr. Snagsby is not to be lured on to his destruction again. Mr. Chadband, leaning forward over the table, pierces what he has got to follow directly into Mr. Snagsby.

"It is," says Chadband, "the ray of rays, the sun of suns, the moon of moons, the star of stars. It is the light of Terewth."

Mr. Chadband draws himself up again, and looks triumphantly at Mr. Snagsby, as if he would be glad to know how he feels after that.

"Of Terewth," says Mr. Chadband, hitting him again. "Say not to me that it is *not* the lamp of lamps. I say to you, it is. I say to you, a million of times over, it is. It is! I say to you that I will proclaim it to you, whether you like it or not—nay, that the less you like it, the more I will proclaim it to you. With a speaking trumpet! I say to you that if you rear yourself against it, you shall fall, you shall be bruised, you shall be battered, you shall be flawed, you shall be smashed."

The present effect of this flight of oratory being not only to make Mr. Chadband unpleasantly warm, but to represent the innocent Mr. Snagsby in the light of a determined enemy to virtue, with a forehead of brass and a heart of adamant, that unfortunate tradesman becomes yet more disconcerted, and is in a very advanced state of low spirits and false position when Mr. Chadband accidentally finishes him.

"My friends," he resumes, after dabbing his fat head for some time, "to pursue the subject we are endeavouring with our lowly gifts to improve, let us in a spirit of love inquire what is that Terewth to which I have alluded. For, my young friends," suddenly addressing the 'prentices and Guster, to their consternation, "if I am told by the doctor that calomel or castor-oil is good for me, I may naturally ask what is calomel, and what is castor-oil. I may wish to be informed of that before I dose myself with either or with both. Now, my young friends, what is this Terewth, then? Firstly (in a spirit of love), what is the common sort of Terewth—the working clothes—the every-day wear, my young friends? Is it deception? Is it suppression? Is it reservation? No, my friends, it is neither of these. Neither of these names belongs to it. When this young Heathen now among us—who is now, my friends, asleep, the seal of indifference, and perdition being set upon his eyelids—but do not wake him, for it is right that I should have to wrestle, and to combat and to struggle, and to conquer, for his sake—when this young hardened Heathen told us a story of a Cock, and of a Bull, and of a lady, and of a sovereign, was *that* the Terewth? No.

Or if it was partly, was it wholly and entirely? No, my friends, no!"

If Mr. Snagsby could withstand his little woman's look as it enters at his eyes, the windows of his soul, and searches the whole tenement, he were other than the man he is. He cowers and droops.

"Or, my juvenile friends," says Chadband, descending to the level of their comprehension, "if the master of this house was to go forth into the city and there see an eel, and was to come back, and was to call untoe him the mistress of this house, and was to say, 'Sarah, rejoice with me, for I have seen an elephant!' would *that* be Terewth?" Mrs. Snagsby in tears. "Or put it, my juvenile friends, that he saw an elephant, and returning said, 'Lo, the city is barren, I have seen but an eel,' would *that* be Terewth?" Mrs. Snagsby sobbing loudly.

"Or put it, my juvenile friends," said Chadband, stimulated by the sound, "that the unnatural parents of this slumbering Heathen—for parents he had, my juvenile friends, beyond a doubt—after casting him forth to the wolves and the vultures, and the wild dogs and the young gazelles, and the serpents, went back to their dwellings and had their pipes, and their pots, and their flutings and their dancings, and their malt liquors, and their butcher's meat and poultry, would *that* be Terewth!"

Mrs. Snagsby replies by delivering herself a prey to spasms; not an unresisting prey, but a crying and a tearing one, so that Cook's Court re-echoes with her shrieks. Finally, becoming cataleptic, she has to be carried up the narrow staircase like a grand piano. After unspeakable suffering, productive of the utmost consternation, she is pronounced, by expresses from the bedroom, free from pain, though much exhausted; in which state of affairs Mr. Snagsby, extremely timid and feeble, ventures to come out from behind the door in the drawing-room.

All this time, Jo has been standing on the spot where he woke up, ever picking his cap, and putting bits of fur in his mouth. He spits them out with a remorseful air, for he feels that it is in his nature to be an unimprovable reprobate, and that it's no good *his* trying to keep awake, for *he* won't never know nothink. Though it may be, Jo, that there is a history so interesting and affecting even to minds as near the brutes as thine, recording deeds done on this earth for common men, that if the Chadbands, removing their own persons from the light, would but show it thee in simple reverence, would but leave it unimproved, would but regard it as being eloquent enough without their modest aid —it might hold thee awake, and thou might learn from it yet!

Jo never heard of any such book. Its compilers and the Reverend Chadband are all one to him—except that he knows the Reverend Chadband, and would rather run away from him for an hour than hear him talk for five minutes. "It an't no good my waiting here no longer," thinks Jo. "Mr. Snagsby an't a-going to say nothink to me tonight." And downstairs he shuffles.

But downstairs is the charitable Guster, holding by the hand-rail of the kitchen stairs and warding off a fit, as yet doubtfully, the same having been induced by Mrs. Snagsby's screaming. She has her own supper of bread and cheese to hand to Jo, with whom she ventures to interchange a word or so, for the first time.

"Here's something to eat, poor boy," says Guster.

"Thank 'ee, mum," says Jo.

"Are you hungry?"

"Jist!" says Jo.

"What's gone of your father and your mother, eh?"

Jo stops in the middle of a bite, and looks petrified. For this orphan charge of the Christian saint whose shrine was at Tooting has patted him on the shoulder, and it is the first time in his life that any decent hand has been so laid upon him.

"I never know'd nothink about 'em," says Jo.

"No more didn't I of mine!" cries Guster. She is repressing symptoms favourable to the fit when she seems to take alarm at something, and vanishes down the stairs.

"Jo," whispers the law-stationer softly.

"Here I am, Mr. Snagsby!"

"I didn't know you were gone—there's another halfcrown. It was quite right of you to say nothing about the lady the other night when we were out together. It would breed trouble. You can't be too quiet, Jo."

"I am fly, master!"

And so good-night.

A ghostly shade, frilled and night-capped, follows the law-stationer to the room he came from, and glides higher up. And henceforth he begins, go where he will, to be attended by another shadow than his own, hardly less constant than his own, hardly less quiet than his own. And into whatsoever atmosphere of secrecy his own shadow may pass, let all concerned in the secrecy beware! For the watchful Mrs. Snagsby is there too—bone of his bone, flesh of his flesh, shadow of his shadow.

# CHAPTER 26

*Sharpshooters*

WINTRY morning, looking with dull eyes and sallow face upon the neighbourhood of Leicester Square, finds its inhabitants unwilling to get out of bed. Many of them are not early risers at the brightest of times, being birds of night who roost when the sun is high and are wide awake and keen for prey when the stars shine out.

The wintry morning wakes Mr. George of the Shooting Gallery, and his familiar. They arise, roll up and stow away their mattresses. Mr. George, having shaved himself before a looking-glass of minute proportions, then marches out, bare-headed and bare-chested, to the pump in the little yard, and anon comes back shining with yellow soap, friction, drifting rain, and exceedingly cold water. As he rubs himself upon a large jack-towel, his crisp hair curling tighter and tighter on his sunburnt temples the more he rubs it, so that it looks as if it never could be loosened by any less coercive instrument than an iron rake or a curry-comb—as he rubs, and puffs, and polishes, and blows, turning his head from side to side, Phil, on his knees lighting a fire, looks round as if it were enough washing for him to see all that done, and sufficient renovation, for one day, to take in the superfluous health his master throws off.

When Mr. George is dry, he goes to work to brush his head with two hard brushes at once. This chafing over, the ornamental part of Mr. George's toilet is soon performed. He fills his pipe, lights it, and marches up and down smoking while Phil, raising a powerful odour of hot rolls and coffee, prepares breakfast. He smokes gravely, and marches in slow time. Perhaps this morning's pipe is devoted to the memory of Gridley in his grave.

"And so, Phil," says George of the Shooting Gallery, after several turns in silence, "you were dreaming of the country last night?"

Phil, by the by, said as much, in a tone of surprise, as he scrambled out of bed.

"Yes, Guv'ner."

"What was it like?"

"I hardly know what it was like, Guv'ner," said Phil, considering.

"How did you know it was the country?"

"On account of the grass, I think," says Phil, after further consideration.

The master resumes his march, and the man resumes his preparation of breakfast. It is not necessarily a lengthened preparation, being limited to the setting forth of very simple breakfast requisites for two, and the broiling of a rasher of bacon at the fire in the rusty grate; but as Phil never brings two objects at once, it takes time under the circumstances. At length the breakfast is ready. Phil announcing it, Mr. George knocks the ashes out of his pipe on the hob, stands his pipe itself in the chimney-corner, and sits down to the meal. When he has helped himself, Phil follows suit, sitting at the extreme end of the little oblong table and taking his plate on his knees.

"The country," says Mr. George, plying his knife and fork—"why, I suppose you never clapped your eyes on the country, Phil?"

"I see the marshes once," says Phil, contentedly eating his breakfast.

"What marshes?"

"I don't know where they are," says Phil, "but I see 'em, Guv'ner. They was flat. And misty."

Governor and Commander are interchangeable terms with Phil, expressive of the same respect and deference, and applicable to nobody but Mr. George.

"I was born in the country, Phil."

"Was you indeed, Commander?"

"Yes. And bred there. There's not a bird's note that I don't know," says Mr. George. "Not many an English leaf or berry that I couldn't name. Not many a tree that I couldn't climb yet, if I was put to it. I was a real country boy once. My good mother lived in the country."

"She must have been a fine old lady, Guv'ner," Phil observes.

"Ay! And not so old either, five and thirty years ago," says Mr. George. "But I'll wager that at ninety she would be near as upright as me, and near as broad across the shoulders."

"Did she die at ninety, Guv'ner?" inquires Phil.

"No. Let her rest in peace, God bless her!" says the trooper. "So you never clapped your eyes upon the country—marshes and dreams excepted. Do you want to see it?"

"N-no, I don't know as I do, particular," says Phil.

"The town's enough for you, eh?"

"Why you see, Commander," says Phil, "I ain't acquainted with anythink else, and I doubt if I ain't a-getting too old to take to novelties."

"How old *are* you, Phil?" asks the trooper, pausing as he conveys his smoking saucer to his lips.

"I'm something with a eight in it," says Phil. "It can't be eighty. Nor yet eighteen. It's betwixt 'em, somewheres." Phil is counting on his dirty fingers. "I was just eight," says Phil, "agreeable to the parish calculation, when I went with the tinker. I was sent on an errand and I see him a sittin under a old buildin with a fire all to himself wery comfortable, and he says, 'Would you like to come along a me, my man?' I says 'Yes,' and him and me and the fire goes home to Clerkenwell together. That was April Fool Day. I was able to count up to ten, and when April Fool Day came round again, I says to myself, 'Now, old chap, you're one and a eight in it.' April Fool Day after that, I says, 'Now, old chap, you're two and a eight in it.' In the course of time, I come to ten and a eight in it; two tens and a eight in it. When it got so high, it got the upper hand of me; but this is how I always know there's a eight in it."

"Ah!" says Mr. George. "And where's the tinker?"

"Drink put him in the hospital, Guv'ner, and the hospital put him—in a glass-case, I *have* heerd," Phil replies mysteriously.

"By that means you got promotion? Took the business, Phil?"

"Yes, Commander, I took the business. Such as it was. It wasn't much of a beat. Most of the tramping tinkers used to come and lodge at our place; that was the best part of my master's earnings. But they didn't come to me. I warn't like him. He could sing 'em a good song. *I* couldn't —never had a note of music in me. Besides, I was too ill-looking, and their wives complained of me."

"They were mighty particular. You would pass muster in a crowd, Phil!" says the trooper with a pleasant smile.

"No, Guv'ner," returns Phil, shaking his head. "No, I shouldn't. I was passable enough when I went with the tinker, though nothing to boast of then: but what with blowing the fire with my mouth when I was young, and spiling my complexion, and singeing my hair off, and swallering the smoke; and what with being nat'rally unfort'nate in the way of running against hot metal, and marking myself by sich means; and what with having turn-ups with the tinker as I got older, my beauty was queer, wery queer, even at that time. As to since, what with being scorched in a accident at a gas-works, and what with being blowed out of winder, case-filling at the firework business, I am ugly enough to be made a show on! It was after the case-filling blow-up when I first see you, Commander. You remember?"

"I remember, Phil. You were walking along in the sun."

"Crawling, Guv'ner, again a wall—in a night-cap!"

"In a night-cap—"

"And hobbling with a couple of sticks!" cries Phil.

"With a couple of sticks. When—"

"When you stops, you know," cries Phil, "and says to me, 'What, comrade! You have been in the wars!' I didn't say much to you, Commander, then, for I was took by surprise that a person so strong and healthy and bold as you was should stop to speak to such a limping bag of bones as I was. But you says to me, says you, 'What accident have you met with? You have been badly hurt. What's amiss, old boy? Cheer up, and tell us about it!' Cheer up! I was cheered already! I says as much to you, you says more to me, I says more to you, you says more to me, and here I am, Commander!" cries Phil, who has started from his chair. "If a mark's wanted or if it will improve the business, let the customers take aim at me. They can't spoil *my* beauty. *I'm* all right. Come on! If they want a man to box at, let 'em box at me. Let 'em knock me well about the head. *I* don't mind! If they want a light-weight to be throwed for practice, Cornwall, Devonshire, or Lancashire, let 'em throw me. They won't hurt *me*. I have been throwed, all sorts of styles, all my life!"

With this unexpected speech, Phil begins to clear away the breakfast.

Mr. George, after laughing cheerfully, and clapping him on the shoulder, assists in these arrangements, and helps to get the gallery into business order. That done, he takes a turn at the dumb-bells; and afterwards weighing himself, and opining that he is getting "too fleshy," engages with great gravity in solitary broadsword practice. Meanwhile, Phil has fallen to work at his usual table, where he screws and unscrews, and cleans, and files, and blackens himself more and more, and seems to do and undo everything that can be done and undone about a gun.

Master and man are at length disturbed by footsteps in the passage, where they make an unusual sound, denoting the arrival of unusual company. These steps, advancing nearer and nearer to the gallery, bring into it a group at first sight scarcely reconcilable with any day in the year but the fifth of November.

It consists of a limp and ugly figure carried in a chair by two bearers, and attended by a lean female with a face like a pinched mask, her lips tightly and defiantly closed as the chair is put down. At which point, the figure in it gasping, "Oh, Lord! Oh dear me! I am shaken!" Mr. George descries in the procession the venerable Mr. Smallweed out for an airing, attended by his grand-daughter Judy as body-guard.

"Mr. George, my dear friend," says Grandfather Smallweed, removing his right arm from the neck of one of his bearers, "how de do? You're surprised to see me, my dear friend."

"I should hardly have been more surprised to have seen your friend in the city," returns Mr. George.

"I am very seldom out," pants Mr. Smallweed. "I haven't been out for months. It's inconvenient—and it comes expensive. But I longed so much to see you, my dear Mr. George. How de do, sir?"

"I am well enough," says Mr. George. "I hope you are the same."

"You can't be too well, my dear friend." Mr. Smallweed takes him by both hands. "I have brought my grand-daughter Judy. I couldn't keep her away. She longed so much to see you. So we got a hackney-cab, and put a chair in it, and just round the corner they lifted me out of the cab and into the chair, and carried me here, that I might see my dear friend in his own establishment! This," says Grandfather Smallweed, "is the driver of the cab. He has nothing extra. It is by agreement included in his fare. This person we engaged in the street outside for a pint of beer. Which is twopence. Judy, give the person twopence. I was not sure you had a workman of your own here, my dear friend, or we needn't have employed this person."

Grandfather Smallweed refers to Phil, with a glance of considerable terror. Nor is his apprehension, on the surface of things, without some reason; for Phil, who has never beheld the apparition in the black-velvet cap before, has stopped short with a gun in his hand, with much of the air of a dead shot intent on picking Mr. Smallweed off as an ugly old bird of the crow species.

"Judy my child," says Grandfather Smallweed, "give the person his twopence. It's a great deal for what he has done."

The person receives his twopence with anything but transport, tosses the money into the air, catches it overhanded, and retires.

"My dear Mr. George," says Grandfather Smallweed, "would you be so kind as help to carry me to the fire? I am accustomed to a fire, and I am an old man, and I soon chill. Oh dear me!"

His closing exclamation is jerked out of the venerable gentleman by the suddenness with which Mr. Squod, like a genie, catches him up, chair and all, and deposits him on the hearthstone.

"Oh, Lord!" says Mr. Smallweed, panting. "Oh dear me! Oh my stars! My dear friend, your workman is very strong—and very prompt. Oh Lord, he is very prompt! Judy, draw me back a little. I'm being scorched in the legs"—which indeed is testified to the noses of all present by the smell of his worsted stockings.

The gentle Judy, having backed her grandfather a little way from the fire, and having shaken him up as usual, and having released his overshadowed eye from its black-velvet extinguisher, Mr. Smallweed again says, "Oh dear me! Oh, Lord!" and meeting Mr. George's glance, again stretches out both hands.

"My dear friend! So happy in this meeting! And this is your establishment? It's a delightful place. It's a picture! You never find that anything goes off here accidentally, do you, my dear friend?" adds Grandfather Smallweed, very ill at ease.

"No, no. No fear of that."

"And your workman. He—Oh dear me!—he never lets anything off without meaning it, does he, my dear friend?"

"He has never hurt anybody but himself," says Mr. George, smiling.

"But he might, you know. He seems to have hurt himself a good deal, and he might hurt somebody else," the old gentleman returns. "He mightn't mean it—or he even might. Mr. George, will you order him to leave his infernal fire-arms alone, and go away?"

Obedient to a nod from the trooper, Phil retires, empty-handed, to the other end of the gallery. Mr. Smallweed, reassured, falls to rubbing his legs.

"And you're doing well, Mr. George?" he says to the trooper. "You are prospering, please the Powers?"

Mr. George answers with a cool nod, adding, "Go on. You have not come to say that, I know."

"You are so sprightly, Mr. George," returns the venerable grandfather. "You are such good company."

"Ha ha! Go on!" says Mr. George. "Now for it!"

"Ho!" cries Mr. Smallweed, rubbing his hands with an artful chuckle. "Yes. Now for it. Now for what, my dear friend?"

"For a pipe," says Mr. George, who with great composure sets his chair in the chimney-corner, takes his pipe from the grate, fills it and lights it, and falls to smoking peacefully.

This tends to the discomfiture of Mr. Smallweed, who finds it so difficult to resume his object, whatever it may be, that he becomes exasperated, and secretly claws the air with impotent vindictiveness. As he continues while he claws to slide down in his chair and to collapse into a shapeless bundle, he becomes such a ghastly spectacle, even in the accustomed eyes of Judy, that that young virgin pounces at him with something more than the ardour of affection, and so shakes him up, and pats and pokes him in divers parts of his body, that in his grievous distress he utters enforced sounds like a paviour's rammer.

When Judy has by these means set him up again in his chair (still clawing), she stretches out her weazen forefinger, and gives Mr. George one poke in the back. The trooper raising his head, she makes another poke at her esteemed grandfather and, having thus brought them together, stares rigidly at the fire.

"Ay, ay! Ho, ho! U—u—u—ugh!" chatters Grandfather Smallweed, swallowing his rage. "My dear friend!"

"I tell you what," says Mr. George. "If you want to converse with me, you must speak out. I am one of the Roughs, and I can't go about and about. I haven't the art to do it. I am not clever enough. It don't suit me. When you go winding round and round me," says the trooper, putting his pipe between his lips again, "damme if I don't feel as if I was being smothered! If you have come to give me a friendly call," continues Mr. George, "I am obliged to you. If you have come to see whether there's any property on the premises, look about you, you are welcome. If you want to out with something, out with it!"

Says Grandfather Smallweed, "My friend in the city, Mr. George, has done a little business with a pupil of yours."

"Has he?" says Mr. George. "I am sorry to hear it."

"Yes, sir." Grandfather Smallweed rubs his legs. "He is a fine young soldier now, Mr. George, by the name of Carstone. Friends came forward, and paid it all up, honourable."

"Did they?" returns Mr. George. "Do you think your friend in the city would like a piece of advice?"

"I think he would, my dear friend. From you."

"I advise him, then, to do no more business in that quarter. There's no more to be got by it. The young gentleman, to my knowledge, is brought to a dead halt."

"No, no, my dear friend. No, no, Mr. George. No, no, no, sir," remonstrates Grandfather Smallweed, cunningly rubbing his spare legs. "Not quite a dead halt, I think. He has good friends, and he is good for his pay, and he is good for the selling price of his commission, and he is good for his chance in a lawsuit, and he is good for his chance in a wife, and—oh, do you know, Mr. George, I think my friend would consider the young gentleman good for something yet?" says Grandfather Smallweed.

Mr. George, who has put aside his pipe and sits with an arm on his chair-back, beats a tattoo on the ground with his right foot, as if he were not particularly pleased with the turn the conversation has taken.

"But to pass from one subject to another," resumes Mr. Smallweed, "to pass, Mr. George, from the ensign to the captain."

"What are you up to now?" asks Mr. George, pausing with a frown in stroking the recollection of his moustache. "What captain?"

"Our captain. The captain we know of. Captain Hawdon."

"Oh that's it, is it?" says Mr. George, with a low whistle. "Well, what about it? Speak!"

"My dear friend," returns the old man, "I was applied—Judy, shake me up a little!—I was applied to yesterday about the Captain, and my opinion still is that the Captain is not dead."

"Bosh!" observes Mr. George.

"Ho!" says Grandfather Smallweed. "Mr. George, of my opinion you can judge for yourself, according to the questions asked of me, and the reasons given for asking 'em. Now what do you think the lawyer making the inquiries wants?"

"A job," says Mr. George.

"Nothing of the kind!"

"Can't be a lawyer, then," says Mr. George.

"My dear friend, he is a lawyer, and a famous one. He wants to see some fragment in Captain Hawdon's writing. He don't want to keep it.

He only wants to see it, and compare it with a writing in his possession."

"Well?"

"Well, Mr. George. Happening to remember the advertisement concerning Captain Hawdon, and any information that could be given respecting him, he looked it up and came to me—just as you did, my dear friend. So glad you came that day! I should have missed forming such a friendship if you hadn't come!"

"Well, Mr. Smallweed?" says Mr. George again.

"I had no such thing. I have nothing but his signature. Plague pestilence, and famine, battle murder and sudden death, upon him," says the old man, making a curse out of one of his few remembrances of a prayer, "I have half a million of his signatures, I think! But you, my dear Mr. George, are likely to have some letter or paper that would suit the purpose. Anything would suit the purpose, written in the hand."

"Some writing in that hand," says the trooper, pondering, "maybe, I have."

"My dearest friend!"

"Maybe I have not."

"Ho!" says Grandfather Smallweed, crest-fallen.

"But if I had bushels of it, I would not show as much as would make a cartridge without knowing why."

"Sir, I have told you why. My dear Mr. George, I have told you why."

"Not enough," says the trooper, shaking his head. "I must know more, and approve it."

"Then will you come to the lawyer? My dear friend, will you come and see the gentleman?" urges Grandfather Smallweed. "I told him it was probable I might call upon him between ten and eleven this forenoon, and it's now half after ten. Will you come and see the gentleman, Mr. George?"

"Hum!" says he, gravely. "I don't mind that. Though why this should concern you so much, I don't know."

"Everything concerns me that has a chance in it of bringing anything to light about him. Didn't he take us all in? Didn't he owe us immense sums, all round? Concern me? Who can anything about him concern more than me? Not, my dear friend," says Grandfather Smallweed, lowering his tone, "that I want *you* to betray anything. Are you ready to come, my dear friend?"

"Ay! I'll come in a moment. I promise nothing, you know."

"No, my dear Mr. George, no."

"And you mean to say that you're going to give me a lift to this place, wherever it is, without charging for it?" Mr. George inquires, getting his hat and thick wash-leather gloves.

This pleasantry so tickles Mr. Smallweed that he laughs, long and

low, before the fire. Mr. George unlocks the padlock of a homely cupboard at the distant end of the gallery, looks here and there upon the
higher shelves, and ultimately takes something out with a rustling of
paper, folds it, and puts it in his breast.

"I am ready," says the trooper, coming back. "Phil, you can carry this
old gentleman to his coach and make nothing of him."

"Oh dear me! Oh, Lord! Stop a moment!" says Mr. Smallweed. "He's
so very prompt! Are you sure you can do it carefully, my worthy man?"

Phil makes no reply, but seizing the chair and its load, sidles away,
tightly hugged by the now speechless Mr. Smallweed, and bolts along
the passage as if he had an acceptable commission to carry the old
gentleman to the nearest volcano. His shorter trust, however, terminating at the cab, he deposits him there; and the fair Judy takes her
place beside him, and the chair embellishes the roof, and Mr. George
takes the vacant place upon the box.

Mr. George is quite confounded by the spectacle he beholds from
time to time as he peeps into the cab through the window behind him,
where the grim Judy is always motionless, and the old gentleman with
his cap over one eye is always sliding off the seat into the straw, and
looking upward at him.

# CHAPTER 27

*More Old Soldiers Than One*

Mr. George has not far to ride with folded arms upon
the box, for their destination is Lincoln's Inn Fields. When the driver
stops his horses, Mr. George alights, and looking in at the window, says:

"What, Mr. Tulkinghorn's your man, is he?"

"Yes, my dear friend. Do you know him, Mr. George?"

"Why, I have heard of him—seen him too, I think. But I don't know
him, and he don't know me."

There ensues the carrying of Mr. Smallweed upstairs, which is done
to perfection with the trooper's help. He is borne into Mr. Tulkinghorn's
great room, and deposited on the Turkey rug before the fire. Mr. Tulkinghorn is not within at the present moment, but will be back directly.

Mr. George is mightily curious in respect of the room. He looks up
at the painted ceiling, looks round at the old law-books, contemplates
the portraits of the great clients, reads aloud the names on the boxes.

" 'Sir Leicester Dedlock, Baronet,' " Mr. George reads thoughtfully. "Ha! 'Manor of Chesney Wold.' Humph!" Mr. George stands looking at these boxes a long while. "Sir Leicester Dedlock, Baronet, and Manor of Chesney Wold, hey?"

"Worth a mint of money, Mr. George!" whispers Grandfather Small-weed, rubbing his legs. "Powerfully rich!"

"Who do you mean? This old gentleman, or the baronet?"

"This gentleman, this gentleman."

"So I have heard, and knows a thing or two, I'll hold a wager. Not bad quarters, either," says Mr. George, looking round again. "See the strong-box yonder!"

This reply is cut short by Mr. Tulkinghorn's arrival. There is no change in him, of course. Rustily drest, with his spectacles in his hand, and their very case worn threadbare. In manner, close and dry. In voice, husky and low. In face, watchful behind a blind, habitually not un-censorious and contemptuous, perhaps. The peerage may have warmer worshippers and faithfuller believers than Mr. Tulkinghorn, after all, if everything were known.

"Good-morning, Mr. Smallweed, good-morning!" he says as he comes in. "You have brought the Sergeant, I see. Sit down, Sergeant."

As Mr. Tulkinghorn takes off his gloves and puts them in his hat, he looks with half-closed eyes across the room to where the trooper stands, and says within himself perchance, "You'll do, my friend!"

"Sit down, Sergeant," he repeats as he comes to his table, which is set on one side of the fire, and takes his easy-chair. "Cold and raw this morning, cold and raw!" Mr. Tulkinghorn warms before the bars, alternately, the palms and knuckles of his hands, and looks at the trio sitting in a little semicircle before him.

"Now I can feel what I am about," (as perhaps he can in two senses) "Mr. Smallweed. You have brought our good friend the Sergeant, I see."

"Yes, sir," returns Mr. Smallweed, very servile to the lawyer's wealth and influence.

"And what does the Sergeant say about this business?"

"Mr. George," says Grandfather Smallweed, with a tremulous wave of his shrivelled hand, "this is the gentleman, sir."

Mr. George salutes the gentleman, but otherwise sits bolt upright and profoundly silent—very forward in his chair, as if the full com-plement of regulation appendages for a field-day hung about him.

Mr. Tulkinghorn proceeds: "Well, George?—I believe your name is George?"

"It is so, sir."

"What do you say, George?"

"I ask your pardon, sir," returns the trooper, "but I should wish to know what *you* say?"

"Do you mean in point of reward?"

"I mean in point of everything, sir."

"I supposed, Sergeant," Mr. Tulkinghorn resumes, "that Mr. Small-weed might have sufficiently explained the matter. It lies in the smallest compass, however. You served under Captain Hawdon at one time, and were his attendant in illness, and rendered him many little services, and were rather in his confidence, I am told. That is so, is it not?"

"Yes sir, that is so," says Mr. George, with military brevity.

"Therefore you may happen to have in your possession something—anything, no matter what—accounts, instructions, orders, a letter, anything—in Captain Hawdon's writing. I wish to compare his writing with some that I have. If you can give me the opportunity, you shall be rewarded for your trouble. Three, four, five, guineas, you would consider handsome, I dare say. If not, say how much more, in your conscience as a soldier, you can demand. There is no need for you to part with the writing against your inclination—though I should prefer to have it."

Mr. George sits squared in exactly the same attitude, looks at the painted ceiling, and says never a word.

"The question is," says Mr. Tulkinghorn in his methodical, subdued, uninterested way, "first, whether you have any of Captain Hawdon's writing."

"First, whether I have any of Captain Hawdon's writing, sir," repeats Mr. George.

"Secondly, what will satisfy you for the trouble of producing it?"

"Secondly, what will satisfy me for the trouble of producing it, sir," repeats Mr. George.

"Thirdly, you can judge for yourself whether it is at all like that," says Mr. Tulkinghorn, suddenly handing him some sheets of written paper tied together.

"Whether it is at all like that, sir. Just so," repeats Mr. George.

All three repetitions Mr. George pronounces in a mechanical manner, looking straight at Mr. Tulkinghorn; nor does he so much as glance at the affidavit in Jarndyce and Jarndyce that has been given to him for his inspection, but continues to look at the lawyer with an air of troubled meditation.

"Well?" says Mr. Tulkinghorn. "What do you say?"

"Well, sir," replies Mr. George, rising erect and looking immense, "I would rather, if you'll excuse me, have nothing to do with this."

Mr. Tulkinghorn, outwardly quite undisturbed, demands, "Why not?"

"Why, sir," returns the trooper, "except on military compulsion, I am not a man of business. Among civilians I am what they call in Scotland a ne'er-do-weel. I have no head for papers, sir. I can stand any fire better than a fire of cross-questions. I mentioned to Mr. Smallweed, only an hour or so ago, that when I come into things of this kind, I feel as if I was being smothered. And that is my sensation," says Mr. George, looking round upon the company, "at the present moment."

With that, he takes three strides forward to replace the papers on the lawyer's table, and three strides backward to resume his former station, where he stands with his hands behind him as if to prevent himself from accepting any other document whatever.

"I do assure you, sir," says Mr. George, "not to say it offensively, that between you and Mr. Smallweed here, I really am being smothered fifty times over. I really am, sir. I am not a match for you gentlemen. Will you allow me to ask why you want to see the Captain's hand, in the case that I could find any specimen of it?"

Mr. Tulkinghorn quietly shakes his head. "No. If you were a man of business, Sergeant, you would not need to be informed that there are confidential reasons, very harmless in themselves, for many such wants, in the profession to which I belong. But if you are afraid of doing any injury to Captain Hawdon, you may set your mind at rest about that."

"Ay! He is dead, sir."

"*Is* he?" Mr. Tulkinghorn quietly sits down to write.

"Well, sir," says the trooper, looking into his hat after another disconcerted pause, "I am sorry not to have given you more satisfaction. If it would be any satisfaction to any one that I should be confirmed in my judgment that I would rather have nothing to do with this, by a friend of mine who has a better head for business than I have, and who is an old soldier, I am willing to consult with him. I—I really am so completely smothered myself at present," says Mr. George, passing his hand hopelessly across his brow, "that I don't know but what it might be a satisfaction to me."

Mr. Smallweed, hearing that this authority is an old soldier, so strongly inculcates the expediency of the trooper's taking counsel with him, and particularly informing him of its being a question of five guineas or more, that Mr. George engages to go and see him. Mr. Tulkinghorn says nothing either way.

"I'll consult my friend, then, by your leave, sir," says the trooper, "and I'll take the liberty of looking in again with the final answer in the course of the day. Mr. Smallweed, if you wish to be carried downstairs—"

"In a moment, my dear friend, in a moment. Will you first let me speak half a word with this gentleman in private?"

"Certainly, sir. Don't hurry yourself on my account." The trooper retires to a distant part of the room, and resumes his curious inspection of the boxes, strong and otherwise.

"If I wasn't as weak as a Brimstone Baby, sir," whispers Grandfather Smallweed, drawing the lawyer down to his level by the lapel of his coat, "I'd tear the writing away from him. He's got it buttoned in his breast. I saw him put it there."

"Violence will not do for me, my friend," Mr. Tulkinghorn then remarks coolly.

"No, no, I know, I know, sir. But it's chafing and galling—it's—it's worse than your smattering chattering Magpie of a grandmother"—to the imperturbable Judy, who only looks at the fire—"to know he has got what's wanted, and won't give it up. He not to give it up! *He!* A vagabond! But never mind, sir, never mind. At the most, he has only his own way for a little while. I have him periodically in a vise. I'll twist him, sir. I'll screw him, sir. If he won't do it with a good grace, I'll make him do it with a bad one, sir!—Now, my dear Mr. George," says Grandfather Smallweed, "I am ready for your kind assistance, my excellent friend!"

Mr. Tulkinghorn, with some shadowy sign of amusement manifesting itself through his self-possession, stands on the hearth-rug with his back to the fire, watching the disappearance of Mr. Smallweed and acknowledging the trooper's parting salute with one slight nod.

It is more difficult to get rid of the old gentleman, Mr. George finds, than to bear a hand in carrying him downstairs; for when he is replaced in his conveyance, he is so loquacious on the subject of the guineas, and retains such an affectionate hold of his button, that some degree of force is necessary on the trooper's part to effect a separation. It is accomplished at last, and he proceeds alone in quest of his adviser.

By the cloisterly Temple, and by Whitefriars, and by Blackfriars Bridge and Blackfriars Road, Mr. George sedately marches to a street of little shops lying somewhere in that ganglion of roads from Kent and Surrey and streets from the bridges of London. To one of the little shops in this street, which is a musician's shop, having a few fiddles in the window and some Pan's pipes and a tambourine, and a triangle, Mr. George directs his massive tread. And halting at a few paces from it as he sees a soldierly-looking woman, with her outer skirts tucked up, come forth with a small wooden tub, and in that tub commence a whisking and a splashing on the margin of the pavement, Mr. George says to himself, "She's, as usual, washing greens. I never saw her, except upon a baggage-waggon, when she wasn't washing greens!"

The subject of this reflection is at all events so occupied in washing greens at present that she remains unsuspicious of Mr. George's approach until, lifting up herself and her tub together, she finds him standing near her. Her reception of him is not flattering.

"George, I never see you but I wish you was a hundred mile away!"

The trooper, without remarking on this welcome, follows into the musical-instrument shop, where the lady places her tub of greens upon the counter, and having shaken hands with him, rests her arms upon it.

"I never," she says, "George, consider Matthew Bagnet safe a minute when you're near him. You are that restless and that roving—"

"Yes! I know I am, Mrs. Bagnet. I know I am."

"You know you are!" says Mrs. Bagnet. "What's the use of that? *Why* are you?"

"The nature of the animal, I suppose," returns the trooper good-humouredly.

"Ah," cried Mrs. Bagnet, something shrilly, "but what satisfaction will the nature of the animal be to me when the animal shall have tempted my Mat away from the musical business to New Zealand or Australy?"

Mrs. Bagnet is not at all an ill-looking woman. Rather large-boned, a little coarse in the grain, and freckled by the sun and wind, but healthy, wholesome, and bright-eyed. A strong, busy, active, honest-faced woman of from forty-five to fifty. Clean, hardy, and so economically dressed (though substantially), that the only article of ornament of which she stands possessed appears to be her wedding-ring, around which her finger has grown to be so large since it was put on that it will never come off again until it shall mingle with Mrs. Bagnet's dust.

"Mrs. Bagnet," says the trooper, "I am on my parole with you. Mat will get no harm from me. You may trust me so far."

"Well, I think I may. But the very looks of you are unsettling," Mrs. Bagnet rejoins. "Ah, George, George! If you had only settled down, and married Joe Pouch's widow when he died in North America, *she'd* have combed your hair for you."

"It was a chance for me, certainly," returns the trooper, half laughingly, half seriously, "but I shall never settle down into a respectable man now. Joe Pouch's widow might have done me good, but I couldn't make up my mind to it. If I had had the luck to meet with such a wife as Mat found!"

Mrs. Bagnet, who seems in a virtuous way to be under little reserve with a good sort of fellow, but to be another good sort of fellow herself for that matter, receives this compliment by flicking Mr. George in the face with a head of greens and taking her tub into the little room behind the shop.

"Why, Quebec my poppet," says George, following, on invitation, into that department. "And little Malta, too! Come and kiss your Bluffy!"

These young ladies—not supposed to have been actually christened by the names applied to them, though always so called in the family, from the places of their birth in barracks—are respectively employed on three-legged stools: the younger (some five or six years old), in learning her letters out of a penny primer; the elder (eight or nine perhaps), in teaching her, and sewing with great assiduity. Both hail Mr. George with acclamations as an old friend, and after some kissing and romping plant their stools beside him.

"And how's young Woolwich?" says Mr. George.

"Ah! There now!" cries Mrs. Bagnet, turning about from her saucepans (for she is cooking dinner), with a bright flush on her face. "Would you believe it? Got an engagement at the theayter, with his father, to play the fife in a military piece."

"Well done, my godson!" cries Mr. George, slapping his thigh.

"I believe you!" says Mrs. Bagnet. "He's a Briton. That's what Woolwich is. A Briton!"

"And Mat blows away at his bassoon, and you're respectable civilians one and all," says Mr. George. "Family people. Children growing up. Mat's old mother in Scotland, and your old father somewhere else, corresponded with, and helped a little; and—well, well! To be sure, I don't know why I shouldn't be wished a hundred mile away, for I have not much to do with all this!"

Mr. George is becoming thoughtful. Sitting before the fire in the whitewashed room—which has a sanded floor, and a barrack smell, and contains nothing superfluous, and has not a visible speck of dirt or dust in it, from the faces of Quebec and Malta to the bright tin pots and pannikins upon the dresser shelves—Mr. George is becoming thoughtful, sitting here while Mrs. Bagnet is busy, when Mr. Bagnet and young Woolwich opportunely come home. Mr. Bagnet is an ex-artilleryman, tall and upright, with shaggy eyebrows, and whiskers like the fibres of a coco-nut, not a hair upon his head, and a torrid complexion. His voice, short, deep, and resonant, is not at all unlike the tones of the instrument to which he is devoted. Young Woolwich is the type and model of a young drummer.

Both father and son salute the trooper heartily. He saying, in due season, that he has come to advise with Mr. Bagnet, Mr. Bagnet hospitably declares that he will hear of no business until after dinner, and that his friend shall not partake of his counsel without first partaking of boiled pork and greens. The trooper yielding to this invitation, he and Mr. Bagnet, not to embarrass the domestic preparations, go forth to take a turn up and down the little street.

"George," says Mr. Bagnet, "you know me. It's my old girl that advises. She has the head. But I never own to it before her. Discipline must be maintained. Wait till the greens is off her mind. Then we'll consult. Whatever the old girl says, do—do it!"

"I intend to, Mat," replies the other. "I would sooner take her opinion than that of a college."

"College," returns Mr. Bagnet, in short sentences, bassoon-like. "What college could you leave. In another quarter of the world. With nothing but grey cloak and an umbrella. To make its way home to Europe? The old girl would do it tomorrow. Did it once!"

"You are right," says Mr. George.

"What college," pursues Bagnet, "could you set up in life. With two penn'orth of white lime. A penn'orth of fuller's earth. A ha'porth of sand. And the rest of the change out of sixpence, in money? That's what the old girl started on. In the present business."

"I am rejoiced to hear it's thriving, Mat."

"The old girl," says Mr. Bagnet, acquiescing, "saves. Has a stocking somewhere. With money in it. I never saw it. But I know she's got it. Wait till the greens is off her mind. Then she'll set you up."

"She is a treasure!" exclaims Mr. George.

"She's more. But I never own to it before her. Discipline must be maintained. It was the old girl that brought out my musical abilities. I should have been in the artillery now but for the old girl. Six years I hammered at the fiddle. Ten at the flute. The old girl said it wouldn't

do. Intention good, but want of flexibility. Try the bassoon. The old girl
borrowed a bassoon from the bandmaster of the Rifle Regiment. I practised in the trenches. Got on, got another, get a living by it!"

George remarks that she looks as fresh as a rose, and as sound as an
apple.

"The old girl," says Mr. Bagnet in reply, "is a thoroughly fine woman.
Consequently, she is like a thoroughly fine day. Gets finer as she gets
on. I never saw the old girl's equal. But I never own to it before her.
Discipline must be maintained!"

Proceeding to converse on indifferent matters, they walk up and down
the little street, keeping step and time, until summoned by Quebec and
Malta to do justice to the pork and greens, over which Mrs. Bagnet, like
a military chaplain, says a short grace. In the distribution of these
comestibles, as in every other household duty, Mrs. Bagnet develops an
exact system—sitting with every dish before her, allotting to every portion of pork its own portion of pot-liquor, greens, potatoes, and even
mustard! and serving it out complete. Having likewise served out the
beer from a can, and thus supplied the mess with all things necessary,
Mrs. Bagnet proceeds to satisfy her own hunger, which is in a healthy
state.

The dinner done, Mrs. Bagnet, assisted by the younger branches
(who polish their own cups and platters, knives and forks), makes all
the dinner garniture shine as brightly as before, and puts it all away,
first sweeping the hearth, to the end that Mr. Bagnet and the visitor may
not be retarded in the smoking of their pipes. These household cares
involve much pattening and counter-pattening in the back yard, and
considerable use of a pail, which is finally so happy as to assist in the
ablutions of Mrs. Bagnet herself. That old girl reappearing by and by
quite fresh, and sitting down to her needlework, then and only then—
the greens being only then to be considered as entirely off her mind—
Mr. Bagnet requests the trooper to state his case.

This Mr. George does with great discretion—appearing to address
himself to Mr. Bagnet, but having an eye solely on the old girl, as
Bagnet has himself. She, equally discreet, busies herself with her needlework. The case fully stated, Mr. Bagnet resorts to his standard artifice
for the maintenance of discipline.

"That's the whole of it, is it, George?" says he.

"That's the whole of it."

"You act according to my opinion?"

"I shall be guided," replies George, "entirely by it."

"Old girl," says Mr. Bagnet, "give him my opinion. You know it. Tell
him what it is."

It is that he cannot have too little to do with people who are too deep for him, and cannot be too careful of interference with matters he does not understand; that the plain rule is to do nothing in the dark, to be a party to nothing underhanded or mysterious, and never to put his foot where he cannot see the ground. This, in effect, is Mr. Bagnet's opinion, as delivered through the old girl; and it so relieves Mr. George's mind, by confirming his own opinion and banishing his doubts, that he composes himself to smoke another pipe on that exceptional occasion, and to have a talk over old times with the whole Bagnet family.

Through these means it comes to pass that Mr. George does not again rise to his full height in that parlour until the time is drawing on when the bassoon and fife are expected by a British public at the theatre; and as it takes time even then for Mr. George, in his domestic character of Bluffy, to take leave of Quebec and Malta, and insinuate a sponsorial shilling into the pocket of his godson, with felicitations on his success in life, it is dark when Mr. George again turns his face towards Lincoln's Inn Fields.

"A family home," he ruminates as he marches along, "however small it is, makes a man like me look lonely. But it's well I never made that evolution of matrimony. I shouldn't have been fit for it, I am such a vagabond still, even at my present time of life, that I couldn't hold to the gallery a month together if it was a regular pursuit, or if I didn't camp there, gipsy fashion. Come! I disgrace nobody and cumber nobody; that's something. I have not done that for many a long year!" So he whistles it off, and marches on.

Arrived in Lincoln's Inn Fields, and mounting Mr. Tulkinghorn's stair, he finds the outer door closed and the chambers shut; but the trooper not knowing much about outer doors, and the staircase being dark besides, he is yet fumbling and groping about, hoping to discover a bell-handle, when Mr. Tulkinghorn comes up the stairs (quietly, of course), and angrily asks:

"Who is that? What are you doing there?"

"I ask your pardon, sir. It's George. The Sergeant."

"And couldn't George, the Sergeant, see that my door was locked?"

"Why no, sir, I couldn't. At any rate, I didn't," says the trooper, rather nettled.

"Have you changed your mind, or are you in the same mind?" Mr. Tulkinghorn demands. But he knows well enough at a glance.

"In the same mind, sir."

"I thought so. That's sufficient. You can go. So you are the man," says Mr. Tulkinghorn, opening his door with the key, "in whose hiding-place Mr. Gridley was found?"

"Yes, I *am* the man," says the trooper, stopping two or three stairs down. "What then, sir?"

"What then? I don't like your associates. You should not have seen the inside of my door this morning if I had thought of your being that man. Gridley? A threatening, murderous, dangerous fellow."

With these words, spoken in an unusually high tone for him, the lawyer goes into his rooms, and shuts the door with a thundering noise.

Mr. George takes his dismissal in great dudgeon, the greater, because the clerk coming up the stairs has heard the last words of all, and evidently applies them to him. "A pretty character to bear," the trooper growls with a hasty oath as he strides downstairs. "A threatening, murderous, dangerous fellow!" and looking up, he sees the clerk looking down at him. This so intensifies his dudgeon that for five minutes he is in an ill-humour. But he whistles that off, like the rest of it, and marches home to the Shooting Gallery.

## CHAPTER 28

*The Ironmaster*

Sir Leicester Dedlock has got the better, for the time being, of the family gout, and is once more, in a literal no less than in a figurative point of view, upon his legs. He is at his place in Lincolnshire; but the waters are out again on the low-lying grounds, and the cold and damp steal into Chesney Wold, though well defended, and eke into Sir Leicester's bones. The blazing fires of faggot and coal that blaze upon the broad wide hearths do not exclude the enemy. The hot-water pipes that trail themselves all over the house, the cushioned doors and windows, and the screens and curtains, fail to supply the fires' deficiencies. Hence the fashionable intelligence proclaims one morning to the listening earth that Lady Dedlock is expected shortly to return to town for a few weeks.

It is a melancholy truth that even great men have their poor relations. Indeed great men have often more than their fair share of poor relations, inasmuch as very red blood of the superior quality, like inferior blood unlawfully shed, *will* cry aloud, and *will* be heard. Sir Leicester's cousins, in the remotest degree, are so many murders, in the respect that they "will out." Among whom there are cousins who are so poor that one might almost dare to think it would have been the happier for them never to have been plated links upon the Dedlock chain of gold, but to have been made of common iron at first, and done base service.

Service, however (with a few limited reservations; genteel but not profitable), they may not do, being of the Dedlock dignity. So they visit their richer cousins, and get into debt when they can and live but shabbily when they can't, and find, the women no husbands, and the men no wives, and ride in borrowed carriages, and sit at feasts that are never of their own making, and so go through high life.

Everybody on Sir Leicester Dedlock's side of the question, and of his way of thinking, would appear to be his cousin more or less. But while he is stately in the cousinship of the Everybodys, he is a kind and generous man, according to his dignified way, in the cousinship of the Nobodys; and at the present time, in despite of the damp, he stays out the visit of several such cousins at Chesney Wold, with the constancy of a martyr.

Of these, foremost in the front rank stands Volumnia Dedlock, a young lady (of sixty), who is doubly highly related, having the honour to be a poor relation by the mother's side to another great family. Miss Volumnia, displaying in early life a pretty talent for cutting ornaments out of coloured paper, and also for singing to the guitar in the Spanish tongue, passed the twenty years of her existence between twenty and forty in a sufficiently agreeable manner. Lapsing then out of date, and being considered to bore mankind by her vocal performances in the Spanish language, she retired to Bath, where she lives slenderly on an annual present from Sir Leicester, and whence she makes occasional resurrections in the country-houses of her cousins. She has an extensive acquaintance at Bath, but she is a little dreaded elsewhere, in consequence of an indiscreet profusion in the article of rouge, and persistency in an obsolete pearl necklace like a rosary of little bird's-eggs.

The rest of the cousins are ladies and gentlemen of various ages and capacities; the major part amiable and sensible, and likely to have done well enough in life if they could have overcome their cousinship; as it is, they are almost all a little worsted by it, and seem to be quite as much at a loss how to dispose of themselves as anybody else can be how to dispose of them.

In this society, and where not? my Lady Dedlock reigns supreme. Beautiful, elegant, accomplished, and powerful in her little world (for the world of fashion does not stretch *all* the way from pole to pole), her influence in Sir Leicester's house, however haughty and indifferent her manner, is greatly to improve it and refine it. The cousins, even those older cousins who were paralyzed when Sir Leicester married her, do her feudal homage; and the Honourable Bob Stables daily repeats to some chosen person, between breakfast and lunch, his favourite original remark that she is the best-groomed woman in the whole stud.

Such the guests in the long drawing-room at Chesney Wold this dismal night, when the step on the Ghost's Walk (inaudible here, however,) might be the step of a deceased cousin shut out in the cold. It is near bedtime. Bedroom fires blaze brightly all over the house. Bedroom candlesticks bristle on the distant table by the door, and cousins yawn on ottomans. Cousins at the piano, cousins at the soda-water tray, cousins rising from the card-table, cousins gathered round the fire. Standing on one side of his own peculiar fire (for there are two), Sir Leicester. On the opposite side of the broad hearth, my Lady at her table. Volumnia, as one of the more privileged cousins, in a luxurious chair between them. Sir Leicester glancing, with magnificent displeasure, at the rouge and the pearl necklace.

"I occasionally meet on my staircase here," drawls Volumnia, "one of the prettiest girls, I think, that I ever saw in my life."

"A protégée of my lady's," observes Sir Leicester.

"I thought so. I felt sure that some uncommon eye must have picked that girl out. She really is a marvel. A dolly sort of beauty, perhaps," says Miss Volumnia, reserving her own sort, "but in its way, perfect; such bloom I never saw!"

"Indeed," remarks my Lady, languidly, "if there is any uncommon eye in the case, it is Mrs. Rouncewell's, and not mine. Rosa is her discovery."

"Your maid, I suppose?"

"No. My anything: pet—secretary—messenger—I don't know what."

"You like to have her about you, as you would like to have a flower, or a bird, or a picture, or a poodle—no, not a poodle, though—or anything else that was equally pretty?" says Volumnia, sympathizing. "Yes, how charming now! And how well that delightful old soul Mrs. Rouncewell is looking. She must be an immense age, and yet she is as active and handsome!—She is the dearest friend I have, positively!"

Sir Leicester feels it to be right and fitting that the housekeeper of Chesney Wold should be a remarkable person. Apart from that, he has a real regard for Mrs. Rouncewell, and likes to hear her praised. So he says, "You are right, Volumnia."

"She has no daughter of her own, has she?"

"Mrs. Rouncewell? No, Volumnia. She has a son. Indeed, she had two. And it is a remarkable example of the confusion into which the present age has fallen—of the obliteration of landmarks, the opening of floodgates, and the uprooting of distinctions," says Sir Leicester with stately gloom—"that I have been informed, by Mr. Tulkinghorn, that Mrs. Rouncewell's son has been invited to go into Parliament."

Miss Volumnia utters a little sharp scream.

"Yes, indeed," repeats Sir Leicester. "Into Parliament."

"I never heard of such a thing! Good gracious, what is the man?" exclaimed Volumnia.

"He is called, I believe—an—ironmaster." Sir Leicester says it slowly, and with gravity and doubt, as not being sure but that he is called a lead-mistress, or that the right word may be some other word expressive of some other relationship to some other metal.

"He has declined the proposal, if my information from Mr. Tulkinghorn be correct, as I have no doubt it is, Mr. Tulkinghorn being always correct and exact. Still," says Sir Leicester, "that does not lessen the anomaly, which is fraught with strange considerations—startling considerations, as it appears to me."

Miss Volumnia rising with a look candlestick-wards, Sir Leicester politely performs the grand tour of the drawing-room, brings one, and lights it at my Lady's shaded lamp.

"I must beg you, my lady," he says while doing so, "to remain a few moments; for this individual of whom I speak arrived this evening shortly before dinner, and requested—in a very becoming note"—Sir Leicester, with his habitual regard to truth, dwells upon it—"I am bound to say in a very becoming and well-expressed note the favour of a short interview with yourself and *my*self, on the subject of this young girl. As it appeared that he wished to depart tonight, I replied that we would see him before retiring."

Miss Volumnia takes flight, wishing her hosts well rid of the—what is it?—ironmaster! The other cousins soon disperse, to the last cousin there. Sir Leicester rings the bell.

"Make my compliments to Mr. Rouncewell, in the housekeeper's apartments, and say I can receive him now."

My Lady, who has heard all this with slight attention outwardly, looks towards Mr. Rouncewell as he comes in. He is a little over fifty perhaps, of a good figure, like his mother, and has a clear voice, a broad forehead from which his dark hair has retired, and a shrewd, though open face. He is a responsible-looking gentleman dressed in black, portly enough, but strong and active. Has a perfectly natural and easy air, and is not in the least embarrassed by the great presence into which he comes.

"Sir Leicester and Lady Dedlock, as I have already apologized for intruding on you, I cannot do better than be very brief. I thank you, Sir Leicester."

The head of the Dedlocks has motioned towards a sofa between himself and my Lady. Mr. Rouncewell quietly takes his seat there.

"In these busy times, when so many great undertakings are in progress, people like myself have so many workmen in so many places that we are always on the flight."

Sir Leicester is content enough that the ironmaster should feel that there is no hurry there—there, in that ancient house, rooted in that quiet park, where the ivy and the moss have had time to mature, and where the sun-dial on the terrace has dumbly recorded for centuries that Time which was as much the property of every Dedlock—while he lasted—as the house and lands. Sir Leicester sits down in an easy-chair, opposing his repose and that of Chesney Wold to the restless flights of ironmasters.

"Lady Dedlock has been so kind," proceeds Mr. Rouncewell, with a respectful glance and a bow that way, "as to place near her a young beauty of the name of Rosa. Now my son has fallen in love with Rosa, and has asked my consent to his proposing marriage to her, and to their becoming engaged if she will take him—which I suppose she will. I have never seen Rosa until today, but I have some confidence in my son's good sense—even in love. I find her what he represents her, to the best of my judgment, and my mother speaks of her with great commendation."

"She in all respects deserves it," says my Lady.

"I am happy, Lady Dedlock, that you say so; and I need not comment on the value to me of your kind opinion of her."

"That," observes Sir Leicester, with unspeakable grandeur, for he thinks the ironmaster a little too glib, "must be quite unnecessary."

"Quite unnecessary, Sir Leicester. Now my son is a very young man, and Rosa is a very young woman. As I made my way, so my son must make his, and his being married at present is out of the question. But supposing I gave my consent to his engaging himself to this pretty girl, if this pretty girl will engage herself to him, I think it a piece of candour to say at once—I am sure, Sir Leicester and Lady Dedlock, you will understand and excuse me—I should make it a condition that she did not remain at Chesney Wold. Therefore, before communicating further with my son I take the liberty of saying that if her removal would be in any way inconvenient or objectionable, I will hold the matter over with him for any reasonable time, and leave it precisely where it is."

Not remain at Chesney Wold! Make it a condition! All Sir Leicester's old misgivings relative to the people in the iron districts who do nothing but turn out by torchlight come in a shower upon his head, the fine grey hair of which, as well as of his whiskers, actually stirs with indignation.

"Am I to understand, sir," says Sir Leicester, "and is my lady to understand"—he brings her in thus specially, first, as a point of gallantry, and next as a point of prudence, having great reliance on her sense—"am I to understand, Mr. Rouncewell, and is my lady to understand, sir, that you consider this young woman too good for Chesney Wold, or likely to be injured by remaining here?"

"Certainly not, Sir Leicester."

"I am glad to hear it." Sir Leicester, very lofty indeed.

"Pray, Mr. Rouncewell," says my Lady, warning Sir Leicester off with the slightest gesture of her pretty hand, as if he were a fly, "explain to me what you mean."

"Willingly, Lady Dedlock. There is nothing I could desire more. I am the son of your housekeeper, Lady Dedlock, and passed my childhood about this house. My mother has lived here half a century, and will die here I have no doubt. She is one of those examples—perhaps as good a one as there is—of love, and attachment, and fidelity in such a station which England may well be proud of, but of which no order can appropriate the whole pride or the whole merit, because such an instance bespeaks high worth on two sides; on the great side, assuredly, on the small one no less assuredly."

Sir Leicester snorts a little to hear the law laid down in this way; but in his honour and his love of truth, he freely, though silently, admits the justice of the ironmaster's proposition.

"Pardon me for saying what is so obvious, but I wouldn't have it hastily supposed"—with the least turn of his eyes towards Sir Leicester—"that I am ashamed of my mother's position here, or wanting in all just respect for Chesney Wold and the family. I certainly may have desired—I certainly have desired, Lady Dedlock—that my mother should retire after so many years, and end her days with me. But as I have found that to sever this strong bond would be to break her heart, I have long abandoned that idea."

Sir Leicester very magnificent again, at the notion of Mrs. Rouncewell being spirited off from her natural home to end her days with an ironmaster.

"I have been," proceeds the visitor, in a modest, clear way, "an apprentice, and a workman. I have lived on workman's wages, years and years, and beyond a certain point have had to educate myself. My wife was a foreman's daughter, and plainly brought up. We have three daughters, besides this son of whom I have spoken, and being fortunately able to give them greater advantages than we have had ourselves, we have educated them well—very well. It has been one of our great cares and pleasures to make them worthy of any station."

A little boastfulness in his fatherly tone here, as if he added in his heart, "even of the Chesney Wold station." Not a little more magnificence, therefore, on the part of Sir Leicester.

"All this is so frequent, Lady Dedlock, where I live, and among the class to which I belong, that what would be generally called unequal marriages are not of such rare occurrence with us as elsewhere. A son will sometimes make it known to his father that he has fallen in love, say, with a young woman in the factory. The father, who once worked in a factory himself, will be a little disappointed at first, very possibly. It may be that he had other views for his son. However, the chances are that having ascertained the young woman to be of unblemished character, he will say to his son: 'I must be quite sure you are in earnest here. This is a serious matter for both of you. Therefore I shall have this girl educated for two years during which you will give me your word and honour to see her only so often. If, at the expiration of that time, when she has so far profited by her advantages as that you may be upon a fair equality, you are both in the same mind, I will do my part to make you happy.' I know of several cases such as I describe, my lady, and I think they indicate to me my own course now."

Sir Leicester's magnificence explodes. Calmly, but terribly.

"Mr. Rouncewell," says Sir Leicester, with his right hand in the breast of his blue coat—the attitude of state in which he is painted in the gallery—"do you draw a parallel between Chesney Wold and a—" here he resists a disposition to choke—"a factory?"

"I need not reply, Sir Leicester, that the two places are very different, but for the purposes of this case, I think a parallel may be justly drawn between them."

Sir Leicester directs his majestic glance down one side of the long drawing-room, and up the other, before he can believe that he is awake.

"Are you aware, sir, that this young woman whom my lady—my lady—has placed near her person was brought up at the village school outside the gates?"

"Sir Leicester, I am quite aware of it. A very good school it is, and handsomely supported by this family."

"Then, Mr. Rouncewell," returns Sir Leicester, "the application of what you have said is, to me, incomprehensible."

"Will it be more comprehensible, Sir Leicester, if I say"—the ironmaster is reddening a little—"that I do not regard the village school as teaching everything desirable to be known by my son's wife?"

From the village school of Chesney Wold, intact as it is this minute, to the whole framework of society; from the whole framework of society to the aforesaid framework receiving tremendous cracks in consequence of people (ironmasters, lead-mistresses, and what not) not minding their catechism, and getting out of the station unto which they are called—necessarily and for ever, according to Sir Leicester's rapid logic, the first station in which they happen to find themselves—and from that to educating other people out of *their* stations, and so obliterating the landmarks, and opening the floodgates, and all the rest of it: this is the swift progress of the Dedlock mind.

"My lady, I beg your pardon. Permit me, for one moment!" She has given a faint indication of intending to speak. "Mr. Rouncewell, our views of duty, and our views of station, and our views of education, and our views of—in short, *all* our views—are so diametrically opposed that to prolong this discussion must be repellant to your feelings, and re-pellant to my own. This young woman is honoured with my lady's notice and favour. If she wishes to withdraw herself from that notice and favour, or if she chooses to place herself under the influence of any one who may in his peculiar opinions withdraw her from that notice and favour, she is at any time at liberty to do so. We are obliged to you for the plainness with which you have spoken. It will have no effect of it-self, one way or other, on the young woman's position here. Beyond this, we can make no terms; and here we beg—if you will be so good—to leave the subject."

The visitor pauses a moment to give my Lady an opportunity, but she says nothing. He then rises and replies:

"Sir Leicester and Lady Dedlock, allow me to thank you for your at-tention, and only to observe that I shall very seriously recommend my son to conquer his present inclinations. Good-night!"

"Mr. Rouncewell," says Sir Leicester, with all the nature of a gentle-man shining in him, "it is late, and the roads are dark. I hope your time is not so precious but that you will allow my lady and myself to offer you the hospitality of Chesney Wold, for tonight at least."

"I hope so," adds my Lady.

"I am much obliged to you, but I have to travel all night in order to reach a distant part of the country punctually at an appointed time in the morning."

Therewith the ironmaster takes his departure, Sir Leicester ringing the bell, and my Lady rising as he leaves the room.

When my Lady goes to her boudoir, she sits down thoughtfully by the fire and, inattentive to the Ghost's Walk, looks at Rosa, writing in an inner room. Presently my Lady calls her.

"Come to me, child. Tell me the truth. Are you in love?"

"Oh, my lady!"

My Lady, looking at the downcast and blushing face, says smiling:

"Who is it? Is it Mrs. Rouncewell's grandson?"

"Yes, if you please, my lady. But I don't know that I am in love with him—yet."

"Yet, you silly little thing! Do you know that he loves *you*, yet?"

"I think he likes me a little, my lady." And Rosa bursts into tears.

Is this Lady Dedlock standing beside the village beauty, smoothing her dark hair with that motherly touch, and watching her with eyes so full of musing interest? Ay, indeed it is!

"Listen to me, child. You are young and true, and I believe you are attached to me."

"Indeed I am, my lady. Indeed there is nothing in the world I wouldn't do to show how much."

"And I don't think you would wish to leave me just yet, Rosa, even for a lover?"

"No, my lady! Oh no!"

"Confide in me, my child. Don't fear me. I wish you to be happy, and will make you so—if I can make anybody happy on this earth."

Rosa, with fresh tears, kneels at her feet and kisses her hand. My Lady takes the hand with which she has caught it and, standing with her eyes fixed on the fire, puts it about and about between her own two hands, and gradually lets it fall. Seeing her so absorbed, Rosa softly withdraws, but still my Lady's eyes are on the fire.

In search of what? Of any hand that is no more, of any hand that never was, of any touch that might have magically changed her life? Or does she listen to the Ghost's Walk, and think what step does it most resemble? A man's? A woman's? The pattering of a little child's feet, ever coming on—on—on? Some melancholy influence is upon her, or why should so proud a lady close the doors, and sit alone upon the earth so desolate?

# CHAPTER 29

## The Young Man

CHESNEY WOLD is shut up, carpets are rolled into great scrolls in corners of comfortless rooms, bright damask does penance in brown holland, carving and gilding puts on mortification, and the Dedlock ancestors retire from the light of day again. Around and around the house the leaves fall thick. Let the gardener sweep and sweep the turf as he will, and press the leaves into full barrows and wheel them off, still they lie ankle-deep. Howls the shrill wind round Chesney Wold, the sharp rain beats, the windows rattle, and the chimneys growl. On all the house there is a cold, blank smell, like the smell of a little church, though something dryer—suggesting that the dead and buried Dedlocks walk there in the long nights, and leave the flavour of their graves behind them.

But the house in town, which is rarely in the same mind as Chesney Wold at the same time—seldom rejoicing when it rejoices, or mourning when it mourns, excepting when a Dedlock dies—the house in town shines out awakened. As warm and bright as so much state may be—as delicately redolent of pleasant scents that bear no trace of winter as hothouse flowers can make it; soft and hushed, so that the ticking of the clocks and the crisp burning of the fires alone disturb the stillness in the rooms—it seems to wrap those chilled bones of Sir Leicester's in rainbow-coloured wool. And Sir Leicester is glad to repose in dignified contentment before the great fire in the library, condescendingly perusing the backs of his books, or honouring the fine arts with a glance of approbation. For he has his pictures, ancient and modern.

Mr. Tulkinghorn comes and goes pretty often, there being estate business to do, leases to be renewed, and so on. He sees my Lady pretty often, too, and he and she are as composed, and as indifferent, and take as little heed of one another, as ever. Yet it may be that my Lady fears this Mr. Tulkinghorn, and that he knows it. It may be that he pursues her doggedly and steadily, with no touch of compunction, remorse, or pity.

It may be that her beauty, and all the state and brilliancy surrounding her, only give him the greater zest for what he is set upon, and make him the more inflexible in it. Whether he be cold and cruel, whether immovable in what he has made his duty, whether absorbed in love of power, whether determined to have nothing hidden from him in ground where he has burrowed among secrets all his life, whether he in his heart despises the splendour of which he is a distant beam, whether he is always treasuring up slights and offences in the affability of his gorgeous clients—whether he be any of this, or all of this, it may be that my Lady had better have five thousand pairs of fashionable eyes upon her in distrustful vigilance than the two eyes of this rusty lawyer.

Sir Leicester sits in my Lady's room, particularly complacent. My Lady sits before the fire with her screen in her hand. Sir Leicester is particularly complacent, because he has found in his newspaper some congenial remarks bearing directly on the floodgates and the framework of society. They apply so happily to the late case that Sir Leicester has come from the library to my Lady's room expressly to read them aloud. "The man who wrote this article," he observes by way of preface, "has a well-balanced mind."

The man's mind is not so well balanced but that he bores my Lady, who, after a languid effort to listen, or rather a languid resignation of herself to a show of listening, becomes distraught, and falls into a contemplation of the fire as if it were her fire at Chesney Wold, and she had never left it. Sir Leicester, quite unconscious, reads on through his double eye-glass, occasionally stopping to remove his glass and express approval as "Very true indeed," "Very properly put," "I have frequently made the same remark myself," invariably losing his place after each observation, and going up and down the column to find it again.

Sir Leicester is reading, with infinite gravity and state, when the door opens, and the Mercury in powder makes this strange announcement:

"The young man, my lady, of the name of Guppy."

Sir Leicester pauses, stares. Looking round, he beholds the young man of the name of Guppy, much discomfited, and not presenting a very impressive letter of introduction in his manner and appearance.

"Pray," says Sir Leicester to Mercury, "what do you mean by announcing with this abruptness a young man of the name of Guppy?"

"I beg your pardon, Sir Leicester, but my lady said she would see the young man whenever he called. I was not aware that you were here, Sir Leicester."

"It's quite right. I gave him those directions," says my Lady. "Let the young man wait."

"By no means, my lady. Since he has your orders to come, I will not interrupt you." Sir Leicester in his gallantry retires, rather declining to accept a bow from the young man as he goes out, and majestically supposing him to be some shoemaker.

Lady Dedlock looks imperiously at her visitor, when the servant has left the room, casting her eyes over him from head to foot. She suffers him to stand by the door, and asks him what he wants.

"That your ladyship would have the kindness to oblige me with a little conversation," returns Mr. Guppy, embarrassed.

"You are, of course, the person who has written me so many letters?"

"Several, your ladyship. Several, before your ladyship condescended to favour me with an answer."

"And could you not take the same means of rendering a conversation unnecessary? Can you not still?" Mr. Guppy screws his mouth into a silent "No!" and shakes his head. "You have been strangely importunate. If it should appear, after all, that what you have to say does not concern me—and I don't know how it can, and don't expect that it will—you will allow me to cut you short with but little ceremony. Say what you have to say, if you please."

My Lady, with a careless toss of her screen, turns herself towards the fire again, sitting almost with her back to the young man of the name of Guppy.

"With your ladyship's permission, then," says the young man, "I will now enter on my business. Hem! I am, as I told your ladyship in my first letter, in the law. Being in the law, I have learnt the habit of not committing myself in writing, and therefore I did not mention to your ladyship the name of the firm with which I am connected, and in which my standing—and I may add income—is tolerably good. I may now state to your ladyship, in confidence, that the name of that firm is Kenge and Carboy, of Lincoln's Inn, which may not be altogether unknown to your ladyship in connexion with the case in Chancery of Jarndyce and Jarndyce."

My Lady's figure begins to be expressive of some attention. She has ceased to toss the screen, and holds it as if she were listening.

"Now I may say to your ladyship at once," says Mr. Guppy, a little emboldened, "it is no matter arising out of Jarndyce and Jarndyce that made me so desirous to speak to your ladyship, which conduct I have no doubt did appear, and does appear, obtrusive—in fact, almost blackguardly." After waiting for a moment to receive some assurance to the contrary, and not receiving any, Mr. Guppy proceeds. "If it had been Jarndyce and Jarndyce, I should have gone at once to your ladyship's solicitor, Mr. Tulkinghorn of the Fields."

My Lady turns a little round, and says, "You had better sit down."

"Thank your ladyship." Mr. Guppy does so. "Now, your ladyship"—Mr. Guppy refers to a little slip of paper on which he has made small notes of his line of argument, and which seems to involve him in the

densest obscurity whenever he looks at it—"I—oh yes!—I place myself
entirely in your ladyship's hands. If your ladyship was to make any complaint to Kenge and Carboy, or to Mr. Tulkinghorn, of the present visit,
I should be placed in a very disagreeable situation. That I openly admit.
Consequently, I rely upon your ladyship's honour."

My Lady, with a disdainful gesture of the hand that holds the screen,
assures him of his being worth no complaint from her.

"Thank your ladyship," says Mr. Guppy, "quite satisfactory. Now—I
—dash it!—The fact is that I put down a head or two here of the order
of the points I thought of touching upon, and they're written short, and
I can't quite make out what they mean. If your ladyship will excuse me
taking it to the window half a moment, I—"

Mr. Guppy, going to the window, murmurs, growing warm and red,
and holding the slip of paper now close to his eyes, now a long way off,
"C. S. What's C. S. for? Oh! 'E. S.!' Oh, I know! Yes, to be sure!" And
comes back enlightened.

"I am not aware," says Mr. Guppy, standing midway between my
Lady and his chair, "whether your ladyship ever happened to hear of,
or to see, a young lady of the name of Miss Esther Summerson."

My Lady's eyes look at him full. "I saw a young lady of that name not long ago. This past autumn."

"Now did it strike your ladyship that she was like anybody?" asks Mr. Guppy.

My Lady removes her eyes from him no more.

"No."

"Not like your ladyship's family?"

"No."

"I think your ladyship," says Mr. Guppy, "can hardly remember Miss Summerson's face?"

"I remember the young lady very well. What has this to do with me?"

"Your ladyship, I do assure you that, having Miss Summerson's image imprinted on my 'art—which I mention in confidence—I found, when I had the honour of going over your ladyship's mansion of Chesney Wold, while on a short out in the county of Lincolnshire with a friend, such a resemblance between Miss Esther Summerson and your ladyship's own portrait that it completely knocked me over, so much so that I didn't at the moment even know what it *was* that knocked me over. And now I have the honour of beholding your ladyship near, it's really more surprising than I thought it."

Young man of the name of Guppy! There have been times, when ladies lived in strongholds and had unscrupulous attendants within call, when that poor life of yours would not have been worth a minute's purchase with those beautiful eyes looking at you as they look at this moment. My Lady, slowly using her little hand-screen as a fan, asks him again what he supposes that his taste for likenesses has to do with her.

"Your ladyship," replies Mr. Guppy, again referring to his paper. "I am coming to that. Dash these notes! Oh! 'Mrs. Chadband.' Yes." Mr. Guppy draws his chair a little forward, and seats himself again. My Lady reclines in her chair composedly, though with a trifle less of graceful ease than usual, perhaps, and never falters in her steady gaze. "A—stop a minute, though!" Mr. Guppy refers again. "E. S. twice? Oh yes, yes I see my way now, right on."

Rolling up the slip of paper as an instrument to point his speech with, Mr. Guppy proceeds.

"Your ladyship, there is a mystery about Miss Esther Summerson's birth and bringing up. I know that fact in the way of my profession at Kenge and Carboy's. Now as I have already mentioned to your ladyship, Miss Summerson's image is imprinted on my 'art. If I could clear this mystery for her, or prove her to be well related, or find that having the honour to be a remote branch of your ladyship's family she had a right to be made a party in Jarndyce and Jarndyce, why, I might make a sort of a claim upon Miss Summerson to look with an eye of more decided favour on my proposals than she has exactly done as yet. In fact, as yet she hasn't favoured them at all."

A kind of angry smile just dawns upon my Lady's face.

"Now it's a very singular circumstance, your ladyship," says Mr. Guppy, "though one of those circumstances that do fall in the way of us professional men—which I may call myself, for though not admitted, yet I have had a present of my articles made to me by Kenge and Carboy —that I have encountered the person who lived as servant with the lady who brought Miss Summerson up before Mr. Jarndyce took charge of her. That lady was a Miss Barbary, your ladyship."

Is the dead colour on my Lady's face reflected from the screen, which has a green silk ground and which she holds in her raised hand as if she had forgotten it, or is it a dreadful paleness that has fallen on her?

"Did your ladyship," says Mr. Guppy, "ever happen to hear of Miss Barbary?"

"I don't know. I think so. Yes."

"Was Miss Barbary at all connected with your ladyship's family?"

My lady's lips move, but they utter nothing. She shakes her head.

"Not connected?" says Mr. Guppy. "Oh! Not to your ladyship's knowledge, perhaps! Ah! But might be? Yes." After each of these interrogatories, she has inclined her head. "Very good! Now this Miss Barbary was extremely close, and my witness never had an idea whether she possessed a single relative. On one occasion, and only one, she seems to have been confidential to my witness, on a single point, and she then told her that the little girl's real name was not Esther Summerson, but Esther Hawdon."

"My God!"

Mr. Guppy stares. Lady Dedlock sits before him, looking him through with the same dark shade upon her face, in the same attitude even to the holding of the screen, with her lips a little apart, her brow a little contracted, but, for the moment, dead. He sees her consciousness return, sees a tremor pass across her frame like a ripple over water, sees her lips shake, sees her compose them by a great effort, sees her force herself back to the knowledge of his presence, and of what he has said. All this so quickly that her exclamation and her dead condition seem to have passed away like the features of those long-preserved dead bodies sometimes opened up in tombs, which, struck by the air like lightning, vanish in a breath.

"Your ladyship is acquainted with the name of Hawdon?"

"I have heard it before."

"Name of any collateral, or remote, branch of your ladyship's family?"

"No."

"Now, your ladyship," says Mr. Guppy, "I come to the last point of the case, so far as I have got it up. It's going on, and I shall gather it up closer and closer as it goes on. Your ladyship must know—if your ladyship don't happen, by any chance, to know already—that there was found dead at the house of a person named Krook, near Chancery Lane, some time ago, a law-writer in great distress. Upon which law-writer there was an inquest, and which law-writer was an anonymous character, his name being unknown. But, your ladyship, I have discovered very lately that that law-writer's name was Hawdon."

"And what is *that* to me?"

"Ay, your ladyship, that's the question! Now, your ladyship, a queer thing happened after that man's death. A lady started up—a disguised lady, your ladyship—who went to look at the scene of action, and went to look at his grave. She hired a crossing-sweeping boy to show it her. If your ladyship would wish to have the boy produced in corroboration of this statement, I can lay my hand upon him at any time."

The wretched boy is nothing to my Lady, and she does *not* wish to have him produced.

"Oh, I assure your ladyship it's a very queer start indeed," says Mr. Guppy. "If you was to hear him tell about the rings that sparkled on her fingers when she took her glove off, you'd think it quite romantic."

There are diamonds glittering on the hand that holds the screen. My Lady trifles with the screen, and makes them glitter more, with that expression which in other times might have been so dangerous to the young man of the name of Guppy.

"It was supposed, your ladyship, that he left no rag or scrap behind him by which he could be possibly identified. But he did. He left a bundle of old letters." The screen still goes, as before. All this time, her eyes never once release him. "They were taken and secreted. And to-morrow night, your ladyship, they will come into my possession."

"Still I ask you, what is this to me?"

"Your ladyship, I conclude with that." Mr. Guppy rises. "If you think there's enough, in this chain of circumstances put together—in the undoubted strong likeness of this young lady to your ladyship, which is a positive fact for a jury; in her having been brought up by Miss Barbary; in Miss Barbary stating Miss Summerson's real name to be Hawdon; in your ladyship's knowing both these names *very well;* and in Hawdon's dying as he did—to give your ladyship a family interest in going further into the case, I will bring these papers here. I don't know what they are, except that they are old letters; I have never had them in my possession yet. I will bring those papers here as soon as I get them, and go over them for the first time with your ladyship. I have told your ladyship my object. I have told your ladyship that I should be placed in a very disagreeable situation if any complaint was made; and all is in strict confidence."

"You may bring the letters," says my Lady, "if you choose."

"Your ladyship is not very encouraging, upon my word and honour," says Mr. Guppy, a little injured.

"You may bring the letters," she repeats, in the same tone, "if you— please."

"It shall be done. I wish your ladyship good-day."

On a table near her is a rich bauble of a casket, barred and clasped like an old strong chest. She, looking at him still, takes it to her and unlocks it.

"Oh! I assure your ladyship I am not actuated by any motives of that sort," says Mr. Guppy; "and I couldn't accept anything of the kind. I wish your ladyship good-day, and am much obliged to you all the same."

So the young man makes his bow, and goes downstairs, where the supercilious Mercury does not consider himself called upon to leave his Olympus by the hall-fire to let the young man out.

As Sir Leicester basks in his library, and dozes over his newspaper, is there no influence in the house to startle him—not to say to make the very trees at Chesney Wold fling up their knotted arms, the very portraits frown, the very armour stir?

No. Words, sobs, and cries are but air; and air is so shut in and shut out throughout the house in town that sounds need be uttered trumpet-tongued indeed by my Lady in her chamber to carry any faint vibration to Sir Leicester's ears. And yet this cry is in the house, going upward from a wild figure on its knees.

"Oh my child, my child! Not dead in the first hours of her life, as my cruel sister told me, but sternly nurtured by her, after she had renounced me and my name! Oh my child, oh my child!"

## CHAPTER 30

*Esther's Narrative*

RICHARD had been gone away some time when a visitor came to pass a few days with us. It was an elderly lady. It was Mrs. Woodcourt, who, having come from Wales to stay with Mrs. Bayham Badger, and having written to my guardian, "by her son Allan's desire," to report that she had heard from him and that he was well, "and sent his kind remembrances to all of us," had been invited by my guardian to make a visit to Bleak House. She stayed with us nearly three weeks. She took very kindly to me, and was extremely confidential, so much so that sometimes she almost made me uncomfortable.

She was such a sharp little lady, and used to sit, with her hands folded in each other, looking so very watchful while she talked to me, that perhaps I found that rather irksome. Or perhaps it was her being so upright and trim, though I don't think it was that, because I thought that quaintly pleasant. Nor can it have been the general expression of her face, which was very sparkling and pretty for an old lady. I don't know what it was. Or at least if I do now, I thought I did not then. Or at least—but it don't matter.

Of a night when I was going upstairs to bed she would invite me into her room, where she sat before the fire in a great chair, and, dear me, she would tell me about Morgan ap Kerrig until I was quite low-spirited! Sometimes she recited a few verses from Crumlinwallinwer and the Mewlinnwillinwodd (if those are the right names, which I dare say they are not), and would become quite fiery with the sentiments they expressed. Though I never knew what they were (being in Welsh), further than that they were highly eulogistic of the lineage of Morgan ap Kerrig.

"So, Miss Summerson," she would say to me with stately triumph, "this you see, is the fortune inherited by my son. Wherever my son goes, he can claim kindred with Ap Kerrig. He may not have money, but he always has what is much better—family, my dear."

I had my doubts of their caring so very much for Morgan ap Kerrig in India and China, but of course I never expressed them. I used to say it was a great thing to be so highly connected.

"It *is*, my dear, a great thing," Mrs. Woodcourt would reply. "It has its disadvantages; my son's choice of a wife, for instance, is limited by it, but the matrimonial choice of the Royal family is limited in much the same manner."

Then she would pat me on the arm and smooth my dress, as much as to assure me that she had a good opinion of me, the distance between us notwithstanding.

"Poor Mr. Woodcourt, my dear," she would say, and always with some emotion, "was descended from a great Highland family, the Mac-Coorts of MacCoort. He served his king and country as an officer in the Royal Highlanders, and he died on the field. My son is one of the last representatives of two old families. With the blessing of Heaven he will set them up again, and unite them with another old family."

It was in vain for me to try to change the subject, as I used to try—only for the sake of novelty, or perhaps because—but I need not be so particular. Mrs. Woodcourt never would let me change it.

"My dear," she said one night, "you have so much sense, and you look at the world in a quiet manner so superior to your time of life, that it is a comfort to me to talk to you about these family matters of mine. You don't know much of my son, my dear, but you know enough of him, I dare say, to recollect him?"

"Yes, ma'am. I recollect him."

"Yes, my dear. Now, my dear, I think you are a judge of character, and I should like to have your opinion of him."

"Oh Mrs. Woodcourt," said I, "that is so difficult!"

"Why is it so difficult, my dear?" she returned. "I don't see it myself."

"To give an opinion—"

"On so slight an acquaintance, my dear. *That's* true."

I didn't mean that, because Mr. Woodcourt had been at our house a good deal altogether, and had become quite intimate with my guardian. I said so, and added that he seemed to be very clever in his profession— we thought—and that his kindness and gentleness to Miss Flite were above all praise.

"You do him justice!" said Mrs. Woodcourt, pressing my hand. "You define him exactly. Allan is a dear fellow, and in his profession faultless. I say it, though I am his mother. Still, I must confess he is not without faults, love."

"None of us are," said I.

"Ah! But his really are faults that he might correct, and ought to correct," returned the sharp old lady, sharply shaking her head. "I am so much attached to you that I may confide in you, my dear, as a third party wholly disinterested, that he is fickleness itself."

I said I should have thought it hardly possible that he could have been otherwise than constant to his profession, and zealous in the pursuit of it, judging from the reputation he had earned.

"You are right again, my dear," the old lady retorted, "but I don't refer to his profession, look you. I refer, my dear, to his social conduct. He is always paying trivial attentions to young ladies, and always has been, ever since he was eighteen. Now, my dear, he has never really cared for any one of them, and has never meant in doing this to do any harm, or to express anything but politeness and good nature. Still, it's not right, you know, is it?"

"No," said I, as she seemed to wait for me.

"And it might lead to mistaken notions, you see, my dear. Therefore I have told him, many times, that he really should be more careful, both in justice to himself and in justice to others. And he has always said, 'Mother, I will be; but you know me better than anybody else does, and you know I mean no harm—in short, mean nothing.' All of which is very true, my dear, but is no justification. However, as he is now gone so far away, and for an indefinite time, and as he will have good opportunities and introductions, we may consider this past and gone. And you, my dear," said the old lady, who was now all nods and smiles, "regarding your dear self, my love?"

"Me, Mrs. Woodcourt?"

"Not to be always selfish, talking of my son, who has gone to seek his fortune, and to find a wife—when do you mean to seek *your* fortune, and to find a husband, Miss Summerson? Hey, look you! Now you blush!"

I don't think I did blush—at all events, it was not important if I did—and I said my present fortune perfectly contented me, and I had no wish to change it.

"Shall I tell you what I always think of you, and the fortune yet to come for you, my love?" said Mrs. Woodcourt.

"If you believe you are a good prophet," said I.

"Why then, it is that you will marry some one very rich and very worthy, much older—five-and-twenty years, perhaps—than yourself. And you will be an excellent wife, and much beloved, and very happy."

"That is a good fortune," said I. "But why is it to be mine?"

"My dear," she returned, "there's suitability in it—you are so busy, and so neat, and so peculiarly situated altogether, that there's suitability in it, and it will come to pass. And nobody, my love, will congratulate you more sincerely on such a marriage than I shall."

It was curious that this should make me uncomfortable, but I think it did. I know it did. It made me for some part of that night uncomfortable. I was so ashamed of my folly that I did not like to confess it even to Ada, and that made me more uncomfortable still. I would have given anything not to have been so much in the bright old lady's confidence, if I could have possibly declined it. It gave me the most inconsistent opinions of her. At one time I thought she was a story-teller, and at another time that she was the pink of truth. Now I suspected that she was very cunning; next moment, I believed her honest Welsh heart to be perfectly innocent and simple. And, after all, what did it matter to me, and why did it matter to me? Why could not I, going up to bed with my basket of keys, stop to sit down by her fire, and not trouble myself about the harmless things she said to me? Impelled towards her, as I certainly was, for I was very anxious that she should like me, and was very glad indeed that she did, why should I harp afterwards, with actual distress and pain, on every word she said, and weigh it over and over again in twenty scales? Why was it so worrying to me to have her in our house, and confidential to me every night, when I yet felt it was better and safer, somehow, that she should be there than anywhere else? There were perplexities and contradictions that I could not account for.

So when Mrs. Woodcourt went away, I was sorry to lose her, but was relieved too. And then Caddy Jellyby came down, and Caddy brought such a packet of domestic news that it gave us abundant occupation.

First, Caddy declared (and would at first declare nothing else) that I was the best adviser that ever was known. This, my pet said, was no news at all; and this, I said, of course, was nonsense. Then Caddy told us that she was going to be married in a month, and that if Ada and I would be her bridesmaids, she was the happiest girl in the world. To be sure, this was news indeed, and I thought we never should have done talking about it, we had so much to say to Caddy, and Caddy had so much to say to us.

It seemed that Caddy's unfortunate Papa had got over his bankruptcy with the general clemency and commiseration of his creditors, and had got rid of his affairs in some blessed manner without succeeding in understanding them; and had given up everything he possessed (which was not worth much, I should think, to judge from the state of the furniture), and had satisfied every one concerned that he could do no more, poor man. So he had been honourably dismissed to "the office," to begin the world again. What he did at the office, I never knew: Caddy said he was a "Custom-House and General Agent."

As soon as her papa had tranquillized his mind by becoming this shorn lamb, and they had removed to a furnished lodging in Hatton Garden, Caddy had brought about a meeting between him and old Mr. Turveydrop; and poor Mr. Jellyby, being very humble and meek, had deferred to Mr. Turveydrop's Deportment so submissively that they had become excellent friends. By degrees, old Mr. Turveydrop, thus familiarized with the idea of his son's marriage, had worked up his parental feelings to the height of contemplating that event as being near at hand, and had given his gracious consent to the young couple commencing housekeeping at the Academy in Newman Street, when they would.

"And your papa, Caddy. What did he say?"

"Oh, poor Pa," said Caddy, "only cried, and said he hoped we might get on better than he and Ma had got on. He didn't say so before Prince, he only said so to me. And he said, 'My poor girl, you have not been very well taught how to make a home for your husband; but unless you mean with all your heart to strive to do it, you had better murder him than marry him—if you really love him.'"

"And how did you reassure him, Caddy?"

"Why, it was very distressing, you know, to see poor Pa so low, and

276 • BLEAK HOUSE

hear him say such terrible things, and I couldn't help crying myself. But I told him that I *did* mean it with all my heart, and that I hoped our house would be a place for him to come and find some comfort in, of an evening. Then I mentioned Peepy's coming to stay with me, and then Pa began to cry again, and said the children were Indians."

"Indians, Caddy?"

"Yes," said Caddy, "Wild Indians. And Pa said" (here she began to sob, poor girl, not at all like the happiest girl in the world) "that he was sensible the best thing that could happen to them was their being all Tomahawked together."

Ada suggested that it was comfortable to know that Mr. Jellyby did not mean these destructive sentiments.

"No, of course I know Pa wouldn't like his family to be weltering in their blood," said Caddy; "but he means that they are very unfortunate in being Ma's children, and that he is very unfortunate in being Ma's husband; and I am sure that's true, though it seems unnatural to say so."

I asked Caddy if Mrs. Jellyby knew that her wedding-day was fixed.

"Oh, you know what Ma is, Esther," she returned. "It's impossible to say whether she knows it or not. She has been told it often enough; and when she is told it, she only gives me a placid look, as if I was I don't know what—a steeple in the distance," said Caddy, with a sudden idea, "and then she shakes her head, and says 'Oh Caddy, Caddy, what a teaze you are!' and goes on with the Borrioboola letters."

"And about your wardrobe, Caddy?" said I.

"Well, my dear Esther," she returned, drying her eyes, "I must do the best I can, and trust to my dear Prince never to have an unkind remembrance of my coming so shabbily to him. If the question concerned an outfit for Borrioboola, Ma would know all about it, and would be quite excited. Being what it is, she neither knows nor cares."

Caddy was not at all deficient in natural affection for her mother, but mentioned this with tears, as an undeniable fact—which I am afraid it was. We were sorry for the poor dear girl, and found so much to admire in the good disposition which had survived under such discouragement that we both at once (I mean Ada and I) proposed a little scheme that made her perfectly joyful. This was her staying with us for three weeks, my staying with her for one, and our all three contriving and cutting out, and repairing, and sewing, and saving, and doing the very best we could think of to make the most of her stock. My guardian being as pleased with the idea as Caddy was, we took her home next day to arrange the matter; and brought her out again in triumph, with her boxes, and all the purchases that could be squeezed out of a ten-pound note, which Mr. Jellyby gave her. What my guardian would not have given her, if we had encouraged him, it would be difficult to say, but we thought it right to compound for no more than her wedding-dress and bonnet. He agreed to this compromise, and if Caddy had ever been happy in her life, she was happy when we sat down to work.

She was clumsy enough with her needle, poor girl, and pricked her fingers as much as she had been used to ink them. She could not help reddening a little, now and then—partly with the smart, and partly with vexation at being able to do no better—but she soon got over that, and began to improve rapidly. So, day after day, she, and my darling, and my little maid Charley, and a milliner out of the town, and I sat hard at work, as pleasantly as possible.

Over and above this, Caddy was very anxious "to learn housekeeping," as she said. Now, mercy upon us! the idea of her learning housekeeping of a person of my vast experience was such a joke that I laughed, and coloured up, when she proposed it. However, I said, "Caddy, I am sure you are very welcome to learn anything that you can learn of *me,* my dear"; and I showed her all my books and methods, and all my fidgety ways. You would have supposed that I was showing her some wonderful inventions, by her study of them; and if you had seen her, whenever I jingled my housekeeping keys, get up and attend me, certainly you might have thought that there never was a greater impostor than I, with a blinder follower than Caddy Jellyby.

So, what with working and housekeeping, and lessons to Charley, and backgammon in the evening with my guardian, and duets with Ada, the three weeks slipped fast away. Then I went home with Caddy, to see what could be done there, and Ada and Charley remained behind to take care of my guardian.

When I say I went home with Caddy, I mean to the furnished lodging in Hatton Garden. We went to Newman Street two or three times, where preparations were in progress—a good many, I observed, for enhancing the comforts of old Mr. Turveydrop, and a few for putting the newly married couple away cheaply at the top of the house—but our great point was to make the furnished lodging decent for the wedding-breakfast, and to imbue Mrs. Jellyby beforehand with some faint sense of the occasion.

The latter was the more difficult thing of the two, because Mrs. Jellyby and an unwholesome boy occupied the front sitting-room, and it was littered down with waste paper and Borrioboolan documents. Mrs. Jellyby sat there all day, drinking strong coffee, dictating, and holding Borrioboolan interviews by appointment. The unwholesome boy took his meals out of the house. When Mr. Jellyby came home, he usually groaned and went down into the kitchen. There he got something to eat, if the servant would give him anything, and then, feeling that he was in the way, went out and walked about Hatton Garden in the wet. The poor children scrambled up and tumbled down the house, as they had always been accustomed to do.

The production of these devoted little sacrifices, in any presentable condition, being quite out of the question at a week's notice, I proposed to Caddy that we should make them as happy as we could on her marriage morning in the attic where they all slept, and should confine our greatest efforts to her mama and her mama's room, and a clean breakfast. In truth Mrs. Jellyby required a good deal of attention, her hair looking like the mane of a dustman's horse. Thinking that the display of Caddy's wardrobe would be the best means of approaching the subject, I invited Mrs. Jellyby to come and look at it spread out on Caddy's bed, in the evening after the unwholesome boy was gone.

"My dear Miss Summerson," said she, rising from her desk, with her usual sweetness of temper, "these are really ridiculous preparations, though your assisting them is a proof of your kindness. There is something so inexpressibly absurd to me in the idea of Caddy being married! Oh Caddy, you silly, silly, silly puss!"

She came upstairs with us notwithstanding, and looked at the clothes in her customary far-off manner. They suggested one distinct idea to her; for she said, with her placid smile, and shaking her head, "My good Miss Summerson, at half the cost this weak child might have been equipped for Africa!"

On our going downstairs again, Mrs. Jellyby asked me whether this troublesome business was really to take place next Wednesday. And on my replying yes, she said, "Will my room be required, my dear Miss Summerson? For it's quite impossible that I can put my papers away." I took the liberty of saying that the room would certainly be wanted, and that I thought we must put the papers away somewhere. "Well, my dear Miss Summerson," said Mrs. Jellyby, "you know best, I dare say. But by obliging me to employ a boy, Caddy has embarrassed me to that extent, overwhelmed as I am with public business, that I don't know which way to turn. We have a Ramification meeting, too, on Wednesday afternoon, and the inconvenience is very serious."

"It is not likely to occur again," said I, smiling. "Caddy will be married but once, probably."

"That's true," Mrs. Jellyby replied, "that's true, my dear. I suppose we must make the best of it!"

The next question was, how Mrs. Jellyby should be dressed on the occasion. I thought it very curious to see her looking on serenely from her writing-table while Caddy and I discussed it; occasionally shaking her head at us with a half-reproachful smile. The state in which her dresses were, and the extraordinary confusion in which she kept them, added not a little to our difficulty; but at length we devised something not very unlike what a commonplace mother might wear on such an occasion. The abstracted manner in which Mrs. Jellyby would deliver herself up to having this attire tried on by the dressmaker, and the sweetness with which she would then observe to me how sorry she was that I had not turned my thoughts to Africa, were consistent with the rest of her behaviour.

The lodging was rather confined as to space, but I fancied that if Mrs. Jellyby's household had been the only lodgers in St. Paul's or St. Peter's, the sole advantage they would have found in the size of the building would have been its affording a great deal of room to be dirty in. I believe that nothing belonging to the family which it had been possible to break was unbroken at the time; that nothing which it had been possible to spoil in any way was unspoilt; and that no domestic object which was capable of collecting dirt, from a dear child's knee to the door-plate, was without as much dirt as could well accumulate upon it.

Poor Mr. Jellyby, who very seldom spoke, and almost always sat when he was at home with his head against the wall, became interested when he saw that Caddy and I were attempting to establish some order among all this waste and ruin, and took off his coat to help. But such wonderful things came tumbling out of the closets when they were opened—bits of mouldy pie, sour bottles, Mrs. Jellyby's caps, letters, tea, forks, odd boots and shoes of children, firewood, wafers, saucepan-lids, damp sugar in odds and ends of paper bags, footstools, bread, Mrs. Jellyby's bonnets, books with butter sticking to the binding, guttered candle-ends, nutshells, heads and tails of shrimps, dinner-mats, gloves, coffee-grounds, umbrellas—that he looked frightened, and left off again. But he came regularly every evening, and sat without his coat, with his head against the wall, as though he would have helped us if he had known how.

"Poor Pa!" said Caddy to me on the night before the great day, when we really had got things a little to rights. "It seems unkind to leave him, Esther. But what could I do if I stayed! Since I first knew you, I have tidied and tidied over and over again, but it's useless. Ma and Africa, together, upset the whole house directly. We never have a servant who don't drink. Ma's ruinous to everything." Mr. Jellyby could not hear what she said, but he seemed very low indeed, and shed tears, I thought. "My heart aches for him; that it does!" sobbed Caddy. "I can't help thinking tonight, Esther, how dearly I hope to be happy with Prince, and how dearly Pa hoped, I dare say, to be happy with Ma. What a disappointed life!"

"My dear Caddy!" said Mr. Jellyby, looking slowly round from the wall. It was the first time, I think, I ever heard him say three words together.

"Yes, Pa!" cried Caddy, going to him and embracing him affectionately.

"My dear Caddy," said Mr. Jellyby. "Never have—"

"Not Prince, Pa?" faltered Caddy. "Not have Prince?"

"Yes, my dear," said Mr. Jellyby. "Have him, certainly. But, never have—"

I mentioned in my account of our first visit in Thavies Inn that Richard described Mr. Jellyby as frequently opening his mouth after dinner without saying anything. It was a habit of his. He opened his mouth now, a great many times, and shook his head in a melancholy manner.

"What do you wish me not to have? Don't have what, dear Pa?" asked Caddy, coaxing him, with her arms round his neck.

"Never have a Mission, my dear child."

Mr. Jellyby groaned, and laid his head against the wall again, and this was the only time I ever heard him make any approach to expressing his sentiments on the Borrioboolan question. I suppose he had been more talkative and lively once, but he seemed to have been completely exhausted long before I knew him.

I thought Mrs. Jellyby never would have left off serenely looking over her papers, and drinking coffee, that night. It was twelve o'clock before we could obtain possession of the room; and the clearance it required then was so discouraging that Caddy, who was almost tired out, sat down in the middle of the dust and cried. But she soon cheered up, and we did wonders with it before we went to bed.

In the morning it looked, by the aid of a few flowers and a quantity of soap and water, and a little arrangement, quite gay. The plain breakfast made a cheerful show, and Caddy was perfectly charming. But when my darling came, I thought—and I think now—that I never had seen such a dear face as my beautiful pet's.

We made a little feast for the children upstairs, and we put Peepy at the head of the table, and we showed them Caddy in her bridal dress, and they clapped their hands and hurrahed, and Caddy cried to think that she was going away from them, and hugged them over and over again, until we brought Prince up to fetch her away—when, I am sorry to say, Peepy bit him. Then there was old Mr. Turveydrop downstairs, in a state of Deportment not to be expressed, benignly blessing Caddy, and giving my guardian to understand that his son's happiness was his own parental work, and that he sacrificed personal considerations to ensure it. "My dear sir," said Mr. Turveydrop, "these young people will live with me; my house is large enough for their accommodation, and they shall not want the shelter of my roof. I could have wished—you will understand the allusion, Mr. Jarndyce, for you remember my illustrious patron the Prince Regent—I could have wished that my son had married into a family where there was more Deportment, but the will of Heaven be done!"

The guests were few, but were, as one might expect at Mrs. Jellyby's, all devoted to public objects only. A party having less in common with such an occasion could hardly have been got together by any ingenuity. Such a mean mission as the domestic mission was the very last thing to be endured among them. Mrs. Jellyby, all the while, sat smiling at the limited vision that could see anything but Borrioboola-Gha.

But I am anticipating now the purport of our conversation on the ride home, instead of first marrying Caddy. We all went to church, and Mr. Jellyby gave her away. Of the air with which old Mr. Turveydrop, with his hat under his left arm, and his eyes creasing themselves up into his wig, stood, stiff and high-shouldered, behind us bridesmaids during the ceremony, and afterwards saluted us, I could never say enough to do it justice. Mrs. Jellyby, with her calm smile and her bright eyes, looked the least concerned of all the company.

We duly came back to breakfast, and Mrs. Jellyby sat at the head of the table, and Mr. Jellyby at the foot. Caddy had previously stolen upstairs, to hug the children again, and tell them that her name was Turveydrop. But this piece of information, instead of being an agreeable surprise to Peepy, threw him on his back in such transports of kicking grief that I could do nothing on being sent for but accede to the proposal that he should be admitted to the breakfast-table. So he came down, and sat in my lap; and Mrs. Jellyby, after saying, in reference to the state of his pinafore, "Oh you naughty Peepy, what a shocking little pig you are!" was not at all discomposed.

My guardian, with his sweet temper and his quick perception and his amiable face, made something agreeable even out of the ungenial company. None of them seemed able to talk about anything but his, or her, own one subject; and none of them seemed able to talk about even that as part of a world in which there was anything else; but my guardian turned it all to the merry encouragement of Caddy, and the honour of the occasion, and brought us through the breakfast nobly. What we should have done without him, I am afraid to think; for all the company despising the bride and bridegroom, and old Mr. Turveydrop—and old Mr. Turveydrop, in virtue of his Deportment, considering himself vastly superior to all the company—it was a very unpromising case.

At last the time came when poor Caddy was to go, and when all her property was packed on the hired coach and pair that was to take her and her husband to Gravesend. It affected us to see Caddy clinging, then, to her deplorable home, and hanging on her mother's neck with the greatest tenderness.

"I am very sorry I couldn't go on writing from dictation, Ma," sobbed Caddy. "I hope you forgive me now?"

"Oh Caddy, Caddy!" said Mrs. Jellyby. "I have told you over and over again that I have engaged a boy, and there's an end of it."

"You are sure you are not the least angry with me, Ma? Say you are sure before I go away, Ma."

"You foolish Caddy," returned Mrs. Jellyby, "do I look angry, or have I inclination to be angry, or time to be angry? How *can* you?"

"Take a little care of Pa while I am gone, Mama!"

Mrs. Jellyby positively laughed at the fancy. "You romantic child," said she, lightly patting Caddy's back. "Go along. I am excellent friends with you. Now, good-bye, Caddy, and be very happy!"

Then Caddy hung upon her father, and nursed his cheek against hers as if he were some poor dull child in pain. All this took place in the hall. Her father released her, took out his pocket-handkerchief, and sat down on the stairs with his head against the wall. I hope he found some consolation in walls. I almost think he did.

And then Prince took her arm in his, and turned with great emotion and respect to his father, whose Deportment at that moment was overwhelming.

"Thank you over and over again, Father!" said Prince, kissing his hand. "I am very grateful for all your kindness and consideration regarding our marriage, and so, I can assure you, is Caddy."

"Very," sobbed Caddy. "Ve-ry!"

"My dear son," said Mr. Turveydrop, "and dear daughter, I have done my duty. If the spirit of a sainted Wooman hovers above us, and looks down on the occasion, that, and your constant affection, will be my recompense. You will not fail in *your* duty, my son and daughter, I believe?"

"Dear Father, never!" cried Prince.

"Never, never, dear Mr. Turveydrop!" said Caddy.

"This," returned Mr. Turveydrop, "is as it should be. My children, my home is yours, my heart is yours, my all is yours. I will never leave you; nothing but Death shall part us. My dear son, you contemplate an absence of a week, I think?"

"A week, dear Father. We shall return home this day week."

"My dear child," said Mr. Turveydrop, "let me, even under the present exceptional circumstances, recommend strict punctuality. It is highly important to keep the connexion together; and schools, if at all neglected, are apt to take offence."

"This day week, Father, we shall be sure to be home to dinner."

"Good!" said Mr. Turveydrop. "You will find fires, my dear Caroline, in your own room, and dinner prepared in my apartment. Yes, yes, Prince!"—anticipating some self-denying objection on his son's part with a great air. "You and our Caroline will be strange in the upper part of the premises, and will therefore dine that day in my apartment. Now, bless ye!"

They drove away, and whether I wondered most at Mrs. Jellyby or at Mr. Turveydrop, I did not know. Ada and my guardian were in the same condition when we came to talk it over. But before we drove away too, I received a most unexpected and eloquent compliment from Mr. Jellyby. He came up to me in the hall, took both my hands, pressed them earnestly, and opened his mouth twice. I was so sure of his meaning that I said, quite flurried, "You are very welcome, sir. Pray don't mention it!"

"I hope this marriage is for the best, Guardian?" said I, when we three were on our road home.

"I hope it is, little woman. Patience. We shall see."

"Is the wind in the east today?" I ventured to ask him.

He laughed heartily, and answered "No."

"But it must have been this morning, I think," said I.

He answered "No" again; and this time my dear girl confidently answered "No" too, and shook the lovely head which, with its blooming flowers against the golden hair, was like the very spring. "Much *you* know of east winds, my ugly darling," said I, kissing her in my admiration—I couldn't help it.

Well! It was only their love for me, I know very well, and it is a long time ago. I must write it, even if I rub it out again, because it gives me so much pleasure. They said there could be no east wind where Somebody was; they said that wherever Dame Durden went, there was sunshine and summer air.

## CHAPTER 31

*Nurse and Patient*

I HAD not been at home again many days when one evening I went upstairs into my own room to take a peep over Charley's shoulder and see how she was getting on with her copy-book. Writing was a trying business to Charley, who seemed to have no natural power over a pen, but in whose hand every pen appeared to become perversely animated, and to go wrong and crooked, and to stop, and splash, and sidle into corners, like a saddle-donkey. It was very odd to see what old letters Charley's young hand had made, they so wrinkled, and shrivelled, and tottering, it, so plump and round. Yet Charley was uncommonly expert at other things, and had as nimble little fingers as I ever watched.

"Well, Charley," said I, looking over a copy of the letter O in which it was represented as square, triangular, pear-shaped, and collapsed in all kinds of ways, "we are improving. If we only get to make it round, we shall be perfect, Charley."

Then I made one, and Charley made one, and the pen wouldn't join Charley's neatly, but twisted it up into a knot.

"Never mind, Charley. We shall do it in time."

Charley laid down her pen, the copy being finished, opened and shut her cramped little hand, looked gravely at the page, half in pride and half in doubt, and got up, and dropped me a curtsey.

"Thank you, miss. If you please, miss, did you know a poor person of the name of Jenny?"

"A brickmaker's wife, Charley? Yes."

"She came and spoke to me when I was out a little while ago, and said you knew her, miss. She asked me if I wasn't the young lady's little maid—meaning you for the young lady, miss—and I said yes."

"I thought she had left this neighbourhood altogether, Charley."

"So she had, miss, but she's come back again to where she used to live—she and Liz. Did you know another poor person of the name of Liz, miss?"

"I think I do, Charley, though not by name."

"That's what she said!" returned Charley. "They have both come back, miss, and have been tramping high and low. And this poor person came about the house three or four days, hoping to get a glimpse of you, miss—all she wanted, she said—but you were away. That was when she saw me. She saw me a-going about, miss," said Charley, with a short laugh of the greatest delight and pride, "and she thought I looked like your maid!"

"Did she though, really, Charley?"

"Yes, miss!" said Charley, "really and truly." And Charley, with another short laugh of the purest glee, made her eyes very round again, and looked as serious as became my maid. I was never tired of seeing Charley in the full enjoyment of that great dignity.

"And where did you see her, Charley?" said I.

My little maid's countenance fell as she replied, "By the doctor's shop, miss." For Charley wore her black frock yet.

I asked if the brickmaker's wife were ill, but Charley said no, it was some one else. Some in in her cottage who had tramped down to Saint Albans, and was tramping he didn't know where. A poor boy, Charley said. No father, no mother, no any one. "Like as Tom might have been, miss, if Emma and me had died after Father," said Charley, her round eyes filling with tears.

"And she was getting medicine for him, Charley?"

"She said, miss," returned Charley, "how that he had once done as much for her."

My little maid's face was so eager, and her quiet hands were folded so closely in one another as she stood looking at me, that I had no great difficulty in reading her thoughts. "Well, Charley," said I, "it appears to me that you and I can do no better than go round to Jenny's and see what's the matter."

The alacrity with which Charley brought my bonnet and veil and, having dressed me, quaintly pinned herself into her warm shawl and made herself look like a little old woman, sufficiently expressed her readiness. So Charley and I, without saying anything to any one, went out. It was a cold, wild night, and the trees shuddered in the wind. The rain had been thick and heavy all day, and with little intermission for many days. None was falling just then, however. The sky had partly cleared, but was very gloomy—even above us, where a few stars were shining.

I had no thought that night—none, I am quite sure—of what was soon to happen to me. But I have always remembered since that when we had stopped at the garden-gate to look up at the sky, and when we went upon our way, I had for a moment an undefinable impression of myself as being something different from what I then was. I know it was then, and there, that I had it.

It was Saturday night, and most of the people belonging to the place where we were going were drinking elsewhere. We found it quieter than I had previously seen it, though quite as miserable. The kilns were

burning, and a stifling vapour set towards us with a pale-blue glare. We came to the cottage, where there was a feeble candle in the patched window. We tapped at the door, and went in. The mother of the little child who had died was sitting in a chair on one side of the poor fire by the bed; and opposite to her a wretched boy, supported by the chimney-piece, was cowering on the floor. He held under his arm, like a little bundle, a fragment of a fur cap, and as he tried to warm himself he shook until the crazy door and window shook. The place was closer than before, and had an unhealthy and a very peculiar smell.

I had not lifted my veil when I first spoke to the woman, which was at the moment of our going in. The boy staggered up instantly, and stared at me with a remarkable expression of surprise and terror. His action was so quick, and my being the cause of it was so evident, that I stood still instead of advancing nearer.

"I won't go no more to the berryin ground," muttered the boy; "I ain't a-going there, so I tell you!"

I lifted my veil and spoke to the woman. She said to me in a low voice, "Don't mind him, ma'am. He'll soon come back to his head," and said to him, "Jo, Jo, what's the matter?"

"I know wot she's come for!" cried the boy.

"Who?"

"The lady there. She's come to get me to go along with her to the berryin ground. I won't go to the berryin ground. I don't like the name on it. She might go a-berryin *me*." His shivering came on again, and as he leaned against the wall, he shook the hovel.

"He has been talking off and on about such-like all day, ma'am," said Jenny softly. "Why, how you stare! This is *my* lady, Jo."

"Is it?" returned the boy doubtfully, and surveying me with his arm held out above his burning eyes. "She looks to me the t'other one. It ain't the bonnet, nor yet it ain't the gownd, but she looks to me the t'other one."

My little Charley, with her premature experience of illness and trouble, had pulled off her bonnet and shawl, and now went quietly up to him with a chair, and sat him down in it like an old sick-nurse. Except that no such attendant could have shown him Charley's youthful face, which seemed to engage his confidence.

"I say!" said the boy. "*You* tell me. Ain't the lady the t'other lady?"

Charley shook her head as she methodically drew his rags about him and made him as warm as she could.

"Oh!" the boy muttered. "Then I s'pose she ain't."

"I came to see if I could do you any good," said I. "What is the matter with you?"

"I'm a-being froze," returned the boy hoarsely, with his haggard gaze wandering about me, "and then burnt up, and then froze, and then burnt up, ever so many times in a hour. And my head's all sleepy, and all a-going mad-like—and I'm so dry—and my bones isn't half so much bones as pain."

"When did he come here?" I asked the woman.

"This morning, ma'am, I found him at the corner of the town. I had known him up in London yonder. Hadn't I, Jo?"

"Tom-all-Alone's," the boy replied.

Whenever he fixed his attention, or his eyes, it was only for a very little while. He soon began to droop his head again, and roll it heavily, and speak as if he were half-awake.

"When did he come from London?" I asked.

"I come from London yes'day," said the boy himself, now flushed and hot. "I'm a-going somewheres."

"Where is he going?" I asked.

"Somewheres," repeated the boy, in a louder tone. "I have been moved on, and moved on, more nor ever I was afore, since the t'other one give me the sov'ring. Mrs. Snagsby, she's always a-watching, and a-driving of me—what have I done to her?—and they're all a-watching and a-driving of me. Every one of 'em's doing of it, from the time when I don't get up to the time when I don't go to bed. And I'm a-going somewheres. That's where I'm a-going."

"What is to be done with him?" said I, taking the woman aside. "He could not travel in this state, even if he had a purpose, and knew where he was going!"

"I know no more, ma'am, than the dead," she replied, glancing compassionately at him. "Perhaps the dead know better, if they could only tell us. I've kept him here all day for pity's sake, and I've given him broth and physic, and Liz has gone to try if any one will take him in (here's my pretty in the bed—her child, but I call it mine); but I can't keep him long, for if my husband was to come home and find him here, he'd be rough in putting him out, and might do him a hurt. Hark! Here comes Liz back!"

The other woman came hurriedly in as she spoke, and the boy got up with a half-obscured sense that he was expected to be going. When the little child awoke, and when and how Charley got at it, took it out of bed, and began to walk about hushing it, I don't know.

The friend had been here and there, and had been played about from hand to hand, and had come back as she went. At first it was too early for the boy to be received into the proper refuge, and at last it was too late. One official sent her to another, and the other sent her back again to the first, and so backward and forward; until it appeared to me as if both must have been appointed for their skill in evading their duties instead of performing them. And now she said, breathing quickly, for she had been running, and was frightened too, "Jenny, your master's on the road home, and mine's not far behind, and the Lord help the boy, for we can do no more for him!" They put a few halfpence together and hurried them into his hand, and so, in an oblivious, half-thankful, half-insensible way, he shuffled out of the house.

"Give me the child, my dear!" said its mother to Charley, "and thank you kindly too! Jenny woman dear, good-night! Young lady, if my master don't fall out with me, I'll look down by the kiln by and by, where the boy will be most-like, and again in the morning!" She hurried off, and presently we passed her hushing and singing to her child at her own door, and looking anxiously along the road for her drunken husband.

I was afraid of staying then to speak to either woman, lest I should bring her into trouble. But I said to Charley that we must not leave the boy to die. Charley, who knew what to do much better than I did, and whose quickness equalled her presence of mind, glided on before me, and presently we came up with Jo, just short of the brick-kiln.

I think he must have begun his journey with some small bundle under his arm, and must have had it stolen, or lost it. For he still carried his wretched fragment of fur cap like a bundle, though he went bare-headed through the rain, which now fell fast. He stopped when we called to him, and again showed a dread of me when I came up, standing with his lustrous eyes fixed upon me, and even arrested in his shivering fit. I asked him to come with us, and we would take care that he had some shelter for the night.

"I don't want no shelter," he said. "I can lay amongst the warm bricks."

"But don't you know that people die there?" replied Charley.

"They dies everywheres," said the boy. "They dies in their lodgings—

she knows where, I showed her—and they dies down in Tom-all-Alone's in heaps. They dies more than they lives, according to what *I* see." Then he hoarsely whispered to Charley, "If she ain't the t'other one, she ain't the forrener. Is there *three* of 'em, then?"

Charley looked at me, a little frightened. I felt half-frightened at myself. But he turned and followed when I beckoned to him; and finding that he acknowledged that influence in me, I led the way straight home. It was not far, only at the summit of the hill. I doubted if we should have got home without assistance, the boy's steps were so uncertain. He made no complaint, and was strangely unconcerned about himself, if I may say so strange a thing.

Leaving him in the hall for a moment, shrunk into the corner of the window-seat and staring with an indifference that scarcely could be called wonder at the comfort and brightness about him, I went into the drawing-room to speak to my guardian. He came out with me directly, to look at the boy. The servants had gathered in the hall, too, and he shivered in the window-seat like some wounded animal that had been found in a ditch.

"This is a sorrowful case," said my guardian, to whom I hastily explained the unavailing efforts of the two women. "Of course, little woman, I can ensure his admission into the proper place by merely going there to enforce it, though it's a bad state of things when, in his condition, that is necessary. But it's growing late, and is a very bad night, and the boy is worn-out already. There is a bed in the wholesome loft-room by the stable; we had better keep him there till morning, when he can be wrapped up and removed. We'll do that."

We explained to Jo what we proposed to do, which Charley explained to him again, and which he received with the languid unconcern I had already noticed, wearily looking on at what was done as if it were for somebody else. The servants compassionating his miserable state, and being very anxious to help, we soon got the loft-room ready, and some of the men about the house carried him across the wet yard, well wrapped up. It was pleasant to observe how kind they were to him, and how there appeared to be a general impression among them that frequently calling him "old chap" was likely to revive his spirits. Charley directed the operations, and went to and fro between the loft-room and the house with such little stimulants and comforts as we thought it safe to give him. My guardian himself saw him before he was left for the night, and reported to me—when he returned to the Growlery to write a letter on the boy's behalf, which a messenger was charged to deliver at daylight in the morning—that he seemed easier, and inclined to sleep. They had fastened his door on the outside, he said, in case of his being delirious, but had so arranged that he could not make any noise without being heard. Charley's last report was that the boy was quiet. I could see from my window the lantern they had left him burning quietly; and I went to bed very happy to think that he was sheltered.

There was more movement and more talking than usual a little before daybreak, and it woke me. As I was dressing, I looked out of my window and asked one of our men who had been among the active sympathizers last night whether there was anything wrong about the house. The lantern was still burning in the loft-window.

"It's the boy, miss," said he.

"Is he worse?" I inquired.

"Gone, miss. Gone clean off."

At what time of the night he had gone, or how, or why, it seemed hopeless ever to divine. The door remaining as it had been left, and the lantern standing in the window, it could only be supposed that he had got out by a trap in the floor which communicated with an empty cart-house below. But he had shut it down again, if that were so. Nothing of any kind was missing. On this fact being clearly ascertained, we all yielded to the painful belief that delirium had come upon him in the night, and that, allured by some imaginary object, or pursued by some imaginary horror, he had strayed away in that worse than helpless state.

Every possible inquiry was made, and every place was searched. The brick-kilns were examined, the cottages were visited, the two women were particularly questioned, but they knew nothing of him, and nobody could doubt that their wonder was genuine. The weather had for some time been too wet, and the night itself had been too wet, to admit of any tracing by footsteps. Hedge and ditch, and wall, and rick and stack, were examined by our men for a long distance round, lest the boy should be lying in such a place insensible or dead; but nothing was seen to indicate that he had ever been near. From the time when he was left in the loft-room, he vanished. The search continued for five days. I do not mean that it ceased, even then, but that my attention was then diverted into a current very memorable to me.

As Charley was at her writing again in my room in the evening, and as I sat opposite to her at work, I felt the table tremble. Looking up, I saw my little maid shivering from head to foot.

"Charley," said I, "are you so cold?"

"I think I am, miss," she replied. "I don't know what it is. I can't hold myself still. I felt so yesterday, at about this same time, miss. Don't be uneasy, I think I'm ill."

I heard Ada's voice outside, and I hurried to the door of communication between my room and our pretty sitting-room and locked it. Just in time, for she tapped at it while my hand was yet upon the key. Ada called to me to let her in; but I said, "Not now, my dearest. Go away.

There's nothing the matter. I will come to you presently." Ah, it was a long, long time before my darling girl and I were companions again!

Charley fell ill. In twelve hours she was very ill. I moved her to my room and laid her in my bed, and sat down quietly to nurse her. I told my guardian all about it, and why I felt it was necessary that I should seclude myself, and my reason for not seeing my darling, above all. At first she came very often to the door, and called to me, and even re-proached me with sobs and tears; but I wrote her a long letter, saying that she made me anxious and unhappy, and imploring her, as she loved me, and wished my mind to be at peace, to come no nearer than the garden. After that, she came beneath the window even oftener than she had come to the door; and if I had learnt to love her dear sweet voice before when we were hardly ever apart, how did I learn to love it then, when I stood behind the window-curtain listening and replying, but not so much as looking out! How did I learn to love it afterwards, when the harder time came!

They put a bed for me in our sitting-room, and by keeping the door wide open, I turned the two rooms into one, now that Ada had vacated that part of the house, and kept them always fresh and airy. There was not a servant in or about the house but was so good that they would all most gladly have come to me at any hour of the day or night, without the least fear or unwillingness; but I thought it best to choose one worthy woman, who was never to see Ada, and whom I could trust to come and go with all precaution. Through her means, I wanted for nothing in the way of attendance, any more than in any other respect.

And thus poor Charley sickened and grew worse, and fell into heavy danger of death, and lay severely ill for many a long round of day and night. So patient she was, so uncomplaining, and inspired by such a gentle fortitude, that very often as I sat by Charley, holding her head in my arms—repose would come to her so when it would come to her in no other attitude—I silently prayed to our Father in Heaven that I might not forget the lesson which this little sister taught me.

I was very sorrowful to think that Charley's pretty looks would change and be disfigured, even if she recovered—she was such a child with her dimpled face—but that thought was, for the greater part, lost in her greater peril. When she was at the worst, and her mind rambled again to the cares of her father's sick-bed, and the little children, she still knew me so far as that she would be quiet in my arms when she could lie quiet nowhere else, and murmur out the wanderings of her mind less rest-lessly. At those times I used to think, how should I ever tell the two remaining babies that the baby who had learned of her faithful heart to be a mother to them in their need was dead!

There were other times when Charley knew me well, and talked to me, telling me that she sent her love to Tom and Emma, and that she was sure Tom would grow up to be a good man. But of all the various times there were in Charley's illness, there was not one when she lost the gentle qualities I have spoken of.

And Charley did not die. She flutteringly and slowly turned the dangerous point, after long lingering there, and then began to mend. The hope that never had been given, from the first, of Charley being in outward appearance Charley any more, soon began to be encouraged; and even that prospered, and I saw her growing into her old childish likeness again.

It was a great morning when I could tell Ada all this as she stood out in the garden, and it was a great evening when Charley and I at last took tea together in the next room. But on that same evening I felt that I was stricken old.

Happily for both of us, it was not until Charley was safe in bed again, and placidly asleep, that I began to think the contagion of her illness was upon me. I had been able easily to hide what I felt at tea-time, but I was past that already now, and I knew that I was rapidly following in Charley's steps.

I was well enough, however, to be up early in the morning, and to return my darling's cheerful blessing from the garden, and to talk with her as long as usual. But I was not free from an impression that I had been walking about the two rooms in the night a little beside myself, though knowing where I was; and I felt confused at times—with a curious sense of fulness, as if I were becoming too large altogether.

In the evening I was so much worse that I resolved to prepare Charley. With which view, I said, "You're getting quite strong, Charley, are you not?"

"Oh, quite!" said Charley.

"Strong enough to be told a secret, I think, Charley?"

"Quite strong enough for that, miss!" cried Charley. But Charley's face fell in the height of her delight, for she saw the secret in *my* face; and she came out of the great chair, and fell upon my bosom and said, "Oh miss, it's my doing! It's my doing!" and a great deal more, out of the fulness of her grateful heart.

"Now, Charley," said I, after letting her go on for a little while, "if I am to be ill, my great trust, humanly speaking, is in you. And unless you are as quiet and composed for me as you always were for yourself, you can never fulfil it, Charley."

"If you'll let me cry a little longer, miss," said Charley. "Oh my dear, my dear! if you'll only let me cry a little longer, Oh my dear!"—how affectionately and devotedly she poured this out, as she clung to my neck, I never can remember without tears—"I'll be good." So I let Charley cry a little longer, and it did us both good.

"Trust in me now, if you please, miss," said Charley, quietly. "I am listening to everything you say."

"It's very little at present, Charley. I shall tell your doctor tonight that I don't think I am well, and that you are going to nurse me." For that the poor child thanked me with her whole heart. "And in the morning, when you hear Miss Ada in the garden, if I should not be quite able to go to the window-curtain as usual, do you go, Charley, and say I am asleep—that I have rather tired myself, and am asleep. At all times keep the room as I have kept it, Charley, and let no one come."

Charley promised, and I lay down, for I was very heavy. I saw the doctor that night, and asked the favour of him that I wished to ask—relative to his saying nothing of my illness in the house as yet. I have a very indistinct remembrance of that night melting into day, and of day melting into night again; but I was just able on the first morning to get to the window and speak to my darling.

On the second morning I heard her dear voice—oh, how dear now!—outside; and I asked Charley, with some difficulty (speech being painful to me), to go and say I was asleep. I heard her answer softly, "Don't disturb her, Charley, for the world!"

"How does my own Pride look, Charley?" I inquired.

"Disappointed, miss," said Charley, peeping through the curtain.

"But I know she is very beautiful this morning."

"She is indeed, miss," answered Charley, peeping. "Still looking up at the window."

With her blue clear eyes, God bless them, always loveliest when raised like that!

I called Charley to me, and gave her her last charge.

"Now, Charley, when she knows I am ill, she will try to make her way into the room. Keep her out, Charley, if you love me truly, to the last! Charley, if you let her in but once, only to look upon me for one moment as I lie here, I shall die."

"I never will! I never will!" she promised me.

"I believe it, my dear Charley. And now come and sit beside me for a little while, and touch me with your hand. For I cannot see you, Charley, I am blind."

# CHAPTER 32

~~~~~~~~~~~~~~~~~~~~~~~~~~~~~~~~~~~~~~~~~~~~~~

## The Appointed Time

IT is night in Lincoln's Inn and fat candles are snuffed out in offices, and clerks have rattled down the crazy wooden stairs and dispersed. The bell that rings at nine o'clock has ceased its doleful clangour about nothing; the gates are shut; and the night-porter, a solemn warder with a mighty power of sleep, keeps guard in his lodge. In dirty upper casements, here and there, hazy little patches of candle-light reveal where some wise draughtsman and conveyancer yet toils for the entanglement of real estate in meshes of sheepskin, in the average ratio of about a dozen of sheep to an acre of land.

In the neighbouring court, where the Lord Chancellor of the rag and bottle shop dwells, there is a general tendency towards beer and supper. Now there is a sound of putting up shop-shutters in the court, and a smell as of the smoking of pipes; and shooting stars are seen in upper windows, further indicating retirement to rest. Now, too, the policeman begins to push at doors, to try fastenings, to be suspicious of bundles, and to administer his beat on the hypothesis that every one is either robbing or being robbed.

It is a close night, though the damp cold is searching too, and there is a laggard mist a little way up in the air. It is a fine steaming night to turn the slaughter-houses, the unwholesome trades, the sewerage, bad water, and burial-grounds to account, and give the Registrar of Deaths some extra business. It may be something in the air—there is plenty of it—or it may be something in himself, that is in fault, but Mr. Weevle, otherwise Jobling, is very ill at ease. He comes and goes between his own room and the open street-door twenty times an hour. He has been doing so ever since it fell dark. Since the Chancellor shut up his shop, which he did very early tonight, Mr. Weevle has been down and up, and down and up (with a cheap tight velvet skull-cap on his head, making his whiskers look out of all proportion), oftener than before.

It is no phenomenon that Mr. Snagsby should be ill at ease too, for he always is so, more or less, under the oppressive influence of the secret that is upon him. Impelled by the mystery of which he is a partaker and yet in which he is not a sharer, Mr. Snagsby haunts what seems to be its fountain-head—the rag and bottle shop in the court. It has an irresistible attraction for him. Even now, coming round by the Sol's Arms with the intention of passing down the court and out at the Chancery Lane end, Mr. Snagsby approaches.

"What, Mr. Weevle?" says the stationer, stopping to speak. "Are *you* there?"

"Ay!" says Weevle. "Here I am, Mr. Snagsby."

"Airing yourself, as I am doing, before you go to bed?"

"Why, there's not much air to be got here, and what there is, is not very freshening," Weevle answers.

"Very true, sir. Don't you observe," says Mr. Snagsby, pausing to sniff and taste the air a little, "that you're—not to put too fine a point upon it—that you're rather greasy here, sir?"

"Why, I have noticed myself that there is a queer kind of flavour in the place tonight," Mr. Weevle rejoins. "I suppose it's chops at the Sol's Arms."

"Chops, do you think? Oh!—Chops, eh?" Mr. Snagsby sniffs and tastes again. "Well, sir, I suppose it is. But I should say their cook at the Sol wanted a little looking after. She has been burning 'em, sir! And I don't think"—Mr. Snagsby sniffs and tastes again, and then spits and wipes his mouth—"I don't think that they were quite fresh when they were shown the gridiron."

"That's very likely. It's a tainting sort of weather."

"It *is* a tainting sort of weather," says Mr. Snagsby, "and I find it sinking to the spirits."

"By George! I find it gives me the horrors," returns Mr. Weevle.

"Then you see you live in a lonesome way, and in a lonesome room, with a black circumstance hanging over it," says Mr. Snagsby, falling back a step to look up at the house. "I couldn't live in that room alone, as you do, sir. I should get so fidgety and worried of an evening, sometimes, that I should be driven to come to the door and stand here, sooner than sit there. But then it's very true that you didn't see in your room what I saw there. That makes a difference."

"I know quite enough about it," returns Tony.

"It's not agreeable, is it?" pursues Mr. Snagsby, coughing his cough of mild persuasion behind his hand. "Mr. Krook ought to consider it in the rent. I hope he does, I am sure."

"I hope he does," says Tony. "But I doubt it."

"You find the rent too high, do you, sir?" returns the stationer. "Rents *are* high about here. I don't know how it is exactly, but the law seems to put things up in price. Not that I mean to say a word against the profession I get my living by."

Mr. Weevle again glances up and down the court, and then looks at the stationer. Mr. Snagsby, blankly catching his eye, looks upward for a star or so, and coughs a cough expressive of not exactly seeing his way out of this conversation.

"It's a curious fact, sir," he observes, slowly rubbing his hands, "that he should have been—"

"Who's he?" interrupts Mr. Weevle.

"The deceased, you know," says Mr. Snagsby, twitching his head and right eyebrow towards the staircase.

"Ah, to be sure!" returns the other, as if he were not overfond of the subject. "I thought we had done with him."

"I was only going to say it's a curious fact, sir, that he should have come and lived here and been one of my writers, and then that you should come and live here and be one of my writers, too."

"It's a curious coincidence, as you say," answers Weevle, once more glancing up and down the court.

"Seems a Fate in it, don't there?" suggests the stationer.

"There does."

"Just so," observes the stationer, with his confirmatory cough. "Quite a Fate in it. Quite a Fate. Well, Mr. Weevle, I am afraid I must bid you good-night. My little woman will be looking for me else. Good-night, sir!"

If Mr. Snagsby hastens home to save his little woman the trouble of looking for him, he might set his mind at rest on that score. His little woman has had her eye upon him round the Sol's Arms all this time, and now glides after him with a pocket-handkerchief wrapped over her head, honouring Mr. Weevle and his doorway with a searching glance as she goes past.

"You'll know me again, ma'am, at all events," says Mr. Weevle to himself, "and I can't compliment you on your appearance, whoever you are, with your head tied up in a bundle. Is this fellow *never* coming!"

This fellow approaches as he speaks. Mr. Weevle softly holds up his finger, and draws him into the passage, and closes the street-door. Then they go upstairs, Mr. Weevle heavily, and Mr. Guppy (for it is he) very lightly indeed. When they are shut into the back room, they speak low.

"I thought you had gone to Jericho at least, instead of coming here," says Tony.

"Why, I said about ten."

"You said about ten," Tony repeats. "Yes, so you did say about ten. But according to my count, it's ten times ten—it's a hundred o'clock. I never had such a night in my life!"

"What has been the matter?"

"That's it!" says Tony. "Nothing has been the matter. But here have

I been stewing and fuming in this jolly old crib till I have had the horrors falling on me as thick as hail."

"Why, what's the matter with you, Tony?" inquires Mr. Guppy, looking at him as he sits down with his elbow on the table.

"William Guppy," replies the other, "I am in the Downs. It's this unbearably dull, suicidal room—and old Boguey downstairs, I suppose." Mr. Weevle leans his head on his hand, puts his feet on the fender, and looks at the fire. Mr. Guppy slightly tosses his head, and sits down on the other side of the table in an easy attitude.

"Wasn't that Snagsby talking to you, Tony?"

"Yes, and be—yes, it was Snagsby," says Mr. Weevle, altering the construction of his sentence.

"On business?"

"No. He was only sauntering by, and stopped to prose."

"I thought it was Snagsby," says Mr. Guppy, "and thought it as well that he shouldn't see me, so I waited till he was gone."

"There we go again, William G.!" cried Tony, looking up for an instant. "So mysterious and secret! By George, if we were going to commit a murder, we couldn't have more mystery about it!"

Mr. Guppy affects to smile; and with the view of changing the conversation, looks with an admiration, real or pretended, round the room at the Galaxy Gallery of British Beauty, terminating his survey with the portrait of Lady Dedlock over the mantel-shelf, in which she is represented on a terrace, with a pedestal upon the terrace, and a vase upon the pedestal, and her shawl upon the vase, and a bracelet on her arm.

"That's very like Lady Dedlock," says Mr. Guppy. "It's a speaking likeness."

"I wish it was," growled Tony, without changing his position. "I should have some fashionable conversation here then."

Finding, by this time, that his friend is not to be wheedled into a more sociable humour, Mr. Guppy puts about upon the ill-used tack and remonstrates with him.

"Tony," says he, "I can make allowances for lowness of spirits, for no man knows what it is when it does come upon a man better than I do; and no man perhaps has a better right to know it than a man who has an unrequited image imprinted on his 'art. But there are bounds to these things when an unoffending party is in question, and I will acknowledge to you, Tony, that I don't think your manner on the present occasion is hospitable, or quite gentlemanly."

"This is strong language, William Guppy," returns Mr. Weevle.

"Sir, it may be," retorts Mr. William Guppy, "but I feel strongly when I use it."

Mr. Weevle admits that he has been wrong, and begs Mr. William Guppy to think no more about it. Mr. William Guppy, however, having got the advantage, cannot quite release it without a little more injured remonstrance.

"No! Dash it, Tony," says that gentleman, "you really ought to be careful how you wound the feelings of a man who has an unrequited image imprinted on his 'art, and who is *not* altogether happy in those chords which vibrate to the tenderest emotions. You, Tony, possess in yourself all that is calculated to charm the eye, and allure the taste. It is not your character to hover around one flower. The 'ole garden is open to you, and your airy pinions carry you through it. Still, Tony, far be it from me, I am sure, to wound even your feelings without a cause!"

"And now," says Tony, stirring the fire, "touching this same bundle of letters. Isn't it an extraordinary thing of Krook to have appointed twelve o'clock tonight to hand 'em over to me?"

"Very. What did he do it for?"

"What does he do anything for? *He* don't know. Said today was his birthday, and he'd hand 'em over tonight at twelve o'clock. He'll have drunk himself blind by that time. He has been at it all day."

"He hasn't forgotten the appointment, I hope?"

"Forgotten? Trust him for that. He never forgets anything. I saw him tonight, about eight—helped him to shut up his shop—and he had got the letters then in his hairy cap. He pulled it off and showed 'em me. When the shop was closed, he took them out of his cap, hung his cap on the chair-back, and stood turning them over before the fire. I heard him a little while afterwards through the floor here, humming, like the wind, the only song he knows—about Bibo, and old Charon, and Bibo being drunk when he died. He has been as quiet since as an old rat asleep in his hole."

"And you are to go down at twelve?"

"At twelve. And, as I tell you, when you came it seemed to me a hundred."

"Tony," says Mr. Guppy, after considering a little with his legs crossed, "he can't read yet, can he?"

"Read! He'll never read. He can make all the letters separately, and he knows most of them separately when he sees them; he has got on that much, under me, but he can't put them together. He's too old to acquire the knack of it now—and too drunk."

"Tony," says Mr. Guppy, uncrossing and recrossing his legs; "how do you suppose he spelt out that name of Hawdon?"

"He never spelt it out. You know what a curious power of eye he has, and how he has been used to employ himself in copying things by eye alone. He imitated it—evidently from the direction of a letter—and asked me what it meant."

"Tony," says Mr. Guppy, uncrossing and recrossing his legs again—"should you say that the original was a man's writing or a woman's?"

"A woman's. Fifty to one a lady's—slopes a good deal, and the end of the letter *n* long and hasty."

Mr. Guppy has been biting his thumb-nail during this dialogue. As he is going to do so again, he happens to look at his coat-sleeve. It takes his attention. He stares at it, aghast.

"Why, Tony, what on earth is going on in this house tonight? Is there a chimney on fire? See how the soot's falling. See here, on my arm! See again, on the table here! Confound the stuff, it won't blow off—smears, like black fat!"

They look at one another, and Tony goes listening to the door, and a little way upstairs, and a little way downstairs. Comes back, and says it's all right, and all quiet, and quotes the remark he lately made to Mr. Snagsby about their cooking chops at the Sol's Arms.

"And it was then," resumes Mr. Guppy, still glancing with remarkable aversion at the coat-sleeve, as they pursue their conversation with their heads very near together, "that he told you of his having taken the bundle of letters from his lodger's portmanteau?"

"That was the time, sir," answers Tony, faintly adjusting his whiskers. "Whereupon I wrote a line to my dear boy, the Honourable William Guppy, informing him of the appointment for tonight, and advising him not to call before, Boguey being a Sly-boots."

The light vivacious tone of fashionable life which is usually assumed by Mr. Weevle sits so ill upon him tonight that he abandons that and his whiskers together, and, after looking over his shoulder, appears to yield himself up a prey to the horrors again.

"You are to bring the letters to your room to read and compare, and to get yourself into a position to tell him all about them. That's the arrangement, isn't it, Tony?" asks Mr. Guppy.

"You can't speak too low. Yes. That's what he and I agreed."

"I tell you what, Tony—"

"You can't speak too low," says Tony once more. Mr. Guppy nods his sagacious head, advances it yet closer, and drops into a whisper.

"I tell you what. The first thing to be done is to make another packet like the real one, so that if he should ask to see the real one while it's in my possession, you can show him the dummy."

"And suppose he detects the dummy as soon as he sees it—which with his biting screw of an eye is about five hundred times more likely than not," suggests Tony.

"Then we'll face it out. They don't belong to him, and they never did. You found that, and you placed them in my hands—a legal friend of yours—for security. If he forces us to it, they'll be producible, won't they?"

"Ye-es," is Mr. Weevle's reluctant admission.

"Why, Tony," remonstrates his friend, "how you look! You don't doubt William Guppy? You don't suspect any harm?"

"I don't suspect anything more than I know, William," returns the other, gravely.

"And what do you know?" urges Mr. Guppy.

"I know three things. First, I know that here we are whispering in secrecy, a pair of conspirators."

"Well," says Mr. Guppy, "and we had better be that than a pair of noodles, which we should be if we were doing anything else; for it's the only way of doing what we want to do. Secondly?"

"Secondly, it's not made out to me how it's likely to be profitable, after all."

Mr. Guppy casts up his eyes at the portrait of Lady Dedlock over the mantel-shelf, and replies, "Tony, you are asked to leave that to the honour of your friend. Besides its being calculated to serve that friend, your friend is no fool—what's that?"

"It's eleven o'clock striking by the bell of St. Paul's. Listen and you'll hear all the bells in the city jangling."

Both sat silent, listening to the metal voices, near and distant, resounding from towers of various heights, in tones more various than their situations. When these at length cease, all seems more mysterious and quiet than before. One disagreeable result of whispering is that it seems to evoke an atmosphere of silence haunted by the ghosts of sound—strange cracks and tickings, the rustling of garments that have no substance in them, and the tread of dreadful feet that would leave no mark on the sea-sand or the winter snow. So sensitive the two friends happen to be that the air is full of these phantoms; and the two look over their shoulders, by one consent, to see that the door is shut.

"Yes, Tony?" says Mr. Guppy, drawing nearer to the fire, and biting his unsteady thumb-nail. "You were going to say, thirdly?"

"It's far from a pleasant thing to be plotting about a dead man in the room where he died, especially when you happen to live in it."

"But we are plotting nothing against him, Tony."

"Maybe not, still I don't like it. Live here by yourself, and see how *you* like it."

"As to dead men, Tony," proceeds Mr. Guppy, evading this proposal, "there have been dead men in most rooms."

"I know there have, but in most rooms you let them alone and—and they let you alone," Tony answers.

The two look at each other again. Mr. Guppy makes a hurried remark to the effect that they may be doing the deceased a service, that he hopes so. There is an oppressive blank, until Mr. Weevle, by stirring the fire suddenly, makes Mr. Guppy start.

"Fah! Here's more of this hateful soot hanging about," says he. "Let us open the window a bit and get a mouthful of air. It's too close."

He raises the sash, and they both rest on the window-sill, half in and half out of the room. The neighbouring houses are too near to admit of their seeing any sky without craning their necks and looking up; but lights in frowsy windows here and there, and the rolling of distant carriages, and the new expression that there is of the stir of men, they find to be comfortable. Mr. Guppy, noiselessly tapping on the window-sill, resumes his whispering in quite a light-comedy tone.

"By the by, Tony, don't forget old Smallweed"—meaning the younger of that name. "I have not let him into this, you know. That grandfather of his is too keen by half. It runs in the family."

"I remember," says Tony. "I am up to all that."

"And as to Krook," resumes Mr. Guppy, "now, do you suppose he really has got hold of any other papers of importance, as he has boasted to you since you have been such allies?"

Tony shakes his head. "I don't know. Can't imagine. If we get through this business without rousing his suspicions, I shall be better informed, no doubt. How can I know without seeing them, when he don't know himself? He is always spelling out words from them, and chalking them over the shop-wall, and asking what this is, and what that is; but his whole stock from beginning to end may easily be the waste paper he bought it as, for anything I can say. It's a monomania with him to think he is possessed of documents."

"How did he first come by that idea, though? that's the question," Mr. Guppy suggests. "He may have found papers in something he bought, where papers were not supposed to be, and may have got it into his shrewd head, from the manner and place of their concealment, that they are worth something."

"Or he may have been taken in in some pretended bargain. Or he may have been muddled altogether, by long staring at whatever he *has* got, and by drink, and by hanging about the Lord Chancellor's Court and hearing of documents for ever," returns Mr. Weevle.

Mr. Guppy sitting on the window-sill, nodding his head and balancing all these possibilities in his mind, continues thoughtfully to tap it, and clasp it, and measure it with his hand, until he hastily draws his hand away.

"What in the devil's name," he says, "is this! Look at my fingers!"

A thick, yellow liquor defiles them, which is offensive to the touch and sight and more offensive to the smell. A stagnant, sickening oil, with some natural repulsion in it that makes them both shudder.

"What have you been doing here? What have you been pouring out of window?"

"I pouring out of window! Nothing, I swear! Never, since I have been here!" cries the lodger.

And yet look here—and look here! When he brings the candle here, from the corner of the window-sill it slowly drips, and creeps away down the bricks; here lies in a little thick nauseous pool.

"This is a horrible house," says Mr. Guppy, shutting down the window. "Give me some water, or I shall cut my hand off."

He so washes, and rubs, and scrubs, and smells and washes, that he has not long restored himself with a glass of brandy when St. Paul's bell strikes twelve, and all those other bells strike twelve from their towers of various heights in the dark air, and in their many tones. When all is quiet again, the lodger says:

"It's the appointed time at last. Shall I go?"

Mr. Guppy nods, and gives him a "lucky touch" on the back; but not with the washed hand, though it is his right hand.

He goes downstairs; and Mr. Guppy tries to compose himself, before the fire for waiting a long time. But in no more than a minute or two the stairs creak, and Tony comes swiftly back.

"Have you got them?"

"Got them! No. The old man's not there."

He has been so horribly frightened in the short interval that his terror seizes the other, who makes a rush at him, and asks loudly, "What's the matter?"

"I couldn't make him hear, and I softly opened the door and looked in. And the burning smell is there—and the soot is there, and the oil is there—and he is not there!" Tony ends this with a groan.

Mr. Guppy takes the light. They go down, more dead than alive, and holding one another, push open the door of the back shop. The cat has retreated close to it and stands snarling—not at them, at something on the ground before the fire. There is a very little fire left in the grate, but there is a smouldering, suffocating vapour in the room, and a dark greasy coating on the walls and ceiling. The chairs and table, and the bottle so rarely absent from the table, all stand as usual. On one chair-back hang the old man's hairy cap and coat.

"Look!" whispers the lodger, pointing his friend's attention to these objects with a trembling finger. "I told you so. When I saw him last, he took his cap off, took out the little bundle of old letters, hung his cap on the back of the chair—his coat was there already, for he had pulled that off before he went to put the shutters up—and I left him turning the letters over in his hand, standing just where that crumbled black thing is upon the floor."

Is he hanging somewhere? They look up. No.

"See!" whispers Tony. "At the foot of the same chair, there lies a dirty bit of thin red cord that they tie up pens with. That went round the letters. He undid it slowly, leering and laughing at me, before he began to turn them over, and threw it there. I saw it fall."

"What's the matter with the cat?" says Mr. Guppy. "Look at her!"

"Mad, I think. And no wonder in this evil place."

They advance slowly, looking at all these things. The cat remains where they found her, still snarling at the something on the ground

before the fire and between the two chairs. What is it? Hold up the light.

Here is a small burnt patch of flooring; here is the tinder from a little bundle of burnt paper, but not so light as usual, seeming to be steeped in something; and here is—is it the cinder of a small charred and broken log of wood sprinkled with white ashes, or is it coal? Oh horror, he *is* here! and this from which we run away, striking out the light and over-turning one another into the street, is all that represents him.

Help, help, help! Come into this house, for Heaven's sake!

Plenty will come in, but none can help. The Lord Chancellor of that Court, true to his title in his last act, has died the death of all Lord Chancellors in all courts, and of all authorities in all places under all names soever where false pretences are made, and where injustice is done. Call the death by any name Your Highness will, attribute it to whom you will, or say it might have been prevented how you will, it is the same death eternally—inborn, inbred, engendered in the corrupted humours of the vicious body itself, and that only—Spontaneous Combustion, and none other of all the deaths that can be died.

## CHAPTER 33

*Interlopers*

Now do those two gentlemen not very neat about the cuffs and buttons who attended the last Coroner's Inquest at the Sol's Arms, reappear in the precincts with surprising swiftness (being, in fact, breathlessly fetched by the active and intelligent beadle), and institute perquisitions through the court, and dive into the Sol's parlour, and write with ravenous little pens on tissue-paper. Now do they note down, in the watches of the night, how the neighbourhood of Chancery Lane was yesterday, at about midnight, thrown into a state of the most intense agitation and excitement by the following alarming and horrible discovery. Now do they set forth how it will doubtless be remembered that some time back a painful sensation was created in the public mind by a case of mysterious death from opium occurring in the first floor of the house occupied as a rag, bottle and general marine-store shop by an eccentric individual of intemperate habits, far advanced in life, named Krook; and how, by a remarkable coincidence, Krook was examined at the Inquest, which it may be recollected was held on that occasion at the Sol's Arms; a well-conducted tavern, immediately adjoining the premises in question, on the west side, and licensed to a highly respectable landlord, Mr. James George Bogsby. Now do they show (in as many words as possible), how during some hours of yesterday evening a very peculiar smell was observed by the inhabitants of the court in which the tragical occurrence which forms the subject of that present account transpired; and which odour was at one time powerful. All this, and a great deal more, the two gentlemen, who have formed an amicable partnership in the melancholy catastrophe, write down on the spot; and the boy population of the court (out of bed in a moment) swarm up the shutters of the Sol's Arms parlour to behold the tops of their heads while they are about it.

The whole court, adult as well as boy, is sleepless for that night, and can do nothing but wrap up its many heads and talk of the ill-fated house, and look at it. Miss Flite has been bravely rescued from her chamber, as if it were in flames, and accommodated with a bed at the Sol's Arms. The Sol neither turns off its gas nor shuts its door, all night; for any kind of public excitement makes good for the Sol, and causes the court to stand in need of comfort. The house has not done so much in the stomachic article of cloves, or in brandy-and-water warm, since the Inquest. The moment the pot-boy heard what had happened, he rolled up his shirt-sleeves tight to his shoulders, and said, "There'll be a run upon us!"

Mr. Weevle and his friend Mr. Guppy are within the bar at the Sol, and are worth anything to the Sol that the bar contains if they will only stay there. "This is not a time," says Mr. Bogsby, "to haggle about money," though he looks something sharply after it, over the counter. "Give your orders, you two gentlemen, and you're welcome to whatever you put a name to."

Thus entreated, the two gentlemen (Mr. Weevle especially) put names to so many things that in course of time they find it difficult to put a name to anything quite distinctly; though they still relate, to all new-comers, some version of the night they have had of it, and of what they said, and what they thought, and what they saw. Meanwhile, one or other of the policemen often flits about the door, and pushing it open a little way at the full length of his arm, looks in from outer gloom. Not that he has any suspicions, but that he may as well know what they are up to in there.

Night at length with slow-retreating steps departs, and the lamp-lighter, going his rounds, like an executioner to a despotic king strikes off the little heads of fire that have aspired to lessen the darkness. Thus the day cometh, whether or no. And the day may discern, even with its dim London eye, that the court has been up all night. Over and above the faces that have fallen drowsily on tables, and the heels that lie prone on hard floors instead of beds, the brick-and-mortar physiognomy of the very court itself looks worn and jaded. And now the neighbourhood, waking up and beginning to hear of what has happened, comes streaming in, half-dressed, to ask questions; and the two policemen have enough to do to keep the door.

"Good gracious, gentlemen!" says Mr. Snagsby, coming up. "What's this I hear!"

"Why, it's true," returns one of the policemen. "That's what it is. Now move on here, come!"

"Why, good gracious, gentlemen," says Mr. Snagsby, somewhat promptly backed away, "I was at this door last night betwixt ten and eleven o'clock, in conversation with the young man who lodges here."

"Indeed?" returns the policeman. "You will find the young man next door, then. Now move on here, some of you."

"Not hurt, I hope?" says Mr. Snagsby.

"Hurt? No. What's to hurt him!"

Mr. Snagsby, wholly unable to answer this, or any question, in his troubled mind, repairs to the Sol's Arms, and finds Mr. Weevle languishing over tea and toast.

"And Mr. Guppy likewise!" quoth Mr. Snagsby. "Dear, dear, dear! What a fate there seems in all this! And my lit—"

Mr. Snagsby's power of speech deserts him in the formation of the words "my little woman." For to see that injured female walk into the Sol's Arms at that hour of the morning and stand before the beer-engine, with her eyes fixed upon him like an accusing spirit, strikes him dumb.

"My dear," says Mr. Snagsby, when his tongue is loosened, "will you take anything? A little drop of shrub?"

"No," says Mrs. Snagsby.

"My love, you know these two gentlemen?"

"Yes!" says Mrs. Snagsby, and in a rigid manner acknowledges their presence, still fixing Mr. Snagsby with her eye.

The devoted Mr. Snagsby cannot bear this treatment. He takes Mrs. Snagsby by the hand, and leads her aside to an adjacent cask.

"My little woman, why do you look at me in that way? Pray don't do it."

"I can't help my looks," says Mrs. Snagsby, "and if I could I wouldn't."

Mr. Snagsby, with his cough of meekness, rejoins, "Wouldn't you really, my dear?" and meditates. Then coughs his cough of trouble, and says, "This is a dreadful mystery, my love!"

"It *is*," returns Mrs. Snagsby, shaking her head, "a dreadful mystery."

"My little woman," urges Mr. Snagsby, in a piteous manner, "don't for goodness' sake speak to me with that bitter expression, and look at me in that searching way! I beg and entreat of you not to do it. Good Lord, you don't suppose that I would go spontaneously combusting any person, my dear?"

"I can't say," returns Mrs. Snagsby.

On a hasty review of his unfortunate position, Mr. Snagsby "can't say" either. He is not prepared positively to deny that he may have had something to do with it. He has had something—he don't know what—to do with so much in this connexion that is mysterious that it is possible he may even be implicated, without knowing it, in the present transaction.

"My life," says the unhappy stationer, "would you have any objections to mention why, being in general so delicately circumspect in your conduct, you come into a wine vaults before breakfast?"

"Why do *you* come here?" inquires Mrs. Snagsby.

"My dear, merely to know the rights of the fatal accident which has happened to the venerable party who has been—combusted." Mr. Snagsby has made a pause to suppress a groan. "I should then have related them to you, my love, over your French roll."

"I dare say you would! You relate everything to me, Mr. Snagsby."

"Every—my lit—?"

"I should be glad," says Mrs. Snagsby, after contemplating his increased confusion with a severe and sinister smile, "if you would come home with me. I think you may be safer there, Mr. Snagsby, than anywhere else."

"My love, I don't know but what I may be. I am ready to go."

Mr. Snagsby casts his eye forlornly round the bar, gives Messrs. Weevle and Guppy good-morning, assures them of the satisfaction with which he sees them uninjured, and accompanies Mrs. Snagsby from the Sol's Arms. Before night, his doubt whether he may not be responsible for some inconceivable part in the catastrophe which is the talk of the whole neighbourhood is almost resolved into certainty by Mrs. Snagsby's pertinacity in that fixed gaze. His mental sufferings are so great that he entertains wandering ideas of delivering himself up to justice, and requiring to be cleared, if innocent, and punished with the utmost rigour of the law, if guilty.

Mr. Weevle and Mr. Guppy, having taken their breakfast, step into Lincoln's Inn to take a little walk about the square and clear as many of the dark cobwebs out of their brains as a little walk may.

"There can be no more favourable time than the present, Tony," says Mr. Guppy, after they have broodingly made out the four sides of the square, "for a word or two between us upon a point on which we must, with very little delay, come to an understanding."

"Now I tell you what, William G.!" returns the other, eyeing his companion with a bloodshot eye. "If it's a point of conspiracy, you needn't take the trouble to mention it. I have had enough of that, and I ain't going to have any more. We shall have *you* taking fire next, or blowing up with a bang."

This supposititious phenomenon is so very disagreeable to Mr. Guppy that his voice quakes as he says in a moral way, "Tony, I should have thought that what we went through last night would have been a lesson to you never to be personal any more as long as you lived." To which

Mr. Weevle returns, "William, I should have thought it would have been a lesson to *you* never to conspire any more as long as you lived." To which Mr. Guppy says, "Who's conspiring?" To which Mr. Jobling replies, "Why, *you* are!" To which Mr. Guppy retorts, "No, I am not." To which Mr. Jobling retorts again, "Yes, you are!" To which Mr. Guppy retorts, "Who says so?" To which Mr. Jobling retorts, "*I* say so!" To which Mr. Guppy retorts, "Oh, indeed?" To which Mr. Jobling retorts, "Yes, indeed!" And both being now in a heated state, they walk on silently for a while, to cool down again.

"Tony," says Mr. Guppy then, "if you heard your friend out, instead of flying at him, you wouldn't fall into mistakes. But your temper is hasty, and you are not considerate. Possessing in yourself, Tony, all that is calculated to charm the eye—"

"Oh! Blow the eye!" cries Mr. Weevle, cutting him short. "Say what you have got to say!"

Finding his friend in this morose and material condition, Mr. Guppy only expresses the finer feelings of his soul through the tone of injury in which he recommences:

"Tony, when I say there is a point on which we must come to an understanding pretty soon, I say so quite apart from any kind of conspiring, however innocent. You know it is professionally arranged beforehand, in all cases that are tried, what facts the witnesses are to prove. Is it, or is it not, desirable that we should know what facts we are to prove on the inquiry into the death of this unfortunate old Mo—— gentleman?" (Mr. Guppy was going to say "Mogul," but thinks "gentleman" better suited to the circumstances.)

"What facts? *The* facts."

"The facts bearing on that inquiry. Those are—" Mr. Guppy tells them off on his fingers—"what we knew of his habits; when you saw him last; what his condition was then; the discovery that we made, and how we made it. We made the discovery in consequence of his having, in his eccentric way, an appointment with you at twelve o'clock at night, when you were to explain some writing to him, as you had often done before, on account of his not being able to read. I, spending the evening with you, was called down—and so forth. The inquiry being only into the circumstances touching the death of the deceased, it's not necessary to go beyond these facts, I suppose."

"No!" returns Mr. Weevle. "I suppose not."

"And this is not a conspiracy, perhaps?" said the injured Guppy.

"No," returns his friend. "If it's nothing worse than this, I withdraw the observation."

"Now, Tony," says Mr. Guppy, taking his arm again, and walking him slowly on, "I should like to know, in a friendly way, whether you have yet thought over the many advantages of your continuing to live at that place."

"What do you mean?" says Tony, stopping.

"Whether you have yet thought over the many advantages of your continuing to live at that place," repeats Mr. Guppy.

"At what place? *That* place?" pointing in the direction of the rag and bottle shop. Mr. Guppy nods. "Why, I wouldn't pass another night there, for any consideration that you could offer me," said Mr. Weevle, haggardly staring.

"Do you mean it though, Tony?"

"Mean it! Do I look as if I mean it? I feel as if I do, I know that," says Mr. Weevle, with a very genuine shudder.

"Then the possibility, or probability—for such it must be considered—of your never being disturbed in possession of those effects lately belonging to a lone old man who seemed to have no relation in the world, and the certainty of your being able to find out what he really had got stored up there, don't weigh with you at all against last night, Tony, if I understand you?" says Mr. Guppy.

"Certainly not. Talk in that cool way of a fellow's living there?" cries Mr. Weevle, indignantly. "Go and live there yourself."

"Oh, I, Tony!" says Mr. Guppy, soothing him. "I have never lived there, and couldn't get a lodging there now; whereas you have got one."

"You are welcome to it," rejoins his friend, "and—ugh!—you may make yourself at home in it."

"Then you really and truly at this point," says Mr. Guppy, "give up the whole thing, if I understand you, Tony?"

"You never," returns Tony, with a most convincing steadfastness, "said a truer word in all your life. I do!"

While they are so conversing, a hackney-coach drives into the square, on the box of which vehicle a very tall hat makes itself manifest to the public. Inside the coach, and consequently not so manifest to the multitude, though sufficiently so to the two friends, for the coach stops almost at their feet, are the venerable Mr. Smallweed and Mrs. Smallweed, accompanied by their grand-daughter Judy. An air of haste and excitement pervades the party, and as the tall hat (surmounting Mr. Smallweed the younger) alights, Mr. Smallweed the elder pokes his head out of window and bawls to Mr. Guppy, "How de do, sir! How de do!"

"What do Chick and his family want here at this time of the morning, I wonder!" says Mr. Guppy, nodding to his familiar.

"My dear sir," cried Grandfather Smallweed, "would you do me a favour? Would you and your friend be so very obleeging as to carry me into the public-house in the court while Bart and his sister bring their grandmother along? Would you do an old man that good turn, sir?"

Mr. Guppy looks at his friend, and they prepare to bear the venerable burden to the Sol's Arms.

"There's your fare!" says the Patriarch to the coachman with a fierce grin. "Ask me for a penny more and I'll have my lawful revenge upon you. My dear young men, be easy with me, if you please. Allow me to catch you round the neck. I won't squeeze you tighter than I can help. Oh, Lord! Oh dear me! Oh my bones!"

It is well that the Sol is not far off, for Mr. Weevle presents an apoplectic appearance before half the distance is accomplished. With no worse aggravation of his symptoms, however, than the utterance of divers croaking sounds, expressive of obstructed respiration, he fulfils his share of the porterage, and the benevolent old gentleman is deposited by his own desire in the parlour of the Sol's Arms.

"Oh Lord!" gasps Mr. Smallweed, looking about him, breathless, from an arm-chair. "Oh dear me! Oh my bones and back! Oh my aches and pains! Sit down, you dancing, prancing, shambling, scrambling pollparrot! Sit down!"

This little apostrophe to Mrs. Smallweed is occasioned by a propensity on the part of that unlucky old lady, whenever she finds herself on her feet, to amble about and "set" to inaminate objects, accompanying herself with a chattering noise, as in a witch dance. A nervous affection has probably as much to do with these demonstrations as any imbecile intention in the poor old woman; but on the present occasion they are so particularly lively in connexion with the Windsor arm-chair, fellow to that in which Mr. Smallweed is seated, that she only quite desists when her grandchildren have held her down in it.

"My dear sir," Grandfather Smallweed then proceeds, addressing Mr. Guppy, "there has been a calamity here. Have you heard of it, either of you!"

"Heard of it, sir? Why, we discovered it."

"You discovered it. You two discovered it! Bart, *they* discovered it!" The two discoverers stare at the Smallweeds, who return the compliment. "My dear friends," whines Grandfather Smallweed, putting out both hands, "I owe you a thousand thanks for discharging the melancholy office of discovering the ashes of Mrs. Smallweed's brother."

"Eh?" says Mr. Guppy.

"Mrs. Smallweed's brother, my dear friend—her only relation. We were not on terms, which is to be deplored now, but he never *would* be on terms. He was not fond of us. He was eccentric—he was very eccentric. Unless he has left a will (which is not at all likely) I shall take out letters of administration. I have come down to look after the property; it must be sealed up, it must be protected. I have come down," repeats Grandfather Smallweed, "to look after the property."

"I think, Small," says the disconsolate Mr. Guppy, "you might have mentioned that the old man was your uncle."

"You two were so close about him that I thought you would like me to be the same," returns that old bird, with a secretly glistening eye. "Besides, I wasn't proud of him."

"Besides which, it was nothing to you, you know, whether he was or not," says Judy. Also with a secretly glistening eye.

"He never saw me in his life, to know me," observed Small. "I don't know why I should introduce *him*, I am sure!"

"No, he never communicated with us—which is to be deplored," the old gentleman strikes in; "but I have come to look after the property—to look over the papers, and to look after the property. We shall make good our title. It is in the hands of my solicitor. Mr. Tulkinghorn, of Lincoln's Inn Fields, over the way there, is so good as to act as my solicitor, and grass don't grow under *his* feet, I can tell ye. Krook was Mrs. Smallweed's only brother; she had no relation but Krook, and Krook had no relation but Mrs. Smallweed. I am speaking of your brother, you brimstone black-beetle, that was seventy-six years of age."

Mrs. Smallweed instantly begins to shake her head and pipe up,

"Seventy-six pound seven and sevenpence! Seventy-six thousand bags of money! Seventy-six hundred thousand million of parcels of bank-notes!"

"Will somebody give me a quart-pot?" exclaims her exasperated husband, looking helplessly about him and finding no missile within his reach. "Will somebody obleege me with a spittoon? Will somebody hand me anything hard and bruising to pelt at her? You hag, you cat, you dog, you brimstone barker!" Here Mr. Smallweed, wrought up to the highest pitch by his own eloquence, actually throws Judy at her grandmother in default of anything else, by butting that young virgin at the old lady with such force as he can muster, and then dropping into his chair in a heap.

"Shake me up, somebody, if you'll be so good," says the voice from within the faintly struggling bundle into which he has collapsed. "I have come to look after the property. Shake me up, and call in the police on duty at the next house, to be explained to about the property. My solicitor will be here presently to protect the property." As his dutiful grandchildren set him up, he still repeats like an echo, "the—the property! The property!—property!"

Mr. Weevle and Mr. Guppy look at each other, the former as having relinquished the whole affair, the latter with a discomfited countenance, as having entertained some lingering expectations yet. But there is nothing to be done in opposition to the Smallweed interest. Mr. Tulking-horn's clerk comes down from his official pew in the chambers, to mention to the police that Mr. Tulkinghorn is answerable for its being all correct about the next of kin, and that the papers and effects will be formally taken possession of in due time and course. Mr. Smallweed is at once permitted so far to assert his supremacy as to be carried on a visit of sentiment into the next house, and upstairs into Miss Flite's deserted room, where he looks like a hideous bird of prey newly added to her aviary.

The arrival of this unexpected heir soon taking wind in the court, still makes good for the Sol, and keeps the court upon its mettle. There is one point connected with the deceased upon which the court is particularly anxious; namely, that the fiction of a full-sized coffin should be preserved, though there is so little to put in it. Upon the undertaker's stating in the Sol's bar in the course of the day that he has received orders to construct "a six-footer," the general solicitude is much relieved, and it is considered that Mr. Smallweed's conduct does him great honour.

Out of the court, and a long way out of it, there is considerable excitement too; for men of science and philosophy come to look, and carriages set down doctors at the corner who arrive with the same intent,

and there is more learned talk about inflammable gases and phosphu-
retted hydrogen than the court has ever imagined. Some of these authorities (of course the wisest) hold with indignation that the deceased had
no business to die in the alleged manner; and being reminded by other
authorities of a certain inquiry into the evidence for such deaths, re-
printed in the sixth volume of the Philosophical Transactions—and also
of a book not quite unknown, on English Medical Jurisprudence; and
likewise of the Italian case of the Countess Cornelia Baudi as set
forth in detail by one Bianchini, prebendary of Verona, who wrote a
scholarly work or so, and was occasionally heard of in his time as having
gleams of reason in him; and also of the testimony of Messrs. Foderé
and Mere, two pestilent Frenchmen who *would* investigate the subject;
and further, of the corroborative testimony of Monsieur Le Cat, a
rather celebrated French surgeon once upon a time, who had the un-
politeness to live in a house where such a case occurred, and even to
write an account of it—still they regard the late Mr. Krook's obstinacy
in going out of the world by any such by-way as wholly unjustifiable
and personally offensive. The less the court understands of all this, the
more the court likes it.

At last come the Coroner and his inquiry, like as before, except that
the Coroner cherishes this case as being out of the common way, and
tells the gentlemen of the jury, in his private capacity, that "that would
seem to be an unlucky house next door, gentlemen, a destined house;
but so we sometimes find it, and these are mysteries we can't account
for!"

In all these proceedings Mr. Guppy has so slight a part, except when
he gives his evidence, that he is moved on like a private individual,
and can only haunt the secret house on the outside, where he has the
mortification of seeing Mr. Smallweed padlocking the door, and of
bitterly knowing himself to be shut out. But before these proceedings
draw to a close—that is to say, on the night next after the catastrophe—
Mr. Guppy has a thing to say that must be said to Lady Dedlock.

For which reason, with a sinking heart, and with that hangdog sense
of guilt upon him which dread and watching enfolded in the Sol's
Arms have produced, the young man of the name of Guppy presents
himself at the town-mansion at about seven o'clock in the evening and
requests to see her ladyship. Mercury replies that she is going out to
dinner; don't he see the carriage at the door? Yes, he does see the carriage at the door but he wants to see my Lady, too. Mercury is disposed,
as he will presently declare to a fellow-gentleman in waiting, "to pitch
into the young man," but his instructions are positive. Therefore he
sulkily supposes that the young man must come up into the library.

There he leaves the young man in a large room, not overlight, while he makes report of him.

Mr. Guppy looks into the shade in all directions, discovering everywhere a certain charred and whitened little heap of coal or wood. Presently he hears a rustling. Is it—? No, it's no ghost, but fair flesh and blood, most brilliantly dressed.

"I have to beg your ladyship's pardon," Mr. Guppy stammers, very downcast. "This is an inconvenient time—"

"I told you you could come at any time." She takes a chair, looking straight at him as on the last occasion.

"Thank your ladyship. Your ladyship is very affable."

"You can sit down." There is not much affability in her tone.

"I don't know, your ladyship, that it's worth while my sitting down and detaining you, for I—I have not got the letters that I mentioned when I had the honour of waiting on your ladyship."

"Have you come merely to say so?"

"Merely to say so, your ladyship." Mr. Guppy, besides being depressed, disappointed, and uneasy, is put at a further disadvantage by the splendour and beauty of her appearance. She knows its influence perfectly, has studied it too well to miss a grain of its effect on any one. As she looks at him so steadily and coldly, he not only feels conscious that he has no guide in the least perception of what is really the complexion of her thoughts, but also that he is being every moment, as it were, removed further and further from her. She will not speak, it is plain. So he must.

"In short, your ladyship," says Mr. Guppy, like a meanly penitent thief, "the person I was to have had the letters of has come to a sudden end, and—" He stops. Lady Dedlock calmly finishes the sentence.

"And the letters are destroyed with the person?"

Mr. Guppy would say no if he could—as he is unable to hide.

"I believe so, your ladyship."

If he could see the least sparkle of relief in her face now? No, he could see no such thing, even if that brave outside did not utterly put him away, and he were not looking beyond it and about it. He falters an awkward excuse or two for his failure.

"Is this all you have to say?" inquires Lady Dedlock, having heard him out—or as nearly out as he can stumble. Mr. Guppy thinks that's all. "You had better be sure that you wish to say nothing more to me, this being the last time you will have the opportunity."

Mr. Guppy is quite sure. And indeed he has no such wish at present, by any means.

"That is enough. I will dispense with excuses. Good-evening to you!"

And she rings for Mercury to show the young man of the name of Guppy out.

But in that house, in that same moment, there happens to be an old man of the name of Tulkinghorn. And that old man, coming with his quiet footstep to the library, has his hand at that moment on the handle of the door—comes in—and comes face to face with the young man as he is leaving the room.

One glance between the old man and the lady, and for an instant the blind that is always down flies up. Suspicion, eager and sharp, looks out. Another instant—close again.

"I beg your pardon, Lady Dedlock. I beg your pardon a thousand times. It is so very unusual to find you here at this hour. I supposed the room was empty. I beg your pardon!"

"Stay!" She negligently calls him back. "Remain here, I beg. I am going out to dinner. I have nothing more to say to this young man!"

The disconcerted young man bows as he goes out, and cringingly hopes that Mr. Tulkinghorn of the Fields is well.

"Ay, ay?" says the lawyer, looking at him from under his bent brows. "From Kenge and Carboy's, surely?"

"Kenge and Carboy's, Mr. Tulkinghorn. Name of Guppy, sir."

"To be sure. Why, thank you, Mr. Guppy, I am very well!"

"Happy to hear it, sir. You can't be too well, sir, for the credit of the profession."

"Thank you, Mr. Guppy!"

Mr. Guppy sneaks away. Mr. Tulkinghorn, such a foil in his old-fashioned rusty black to Lady Dedlock's brightness, hands her down the staircase to her carriage. He returns rubbing his chin, and rubs it a good deal in the course of the evening.

# CHAPTER 34

## A Turn of the Screw

"Now what," says Mr. George, "may this be? Is it blank cartridge, or ball? A flash in the pan, or a shot?"

An open letter is the subject of the trooper's speculations, and it seems to perplex him mightily. He looks at it at arm's length, brings it close to him, holds it in his right hand, holds it in his left hand, reads it with his head on this side, with his head on that side, contracts his eyebrows, elevates them, still cannot satisfy himself. He smooths it out upon the table with his heavy palm, and thoughtfully walking up and down the gallery, makes a halt before it every now and then, to come upon it with a fresh eye. Even that won't do. "Is it," Mr. George still muses, "blank cartridge or ball?"

Phil Squod, with the aid of brush and paint-pot, is employed in the

distance whitening the targets, softly whistling, in quick-march time and in drum-and-fife manner, that he must and will go back again to the girl he left behind him.

"Phil!" The trooper beckons as he calls him.

Phil approaches. Certain splashes of white show in high relief upon his dirty face, and he scrapes his one eyebrow with the handle of the brush.

"Attention, Phil! Listen to this."

"Steady, Commander, steady."

" 'Sir. Allow me to remind you (though there is no legal necessity for my doing so, as you are aware) that the bill at two months' date drawn on yourself by Mr. Matthew Bagnet, and by you accepted, for the sum of ninety-seven pounds four shillings and ninepence, will become due tomorrow, when you will please be prepared to take up the same on presentation. Yours, Joshua Smallweed.'—What do you make of that, Phil?"

"Mischief, Guv'ner. I think," replies Phil, aften pensively tracing out a cross-wrinkle in his forehead with the brush-handle, "that mischeevious consequences is always meant when money's asked for."

"Lookye, Phil," says the trooper, sitting on the table. "First and last, I have paid, I may say, half as much again as this principal, in interest and one thing and another."

Phil intimates, by sidling back a pace or two, with a very unaccountable wrench of his wry face, that he does not regard the transaction as being made more promising by this incident.

"And lookye further, Phil," says the trooper, staying his premature conclusions with a wave of his hand. "There has always been an understanding that this bill was to be what they call renewed. And it has been renewed, no end of times. What do you say now?"

"I say that I think the times is come to a end at last."

"You do? Humph! I am much of the same mind myself."

"Joshua Smallweed is him that was brought here in a chair?"

"The same."

"Guv'ner," says Phil, with exceeding gravity, "he's a leech in his dispositions, he's a screw and a wice in his actions, a snake in his twistings, and a lobster in his claws."

Having thus expressively uttered his sentiments, Mr. Squod, after waiting a little to ascertain if any further remark be expected of him, gets back to the target he has in hand. George, having folded the letter, walks in that direction.

"There *is* a way, Commander," says Phil, looking cunningly at him, "of settling this."

"Paying the money, I suppose? I wish I could."

Phil shakes his head. "No, Guv'ner, no, not so bad as that. There *is* a way," says Phil, with a highly artistic turn of his brush—"what I'm a-doing at present."

"Whitewashing."

Phil nods.

"A pretty way that would be! Do you know what would become of the Bagnets in that case? Do you know they would be ruined to pay off my old scores? *You're* a moral character," says the trooper, eyeing him in his large way with no small indignation, "upon my life you are, Phil!"

Phil, on one knee at the target, is in course of protesting earnestly when steps are audible in the long passage without, and a cheerful voice is heard to wonder whether George is at home. Phil, with a look at his master, hobbles up, saying, "Here's the Guv'ner, Mrs. Bagnet! Here he is!" and the old girl herself, accompanied by Mr. Bagnet, appears. The old girl never appears in walking trim, in any season of the year, without a grey-cloth cloak, coarse and much worn but very clean, which is undoubtedly the identical garment rendered so interesting to Mr. Bagnet by having made its way home to Europe from another quarter of the globe, in company with Mrs. Bagnet and an umbrella. The latter faithful appendage is also invariably a part of the old girl's presence out of doors. It is of no colour known in this life, and has a corrugated wooden crook for a handle, with a metallic object let into its prow or beak, resembling a little model of a fan-light over a street-door, or one of the oval glasses out of a pair of spectacles—which ornamental object has not that tenacious capacity of sticking to its post that might be desired in an article long associated with the British army. The old girl's umbrella is of a flabby habit of waist—an appearance that is possibly referable to its having served, through a series of years, at home as a cupboard, and on journeys as a carpet-bag. She never puts it up, having the greatest reliance on her well-proved cloak with its capacious hood, but generally uses the instrument as a wand with which to point out joints of meat or bunches of greens in marketing, or to arrest the attention of tradesmen by a friendly poke. Without her market-basket, which is a sort of wicker well with two flapping lids, she never stirs abroad. Attended by these her trusty companions, therefore, her honest sunburnt face looking cheerily out of a rough straw bonnet, Mrs. Bagnet now arrives, fresh-coloured and bright, in George's Shooting Gallery.

"Well, George old fellow," says she, "and how do *you* do this sunshiny morning?"

Giving him a friendly shake of the hand, Mrs. Bagnet draws a long breath after her walk, and sits down to enjoy a rest. Having a faculty, matured on the tops of baggage-waggons and in other such positions, of resting easily anywhere, she perches on a rough bench, unties her bonnet-strings, pushes back her bonnet, crosses her arms, and looks perfectly comfortable. Mr. Bagnet, in the meantime, has shaken hands with his old comrade, and with Phil, on whom Mrs. Bagnet likewise bestows a good-humoured nod and smile.

"Now, George," said Mrs. Bagnet, briskly, "here we are, Lignum and myself"—she often speaks of her husband by this appellation, on account, as it is supposed, of Lignum Vitae having been his old regimental nickname when they first became acquainted, in compliment to the extreme hardness and toughness of his physiognomy—"just looked in, we have, to make it all correct as usual about that security. Give him the new bill to sign, George, and he'll sign it like a man."

"I was coming to you this morning," observes the trooper, reluctantly.

"Yes, we thought you'd come to us this morning, but we turned out early, and left Woolrich, the best of boys, to mind his sisters, and came to you instead—as you see! For Lignum, he's tied so close now, and gets so little exercise, that a walk does him good. But what's the matter, George?" asks Mrs. Bagnet, stopping in her cheerful talk. "You don't look yourself."

"I am not quite myself," returns the trooper. "I have been a little put out, Mrs. Bagnet."

Her bright, quick eye catches the truth directly. "George!"—holding up her forefinger. "Don't tell me there's anything wrong about that security of Lignum's! Don't do it, George, on account of the children!" The trooper looks at her with a troubled visage. "George," says Mrs. Bagnet, using both her arms for emphasis, and occasionally bringing down her open hands upon her knees. "If you have allowed anything wrong to come to that security of Lignum's, and if you have let him in for it, and if you have put us in danger of being sold up—and I see sold up in your face, George, as plain as print—you have done a shameful action, and have deceived us cruelly. I tell you cruelly, George. There!"

Mr. Bagnet, otherwise as immovable as a pump or a lamp-post, puts his large right hand on the top of his bald head, as if to defend it from a shower-bath, and looks with great uneasiness at Mrs. Bagnet.

"George," says that old girl, "I wonder at you! George, I am ashamed of you! George, I couldn't have believed you would have done it! I always knew you to be a rolling stone that gathered no moss, but I never thought you would have taken away what little moss there was for Bagnet and the children to lie upon. You know what a hard-working, steady-going chap he is. You know what Quebec and Malta and Woolwich are—and I never did think you would, or could, have had the heart to serve us so. O George, how could you do it?"

Mrs. Bagnet ceasing, Mr. Bagnet removes his hand from his head, as if the shower-bath were over, and looks disconsolately at Mr. George, who has turned quite white, and looks distressfully at the grey cloak and straw bonnet.

"Mat," says the trooper, in a subdued voice, addressing him, but still looking at his wife, "I am sorry you take it so much to heart, because I do hope it's not so bad as that comes to. I certainly have, this morning, received this letter"—which he reads aloud—"but I hope it may be set right yet. As to a rolling stone, why, what you say is true. I *am* a rolling stone, and I never rolled in anybody's way, I fully believe, that I rolled the least good to. But it's impossible for an old vagabond comrade to like your wife and family better than *I* like 'em, Mat, and I trust you'll look upon me as forgivingly as you can. Don't think I've kept anything from you. I haven't had the letter more than a quarter of an hour."

"Old girl!" murmurs Mr. Bagnet, after a short silence, "will you tell him my opinion?"

"Oh! Why didn't he marry," Mrs. Bagnet answers, half laughing and half crying, "Joe Pouch's widder in North America? Then he wouldn't have got himself into these troubles."

"The old girl," says Mr. Bagnet, "puts it correct—why didn't you?"

"Well, she has a better husband by this time, I hope," returns the trooper. "Anyhow, here I stand, this present day, *not* married to Joe Pouch's widder. What shall I do? You see all I have got about me. It's not mine, it's yours. Give the word and I'll sell off every morsel. If I could have hoped it would have brought in nearly the sum wanted, I'd have sold all long ago. Don't believe that I'll leave you or yours in the lurch, Mat. I'd sell myself first. I only wish," says the trooper, giving himself a disparaging blow in the chest, "that I knew of any one who'd buy such a second-hand piece of old stores."

"Old girl," murmurs Mr. Bagnet, "give him another bit of my mind."

"George," says the old girl, "you are not so much to be blamed, on full consideration, except for ever taking this business without the means."

"And that was like me!" observes the penitent trooper, shaking his head. "Like me, I know."

"Silence! The old girl," says Mr. Bagnet, "is correct—in her way of giving my opinions—hear me out!"

"That was when you ought to have asked for the security, George, and when you never ought to have got it, all things considered. But what's done can't be undone. You are always an honourable and straightforward fellow, as far as lays in your power, though a little flighty. On the other hand, you can't admit but what it's natural in us to be anxious, with such a thing hanging over our heads. So forget and forgive all round, George. Come! Forget and forgive all round!"

Mrs. Bagnet giving him one of her honest hands, and giving her husband the other, Mr. George gives each of them one of his, and holds them while he speaks.

"I do assure you both there's nothing I wouldn't do to discharge this obligation. But whatever I have been able to scrape together has gone every two months in keeping it up. We have lived plainly enough here, Phil and I. But the Gallery don't quite do what was expected of it, and it's not—in short, it's not the Mint. It was wrong in me to take it? Well, so it was. But I was in a manner drawn into that step, and I thought it might steady me, and set me up, and you'll try to overlook my having such expectations, and upon my soul, I am very much obliged to you, and very much ashamed of myself." With these concluding words, Mr. George gives a shake to each of the hands he holds, and, relinquishing them, backs a pace or two, in a broad-chested upright attitude, as if he had made a final confession, and were immediately going to be shot with all military honours.

"George, hear me out!" says Mr. Bagnet, glancing at his wife. "Old girl, go on!"

Mr. Bagnet, being in this singular manner heard out, has merely to observe that the letter must be attended to without any delay; that it is advisable that George and he should immediately wait on Mr. Smallweed in person; and that the primary object is to save and hold harmless Mr. Bagnet, who had none of the money. Mr. George, entirely assenting, puts on his hat, and prepares to march with Mr. Bagnet to the enemy's camp.

"Don't you mind a woman's hasty word, George," says Mrs. Bagnet, patting him on the shoulder. "I trust by old Lignum to you, and I am sure you'll bring him through it."

The trooper returns that this is kindly said, and that he *will* bring Lignum through it somehow. Upon which Mrs. Bagnet, with her cloak, basket, and umbrella, goes home, bright-eyed again, to the rest of her family, and the comrades sally forth on the hopeful errand of mollifying Mr. Smallweed.

Whether there are two people in England less likely to come satisfactorily out of any negotiation with Mr. Smallweed than Mr. George and Mr. Matthew Bagnet may be very reasonably questioned. Also, notwithstanding their martial appearance, broad square shoulders, and heavy tread, whether there are, within the same limits, two more simple and unaccustomed children in all the Smallweedy affairs of life. As they proceed with great gravity through the streets towards the region of Mount Pleasant, Mr. Bagnet, observing his companion to be thoughtful, considers it a friendly part to refer to Mrs. Bagnet's late sally.

"George, you know the old girl—she's as sweet and as mild as milk. But touch her on the children—or myself—and she's off like gunpowder."

"It does her credit, Mat!"

"George," says Mr. Bagnet, looking straight before him, "the old girl. Can't do anything. That don't do her credit. More or less. I never say so. Discipline must be maintained."

"She's worth her weight in gold," says the trooper.

"In gold?" says Mr. Bagnet. "I'll tell you what. The old girl's weight. Is twelve stone six. Would I take that weight. In any metal. *For* the old girl? No. Why not? Because the old girl's metal is far more precious. Than the preciousest metal. And she's *all* metal!"

"You are right, Mat!"

"When she took me. And accepted of the ring. She 'listed under me and the children. Heart and head. For life. She's that earnest," says Mr. Bagnet, "and true to her colours. That, touch us with a finger. And she turns out. And stands to her arms. If the old girl fires wide. Once in a way. At the call of duty. Look over it, George. For she's loyal!"

"Why, bless her, Mat," returns the trooper, "I think the higher of her for it!"

"You are right!" says Mr. Bagnet with the warmest enthusiasm, though without relaxing the rigidity of a single muscle. "Think as high of the old girl. As the rock of Gibraltar. And still you'll be thinking low. Of such merits. But I never own to it before her. Discipline must be maintained."

These encomiums bring them to Mount Pleasant, and to Grandfather Smallweed's house. The door is opened by the perennial Judy, who, having surveyed them from top to toe, leaves them standing there while she consults the oracle as to their admission. The oracle may be inferred to give consent from the circumstance of her returning with the words on her honey lips that "they can come in if they want to it." Thus privileged, they come in, and find Mr. Smallweed with his feet in the drawer of his chair as if it were a paper foot-bath, and Mrs. Smallweed obscured with the cushion like a bird that is not to sing.

"My dear friend," says Grandfather Smallweed, with those two lean affectionate arms of his stretched forth. "How de do? How de do? Who is our friend, my dear friend?"

"Why this," returns George, "is Matthew Bagnet, who has obliged me in that matter of ours, you know."

"Oh! Mr. Bagnet? Surely!" The old man looks at him under his hand. "Hope you're well, Mr. Bagnet? Fine man, Mr. George! Military air, sir!"

No chairs being offered, Mr. George brings one forward for Bagnet and one for himself. They sit down, Mr. Bagnet as if he had no power of bending himself, except at the hips, for that purpose.

"Judy," says Mr. Smallweed, "bring the pipe."

"Why, I don't know," Mr. George interposes, "that the young woman need give herself that trouble, for to tell you the truth, I am not inclined to smoke it today."

"Ain't you?" returns the old man. "Judy, bring the pipe."

"The fact is, Mr. Smallweed," proceeds George, "that I find myself in rather an unpleasant state of mind. It appears to me, sir, that your friend in the city has been playing tricks."

"Oh dear no!" says Grandfather Smallweed. "He never does that!"

"Don't he? Well, I am glad to hear it, because I thought it might be *his* doing. This, you know, I am speaking of. This letter." Grandfather Smallweed smiles in a very ugly way, in recognition of the letter.

"What does it mean?" asks Mr. George.

"Judy," says the old man, "have you got the pipe? Give it to me. Did you say what does it mean, my good friend?"

"Ay! Now, come, come, you know, Mr. Smallweed," urges the trooper, constraining himself to speak as smoothly and confidentially as he can, holding the open letter in one hand, "a good lot of money has passed between us, and we are face to face at the present moment, and are both well aware of the understanding there has always been. I am prepared to do the usual thing which I have done regularly, and to keep this matter going. I never got a letter like this from you before, and I have been a little put about by it this morning; because here's my friend Matthew Bagnet, who, you know, had none of the money—"

"I *don't* know it, you know," says the old man, quietly.

"Why, con-found you—it, I mean—I tell you so, don't I?"

"Oh yes, you tell me so," returns Grandfather Smallweed. "But I don't know it."

"Well!" says the trooper, swallowing his fire. "*I* know it."

Mr. Smallweed replies with excellent temper, "Ah, that's quite another thing!" And adds, "But it don't matter. Mr. Bagnet's situation is all one, whether or no."

The unfortunate George makes a great effort to arrange the affair comfortably, and to propitiate Mr. Smallweed by taking him upon his own terms.

"That's just what I mean. As you say, Mr. Smallweed, here's Matthew Bagnet liable to be fixed whether or no. Now, you see, that makes his good lady very uneasy in her mind, and me too; for whereas I'm a harum-scarum sort of a good-for-nought, he's a steady family man, don't you see? Now, Mr. Smallweed," says the trooper, gaining confidence as he proceeds in his soldierly mode of doing business, "although you and I are good friends enough in a certain sort of a way, I am well aware that I can't ask you to let my friend Bagnet off entirely."

"Oh dear, you are too modest. You can *ask* me anything, Mr. George."

"And you can refuse, you mean, eh? Or not you so much, perhaps, as your friend in the city? Ha ha ha!"

"Ha ha ha!" echoes Grandfather Smallweed. In such a very hard manner, and with eyes so particularly green, that Mr. Bagnet's natural gravity is much deepened by the contemplation of that venerable man.

"Come," says the sanguine George, "I am glad to find we can be pleasant, because I want to arrange this pleasantly. Here's my friend Bagnet, and here am I. We'll settle the matter on the spot, if you please, Mr. Smallweed, in the usual way. And you'll ease my friend Bagnet's mind, and his family's mind, a good deal if you'll just mention to him what our understanding is."

"But I think you asked me, Mr. George"—old Smallweed, who all this time has had the pipe in his hand, is the speaker now—"I think you asked me what did the letter mean."

"Why yes, I did," returns the trooper, in his offhand way: "but I don't care to know particularly if it's all correct and pleasant."

Mr. Smallweed, purposely balking himself in an aim at the trooper's head, throws the pipe on the ground and breaks it to pieces.

"That's what it means, my dear friend. I'll smash you. I'll crumble you. I'll powder you. Go to the devil!" The two friends rise and look at one another. "I'll have no more of your pipe-smoking and swaggerings. What? You're an independent dragoon, too! Go to my lawyer (you remember where, you have been there before) and show your independence now, will you? Come, my dear friend, there's a chance for you. Open the street-door, Judy, put these blusterers out! Call in help if they don't go. Put 'em out!"

He vociferates this so loudly that Mr. Bagnet, laying his hands on the shoulders of his comrade before the latter can recover from his amazement, gets him on the outside of the street-door, which is instantly slammed by the triumphant Judy. Utterly confounded, Mr. George awhile stands looking at the knocker. Mr. Bagnet, in a perfect abyss of gravity, walks up and down before the little parlour window like a sentry, and looks in every time he passes, apparently revolving something in his mind.

"Come, Mat," says Mr. George, when he has recovered himself, "we must try the lawyer. Now what do you think of this rascal?"

Mr. Bagnet, stopping to take a farewell look into the parlour replies, with one shake of his head directed at the interior, "If my old girl had been here—I'd have told him!" Having so discharged himself of the subject of his cogitations, he falls into step, and marches off with the trooper, shoulder to shoulder.

When they present themselves in Lincoln's Inn Fields, Mr. Tulkinghorn is engaged, and not to be seen. He is not at all willing to see them; for when they have waited a full hour, the clerk, on his bell being run brings forth no more encouraging message than that Mr. Tulkinghorn has nothing to say to them, and they had better not wait. They do wait, however, with the perseverance of military tactics; and at last the bell rings again, and the client in possession comes out of Mr. Tulkinghorn's room.

The client is a handsome old lady, no other than Mrs. Rouncewell, housekeeper at Chesney Wold. She comes out of the sanctuary with a fair old-fashioned curtsey, and softly shuts the door. She is treated with some distinction there, for the clerk steps out of his pew to let her out. The old lady is thanking him for his attention when she observes the comrades in waiting.

"I beg your pardon, sir, but I think those gentlemen are military?"

The clerk referring the question to them with his eye, and Mr. George not turning round from the almanack over the fireplace, Mr. Bagnet takes upon himself to reply, "Yes, ma'am. Formerly."

"I thought so. I was sure of it. My heart warms, gentlemen, at the sight of you. It always does at the sight of such. God bless you, gentlemen! You'll excuse an old woman, but I had a son once who went for a soldier. A fine handsome youth he was, and good in his bold way, though some people did disparage him to his poor mother. I ask your pardon for troubling you, sir. God bless you, gentlemen!"

"Same to you, ma'am!" returns Mr. Bagnet, with right good will.

There is something very touching in the earnestness of the old lady's voice, and in the tremble that goes through her quaint old figure. But Mr. George is so occupied with the almanack over the fireplace that he does not look round until she has gone away and the door is closed upon her.

"George," Mr. Bagnet gruffly whispers, when he does turn from the almanack at last. "Don't be cast down! 'Why, soldiers, why. Should we be melancholy, boys?' Cheer up, my hearty!"

The clerk having now again gone in to say that they are still there, and Mr. Tulkinghorn being heard to return with some irascibility, "Let 'em come in then!" they pass into the great room with the painted ceiling, and find him standing before the fire.

"Now, you men, what do you want? Sergeant, I told you the last time I saw you that I don't desire your company here."

Sergeant replies—dashed within the last few minutes as to his usual manner of speech, and even as to his usual carriage—that he has received this letter, has been to Mr. Smallweed about it, and has been referred there.

"I have nothing to say to you," rejoins Mr. Tulkinghorn. "If you get into debt, you must pay your debts or take the consequences. You have no occasion to come here to learn that, I suppose?"

Sergeant is sorry to say that he is not prepared with the money.

"Very well! Then the other man—this man, if this is he—must pay it for you."

Sergeant is sorry to add that the other man is not prepared with the money either.

"Very well! Then you must pay it between you, or you must both be sued for it, and both suffer. You have had the money and must refund it. You are not to pocket other people's pounds, shillings, and pence and escape scot-free."

The lawyer sits down in his easy-chair and stirs the fire. Mr. George hopes he will have the goodness to—

"I tell you, Sergeant, I have nothing to say to you. I don't like your associates, and don't want you here. This matter is not at all in my course of practice, and is not in my office. Mr. Smallweed is good enough to offer these affairs to me, but they are not in my way. You must go to Melchisedech's in Clifford's Inn."

"I must make an apology to you, sir," says Mr. George, "for pressing myself upon you with so little encouragement—which is almost as unpleasant to me as it can be to you—but would you let me say a private word to you?"

Mr. Tulkinghorn rises with his hands in his pockets, and walks into one of the window-recesses. "Now! I have no time to waste." In the midst of his perfect assumption of indifference, he directs a sharp look at the trooper, taking care to stand with his own back to the light and to have the other with his face towards it.

"Well, sir," says Mr. George, "this man with me is the other party implicated in this unfortunate affair—nominally, only nominally—and my sole object is to prevent his getting into trouble on my account. He is a most respectable man with a wife and family, formerly in the Royal Artillery—"

"My friend, I don't care a pinch of snuff for the whole Royal Artillery establishment—officers, men, tumbrils, waggons, horses, guns, and ammunition."

" 'Tis likely, sir. But I care a good deal for Bagnet and his wife and family being injured on my account. And if I could bring them through this matter, I should have no help for it but to give up what you wanted of me the other day."

"Have you got it here?"

"I have got it here, sir."

"Sergeant," the lawyer proceeds in his dry passionless manner, far more hopeless in the dealing with than any amount of vehemence, "make up your mind while I speak to you, for this is final. After I have finished speaking I have closed the subject, and I won't reopen it. Understand that. You can leave here, for a few days, what you say you have brought here, if you choose; you can take it away at once, if you choose. In case you choose to leave it here, I can do this for you—I can replace this matter on its old footing, and I can go so far besides as to give you a written undertaking that this man Bagnet shall never be troubled in any way until you have been proceeded against to the utmost—that your means shall be exhausted before the creditor looks to his. This is in fact all but freeing him. Have you decided?"

The trooper puts his hand into his breast, and answers with a long breath, "I must do it, sir."

So Mr. Tulkinghorn, putting on his spectacles, sits down and writes the undertaking, which he slowly reads and explains to Bagnet, who puts his hand on his bald head under this new verbal shower-bath, and seems exceedingly in need of the old girl through whom to express his sentiments. The trooper then takes from his breast-pocket a folded paper, which he lays with an unwilling hand at the lawyer's elbow. " 'Tis only a letter of instructions, sir. The last I ever had from him."

Look at a millstone, Mr. George, for some change in its expression and you will find it quite as soon as in the face of Mr. Tulkinghorn when he opens and reads the letter! He refolds it, and lays it in his desk, with a countenance as imperturbable as Death.

Nor has he anything more to say or do but to nod once in the same frigid and discourteous manner, and to say briefly, "You can go. Show these men out, there!" Being shown out, they repair to Mr. Bagnet's residence to dine.

Boiled beef and greens constitute the day's variety on the former repast of boiled pork and greens; and Mrs. Bagnet serves out the meal in the same way, and seasons it with the best of temper, being that rare sort of old girl that she receives Good to her arms without a hint that it might be Better, and catches light from any little spot of darkness near her. The spot on this occasion is the darkened brow of Mr. George; he is unusually thoughtful and depressed. At first Mrs. Bagnet trusts to the combined endearments of Quebec and Malta to restore him; but finding those young ladies sensible that their existing Bluffy is not the Bluffy of their usual frolicsome acquaintance, she winks off the light infantry, and leaves him to deploy at leisure on the open ground of the domestic hearth. But he does not. He remains in close order, clouded and depressed. During the lengthy cleaning-up and pattening process, when he and Mr. Bagnet are supplied with their pipes, he is no better than he was at dinner. He forgets to smoke, looks at the fire and ponders, lets his pipe out, fills the breast of Mr. Bagnet with perturbation and dismay by showing that he has no enjoyment of tobacco. Therefore when Mrs. Bagnet at last appears, rosy from the invigorating pail, and sits down to her work, Mr. Bagnet growls, "Old girl!" and winks monitions to her to find out what's the matter.

"Why, George," says Mrs. Bagnet, quietly threading her needle, "how low you are!"

"Am I? Not good company? Well, I am afraid I am not."

"He ain't at all like Bluffy, Mother!" cries little Malta.

"Sure that's a bad sign not to be like Bluffy," returns the trooper. "But it's true"—with a sigh—"true, I am afraid."

"George," says Mrs. Bagnet, working busily, "if I thought you cross enough to think of anything that a shrill old soldier's wife—who could have bitten her tongue off afterwards, and ought to have done it almost

—said this morning, I don't know what I shouldn't say to you now."

"My kind soul of a darling," returns the trooper, "not a morsel of it."

"Because really and truly, George, what I said, and meant to say, was that I trusted Lignum to you, and was sure you'd bring him through it. And you *have* brought him through it, noble!"

"Thank'ee, my dear!" says George. "I am glad of your good opinion."

In giving Mrs. Bagnet's hand, with her work in it, a friendly shake—for she took her seat beside him—the trooper's attention is attracted to her face. After looking at it for a little while as she plies her needle, he looks to young Woolwich, sitting on his stool in the corner, and beckons that fifer to him.

"See there, my boy," says George, very gently smoothing the mother's hair with his hand, "there's a good loving forehead for you! All bright with love of you, my boy. A little touched by the sun and the weather through following your father about and taking care of you, but as fresh and wholesome as a ripe apple on a tree. The time will come, my boy, when this hair of your mother's will be grey, and this forehead all crossed and recrossed with wrinkles—and a fine old lady she'll be then. Take care, while you are young, that you can think in those days, 'I never whitened a hair of her dear head—I never marked a sorrowful line in her face!' For of all the many things that you can think of when you are a man, you had better have *that* by you, Woolwich!"

Mr. George concludes by rising from his chair, seating the boy beside his mother in it, and saying, with something of a hurry about him, that he'll smoke his pipe in the street a bit.

# CHAPTER 35

*Esther's Narrative*

I LAY ill through several weeks, and the usual tenor of my life became like an old remembrance. But this was not the effect of time so much as of the change in all my habits made by the helplessness and inaction of a sick-room. Before I had been confined to it many days, everything else seemed to have retired into a remote distance, where there was little or no separation between the various stages of my life. In falling ill, I seemed to have crossed a dark lake, and to have left all my experiences mingled together by the great distance on the healthy shore.

My housekeeping duties, though at first it caused me great anxiety to think that they were unperformed, were soon as far off as the oldest of the old duties at Greenleaf, or the summer afternoons when I went home from school with my portfolio under my arm, to my godmother's house. I had never known before how short life really was, and into how small a space the mind could put it.

While I was very ill, the way in which these divisions of time became confused with one another distressed my mind exceedingly. At once a

child, an elder girl, and the little woman I had been so happy as, I was not only oppressed by cares and difficulties adapted to each station, but by the great perplexity of endlessly trying to reconcile them. I suppose that few who have not been in such a condition can quite understand what I mean, or what painful unrest arose from this source.

For the same reason I am almost afraid to hint at that time in my disorder—it seemed one long night, but I believe there were both nights and days in it—when I laboured up colossal staircases, ever striving to reach the top and ever turned, as I have seen a worm in a garden path, by some obstruction, and labouring again. I knew perfectly at intervals, and I think vaguely at most times, that I was in my bed; and I talked with Charley, and felt her touch, and knew her very well; yet I would find myself complaining "Oh, more of these never-ending stairs, Charley —more and more—piled up to the sky, I think!" and labouring on again.

The repose that succeeded, the long delicious sleep, the blissful rest, when in my weakness I was too calm to have any care for myself and could have heard (or so I think now) that I was dying with no other emotion than with a pitying love for those I left behind—this state can be perhaps more widely understood. I was in this state when I first shrank from the light as it twinkled on me once more, and knew with a boundless joy for which no words are rapturous enough that I should see again.

I had heard my Ada crying at the door, day and night; I had heard her calling to me that I was cruel and did not love her; I had heard her praying and imploring to be let in to nurse and comfort me, and to leave my bedside no more; but I had only said, when I could speak, "Never, my sweet girl, never!" and I had over and over again reminded Charley that she was to keep my darling from the room, whether I lived or died.

But now, my sight strengthening and the glorious light coming every day more fully and brightly on me, I could read the letters that my dear wrote to me every morning and evening, and could put them to my lips and lay my cheek upon them with no fear of hurting her. I could see my little maid, so tender and so careful, going about the two rooms setting everything in order, and speaking cheerfully to Ada from the open window again. I could understand the stillness in the house, and the thoughtfulness it expressed on the part of all those who had always been so good to me. I could weep in the exquisite felicity of my heart, and be as happy in my weakness as ever I had been in my strength.

By and by, my strength began to be restored. Instead of lying with so strange a calmness watching what was done for me as if it were done for some one else whom I was quietly sorry for, I helped it a little, and a little more and much more, until I became useful to myself, and interested, and attached to life again.

How well I remember the pleasant afternoon when I was raised in bed with pillows for the first time, to enjoy a great tea-drinking with Charley! The little creature was so happy, and so busy, and stopped so often in her preparations to fondle me, and cry with joyful tears she was so glad, she was so glad! that I was obliged to say, "Charley, if you go on in this way, I must lie down again, my darling, for I am weaker than I thought I was!" So Charley became as quiet as a mouse, and took her bright face here and there across and across the two rooms, while I watched her peacefully. When all her preparations were concluded and the pretty tea-table, with its little delicacies to tempt me, and its white cloth, and its flowers, and everything so lovingly and beautifully arranged for me by Ada downstairs, was ready at the bedside, I felt sure I was steady enough to say something to Charley that was not new to my thoughts.

First, I complimented Charley on the room, and indeed it was so fresh and airy, so spotless and neat, that I could scarce believe I had been lying there so long.

"Yet, Charley," said I, looking round, "I miss something, surely, that I am accustomed to?"

Poor little Charley looked round too, and pretended to shake her head, as if there were nothing absent.

"Are the pictures all as they used to be?" I asked her.

"Every one of them, miss," said Charley.

"And the furniture, Charley?"

"Except where I have moved it about, to make more room, miss."

"And yet," said I, "I miss some familiar object. Ah, I know what it is, Charley! It's the looking-glass."

Charley got up from the table, making as if she had forgotten something, and went into the next room, and I heard her sob there.

I had thought of this very often. I was not certain of it. I could thank God that it was not a shock to me now. I called Charley back; and when she came, looking grieved, I took her in my arms and said, "It matters very little, Charley. I hope I can do without my old face very well."

I was presently so far advanced as to be able to sit up in a great chair, and even giddily to walk into the adjoining room, leaning on Charley. The mirror was gone from its usual place in that room too, but what I had to bear was none the harder to bear for that.

My guardian had throughout been earnest to visit me, and there was now no good reason why I should deny myself that happiness. He came one morning, and when he first came in could only hold me in his embrace and say, "My dear, dear girl!" I had long known—who could know better?—what a deep fountain of affection and generosity his heart was, and was it not worth my trivial suffering and change to fill such a place in it? "Oh yes!" I thought, "he has seen me, and is even fonder of me than he was before, and what have I to mourn for!"

He sat down by me on the sofa, supporting me with his arm. For a little while he sat with his hand over his face, but when he removed it, fell into his usual manner. There never can have been, there never can be, a pleasanter manner.

"My little woman," said he, "what a sad time this has been! Such an inflexible little woman, too, through all!"

"Only for the best, Guardian," said I.

"For the best?" he repeated, tenderly. "Of course for the best. But here have Ada and I been perfectly forlorn and miserable; here has your friend Caddy been coming and going late and early; here has every one about the house been utterly lost and dejected; here has even poor Rick been writing—to *me* too—in his anxiety for you!"

I had read of Caddy in Ada's letters, but not of Richard. I told him so.

"Why no, my dear," he replied. "I have thought it better not to mention it to her."

"And you speak of his writing to *you*," said I, repeating his emphasis. "As if it were not natural for him to do so, Guardian, as if he could write to a better friend!"

"He thinks he could, my love," returned my guardian, "and to many a better. The truth is, he wrote to me under a sort of protest, while unable to write to you with any hope of an answer—wrote coldly, haughtily, distantly, resentfully. Well, dearest little woman, we must look forbearingly on it. He is not to blame. Jarndyce and Jarndyce has warped him out of himself, and perverted me in his eyes. I have known it do as bad deeds, and worse, many a time. If two angels could be concerned in it, I believe it would change their nature."

"It has not changed yours, Guardian."

"Oh yes it has, my dear," he said, laughingly. "It has made the south wind easterly, I don't know how often. Rick mistrusts and suspects me —goes to lawyers, and is taught to mistrust and suspect me. Hears I have conflicting interests, claims clashing against his, and what not. Whereas Heaven knows that if I could get out of the mountains of Wiglomeration on which my unfortunate name has been so long bestowed (which I can't), or could level them by the extinction of my own original right (which I can't either, and no human power ever can, anyhow, I believe, to such a pass have we got), I would do it this hour. I would rather restore to poor Rick his proper nature than be endowed with all the money that dead suitors, broken heart and soul upon the wheel of Chancery, have left unclaimed with the Accountant-General—and that's money enough, my dear, to be cast into a pyramid in memory of Chancery's transcendent wickedness."

"Is it possible, Guardian," I asked, amazed, "that Richard can be suspicious of you?"

"Ah, my love, my love," he said, "it is in the subtle poison of such abuses to breed such diseases. His blood is infected, and objects lose their natural aspects in his sight. It is not *his* fault."

"But it is a terrible misfortune, Guardian."

"It is a terrible misfortune, little woman, to be ever drawn within the influences of Jarndyce and Jarndyce. I know none greater. By little and little he has been induced to trust in that rotten reed, and it communicates some portion of its rottenness to everything around him. But again, I say, with all my soul, we must be patient with poor Rick, and not blame him. What a troop of fine fresh hearts, like his, have I seen turned by the same means!"

I could not help expressing something of my wonder and regret that his benevolent disinterested intentions had prospered so little.

"We must not say so, Dame Durden," he cheerfully replied. "Ada is the happier, I hope, and that is much. I did think that I and both these young creatures might be friends, instead of distrustful foes, and that we might so far counteract the suit, and prove too strong for it. But it was too much to expect. Jarndyce and Jarndyce was the curtain of Rick's cradle."

"But Guardian, may we not hope that a little experience will teach him what a false and wretched thing it is?"

"We *will* hope so, my Esther," said Mr. Jarndyce, "and that it may not teach him so too late. In any case we must not be hard on him. There are not many grown and matured men living while we speak, good men too, who, if they were thrown into this same Court as suitors, would not be vitally changed within three years—within two—within one. How can we stand amazed at poor Rick? A young man so unfortunate"—here he fell into a lower tone, as if he were thinking aloud—"cannot at first believe (who could?) that Chancery is what it is. He looks to it, flushed and fitfully, to do something with his interests, and bring them to some settlement. It procrastinates, disappoints, tries, tortures him, wears out his sanguine hopes and patience, thread by thread; but he still looks to it, and hankers after it, and finds his whole world treacherous and hollow. Well, well, well! Enough of this, my dear!"

I resolved in my own mind by some means to see Richard when I grew strong, and try to set him right.

"There are better subjects than these," said my guardian, "for such a joyful time as the time of our dear girl's recovery. And I had a commission to broach one of them as soon as I should begin to talk. When shall Ada come to see you, my love?"

I had been thinking of that too. A little in connexion with the absent mirrors, but not much; for I knew my loving girl would be changed by no change in my looks.

"Dear Guardian," said I, "as I have shut her out so long—though indeed, indeed, she is like the light to me—"

"I know it well, Dame Durden, well."

He was so good, his touch expressed such endearing compassion and affection, and the tone of his voice carried such comfort into my heart, that I stopped for a little while, quite unable to go on. "Yes, yes, you are tired," said he. "Rest a little."

"As I have kept Ada out so long," I began afresh after a short while, "I think I should like to have my own way a little longer, Guardian. It would be best to be away from here before I see her. If Charley and I were to go to some country lodging as soon as I can move, and if I had a week there in which to grow stronger and to look forward to the happiness of having Ada with me again, I think it would be better for us."

I hope it was not a poor thing in me to wish to be a little more used to my altered self before I met the eyes of the dear girl I longed so ardently to see; but it is the truth. I did. He understood me, I was sure, but I was not afraid of that.

"Our spoilt little woman," said my guardian, "shall have her own way even in her inflexibility, though at the price, I know, of tears downstairs. And see here! Here is Boythorn, heart of chivalry, breathing such ferocious vows as never were breathed on paper before that if you don't go and occupy his whole house, he having already turned out of it expressly for that purpose, by Heaven and by earth he'll pull it down, and not leave one brick standing on another!"

And my guardian put a letter in my hand—without any ordinary beginning such as "My dear Jarndyce," but rushing at once into the words "I swear if Miss Summerson do not come down and take possession of my house, which I vacate for her this day at one o'clock, p.m.," and then with the utmost seriousness, and in the most emphatic terms, going on to make the extraordinary declaration he had quoted. We did not appreciate the writer less for laughing heartily over it, and we settled that I should send him a letter of thanks on the morrow, and accept his offer. It was a most agreeable one to me, for of all the places I could have thought of, I should have liked to go to none so well as Chesney Wold.

"Now, little housewife," said my guardian, looking at his watch, "I was strictly timed before I came upstairs, for you must not be tired too soon, and my time has waned away to the last minute. I have one other petition. Little Miss Flite, hearing a rumour that you were ill, made nothing of walking down here—twenty miles, poor soul, in a pair of dancing-shoes—to inquire. It was Heaven's mercy we were at home, or she would have walked back again."

The old conspiracy to make me happy! Everybody seemed to be in it!

"Now, pet," said my guardian, "if it would not be irksome to you to admit the harmless little creature one afternoon before you save Boythorn's house from demolition, I believe you would make her prouder and better pleased with herself than I—though my eminent name *is* Jarndyce—could do in a lifetime."

I have no doubt he knew there would be something in the simple image of the poor afflicted creature that would fall like a gentle lesson on my mind at that time. I felt it as he spoke to me. I could not tell him heartily enough how ready I was to receive her. I had always pitied her, never so much as now. I had always been glad of my little power to soothe her under her calamity, but never, never, half so glad before.

We arranged a time for Miss Flite to come out by the coach and share my early dinner. When my guardian left me, I turned my face away upon my couch, and prayed to be forgiven if I, surrounded by such blessings, had magnified to myself the little trial that I had to undergo. The childish prayer of that old birthday, when I had aspired to be industrious, contented, and true-hearted, and to do good to some one, and win some love to myself if I could, came back into my mind with a reproachful sense of all the happiness I had since enjoyed, and all the affectionate hearts that had been turned towards me. I repeated the old childish prayer in its old childish words, and found that its old peace had not departed from it.

My guardian now came every day. In a week or so more, I could walk about our rooms, and hold long talks with Ada, from behind the window-curtain. Yet I never saw her; for I had not as yet the courage to look at the dear face, though I could have done so easily without her seeing me.

On the appointed day Miss Flite arrived. The poor little creature ran into my room quite forgetful of her usual dignity, and, crying from her very heart of hearts, "My dear Fitz-Jarndyce!" fell upon my neck and kissed me twenty times.

"Dear me!" said she, putting her hand into her reticule, "I have nothing here but documents, my dear Fitz-Jarndyce; I must borrow a pocket-handkerchief."

Charley gave her one, and the good creature certainly made use of it, for she sat so, shedding tears, for the next ten minutes.

"With pleasure, my dear Fitz-Jarndyce," she was careful to explain. "Not the least pain. Pleasure to see you well again. Pleasure at having the honour of being admitted to see you. I am so much fonder of you, my love, than of the Chancellor. Though I *do* attend Court regularly. By the by, my dear, mentioning pocket-handkerchiefs—"

Miss Flite here looked at Charley, who had been to meet her at the place where the coach stopped. Charley glanced at me, and looked unwilling to pursue the suggestion.

"Ve-ry right!" said Miss Flite, "ve-ry correct. Truly! Highly indiscreet of me to mention it, but my dear Miss Fitz-Jarndyce, I am afraid I am at times (between ourselves, you wouldn't think it) a little—rambling you know," said Miss Flite, touching her forehead. "Nothing more."

"What were you going to tell me?" said I, smiling, for I saw she wanted to go on. "You have roused my curiosity, and now you must gratify it."

Miss Flite looked at Charley for advice in this important crisis, who

said, "If you please, ma'am, you had better tell then," and therein gratified Miss Flite beyond measure.

"So sagacious, our young friend," said she to me, in her mysterious
way. "Diminutive. But ve-ry sagacious! Well, my dear, it's a pretty anecdote. Nothing more. Still I think it charming. Who should follow us
down the road from the coach, my dear, but a poor person in a very un-
genteel bonnet."

"Jenny, if you please, miss," said Charley.

"Just so!" Miss Flite acquiesced with the greatest suavity. "Jenny.
Ye-es! And what does she tell our young friend, but that there has been
a lady with a veil inquiring at her cottage after my dear Fitz-Jarndyce's
health, and taking a handkerchief away with her as a little keepsake,
merely because it was my amiable Fitz-Jarndyce's!"

"If you please, miss," said Charley, to whom I looked in some astonishment, "Jenny says that when her baby died, you left a handkerchief
there, and that she put it away and kept it with the baby's little things.
I think, if you please, partly because it was yours, miss, and partly because it had covered the baby."

"Yes, Charley," I returned. "I remember it. Well?"

"Well, miss," said Charley, "and that's the handkerchief the lady
took. And Jenny wants you to know that she wouldn't have made away
with it herself for a heap of money, but that the lady took it, and left
some money instead. Jenny don't know her at all, if you please, miss?"

I did not think very much about this lady then, for I had an impression that it might be Caddy. Besides, my attention was diverted by my
visitor, who was cold after her ride, and looked hungry, and who, our
dinner being brought in, required some little assistance in arraying herself with great satisfaction in a pitiable old scarf and a much-worn and
often-mended pair of gloves, which she had brought down in a paper
parcel. I had to preside, too, over the entertainment, consisting of a
dish of fish, a roast fowl, a sweetbread, vegetables, pudding, and Ma-
deira; and it was so pleasant to see how she enjoyed it that I was soon
thinking of nothing else.

When we had finished, and had our little dessert before us, Miss
Flite was so very chatty and happy that I thought I would lead her to her
own history, as she was always pleased to talk about herself. I began by
saying "You have attended on the Lord Chancellor many years, Miss
Flite?"

"Oh many, many, many years, my dear. But I expect a judgment.
Shortly. My father expected a judgment," said Miss Flite. "My brother.
My sister. They all expected a judgment. The same that I expect."

"They are all—"

"Ye-es. Dead of course, my dear," said she.

"Would it not be wiser," said I, "to expect this judgment no more?"

"Why, my dear," she answered promptly, "of course it would!"

"And to attend the Court no more?"

"Equally of course," said she. "Very wearing to be always in expectation of what never comes, my dear Fitz-Jarndyce! But, my dear," she went on, in her mysterious way, "there's a dreadful attracton in that place. There's a cruel attraction in the place. You *can't* leave it. And you *must* expect."

I tried to assure her that this was not so. She heard me patiently and smilingly, but was ready with her own answer.

"Ay, ay, ay! You think so because I am a little rambling. Ve-ry absurd, to be a little rambling, is it not? Ve-ry confusing, too. To the head. I find it so. But, my dear, I have been there many years, and I have noticed. It's the Mace and Seal upon the table."

What could they do, did she think? I mildly asked her.

"Draw," returned Miss Flite. "Draw people on, my dear. Draw peace out of them. Sense out of them. Good looks out of them. Good qualities out of them. I have felt them even drawing my rest away in the night. Cold and glittering devils!"

She tapped me several times upon the arm, and nodded good-humouredly, as if she were anxious I should understand that I had no cause to fear her, though she spoke so gloomily and confided these awful secrets to me.

"Let me see," said she. "I'll tell you my own case. Before they ever drew me—before I had ever seen them—what was it I used to do? Tambourine playing? No. Tambour-work. I and my sister worked at tambour-work. Our father and our brother had a builder's business. We all lived together. Ve-ry respectably, my dear! First, our father was drawn—slowly. Home was drawn with him. In a few years, he was a fierce, sour, angry bankrupt, without a kind word or a kind look for any one. He had been so different, Fitz-Jarndyce. He was drawn to a debtor's prison. There he died. Then our brother was drawn—swiftly—to drunkenness. And rags. And death. Then my sister was drawn. Hush! Never ask to what! Then I was ill, and in misery, and heard, as I had often heard before, that this was all the work of Chancery. When I got better, I went to look at the Monster. And then I found out how it was, and I was drawn to stay there."

Having got over her own short narrative, in the delivery of which she had spoken in a low, strained voice as if the shock were fresh upon her, she gradually resumed her usual air of amiable importance.

"You don't quite credit me, my dear! Well, well! You will, some day. I am a little rambling. But I have noticed. I have seen many new faces come, unsuspicious, within the influence of the Mace and Seal, in these many years. As my father's came there. As my brother's. As my sister's. As my own. I hear Conversation Kenge, and the rest of them, say to the new faces, 'Here's little Miss Flite. Oh, you are new here, and you must come and be presented to little Miss Flite!' Ve-ry good. Proud I am sure to have the honour! And we all laugh. But, Fitz-Jarndyce, I know what will happen. I know, far better than they do, when the attraction has begun. I know the signs, my dear. I saw them begin in Gridley. And I saw them end. Fitz-Jarndyce, my love," speaking low again, "I saw them beginning in our friend the ward in Jarndyce. Let some one hold him back. Or he'll be drawn to ruin."

She looked at me in silence for some moments, with her face gradually softening into a smile. Seeming to lose the connexion in her mind, she said politely as she sipped her glass of wine, "Yes, my dear, as I was saying, I expect a judgment. Shortly. Then I shall release my birds, you know, and confer estates."

I was much impressed by her allusion to Richard, and by the sad meaning that made its way through all her incoherence. But happily for her, she was quite complacent again now, and beamed with nods and smiles.

"But, my dear," she said, gaily, "you have not congratulated me on my physician. Positively not once, yet! My physician, Mr. Woodcourt, my dear, who was so exceedingly attentive to me. Though his services were rendered quite gratuitously. Until the Day of Judgment. I mean *the* judgment that will dissolve the spell upon me of the Mace and Seal."

"Mr. Woodcourt is so far away, now," said I, "that I thought the time for such congratulation was past, Miss Flite."

"But my child," she returned, "is it possible that you don't know what has happened? what everybody has been talking of, my beloved Fitz-Jarndyce!"

"No," said I. "You forget how long I have been here."

"True! I blame myself. But my memory has been drawn out of me by what I mentioned. Ve-ry strong influence, is it not? Well, my dear, there has been a terrible shipwreck over in those East Indian seas."

"Mr. Woodcourt shipwrecked!"

"Don't be agitated, my dear. He is safe. An awful scene. Death in all shapes. Hundreds of dead and dying. Fire, storm, and darkness. Numbers of the drowning thrown upon a rock. There, and through it all, my dear physician was a hero. Calm and brave through everything. Saved many lives, never complained in hunger and thirst, wrapped naked people in his spare clothes, took the lead, showed them what to do, governed them, tended the sick, buried the dead, and brought the poor survivors safely off at last! My dear, the poor emaciated creatures fell down at his feet when they got to the land, and blessed him. The whole country rings with it. Stay! Where's my bag of documents? I have got it there, and you shall read it, you shall read it!"

And I *did* read all the noble history; though very slowly and imperfectly then, for my eyes were so dimmed that I could not see the words, and I cried so much that I was many times obliged to lay down the long account she had cut out of the newspaper. I felt so triumphant ever to have known the man who had done such generous and gallant deeds, I felt such glowing exultation in his renown, I so admired and loved what he had done, that I envied the storm-worn people who had fallen at his feet and blessed him as their preserver. I could myself have kneeled down then, so far away, and blessed him, in my rapture that he should be so truly good and brave.

My poor little visitor made me a present of the account, and when, as the evening began to close in, she rose to take her leave, lest she should miss the coach by which she was to return, she was still full of the shipwreck.

"My dear," said she, as she carefully folded up her scarf and gloves, "my brave physician ought to have a title bestowed upon him. And no doubt he will. You are of that opinion?"

That he well deserved one, yes. That he would have one, no.

"Why not, Fitz-Jarndyce?" she asked, rather sharply.

I said it was not the custom in England to confer titles on men distinguished by peaceful services, however good and great, unless occasionally, when they consisted of the accumulation of some very large amount of money.

"Why, good gracious," said Miss Flite, "how can you say that? Surely you know, my dear, that all the greatest ornaments of England in knowledge, imagination, active humanity, and improvement of every sort are added to its nobility! Look round you, my dear, and consider. *You* must be rambling a little now, I think, if you don't know that this is the great reason why titles will always last in the land!"

I am afraid she believed what she said, for there were moments when she was very mad indeed.

And now I must part with the little secret I have thus far tried to keep. I had thought, sometimes, that Mr. Woodcourt loved me, and that if he had been richer, he would perhaps have told me that he loved me before he went away. I had thought, sometimes, that if he had done so, I should have been glad of it. But how much better it was now that this had never happened! What should I have suffered if I had had to write to him and tell him that the poor face he had known as mine was quite gone from me, and that I freely released him from his bondage to one whom he had never seen!

Oh, it was so much better as it was!

# CHAPTER 36

*Chesney Wold*

CHARLEY and I did not set off alone upon our expedition into Lincolnshire. My guardian had made up his mind not to lose sight of me until I was safe in Mr. Boythorn's house, so he accompanied us, and we were two days upon the road. I found every breath of air, and every scent, and every flower and leaf and blade of grass, and every passing cloud, and everything in nature, more beautiful and wonderful to me than I had ever found it yet. This was my first gain from my illness.

My guardian intending to go back immediately, we appointed, on our way down, a day when my dear girl should come. I wrote her a letter, of which he took charge, and he left us within half an hour of our arrival at our destination, on a delightful evening in the early summer.

If a good fairy had built the house for me with a wave of her wand, and I had been a princess and her favoured godchild, I could not have been more considered in it. So many preparations were made for me, and such an endearing remembrance was shown of all my little tastes and likings, that I could have sat down, overcome, a dozen times before I had revisited half the rooms. I did better than that, however, by showing them all to Charley instead. Charley's delight calmed mine, and after we had had a walk in the garden I was as tranquilly happy as I ought to have been. It was a great comfort to be able to say to myself after tea, "Esther, my dear, I think you are quite sensible enough to sit down now, and write a note of thanks to your host." He had left a note of welcome for me, as sunny as his own face, and had confided his bird to my care, which I knew to be his highest mark of confidence. Accordingly I wrote a little note to him in London, telling him how all his favourite plants and trees were looking, and how the most astonishing of birds had chirped the honours of the house to me in the most hospitable manner, and how he was then at roost in the usual corner of his cage, but whether dreaming or no I could not report. My note finished and sent off to the post, I made myself very busy in unpacking and arranging, and I sent

Charley to bed in good time and told her I should want her no more that night.

For I had not yet looked in the glass, and had never asked to have my own restored to me. I knew this to be a weakness which must be overcome, but I had always said to myself that I would begin afresh when I got to where I now was. Therefore I had wanted to be alone, and therefore I said, now alone, in my own room, "Esther, if you are to be happy, if you are to have any right to pray to be true-hearted, you must keep your word, my dear." I was quite resolved to keep it, but I sat down for a little while first, to reflect upon all my blessings. And then I said my prayers and thought a little more.

My hair had not been cut off, though it had been in danger more than once. It was long and thick. I let it down and shook it out, and went up to the glass upon the dressing-table. There was a little muslin curtain drawn across it. I drew it back, and stood for a moment looking through such a veil of my own hair that I could see nothing else. Then I put my hair aside and looked at the reflection in the mirror. I was very much changed—oh very, very much. At first, my face was strange to me, but very soon it became more familiar, and then I knew the extent of the alteration in it better than I had done at first. It was not like what I had expected; but I had expected nothing definite. I had never been a beauty, and had never thought myself one, but I had been very different from this. It was all gone now. Heaven was so good to me that I could let it go with a few not bitter tears, and could stand there arranging my hair for the night quite thankfully.

One thing troubled me, and I considered it for a long time before I went to sleep. I had kept Mr. Woodcourt's flowers. When they were withered I had dried them, and put them in a book that I was fond of. Nobody knew this, not even Ada. I was doubtful whether I had a right to preserve what he had sent to one so different—whether it was generous towards him to do it. At last I came to the conclusion that I might keep them, if I treasured them only as a remembrance of what was irrevocably past and gone, never to be looked back on any more. I hope this may not seem trivial. I was very much in earnest.

I took care to be up early in the morning, and to be before the glass when Charley came in on tiptoe.

"Dear, dear, miss!" cried Charley, starting. "Is that you?"

"Yes, Charley," said I, quietly putting up my hair. "And I am very well indeed, and very happy."

I saw it was a weight off Charley's mind, but it was a greater weight off mine. I knew the worst now, and was composed to it. I shall not conceal, as I go on, the weaknesses I could not quite conquer, but they always passed from me soon, and the happier frame of mind stayed by me faithfully.

Wishing to be fully re-established in my strength and my good spirits before Ada came, I now laid down a little series of plans with Charley for being in the fresh air all day long. We were to be out before breakfast, and were to dine early, and were to be out again before and after dinner, and were to walk in the garden after tea, and were to go to rest betimes, and were to climb every hill and explore every road, lane, and field in the neighbourhood. As to restoratives and strengthening delicacies, Mr. Boythorn's good housekeeper was for ever trotting about with something to eat or drink in her hand. Then there was a pony expressly for my riding, a chubby pony with a short neck and a mane all over his eyes, who could canter—when he would—so easily and quietly that he was a treasure. In a very few days, he would come to me in the paddock when I called him, and eat out of my hand, and follow me about—Stubbs. We drove him triumphantly through the green lanes, and to the village.

Charley and I had reason to call it the most friendly of villages, I am sure; for in a week's time the people were so glad to see us go by, though ever so frequently in the course of a day, that there were faces of greeting in every cottage. I had known many of the grown people before, and almost all the children; but now the very steeple began to wear a familiar and affectionate look.

Thus, what with being so much in the air, playing with so many children, gossiping with so many people, sitting on invitation in so many cottages, going on with Charley's education, and writing long letters to Ada every day, I had scarcely any time to think about that little loss of mine, and was almost always cheerful. If I did think of it at odd moments now and then, I had only to be busy and forget it.

There was a favourite spot of mine in the park-woods of Chesney Wold, where a seat had been erected commanding a lovely view. The wood had been cleared and opened, to improve this point of sight, and the bright sunny landscape beyond was so beautiful that I rested there at least once every day. A picturesque part of the Hall, called the Ghost's Walk, was seen to advantage from this higher ground; and the startling name, and the old legend in the Dedlock family which I had heard from Mr. Boythorn accounting for it, mingled with the view and gave it something of a mysterious interest in addition to its real charms.

It would be idle to inquire now why I never went close to the house, or never went inside it. The family were not there, I had heard on my arrival, and were not expected. I was far from being incurious or uninterested about the building; on the contrary, I often sat in this place wondering how the rooms ranged, and whether any echo like a footstep really did resound at times, as the story said, upon the lonely Ghost's Walk. The indefinable feeling with which Lady Dedlock has impressed me may have had some influence in keeping me from the house even when she was absent. I am not sure. Her face and figure were associated with it, naturally, but I cannot say that they repelled me from it, though

something did. For whatever reason or no reason, I had never once gone near it down to the day at which my story now arrives.

I was resting at my favourite point, after a long ramble, and Charley was gathering violets at a little distance from me. I had been looking at the Ghost's Walk lying in a deep shade of masonry afar off, and picturing to myself the female shape that was said to haunt it, when I became aware of a figure approaching through the wood. The perspective was so long, and so darkened by leaves, that at first I could not discern what figure it was. By little and little, it revealed itself to be a woman's—a lady's—Lady Dedlock's. She was alone, and coming to where I sat with a much quicker step, I observed to my surprise, than was usual with her.

I was fluttered by her being unexpectedly so near (she was almost within speaking distance before I knew her), and would have risen to continue my walk. But I could not. I was rendered motionless. Not so much by her hurried gesture of entreaty, not so much by her quick advance and outstretched hands, not so much by the great change in her manner and the absence of her haughty self-restraint, as by a something in her face that I had pined for and dreamed of when I was a little child—something I had never seen in any face, something I had never seen in hers before.

A dread and faintness fell upon me, and I called to Charley. Lady Dedlock stopped upon the instant, and changed back almost to what I had known her.

"Miss Summerson, I am afraid I have startled you," she said, now advancing slowly. "You can scarcely be strong yet. You have been very ill, I know. I have been much concerned to hear it."

I could no more have removed my eyes from her pale face than I could have stirred from the bench on which I sat. She gave me her hand, and its deadly coldness, so at variance with the enforced composure of her features, deepened the fascination that overpowered me. I cannot say what was in my whirling thoughts.

"You are recovering again?" she asked kindly.

"I was quite well but a moment ago, Lady Dedlock."

"Is this your young attendant?"

"Yes."

"Will you send her on before, and walk towards your house with me?"

"Charley," said I, "take your flowers home, and I will follow you directly."

Charley, with her best curtsey, blushingly tied on her bonnet and went her way. When she was gone, Lady Dedlock sat down on the seat beside me. I cannot tell in any words what the state of my mind was when I saw in her hand my handkerchief, with which I had covered the dead baby.

I looked at her, but I could not see her, I could not hear her, I could not draw my breath. The beating of my heart was so violent and wild that I felt as if my life were breaking from me. But when she caught me to her breast, kissed me, wept over me, compassionated me, and called me back to myself—when she fell down on her knees and cried to me, "Oh my child, my child, I am your wicked and unhappy mother! Oh, try to forgive me!" when I saw her at my feet on the bare earth in her great agony of mind—I felt, through all my tumult of emotion, a burst of gratitude to the Providence of God that I was so changed that I never could disgrace her by any trace of likeness, that nobody could ever now look at me and look at her, and remotely think of any near tie between us.

I raised my mother up, praying and beseeching her not to stoop before me in such affliction and humiliation. I did so in broken incoherent words, for, besides the trouble I was in, it frightened me to see her at *my* feet. I told her—or I tried to tell her—that if it were for me, her child, under any circumstances to take upon me to forgive her, I did it, and had done it, many, many years. I told her that my heart overflowed with love for her; that it was natural love, which nothing in the past had changed, or could change. That it was not for me to take her to account for having given me life; but that my duty was to bless her and receive her, though the whole world turned from her, and that I only asked her leave to do it. I held my mother in my embrace, and she held me in hers, and among the still woods in the silence of the summer day, there seemed to be nothing but our own two troubled minds that was not at peace.

"To bless and receive me," groaned my mother, "it is far too late. I must travel my dark road alone, and it will lead me where it will. From day to day, sometimes from hour to hour, I do not see the way before my guilty feet. This is the earthly punishment I have brought upon myself. I bear it, and I hide it. I must keep this secret, if by any means it can be kept, not wholly for myself. I have a husband, wretched and dishonouring creature that I am!"

These words she uttered with a suppressed cry of despair, more terrible in its sound than any shriek. Covering her face with her hands, she shrank down in my embrace as if she were unwilling that I should touch her; nor could I, by my utmost persuasions, or by any endearments I could use, prevail upon her to rise. She said no, no, no, she could only speak to me so; she must be proud and disdainful everywhere else, she would be humbled and ashamed there, in the only natural moments of her life.

My unhappy mother told me that in my illness she had been nearly frantic. She had but then known that her child was living. She could not have suspected me to be that child before. She had followed me down here, to speak to me but once in all her life. We never could associate, never could communicate, never probably from that time forth could interchange another word. She put into my hands a letter she had written for my reading only, and said when I had read it and destroyed it—but not so much for her sake, since she asked nothing, as for her husband's and my own—I must evermore consider her as dead. If I could believe that she loved me, in this agony in which I saw her, with a mother's love, she asked me to do that; for then I might think of her with a greater pity, imagining what she suffered. She had put herself beyond all hope, and beyond all help. Whether she preserved her secret until death, or it came to be discovered and she brought dishonour and disgrace upon the name she had taken, it was her solitary struggle always, and no affection could come near her, and no human creature could render her any aid.

"But is the secret safe so far?" I asked. "Is it safe now, dearest Mother?"

"No," replied my mother. "It has been very near discovery. It was

saved by an accident. It may be lost by another accident—tomorrow, any day."

"Do you dread a particular person?"

"I dread one person very much."

"An enemy?"

"Not a friend. One who is too passionless to be either. He is Sir Leicester Dedlock's lawyer, mechanically faithful without attachment, and very jealous of the profit, privilege, and reputation of being master of the mysteries of great houses."

"Has he any suspicions?"

"Many."

"Not of you?" I said alarmed.

"Yes! He is always vigilant, and always near me. I may keep him at a standstill, but I can never shake him off."

"Has he so little pity or compunction?"

"He has none, and no anger. He is indifferent to everything but his calling. His calling is the acquisition of secrets, and the holding possession of such power as they give him."

"Could you trust in him?"

"I shall never try. The dark road I have trodden for so many years will end where it will. I follow it alone to the end, whatever the end be. It may be near, it may be distant; while the road lasts, nothing turns me."

"Dear Mother, are you so resolved?"

"I *am* resolved. I have long outbidden folly with folly, pride with pride, scorn with scorn, insolence with insolence, and have outlived many vanities with many more. I will outlive this danger, and outdie it, if I can. It has closed around me, almost as awfully as if these woods of Chesney Wold had closed around the house; but my course through it is the same. I have but one, I can have but one."

"Mr. Jarndyce—" I was beginning, when my mother hurriedly inquired:

"Does *he* suspect?"

"No," said I. "No indeed! Be assured that he does not!" And I told her what he had related to me as his knowledge of my story. "But he is so good and sensible," said I, "that perhaps if he knew—"

My mother, who until this time had made no change in her position, raised her hands up to my lips and stopped me.

"Confide fully in him," she said, after a little while. "You have my free consent—a small gift from such a mother to her injured child!—but do not tell me of it. Some pride is left in me, even yet."

I explained, or tried to do it, how I had only hoped that Mr. Jarndyce, who had been the best of fathers to me, might be able to afford some counsel and support to her. But my mother answered no, it was impossible; no one could help her. Through the desert that lay before her, she must go alone.

"My child, my child!" she said. "For the last time! These kisses for the last time! These arms upon my neck for the last time! We shall meet no more. To hope to do what I seek to do, I must be what I have been so long. Such is my reward and doom. If you hear of Lady Dedlock, brilliant, prosperous, and flattered, think of your wretched mother, conscience-stricken underneath that mask! Think that the reality is in her suffering, in her useless remorse, in her murdering within her breast the only love and truth of which it is capable! And then forgive her, if you can, and cry to Heaven to forgive her, which it never can!"

We held one another for a little space yet, but she was so firm that she took my hands away and put them back against my breast and, with a last kiss as she held them there, released them, and went from me into the wood. I was alone; calm and quiet below me in the sun and shade lay the old house, with its terraces and turrets, on which there had seemed to me to be such complete repose when I first saw it, but which now looked like the obdurate and unpitying watcher of my mother's misery.

Stunned as I was, as weak and helpless at first as I had ever been in my sick-chamber, the necessity of guarding against the danger of discovery, or even of the remotest suspicion, did me service. I took such precautions as I could to hide from Charley that I had been crying, and I constrained myself to think of every sacred obligation that there was upon me to be careful and collected. After an hour or so I was better, and felt that I might return. I went home very slowly, and told Charley, whom I found at the gate looking for me, that I had been tempted to extend my walk after Lady Dedlock had left me, and that I was over-tired, and would lie down. Safe in my own room, I read the letter. I clearly derived from it—and that was much, then—that I had not been abandoned by my mother. Her elder and only sister, the godmother of my childhood, discovering signs of life in me when I had been laid aside as dead, had in her stern sense of duty, with no desire or willing-ness that I should live, reared me in rigid secrecy, and had never again beheld my mother's face from within a few hours of my birth. So strangely did I hold my place in this world that until within a short time back I had never, to my own mother's knowledge, breathed—had been buried—had never been endowed with life—had never borne a name. When she had first seen me in the church, she had been startled, and had thought of what would have been like me, if it had ever lived and had lived on; but that was all, then.

What more the letter told me, needs not to be repeated here. It has its own times and places in my story.

My first care was to burn what my mother had written. I hope it may not appear very unnatural or bad in me that I then became heavily sorrowful to think I had ever been reared. That I felt as if I knew it would have been better and happier for many people if indeed I had never breathed. That I had a terror of myself, as the danger and the possible disgrace of my own mother, and of a proud family name. That I was so confused and shaken as to be possessed by a belief that it was right, and had been intended, that I should die at my birth; and that it was wrong, and not intended, that I should be then alive.

These are the real feelings that I had. I fell asleep, worn out, and when I awoke, I cried afresh to think that I was back in the world, with my load of trouble for others. I was more than ever frightened of myself, thinking anew of her, against whom I was a witness, of the owner of Chesney Wold.

The day waned into a gloomy evening, overcast and sad, and I still contended with the same distress. I went out alone, and after walking a little in the park, watching the dark shades falling on the trees and the fitful flight of the bats, which sometimes almost touched me, was attracted to the house for the first time. Perhaps I might not have gone near it if I had been in a stronger frame of mind. As it was, I took the path that led close by it.

I did not dare to linger or to look up, but I passed before the terrace-garden with its fragrant odours, and its broad walks, and its well-kept beds and smooth turf; and I saw how beautiful and grave it was, and how the old stone balustrades and parapets, and wide flights of shallow steps, were seamed by time and weather; and how the trained moss and ivy grew about them, and around the old stone pedestal of the sun-dial; and I heard the fountain falling. Then the way went by long lines of dark windows, diversified by turreted towers, and porches of eccentric shapes. Thence the path wound underneath a gateway, and through a courtyard where the principal entrance was. So, encountering presently a sweet smell of limes, I turned with the turning of the path, to the south front; and there, above me, were the balustrades of the Ghost's Walk, and one lighted window that might be my mother's.

The way was paved here, like the terrace overhead, and my foot-steps from being noiseless made an echoing sound upon the flags. Stopping to look at nothing, but seeing all I did see as I went, I was passing quickly on, and in a few moments should have passed the lighted window, when my echoing footsteps brought it suddenly into my mind that there was a dreadful truth in the legend of the Ghost's Walk; that it was I who was to bring calamity upon the stately house, and that my warning feet were haunting it even then. Seized with an augmented terror of myself which turned me cold, I ran from myself and everything, retraced the way by which I had come, and never paused until I had gained the lodge-gate, and the park lay sullen and black behind me.

Not before I was alone in my own room for the night, and had again been dejected and unhappy there, did I begin to know how wrong and thankless this state was. But from my darling, who was coming on the morrow, I found a joyful letter full of such loving anticipation that I must have been of marble if it had not moved me; from my guardian I found another letter, asking me to tell Dame Durden, if I should see that little woman anywhere, that they had moped most pitiably without her, that the housekeeping was going to rack and ruin, that nobody else could manage the keys, and that everybody in and about the house declared it was not the some house, and was becoming rebellious for her return. Two such letters together made me think how far beyond my deserts I was beloved, and how happy I ought to be. That made me think of all my past life; and that brought me, as it ought to have done before, into a better condition.

For I saw very well that I could not have been intended to die, or I should never have lived, not to say should never have been reserved for such a happy life. I saw very well how many things had worked together for my welfare, and that if the sins of the fathers were sometimes visited upon the children, the phrase did not mean what I had in the morning feared it meant. I knew I was as innocent of my birth as a queen of hers, and that before my Heavenly Father I should not be punished for birth, nor a queen rewarded for it. I had had experience, in the shock of that very day, that I could, even thus soon, find comforting reconcilements to the change that had fallen on me. I renewed my resolutions, and prayed to be strengthened in them, pouring out my heart for myself and for my unhappy mother, and feeling that the darkness of the morning was passing away. It was not upon my sleep, and when the next day's light woke me, it was gone.

My dear girl was to arrive at five o'clock in the afternoon. How to help myself through the intermediate time better than by taking a long walk along the road by which she was to come, I did not know, so Charley and I and Stubbs made a long expedition along that road and back. On our return, we held a great review of the house and garden, and saw that everything was in its prettiest condition, and had the bird out ready as an important part of the establishment.

There were more than two full hours yet to elapse before she could come, and in that interval, which seemed a long one, I must confess I was nervously anxious about my altered looks. I loved my darling so well that I was more concerned for their effect on her than on any one. I was not in this slight distress because I at all repined, but I thought, would she be wholly prepared? When she first saw me, might she not be a little shocked and disappointed? Might it not prove a little worse than she expected?

I knew the various expressions of my sweet girl's face so well, and it was such an honest face in its loveliness, that I was sure beforehand she could not hide that first look from me. And I considered whether, if it should signify any one of these meanings, which was so very likely, could I quite answer for myself? Well, I thought I could. After last night, I thought I could.

At last, when I believed there was at least a quarter of an hour more yet, Charley all at once cried out to me as I was trembling in the garden, "Here she comes, miss! Here she is!"

I did not mean to do it, but I ran upstairs into my room and hid myself behind the door. There I stood trembling, even when I heard my darling calling as she came upstairs, "Esther, my dear, my love, where are you? Little woman, dear Dame Durden!"

She ran in, and was running out again when she saw me. Ah, my angel girl! the old dear look, all love, all fondness, all affection. Nothing else in it—no, nothing, nothing!

Oh how happy I was, down upon the floor, with my sweet beautiful girl down upon the floor too, holding my scarred face to her lovely cheek, bathing it with tears and kisses, rocking me to and fro like a child, calling me by every tender name that she could think of, and pressing me to her faithful heart!

## CHAPTER 37

*Jarndyce and Jarndyce*

IF the secret I had to keep had been mine, I must have confided it to Ada before we had been long together. But it was not mine; and I did not feel that I had a right to tell it, even to my guardian, unless some great emergency arose. It was a weight to bear alone; still my present duty appeared to be plain and, blest in the attachment of my dear, I did not want an impulse and encouragement to do it. Though often when she was asleep, and all was quiet, the remembrance of my mother kept me waking, and made the night sorrowful, I did not yield to it at another time, and Ada found me what I used to be—except, of course, in that particular of which I have said enough, and which I have no intention of mentioning any more just now, if I can help it.

The difficulty that I felt in being quite composed that first evening, when Ada asked me, over our work, if the family were at the house, and when I was obliged to answer yes, I believed so, for Lady Dedlock had spoken to me in the woods the day before yesterday, was great. Greater still when Ada asked me what she had said, and when I replied that she had been kind and interested; and when Ada, while admitting her beauty and elegance, remarked upon her proud manner, and her imperious chilling air. But Charley helped me through unconsciously by telling us that Lady Dedlock had only stayed at the House two nights, on her way from London to visit at some other great house in the next county, and that she had left early on the morning after we had seen her at our view, as we called it. Charley verified the adage about little pitchers, I am sure; for she heard of more sayings and doings in a day than would have come to my ears in a month.

We were to stay a month at Mr. Boythorn's. My pet had scarcely been there a bright week, as I recollect the time, when one evening just as the candles were lighted, Charley, appearing with a very important air behind Ada's chair, beckoned me mysteriously out of the room.

"Oh, if you please, miss," said Charley, in a whisper, "you're wanted at the Dedlock Arms."

"Why, Charley," said I, "who can possibly want me at the public-house?"

"I don't know, miss," returned Charley, "but it's a gentleman, miss, and his compliments, and will you please to come without saying anything about it."

"Whose compliments, Charley?"

"His'n, miss," returned Charley, whose grammatical education was advancing, but not very rapidly.

"And how do you come to be the messenger, Charley?"

"I am not the messenger, if you please, miss," returned my little maid. "It was W. Grubble, miss."

"Ay? The landlord, Charley?"

"Yes, miss. If you please, miss."

Not knowing what might be the matter, and being easily apprehensive now, I thought it best to go to this place by myself. I bade Charley be quick with my bonnet and veil and shawl, and having put them on, went away down the little hilly street, where I was as much at home as in Mr. Boythorn's garden.

Mr. Grubble was standing in his shirt-sleeves at the door of his very clean little tavern, waiting for me. He lifted off his hat with both hands when he saw me coming, and carrying it so, as if it were an iron vessel (it looked as heavy), preceded me along the sanded passage to his best parlour: a neat carpeted room, with more plants in it than were quite convenient, a coloured print of Queen Caroline, several shells, a good many tea-trays, two stuffed and dried fish in glass cases, and either a curious egg or a curious pumpkin (but I don't know which, and I doubt if many people did) hanging from his ceiling. I knew Mr. Grubble very well by sight, from his often standing at his door. A pleasant-looking, stoutish, middle-aged man, who never seemed to consider himself cosily dressed for his own fireside without his hat and top-boots, but who never wore a coat except at church.

He snuffed the candle, and backing away a little to see how it looked, backed out of the room. The door of the opposite parlour being open, I heard some voices, familiar in my ears, I thought. A quick light step approached the room in which I was, and who should stand before me but Richard!

"My dear Esther!" he said, "my best friend!" and he really was so warm-hearted and earnest that in the first surprise and pleasure of his brotherly greeting I could scarcely find breath to tell him that Ada was well.

"Answering my very thoughts—always the same dear girl!" said

Richard, leading me to a chair, and seating himself beside me. I put my veil up, but not quite. "Always the same dear girl!" said Richard, just as heartily as before.

I put up my veil altogether, and laying my hand on Richard's sleeve, and looking in his face, told him how much I thanked him for his kind welcome, and how greatly I rejoiced to see him, the more so because of the determination I had made in my illness, which I now conveyed to him.

"My love," said Richard, "there is no one with whom I have a greater wish to talk than you, for I want you to understand me."

"And I want you, Richard," said I, shaking my head, "to understand some one else."

"Since you refer so immediately to John Jarndyce," said Richard, "I suppose you mean him?"

"Of course I do."

"Then I may say at once that I am glad of it, because it is on that subject that I am anxious to be understood. By you, mind—you, my dear! I am not accountable to Mr. Jarndyce, or Mr. Anybody." I was pained to find him taking this tone, and he observed it. "Well, well, my dear," said Richard, "we won't go into that now. I want to appear quietly in your country-house here, with you under my arm, and give my charming cousin a surprise. I suppose your loyalty to John Jarndyce will allow that?"

"My dear Richard," I returned, "you know you would be heartily welcome at his house—your home, if you will but consider it so—and you are as heartily welcome here!"

"Spoken like the best of little women!" cried Richard gaily.

I asked him how he liked his profession.

"Oh, I like it well enough!" said Richard. "It's all right. It does as well as anything else, for a time. I don't know that I shall care about it when I come to be settled, but I can sell out then, and—however, never mind all that botheration at present."

So young and handsome, and in all respects so perfectly the opposite of Miss Flite! And yet, in the clouded, eager, seeking look that passed over him, so dreadfully like her!

"I am in town on leave, just now," said Richard. "I have run over to look after my—my Chancery interests, before the long vacation," said Richard, forcing a careless laugh. "We are beginning to spin along with that old suit at last, I promise you."

No wonder that I shook my head!

"As you say, it's not a pleasant subject." Richard spoke with the same shade crossing his face as before. "Let it go to the four winds tonight.—Puff! Gone!"

I walked softly in with Richard, and said, "Ada, my love, I have brought a gentleman to visit you." It was not difficult to read the blushing, startled face. She loved him dearly, and he knew it, and I knew it. It was a very transparent business, that meeting as cousins only.

I almost mistrusted myself, as growing quite wicked in my suspicions, but I was not so sure that Richard loved her dearly. He admired her very much—any one must have done that—and I dare say would have renewed their youthful engagement with great pride and ardour but that he knew how she would respect her promise to my guardian. Still, I had a tormenting idea that the influence upon him extended even here: that he was postponing his best truth and earnestness, in this as in all things, until Jarndyce and Jarndyce should be off his mind. Ah me, what Richard would have been without that blight I never shall know now!

He told Ada, in his most ingenuous way, that he had not come to make any secret inroad on the terms she had accepted (rather too implicitly and confidingly, he thought) from Mr. Jarndyce; that he had come openly to see her, and to see me, and to justify himself for the present terms on which he stood with Mr. Jarndyce. He begged that I would make an appointment for the morning, when he might set himself right, through the means of an unreserved conversation with me. I proposed to walk with him in the park at seven o'clock, and this was arranged.

Richard was a little late, but I had not to wait for him long, and we turned into the park. The air was bright and dewy, and the sky without a cloud.

"This is a lovely place," said Richard, looking round. "None of the jar and discord of law-suits here!"

But there was other trouble.

"I tell you what, my dear girl," said Richard, "when I get affairs in general settled, I shall come down here, I think, and rest."

"Would it not be better to rest now?" I asked.

"Oh, as to resting *now,*" said Richard, "or as to doing anything very definite *now,* that's not easy. In short, it can't be done. *I* can't do it at least."

"Why not?" said I.

"You know why not, Esther. If you were living in an unfinished house, liable to have the roof put on or taken off tomorrow, next day, next week, next month, next year—you would find it hard to rest or settle. So do I. Now? There's no now for us suitors."

"My dear Richard," said I, "this is a bad beginning of our conversation."

"I knew you would tell me so, Dame Durden."

"And not I alone, dear Richard. It was not I who cautioned you once never to found a hope or expectation on the family curse."

"There you come back to John Jarndyce!" said Richard, impatiently. "Well! We must approach him sooner or later, for he is the staple of what I have to say, and it's as well at once. My dear Esther, how can you be so blind? Don't you see that he is an interested party, and that it may be very well for him to wish me to know nothing of the suit, and care nothing about it, but that it may not be quite so well for me?"

"O Richard," I remonstrated, "is it possible that you can ever have seen him and heard him, that you can ever have lived under his roof and known him, and can yet breathe such unworthy suspicions?"

He reddened deeply, as if his natural generosity felt a pang of reproach. He was silent for a little while before he replied in a subdued voice:

"Esther, I am sure you know that I am not a mean fellow, and that I have some sense of suspicion and distrust being poor qualities in one of my years."

"I know it very well," said I. "I am not more sure of anything."

"That's a dear girl!" retorted Richard. "And like you, because it gives me comfort. I had need to get some scrap of comfort out of all this business, for it's a bad one at the best, as I have no occasion to tell you."

"I know," said I, "I know as well, Richard—what shall I say?—as well as you do that such misconstructions are foreign to your nature. And I know, as well as you know, what so changes it."

"Come, sister, come," said Richard, a little more gaily, "you will be fair with me, at all events. If I have the misfortune to be under that influence, so has he. If it has a little twisted me, it may have a little twisted him, too. I don't say that he is not an honourable man, I am sure he is. But it taints everybody. You have heard him say so fifty times. Then why should *he* escape?"

"Because," said I, "his is an uncommon character, and he has resolutely kept himself outside the circle, Richard."

"Oh, because and because!" replied Richard, in his vivacious way. "I am not sure, my dear girl, but that it may be wise and specious to preserve that outward indifference. It may cause other parties interested to become lax about their interests—and people may die off, and points may drag themselves out of memory, and many things may smoothly happen that are convenient enough."

I was so touched with pity for Richard that I could not reproach him any more, even by a look. I remembered my guardian's gentleness towards his errors, and with what perfect freedom from resentment he had spoken of them.

"Esther," Richard resumed, "you are not to suppose that I have come here to make underhand charges against John Jarndyce. I have only come to justify myself. What I say is, it was all very well, and we got on very well, while I was a boy, utterly regardless of this same suit; but as soon as I began to take an interest in it, and look into it, then it was quite another thing. Then John Jarndyce discovers that Ada and I must break off, and that if I don't amend that very objectionable course, I am not fit for her. Now, Esther, I don't mean to amend that very objectionable course—I will not hold John Jarndyce's favour on those unfair terms of compromise, which he has no right to dictate. Whether it pleases him or displeases him, I must maintain my rights, and Ada's. I have been thinking about it a good deal, and this is the conclusion I have come to."

Poor dear Richard! He had indeed been thinking about it a good deal. His face, his voice, his manner all showed that, too plainly.

"So I tell him honourably (you are to know I have written to him about all this) that we are at issue, and that we had better be at issue openly than covertly. I thank him for his goodwill and his protection, and he goes his road and I go mine. The fact is, our roads are not the same. Under one of the wills in dispute, I should take much more than he. I don't mean to say that it is the one to be established; but there it is, and it has its chance."

"I have not to learn from you, my dear Richard," said I, "of your letter. I had heard of it already, without an offended or angry word."

"Indeed?" replied Richard, softening. "I am glad I said he was an honourable man, out of all this wretched affair. But I always say that, and have never doubted it. Now, my dear Esther, I know these views of mine appear extremely harsh to you, and will to Ada when you tell her what has passed between us. But if you had gone into the case as I have, if you had only applied yourself to the papers as I did when I was at Kenge's, if you only knew what an accumulation of charges and countercharges, and suspicions and cross-suspicions, they involve, you would think me moderate in comparison."

"Perhaps so," said I. "But do you think that among those many papers there is much truth and justice, Richard?"

"There is truth and justice somewhere in the case, Esther."

"Or was once, long ago," said I.

"Is—is—must be somewhere," pursued Richard impetuously, "and must be brought out. To allow Ada to be made a bribe and hush-money of is not the way to bring it out. You say the suit is changing me; John Jarndyce says it changes, has changed, and will change, everybody who has any share in it. Then the greater right I have on my side when I resolve to do all I can to bring it to an end."

"All you can, Richard! Do you think that in these many years no others have done all they could? Has the difficulty grown easier because of so many failures?"

"It can't last for ever," returned Richard, with a fierceness kindling in him which again presented to me that last sad reminder. "I am young and earnest, and energy and determination have done wonders many a time. Others have only half thrown themselves into it. I devote myself to it. I make it the object of my life."

"O Richard my dear, so much the worse, so much the worse!"

"No, no, no, don't you be afraid for me," he returned, affectionately. "You're a dear, good, wise, quiet, blessed girl; but you have your pre-possessions. So I come round to John Jarndyce. I tell you, my good

Esther, when he and I were on those terms which he found so convenient, we were not on natural terms."

"Are division and animosity your natural terms, Richard?"

"No, I don't say that. I mean that all this business puts us on unnatural terms. See another reason for urging it on! I may find out, when it's over, that I have been mistaken in John Jarndyce. My head may be clearer when I am free of it, and I may then agree with what you say today. Very well. Then I shall acknowledge it, and make him reparation."

Everything postponed to that imaginary time! Everything held in confusion and indecision until then!

"Now, my best of confidantes," said Richard, "I want my cousin, Ada to understand that I am not captious, fickle, and wilful about John Jarndyce, but that I have this purpose and reason at my back. I wish to represent myself to her through you, because she has a great esteem and respect for her cousin John, and I know you will soften the course I take, even though you disapprove of it, and—and in short," said Richard, who had been hesitating through these words, "I—I don't like to represent myself in this contentious, doubting character to a confiding girl like Ada."

I told him that he was more like himself in those latter words than in anything he had said yet.

"Why," acknowledged Richard, "that may be true enough, my love. I rather feel it to be so. But I shall be able to give myself fair play by and by. I shall come all right again, then, don't you be afraid."

I asked him if this were all he wished me to tell Ada.

"Not quite," said Richard. "I am bound not to withhold from her that John Jarndyce answered my letter in his usual manner, addressing me as 'My dear Rick,' trying to argue me out of my opinions, and telling me that they should make no difference in him. I also want Ada to know that if I see her seldom just now, I am looking after her interests as well as my own—we two being in the same boat exactly—and that I hope she will not suppose, from any flying rumours she may hear, that I am at all light-headed or imprudent. On the contrary, I am always looking forward to the termination of the suit, and always planning in that direction. Being of age now, and having taken the step I have taken, I consider myself free from any accountability to John Jarndyce; but Ada being still a ward of the Court, I don't yet ask her to renew our engagement. When she is free to act for herself, I shall be myself once more, and we shall both be in very different worldly circumstances, I believe. If you tell her all this with the advantage of your considerate way, you will do me a very great and a

very kind service, my dear Esther; and I shall knock Jarndyce and Jarndyce on the head with greater vigour. Of course I ask for no secrecy at
Bleak House."

"Richard," said I, "you place great confidence in me, but I fear you
will not take advice from me."

"It's impossible that I can on this subject, my dear girl. On any other,
readily."

As if there were any other in his life!

"But I may ask you a question, Richard?"

"I think so," said he, laughing. "I don't know who may not if you
may not."

"You say yourself you are not leading a very settled life."

"How can I, my dear Esther, with nothing settled!"

"Are you in debt again?"

"Why, of course I am," said Richard, astonished at my simplicity.

"Is it of course?"

"My dear child, certainly. I can't throw myself into an object so completely without expense. You forget, or perhaps you don't know, that
under either of the wills Ada and I take something. It's only a question
between the larger sum and the smaller. I shall be within the mark
anyway. Bless your heart, my excellent girl," said Richard, quite amused
with me, "I shall be all right! I shall pull through, my dear!"

I felt so deeply sensible of the danger in which he stood that I tried,
in Ada's name, in my guardian's, in my own, by every fervent means
that I could think of, to warn him of it, and to show him some of his
mistakes. He received everything I said with patience and gentleness,
but it all rebounded from him without taking the least effect. I could
not wonder at this, after the reception his preoccupied mind had given
to my guardian's letter; but I determined to try Ada's influence yet.

So when our walk brought us round to the village again, and I went
home to breakfast, I prepared Ada for the account I was going to give
her, and told her exactly what reason we had to dread that Richard
was losing himself, and scattering his whole life to the winds. It made
her very unhappy, of course, though she had a far, far greater reliance
on his correcting his errors than I could have, she presently wrote him
this little letter:

My Dearest Cousin,
    Esther has told me all you said to her this morning. I write this to
repeat most earnestly for myself all that she said to you, and to let you
know how sure I am that you will sooner or later find our cousin John a
pattern of truth, sincerity, and goodness, when you will deeply deeply
grieve to have done him (without intending it) so much wrong.

I do not quite know how to write what I wish to say next, but I trust you will understand it as I mean it. I have some fears, my dearest Cousin, that it may be partly for my sake you are now laying up so much unhappiness for yourself—and if for yourself, for me. In case this should be so, or in case you should entertain much thought of me in what you are doing, I most earnestly entreat and beg you to desist. You can do nothing for my sake that will make me half so happy as for ever turning your back upon the shadow in which we both were born. Do not be angry with me for saying this. Pray, pray, dear Richard, for my sake, and for your own, and in a natural repugnance for that source of trouble which had its share in making us both orphans when we were very young, pray, pray, let it go for ever. We have reason to know, by this time, that there is no good in it, and no hope, that there is nothing to be got from it but sorrow.

My dearest Cousin, it is needless for me to say that you are quite free, and that it is very likely you may find some one whom you will love much better than your first fancy. I am quite sure, if you will let me say so, that the object of your choice would greatly prefer to follow your fortunes far and wide, however moderate or poor, and see you happy, doing your duty and pursuing your chosen way, than to have the hope of being, or even to be, very rich with you at the cost of dragging years of procrastination and anxiety, and of your indifference to other aims. You may wonder at my saying this so confidently with so little knowledge or experience, but I know it for a certainty from my own heart.

Ever, my dearest Cousin, your most affectionate,

ADA

This note brought Richard to us very soon; but it made little change in him, if any. We would fairly try, he said, who was right and who was wrong—he would show us—we should see! He was animated and glowing, as if Ada's tenderness had gratified him; but I could only hope that the letter might have stronger effect upon his mind on reperusal than it assuredly had then.

I felt it a relief when Richard, with an exclamation of surprise, hurried away to meet a stranger, whom he first descried coming slowly towards us, and coming back to us in an excited state, presented Mr. Vholes—a sallow man with pinched lips that looked as if they were cold, a red eruption here and there upon his face, tall and thin, about fifty years of age, high-shouldered, and stooping, dressed in black, black-gloved, and buttoned to the chin.

"I hope I don't disturb you, ladies," said Mr. Vholes; and now I observed that he was further remarkable for an inward manner of speaking. "I arranged with Mr. Carstone that he should always know when his cause was in the Chancellor's paper, and being informed by one of my clerks last night after post-time that it stood in the paper for tomorrow, I put myself into the coach early this morning and came down to confer with him."

"Yes," said Richard, flushed, and looking triumphantly at Ada and me, "we don't do these things in the old slow way, now! We spin along, now! Mr. Vholes, we must hire something to get over to the post town in, and catch the mail tonight and go up by it!"

"Anything you please, sir," returned Mr. Vholes. "I am quite at your service."

"Let me see," said Richard, looking at his watch. "If I run down to the Dedlock and get my portmanteau fastened up, and order a gig, or a chaise, or whatever's to be got, we shall have an hour then before starting. I'll come back to tea. Cousin Ada, will you and Esther take care of Mr. Vholes when I am gone?"

He was away directly, in his heat and hurry, and was soon lost in the dusk of evening. We who were left walked on towards the house.

"Is Mr. Carstone's presence necessary tomorrow, sir?" said I. "Can it do any good?"

"No, miss," Mr. Vholes replied. "I am not aware that it can. Mr. Carstone has laid down the principle of watching his own interests, and when a client lays down his own principle, and it is not immoral, it devolves upon me to carry it out. I wish in business to be exact and open. I am a widower with three daughters—Emma, Jane, and Caroline —and my desire is so to discharge the duties of life as to leave them a good name— This appears to be a pleasant spot, miss."

The remark being made to me, in consequence of my being next him as we walked, I assented, and enumerated its chief attractions.

"Indeed?" said Mr. Vholes. "I have the privilege of supporting an aged father in the Vale of Taunton—his native place—and I admire that country very much. I had no idea there was anything so attractive here."

To keep up the conversation, I asked Mr. Vholes if he would like to live altogether in the country.

"There, miss," said he, "you touch me on a tender string. My health is not good (my digestion being much impaired), and if I had only myself to consider, I should take refuge in rural habits; especially as the cares of business have prevented me from ever coming much into contact with general society, and particularly with ladies' society, which I have most wished to mix in. But with my three daughters, Emma, Jane, and Caroline, and my aged father, I cannot afford to be selfish."

It required some attention to hear him, on account of his inward speaking and his lifeless manner.

We now arrived at Mr. Boythorn's house, where the tea-table, all prepared, was awaiting us. Richard came in restless and hurried shortly afterwards, and leaning over Mr. Vholes's chair whispered something in his ear. Mr. Vholes replied aloud—or as nearly aloud I suppose as he had ever replied to anything—"You will drive me, will you, sir? It is all the same to me, sir. Anything you please. I am quite at your service."

Richard's high spirits carrying everything before them, we all went out together to the top of the hill above the village, where he had ordered a gig to wait. I never shall forget those two seated side by side in the lantern's light; Richard, all flush and fire and laughter, with the reins in his hand; Mr. Vholes, quite still, black-gloved, and buttoned-up, looking at him as if he were looking at his prey and charming it.

# CHAPTER 38

## A Struggle

WHEN our time came for returning to Bleak House again, we were punctual to the day, and were received with an overpowering welcome. I was perfectly restored to health and strength, and finding my housekeeping keys laid ready for me in my room, rang myself in as if I had been a new year, with a merry little peal. The first few mornings were mornings of so much bustle and business, devoted to such settlements of accounts, such repeated journeys to and fro between the Growlery and all other parts of the house, so many re-arrangements of drawers and presses, that I had not a moment's leisure. But when everything was in order, I paid a visit of a few hours to London, which something in the letter I had destroyed at Chesney Wold had induced me to decide upon in my own mind.

I made Caddy Jellyby—her maiden name was so natural to me that I always called her by it—the pretext for this visit, and wrote her a note previously, asking the favour of her company on a little business expedition. Leaving home very early in the morning, I got to London by stage-coach in such good time that I got to Newman Street with the day before me.

Caddy, who had not seen me since her wedding-day, was so glad and so affectionate that I was half inclined to fear I should make her husband jealous. But he was, in his way, just as bad—I mean as good; and in short it was the old story, and nobody would leave me any possibility of doing anything meritorious.

The elder Mr. Turveydrop was in bed, I found, and Caddy was

milling his chocolate, which a melancholy little boy who was an apprentice—it seemed such a curious thing to be apprenticed to the trade of dancing—was waiting to carry upstairs. Her father-in-law was extremely kind and considerate, Caddy told me, and they lived most happily together.

"And how is your mama, Caddy?" said I.

"Why, I hear of her, Esther," replied Caddy, "through Pa, but I see very little of her. We are good friends, I am glad to say, but Ma thinks there is something absurd in my having married a dancing-master, and she is rather afraid of its extending to her."

"And your papa, Caddy?"

"He comes here every evening," returned Caddy, "and is so fond of sitting in the corner there that it's a treat to see him."

Looking at the corner, I plainly perceived the mark of Mr. Jellyby's head against the wall. It was consolatory to know that he had found such a resting-place for it.

"And you, Caddy," said I, "you are always busy, I'll be bound?"

"Well, my dear," returned Caddy, "I am indeed, for to tell you a grand secret, I am qualifying myself to give lessons. Prince's health is not strong, and I want to be able to assist him. What with schools, and classes here, and private pupils, *and* the apprentices, he really has too much to do, poor fellow! You see, my dear, to save expense, I ought to know something of the piano, and I ought to know something of the kit too, and consequently I have to practise those two instruments as well as the details of our profession. If Ma had been like anybody else, I might have had some little musical knowledge to begin upon. However, I hadn't any, and that part of the work is, at first, a little discouraging, I must allow. But I have a very good ear, and I am used to drudgery—I have to thank Ma for that, at all events—and where there's a will there's a way, you know, Esther, the world over." Saying these words, Caddy laughingly sat down at a little jingling square piano, and really rattled off a quadrille with great spirit. Then she good-humouredly and blushingly got up again, and while she still laughed herself, said, "Don't laugh at me, please, that's a dear girl!"

I would sooner have cried, but I did neither. I encouraged her and praised her with all my heart. For I conscientiously believed, dancing-master's wife though she was, and dancing-mistress though in her limited ambition she aspired to be, she had struck out a natural, wholesome, loving course of industry and perseverance that was quite as good as a Mission.

"My dear," said Caddy, delighted, "you can't think how you cheer me. I shall owe you you don't know how much. What changes, Esther,

even in my small world! You recollect that first night, when I was so unpolite and inky? Who would have thought then of my ever teaching
people to dance, of all other possibilities and impossibilities!"

Her husband, who had left us while we had this chat, now coming
back, preparatory to exercising the apprentices in the ballroom, Caddy
informed me she was quite at my disposal. But it was not my time yet, I
was glad to tell her, for I should have been vexed to take her away then.
Therefore we three adjourned to the apprentices together, and I made
one in the dance. Caddy, while she was observant of her husband, and
was evidently founded upon him, had acquired a grace and self-possession of her own which, united to her pretty face and figure, was uncommonly agreeable. She already relieved him of much of the instruction
of these young people, and he seldom interfered, except to walk his part
in the figure if he had anything to do in it. He always played the tune.
And thus we danced an hour by the clock.

When the practice was concluded, Caddy's husband made himself
ready to go out of town to a school, and Caddy ran away to get ready to
go out with me. I sat in the ballroom in the interval, contemplating the
apprentices.

"Old Mr. Turveydrop is so sorry," said Caddy, "that he has not finished dressing yet and cannot have the pleasure of seeing you before you
go. You are such a favourite of his, Esther."

I expressed myself much obliged to him, but did not think it necessary
to add that I readily dispensed with this attention.

"It takes him a long time to dress," said Caddy, "because he is very
much looked up to in such things, you know, and has a reputation to
support. You can't think how kind he is to Pa. He talks to Pa of an evening about the Prince Regent, and I never saw Pa so interested."

There was something in the picture of Mr. Turveydrop bestowing his
Deportment on Mr. Jellyby that quite took my fancy. I asked Caddy if
he brought her papa out much.

"No," said Caddy, "I don't know that he does that; but he talks to Pa,
and Pa greatly admires him, and listens, and likes it. Of course I am
aware that Pa has hardly any claims to Deportment, but they get on together delightfully. You can't think what good companions they make.
I never saw Pa take snuff before in my life, but he takes one pinch out of
Mr. Turveydrop's box regularly, and keeps putting it to his nose and
taking it away again all the evening."

That old Mr. Turveydrop should ever, in the chances and changes of
life, have come to the rescue of Mr. Jellyby from Borrioboola-Gha appeared to me to be one of the pleasantest of oddities.

"As to Peepy," said Caddy, with a little hesitation, "whom I was most afraid of—next to having any family of my own, Esther—as an inconvenience to Mr. Turveydrop, the kindness of the old gentleman to that child is beyond everything. He asks to see him, my dear! He lets him take the newspaper up to him in bed; he gives him the crusts of his toast to eat; he sends him on little errands about the house; he tells him to come to me for sixpences. In short," said Caddy, cheerily, "I am a very fortunate girl, and ought to be very grateful. Where are we going, Esther?"

"To the Old Street Road," said I, "where I have a few words to say to the solicitor's clerk who was sent to meet me at the coach-office on the very day when I came to London and first saw you, my dear. Now I think of it, the gentleman who brought us to your house."

"Then indeed I seem to be naturally the person to go with you," returned Caddy.

To the Old Street Road we went, and there inquired at Mrs. Guppy's residence for Mrs. Guppy. Mrs. Guppy, occupying the parlours, immediately presented herself, and requested us to walk in. She was an old lady in a large cap, with rather a red nose and rather an unsteady eye, but smiling all over. Her close little sitting-room was prepared for a visit, and there was a portrait of her son in it. Not only was the portrait there, but we found the original there too. He was dressed in a great many colours, and was discovered at a table reading law-papers with his fore-finger to his forehead.

"Miss Summerson," said Mr. Guppy, rising, "this is indeed an Oasis. Mother, will you be so good as to put a chair for the other lady, and get out of the gangway?"

Mrs. Guppy, whose incessant smiling gave her quite a waggish ap-pearance, did as her son requested, and then sat down in a corner. I pre-sented Caddy, and Mr. Guppy said that any friend of mine was more than welcome. I then proceeded to the object of my visit.

"I took the liberty of sending you a note, sir," said I.

Mr. Guppy acknowledged the receipt by taking it out of his breast-pocket, putting it to his lips, and returning it to his pocket with a bow.

"Could I speak to you alone for a moment?" said I.

Anything like the jocoseness of Mr. Guppy's mother just now, I think I never saw. She was so unspeakably entertained altogether that it was with some difficulty she could marshal Caddy through the little folding-door into her bedroom adjoining.

I could hardly have believed that anybody could in a moment have turned so red, or changed so much, as Mr. Guppy did when I now put up my veil.

"I asked the favour of seeing you for a few moments here," said I, "in preference to calling at Mr. Kenge's, because, remembering what you said on an occasion when you spoke to me in confidence, I feared I might otherwise cause you some embarrassment."

I caused him embarrassment enough as it was, I am sure. I never saw such faltering, such confusion, such amazement and apprehension.

"Miss Summerson," stammered Mr. Guppy, "I—I—beg your pardon, but in our profession—we—we—find it necessary to be explicit. You have referred to an occasion, miss, when I—when I did myself the honour of making a declaration which—"

Something seemed to rise in his throat that he could not possibly swallow. He put his hand there, coughed, made faces, tried again to swallow it, coughed again, made faces again, looked all round the room, and fluttered his papers. I gave him a little time to recover. He consumed it in putting his hand to his forehead and taking it away again, and in backing his chair into the corner behind him.

"My intention was to remark, miss," said Mr. Guppy, "that you was so good on that occasion as to repel and repudiate that declaration. You—you wouldn't perhaps object to admit that? Though no witnesses are present, it might be a satisfaction to—to your mind—if you was to put in that admission."

"There can be no doubt," said I, "that I declined your proposal without any reservation or qualification whatever, Mr. Guppy."

"Thank you, miss," he returned. "So far that's satisfactory, and it does you credit. Er—er—you wouldn't perhaps be offended if I was to mention —not that it's necessary, for your own good sense or any person's sense must show 'em that—if I was to mention that such declaration on my part was final, and there terminated?"

"I quite understand that," said I.

"Perhaps—er—it may not be worth the form, but it might be a satisfaction to your mind—perhaps you wouldn't object to admit that, miss?" said Mr. Guppy.

"I admit it most fully and freely," said I.

"Thank you," returned Mr. Guppy. "Very honourable, I am sure. I regret that my arrangements in life, combined with circumstances over which I have no control, will put it out of my power ever to fall back upon that offer, or to renew it in any shape or form whatever; but it will ever be a retrospect entwined—er—with friendship's bowers."

"I may now perhaps mention what I wished to say to you?" I began.

"I shall be honoured, I am sure," said Mr. Guppy. "I am so persuaded that your own good sense and right feeling, miss, will—will keep you as square as possible—that I can have nothing but pleasure in hearing any observations you may wish to offer."

"You were so good as to imply, on that occasion—"

"Excuse me, miss," said Mr. Guppy, "but we had better not travel out of the record into implication. I cannot admit that I implied anything."

"You said on that occasion," I recommenced, "that you might possibly have the means of advancing my interests, and promoting my fortunes, by making discoveries of which I should be the subject. I presume that you founded that belief upon your general knowledge of my being an orphan girl, indebted for everything to the benevolence of Mr. Jarndyce. Now the beginning and the end of what I have come to beg of you is, Mr. Guppy, that you will have the kindness to relinquish all idea of so serving me. I have thought of this sometimes, and I have thought of it most lately—since I have been ill. At length I have decided, in case you should at any time recall that purpose, and act upon it in any way, to come to you and assure you that you are altogether mistaken. You could make no discovery in reference to me that would do me the least service, or give me the least pleasure. I am acquainted with my personal history, and I have it in my power to assure you that you never can advance my welfare by such means. You may, perhaps, have abandoned this project a long time. If so, excuse my giving you unnecessary trouble. If not, I entreat you, on the assurance I have given you, henceforth to lay it aside."

"I am bound to confess," said Mr. Guppy, "that you express yourself, miss, with that good sense and right feeling for which I gave you credit. Nothing can be more satisfactory than such right feeling, and if I mistook any intentions on your part just now, I am prepared to tender a full apology. I should wish to be understood, miss, as hereby offering that apology."

I must say for Mr. Guppy that the shuffling manner he had had upon him improved very much. He seemed truly glad to be able to do something I asked, and he looked ashamed.

"If you will allow me to finish what I have to say at once, so that I may have no occasion to resume," I went on, seeing him about to speak, "you will do me a kindness, sir. I come to you as privately as possible, because you announced this impression of yours to me in a confidence which I have really wished to respect—and which I always have respected, as you remember. I have mentioned my illness. There really is no reason why I should hesitate to say that I know very well that any little delicacy I might have had in making a request to you is quite removed. Therefore I make the entreaty I have now preferred, and I hope you will have sufficient consideration for me to accede to it."

I must do Mr. Guppy the further justice of saying that he had looked more and more ashamed, and that he looked most ashamed, and very earnest, when he now replied with a burning face:

"Upon my word and honour, upon my soul, Miss Summerson, as I am a living man, I'll act according to your wish! I'll never go another step in opposition to it. I'll take my oath to it, if it will be any satisfaction to you. In what I promise at this present time touching the matters now in question," continued Mr. Guppy rapidly, as if he were repeating a familiar form of words, "I speak the truth, the whole truth, and nothing but the truth, so—"

"I am quite satisfied," said I, rising at this point, "and I thank you very much. Caddy, my dear, I am ready!"

Mr. Guppy's mother returned with Caddy and we took our leave. Mr. Guppy saw us to the door with the air of one who was either imperfectly awake or walking in his sleep, and we left him there, staring. But in a minute he came after us down the street without any hat, and with his long hair all blown about, and stopped us, saying fervently:

"Miss Summerson, upon my honour and soul, you may depend upon me!"

"I do," said I, "quite confidently."

"I beg your pardon, miss," said Mr. Guppy, going with one leg and staying with the other, "but this lady being present—your own witness —it might be a satisfaction to your mind (which I should wish to set at rest) if you was to repeat those admissions."

"Well, Caddy," said I, turning to her, "perhaps you will not be surprised when I tell you, my dear, that there never has been any engagement—"

"No proposal or promise of marriage whatsoever," suggested Mr. Guppy.

"No proposal or promise of marriage whatsoever," said I, "between this gentleman—"

"William Guppy of Penton Place, Pentonville, in the County of Middlesex," he murmured.

"Between this gentleman, Mr. William Guppy, of Penton Place, Pentonville, in the County of Middlesex, and myself."

"Thank you, miss," said Mr. Guppy. "Very full,—er—excuse me—lady's name, Christian and surname both?" I gave them. "Married woman, I believe?" said Mr. Guppy. "Married woman. Thank you. Formerly Caroline Jellyby, spinster, then of Thavies Inn, within the City of London, but extra-parochial; now of Newman Street, Oxford Street. Much obliged."

He ran home and came running back again.

"Touching that matter, you know, I really and truly am very sorry that my arrangements in life, combined with circumstances over which I have no control, should prevent a renewal of what was wholly terminated some time back," said Mr. Guppy to me forlornly, "but it couldn't be. Now *could* it, you know!"

I replied it certainly could not. The subject did not admit of a doubt. He thanked me, and ran to his mother's again—and back again.

"It's very honourable of you, miss, I am sure," said Mr. Guppy. "If an altar could be erected in the bowers of friendship—but, upon my soul, you may rely upon me in every respect, save and except the tender passion only!"

The struggle in Mr. Guppy's breast, and the numerous oscillations it occasioned him between his mother's door and us, were sufficiently conspicuous in the windy street (particularly as his hair wanted cutting), to make us hurry away. I did so with a lightened heart, but when we last looked back, Mr. Guppy was still oscillating in the same troubled state of mind.

# CHAPTER 39

~~~~~~~~~~~~~~~~~~~~~~~~~~~~~~~~~~~~~~~~~~~~~~~~~~~~~~

*Attorney and Client*

THE name of MR. VHOLES, preceded by the legend GROUND FLOOR, is inscribed upon a door-post in Symond's Inn, Chancery Lane: a little, pale, wall-eyed, woe-begone inn, like a large dust-bin of two compartments and a sifter. Mr. Vholes's office, in disposition retiring and in situation retired, is squeezed up in a corner, and blinks at a dead wall. Three feet of knotty-floored dark passage bring the client to Mr. Vholes's jet-black door, in an angle profoundly dark on the brightest midsummer morning. Mr. Vholes's chambers are on so small a scale that one clerk can open the door without getting off his stool while the other who elbows him at the same desk has equal facilities for poking the fire. The place was last painted or whitewashed beyond the memory of man, and the two chimneys smoke, and there is a loose outer surface of soot everywhere, and the dull cracked windows in their heavy frames have but one piece of character in them, which is a determination to be always dirty, and always shut, unless coerced.

Mr. Vholes is a very respectable man. He has not a large business, but he is a very respectable man. He is allowed by the greater attorneys who have made good fortunes, or are making them, to be a most respectable man. He never misses a chance in his practice, which is a mark of respectability. He never takes any pleasure, which is another mark of respectability. He is reserved and serious, which is another mark of respectability. His digestion is impaired, which is highly respectable. And he is making hay of the grass which is flesh, for his three daughters. And his father is dependent on him in the Vale of Taunton.

The one great principle of the English law is to make business for itself. There is no other principle distinctly, certainly, and consistently maintained through all its narrow turnings. Viewed by this light it becomes a coherent scheme and not the monstrous maze the laity are apt to think it. Let them but once clearly perceive that its grand principle is to make business for itself at their expense, and surely they will cease to grumble.

The Chancellor is, within these ten minutes, "up" for the long vacation. Mr. Vholes, and his young client, and several blue bags hastily stuffed out of all regularity of form, as the larger sort of serpents are in their first gorged state, have returned to the official den. Mr. Vholes, quiet and unmoved, as a man of so much respectability ought to be, takes off his close black gloves as if he were skinning his hands, lifts off his tight hat as if he were scalping himself, and sits down at his desk. The client throws his hat and gloves upon the ground—tosses them anywhere, without looking after them or caring where they go—flings himself into a chair, half sighing and half groaning, rests his aching head upon his hand, and looks the portrait of Young Despair.

"Again nothing done!" says Richard. "Nothing, nothing done!"

"Don't say nothing done, sir," returns the placid Vholes. "That is scarcely fair, sir, scarcely fair!"

"Why, what *is* done?" says Richard, turning gloomily upon him.

"That may not be the whole question," returns Vholes. "The question may branch off into what is doing, what is doing?"

"And what is doing?" asks the moody client.

Vholes, sitting with his arms on the desk, and fixedly and slowly looking at his client, replies:

"A good deal is doing, sir. We have put our shoulders to the wheel, Mr. Carstone, and the wheel is going round."

"Yes, with Ixion on it. How am I to get through the next four or five accursed months?" exclaims the young man, rising from his chair and walking about the room.

"Mr. C.," returns Vholes, following him close with his eyes wherever he goes, "your spirits are hasty, and I am sorry for it on your account. Excuse me if I recommend you not to chafe so much, not to be so impetuous, not to wear yourself out so. You should have more patience. You should sustain yourself better."

"I ought to imitate you, in fact, Mr. Vholes?" says Richard, sitting down again with an impatient laugh, and beating the devil's tattoo with his boot on the patternless carpet.

"Sir," returns Vholes, with his inward manner of speech and his bloodless quietude, "I should not have had the presumption to propose myself as a model for your imitation, or any man's. Let me but leave my good name to my three daughters and that is enough for me; I am not a self-seeker. But, since you mention me so pointedly, I will acknowledge that I should like to impart to you a little of my—come, sir, you are disposed to call it insensibility—say a little of my insensibility."

"Mr. Vholes," explains the client, somewhat abashed, "I had no intention to accuse you of insensibility."

"I think you had, sir, without knowing it," returns the equable Vholes. "Very naturally. It is my duty to attend to your interests with a cool head, and I can quite understand that to your excited feelings I may appear, at such times as the present, insensible. Not that I complain, sir, of the eye of business being distrustful, quite the contrary. In attending to your interests, I wish to have all possible checks upon me; it is right that I should have them, I court inquiry. But your interests demand that I should be cool and methodical, Mr. Carstone, and I cannot be otherwise —no, sir, not even to please you."

Mr. Vholes, after glancing at the official cat, who is patiently watching a mouse's hole, fixes his charmed gaze again on his young client and proceeds in his buttoned-up, half-audible voice:

"What are you to do, sir, you inquire, during the vacation. I should hope you gentlemen of the Army may find many means of amusing yourselves, if you give your minds to it. If you had asked me what *I* was to do during the vacation, I could have answered you more readily. I am to attend to your interests. I am to be found here, day by day, attending to your interests. That is my duty, Mr. C.; and term-time or vacation makes no difference to me. If you wish to consult me as to your interests, you will find me here at all times alike. Other professional men go out of town. I don't. This desk is your rock, sir!"

Mr. Vholes gives it a rap, and it sounds as hollow as a coffin. Not to Richard, though. There is encouragement in the sound to him. Perhaps Mr. Vholes knows there is.

"I am perfectly aware, Mr. Vholes," says Richard, more familiarly and good-humouredly, "that you are the most reliable fellow in the world, and that to have to do with you is to have to do with a man of business who is not to be hoodwinked. But put yourself in my case, dragging on this dislocated life, sinking deeper and deeper into difficulty every day, continually hoping and continually disappointed, conscious of change upon change for the worse in myself and of no change for the better in anything else; and you will find it a dark-looking case sometimes, as I do."

"You know," says Mr. Vholes, "that I never give hopes, sir. I told you from the first, Mr. C., that I never give hopes. Particularly in a case like this, where the greater part of the costs comes out of the estate, I should not be considerate of my good name if I gave hopes. It might seem as if costs were my object. Still, when you say there is no change for the better, I must, as a bare matter of fact, deny that."

"Ay?" returns Richard, brightening. "But how do you make it out?"

"Mr. Carstone, you are separately represented, and no longer hidden and lost in the interests of others. *That's* something. The suit does not sleep, we wake it up, we air it, we walk it about. *That's* something. It's not all Jarndyce, in fact as well as in name. *That's* something. Nobody has it all his own way now, sir. And *that's* something, surely."

Richard, his face flushing suddenly, strikes the desk with his clenched hand.

"Mr. Vholes! If any man had told me when I first went to John Jarndyce's house that he was anything but the disinterested friend he seemed —that he was what he has gradually turned out to be—I could have found no words strong enough to repel the slander, I could not have defended hm too ardently. So little did I know of the world! Whereas now I do declare to you that he becomes to me the embodiment of the suit; that in place of its being an abstraction, it is John Jarndyce; that the more I suffer, the more indignant I am with him; that every new delay, and every new disappointment, is only a new injury from John Jarndyce's hand."

"No, no," says Vholes. "Don't say so. We ought to have patience, all of us. Besides, I never disparage, sir. I never disparage."

"Mr. Vholes," returns the angry client. "You know as well as I that he would have strangled the suit if he could."

"He was not active in it," Mr. Vholes admits, with an appearance of reluctance. "He certainly was not active in it. However, he might have had amiable intentions. Who can read the heart, Mr. C.!"

"You can," returns Richard. "Well enough to know what his intentions were. Are, or are not, our interests conflicting? Tell—me—that?" says Richard, accompanying his last three words with three raps on his rock of trust.

"Mr. C.," returns Vholes, immovable in attitude and never winking his hungry eyes, "I should be wanting in my duty as your professional adviser, I should be departing from my fidelity to your interests, if I represented those interests as identical with the interests of Mr. Jarndyce. They are no such thing, sir. I never impute motives. But I must not shrink from a professional duty, even if it sows dissensions in families. I understand you to be now consulting me professionally as to your interests? You are so? I reply, then, they are not identical with those of Mr. Jarndyce."

"Of course they are not!" cries Richard. "You found that out, long ago."

"Mr. C.," returns Vholes, "I wish to say no more of any third party than is necessary. I wish to leave my good name unsullied, together with any little property of which I may become possessed through industry and perseverance, to my daughters Emma, Jane, and Caroline. I also desire to live in amity with my professional brethren. When Mr. Skimpole did me the honour, sir, of bringing us together in this room, I mentioned to you that I could offer no opinion or advice as to your interests while those interests were entrusted to another member of the profession. And I spoke in such terms as I was bound to speak of Kenge and Carboy's office, which stands high. You, sir, thought fit to withdraw your interests from that keeping nevertheless, and to offer them to me. You brought them with clean hands, sir, and I accepted them with clean hands.

Those interests are now paramount in this office. I shall not rest, sir, while I am your representative. Whenever you want me, you will find me here. Summon me anywhere and I will come. During the long vacation, sir, I shall devote my leisure to studying your interests more and more closely, and to making arrangements for moving heaven and earth (including, of course the Chancellor) after Michaelmas term; and when I ultimately congratulate you, sir," says Mr. Vholes, with the severity of a determined man, "when I ultimately congratulate you, sir, with all my heart, on your accession to fortune, you will owe me nothing beyond whatever little balance may be then outstanding of the costs as between solicitor and client, not included in the taxed costs allowed out of the estate. My duty prosperously ended, all between us is ended."

Vholes finally adds, by way of rider to this declaration of his principles, that as Mr. Carstone is about to rejoin his regiment, perhaps Mr. C. will favour him with an order on his agent for twenty pounds on account. The client, with his dejection insensibly relieved, and his vague hopes rekindled, takes pen and ink and writes the draft, not without perplexed consideration and calculation of the date it may bear, implying scant effects in the agent's hands. All the while Vholes, buttoned-up in body and mind, looks at him attentively. All the while Vholes's official cat watches the mouse's hole. Thus they part; and Vholes, left alone, employs himself in carrying sundry little matters out of his Diary into his draft-bill book, for the ultimate behoof of his three daughters.

Richard, emerging from the heavy shade of Symond's Inn into the sunshine of Chancery Lane—for there happens to be sunshine there to-day—walks thoughtfully on, and turns into Lincoln's Inn, and passes under the shadow of the Lincoln's Inn trees. On many such loungers have the speckled shadows of those trees often fallen—on the like bent head, the bitten nail, the lowering eye, the lingering step, the purposeless and dreamy air, the good consuming and consumed, the life turned sour. This lounger is not shabby yet, but that may come. Chancery, which knows no wisdom but in Precedent, is very rich in such Precedents; and why should one be different from ten thousand?

Yet the time is so short since his depreciation began that as he saunters away, reluctant to leave the spot for some long months together, though he hates it, Richard himself may feel his own case as if it were a startling one. While his heart is heavy with corroding care, suspense, distrust, and doubt, it may have room for some sorrowful wonder when he recalls how different his first visit there, how different he, how different all the colours of his mind. But injustice breeds injustice; the fighting with shadows and being defeated by them necessitates the setting up of substances to combat; from the impalpable suit which no man alive can understand, the time for that being long gone by, it has become a gloomy relief to turn to the palpable figure of the friend who would have saved him from this ruin, and make *him* his enemy. Richard has told Vholes the truth. Is he in a hardened or a softened mood, he still lays his injuries equally at that door; he was thwarted, in that quarter, of a set purpose, and that purpose could only originate in the one subject that is resolving his existence into itself; besides, it is a justification to him in his own eyes to have an embodied antagonist and oppressor.

Is Richard a monster in all this—or would Chancery be found rich in such Precedents too, if they could be got for citation from the Recording Angel?

Never, since it has been a court, has it had such a Fortunatus's purse of gossip as in the proceedings at the rag and bottle shop. Regularly, every morning at eight, is the elder Mr. Smallweed brought down to the corner and carried in, accompanied by Mrs. Smallweed, Judy, and Bart; and regularly, all day, do they all remain there until nine at night, solaced by gipsy dinners, not abundant in quantity, from the cook's shop; rummaging and searching, digging, delving, and diving among the treasures of the late lamented. What those treasures are they keep so secret that the court is maddened. In its delirium it imagines guineas pouring out of tea-pots, crown-pieces overflowing punch-bowls, old chairs and mattresses stuffed with Bank of England notes. Twice when the dustman is called in to carry off a cartload of old paper, ashes, and broken bottles, the whole court assembles and pries into the baskets as they come forth. Many times the two gentlemen who write with the ravenous little pens on the tissue-paper are seen prowling in the neighbourhood.

Mr. Weevle and Mr. Guppy, with every eye in the court's head upon them, knock at the closed door of the late lamented's house in a high state of popularity. But being, contrary to the court's expectation, admitted, they immediately become unpopular, and are considered to mean no good.

The shutters are more or less closed all over the house, and the ground floor is sufficiently dark to require candles. Introduced into the back shop by Mr. Smallweed the younger, they, fresh from the sunlight, can at first see nothing save darkness and shadows; but they gradually discern the elder Mr. Smallweed seated in his chair upon the brink of a well or grave of waste paper; the virtuous Judy groping therein, like a female sexton; and Mrs. Smallweed on the level ground in the vicinity, snowed up in a heap of paper fragments, print and manuscript, which would appear to be the accumulated compliments that have been sent flying at her in the course of the day. The whole party, Small included, are blackened with dust and dirt, and present a fiendish appearance not relieved by the general aspect of the room.

On the entrance of visitors, Mr. Smallweed and Judy simultaneously fold their arms and stop in their researches.

"Aha!" croaks the old gentleman. "How de do, gentlemen, how de do! Come to fetch your property, Mr. Weevle? That's well, that's well. Ha! ha! We should have been forced to sell you up, sir, to pay your warehouse room, if you had left it here much longer. You feel quite at home here again, I dare say? Glad to see you, glad to see you!"

Mr. Weevle, thanking him, casts an eye about. Mr. Guppy's eye follows Mr. Weevle's eye. Mr. Weevle's eye comes back without any new intelligence in it. Mr. Guppy's eye comes back and meets Mr. Smallweed's eye. That engaging old gentleman is still murmuring, like some wound-up instrument running down, "How de do, sir—how de—how—" And then having run down, he lapses into grinning silence as Mr. Guppy starts at seeing Mr. Tulkinghorn standing in the darkness opposite, with his hands behind him.

"Gentleman so kind as to act as my solicitor," says Grandfather Smallweed. "I am not the sort of client for a gentleman of such note, but he is so good!"

Mr. Guppy, slightly nudging his friend to take another look, makes a shuffling bow to Mr. Tulkinghorn, who returns it with an easy nod. Mr. Tulkinghorn is looking on as if he had nothing else to do, and were rather amused by the novelty.

"A good deal of property here, sir, I should say," Mr. Guppy observes to Mr. Smallweed.

"Principally rags and rubbish, my dear friend, rags and rubbish! Me and Bart, and my grand-daughter Judy, are endeavouring to make out an inventory of what's worth anything to sell. But we haven't come to much as yet, we—haven't—come—to—hah!"

Mr. Smallweed has run down again, while Mr. Weevle's eye, attended by Mr. Guppy's eye, has again gone round the room and come back.

"Well, sir," says Mr. Weevle. "We won't intrude any longer, if you'll allow us to go upstairs."

"Anywhere, my dear sir, anywhere! You're at home. Make yourself so, pray!"

As they go upstairs Mr. Guppy lifts his eyebrows inquiringly, and looks at Tony. Tony shakes his head. They find the old room very dull and dismal. They have a great disinclination to touch any object, and carefully blow the dust from it first. Nor are they desirous to prolong their visit, packing the few movables with all possible speed, and never speaking above a whisper.

"Look here," says Tony, recoiling. "Here's that horrible cat coming in!"

Mr. Guppy retreats behind a chair. "Small told me of her. She went leaping and bounding and tearing about that night like a Dragon, and got out on the house-top, and roamed about up there for a fortnight, and then came tumbling down the chimney very thin. Did you ever see such a brute? Looks as if she knew all about it, don't she? Shoohoo! Get out, you goblin!"

Lady Jane in the doorway, with her tiger-snarl from ear to ear and her club of a tail, shows no intention of obeying; but Mr. Tulkinghorn stumbling over her, she spits at his rusty legs, and swearing wrathfully, takes her arched back upstairs. Possibly to roam the house-tops again, and return by the chimney.

"Mr. Guppy," says Mr. Tulkinghorn, "could I have a word with you?"

Mr. Guppy is engaged in collecting the Galaxy Gallery of British Beauty from the wall and depositing those works of art in their old ignoble bandbox. "Sir," he returns, reddening, "I wish to act with courtesy towards every member of the profession, and especially, I am sure, towards a member of it so well known as yourself—I will truly add, sir, so distinguished as yourself. Still, Mr. Tulkinghorn, sir, I must stipulate that if you have any word with me, that word is spoken in the presence of my friend."

"Oh, indeed?" says Mr. Tulkinghorn.

"Yes sir. My reasons are not of a personal nature at all, but they are amply sufficient for myself."

"No doubt, no doubt." Mr. Tulkinghorn is as imperturbable as the hearthstone to which he has quietly walked. "The matter is not of that consequence that I need put you to the trouble of making any conditions, Mr. Guppy." He pauses here to smile, and his smile is as dull and rusty as his pantaloons. "You are to be congratulated, Mr. Guppy, you are a fortunate young man, sir."

"Pretty well so, Mr. Tulkinghorn. I don't complain."

"Complain? High friends, free admission to great houses, and access to elegant ladies! Why, Mr. Guppy, there are people in London who would give their ears to be you."

Mr. Guppy, looking as if he would give his own reddening and still reddening ears to be one of those people at present instead of himself, replies, "Sir, if I attend to my profession, and do what is right by Kenge and Carboy, my friends and acquaintances are of no consequence to them, nor to any member of the profession, not excepting Mr. Tulkinghorn of the Fields. I am not under any obligation to explain myself further, and with all respect for you, sir, and without offence—I repeat, without offence—I don't intend to do it."

"Quite so," says Mr. Tulkinghorn, with a calm nod. "Very good. I see by these portraits that you take a strong interest in the fashionable great, sir?"

He addresses this to the astounded Tony, who admits the soft impeachment.

"A virtue in which few Englishmen are deficient," observes Mr. Tulkinghorn. He has been standing on the hearthstone, with his back to the smoked chimney-piece, and now turns round, with his glasses to his eyes. "Who is this? 'Lady Dedlock.' Ha! A very good likeness in its way, but it wants force of character. Good-day to you, gentlemen, good-day!"

When he has walked out, Mr. Guppy, in a great perspiration, nerves himself to the hasty completion of the taking down of the Galaxy Gallery, concluding with Lady Dedlock.

"Tony," he says hurriedly to his astonished companion, "let us be quick in putting the things together and in getting out of this place. It were in vain longer to conceal from you, Tony, that between myself and one of the members of a swanlike aristocracy whom I now hold in my hand, there has been undivulged communication and association. The time might have been when I might have revealed it to you. It never will be more. It is due alike to the oath I have taken, alike to the shattered idol, and alike to circumstances over which I have no control, that the whole should be buried in oblivion. I charge you as a friend, by the interest you have ever testified in the fashionable intelligence, and by any little advances with which I may have been able to accommodate you, so to bury it without a word of inquiry!"

This charge Mr. Guppy delivers in a state little short of forensic lunacy, while his friend shows a dazed mind in his whole head of hair, and even in his cultivated whiskers.

# CHAPTER 40

*National and Domestic*

ENGLAND has been in a dreadful state for some weeks. Lord Coodle would go out, Sir Thomas Doodle wouldn't come in, and there being nobody in Great Britain (to speak of) except Coodle and Doodle, there has been no Government. It is a mercy that the hostile meeting between those two great men, which at one time seemed inevitable, did not come off, because if both pistols had taken effect, and Coodle and Doodle had killed each other, it is to be presumed that England must have waited to be governed until young Coodle and young Doodle, now in frocks and long stockings, were grown up. This stupendous national calamity, however, was averted by Lord Coodle's making the timely discovery that if in the heat of debate he had said that he scorned and despised the whole ignoble career of Sir Thomas Doodle, he had merely meant to say that party differences should never induce him to withhold from it the tribute of his warmest admiration, while it as opportunely turned out that Sir Thomas Doodle had in his own bosom expressly booked Lord Coodle to go down to posterity as the mirror of virtue and honour. Still, England has been some weeks in the dismal strait of having no pilot to weather the storm, and the marvellous part of the matter is that England has not appeared to care very much about it, but has gone on eating and drinking and marrying and giving in marriage as the old world did in the days before the flood. At last Sir Thomas Doodle has not only condescended to come in, but has done it handsomely, bringing in with him all his nephews, all his male cousins, and all his brothers-in-law. So there is hope for the old ship yet.

Doodle has found that he must throw himself upon the country— chiefly in the form of sovereigns and beer. In this metamorphosed state he is available in a good many places simultaneously, and can throw himself upon a considerable portion of the country at one time. Britannia be-

ing much occupied in pocketing Doodle in the form of sovereigns, and
swallowing Doodle in the form of beer, and in swearing herself black in
the face that she does neither—plainly to the advancement of her glory
and morality—the London season comes to a sudden end, through all the
Doodleites and Coodleites dispersing to assist Britannia in those religious
exercises.

Hence Mrs. Rouncewell, housekeeper at Chesney Wold, foresees,
though no instructions have yet come down, that the family may shortly
be expected, together with a pretty large accession of cousins and others
who can in any way assist the great Constitutional work. And hence the
stately old dame, taking Time by the forelock, leads him up and down
the staircases, and along the galleries and passages, and through the
rooms, to witness before he grows any older that everything is prepared
as beseems the Dedlock dignity.

This present summer evening, as the sun goes down, the preparations
are complete. Dreary and solemn the old house looks, with so many appliances of habitation and with no inhabitants except the pictured forms
upon the walls.

Through some of the fiery windows beautiful from without, and set,
at this sunset hour, not in dull grey stone but in a glorious house of
gold, the light excluded at other windows pours in, rich, lavish, overflowing like the summer plenty in the land. Then do the frozen Dedlocks thaw. Strange movements come upon their features, as the shadows
of leaves play there. A dense Justice in a corner is beguiled into a wink.
A staring Baronet with a truncheon gets a dimple in his chin. Down into
the bosom of a stony shepherdess there steals a fleck of light and warmth
that would have done it good a hundred years ago.

But the fire of the sun is dying. Even now the floor is dusky, and
shadow slowly mounts the walls, bringing the Dedlocks down like age
and death. And now upon my Lady's picture over the great chimney-
piece a weird shade falls from some old tree that turns it pale, and flutters it, and looks as if a great arm held a veil or hood, watching an
opportunity to draw it over her. Higher and darker rises shadow on the
wall—now a red gloom on the ceiling—now the fire is out.

All that prospect which from the terrace looked so near has moved
solemnly away, and changed into a distant phantom. Light mists arise,
and the dew falls, and all the sweet scents in the garden are heavy in the
air. Now the woods settle into great masses as if they were each one profound tree. And now the moon rises, to separate them and to make the
avenue a pavement of light among high cathedral arches fantastically
broken.

Now the moon is high, and the great house, needing habitation more
than ever, is like a body without life. Now it is even awful, stealing

through it, to think of the live people who have slept in the solitary bed-rooms, to say nothing of the dead. Now is the time for shadow, when every corner is a cavern, and every downward step a pit, when the stained glass is reflected in pale and faded hues upon the floors, when anything and everything can be made of the heavy staircase beams ex-cepting their own proper shapes, when the armour has dull lights upon it not easily to be distinguished from stealthy movement. But of all the shadows in Chesney Wold, the shadow in the long drawing-room upon my Lady's picture is the first to come, the last to be disturbed. At this hour and by this light it changes into threatening hands raised up, and menacing the handsome face with every breath that stirs.

"She is not well, ma'am," says a groom in Mrs. Rouncewell's audience-chamber.

"My lady not well! What's the matter?"

"Why, my lady has been but poorly, ma'am, since she was last here—I don't mean with the family, ma'am, but when she was here as a bird of passage-like. My lady has not been out much for her, and has kept her room a good deal."

"Chesney Wold, Thomas," rejoins the housekeeper, with proud com-placency, "will set my lady up! There is no finer air, and no healthier soil, in the world!"

Thomas may have his own personal opinions on this subject, but he forbears to express them further, and retires to the servants' hall to regale on cold meat-pie and ale. This groom is the pilot-fish before the nobler shark. Next evening, down come Sir Leicester and my Lady with their largest retinue, and down come the cousins and others from all the points of the compass. Thenceforth for some weeks, backward and for-ward rush mysterious men with no names, who fly about all those par-ticular parts of the country on which Doodle is at present throwing himself in an auriferous and malty shower, but who are merely persons of a restless disposition and never do anything anywhere.

On these national occasions, Sir Leicester finds the cousins useful. A better man than the Honourable Bob Stables to meet the Hunt at dinner there could not possibly be. Better got-up gentlemen than the other cousins to ride over to polling-booths and hustings here and there, and show themselves on the side of England, it would be hard to find. Volumnia is a little dim, but she is of the true descent; and there are many who appreciate her sprightly conversation, the honour of taking the fair Dedlock in to dinner, or even the privilege of her hand in the dance. On these national occasions, dancing may be a patriotic service, and Volumnia is constantly seen hopping about for the good of an un-grateful and unpensioning country.

My Lady takes no great pains to entertain the numerous guests and, being still unwell, rarely appears until late in the day. But at all the dismal dinners, leaden lunches, basilisk balls, and other melancholy pageants, her mere appearance is a relief. As to Sir Leicester, he conceives it utterly impossible that anything can be wanting, in any direction, by any one who has the good fortune to be received under that roof; and in a state of sublime satisfaction he moves among the company, a magnificent refrigerator.

Daily the cousins trot through dust, and canter over roadside turf, away to hustings and polling-booths, and daily bring back reports on which Sir Leicester holds forth after dinner. Daily the restless men who have no occupation in life present the appearance of being rather busy. Daily Volumnia has a little cousinly talk with Sir Leicester on the state of the nation, from which Sir Leicester is disposed to conclude that Volumnia is a more reflecting woman than he had thought her.

"How are we getting on?" says Miss Volumnia, clasping her hands. "*Are* we safe?"

"Volumnia," replies Sir Leicester, "we are doing tolerably."

"At least there is no opposition to *you*," Volumnia asserts with confidence.

"No, Volumnia. This distracted country has lost its senses in many respects, I grieve to say, but—"

"It is not so mad as that. I am glad to hear it!"

Volumnia's finishing the sentence restores her to favour. Sir Leicester, with a gracious inclination of his head, seems to say to himself, "A sensible woman this, on the whole, though occasionally precipitate."

In fact, as to this question of opposition, the fair Dedlock's observation was superfluous, Sir Leicester, on these occasions, always delivering in his own candidateship as a kind of handsome wholesale order to be promptly executed. Two other little seats that belong to him, he treats as retail orders of less importance, merely sending down the men, and signifying to the tradespeople, "You will have the goodness to make these materials into two Members of Parliament, and to send them home when done."

"I regret to say, Volumnia, that in many places the people have shown a bad spirit, and that this opposition to the Government has been of a most determined and most implacable description."

"W-r-retches!" says Volumnia.

"Even," proceeds Sir Leicester, glancing at the circumjacent cousins on sofas and ottomans, "even in many—in fact, in most—of those places in which the Government has carried it against a faction—"

(Note, by the way, that the Coodleites are always a faction with the Doodleites, and that the Doodleites occupy exactly the same position towards the Coodleites.)

"—even in them I am shocked, for the credit of Englishmen, to be constrained to inform you that the party has not triumphed without being put to an enormous expense. Hundreds," says Sir Leicester, eyeing the cousins with increasing dignity and swelling indignation, "hundreds of thousands of pounds!"

If Volumnia have a fault, it is the fault of being a trifle too innocent. Impelled by innocence, she asks:

"What for?"

"Volumnia," remonstrates Sir Leicester, with his utmost severity. "Volumnia!"

"No, no, I don't mean what for," cries Volumnia, with her favourite little scream. "How stupid I am! I mean what a pity!"

"I am glad," returns Sir Leicester, "that you do mean what a pity. It is disgraceful to the electors. But as you, though inadvertently, and without intending so unreasonable a question, asked me 'What for?' let me reply to you. For necessary expenses. And I trust to your good sense, Volumnia, not to pursue the subject, here or elsewhere."

Sir Leicester feels it incumbent on him to observe a crushing aspect towards Volumnia, because it is whispered abroad that these necessary expenses will, in some two hundred election petitions, be unpleasantly connected with the word "bribery."

"I suppose," observes Volumnia, "Mr. Tulkinghorn has been worked to death."

"I don't know," says Sir Leicester, opening his eyes, "why Mr. Tulkinghorn should be worked to death. I don't know what Mr. Tulkinghorn's engagements may be. He is not a candidate."

Lady Dedlock, seated at an open window with her arm upon its cushioned ledge and looking out at the evening shadows falling on the park, has seemed to attend since the lawyer's name was mentioned.

A languid cousin with a moustache, in a state of extreme debility, now observes from his couch that man told him "ya'as'dy that Tulkinghorn had gone down t' that iron place t' give legal 'pinion 'bout something"; and that, "contest being over t' day, 'twould be highly jawly thing if Tulkinghorn should pear with news that Coodle man was floored."

Mercury in attendance with coffee informs Sir Leicester, hereupon, that Mr. Tulkinghorn has arrived, and is taking dinner. My Lady turns her head inward for the moment, then looks out again as before.

"Mr. Tulkinghorn," says Sir Leicester, "is always welcome here, and always discreet wheresoever he is. A very valuable person, and deservedly respected." The debilitated cousin supposes he is " 'normously rich fler." "He has a stake in the country," says Sir Leicester, "I have no doubt. He is, of course, handsomely paid, and he associates almost on a footing of equality with the highest society."

Everybody starts. For a gun is fired close by.

"Good gracious, what's that?" cries Volumnia with her little withered scream.

"A rat," says my Lady. "And they have shot him."

Enter Mr. Tulkinghorn, followed by Mercuries with lamps and candles.

"No, no," says Sir Leicester, "I think not. My lady, do you object to the twilight?"

On the contrary, my Lady prefers it.

"Then take them away," says Sir Leicester. "Tulkinghorn, I beg your pardon. How do you do?"

Mr. Tulkinghorn with his usual leisurely ease advances, renders his passing homage to my Lady, shakes Sir Leicester's hand, and subsides into the chair proper to him when he has anything to communicate, on the opposite side of the baronet's little newspaper-table. Sir Leicester is apprehensive that my Lady, not being very well, will take cold at that open window. My Lady is obliged to him, but would rather sit there, for the air. Sir Leicester rises, adjusts her scarf about her, and returns to his seat. Mr. Tulkinghorn in the meanwhile takes a pinch of snuff.

"Now," says Sir Leicester. "How has that contest gone?"

"Oh, hollow from the beginning. Not a chance. They have brought in both their people. You are beaten out of all reason. Three to one."

It is a part of Mr. Tulkinghorn's policy and mastery to have no political opinions—indeed, *no* opinions. Therefore he says "you" are beaten, and not "we." Sir Leicester is majestically wroth. Volumnia never heard of such a thing. "It's the place, you know," Mr. Tulkinghorn goes on to say in the fast-increasing darkness, "where they wanted to put up Mrs. Rouncewell's son."

"A proposal which, as you correctly informed me at the time, he had the becoming taste and perception," observes Sir Leicester, "to decline. I cannot say that I by any means approve of the sentiments expressed by Mr. Rouncewell when he was here for some half-hour in this room, but there was a sense of propriety in his decision which I am glad to acknowledge."

"Ha!" says Mr. Tulkinghorn. "It did not prevent him from being very active in this election, though."

Sir Leicester is distinctly heard to gasp before speaking. "Did I understand you? Did you say that Mr. Rouncewell had been very active in this election?"

"Uncommonly active."

"Against—"

"Oh dear yes, against you. He is a very good speaker. Plain and emphatic. He made a damaging effect, and has great influence. In the business-part of the proceedings he carried all before him." It is evident to the whole company, though nobody can see him, that Sir Leicester is staring majestically. "And he was much assisted," says Mr. Tulkinghorn, as a wind-up, "by his son."

"By his son, sir?" repeats Sir Leicester, with awful politeness. "The son who wished to marry the young woman in my lady's service?"

"That son. He has but one."

"Then upon my honour," says Sir Leicester, after a terrific pause, during which he has been heard to snort and felt to stare, "upon my reputation and principles, the floodgates of society are burst open, and the waters have—a—obliterated the landmarks of the framework of the cohesion by which things are held together!" General burst of cousinly indignation. "I beg," says Sir Leicester, in a breathless condition, "that we may not comment further on this circumstance. Comment is superfluous. My lady, let me suggest in reference to that young woman—"

"I have no intention," observes my Lady from her window, in a low but decided tone, "of parting with her."

"That was not my meaning," returns Sir Leicester. "I am glad to hear you say so. I would suggest that as you think her worthy of your patronage, you should exert your influence to keep her from these dangerous hands. You might show her what violence would be done, in such association, to her duties and principles, and you might preserve her for a better fate. You might point out to her that she probably would, in good time, find a husband at Chesney Wold by whom she would not be—" Sir Leicester adds, after a moment's consideration—"dragged from the altars of her forefathers."

These remarks he offers with his unvarying politeness and deference when he addresses himself to his wife. She merely moves her head in reply. The moon is rising, and where she sits there is a little stream of cold pale light, in which her head is seen.

"It is worthy of remark," says Mr. Tulkinghorn, "however, that these people are, in their way, very proud."

"Proud?" Sir Leicester doubts his hearing.

"I should not be surprised if they all voluntarily abandoned the girl— yes, lover and all—instead of her abandoning them, supposing she remained at Chesney Wold under such circumstances."

"Well," says Sir Leicester, tremulously, "well! You should know Mr. Tulkinghorn. You have been among them."

"Really, Sir Leicester," returns the lawyer, "I state the fact. Why, I could tell you a story—with Lady Dedlock's permission." Her head concedes it. "Sir Leicester, these particulars have only lately become known to me. They are very brief. They exemplify what I have said. I suppress names for the present. Lady Dedlock will not think me ill-bred, I hope?"

By the light of the fire, which is low, he can be seen looking towards the moonlight. By the light of the moon Lady Dedlock can be seen, perfectly still.

"A townsman of this Mr. Rouncewell, a man in exactly parallel circumstances as I am told, had the good fortune to have a daughter who attracted the notice of a great lady. I speak of really a great lady, not merely great to him, but married to a gentleman of your condition, Sir Leicester."

Sir Leicester condescendingly says, "Yes, Mr. Tulkinghorn"; implying that then she must have appeared of very considerable moral dimensions indeed in the eyes of an ironmaster.

"The lady was wealthy and beautiful, and had a liking for the girl, and treated her with great kindness, and kept her always near her. Now this lady preserved a secret under all her greatness, which she had preserved for many years. In fact, she had in early life been engaged to marry a young rake—he was a captain in the army—nothing connected with whom came to any good. She never did marry him, but she gave birth to a child of which he was the father."

By the light of the fire he can be seen looking towards the moonlight. By the moonlight, Lady Dedlock can be seen in profile, perfectly still.

"The captain in the army being dead, she believed herself safe; but a train of circumstances with which I need not trouble you led to discovery. As I received the story, they began in an imprudence on her own part one day, when she was taken by surprise; which shows how difficult it is for the firmest of us (she was very firm) to be always guarded.

There was great domestic trouble and amazement, you may suppose; I leave you to imagine, Sir Leicester, the husband's grief. But that is not the present point. When Mr. Rouncewell's townsman heard of the disclosure, he no more allowed the girl to be patronized and honoured than he would have suffered her to be trodden underfoot before his eyes. Such was his pride that he indignantly took her away, as if from reproach and disgrace. He had no sense of the honour done him and his daughter by the lady's condescension, not the least. He resented the girl's position as if the lady had been the commonest of commoners. That is the story. I hope Lady Dedlock will excuse its painful nature."

There is not much conversation, for late hours have been kept at Chesney Wold since the necessary expenses elsewhere began, and this is the first night in many on which the family have been alone. It is past ten when Sir Leicester begs Mr. Tulkinghorn to ring for candles. Then the stream of moonlight has swelled into a lake, and then Lady Dedlock for the first time moves, and rises, and comes forward to a table for a glass of water. Winking cousins, batlike in the candle glare, crowd round to give it; Volumnia takes another, a very mild sip of which contents her. Lady Dedlock, graceful, self-possessed, looked after by admiring eyes, passes away slowly down the long perspective by the side of that nymph, not at all improving her as a question of contrast.

# CHAPTER 41

*In Mr. Tulkinghorn's Room*

MR. TULKINGHORN arrives in his turret-room a little breathed by the journey up, though leisurely performed. There is an expression on his face as if he had discharged his mind of some grave matter, and were, in his close way, satisfied. To say of a man so severely and strictly self-repressed that he is triumphant would be to do him as great an injustice as to suppose him troubled with love or sentiment, or any romantic weakness. He is sedately satisfied. Perhaps there is a rather increased sense of power upon him as he loosely grasps one of his veinous wrists with his other hand, and holding it behind his back, walks noiselessly up and down.

There is a capacious writing-table in the room, on which is a pretty large accumulation of papers. The green lamp is lighted, his reading-glasses lie upon the desk, the easy-chair is wheeled up to it, and it would seem as though he had intended to bestow an hour or so upon these claims on his attention before going to bed. But he happens not to be in a business mind. After a glance at the documents awaiting his notice, he opens the French window and steps out upon the leads. There he again walks slowly up and down in the same attitude; subsiding, if a man so cool may have any need to subside, from the story he has related downstairs.

As he paces the leads, with his eyes most probably as high above his thoughts as they are high above the earth, he is suddenly stopped in passing the window by two eyes that meet his own. The ceiling of his room is rather low, and the upper part of the door, which is opposite the window, is of glass. There is an inner baize door, too, but the night being warm, he did not close it when he came upstairs. These eyes that meet his own are looking in through the glass from the corridor outside. He knows them well. The blood has not flushed into his face so suddenly and redly for many a long year as when he recognizes Lady Dedlock.

He steps into the room, and she comes in too, closing both the doors behind her. There is a wild disturbance—is it fear or anger?—in her eyes. In her carriage and all else, she looks as she looked downstairs two hours ago. Is it fear, or is it anger, now? He cannot be sure. Both might be as pale, both as intent.

"Lady Dedlock?"

She does not speak at first, nor even when she has slowly dropped into the easy-chair by the table. They look at each other, like two pictures.

"Why have you told my story to so many persons?"

"Lady Dedlock, it was necessary for me to inform you that I knew it."

"How long have you known it?"

"I have suspected it a long while—fully known it, a little while."

"Months?"

"Days."

He stands before her, with one hand on a chair-back and the other in his old-fashioned waistcoat and shirt-frill, exactly as he has stood before her at any time since her marriage. The same formal politeness, the same composed deference that might as well be defiance—the whole man the same dark, cold object, at the same distance, which nothing has ever diminished.

"Is this true concerning the poor girl?"

He slightly inclines and advances his head, as not quite understanding the question.

"You know what you related. Is it true? Do her friends know my story also? Is it the town-talk yet? Is it chalked upon the walls and cried in the streets?"

So! Anger, and fear, and shame. All three contending. What power this woman has to keep these raging passions down! Mr. Tulkinghorn's thoughts take such form as he looks at her with his ragged grey eyebrows a hair's-breadth more contracted than usual under her gaze.

"No, Lady Dedlock. That was a hypothetical case, arising out of Sir Leicester's unconsciously carrying the matter with so high a hand. But it would be a real case if they knew—what we know."

"Then they do not know it yet?"

"No."

"Can I save the poor girl from injury before they know it?"

"Really, Lady Dedlock," Mr. Tulkinghorn replies, "I cannot give a satisfactory opinion on that point."

And he thinks, with the interest of attentive curiosity, as he watches the struggle in her breast, "The power and force of this woman are astonishing!"

"Sir," she says, "I will make it plainer. I do not dispute your hypothetical case. I anticipated it, and felt its truth as strongly as you can do when I saw Mr. Rouncewell here. I knew very well that if he could have had the power of seeing me as I was, he would consider the poor girl tarnished by having for a moment been, although most innocently, the subject of my great and distinguished patronage. But I have an interest in her, or I should rather say—no longer belonging to this place—I had; and if you can find so much consideration for the woman under your foot as to remember that, she will be very sensible of your mercy."

Mr. Tulkinghorn, profoundly attentive, throws this off with a shrug of self-depreciation, and contracts his eyebrows a little more.

"You have prepared me for my exposure, and I thank you for that too. Is there anything that you require of me? Is there any claim that I can release, or any charge or trouble that I can spare my husband in obtaining *his* release, by certifying to the exactness of your discovery? I will write anything, here and now, that you will dictate. I am ready to do it."

And she would do it! thinks the lawyer, watchful of the firm hand with which she takes the pen.

"I will not trouble you, Lady Dedlock. Pray spare yourself."

"I have long expected this, as you know. I neither wish to spare myself, nor to be spared. You can do nothing worse to me than you have done. Do what remains, now."

"Lady Dedlock, there is nothing to be done. I will take leave to say a few words, when you have finished."

Their need for watching one another should be over now, but they do it all this time, and the stars watch them both through the opened window.

"Of repentance or remorse, or any feeling of mine," Lady Dedlock presently proceeds, "I say not a word. If I were not dumb, you would be deaf. Let that go by. It is not for your ears."

He makes a feint of offering a protest, but she sweeps it away with her disdainful hand.

"Of other and very different things I come to speak to you. My jewels are all in their proper places of keeping. They will be found there. So, my dresses. So, all the valuables I have. Some ready money I had with me, please to say, but no large amount. I did not wear my own dress, in order that I might avoid observation. I went, to be henceforward lost. Make this known. I leave no other charge with you."

"Excuse me, Lady Dedlock," says Mr. Tulkinghorn, quite unmoved. "I am not sure that I understand you. You went?"

"To be lost to all here. I leave Chesney Wold tonight. I go this hour."

Mr. Tulkinghorn shakes his head. She rises, but he, without moving hand from chair-back or from old-fashioned waistcoat and shirt-frill, shakes his head.

"What? Not go as I have said?"

"No, Lady Dedlock," he very calmly replies.

"Do you know the relief that my disappearance will be? Have you forgotten the stain and blot upon this place, and where it is, and who it is?"

"No, Lady Dedlock, not by any means."

Without deigning to rejoin, she moves to the inner door, and has it in her hand when he says to her, without himself stirring hand or foot, or raising his voice:

"Lady Dedlock, have the goodness to stop and hear me, or before you reach the staircase I shall ring the alarm-bell and rouse the house. And then I must speak out, before every guest and servant, every man and woman, in it."

He has conquered her. She falters, trembles, and puts her hand confusedly to her head. Slight tokens these in any one else, but when so practised an eye as Mr. Tulkinghorn's sees indecision for a moment in such a subject, he thoroughly knows its value.

He promptly says again, "Have the goodness to hear me, Lady Dedlock," and motions to the chair from which she has risen. She hesitates, but he motions again, and she sits down. "The relations between us are of an unfortunate description, Lady Dedlock, but as they are not of my making, I will not apologize for them. The position I hold in reference to Sir Leicester is so well known to you that I can hardly imagine but that I must long have appeared in your eyes the natural person to make this discovery."

"Sir," she returns, without looking up from the ground, on which her eyes are now fixed, "I had better have gone. It would have been far better not to have detained me. I have no more to say."

"Excuse me, Lady Dedlock, if I add, a little more to hear."

"I wish to hear it at the window, then. I can't breathe where I am."

His jealous glance as she walks away betrays an instant's misgiving that she may have it in her thoughts to leap over, and dashing against ledge and cornice, strike her life out upon the terrace below. But a moment's observation of her figure as she stands in the window without any support, looking out at those stars which are low in the heavens, reassures him. By facing round as she has moved, he stands a little behind her.

"Lady Dedlock, I have not yet been able to come to a decision satisfactory to myself on the course before me. I am not clear what to do, or how to act next. I must request you, in the meantime, to keep your

secret as you have kept it so long, and not to wonder that I keep it too."
He pauses, but she makes no reply. "Pardon me, Lady Dedlock. This
is an important subject. You are honouring me with your attention?"

"I am."

"Thank you. I might have known it, from what I have seen of your
strength of character. I ought not to have asked the question, but I have
the habit of making sure of my ground, step by step, as I go on. The
sole consideration in this unhappy case is Sir Leicester."

"Then why," she asks in a low voice, and without removing her
gloomy look from those distant stars, "do you detain me in this house?"

"Because he *is* the consideration. Lady Dedlock, I have no occasion
to tell you that Sir Leicester is a very proud man; that his reliance upon
you is implicit; that the fall of that moon out of the sky would not
amaze him more than your fall from your high position as his wife."
She breathes quickly and heavily, but she stands as unflinchingly as
ever he has seen her in the midst of her grandest company. "I declare to
you, Lady Dedlock, that with anything short of this case that I have,
I would as soon have hoped to root up, by means of my own strength
and my own hands, the oldest tree on this estate as to shake your hold
upon Sir Leicester, and Sir Leicester's trust and confidence in you.
And even now, with this case, I hesitate. Not that he could doubt, but
that nothing can prepare him for the blow."

"Not my flight?" she returned. "Think of it again."

"Your flight, Lady Dedlock, would spread the whole truth, and a
hundred times the whole truth, far and wide. It would be impossible to
save the family credit for a day. It is not to be thought of." There is a
quiet decision in his reply, which admits of no remonstrance. "When
I speak of Sir Leicester being the sole consideration, he and the family
credit are one. Sir Leicester and the baronetcy, Sir Leicester and Chesney Wold, Sir Leicester and his ancestors and his patrimony"—Mr.
Tulkinghorn very dry here—"are, I need not say to you, Lady Dedlock,
inseparable."

"Go on!"

"Therefore," says Mr. Tulkinghorn, pursuing his case in his jog-trot
style, "I have much to consider. This is to be hushed up, if it can be.
How can it be if Sir Leicester is driven out of his wits, or laid upon a
death-bed? If I inflicted this shock upon him tomorrow morning, how
could the immediate change in him be accounted for? What could
have caused it? What could have divided you? Lady Dedlock, the wall-
chalking and the street-crying would come on directly, and you are to
remember that it would not affect you merely (whom I cannot at all
consider in this business) but your husband, Lady Dedlock, your
husband."

He gets plainer as he gets on, but not an atom more emphatic or animated.

"There is another point of view," he continues, "in which the case presents itself. Sir Leicester is devoted to you almost to infatuation. He might not be able to overcome that infatuation, even knowing what we know. I am putting an extreme case, but it might be so. If so, it were better that he knew nothing. Better for common sense, better for him, better for me. I must take all this into account, and it combines to render a decision very difficult."

She stands looking out at the same stars without a word. They are beginning to pale, and she looks as if their coldness froze her.

"My experience teaches me," says Mr. Tulkinghorn, going on in his business consideration of the matter like a machine. "My experience teaches me, Lady Dedlock, that most of the people I know would do far better to leave marriage alone. It is at the bottom of three-fourths of their troubles. So I thought when Sir Leicester married, and so I always have thought since. No more about that. I must now be guided by circumstances. In the meanwhile I must beg you to keep your own council, and I will keep mine."

"I am to drag my present life on, holding its pains at your pleasure, day by day?" she asks, still looking at the distant sky.

"Yes, I am afraid so, Lady Dedlock."

"It is necessary, you think, that I should be so tied to the stake?"

"I am sure that what I recommend is necessary."

"I am to remain on this gaudy platform, on which my miserable deception has been so long acted, and it is to fall beneath me when you give the signal?" she said slowly.

"Not without notice, Lady Dedlock. I shall take no step without forewarning you."

She asks all her questions as if she were repeating them from memory, or calling them over in her sleep.

"We are to meet as usual?"

"Precisely as usual, if you please."

"And I am to hide my guilt, as I have done so many years?"

"As you have done so many years. I should not have made that reference myself, Lady Dedlock, but I may now remind you that your secret can be no heavier to you than it was, and is no worse and no better than it was. I know it certainly, but I believe we have never wholly trusted each other."

She stands absorbed in the same frozen way for some little time, before asking:

"Is there anything more to be said tonight?"

"Why," Mr. Tulkinghorn returns, "I should like to be assured of your acquiescence in my arrangements, Lady Dedlock."

"You may be assured of it."

"Good. And I would wish in conclusion to remind you, as a business precaution, in case it should be necessary to recall the fact in any communication with Sir Leicester, that throughout our interview I have expressly stated my sole consideration to be Sir Leicester's feelings and honour, and the family reputation. I should have been happy to have made Lady Dedlock a prominent consideration, too, if the case had admitted of it, but unfortunately it does not."

"I can attest your fidelity, sir."

Both before and after saying it she remains absorbed, but at length moves, and turns, unshaken in her natural and acquired presence, towards the door. Mr. Tulkinghorn opens both the doors exactly as he would have done yesterday, or as he would have done ten years ago, and makes his old-fashioned bow as she passes out. It is not an ordinary look that he receives from the handsome face as it goes into the darkness, and it is not an ordinary movement, though a very slight one, that acknowledges his courtesy. But, as he reflects when he is left alone, the woman has been putting no common constraint upon herself.

He would know it all the better if he saw the woman pacing her own rooms with her hair wildly thrown from her flung-back face, her hands clasped behind her head, her figure twisted as if by pain. He would think so all the more if he saw the woman thus hurrying up and down for hours, without fatigue, without intermission, followed by the faithful step upon the Ghost's Walk. But he shuts out the now chilled air, draws the window-curtain, goes to bed, and falls asleep.

CHAPTER 42

*In Mr. Tulkinghorn's Chambers*

FROM the verdant undulations and the spreading oaks of the Dedlock property, Mr. Tulkinghorn transfers himself to the stale heat and dust of London. His manner of coming and going between the two places is one of his impenetrabilities. He walks into Chesney Wold as if it were next door to his chambers, and returns to his chambers as if he had never been out of Lincoln's Inn Fields. He neither changes his dress before the journey, nor talks of it afterwards. He melted out of his turret-room this morning just as now, in the late twilight, he melts into his own square.

Like a dingy London bird among the birds at roost in these pleasant fields, where the sheep are all made into parchment, the goats into wigs, and the pasture into chaff, the lawyer—smoke-dried and faded, dwelling among mankind but not consorting with them, aged without experience of genial youth, and so long used to make his cramped nest in holes and corners of human nature that he has forgotten its broader and better range—comes sauntering home.

The lamplighter is skipping up and down his ladder on Mr. Tulkinghorn's side of the Fields when that high priest of noble mysteries arrives at his own dull courtyard. He ascends the door-steps, and is gliding into the dusky hall when he encounters, on the top step, a bowing and propitiatory little man.

"Is that Snagsby?"

"Yes, sir. I hope you are well, sir. I was just giving you up, sir, and going home."

"Ay? What is it? What do you want with me?"

"Well, sir," says Mr. Snagsby, holding his hat at the side of his head, "I was wishful to say a word to you, sir."

"Can you say it here?"

"Perfectly, sir."

"Say it, then." The lawyer turns, leans his arms on the iron railing at the top of the steps, and looks at the lamplighter lighting the courtyard.

"It is relating," says Mr. Snagsby, in a mysterious low voice, "not to put too fine a point upon it—to the foreigner, sir."

Mr. Tulkinghorn eyes him with some surprise. "What foreigner?"

"The foreign female, sir. French, if I don't mistake? I am not acquainted with that language myself, but I should judge from her manners and appearance that she was French; anyways, certainly foreign. Her that was upstairs, sir, when Mr. Bucket and me had the honour of waiting upon you with the sweeping-boy that night."

"Oh, yes, yes! Mademoiselle Hortense."

"Indeed, sir?" Mr. Snagsby coughs his cough of submission behind his hat. "I am not acquainted myself with the names of foreigners in general, but I have no doubt it *would* be that."

"And what can you have to say, Snagsby," demands Mr. Tulkinghorn, "about her?"

"Well, sir," returns the stationer, shading his communication with his hat, "it falls a little hard upon me. My domestic happiness is very great —at least, it's as great as can be expected, I'm sure—but my little woman is rather given to jealousy. Not to put too fine a point upon it, she is very much given to jealousy. And you see, a foreign female of that genteel appearance coming into the shop, and hovering—hovering, sir— in the court—you know it is—now ain't it? I only put it to yourself, sir."

Mr. Snagsby having said this in a very plaintive manner, throws in a cough of general application to fill up all the blanks.

"Why, what do you mean?" asks Mr. Tulkinghorn.

"Just so, sir," returns Mr. Snagsby; "I was sure you would feel it yourself, and would excuse the reasonableness of *my* feelings when coupled with the known excitableness of my little woman. You see, the foreign female caught up the word Snagsby that night, being uncommon quick, and made inquiry, and got the direction and come at dinner-time. Now Guster, our young woman, is timid and has fits, and she, taking fright at the foreigner's looks—which are fierce—and at a grinding manner that she has of speaking—which is calculated to alarm a weak mind—gave way to it, instead of bearing up against it, and tumbled down the kitchen stairs out of one into another, such fits as I do sometimes think are never gone into, or come out of, in any house but ours. Consequently there was by good fortune ample occupation for my little woman, and only me to answer the shop. When she *did* say that Mr. Tulkinghorn being always denied to her, she would do herself the pleasure of continually calling at my place until she was let in here. Since then she has been, as I began by saying, hovering—hovering, sir," Mr. Snagsby repeats the word with pathetic emphasis, "in the court. The effects of which movement it is impossible to calculate. I shouldn't wonder if it might have already given rise to the painfullest mistakes even in the neighbours' minds, not mentioning my little woman. Whereas, goodness knows," says Mr. Snagsby, shaking his head, "I never had an idea of a foreign female, except as being formerly connected with a bunch of brooms and a baby, or at the present time with a tambourine and ear-rings. I never had, I do assure you, sir!"

Mr. Tulkinghorn had listened gravely to this complaint, and inquires, when the stationer has finished, "And that's all, is it, Snagsby?"

"Why yes, sir, that's all," says Mr. Snagsby, ending with a cough that plainly adds, "and it's enough too—for me."

"I don't know what Mademoiselle Hortense may want or mean, unless she is mad," says the lawyer.

"Even if she was, you know, sir," Mr. Snagsby pleads, "it wouldn't be a consolation to have some weapon or another, in the form of a foreign dagger, planted in the family."

"No," says the other. "Well, well! This shall be stopped. I am sorry you have been inconvenienced. If she comes again, send her here."

Mr. Snagsby, with much bowing and short apologetic coughing, takes his leave, lightened in heart. Mr. Tulkinghorn goes upstairs, saying to himself. "These women were created to give trouble, the whole earth over. The mistress not being enough to deal with, here's the maid now! But I will be short with *this* jade at least!"

So saying he unlocks his door, gropes his way into his murky rooms, lights his candles, and looks about him. Mr. Tulkinghorn takes a small key from his pocket, unlocks a drawer in which there is another key, which unlocks a chest in which there is another, and so comes to the cellar-key, with which he prepares to descend to the regions of old wine. He is going towards the door with a candle in his hand when a knock comes.

"Who's this?—Ay, ay, mistress, it's you, is it? You appear at a good time. I have just been hearing of you. Now! What do you want?"

He stands the candle on the chimney-piece in the clerk's hall and taps his dry cheek with the key as he addresses these words of welcome to Mademoiselle Hortense. That feline personage, with her lips tightly shut and her eyes looking out at him sideways, softly closes the door before replying.

"I have had great deal of trouble to find you, sir."

"*Have* you!"

"I have been here very often, sir. It has always been said to me, he is not at home, he is engage, he is not for you."

"Quite right, and quite true."

"Not true. Lies!"

At times, there is a suddenness in the manner of Mademoiselle Hortense so like a bodily spring upon the subject of it that such subject involuntarily starts and falls back. It is Mr. Tulkinghorn's case at present, although Mademoiselle Hortense, with her eyes almost shut up (but still looking out sideways), is only smiling contemptuously and shaking her head.

"Now, mistress," says the lawyer, tapping the key hastily upon the chimney-piece. "If you have anything to say, say it, say it."

"Sir, you have not use me well. You have been mean and shabby."

"Mean and shabby, eh?" returns the lawyer.

"Yes. What is it that I tell you? You know you have. You have attrapped me—catched me—to give you information; you have asked me to show you the dress of mine my lady must have wore that night; you have prayed me to come in it here to meet that boy—Say! Is it not?" Mademoiselle Hortense makes another spring.

"You are a vixen, a vixen!" he replies. "Well, wench, well. I paid you."

"You paid me!" she repeats, with fierce disdain. "Two sovereign!

I have not change them, I ref-use them, I despise them, I throw them from me!" Which she literally does, taking them out of her bosom as she speaks and flinging them with such violence on the floor that they jerk up again into the light before they roll away and slowly settle down after spinning vehemently.

"Now!" says Mademoiselle Hortense, darkening her large eyes again. "You have paid me? Eh my God, oh yes!"

Mr. Tulkinghorn rubs his head with the key while she entertains herself with a sarcastic laugh.

"You must be rich, my fair friend," he composedly observes, "to throw money about in that way!"

"I *am* rich," she returns, "I am very rich in hate. I hate my lady, of all my heart. You know that."

"Know it? How should I know it?"

"Because you have known it perfectly before you prayed me to give you that information. Because you have known perfectly that I was en-r-r-r-raged!" It appears impossible for Mademoiselle to roll the letter *r* sufficiently in this word, notwithstanding that she assists her energetic delivery by clenching both her hands, and setting all her teeth.

"Oh! I knew that, did I?" says Mr. Tulkinghorn.

"Yes, without doubt. I am not blind. You have made sure of me because you knew that. You had reason! I det-est her." Mademoiselle throws this at him over one of her shoulders.

"Having said this, have you anything else to say, mademoiselle?"

"I am not yet placed. Place me well. Find me a good condition! If you cannot, or do not choose to do that, employ me to pursue her, to chase her, to disgrace and to dishonour her. I will help you well, and with a good will. It is what *you* do. Do I not know that?"

"You appear to know a good deal," Mr. Tulkinghorn retorts.

"Do I not? Is it that I am so weak as to believe, like a child, that I come here in that dress to rec-eive that boy only to decide a little bet, a wager?—Eh my God, oh yes!" In this reply, down to the word "wager" inclusive, Mademoiselle has been ironically polite and tender, then as suddenly dashed into the bitterest and most defiant scorn, with her black eyes in one and the same moment very nearly shut and staringly wide open.

"Now let us see," says Mr. Tulkinghorn, tapping his chin with the key, and looking imperturbably at her, "how this matter stands."

"Ah! Let us see," Mademoiselle assents, with many angry and tight nods of her head.

"You come here to make a remarkably modest demand, which you have just stated, and it not being conceded, you will come again."

"And again," says Mademoiselle, with more tight and angry nods. "And yet again. And many times again. In effect, for ever!"

"And not only here, but you will go to Mr. Snagsby's too, perhaps? That visit not succeeding either, you will go again perhaps?"

"And again," repeats Mademoiselle, cataleptic with determination. "And yet again. And many times again. In effect, for ever!"

"Very well. Now, Mademoiselle Hortense, let me recommend you to take the candle and pick up that money of yours."

She merely throws a laugh over her shoulder, and stands her ground with folded arms.

"You will not, eh?"

"No, I will not!"

"So much the poorer you, so much the richer I! Look, mistress, this is the key of my wine-cellar. It is a large key, but the keys of prisons are larger. In this city, there are houses of correction (where the tread-mills are, for women) the gates of which are very strong and heavy, and no doubt the keys too. I am afraid a lady of your spirit would find it an inconvenience to have one of those keys turned upon her for any length of time. What do you think?"

"I think," Mademoiselle replies, without any action, and in a clear, obliging voice, "that you are a miserable wretch."

"Probably," returns Mr. Tulkinghorn quietly. "But I don't ask what you think of myself, I ask what you think of the prison."

"Nothing. What does it matter to me?"

"Why, it matters this much, mistress," says the lawyer, deliberately adjusting his frill, "the law is so despotic here that it interferes to prevent any of our good English citizens from being troubled, even by a lady's visits, against his desire. And on his complaining that he is so troubled, it takes hold of the troublesome lady and shuts her up in prison under hard discipline. Turns the key upon her, mistress." Illustrating with the cellar-key.

"Truly!" returns Mademoiselle, in the same pleasant voice. "That is droll! But—my faith!—still what does it matter to me?"

"My fair friend," says Mr. Tulkinghorn, "make another visit here, or at Mr. Snagsby's and you shall learn."

"In that case you will send Me to the prison, perhaps?"

"Perhaps." It would be contradictory for one in Mademoiselle's state of agreeable jocularity to foam at the mouth, otherwise a tigerish expansion thereabouts might look as if a very little more would make her do it. "In a word, mistress," says Mr. Tulkinghorn, "I am sorry to be unpolite, but if you ever present yourself uninvited here—or there —again, I will give you over to the police. Their gallantry is great, but they carry troublesome people through the streets in an ignominious manner—strapped down on a board, my good wench."

"I will prove you," whispers Mademoiselle, stretching out her hand, "I will try if you dare to do it!"

"And if," pursues the lawyer, without minding her, "I place you in that good position of being locked up in jail, it will be some time before you find yourself at liberty again."

"I will prove you," repeats Mademoiselle in her former whisper.

"And now," proceeds the lawyer, still without minding her, "you had better go. Think twice before you come here again."

"Think you," she answers, "twice two hundred times!"

"You were dismissed by your lady, you know," Mr. Tulkinghorn observes, following her out upon the staircase, "as the most implacable and unmanageable of women. Now turn over a new leaf, and take warning by what I say to you. For what I say I mean; and what I threaten I will do, mistress."

She goes down without answering or looking behind her. When she is gone, he goes down too, and returning with his cobweb-covered bottle, devotes himself to a leisurely enjoyment of its contents, now and then, as he throws his head back in his chair, catching sight of the pertinacious Roman pointing from the ceiling.

## CHAPTER 43

*Esther's Narrative*

It matters little now how much I thought of my living mother who had told me evermore to consider her dead. I could not venture to approach her, or to communicate with her in writing, for my sense of the peril in which her life was passed was only to be equalled by my fears of increasing it. Knowing that my mere existence as a living creature was an unforeseen danger in her way, I could not always conquer that terror of myself which had seized me when I first knew the secret. At no time did I dare to utter her name. I felt as if I did not even dare to hear it. If the conversation anywhere, when I was present, took that direction, as it sometimes naturally did, I tried not to hear—I mentally counted, repeated something that I knew, or went out of the room.

It matters little now how often I recalled the tones of my mother's voice, wondered whether I should ever hear it again as I so longed to do. It matters little that I watched for every public mention of my mother's name; that I passed and repassed the door of her house in town, loving it but afraid to look at it; that I once sat in the theatre when my mother was there and saw me, and when we were so wide asunder, before the great company of all degrees, that any link or confidence between us seemed a dream. It is all, all over. My lot has been so blest that I can relate little of myself which is not a story of goodness and generosity in others.

When we were settled at home again, Ada and I had many conversations with my guardian of which Richard was the theme. My dear girl was deeply grieved that he should do their kind cousin so much wrong; but she was so faithful to Richard that she could not bear to blame him, even for that. My guardian was assured of it, and never coupled his name with a word of reproof. "Rick is mistaken, my dear," he would say to her. "Well, well, we have all been mistaken over and over again! We must trust to you and time to set him right."

We knew afterwards what we suspected then, that he did not trust to time until he had often tried to open Richard's eyes. That he had written to him, gone to him, talked with him, tried every gentle and persuasive art his kindness could devise. Our poor devoted Richard was deaf and blind to all. If he were wrong, he would make amends when the Chancery suit was over. Suspicion and misunderstanding were the fault of the suit? Then let him work the suit out, and come through it to his right mind. This was his unvarying reply. Jarndyce and Jarndyce had obtained such possession of his whole nature that it was impossible to place any consideration before him which he did not make a new argument in favour of his doing what he did. "So that it is even more mischievous," said my guardian once to me, "to remonstrate with the poor dear fellow, than to leave him alone." By that time I had made up my mind that the period was come when I must tell my guardian what I knew. When we had retired for the night, and Ada and I had had our usual talk in our pretty room, I went out at my door again, and sought my guardian among his books. I knew he always read at that hour, and as I drew near I saw the light shining out into the passage from his reading-lamp.

"May I come in, Guardian?"

"Surely, little woman. What's the matter?"

"Nothing is the matter. I thought I would like to take this quiet time of saying a word to you about myself."

He put a chair for me, shut his book and put it by, and turned his kind attentive face towards me. I could not help observing that it wore that curious expression I had observed in it once before—on that night when he had said that he was in no trouble which I could readily understand.

"What concerns you, my dear Esther," said he, "concerns us all. You cannot be more ready to speak than I am to hear."

"I know that, Guardian. But I have such need of your advice and support. Oh, you don't know how much need I have tonight." He looked unprepared for my being so earnest, and even a little alarmed.

"Guardian," said I, "do you remember, when we were overtaken by the thunderstorm, Lady Dedlock's speaking to you of her sister?"

"Of course. Of course I do."

"And reminding you that she and her sister had differed; had 'gone their several ways'?"

"Of course."

"Why did they separate, Guardian?"

His face quite altered as he looked at me. "My child, what questions are these! I never knew. No one but themselves ever did know, I believe. Who could tell what the secrets of those two handsome and proud women were! You have seen Lady Dedlock. If you had ever seen her sister, you would know her to have been as resolute and haughty as she."

"O Guardian, I have seen her many and many a time!"

"Seen her?" He paused a little, biting his lip. "Then, Esther, when you spoke to me long ago of Boythorn, and when I told you that he was all but married once, and that the lady did not die, but died to him, and that that time had had its influence on his later life—did you know it all, and know who the lady was?"

"No, Guardian," I returned, fearful of the light that dimly broke upon me. "Nor do I know yet."

"Lady Dedlock's sister."

"And why," I could scarcely ask him, "why, Guardian, pray tell me why were *they* parted?"

"It was her act, and she kept its motives in her inflexible heart. He afterwards did conjecture that some injury which her haughty spirit had received in her cause of quarrel with her sister, had wounded her beyond all reason; but she wrote him that from the date of that letter she died to him, and that the resolution was exacted from her by her knowledge of his proud temper and his strained sense of honour, which were both her nature too. In consideration for those master points in him, and even in consideration for them in herself, she made the sacrifice, she said, and would live in it and die in it. She did both, I fear: certainly he never saw her, never heard of her from that hour. Nor did any one."

"O Guardian, what have I done!" I cried, giving way to my grief. "What sorrow have I innocently caused!"

"You caused, Esther?"

"Yes, Guardian. Innocently, but most surely. That secluded sister is my first remembrance."

"No, no!" he cried, starting.

"Yes, Guardian, yes! And *her* sister is my mother!"

I would have told him all my mother's letter, but he would not hear it then. He spoke so tenderly and wisely to me, and he put so plainly before me all I had myself imperfectly thought and hoped in my better state of mind, that, penetrated as I had been with fervent gratitude towards him through so many years, I believed I had never loved him so dearly, never thanked him in my heart so fully, as I did that night. And when he had taken me to my room and kissed me at the door, and when at last I lay down to sleep, my thought was how could I ever be busy enough, how could I ever be good enough, devoted enough to him, and useful enough to others, to show him how I blessed and honoured him!

# CHAPTER 44

~~~~~~~~~~~~~~~~~~~~~~~~~~~~~~~~~~~~~~~~~~~~~~~~~~~~~~~~

*The Letter and the Answer*

MY guardian called me into his room next morning, and then I told him what had been left untold on the previous night. There was nothing to be done, he said, but to keep the secret. He understood my feeling, and entirely shared it. One person whom he need not name to me, it was not now possible for him to advise or help. He wished it were, but no such thing could be. If her mistrust of the lawyer whom she had mentioned were well-founded, which he scarcely doubted, he dreaded discovery. He knew something of him, both by sight and by reputation, and it was certain that he was a dangerous man. Whatever happened, he repeatedly impressed upon me with anxious affection and kindness, I was as innocent of as himself, and as unable to influence.

"Nor do I understand," said he, "that any doubts tend towards you, my dear. Much suspicion may exist without that connexion."

"With the lawyer," I returned. "But two other persons have come into my mind since I have been anxious." Then I told him all about Mr. Guppy, who I feared might have had his vague surmises when I little understood his meaning, but in whose silence after our last interview I expressed perfect confidence.

"Well," said my guardian, "then we may dismiss him for the present. Who is the other?"

I called to his recollection the French maid, and the eager offer of herself she had made to me.

"Ha," he returned thoughtfully, "that is a more alarming person than the clerk! But after all, my dear, it was but seeking for a new service. She had seen you and Ada a little while before, and it was natural that you should come into her head. She merely proposed herself for your maid, you know. She did nothing more."

"Her manner was strange," said I.

"Yes, and her manner was strange when she took her shoes off, and showed that cool relish for a walk that might have ended in her death-bed," said my guardian. "It would be useless self-distress and torment to reckon up such chances and possibilities. Be hopeful, little woman. You can be nothing better than yourself; be that, through this knowledge as you were before you had it. It is the best you can do for every-body's sake. I sharing the secret with you—"

"And lightening it, Guardian, so much," said I.

"—will be attentive to what passes in that family, so far as I can observe it from my distance. And if the time should come when I can stretch out a hand to render the least service to one whom it is better not to name even here, I will not fail to do it for her dear daughter's sake."

I thanked him with my whole heart. What could I ever do but thank him! I was going out at the door when he asked me to stay a moment. Quickly turning round, I saw that same expression on his face again, and all at once, I don't know how, it flashed upon me as a new and far-off possibility that I understood it.

"My dear Esther," said my guardian, "I have long had something in my thoughts that I have wished to say to you. I have had some difficulty in approaching it, and I still have. I should wish it to be so deliberately said, and so deliberately considered. Would you object to my writing it?"

"Dear Guardian, how could I object to your writing anything for *me* to read?"

"Then see, my love," said he, with his cheery smile, "am I at this moment quite as plain and easy—do I seem as open, as honest and old-fashioned—as I am at any time?"

I answered, in all earnestness, "Quite." With the strictest truth, for his momentary hesitation was gone (it had not lasted a minute), and his fine, sensible, cordial, sterling manner was restored.

"Do I look as if I suppressed anything, meant anything but what I said, had any reservation at all, no matter what?" said he, with his bright clear eyes on mine. I answered, most assuredly he did not. "Can you fully trust me, and thoroughly rely on what I profess, Esther?"

"Most thoroughly," said I, with my whole heart.

"My dear girl," returned my guardian, "give me your hand."

He took it in his, holding me lightly with his arm, and, looking down into my face with the same genuine freshness and faithfulness of manner—the old protecting manner which had made that house my home in a moment—said, "You have wrought changes in me, little woman, since the winter day in the stage-coach. First and last you have done me a world of good since that time."

"Ah, Guardian, what have you done for me since that time!"

"But," said he, "that is not to be remembered now."

"It never can be forgotten."

"Yes, Esther," said he with a gentle seriousness, "it is to be forgotten now—to be forgotten for a while. You are only to remember now that nothing can change me as you know me. Can you feel quite assured of that, my dear?"

"I can, and I do," I said.

"That's much," he answered. "That's everything. But I must not take that at a word. I will not write this something in my thoughts until you have quite resolved within yourself that nothing can change me as you know me. If you doubt that in the least degree, I will never write it. If you are sure of that, on good consideration, send Charley to me this night week—'for the letter.' But if you are not quite certain, never send."

"Guardian," said I, "I am already certain. I can no more be changed in that conviction than you can be changed towards me. I shall send Charley for the letter."

He shook my hand and said no more. Nor was any more said in reference to this conversation, either by him or me, through the whole week. When the appointed night came, I said to Charley as soon as I was alone, "Go and knock at Mr. Jarndyce's door, Charley, and say you have come from me—'for the letter.'" Charley went and came back, and brought the letter. "Lay it on the table, Charley," said I. So Charley laid it on the table and went to bed, and I sat looking at it without taking it up, thinking of many things.

I began with my overshadowed childhood, and passed through those timid days to the heavy time when my aunt lay dead, and when I was more solitary with Mrs. Rachael than if I had had no one in the world to speak to or to look at. I passed to the altered days when I was so blest as to find friends in all around me, and to be beloved. I came to the time when I first saw my dear girl, and was received into that sisterly affection which was the grace and beauty of my life. I recalled the first bright gleam of welcome which had shone out of those very windows upon our expectant faces on that cold bright night, and which had never paled. I lived my happy life there over again, I went through my illness and recovery, I thought of myself so altered and of those around me so unchanged; and all this happiness shone like a light from one central figure, represented before me by the letter on the table.

I opened it and read it. It was so impressive in its love for me, and in the unselfish caution it gave me, and the consideration it showed for me in every word, that my eyes were too often blinded to read much at a time. But I read it through three times, before I laid it down. I had thought beforehand that I knew its purport, and I did. It asked me—would I be the mistress of Bleak House.

It was not a love-letter though it expressed so much love, but was written just as he would at any time have spoken to me. I saw his face, and heard his voice, and felt the influence of his kind protecting manner, in every line. It addressed me as if our places were reversed, as if

all the good deeds had been mine and all the feelings they had awakened, his. It dwelt on my being young and he past the prime of life,
on his having attained a ripe age, while I was a child, knowing all
this so well as to set it in full before me for mature deliberation. It
told me that I would gain nothing by such a marriage, and lose nothing
by rejecting it; for no new relation could enhance the tenderness in
which he held me, and whatever my decision was, he was certain
it would be right. But he had considered this step anew since our
late confidence, and had decided on taking it—if it only served to
show me, through one poor instance, that the whole world would
readily unite to falsify the stern prediction of my childhood. I was
the last to know what happiness I could bestow upon him, but of that
he said no more, for I was always to remember that I owed him nothing
and that he was my debtor, and for very much. If I felt that I could
ever give him the best right he could have to be my protector, and if
I felt that I could happily and justly become the dear companion of
his remaining life, even then he could not have me bind myself
irrevocably while this letter was yet so new to me, but, even then, I
must have ample time for reconsideration. In that case, or in the opposite case, let him be unchanged in his old relation, in his old manner,
in the old name by which I called him. And as to his bright Dame
Durden and little housekeeper, she would ever be the same, he knew.

This was the substance of the letter, written throughout with a justice and a dignity as if he were indeed my responsible guardian, im-
partially representing the proposal of a friend against whom in his
integrity he stated the full case.

But he did not hint to me that when I had been better-looking he
had had this same proceeding in his thoughts, and had refrained from
it. That when my old face was gone from me, and I had no attractions,
he could love me just as well as in my fairer days. That the discovery of
my birth gave him no shock. That his generosity rose above my dis-
figurement, and my inheritance of shame. But I knew it, I knew it well
now. It came upon me as the close of the benignant history I had been
pursuing, and I felt that I had but one thing to do. To devote my life
to his happiness was to thank him poorly, and what had I wished for
the other night but some new means of thanking him?

Still, I cried very much, not only in the fulness of my heart after
reading the letter, not only in the strangeness of the prospect—for it
was strange, though I had expected the contents—but as if something
for which there was no name or distinct idea were indefinitely lost to
me. I was very happy, very thankful, very hopeful; but I cried very
much.

By and by I went to my old glass. My eyes were red and swollen, and

I said, "O Esther, Esther, can that be you!" I am afraid the face in the glass was going to cry again at this reproach, but I held up my finger at it, and it stopped.

"That is more like the composed look you comforted me with, my dear, when you showed me such a change!" said I, beginning to let down my hair. "When you are mistress of Bleak House, you are to be as cheerful as a bird. In fact, you are always to be cheerful; so let us begin for once and for all."

I thought, all at once, if my guardian had married some one else, how should I have felt, and what should I have done! That would have been a change indeed. It presented my life in such a new and blank form that I rang my housekeeping keys and gave them a kiss before I laid them down in their basket again.

Then I went on to think, as I dressed my hair before the glass, how often had I considered within myself that the deep traces of my illness, and the circumstances of my birth, were only new reasons why I should be busy, busy, busy—useful, amiable, serviceable, in all honest, unpretending ways. This was a good time, to be sure, to sit down morbidly and cry! As to its seeming at all strange to me at first that I was one day to be the mistress of Bleak House, why should it seem strange? Other people had thought of such things, if I had not. "Don't you remember, my plain dear," I asked myself, looking at the glass, "what Mrs. Woodcourt said before those scars were there, about your marrying—?"

Perhaps the name brought them to my remembrance. The dried remains of the flowers. It would be better not to keep them now. They had only been preserved in memory of something wholly past and gone, but it would be better not to keep them now.

They were in a book, and it happened to be in the next room—our sitting-room, dividing Ada's chamber from mine. I took a candle, and went softly in to fetch it from its shelf. After I had it in my hand, I saw my beautiful darling through the open door, lying asleep, and I stole in to kiss her. It was weak in me, I know, and I could have no reason for crying, but I dropped a tear upon her dear face, and another and another. Weaker than that, I took the withered flowers out, and put them for a moment to her lips. Then I took them into my own room, and burned them at the candle, and they were dust in an instant.

On entering the breakfast-room next morning, I found my guardian just as usual, quite as frank, as open, and free. There being not the least constraint in his manner, there was none (or I think there was none) in mine. I was with him several times in the course of the morning, in and out, when there was no one there, and I thought it not unlikely that he might speak to me about the letter; but he did not say a word.

So, on the next morning, and the next, and for at least a week. I expected every day that my guardian might speak to me about the letter; but he never did.

I thought then, growing uneasy, that I ought to write an answer. I tried over and over again in my own room at night, but I could not write an answer that at all began like a good answer, so I thought each night I would wait one more day. And I waited seven more days, and he never said a word.

At last we three were one afternoon going out for a ride, and I being dressed before Ada, and going down, came upon my guardian, with his back towards me, standing at the drawing-room window looking out. He turned on my coming in, and said, smiling, "Ay, it's you, little woman, is it?" and looked out again.

I had made up my mind to speak to him now. In short, I had come down on purpose. "Guardian," I said, rather hesitating and trembling, "when would you like to have the answer to the letter Charley came for?"

"When it's ready, my dear," he replied.

"I think it is ready," said I.

"Is Charley to bring it?" he asked pleasantly.

"No. I have brought it myself, Guardian," I replied.

I put my two arms round his neck and kissed him; and he said was this the mistress of Bleak House? and I said yes, and it made no difference presently, and we all went out together, and I said nothing to my precious pet about it.

## CHAPTER 45

*In Trust*

ONE morning when I had done jingling about with my basket of keys, as my beauty and I were walking round and round the garden I happened to turn my eye towards the house and saw a long thin shadow going in which looked like Mr. Vholes. Presently came Charley, tripping along the paths, saying, "Oh if you please, miss, would you step and speak to Mr. Jarndyce!"

I told Ada I would make haste back, and inquired of Charley as we went in whether there was not a gentleman with Mr. Jarndyce. To which Charley, whose grammar, I confess to my shame, never did any credit to my educational powers, replied, "Yes, miss. Him as come down in the country with Mr. Richard."

A more complete contrast than my guardian and Mr. Vholes, I suppose there could not be. I found them looking at one another across the table, the one so open and the other so close, the one giving out what he had to say in such a rich ringing voice and the other keeping it in in such a cold-blooded, gasping, fishlike manner, that I thought I never had seen two people so unmatched.

"You know Mr. Vholes, my dear," said my guardian.

Mr. Vholes rose, gloved and buttoned-up as usual, and seated himself again, just as he had seated himself beside Richard in the gig. Not having Richard to look at, he looked straight before him.

"Mr. Vholes," said my guardian, eying his black figure as if he were a bird of ill-omen, "has brought an ugly report of our most unfortunate Rick." Laying a marked emphasis on "most unfortunate," as if the words were rather descriptive of his connexion with Mr. Vholes. I sat down between them; Mr. Vholes remained immovable, except that he secretly picked at one of the red pimples on his yellow face with his black glove. "And as Rick and you are happily good friends, I should like to know," said my guardian, "what you think, my dear. Would you be so good as to—as to speak up, Mr. Vholes?"

Doing anything but that, Mr. Vholes observed:

"I have been saying that I have reason to know, Miss Summerson, as Mr. C.'s professional adviser, that Mr. C.'s circumstances are at the present moment in an embarrassed state. Not so much in point of amount as owing to the peculiar and pressing nature of liabilities Mr. C. has incurred, and the means he has of liquidating or meeting the same. I have staved off many little matters for Mr. C., but there is a limit to staving off, and we have reached it. I have made some advances out of pocket to accommodate these unpleasantnesses, but I necessarily look to being repaid. My apprehension is, Mr. C.'s circumstances being such, lest it should end in his obtaining leave to part with his commission, which at all events is desirable to be made known to his connexions."

"Imagine the poor fellow without even his present resource," said my guardian to me. "Yet what can I do? You know him, Esther. He would never accept of help from me now. To offer it, or hint at it, would be to drive him to an extremity, if nothing else did."

Mr. Vholes hereupon addressed me again.

"What Mr. Jarndyce remarks, miss, is no doubt the case, and is the difficulty. I do not see that anything is to be done. I do not say that anything is to be done. Far from it. I merely come down here under the seal of confidence and mention it in order that everything may be openly carried on, and that it may not be said afterwards that everything was not openly carried on. I desire to leave a good name behind me. If I consulted merely my own interests with Mr. C., I should not be here. So insurmountable, as you must well know, would be his objections. This is not a professional attendance."

It appeared to us that Mr. Vholes said neither more nor less than the truth in intimating that he sought to divide the responsibility, such as it was, of knowing Richard's situation. I could only suggest that I should go down to Deal, where Richard was then stationed, and see him, and try if it were possible to avert the worst. Without consulting Mr. Vholes on this point, I took my guardian aside to propose it while Mr. Vholes gauntly stalked to the fire and warmed his funeral gloves. The fatigue of the journey formed an immediate objection on my guardian's part; but as I saw he had no other, and as I was only too happy to go, I got his consent. We had then merely to dispose of Mr. Vholes.

"Well, sir," said Mr. Jarndyce, "Miss Summerson will communicate with Mr. Carstone, and we can only hope that his position may be yet retrievable. You will allow me to order you lunch after your journey, sir."

"I thank you, Mr. Jarndyce," said Mr. Vholes, putting out his long black sleeve to check the ringing of the bell, "not any. I thank you, no, not a morsel. Everything having been openly carried on, sir, I will now with your permission take my leave."

"And I would that you could take your leave, and we could all take our leave, Mr. Vholes," returned my guardian, bitterly, "of a Cause you know of."

Mr. Vholes made a short one-sided inclination of his head from the neck, and slowly shook it.

"We whose ambition it is to be looked upon in the light of respectable practitioners, sir, can but put our shoulders to the wheel. We do it, sir. At least, I do it myself, and I wish to think well of my professional brethren, one and all. You are sensible of an obligation not to refer to me, miss, in communicating with Mr. C.?" I said I would be careful not to do it. "Just so, miss. Good-morning. Mr. Jarndyce, good-morning, sir." Mr. Vholes put his dead glove, which scarcely seemed to have any hand in it, on my fingers, and then on my guardian's fingers, and took his long thin shadow away.

Of course it became necessary to tell Ada where I was going, and why I was going, and of course she was anxious and distressed. But she was too true to Richard to say anything but words of pity and words of excuse, and in a more loving spirit still—my dear devoted girl!—she wrote him a long letter, of which I took charge.

Charley was to be my travelling companion, though I am sure I wanted none and would willingly have left her at home. We all went to London that afternoon, and finding two places in the mail, secured them. At our usual bedtime, Charley and I were rolling away seaward, with the Kentish letters.

It was a night's journey in those coach times, but we had the mail to ourselves, and did not find the night very tedious. It passed with me as I suppose it would with most people under such circumstances. At one while, my journey looked hopeful, and at another hopeless. Now I thought I should do some good, and now I wondered how I could ever have supposed so. In what state I should find Richard, what I should say to him, and what he would say to me, occupied my mind by turns, and the wheels seemed to play one tune over and over again all night.

At last we came into the narrow streets of Deal, and very gloomy they were upon a raw misty morning. The long flat beach, with its little irregular houses, wooden and brick, and its litter of capstans, and great boats, and sheds, and bare upright poles with tackle and blocks, wore as dull an appearance as any place I ever saw. The sea was heaving under a thick white fog.

But when we got into a warm room in an excellent hotel, and sat down, comfortably washed and dressed, to an early breakfast (for it was too late to think of going to bed), Deal began to look more cheerful. Our little room was like a ship's cabin, and that delighted Charley very much. Then the fog began to rise like a curtain, and numbers of ships, that we had had no idea were near, appeared. Some of these vessels were of grand size—one was a large Indiaman just come home—and when the sun shone through the clouds, making silvery pools in the dark sea, the way in which these ships brightened, and shadowed, and changed, amid a bustle of boats pulling off from the shore to them and from them to the shore, was most beautiful.

The large Indiaman was our great attraction, because she had come into the Downs in the night. Charley was curious about the voyage, and about the heat in India, and the serpents and the tigers; and as she picked up such information much faster than grammar, I told her what I knew on those points. I told her, too, how people in such voyages were sometimes wrecked and cast on rocks, where they were saved by the intrepidity and humanity of one man. And Charley asking how that could be, I told her how we knew at home of such a case.

I had thought of sending Richard a note saying I was there, but it seemed so much better to go to him without preparation. As he lived in barracks, I was a little doubtful whether this was feasible, but we went out to reconnoitre. Peeping in at the gate of the barrack-yard, we found everything very quiet, and I asked a sergeant standing on the guard-house-steps, where he lived. He sent a man before to show me, who went up some bare stairs and knocked with his knuckles at a door, and left us.

"Now then!" cried Richard from within. So I left Charley in the little passage, and going on to the half-open door, said, "Can I come in, Richard? It's only Dame Durden."

He was writing at a table, with a great confusion of clothes, tin cases, books, boots, brushes, and portmanteaus strewn all about the floor. He was only half-dressed—in plain clothes, I observed, not in uniform—and his hair was unbrushed, and he looked as wild as his room. All this I saw after he had heartily welcomed me and I was seated near him, for he started upon hearing my voice and caught me in his arms in a moment. Dear Richard! He was ever the same to me. Down to—ah, poor poor fellow!—to the end, he never received me but with something of his old merry boyish manner.

"Good heaven, my dear little woman," said he, "how do you come here? Nothing the matter? Ada is well?"

"Quite well. Lovelier than ever, Richard!"

"Ah!" he said, leaning back in his chair. "My poor cousin! I was writing to you, Esther."

So worn and haggard as he looked, even in the fulness of his handsome youth, leaning back in his chair and crushing the closely written sheet of paper in his hand!

"Have you been at the trouble of writing all that and am I not to read it after all?" I asked.

"Oh my dear," he returned, with a hopeless gesture. "You may read it in the whole room. It is all over here."

I mildly entreated him not to be despondent. I told him that I had heard by chance of his being in difficulty, and had come to consult with him what could best be done.

"Like you, Esther, but useless, and so *not* like you!" said he with a melancholy smile. "I am away on leave this day—should have been gone in another hour—and that is to smooth it over for my selling-out. Well! Let bygones be bygones. So this calling follows the rest. I only want to have been in the Church to have made the round of all the professions."

"Richard," I urged, "it is not so hopeless as that?"

"Esther," he returned, "it is indeed. I am just so near disgrace as that those who are put in authority over me (as the catechism goes) would far rather be without me than with me. And they are right. Apart from debts and duns, and all such drawbacks, I am not fit even for this employment. I have no care, no mind, no heart, no soul, but for one thing. Why, if this bubble hadn't broken now," he said, tearing the letter he had written into fragments, "how could I have gone abroad? I must have been ordered abroad; but how could I have gone? How could I, with my experience of that thing, trust even Vholes unless I was at his back!"

I suppose he knew by my face what I was about to say, but he caught the hand I had laid upon his arm and touched my own lips with it to prevent me from going on.

"No, Dame Durden! Two subjects I forbid—must forbid. The first is John Jarndyce. The second, you know what. Call it madness, and I tell you I can't help it now, and can't be sane. But it is no such thing; it is the one object I have to pursue. It is a pity I ever was prevailed upon to turn out of my road for any other. It would be wisdom to abandon it now, after all the time, anxiety, and pains I have bestowed upon it! Oh yes, true wisdom. It would be very agreeable, too, to some people; but I never will."

He was in that mood in which I thought it best not to increase his determination (if anything could increase it) by opposing him. I took out Ada's letter, and put it in his hand.

"Am I to read it now?" he asked.

As I told him yes, he laid it on the table and, resting his head upon his hand, began. He had not read far when he rested his head upon his two hands—to hide his face from me. In a little while he rose as if the light were bad, and went to the window. He finished reading it there, with his back towards me, and after he had finished and had folded it up, stood there for some minutes with the letter in his hand. When he came back to his chair, I saw tears in his eyes.

"Of course, Esther, you know what she says here?" He spoke in a softened voice, and kissed the letter as he asked me.

"Yes, Richard."

"Offers me," he went on, tapping his foot upon the floor, "the little inheritance she is certain of so soon—just as little and as much as I have wasted—and begs and prays me to take it, set myself right with it, and remain in the service."

"I know your welfare to be the dearest wish of her heart," said I. "And oh my dear Richard, Ada's is a noble heart."

"I am sure it is. I—I wish I was dead!"

He went back to the window, and laying his arm across it, leaned his head down on his arm. It greatly affected me to see him so; but I hoped he might become more yielding, and I remained silent. My experience was very limited; I was not at all prepared for his rousing himself out of this emotion to a new sense of injury.

"And this is the heart that the same John Jarndyce, who is not otherwise to be mentioned between us, stepped in to estrange from me!" said he indignantly. "And the dear girl makes me this generous offer from under the same John Jarndyce's roof, and with the same John Jarndyce's gracious consent and connivance, I dare say, as a new means of buying me off."

"Richard," I cried out, rising hastily, "I will not hear you say such shameful words!" I was very angry with him indeed, for the first time in my life; but it only lasted a moment. When I saw his worn young face looking at me as if he were sorry, I put my hand on his shoulder and said, "If you please, my dear Richard, do not speak in such a tone to me. Consider!"

He blamed himself exceedingly, and told me in the most generous manner that he had been very wrong, and that he begged my pardon a thousand times.

"To accept this offer, my dear Esther," said he, sitting down beside me—"once more, pray, pray, forgive me—is, I need not say, impossible. Besides, I have letters and papers that I could show you which would convince you it is all over here. I have done with the red coat, believe me. But it is some satisfaction, in the midst of my troubles and perplexities, to know that I am pressing Ada's interests in pressing my own. Vholes has his shoulder to the wheel, and he cannot help urging it on as much for her as for me, thank God!"

His sanguine hopes were rising within him and lighting up his features, but they made his face more sad to me than it had been before.

"No, no!" cried Richard, exultingly. "If every farthing of Ada's little fortune were mine, no part of it should be spent in retaining me in what I am not fit for, can take no interest in, and am weary of. It should be devoted to what promises a better return, and should be used where she has a larger stake. Don't be uneasy for me! I shall now have only one thing on my mind, and Vholes and I will work it. I shall not be without means. Free of my commission, I shall be able to compound with some small usurers who will hear of nothing but their bond now— Vholes says so. I should have a balance in my favour anyway, but that would swell it. Come, come! You shall carry a letter to Ada from me, Esther, and you must both of you be more hopeful of me, and not believe that I am quite cast away just yet, my dear."

I will not repeat what I said to Richard. I know it was tiresome, and nobody is to suppose for a moment that it was at all wise. It only came from my heart. He heard it patiently and feelingly, but I saw that on the two subjects he had reserved it was at present hopeless to make any representation to him. I saw, too, the sense of my guardian's remark that it was even more mischievous to use persuasion with him than to leave him as he was.

Therefore I was driven at last to asking Richard if he would mind convincing me that it really was all over there, as he had said, and that it was not his mere impression. He showed me without hesitation a correspondence making it quite plain that his retirement was arranged. He told me that Mr. Vholes had copies of these papers, and had been in consultation with him throughout. Beyond ascertaining this, and having been the bearer of Ada's letter, and being (as I was going to be) Richard's companion back to London, I had done no good by coming down. Admitting this to myself with a reluctant heart, I said I would return to the hotel and wait until he had joined me there; so he saw me to the gate, and Charley and I went back.

There was a concourse of people in one spot, surrounding some naval officers who were landing from a boat, and pressing about them with unusual interest. The gentlemen came slowly up from the waterside, speaking good-humouredly to each other and to the people around, and glancing about them as if they were glad to be in England again. "Charley, Charley," said I, "come away!" And I hurried on so swiftly that my little maid was surprised.

It was not until we were shut up in our cabin-room, and I had had time to take breath, that I began to think why I had made such haste. In one of the sunburnt faces I had recognized Mr. Allan Woodcourt, and I had been afraid of his recognizing me. I had been unwilling that he should see my altered looks. I had been taken by surprise, and my courage had quite failed me.

But I knew this would not do, and I now said to myself, "My dear, there is no reason—there is and there can be no reason at all—why it should be worse for you now than it ever has been. What you were last month, you are today; you are no worse, you are no better. This is not your resolution; call it up, Esther, call it up!" I was in a great tremble and at first was quite unable to calm myself, but I got better, and I was very glad to know it.

The party came to the hotel. I heard them speaking on the staircase. I was sure it was the same gentlemen because I knew their voices again —I mean I knew Mr. Woodcourt's. It would still have been a great relief to me to have gone away without making myself known, but I was determined not to do so. I untied my bonnet, and put my veil half up, wrote on one of my cards that I happened to be there with Mr. Richard Carstone, and sent it in to Mr. Woodcourt. He came immediately. I told him I was rejoiced to be by chance among the first to welcome him home to England. And I saw that he was very sorry for me.

"You have been in shipwreck and peril since you left us, Mr. Woodcourt," said I, "but we can hardly call that a misfortune which enabled you to be so useful and so brave. We read of it with the truest interest. It first came to my knowledge through your old patient, poor Miss Flite, when I was recovering from my severe illness."

"Ah! little Miss Flite!" he said. "She lives the same life yet?"

"Just the same." I was so comfortable with myself now as not to mind the veil, and to be able to put it aside. "Her gratitude to you, Mr. Woodcourt, is delightful. She is a most affectionate creature, as I have reason to say."

"You—you have found her so?" he returned. "I—I am glad of that." He was so very sorry for me that he could scarcely speak.

"I assure you," said I, "that I was deeply touched by her sympathy and pleasure at the time I have referred to."

"I was grieved to hear that you had been very ill, but you have quite recovered?"

"I have quite recovered my health and my cheerfulness," said I. "You know how good my guardian is, and what a happy life we lead; and I have everything to be thankful for, and nothing in the world to desire."

I felt as if he had greater commiseration for me than I had ever had for myself. It inspired me with new fortitude, and new calmness, to find that it was I who was under the necessity of reassuring him. I spoke to him of his voyage out and home, and of his future plans, and of his probable return to India. He said that was very doubtful. He had gone out a poor ship's surgeon, and had come home nothing better. While we were talking, and when I was glad to believe that I had alleviated (if I may use such a term) the shock he had had in seeing me, Richard came in. He had heard downstairs who was with me, and they met with cordial pleasure.

I saw that after their first greetings were over, and when they spoke of Richard's career, Mr. Woodcourt had a perception that all was not going well with him. He frequently glanced at his face as if there were something in it that gave him pain, and more than once he looked towards me, as though he sought to ascertain whether I knew what the truth was. Yet Richard was in one of his sanguine states and in good spirits, and was thoroughly pleased to see Mr. Woodcourt again, whom he had always liked.

Richard proposed that we all should go to London together, but Mr. Woodcourt, having to remain by his ship a little longer, could not join us. He dined with us, however, at an early hour; and became so much more like what he used to be that I was still more at peace to think I had been able to soften his regrets. Yet his mind was not relieved of Richard. When the coach was almost ready, and Richard ran down to look after his luggage, he spoke to me about him. I was not sure that I had a right to lay his whole story open; but I referred in a few words to his estrangement from Mr. Jarndyce, and to his being entangled in the ill-fated Chancery suit. Mr. Woodcourt expressed his regret.

"I saw you observe him rather closely," said I. "Do you think him so changed?"

"He is changed," he returned, shaking his head. "It is not his being so much younger or older, or thinner or fatter, or paler or ruddier, as there being upon his face such a singular expression. I never saw so remarkable a look in a young person. One cannot say that it is all anxiety, or all weariness; yet it is both, and like ungrown despair."

"You do not think he is ill?" said I. No. He looked robust in body. "That he cannot be at peace in mind, we have too much reason to know," I proceeded. "Mr. Woodcourt, you are going to London?"

"Tomorrow or the next day."

"There is nothing Richard wants so much as a friend. He always liked you. Pray help him sometimes with your companionship, if you can. You do not know of what service it might be. You cannot think how Ada, and Mr. Jarndyce, and even I—how we should all thank you, Mr. Woodcourt!"

"Miss Summerson," he said, more moved than he had been from the first, "before Heaven, I will be a true friend to him! I will accept him as a trust, and it shall be a sacred one!"

"God bless you!" said I, with my eyes filling fast, but I thought they might when it was not for myself. "Ada loves him—we all love him, but Ada loves him as we cannot. I will tell her what you say. Thank you, and God bless you, in her name!"

Richard came back as we finished exchanging these hurried words, and gave me his arm to take me to the coach.

"Woodcourt," he said, unconscious with what application, "pray let us meet in London!"

"Meet?" returned the other. "I have scarcely a friend there now but you. Where shall I find you?"

"Why, I must get a lodging of some sort," said Richard, pondering. "Say at Vholes's, Symond's Inn."

"Good! Without loss of time."

They shook hands heartily. When I was seated in the coach, and Richard was yet standing in the street, Mr. Woodcourt laid his friendly hand on Richard's shoulder and looked at me. I understood him, and waved mine in thanks.

And in his last look as we drove away, I saw that he was very sorry for me. I was glad to see it. I felt for my old self as the dead may feel if they ever revisit these scenes. I was glad to be tenderly remembered, to be gently pitied, not to be quite forgotten.

CHAPTER 46

*Stop Him!*

DARKNESS rests upon Tom-all-Alone's. Dilating and di-
lating since the sun went down last night, it has gradually swelled until
it fills every void in the place. For a time there were some dungeon
lights burning, as the lamp of Life burns in Tom-all-Alone's, heavily,
heavily, in the nauseous air, and winking at many horrible things. But
they are blotted out. The moon has eyed Tom with a dull cold stare, as
admitting some puny emulation of herself in his desert region unfit for
life and blasted by volcanic fires; but she has passed on. Tom-all-Alone's
is fast asleep.

It is a moot point whether Tom-all-Alone's be uglier by day or by
night; but on the argument that the more that is seen of it the more
shocking it must be, day carries it. The day begins to break now.

A brown sunburnt gentleman, who appears in some inaptitude for
sleep to be wandering abroad rather than counting the hours on a restless pillow, strolls hitherward at this quiet time. Attracted by curiosity,
he often pauses and looks about him, up and down the miserable by-
ways. Nor is he merely curious, for in his bright dark eye there is compassionate interest, and as he looks here and there, he seems to understand such wretchedness, and to have studied it before.

No waking creature save himself appears, except in one direction,
where he sees the solitary figure of a woman sitting on a doorstep. He
walks that way. Approaching, he observes that she has journeyed a long
distance, and is footsore and travel-stained. She sits on the doorstep in
the manner of one who is waiting, with her elbow on her knee and her
head upon her hand. Beside her is a canvas bag, or bundle, she has
carried. She is dozing, probably, for she gives no heed to his steps as he
comes toward her. The broken footway is so narrow that when Allan
Woodcourt comes to where the woman sits, he has to turn into the road
to pass her. Looking down at her face, his eye meets hers, and he stops.

"What is the matter?"

"Nothing, sir."

"Can't you make them hear? Do you want to be let in?"

"I'm waiting till they get up at another house—a lodging-house, not
here," the woman patiently returns. "I'm waiting here because there
will be sun here presently to warm me."

"I am afraid you are tired. I am sorry to see you sitting in the street."

"Thank you, sir. It don't matter."

A habit in him of speaking to the poor, and of avoiding patronage or condescension, has put him on good terms with the woman easily.

"Let me look at your forehead," he says, bending down. "I am a doctor. Don't be afraid. I wouldn't hurt you for the world." He knows that by touching her with his skilful and accustomed hand, he can soothe her yet more readily. "Ay! A bad bruise, and the skin sadly broken. This must be very sore."

"It do ache a little, sir," returns the woman.

"Let me try to make it more comfortable. My handkerchief won't hurt you."

"Oh dear no, sir, I'm sure of that!"

He cleanses the injured place and dries it; and having carefully examined it and gently pressed it with the palm of his hand, takes a small case from his pocket, dresses it, and binds it up. While he is thus employed, he says:

"And so your husband is a brickmaker?"

"How do you know that, sir?" asked the woman, astonished.

"Why, I suppose so from the colour of the clay upon your bag and on your dress. And I know brickmakers go about working at piecework in different places. And I am sorry to say I have known them cruel to their wives too. Where is he now?"

"He got into trouble last night, sir, but he'll look for me at the lodging-house."

"He will get into worse trouble if he often misuses his large and heavy hand as he has misused it here. But you forgive him, brutal as he is, and I say no more of him, except that I wish he deserved it. You have no young child?"

The woman shakes her head. "One as I calls mine, sir, but it's Liz's."

"Your own is dead. I see! Poor little thing!" By this time he has finished, and is putting up his case. "I suppose you have some settled home. Is it far from here?" he asks, good-humouredly making light of what he has done, as she gets up and curtseys.

"It's good two or three and twenty mile from here, sir. At Saint Albans. You know Saint Albans, sir?"

"Yes, I know something of it. And now I will ask you a question in return. Have you money for your lodging?"

"Yes, sir," she says, "really and truly." And she shows it. He tells her, in acknowledgment of her many subdued thanks, that she is very welcome, gives her good-day, and walks away. Tom-all-Alone's is still asleep, and nothing is astir.

Yes, something is! As he retraces his way to the point from which he descried the woman at a distance sitting on the step, he sees a ragged figure coming very cautiously along, crouching close to the soiled walls and furtively thrusting a hand before it. It is the figure of a youth whose face is hollow, and whose eyes have an emaciated glare. He is so intent on getting along unseen that even the apparition of a stranger in whole garments does not tempt him to look back. He shades his face with his ragged elbow as he passes on the other side of the way, and goes shrinking and creeping on, with his anxious hand before him, and his shapeless clothes hanging in shreds.

Allan Woodcourt pauses to look after him and note all this, with a shadowy belief that he has seen the boy before. He cannot recall how, or where, but there is some association in his mind with such a form. He imagines that he must have seen it in some hospital or refuge. He is gradually emerging from Tom-all-Alone's in the morning light, thinking about it, when he hears running feet behind him, and looking round, sees the boy scouring towards him at great speed, followed by the woman.

"Stop him, stop him!" cries the woman, almost breathless. "Stop him, sir!"

He darts across the road into the boy's path, but the boy is quicker than he—makes a curve—ducks—dives under his hands—comes up half a dozen yards beyond him, and scours away again. Still the woman follows, crying, "Stop him, sir, pray stop him!" Allan, not knowing but that he has just robbed her of her money, follows in chase, and runs so hard that he runs the boy down a dozen times; but each time he repeats the curve, the duck, the dive, and scours away again. To strike at him, on any of these occasions, would be to fell and disable him, but the pursuer cannot resolve to do that, and so the grimly ridiculous pursuit continues. At last the fugitive, hard-pressed, takes to a narrow passage, which has no thoroughfare. Here, against a hoarding of decaying timber, he is brought to bay and tumbles down, lying gasping at his pursuer, who stands and gasps at him until the woman comes up.

"Oh you Jo!" cries the woman. "What? I have found you at last!"

"Jo," repeats Allan, looking at him with attention, "Jo! Stay. To be sure! I recollect this lad some time ago being brought before the Coroner."

"Yes, I see you once afore at the Inkwhich," whimpers Jo. "What of that? Can't you never let such an unfortnet as me alone? An't I unfortnet enough for you yet? How unfortnet do you want me fur to be? I've been a-chivied and a-chivied, fust by one on you and nixt by another on you, till I'm worritted to skins and bones. The Inkwhich warn't *my* fault. *I* done nothink. He wos wery good to me, he wos, he wos the only one I knowed to speak to as ever come across my crossing. It ain't wery likely I should want him to be Inkwhich'd. I only wish I wos myself. I don't know why I don't go and make a hole in the water, I'm sure I don't."

He says it with such a pitiable air, and his grimy tears appear so real, and he lies in the corner up against the hoarding so like a growth of fungus produced there in neglect and impurity, that Allan Woodcourt is softened towards him. He says to the woman, "Miserable creature, what has he done?"

To which she only replies, shaking her head at the prostrate figure more amazedly than angrily, "O you Jo, you Jo, I have found you at last!"

"What has he done?" says Allan. "Has he robbed you?"

"No, sir, no. Robbed me? He did nothing but what was kind-hearted by me, and that's the wonder of it. But he was along with me, sir," says the woman, "down at Saint Albans, ill, and a young lady Lord bless her for a good friend to me took pity on him when I durstn't, and took him home—"

Allan shrinks back from him with a sudden horror.

"Yes, sir, yes. Took him home, and made him comfortable, and like a thankless monster he ran away in the night and never has been seen or heard of since till I set eyes on him just now. And that young lady that was such a pretty dear caught his illness, lost her beautiful looks, and wouldn't hardly be known for the same young lady now if it wasn't for her angel temper, and her pretty shape, and her sweet voice. Do you know it? You ungrateful wretch, do you know that this is all along of you and of her goodness to you?" demands the woman, breaking into passionate tears.

The boy, in rough sort stunned by what he hears, falls to smearing his dirty forehead with his dirty palm, and to shaking from head to foot until the crazy hoarding against which he leans rattles.

Allan restrains the woman, merely by a quiet gesture, but effectually.

"Richard told me," he falters. "—I mean, I have heard of this—don't mind me for a moment, I will speak presently."

He turns away, and stands for a while looking out at the covered passage. When he comes back, he has recovered his composure, except that he contends against an avoidance of the boy, which is so very remarkable that it absorbs the woman's attention.

"You hear what she says. But get up, get up!"

Jo, shaking and chattering, slowly rises, and stands, after the manner of his tribe in a difficulty, sideways against the hoarding, resting one of his high shoulders against it and covertly rubbing his right hand over his left, and his left foot over his right.

"You hear what she says, and I know it's true. Have you been here ever since?"

"Wishermaydie if I seen Tom-all-Alone's till this blessed morning," replies Jo, hoarsely.

"Why have you come here now?"

"I don't know how to do nothink, and I can't get nothink to do. I'm wery poor and ill, and I thought I'd come back here when there warn't nobody about, and lay down and hide somewheres as I knows on till arter dark, and then go and beg a trifle of Mr. Snagsby. He wos allus willin fur to give me somethink he wos, though Mrs. Snagsby she was allus a chivying on me—like everybody everywheres."

"Now tell me," proceeds Allan, making a strong effort to overcome his repugnance, going very near to him, and leaning over him with an expression of confidence, "tell me how it came about that you left that house when the good young lady had been so unfortunate as to pity you, and take you home."

Jo suddenly comes out of his resignation, and excitedly declares, addressing the woman, that he never known about the young lady, that he never heern about it, that he never went fur to hurt her, that he would sooner have hurt his own self, that he'd sooner have had his unfortnet 'ed chopped off than ever gone a-nigh her, and that she wos wery good to him, she wos. Conducting himself throughout as if in his poor fashion he really meant it, and winding up with some very miserable sobs.

Allan Woodcourt sees that this is not a sham. He constrains himself to touch him. "Come, Jo. Tell me."

"No. I dustn't," says Jo, relapsing into the profile state. "I dustn't, or I would."

"But I must know," returns the other, "all the same. Come, Jo."

After two or three such adjurations, Jo lifts up his head again, and says in a low voice, "Well, I'll tell you something. I was took away. There!"

"Took away? In the night?"

"Ah!" Very apprehensive of being overheard, Jo looks about him, and even glances up some ten feet at the top of the hoarding and through the cracks in it, lest the object of his distrust should be looking over, or hidden on the other side.

"Who took you away?"

"I dustn't name him," says Jo. "I dustn't do it, sir."

"But I want, in the young lady's name, to know. You may trust me. No one else shall hear."

"Ah, but I don't know," replies Jo, shaking his head fearfully, "as he *don't* hear."

"Why, he is not in this place."

"Oh, ain't he though?" says Jo. "He's in all manner of places, all at wanst."

Allan looks at him in perplexity, but discovers some real meaning and good faith at the bottom of this bewildering reply. He patiently awaits an explicit answer; and Jo, more baffled by his patience than by anything else, at last desperately whispers a name in his ear.

"Ay!" says Allan. "Why, what had you been doing?"

"Nothink, sir. Never done nothink to get myself into no trouble, 'sept in not moving on and the Inkwhich. But I'm a-moving on now to the berryin-ground—that's the move as I'm up to."

"No, no, we will try to prevent that. But what did he do with you?"

"Put me in a horsepittle," replied Jo, whispering, "till I was discharged, then giv me a little money and ses, 'Hook it! Nobody wants you here,' he ses. 'You hook it. You go and tramp,' he ses. 'You move on,' he ses. 'Don't let me ever see you nowheres within forty mile of London, or you'll repent it.' And he'll see me if I'm above ground."

Allan considers a little, then remarks, turning to the woman but keeping an encouraging eye on Jo, "He is not so ungrateful as you suppose. He had a reason for going away, though it was an insufficient one."

428 · BLEAK HOUSE

"Thank 'ee, sir, thank 'ee!" exclaims Jo. "There now! See how hard you wos upon me. But ony you tell the young lady wot the genlmn ses and it's all right. For *you* wos wery good to me too, and I knows it."

"Now Jo," says Allan, keeping his eye upon him, "come with me, and I will find you a better place than this to lie down and hide in. If I take one side of the way and you the other to avoid observation, you will not run away, I know very well, if you make me a promise."

"I won't, not unless I wos to see *him* a-coming, sir."

"Very well. I take your word. Half the town is getting up by this time, and the whole town will be broad awake in another hour. Come along. Good-day again, my good woman."

"Good-day again, sir, and I thank you kindly many times again."

Jo, repeating, "Ony you tell the young lady as I never went fur to hurt her and wot the genlmn ses!" nods and shambles and shivers, and takes his creeping way along after Allan Woodcourt, close to the houses on the opposite side of the street. In this order, the two come up out of Tom-all-Alone's into the broad rays of the sunlight and the purer air.

## CHAPTER 47

### Jo's Will

As Allan Woodcourt and Jo proceed along the streets Allan revolves in his mind how and where he shall bestow his companion. "It surely is a strange fact," he considers, "that in the heart of a civilized world this creature in human form should be more difficult to dispose of than an unowned dog."

At first he looks behind him often, to assure himself that Jo is still really following. But look where he will, he still beholds him close to the opposite houses, making his way with his wary hand from brick to brick and from door to door, and often, as he creeps along, glancing over at him watchfully.

A breakfast-stall at a street-corner suggests the first thing to be done. He stops there, looks round, and beckons Jo. Jo crosses, and comes halting and shuffling up, slowly scooping the knuckles of his right hand round and round in the hollowed palm of his left—kneading dirt with a natural pestle and mortar. What is a dainty repast to Jo is then set before him, and he begins to gulp the coffee, and to gnaw the bread and butter, looking anxiously about him in all directions as he eats and drinks, like a scared animal.

But he is so sick and miserable that even hunger has abandoned him. "I thought I was almost a-starvin, sir," said Jo, soon putting down his food, "but I don't know nothink—not even that. I don't care for eating wittles nor yet for drinking on 'em." And Jo stands shivering and looking at the breakfast wonderingly.

Allan Woodcourt lays his hand upon his pulse, and on his chest. "Draw breath, Jo!" "It draws," says Jo, "as heavy as a cart." He might add, "and rattles like it," but he only mutters, "I'm a-moving on, sir."

Allan looks about for an apothecary's shop. There is none at hand, but a tavern does as well or better. He obtains a little measure of wine, and gives the lad a portion of it very carefully. He begins to revive almost as soon as it passes his lips. "We may repeat that dose, Jo," observes Allan, after watching him with his attentive face. "So! Now we will take five minutes' rest, and then go on again."

Leaving the boy sitting on the bench of the breakfast-stall, with his back against an iron railing, Allan Woodcourt paces up and down in the early sunshine, casting an occasional look towards him without appearing to watch him. It requires no discernment to perceive that he is warmed and refreshed. If a face so shaded can brighten, his face brightens somewhat, and, by little and little, he eats the slice of bread he had so hopelessly laid down. Observant of these signs of improvement, Allan engages him in conversation; and elicits to his no small wonder the adventure of the lady in the veil, with all its consequences. When he has finished his story and his bread, they go on again.

Intending to refer his difficulty in finding a temporary place of refuge for the boy to his old patient, zealous little Miss Flite, Allan leads the way to the court where he and Jo first forgathered. But all is changed at the rag and bottle shop; Miss Flite no longer lodges there; it is shut up, and a hard-featured female, much obscured by dust—who is no other than the interesting Judy—is tart and spare in her replies. These sufficing, however, to inform the visitor that Miss Flite and her birds are domiciled with a Mrs. Blinder, in Bell Yard, he repairs to that neighbouring place, where Miss Flite (who rises early that she may be punctual at the Divan of Justice held by her excellent friend the Chancellor) comes running downstairs with tears of welcome and with open arms.

"My dear physician!" cried Miss Flite. "My meritorious, distinguished, honourable officer!" She uses some odd expressions, but is as cordial and full of heart as sanity itself can be—more so than it often is. Allan, very patient with her, waits until she has no more raptures to express, then points out Jo, trembling in a doorway, and tells her how he comes there.

"Where can I lodge him hereabouts for the present? Now you have a fund of knowledge and good sense, and can advise me."

Miss Flite, mighty proud of the compliment, sets herself to consider; but it is long before a bright thought occurs to her. Mrs. Blinder is entirely let, and she herself occupies poor Gridley's room. "Gridley!" exclaims Miss Flite, clapping her hands, after a twentieth repetition of this remark. "Gridley! To be sure! Of course! My dear physician! General George will help us out."

It is hopeless to ask for any information about General George, and would be though Miss Flite had not already run upstairs to put on her pinched bonnet and her poor little shawl, and to arm herself with her reticule of documents. But as she informs her physician, in her disjointed manner, on coming down in full array, that General George, whom she often calls upon, knows her dear Fitz-Jarndyce, and takes a great interest in all connected with her, Allan is induced to think that they may be in the right way. So he tells Jo, for his encouragement, that this walking about will soon be over now, and they repair to the General's. Fortunately it is not far.

From the exterior of George's Shooting Gallery, and the long entry, and the bare perspective beyond it, Allan Woodcourt augurs well. He also descries promise in the figure of Mr. George himself, striding towards them in his morning exercise with his pipe in his mouth.

"Your servant, sir," says Mr. George, with a military salute. Good-humouredly smiling all over his broad forehead up into his crisp hair, he then defers to Miss Flite as, with great stateliness, and at some length, she performs the courtly ceremony of presentation. He winds it up with another "Your servant, sir!" and another salute.

"Excuse me, sir. A sailor, I believe?" says Mr. George.

"I am proud to find I have the air of one," returns Allan, "but I am only a seagoing doctor."

"Indeed, sir! I should have thought you was a regular blue-jacket, myself."

Allan hopes Mr. George will forgive his intrusion the more readily on that account, and proceeds to tell him all he knows about Jo, unto which the trooper listens with a grave face.

"And that's the lad, sir, is it?" he inquires, looking along the entry to where Jo stands staring up at the great letters on the whitewashed front, which have no meaning in his eyes.

"That's he," says Allan. "And, Mr. George, I am in this difficulty about him. I am unwilling to place him in a hospital, even if I could procure him immediate admission, because I foresee that he would not stay there many hours, if he could be so much as got there. The same objection applies to a workhouse. I am convinced that he would not remain in either place, because he is possessed by an extraordinary terror of this person who ordered him to keep out of the way; in his ignorance, he believes this person to be everywhere, and cognizant of everything."

"I ask your pardon, sir," says Mr. George, "but you have not mentioned that party's name. Is it a secret, sir?"

"The boy makes it one. But his name is Bucket."

"Bucket the Detective, sir?"

"The same man."

"The man is known to me, sir," returns the trooper, after blowing out a cloud of smoke and squaring his chest, "and the boy is so far correct that he undoubtedly is a—rum customer."

"Now I wish Mr. Jarndyce and Miss Summerson at least to know that this Jo, who tells so strange a story, has reappeared, and to have it in their power to speak with him, if they should desire to do so. Therefore I want to get him, for the present moment, into any poor lodging kept by decent people where he would be admitted. Decent people and Jo, Mr. George," says Allan, following the direction of the trooper's eyes along the entry, "have not been much acquainted, as you see. Hence the difficulty. Do you happen to know any one in this neighbourhood who would receive him for a while, on my paying for him beforehand?"

As he puts the question, he becomes aware of a dirty-faced little man standing at the trooper's elbow and looking up, with an oddly twisted figure and countenance, into the trooper's face. After a few more puffs at his pipe, the trooper looks down askant at the little man and the little man winks up at the trooper.

"Well, sir," says Mr. George, "I can assure you that I would willingly be knocked on the head at any time if it would be at all agreeable to Miss Summerson, and consequently I esteem it a privilege to do that young lady any service, however small. We are naturally in the vaga-bond way here, sir, both myself and Phil. You see what the place is. You are welcome to a quiet corner of it for the boy, if the same would meet your views. No charge made, except for rations. We are not in a flourish-ing state of circumstances here, sir. We are liable to be tumbled out, neck and crop, at a moment's notice. However, sir, such as the place is, and so long as it lasts, here it is at your service. I take it for granted, sir," he adds, "you being one of the medical staff, that there is no present in-fection about this unfortunate subject?" Allan is quite sure of it. "Be-cause, sir," says Mr. George, shaking his head sorrowfully, "we have had enough of that."

His tone is no less sorrowfully echoed by his new acquaintance. "Still, I am bound to tell you," observes Allan, after repeating his former assur-ance, "that the boy is deplorably low and reduced, and that he may be—I do not say that he is—too far gone to recover."

"Do you consider him in present danger, sir?" inquires the trooper.

"Yes, I fear so."

"Then, sir," returns the trooper, in a decisive manner, "it appears to me that the sooner he comes out of the street, the better. You Phil! Bring him in!"

Mr. Squod tacks out, all on one side, to execute the word of com-mand, and the trooper, having smoked his pipe, lays it by. Jo is brought in. He is not one of Mr. Jellyby's lambs, being wholly unconnected with Borrioboola-Gha; he is not softened by distance and unfamiliarity; he is not a genuine foreign-grown savage; he is the ordinary home-made article. Dirty, ugly, disagreeable to all the senses, in body a common creature of the common streets, only in soul a heathen. Homely filth begrimes him, homely parasites devour him, homely rags are on him: native ignorance, the growth of English soil and climate, sinks his im-mortal nature lower than the beasts that perish. Stand forth, Jo, in un-compromising colour! From the sole of thy foot to the crown of thy head, there is nothing interesting about thee.

He shuffles slowly into Mr. George's gallery, and stands huddled together in a bundle, looking all about the floor. He seems to know that they have an inclination to shrink from him, partly for what he is, and partly for what he has caused. He, too, shrinks from them. He is not of the same order of things, not the same place in creation. He is of no order and no place, neither of the beasts nor of humanity.

"Look here, Jo!" says Allan. "This is Mr. George." Jo searches the floor for some time longer, then looks up for a moment, and then down again. "He is a kind friend to you, for he is going to give you lodging-room here."

Jo makes a scoop with one hand, which is supposed to be a bow. After a little more consideration, and some backing and changing of the foot on which he rests, he mutters that he is "wery thankful."

"You are quite safe here. All you have to do at present is to be obedient, and to get strong. And mind you tell us the truth here, whatever you do, Jo."

"Wishermaydie if I don't, sir," says Jo, reverting to his favourite declaration. "I never done nothink yit but wot you knows on to get myself into no trouble. I never was in no other trouble at all, sir—'sept not knowin' nothink and starwation."

"I believe it. Now attend to Mr. George. I see he is going to speak to you."

"My intention merely was, sir," observes Mr. George, amazingly broad and upright, "to point out to him where he can lie down, and get a thorough good dose of sleep. Now, look here." As the trooper speaks, he conducts them to the other end of the gallery, and opens one of the little cabins. "There you are, you see! Here is a mattress, and here you may rest, on good behaviour, as long as Mr.—I ask your pardon, sir"; he refers apologetically to the card Allan has given him—"Mr. Woodcourt pleases. Don't you be alarmed if you hear shots; they'll be aimed at the target, and not you. Now, there's another thing I would recommend, sir," says the trooper, turning to his visitor. "Phil, come here!" Phil bears down upon them, according to his usual tactics. "Here is a man, sir, who was found, when a baby, in the gutter. Consequently, it is to be expected that he takes a natural interest in this poor creature. You do, don't you, Phil?"

"Certainly and surely I do, Guv'ner," is Phil's reply.

"Now I was thinking, sir," says Mr. George, "that if this man was to take him to a bath, and was to lay out a few shillings in getting him one or two coarse articles—"

"Mr. George, my considerate friend," returns Allan, taking out his purse, "it is the very favour I would have asked."

Phil Squod and Jo are sent out immediately on this work of improvement. Miss Flite, quite enraptured by her success, makes the best of her way to Court, having great fears that otherwise her friend the Chancellor may be uneasy about her, or may give the judgment she has so long expected in her absence. Allan takes the opportunity of going out to procure some restorative medicines, and obtaining them near at hand, soon returns, to find the trooper walking up and down the gallery, and to fall into step and walk with him.

"I take it, sir," says Mr. George, "that you know Miss Summerson pretty well?" Yes, it appears. "Not related to her, sir?" No, it appears.

"Excuse the apparent curiosity," says Mr. George. "It seemed to me probable that you might take more than a common interest in this poor creature because Miss Summerson had taken that unfortunate interest in him. 'Tis *my* case, sir, I assure you."

"And mine, Mr. George."

The trooper looks sideways at Allan's sunburnt cheek and bright dark eye, rapidly measures his height and build, and seems to approve of him.

"Since you have been out, sir, I have been thinking that I unquestionably know the rooms in Lincoln's Inn Fields where Bucket took the lad, according to his account. Though he is not acquainted with the name, I can help you to it. It's Tulkinghorn. That's what it is." Allan looks at him inquiringly, repeating the name. "Tulkinghorn. That's the name, sir. I know the man, and know him to have been in communication with Bucket before, respecting a deceased person who had given him offence. *I* know the man, sir. To my sorrow."

Allan naturally asks what kind of man he is.

"What kind of man! Do you mean to look at?"

"I think I know that much of him. I mean to deal with. Generally, what kind of man?"

"Why then, I'll tell you, sir," returns the trooper, stopping short and folding his arms on his square chest so angrily that his face fires and flushes all over. "He is a confoundedly bad kind of man. He is a slow-torturing kind of man. He is no more like flesh and blood than a rusty old carbine is. He is a kind of man—by George!—that has caused me more restlessness, and more uneasiness, and more dissatisfaction with myself, than all other men put together. That's the kind of man Mr. Tulkinghorn is!"

"I am sorry," says Allan, to have touched so sore a place."

"Sore? It's no fault of yours, sir; but you shall judge. He has got a power over me. He is the man I spoke of just now as being able to tumble me out of this place neck and crop. He keeps me on a constant seesaw. He won't hold off, and he won't come on. If I have a payment to make him, or time to ask him for, or anything to go to him about, he don't see me, don't hear me—passes me on to Melchisedech's in Clifford's Inn,

Melchisedech's in Clifford's Inn passes me back again to him—he keeps me prowling and dangling about him as if I was made of the same stone as himself. Why, I spend half my life now, pretty well, loitering and dodging about his door. What does he care? Nothing. He chafes and goads me till—Bah! nonsense—I am forgetting myself. Mr. Woodcourt, all I say is, he is an old man; but I am glad I shall never have the chance of setting spurs to my horse and riding at him in a fair field. For if I had the chance, in one of the humours he drives me into—he'd go down, sir!"

Mr. George has been so excited that he finds it necessary to wipe his forehead on his shirt-sleeve. Even while he whistles his impetuosity away with the National Anthem, some involuntary shakings of his head and heavings of his chest still linger behind, not to mention an occasional hasty adjustment with both hands of his open shirt-collar, as if it were scarcely open enough to prevent his being troubled by a choking sensation. In short, Allan Woodcourt has not much doubt about the going-down of Mr. Tulkinghorn on the field referred to.

Jo and his conductor presently return, and Jo is assisted to his mattress by the careful Phil, to whom, after due administration of medicine by his own hands, Allan confides all needful means and instructions. The morning is by this time getting on apace. He repairs to his lodgings to dress and breakfast, and then, without seeking rest, goes away to Mr. Jarndyce to communicate his discovery.

With him Mr. Jarndyce returns alone, confidentially telling him that there are reasons for keeping this matter very quiet indeed, and showing a serious interest in it. To Mr. Jarndyce, Jo repeats in substance what he said in the morning. Only, that cart of his is heavier to draw, and draws with a hollower sound.

"Let me lay here quiet, and not be chivied no more," falters Jo; "and be so kind any person as is a-passin' nigh where I used fur to sweep as jist to say to Mr. Snagsby that Jo, wot he known once, is a-moving on right forards with his duty, and I'll be wery thankful."

He makes so many of these references to the law-stationer in the course of a day or two, that Allan, after conferring with Mr. Jarndyce, good-naturedly resolves to call in Cook's Court, the rather as the cart seems to be breaking down. To Cook's Court, therefore, he repairs. Mr. Snagsby is behind his counter in his grey coat and sleeves, inspecting an indenture of several skins which has just come in from the engrosser's. Mr. Snagsby greets the stranger with his cough of general preparation for business.

"You don't remember me, Mr. Snagsby?"

The stationer's heart begins to thump heavily, for his old apprehensions have never abated. It is as much as he can do to answer, "No,

436 • BLEAK HOUSE

sir, I can't say I do. I should have considered—not to put too fine a
point upon it—that I never saw you before, sir."

"Twice before," says Allan Woodcourt. "Once at a poor bedside, and
once—"

"It's come at last!" thinks the afflicted stationer as recollection breaks
upon him. "It's got to a head now, and is going to burst!" But he has
sufficient presence of mind to conduct his visitor into the little counting-
house, and to shut the door.

"Are you a married man, sir?"

"No, I am not."

"Would you make the attempt, though single," says Mr. Snagsby in
a melancholy whisper, "to speak as low as you can? For my little woman
is a-listening somewheres, or I'll forfeit the business and five hundred
pound!" In deep dejection Mr. Snagsby sits down on his stool, with his
back against his desk, protesting: "I never had a secret of my own, sir. I
can't charge my memory with ever having once attempted to deceive my
little woman on my own account, since she named the day. I wouldn't
have done it, sir. Not to put too fine a point upon it, I couldn't have
done it, I dursn't have done it. Whereas, and nevertheless, I find myself
wrapped round with secrecy and mystery till my life is a burden to me."

His visitor professes his regret to hear it, and asks him does he remember Jo? Mr. Snagsby answers with a suppressed groan, Oh, don't he!

"You couldn't name an individual human being—except myself—that
my little woman is more set and determined against than Jo," says Mr.
Snagsby. Allan asks why? "Why?" repeats Mr. Snagsby, in his desperation clutching at the clump of hair at the back of his bald head, "How
should I know why? But you are a single person, sir, and may you long
be spared to ask a married person such a question!"

With this beneficent wish, Mr. Snagsby coughs a cough of dismal
resignation, and submits himself to hear what the visitor has to communicate.

"There again!" says Mr. Snagsby. "At it again, in a new direction! A
certain person charges me, in the solemnest way, not to talk of Jo to
any one, even my little woman. Then comes another certain person, in
the person of yourself, and charges me, in an equally solemn way, not to
mention Jo to that other certain person above all other persons. Why,
this is a private asylum! Why, not to put too fine a point upon it, this
is Bedlam, sir!" says Mr. Snagsby.

But, being tender-hearted, and affected by the account he hears of
Jo's condition, he readily engages to "look round" as early in the evening
as he can manage it quietly. He looks round very quietly, when the evening comes; but it may turn out that Mrs. Snagsby is as quiet a manager
as he.

Jo is very glad to see his old friend, and says, when they are left alone, that he takes it uncommon kind as Mr. Snagsby should come so far out of his way on account of sich as him. Mr. Snagsby, touched by the spectacle before him, immediately lays upon the table half a crown, that magic balsam of his for all kinds of wounds.

"And how do you find yourself, my poor lad?" inquires the stationer, with his cough of sympathy.

"I am in luck, Mr. Snagsby, I am," returns Jo, "and don't want for nothink. I'm more cumfbler nor you can't think. Mr. Snagsby! I'm wery sorry that I done it, but I didn't go fur to do it, sir."

The stationer softly lays down another halfcrown, and asks him what it is that he is sorry for having done.

"Mr. Snagsby," says Jo, "I went and giv a illness to the lady as wos and yit as warn't the t'other lady, and none of 'em never says nothink to me for having done it, on accounts of their being ser good and my having been s'unfortnet. The lady come herself and see me yesday, and she ses, 'Ah, Jo,' she ses, 'we thought we'd lost you, Jo!' she ses. And she sits down a-smilin so quiet, and don't pass a word nor yit a look upon me for having done it, she don't, and I turns agin the wall, I doos, Mr. Snagsby. And Mr. Jarnders, I see him a-forced to turn away his own self. And Mr. Woodcot, he come fur to giv me somethink fur to ease me, wot he's allus a-doing, and wen he come a-bendin over me and a-speakin' up so bold, I see his tears a-fallin, Mr. Snagsby."

The softened stationer deposits another halfcrown on the table. Nothing less than a repetition of that infallible remedy will relieve his feelings.

"Wot I was a-thinkin on, Mr. Snagsby," proceeds Jo, "wos, as you wos able to write wery large, p'raps?"

"Yes, Jo, please God," returns the stationer.

"Uncommon precious large, p'raps?" says Jo, with eagerness.

"Yes, my poor boy."

Jo laughs with pleasure. "Wot I wos a-thinkin on then, Mr. Snagsby, wos that when I was moved on as fur as ever I could go and couldn't be moved no furder, whether you might be so good, p'raps, as to write out, wery large so that any one could see it anywheres, as that I wos wery truly hearty sorry that I done it and that I never went fur to do it, and that though I didn't know nothink at all, I knowd as Mr. Woodcot once cried over it and wos allus grieved over it, and that I hoped as he'd be able to forgive me in his mind. If the writin could be made to say it wery large, he might."

"It shall say it, Jo. Very large."

Jo laughs again. "Thankee, Mr. Snagsby. It's wery kind of you, sir, and it makes me more cumfbler nor I was afore."

The meek little stationer, with a broken and unfinished cough, slips down his fourth halfcrown—he has never been so close to a case requiring so many—and is fain to depart. And Jo and he, upon this little earth, shall meet no more. No more.

For the cart so hard to draw is near its journey's end, and drags over stony ground. All round the clock it labours up the broken steps, shattered and worn. Not many times can the sun rise and behold it still upon its weary road.

Phil Squod, with his smoky gunpowder visage, at once acts as nurse and works as armourer at his little table in a corner, often looking round, and saying with a nod of his green-baize cap, and an encouraging elevation of his one eyebrow, "Hold up, my boy! Hold up!" There, too, is Mr. Jarndyce many a time, and Allan Woodcourt almost always, both thinking much how strangely Fate has entangled this rough outcast in the web of very different lives. There, too, the trooper is a frequent visitor, filling the doorway with his athletic figure and, from his superfluity of life and strength, seeming to shed down temporary vigour upon Jo, who never fails to speak more robustly in answer to his cheerful words.

Jo is in a sleep or in a stupor today, and Allan Woodcourt, newly arrived, stands by him looking down upon his wasted form. After a while, he softly seats himself upon the bedstead with his face towards him—just as he sat in the law-writer's room—and touches his chest and heart. The cart had very nearly given up, but labours on a little more.

The trooper stands in the doorway, still and silent. Phil has stopped in a low clinking noise, with his little hammer in his hand. Mr. Woodcourt looks round with that grave professional interest and attention on his face, and, glancing significantly at the trooper, signs to Phil to carry his table out. When the little hammer is next used, there will be a speck of rust upon it.

"Well, Jo! What is the matter? Don't be frightened."

"I thought," says Jo, who has started and is looking round, "I thought I was in Tom-all-Alone's agin. Ain't there nobody here but you, Mr. Woodcot?"

"Nobody."

"And I ain't took back to Tom-all-Alone's. Am I, sir?"

"No." Jo closes his eyes, muttering, "I'm wery thankful."

After watching him closely a little while, Allan puts his mouth very near his ear, and says to him in a low, distinct voice:

"Jo! Did you ever know a prayer?"

"Never knowd nothink, sir."

"Not so much as one short prayer?"

"No, sir. Nothink at all. Mr. Chadbands he wos a-prayin wunst at

Mr. Snagsby's and I heerd him, but he sounded as if he wos a-speakin' to hisself, and not to me. He prayed a lot, but *I* couldn't make out nothink on it. Different times, there was other genlmen come down Tom-all-Alone's a-prayin, but they all mostly sed as the t'other wuns prayed wrong, and all mostly sounded to be a-talkin to theirselves, or a-passing blame on the t'others, and not a-talkin to us. *I* never knowd what it wos all about."

It takes him a long time to say this. After a short relapse into sleep or stupor, he makes, of a sudden, a strong effort to get out of bed.

"Stay, Jo! What now?"

"It's time for me to go to that there berryin-ground, sir," he returns with a wild look.

"Lie down. What burying ground, Jo?"

"Where they laid him as wos wery good to me, wery good to me indeed, he wos. It's time fur me to go down to that there berryin-ground, sir, and ask to be put along with him. I wants to go there and be berried. He used fur to say to me, 'I am as poor as you today, Jo,' he ses. I wants to tell him that I am as poor as him now, and have come there to be laid along with him."

"By and by, Jo. By and by."

"Ah! P'raps they wouldn't do it if I wos to go myself. But will you promise to have me took there, sir, and laid along with him?"

"I will indeed."

"Thank'ee, sir. Thank'ee, sir. They'll have to get the key of the gate afore they can take me in, for it's allus locked. And there's a step there as I used for to clean with my broom.—It's turned wery dark, sir. Is there any light a-comin?"

"It is coming fast, Jo."

Fast. The cart is shaken all to pieces, and the rugged road is very near its end.

"Jo, my poor fellow!"

"I hear you, sir, in the dark, but I'm a-gropin—a-gropin—let me catch hold of your hand."

"Jo, can you say what I say?"

"I'll say anythink as you say, sir, for I knows it's good."

"Our Father."

"Our Father!—yes, that's wery good, sir."

"Which art in Heaven."

"Art in Heaven—is the light a-comin, sir?"

"It is close at hand. Hallowed be thy name!"

"Hallowed be—thy—"

The light is come upon the dark benighted way. Dead!

Dead, your Majesty. Dead, my lords and gentlemen. Dead, Right

Reverends and Wrong Reverends of every order. Dead, men and women born with Heavenly compassion in your hearts. And dying thus around us every day.

## CHAPTER 48

### *Closing In*

THE place in Lincolnshire has shut its many eyes again, and the house in town is awake. In Lincolnshire, the Dedlocks of the past doze in their picture-frames, and the low wind murmurs through the long drawing-room as if they were breathing pretty regularly. In town, the Dedlocks of the present rattle in their fire-eyed carriages through the darkness of the night, and the Dedlock Mercuries loll away the drowsy mornings in the little windows of the hall. The fashionable world—tremendous orb, nearly five miles round—is in full swing, and the solar system works respectfully at its appointed distances.

Where the throng is thickest, where the lights are brightest, where all the senses are ministered to with the greatest delicacy and refinement, Lady Dedlock is. From the shining heights she has scaled and taken she is never absent. Though the belief she of old reposed in herself, as one able to reserve whatsoever she would under her mantle of pride, is beaten down—though she has no assurance that what she is to those around her she will remain another day—it is not in her nature, when envious eyes are looking on, to yield or to droop. They say of her that she has lately grown more handsome and more haughty.

Mr. Tulkinghorn says nothing, looks nothing. Now, as heretofore, he is to be found in doorways of rooms, receiving patronage from the Peerage, and making no sign. Of all men he is still the last who might be supposed to have any influence upon my Lady. Of all women she is still the last who might be supposed to have any dread of him.

One thing has been much on her mind since their late interview in his turret-room at Chesney Wold. She is now decided, and prepared to throw it off. It is morning in the great world, afternoon according to the little sun. The Mercuries, exhausted by looking out of window, are reposing in the hall, and hang their heavy heads, the gorgeous creatures, like overblown sunflowers. Sir Leicester, in the library, has fallen asleep, for the good of the country, over the report of a Parliamentary committee. My Lady sits in the room in which she gave audience to the young man of the name of Guppy. Rosa is with her, and has been writing for her and reading to her. Rosa is now at work upon embroidery, and as she bends her head over it, my Lady watches her in silence. Not for the first time today.

"Rosa." The pretty village face looks brightly up. Then, seeing how serious my Lady is, looks puzzled and surprised. "See to the door. Is it shut?"

Yes. She goes to it and returns, and looks yet more surprised.

"I am about to place confidence in you, child, for I know I may trust your attachment, if not your judgment. In what I am going to do, I will not disguise myself to you at least. But I confide in you. Say nothing to any one of what passes between us." The timid little beauty promises in all earnestness to be trustworthy. "Do you know," Lady Dedlock asks her, signing to her to bring her chair nearer, "do you know, Rosa, that I am different to you from what I am to any one?"

"Yes, my lady. Much kinder. But then I often think I know you as you really are."

"You often think you know me as I really am? Poor child, poor child!" She says it with a kind of scorn—though not of Rosa—and sits brooding, looking dreamily at her. "Do you think, Rosa, you are any relief or comfort to me? Do you suppose your being young and natural, and fond of me and grateful to me, makes it any pleasure to me to have you near me?"

"I don't know, my lady; I can scarcely hope so. But, with all my heart, I wish it was so."

"It is so, little one. And if I were to say today, Go! Leave me! I should say what would give me great pain and disquiet, child, and what would leave me very solitary."

"My lady! Have I offended you?"

"In nothing. Come here."

Rosa bends down on the footstool at my Lady's feet. My Lady, with that motherly touch of the famous ironmaster night, lays her hand upon her dark hair, and gently keeps it there.

"I told you, Rosa, that I wished you to be happy, and that I would make you so if I could make anybody happy on this earth. I cannot. There are reasons now known to me, reasons in which you have no part, rendering it far better for you that you should not remain here. You must not remain here. I have determined that you shall not. I have written to the father of your lover, and he will be here today. All this I have done for your sake."

The weeping girl covers her hand with kisses, and says what shall she do, what shall she do, when they are separated! Her mistress kisses her on the cheek, and makes no other answer.

"Now be happy, child, under better circumstances. Be beloved and happy!"

"Ah, my lady, I have sometimes thought—forgive my being so free—that *you* are not happy."

"I!"

"Will you be more so when you have sent me away? Pray, pray, think again. Let me stay a little while!"

"I have said, my child, that what I do, I do for your sake, not my own. It is done. What I am towards you, Rosa, is what I am now—not what I shall be a little while hence. Remember this, and keep my confidence. Do so much for my sake, and thus all ends between us!"

She detaches herself from her simple-hearted companion, and leaves the room. Late in the afternoon, when she next appears upon the staircase, she is in her haughtiest and coldest state. As indifferent as if all passion, feeling, and interest had been worn out in the earlier ages of the world, and had perished from its surface with its other departed monsters.

Mercury has announced Mr. Rouncewell, which is the cause of her appearance. Mr. Rouncewell is not in the library, but she repairs to the library. Sir Leicester is there, and she wishes to speak to him first.

"Sir Leicester, I am desirous—but you are engaged."

Oh dear no! Not at all. Only Mr. Tulkinghorn.

Always at hand. Haunting every place. No relief or security from him for a moment.

"I beg your pardon, Lady Dedlock. Will you allow me to retire?"

With a look that plainly says, "You know you have the power to remain if you will," she tells him it is not necessary, and moves towards a chair. Mr. Tulkinghorn brings it a little forward for her with his clumsy bow, and retires into a window opposite. Interposed between her and the fading light of day in the now quiet street, his shadow falls upon her, and he darkens all before her. Even so does he darken her life.

Sir Leicester begs his lady's pardon. She was about to say?

"Only that Mr. Rouncewell is here (he has called by my appointment), and that we had better make an end of the question of that girl. I am tired to death of the matter."

"What can I do—to—assist?" demands Sir Leicester, in some considerable doubt.

"Let us see him here, and have done with it. Will you tell them to send him up?"

"Mr. Tulkinghorn, be so good as to ring. Thank you. Request," says Sir Leicester, to Mercury, not immediately remembering the business term, "request the iron gentleman to walk this way."

Mercury departs in search of the iron gentleman, finds and produces him. Sir Leicester receives that ferruginous person graciously.

"I hope you are well, Mr. Rouncewell. Be seated. (My solicitor, Mr. Tulkinghorn.) My lady was desirous, Mr. Rouncewell, to speak with you. Hem!"

"I shall be very happy," returns the iron gentleman, "to give my best attention to anything Lady Dedlock does me the honour to say."

As he turns towards her, he finds that the impression she makes upon him is less agreeable than on the former occasion. A distant supercilious air makes a cold atmosphere about her, and there is nothing in her bearing, as there was before, to encourage openness.

"Pray, sir," says Lady Dedlock, listlessly, "may I be allowed to inquire whether anything has passed between you and your son, respecting your son's fancy?"

"If my memory serves me, Lady Dedlock, I said, when I had the pleasure of seeing you before, that I should seriously advise my son to conquer that—fancy." The ironmaster repeats her expression with a little emphasis.

"And did you?"

"Oh, of course I did."

Sir Leicester gives a nod, approving and confirmatory. Very proper. The iron gentleman having said he would do it, was bound to do it. No difference in this respect between the base metals and the precious. Highly proper.

"And pray has he done so?"

"Really, Lady Dedlock, I cannot make you a definite reply. I fear not. Probably not yet. In our condition of life, we sometimes couple an intention with our—our fancies which renders them not altogether easy to throw off. I think it is rather our way to be in earnest."

Sir Leicester has a misgiving that there may be a hidden meaning in this expression, and fumes a little. Mr. Rouncewell is perfectly good-humoured and polite, but, within such limits, evidently adapts his tone to his reception.

"Because," proceeds my Lady, "I have been thinking of the subject—which is tiresome to me."

"I am very sorry, I am sure."

"And also of what Sir Leicester said upon it, in which I quite concur"—Sir Leicester flattered—"and if you cannot give us the assurance that this fancy is at an end, I have come to the conclusion that the girl had better leave me."

"I can give no such assurance, Lady Dedlock."

"Then she had better go."

"Excuse me, my lady," Sir Leicester considerately interposes, "but perhaps this may be doing an injury to the young woman, which she has not merited. Here is a young woman," says Sir Leicester, magnificently laying out the matter with his right hand, like a service of plate, "whose good fortune it is to have attracted the notice and favour of an eminent lady, and to live, under the protection of that eminent lady, surrounded by the various advantages which such a position confers, and which are unquestionably very great—I believe unquestionably very great, sir—for a young woman in that station of life. The question then arises, should that young woman be deprived of these many advantages and that good fortune simply because she has attracted the notice of Mr. Rouncewell's son? Now, has she deserved this punishment? Is this just towards her? Is this our previous understanding?"

"I beg your pardon," interposes Mr. Rouncewell's son's father. "Sir Leicester, will you allow me? I think I may shorten the subject. Pray dismiss that from your consideration. If you remember anything so unimportant—which is not to be expected—you would recollect that my first thought in the affair was directly opposed to her remaining here."

Dismiss the Dedlock patronage from consideration? Oh! Sir Leicester is bound to believe a pair of ears that have been handed down to him through such a family, or he really might have mistrusted their report of the iron gentleman's observations.

"It is not necessary," observes my Lady, in her coldest manner, before he can do anything but breathe amazedly, "to enter into these matters on either side. The girl is a very good girl, I have nothing whatever to say against her; but she is so far insensible to her many advantages and her good fortune that she is in love—or supposes she is, poor little fool—and unable to appreciate them."

Sir Leicester begs to observe that wholly alters the case. He might have been sure that my Lady had the best grounds and reasons in support of her view. He entirely agrees with my Lady. The young woman had better go.

"As Sir Leicester observed, Mr. Rouncewell, on the last occasion when we were fatigued by this business," Lady Dedlock languidly proceeds, "we cannot make conditions with you. Without conditions, and under present circumstances, the girl is quite misplaced here, and had better go. I have told her so. Do I understand that you will take her with you?"

The iron gentleman makes an iron bow.

"Sir Leicester, will you ring?" Mr. Tulkinghorn steps forward from his window and pulls the bell. "I had forgotten you. Thank you." He makes his usual bow, and goes quietly back again. Mercury, swift-responsive, appears, receives instructions whom to produce, skims away, produces the aforesaid, and departs.

Rosa has been crying, and is yet in distress. On her coming in, the ironmaster leaves his chair, takes her arm in his, and remains with her near the door ready to depart.

"You are taken charge of, you see," says my Lady, in her weary manner, "and are going away well protected. I have mentioned that you are a very good girl, and you have nothing to cry for."

Rosa sobs out that she is very sorry to leave my Lady, and that she was happy at Chesney Wold, and has been happy with my Lady, and that she thanks my Lady over and over again. "Out, you silly little puss!" says the ironmaster, checking her in a low voice, though not angrily. "Have a spirit, if you're fond of Watt!" My Lady merely waves her off with indifference, saying, "There, there, child! You are a good girl. Go away!" Sir Leicester has magnificently disengaged himself from the subject. Mr. Tulkinghorn, an indistinct form against the dark street now dotted with lamps, looms in my Lady's view, bigger and blacker than before.

"Sir Leicester and Lady Dedlock," says Mr. Rouncewell, after a pause of a few moments, "I beg to take my leave, with an apology for having again troubled you, though not of my own act, on this tiresome subject. I can very well understand, I assure you, how tiresome so small a matter must have become to Lady Dedlock. If I am doubtful of my dealing with it, it is only because I did not at first quietly exert my influence to take my young friend here away without troubling you at all. But it appeared to me that it was respectful to explain to you how the matter stood, and candid to consult your wishes and convenience. I hope you will excuse my want of acquaintance with the polite world."

Sir Leicester considers himself evoked out of the sanctuary by these remarks. "Mr. Rouncewell," he returns, "do not mention it. Justifications are unnecessary, I hope, on either side."

"I am glad to hear it, Sir Leicester, and if I may, by way of a last word, revert to what I said before of my mother's long connexion with the family, and the worth it bespeaks on both sides, I would point out this little instance here on my arm, who shows herself so affectionate and faithful in parting, and in whom my mother, I dare say, has done something to awaken such feelings—though of course Lady Dedlock, by her heartfelt interest and her genial condescension, has done much more."

If he mean this ironically, it may be truer than he thinks. He points it, however, by no deviation from his straightforward manner of speech, though in saying it he turns towards that part of the dim room where my Lady sits. Sir Leicester stands to return his parting salutation, Mr. Tulkinghorn again rings, Mercury takes another flight, and Mr. Rouncewell and Rosa leave the house.

Then lights are brought in, discovering Mr. Tulkinghorn still standing in his window with his hands behind him, and my Lady still
sitting with his figure before her, closing up her view of the night as
well as of the day. She is very pale. Mr. Tulkinghorn, observing it as
she rises to retire, thinks, "Well she may be! The power of this woman
is astonishing. She has been acting a part the whole time." But he
can act a part too, and as he holds the door open for this woman, fifty
pairs of eyes, each fifty times sharper than Sir Leicester's pair, should
find no flaw in him.

Lady Dedlock dines alone in her own room today. Sir Leicester is
whipped in to the rescue of the Doodle Party. Lady Dedlock asks, on
sitting down to dinner, still deadly pale, whether he is gone out. Yes.
Whether Mr. Tulkinghorn is gone yet. No. Presently she asks again,
is he gone *yet*? No. What is he doing? Mercury thinks he is writing
letters in the library. Would my Lady wish to see him? Anything but
that. But he wishes to see my Lady. Within a few more minutes he is
reported as sending his respects, and could my Lady please to receive
him for a word or two after her dinner? My Lady will receive him now.
He comes now, apologizing for intruding, even by her permission,
while she is at table. When they are alone, my Lady waves her hand
to dispense with such mockeries.

"What do you want, sir?"

"Why, Lady Dedlock," says the lawyer, taking a chair at a little distance from her, "I am rather surprised by the course you have taken."

"Indeed?"

"Yes, decidedly. I was not prepared for it. I consider it a departure
from our agreement and your promise. It puts us in a new position,
Lady Dedlock. I feel myself under the necessity of saying that I don't
approve of it."

He looks at her, with his hands on his knees. Imperturbable and
unchangeable as he is, there is still an indefinable freedom in his
manner, which is new, and which does not escape this woman's observation.

"I do not quite understand you."

"Oh yes you do, I think. I think you do. Come, come, Lady Dedlock,
we must not fence now. You know you like this girl."

"Well, sir?"

"And you know—and I know—that you have not sent her away for
the reasons you have assigned, but for the purpose of separating her as
much as possible from any reproach and exposure that impend over
yourself."

"Well, sir?"

"Well, Lady Dedlock," returns the lawyer, crossing his legs, and nursing the uppermost knee, "I object to that. I consider that a dangerous proceeding. I know it to be unnecessary, and calculated to awaken speculation, doubt, rumour, I don't know what, in the house. Besides, it is a violation of our agreement. You were to be exactly what you were before. Whereas it must be evident to yourself, as it is to me, that you have been this evening very different from what you were before. Why, bless my soul, Lady Dedlock, transparently so!"

"If, sir," she begins, "in my knowledge of my secret—" But he interrupts her.

"Now Lady Dedlock, this is a matter of business, and in a matter of business the ground cannot be kept too clear. It is no longer your secret. Excuse me. That is just the mistake. It is my secret, in trust for Sir Leicester and the family. If it were your secret, Lady Dedlock, we should not be here, holding this conversation."

"That is very true. If, in my knowledge of *the* secret, I do what I can to spare an innocent girl from the taint of my impending shame, I act upon a resolution I have taken. Nothing in the world, and no one in the world, could shake it, or could move me." This she says with great deliberation and distinctness, and with no more outward passion than himself. As for him, he methodically discusses his matter of business as if she were any insensible instrument used in business.

"Really? Then you see, Lady Dedlock," he returns, "you are not to be trusted. You have put the case in a perfectly plain way, and according to the literal fact, and that being the case, you are not to be trusted."

"Perhaps you may remember that I expressed some anxiety on this same point when we spoke at night at Chesney Wold?"

"Yes," says Mr. Tulkinghorn, coolly getting up and standing on the hearth. "Yes. I recollect, Lady Dedlock, that you certainly referred to the girl; but that was before we came to our arrangement, and both the letter and the spirit of our arrangement altogether precluded any action on your part founded upon my discovery. There can be no doubt about that. As to sparing the girl, of what importance or value is she? Spare! Lady Dedlock, here is a family name compromised. One might have supposed that the course was straight on—over everything, neither to the right nor to the left, regardless of all considerations in the way, sparing nothing, treading everything under foot."

She has been looking at the table. She lifts up her eyes and looks at him. There is a stern expression on her face, and a part of her lower lip is compressed under her teeth. "This woman understands me," Mr. Tulkinghorn thinks, as she lets her glance fall again. "*She* cannot be spared. Why should she spare others?"

For a little while they are silent. Lady Dedlock has eaten no dinner, but has twice or thrice poured out water with a steady hand and drunk it. She rises from table, takes a lounging-chair, and reclines in it, shading her face. There is nothing in her manner to express weakness or excite compassion. It is thoughtful, gloomy, concentrated. "This woman," thinks Mr. Tulkinghorn, standing on the hearth, "is a study."

He studies her at his leisure, not speaking for a time. She too studies something at her leisure. She is not the first to speak, appearing indeed so unlikely to be so, though he stood there until midnight, that even he is driven upon breaking silence.

"Lady Dedlock, the most disagreeable part of this business interview remains, but it is business. Our agreement is broken. A lady of your sense and strength of character will be prepared for my now declaring it void, and taking my own course."

"I am quite prepared."

Mr. Tulkinghorn inclines his head. "That is all I have to trouble you with, Lady Dedlock."

She stops him as he is moving out of the room, by asking, "This is the notice I was to receive? I wish not to misapprehend you."

"Not exactly the notice you were to receive, Lady Dedlock, because the contemplated notice supposed the agreement to have been observed. But virtually the same, virtually the same. The difference is merely in a lawyer's mind."

"You intend to give me no other notice?"

"You are right. No."

"Do you contemplate undeceiving Sir Leicester tonight?"

"A home question!" says Mr. Tulkinghorn, with a slight smile, "No, not tonight."

"Tomorrow?"

"All things considered, I had better decline answering that question, Lady Dedlock. If I were to say I don't know when, exactly, you would not believe me, and it would answer no purpose. It may be tomorrow. I would rather say no more. You are prepared, and I hold out no expectations which circumstances might fail to justify. I wish you good-evening."

She removes her hand, turns her pale face towards him as he walks silently to the door, and stops him once again as he is about to open it.

"Do you intend to remain in the house any time? I heard you were writing in the library. Are you going to return there?"

"Only for my hat. I am going home."

She bows her eyes rather than her head, the movement is so slight and curious, and he withdraws. Clear of the room, he looks at his watch, but is inclined to doubt it by a minute or thereabouts. There is a splendid clock upon the staircase, famous for its accuracy. "And what do *you* say?" Mr. Tulkinghorn inquires. What a famous clock hereafter if it said tonight of all nights that it has counted off to this old man of all the young and old men who have ever stood before it, "Don't go home!" With its sharp clear bell, it strikes three-quarters after seven, and ticks on again. "Why, you are worse than I thought you," says Mr. Tulkinghorn, muttering reproof to his watch. "Two minutes wrong? At this rate you won't last my time." What a watch to return good for evil if it ticked in answer "Don't go home!"

He passes out into the streets, and walks on, with his hands behind

him, under the shadow of the lofty houses, many of whose mysteries, difficulties, mortgages, delicate affairs of all kinds, are treasured up within his old black satin waistcoat. He is in the confidence of the very bricks and mortar. The high chimney-stacks telegraph family secrets to him. Yet there is not a voice in a mile of them to whisper, "Don't go home!"

Arrived at last in his dull room, to light his candles, and look round and up, and see the Roman pointing from the ceiling, there is no new significance in the Roman's hand tonight to give him the late warning, "Don't come here!"

It is a moonlight night; but the moon being past the full, is only now rising over the great wilderness of London. The stars are shining as they shone above Chesney Wold. This woman, as he has of late been so accustomed to call her, looks out upon them. Her soul is turbulent within her, she is sick at heart, and restless. The large rooms are too cramped and close. She cannot endure their restraint, and will walk alone in a neighbouring garden.

Too capricious and imperious in all she does to be the cause of much surprise in those about her as to anything she does, this woman, loosely muffled, goes out into the moonlight. Mercury attends with the key. Having opened the garden-gate, he delivers the key into his Lady's hands at her request, and is bidden to go back. She will walk there some time, to ease her aching head. She may be an hour, she may be more. She needs no further escort. The gate shuts upon its spring with a clash, and he leaves her passing on into the dark shade of some trees.

A fine night, and a bright large moon, and multitudes of stars. Mr. Tulkinghorn, in repairing to his cellar, and in opening and shutting those resounding doors, has to cross a little prisonlike yard. He looks up casually, thinking what a fine night, with a bright large moon, what multitudes of stars! A quiet night, too.

A very quiet night. When the moon shines very brilliantly, a solitude and stillness seem to proceed from her that influence even crowded places full of life. Even on this stranger's wilderness of London there is some rest. Its steeples and towers, and its one great dome, grow more ethereal; its smoky house-tops lose their grossness in the pale effulgence; the noises that arise from the streets are fewer and are softened, and the footsteps on the pavements pass more tranquilly away. In these fields of Mr. Tulkinghorn's inhabiting, where the shepherds play on Chancery pipes that have no stop, and keep their sheep in the fold by hook and by crook until they have shorn them exceedingly close, every noise is merged, this moonlight night, into a distant ringing hum, as if the city were a vast glass, vibrating.

What's that? Who fired a gun or pistol? Where was it?

The few foot-passangers start, stop, and stare about them. Some windows and doors are opened, and people come out to look. It was a loud report, and echoed and rattled heavily. It has aroused all the dogs in the neighbourhood, who bark vehemently. Terrified cats scamper across the road. The church-clocks, as if they were startled too, begin to strike. The hum from the streets seems to swell into a shout. But it is soon over. Before the last clock begins to strike ten, there is a lull. When it has ceased, the fine night, the bright large moon, and multitudes of stars are left at peace again.

Has Mr. Tulkinghorn been disturbed? His windows are dark and quiet, and his door is shut. It must be something unusual indeed to bring him out of his shell. Nothing is heard of him, nothing is seen of him. What power of cannon might it take to shake that rusty old man out of his immovable composure?

For many years the persistent Roman has been pointing, with no particular meaning, from that ceiling. It is not likely that he has any new meaning in him tonight. Moonlight, darkness, dawn, sunrise, day. There he is still, eagerly pointing, and no one minds him.

But a little after the coming of the day, come people to clean the rooms. And either the Roman has some new meaning in him, not expressed before, or the foremost of them goes wild, for, looking up at his outstretched hand and looking down at what is below it, that person shrieks and flies. The others, looking in as the first one looked, shriek and fly too, and there is an alarm in the street.

What does it mean? No light is admitted into the darkened chamber, and people unaccustomed to it enter and, treading softly but heavily, carry a weight into the bedroom, and lay it down. There is whispering and wondering all day, strict search of every corner, careful tracing of steps, and careful noting of the disposition of every article of furniture. All eyes look up at the Roman, and all voices murmur, "If he could only tell what he saw!"

He is pointing at a table, with a bottle (nearly full of wine) and a glass upon it, and two candles that were blown out suddenly soon after being lighted. He is pointing at an empty chair, and at a stain upon the ground before it that might be almost covered with a hand.

For Mr. Tulkinghorn's time is over for evermore, and the Roman pointed at the murderous hand uplifted against his life, and pointed helplessly at him, from night to morning, lying face downward on the floor, shot through the heart.

# CHAPTER 49

## *Dutiful Friendship*

A GREAT annual occasion has come round in the establishment of Mr. Matthew Bagnet, otherwise Lignum Vitae, ex-artillery-man and present bassoon-player. An occasion of feasting and festival. The celebration of a birthday in the family.

It is not Mr. Bagnet's birthday. Mr. Bagnet merely distinguishes that epoch in the musical instrument business by kissing the children with an extra smack before breakfast and by smoking an additional pipe after dinner. It is not the birthday of one of the three children. Those occasions are kept with some marks of distinction, but they rarely overleap the bounds of happy returns and a pudding.

It is the old girl's birthday, and that is the greatest holiday and reddest-letter day in Mr. Bagnet's calendar. The auspicious event is always commemorated according to certain forms settled and prescribed by Mr. Bagnet some years since. Mr. Bagnet, being deeply convinced that to have a pair of fowls for dinner is to attain the highest pitch of imperial luxury, invariably goes forth himself very early in the morning of this day to buy a pair; he is, as invariably, taken in by the vendor, and installed in the possession of the oldest inhabitants of any coop in Europe. Returning with these triumphs of toughness tied up in a clean blue-and-white cotton handkerchief (essential to the arrangements), he in a casual manner invites Mrs. Bagnet to declare at breakfast what she would like for dinner. Mrs. Bagnet, by a coincidence never known to fail, replying "Fowls," Mr. Bagnet instantly produces his bundle from a place of concealment, amidst general amazement and rejoicing. He further requires that the old girl shall do nothing all day long but sit in her very best gown and be served by himself and the young people. As he is not illustrious for his cookery, this may be supposed to be a matter of state rather than enjoyment on the old girl's part; but she keeps her state with all imaginable cheerfulness.

On this present birthday, Mr. Bagnet has accomplished the usual preliminaries. He has bought two specimens of poultry, to be prepared for the spit; he has amazed and rejoiced the family by their unlooked-for production; he is himself directing the roasting of the poultry; and Mrs. Bagnet, with her wholesome brown fingers itching to prevent what she sees going wrong, sits in her gown of ceremony, an honoured guest. Quebec and Malta lay the cloth for dinner while Woolwich, serving, as beseems him, under his father, keeps the fowls revolving.

"George will look us up," says Mr. Bagnet. "At half-after four. To the moment. How many years, old girl. Has George looked us up. This afternoon?"

"Ah, Lignum, Lignum, as many as make an old woman of a young one, I begin to think. Just about that, and no less."

"Old girl," says Mr. Bagnet, "Never mind. You'd be as young as ever you was. If you wasn't younger. Which you are. As everybody knows."

Quebec and Malta here exclaim, with clapping of hands, that Bluffy is sure to bring Mother something, and begin to speculate on what it will be.

"Do you know, Lignum," says Mrs. Bagnet, "I begin to think George is in the roving way again."

"George," returns Mr. Bagnet, "will never desert. And leave his old comrade. In the lurch. Don't be afraid of it."

"No, Lignum. No. I don't say he will. I don't think he will. But if he could get over this money-trouble of his, I believe he would be off." Mr. Bagnet asks why? "Well," returns his wife, considering. "George seems to me to be getting not a little impatient and restless. I don't say but what he's as free as ever. Of course he must be free, or he wouldn't be George; but he smarts, and seems put out."

"He's extra-drilled," says Mr. Bagnet. "By a lawyer. Who would put the devil out."

"There's something in that," his wife assents.

Further conversation is prevented, for the time, by the necessity under which Mr. Bagnet finds himself of directing the whole force of his mind to the dinner, which is a little endangered by the dry humour of the fowls in not yielding any gravy, and also by the made-gravy acquiring no flavour, and turning out of a flaxen complexion.

With a similar perverseness, the potatoes crumble off forks in the process of peeling, upheaving from their centres in every direction, as if they were subject to earthquakes. Overcoming these disadvantages to the best of his ability, Mr. Bagnet at last dishes, and they sit down at table; Mrs. Bagnet occupying the guest's place at his right hand.

It is well for the old girl that she has but one birthday in a year, for two such indulgences in poultry might be injurious. Every kind of finer tendon and ligament that is in the nature of poultry to possess is developed in these specimens in the singular form of guitar-strings. Their legs are so hard as to encourage the idea that they must have devoted the greater part of their long and arduous lives to pedestrian exercises. But Mr. Bagnet, unconscious of these little defects, sets his heart on Mrs. Bagnet eating a most severe quantity of the delicacies before her; and as that good old girl would not cause him a moment's disappointment on any day, least of all on such a day, for any consideration, she imperils her digestion fearfully.

The old girl has another trial to undergo after the conclusion of the repast, in sitting in state to see the room cleared, the hearth swept, and the dinner-service washed up and polished in the back yard. The great delight and energy with which the two young ladies apply themselves to these duties, turning up their skirts in imitation of their mother and skating in and out on little scaffolds of pattens, inspire the highest hopes for the future, but some anxiety for the present. The same causes lead to confusion of tongues, a clattering of crockery, a rattling of tin mugs, a whisking of brooms, and an expenditure of water, all in excess. At last the various cleansing processes are triumphantly completed. Quebec and Malta appear in fresh attire, smiling and dry; pipes, tobacco, and something to drink, are placed upon the table; and the old girl enjoys the first peace of mind she ever knows on the day of this delightful entertainment.

When Mr. Bagnet takes his usual seat, the hands of the clock are very near to half-past four. As they mark it accurately, Mr. Bagnet announces:

"George! Military time."

It is George, and he has hearty congratulations for the old girl (whom he kisses on the great occasion), and for the children, and for Mr. Bagnet. "Happy returns to all!" says Mr. George.

"But, George old man!" cries Mrs. Bagnet, looking at him curiously. "What's come to you?"

"Come to me?"

"Ah, you are so white, George—for you—and look so shocked. Now don't he, Lignum?"

"George," says Mr. Bagnet, "tell the old girl. What's the matter."

"I didn't know I looked white," says the trooper, passing his hand over his brow, "and I didn't know I looked shocked, and I'm sorry I do. But the truth is, that boy who was taken in my place died yesterday afternoon, and it has rather knocked me over."

"Pood creetur!" says Mrs. Bagnet, with a mother's pity. "Is he gone? Dear, dear!"

"I didn't mean to say anything about it, for it's not birthday talk, but you have got it out of me, you see, before I sit down. I should have roused up in a minute," says the trooper, making himself speak more gaily, "but you're so quick, Mrs. Bagnet."

"You're right. The old girl," says Mr. Bagnet. "Is as quick. As powder."

"And what's more, she's the subject of the day, and we'll stick to her!" cries Mr. George. "See here, I have brought a little brooch along with me. It's a poor thing, you know, but it's a keepsake. That's all the good it is, Mrs. Bagnet."

Mr. George produces his present, which is greeted with admiring leapings and clappings by the young family, and with a species of reverential admiration by Mr. Bagnet. "Old girl," says Mr. Bagnet. "Tell him my opinion of it."

"Why, it's a wonder, George!" Mrs. Bagnet exclaims. "It's the beautifullest thing that ever was seen!"

"Good!" says Mr. Bagnet. "My opinion."

"It's so pretty, George," cries Mrs. Bagnet, turning it on all sides, and holding it out at arm's length, "that it seems too choice for me."

"Bad!" says Mr. Bagnet. "Not my opinion."

"But whatever it is, a hundred thousand thanks, old fellow," says Mrs. Bagnet, her eyes sparkling with pleasure, and her hand stretched out to him, "and though I have been a cross-grained soldier's wife to you sometimes, George, we are as strong friends, I am sure, in reality as ever can be. Now you shall fasten it on yourself, for good luck, if you will, George."

The children close up to see it done, and Mr. Bagnet looks over young Woolwich's head to see it done, with an interest so maturely wooden, yet pleasantly childish, that Mrs. Bagnet cannot help laughing in her airy way, and saying, "O Lignum, Lignum, what a precious old chap you are!" But the trooper fails to fasten the brooch. His hand shakes, he is nervous, and it falls off. "Would any one believe this?" says he, catching it as it drops, and looking round. "I am so out of sorts that I bungle at an easy job like this!"

Mrs. Bagnet concludes that for such a case there is no remedy like a pipe, and fastening the brooch herself in a twinkling, causes the trooper to be inducted into his usual snug place, and the pipes to be got into action. "If that don't bring you round, George," says she, "just throw your eye across here at your present now and then, and the two together *must* do it."

"You ought to do it of yourself," George answers, "I know that very well, Mrs. Bagnet. I'll tell you how the blues have got to be too many for me. Here was this poor lad. 'Twas dull work to see him dying as he did and not be able to help him."

"What do you mean, George? You did help him. You took him under your roof."

"I helped him so far, but that's little. I mean, Mrs. Bagnet, there he was, dying without ever having been taught much more than to know his right hand from his left. And he was too far gone to be helped out of that."

"Ah, poor creetur!" says Mrs. Bagnet.

"Then," says the trooper, not yet lighting his pipe, "that brought up Gridley in a man's mind. His was a bad case too, in a different way. Then the two got mixed up in a man's mind with a flinty old rascal who had to do with both. And to think of that rusty carbine, stock and barrel, standing up on end in his corner, hard, indifferent, taking everything so evenly—it made flesh and blood tingle, I do assure you."

"My advice to you," returns Mrs. Bagnet, "is to light your pipe, and tingle that way. It's wholesomer and comfortabler, and better for the health altogether."

"You're right," says the trooper, "and I'll do it."

So he does it, though still with an indignant gravity that impresses the young Bagnets, and even causes Mr. Bagnet to defer the ceremony of drinking Mrs. Bagnet's health—always given by himself, on these occasions, in a speech of exemplary terseness. But the young ladies having composed what Mr. Bagnet is in the habit of calling "the mixtur," and George's pipe being now in a glow, Mr. Bagnet considers it his duty to proceed to the toast of the evening. He addresses the assembled company in the following terms.

"George. Woolwich. Quebec. Malta. This is her birthday. Take a day's march. And you won't find such another. Here's towards her!"

The toast having been drunk with enthusiasm, Mrs. Bagnet returns thanks in a neat address of corresponding brevity. This model composition is limited to the three words "And wishing yours!" which the old girl follows up with a nod at everybody in succession, and a well-regulated swig of the mixture. This she again follows up, on the present occasion, by the wholly unexpected exclamation, "Here's a man!"

Here *is* a man, much to the astonishment of the little company, looking in at the parlour-door. He is a sharp-eyed man and he takes in everybody's look at him all at once, individually and collectively, in a manner that stamps him a remarkable man.

"George," says the man, nodding, "how do you find yourself?"

"Why, it's Bucket!" cries Mr. George.

"Yes," says the man, coming in and closing the door. "I was going down the street here when I happened to stop and look in at the musical instruments in the shop-window—a friend of mine is in want of a second-hand wiolinceller, of a good tone—and I saw a party enjoying themselves, and I thought it was you in the corner, I thought I couldn't be mistaken. How goes the world with you, George, at the present moment? Pretty smooth? And with you, ma'am? And with you, Governor? And Lord," says Mr. Bucket, opening his arms, "here's children too! You may do anything with me if you only show me children. Give us a kiss, my pets."

Mr. Bucket, not unwelcome, has sat himself down next to Mr. George and taken Quebec and Malta on his knees. "You pretty dears," says Mr. Bucket, "give us another kiss; it's the only thing I'm greedy in. Lord bless you, how healthy you look! And what do you call these, my darling?" pursues Mr. Bucket, pinching Malta's cheeks. "These are peaches, these are. Bless your heart! My name's Bucket. Ain't that a funny name?"

These blandishments have entirely won the family heart. Mrs. Bagnet forgets the day to the extent of filling a pipe and glass for Mr. Bucket and waiting upon him hospitably. She would be glad to receive so pleasant a character under any circumstances, but she tells him that as a friend of George's she is particularly glad to see him this evening, for George has not been in his usual spirits.

"Not in his usual spirits?" exclaims Mr. Bucket. "Why, I never heard of such a thing! What's the matter, George? You don't intend to tell me you've been out of spirits! What should you be out of spirits for? You haven't got anything on your mind, you know."

"Nothing particular," returns the trooper.

"I should think not," rejoins Mr. Bucket. "What could you have on your mind, you know! And have these pets got anything on *their* minds, eh? Not they; but they'll be upon the minds of some of the young fellows, some of these days. I ain't much of a prophet, but I can tell you that, ma'am."

Mrs. Bagnet, quite charmed, hopes Mr. Bucket has a family of his own.

"There, ma'am," says Mr. Bucket, "would you believe it? No, I haven't. My wife and a lodger constitute my family. Mrs. Bucket is as fond of children as myself, and as wishful to have 'em, but no. So it is. What a very nice back yard, ma'am! Any way out of that yard, now?"

There is no way out of that yard.

"Ain't there really?" says Mr. Bucket. "I should have thought there might have been. Well, I don't know as I ever saw a back yard that took my fancy more. Would you allow me to look at it? Thank you. No, I see there's no way out. But what a very good-proportioned yard it is!"

Having cast his sharp eye all about it, Mr. Bucket returns to his chair next his friend Mr. George, and pats Mr. George affectionately on the shoulder.

"How are your spirits, now, George?"

"All right now," returns the trooper.

"That's your sort!" says Mr. Bucket. "Why should you ever have been otherwise? A man of your fine figure and constitution has no right to be out of spirits. And you haven't got anything on your mind, you know, George; what could you have on your mind!"

Somewhat harping on this phrase, considering the extent and variety of his conversational powers, Mr. Bucket twice or thrice repeats it to the pipe he lights, and with a listening face that is particularly his own.

This sparkling stranger is such a new and agreeable feature in the evening that Mr. George, who testified no great emotions of pleasure on his entrance, begins, in spite of himself, to be rather proud of him. He is so friendly, is a man of so many resources, and so easy to get on with, that it is something to have made him known there. Mr. Bagnet becomes, after another pipe, so sensible of the value of his acquaintance that he solicits the honour of his company on the old girl's next birthday. If anything can more closely cement and consolidate the esteem which Mr. Bucket has formed for the family, it is the discovery of the nature of the occasion. He drinks to Mrs. Bagnet with a warmth approaching to rapture, engages himself for that day twelvemonth more than thankfully, makes a memorandum of the day in a large black pocket-book with a girdle to it.

It is natural, under these circumstances, that he, in his turn, should remember the friend to whom he is indebted for so promising an acquaintance. And he does. He keeps very close to him. Whatever the subject of the conversation, he keeps a tender eye upon him. He waits to walk home with him. He is interested in his very boots, and observes even them attentively as Mr. George sits smoking cross-legged in the chimney-corner. At length, Mr. George rises to depart. At the same moment Mr. Bucket, with the secret sympathy of friendship, also rises. He remembers the commission he has undertaken for an absent friend.

"Respecting that second-hand wiolinceller, Governor—could you recommend me such a thing?"

"Scores," says Mr. Bagnet.

"I am obliged to you," returns Mr. Bucket, squeezing his hand. "You're a friend in need. A good tone, mind you! My friend is a regular dab at it. And you needn't," says Mr. Bucket, in a considerate and private voice, "you needn't commit yourself to too low a figure, Governor. I don't want to pay too large a price for my friend, but I want you to have your proper percentage, and be remunerated for your loss of time. That is but fair. Every man must live, and ought to it."

Mr. Bagnet shakes his head at the old girl, to the effect that they have found a jewel of price.

"Suppose I was to give you a look in, say at half-arter ten tomorrow morning. Perhaps you could name the figures of a few wiolincellers of a good tone?" says Mr. Bucket.

Nothing easier. Mr. and Mrs. Bagnet both engage to have the requisite information ready, and even hint to each other at the practicability of having a small stock collected there for approval.

"Thank you," says Mr. Bucket, "thank you. Good-night, ma'am. Good-night, Governor. Good-night, darlings. I am much obliged to you for one of the pleasantest evenings I ever spent in my life."

They, on the contrary, are much obliged to him for the pleasure he has given them in his company, and so they part with many expressions of goodwill on both sides. "Now George old boy," says Mr. Bucket, taking his arm at the shop-door, "come along!" As they go down the little street, and the Bagnets pause for a minute looking after them, Mrs. Bagnet remarks to the worthy Lignum that Mr. Bucket "almost clings to George like, and seems to be really fond of him."

The neighbouring streets being narrow and ill-paved, it is a little inconvenient to walk there two abreast and arm in arm. Mr. George therefore soon proposes to walk singly. But Mr. Bucket who cannot make up his mind to relinquish his friendly hold, replies, "Wait half a minute, George. I should wish to speak to you first." Immediately afterwards, he twists him into a public-house and into a parlour, where he confronts him, and claps his own back against the door.

"Now, George," says Mr. Bucket. "Duty is duty, and friendship is friendship. I never want the two to clash, if I can help it. I have endeavoured to make things pleasant tonight, and I put it to you whether I have done it or not. You must consider yourself in custody, George."

"Custody? What for?" returns the trooper, thunderstruck.

"Now, George," says Mr. Bucket, "duty, as you know very well, is one thing, and conversation is another. It's my duty to inform you that any observations you may make will be liable to be used against you. Therefore, George, be careful what you say. You don't happen to have heard of a murder?"

"Murder!"

"Now, George," says Mr. Bucket, "bear in mind what I've said to you. I ask you nothing. You've been in low spirits this afternoon. I say, you don't happen to have heard of a murder?"

"No. Where has there been a murder?"

"Now, George," says Mr. Bucket, "don't you go and commit yourself. I'm a-going to tell you what I want you for. There has been a murder in Lincoln's Inn Fields—gentleman of the name of Tulkinghorn. He was shot last night. I want you for that."

The trooper sinks upon a seat behind him, and great drops start out upon his forehead, and a deadly pallor overspreads his face.

"Bucket! It's not possible that Mr. Tulkinghorn has been killed, and that you suspect *me?*"

"George," returns Mr. Bucket, "it is certainly possible, because it's the case. This deed was done last night at ten o'clock. Now you know where you were last night at ten o'clock, and you'll be able to prove it, no doubt."

"Last night! Last night?" repeats the trooper thoughtfully. Then it flashes upon him. "Why, great heaven, I was there last night!"

"So I have understood, George," returns Mr. Bucket, with great deliberation. "So I have understood. Likewise you've been very often there. You've been seen hanging about the place, and you've been heard more than once in a wrangle with him, and it's possible—I don't say it's certainly so, mind you, but it's possible—that he may have been heard to call you a threatening, murdering, dangerous fellow."

The trooper gasps as if he would admit it all, if he could speak.

"Now, George," continues Mr. Bucket, putting his hat upon the table, "my wish is, as it has been all the evening, to make things pleasant. I tell you plainly there's a reward out, of a hundred guineas, offered by Sir Leicester Dedlock, Baronet. You and me have always been pleasant together, but I have got a duty to discharge, and if that hundred guineas is to be made, it may as well be made by me as any other man. On all of which accounts, I should hope it was clear to you that I must have you, and that I'm damned if I don't have you. Am I to call in any assistance, or is the trick done?"

Mr. George has recovered himself, and stands up like a soldier. "Come," he says; "I am ready."

"George," continues Mr. Bucket, "wait a bit!" With his upholsterer manner, as if the trooper were a window to be fitted up, he takes from his pocket a pair of handcuffs. "This is a serious charge, George, and such is my duty."

The trooper flushes angrily, and hesitates a moment, but holds out his two hands, clasped together, and says, "There! Put them on!"

Mr. Bucket adjusts them in a moment. "How do you find them? Are they comfortable? If not, say so, for I wish to make things as pleasant as is consistent with my duty, and I've got another pair in my pocket. They'll do as they are? Very well! Now, you see, George"—he takes a cloak from a corner, and begins adjusting it about the trooper's neck—"I was mindful of your feelings when I come out, and brought this on purpose. There! Who's the wiser?"

"Only I," returns the trooper; "but as I know it, do me one more good turn and pull my hat over my eyes."

"Really, though! Do you mean it? Ain't it a pity? It looks so."

"I can't look chance men in the face with these things on," Mr. George replies. "Do, for God's sake, pull my hat forward."

So strongly entreated, Mr. Bucket complies, puts his own hat on, and conducts his prize into the streets, the trooper marching on as steadily as usual, though with his head less erect, and Mr. Bucket steering him with his elbow over the crossings and up the turnings.

## CHAPTER 50

*Esther's Narrative*

IT happened that when I came home from Deal, I found a note from Caddy Jellyby (as we always continued to call her), informing me that her health, which had been for some time very delicate, was worse, and that she would be more glad than she could tell me if I would go to see her. It was a note of a few lines, written from the couch on which she lay, and enclosed to me in another from her husband, in which he seconded her entreaty with much solicitude. Caddy was now the mother, and I the godmother, of such a poor little baby— such a tiny old-faced mite, with a countenance that seemed to be scarcely anything but cap-border, and a little lean, long-fingered hand, always clenched under its chin. It would lie in this attitude all day, with its bright specks of eyes open. Whenever it was moved it cried, but at all other times it was so patient that the sole desire of its life appeared to be to lie quiet, and think. It had curious little dark veins in its face, and curious little dark marks under its eyes, like faint remembrances of poor Caddy's inky days; and altogether, to those who were not used to it, it was quite a piteous little sight.

But it was enough for Caddy that *she* was used to it. The projects with which she beguiled her illness, for little Esther's education, and little Esther's marriage, and even for her own old age, as the grandmother of little Esther's little Esthers, was prettily expressive of devotion to this pride of her life.

To return to the letter. Caddy had a superstition about me, which had been strengthening in her mind ever since that night long ago when she had lain asleep with her head in my lap. She almost—I think I must say quite—believed that I did her good whenever I was near her. Now although this was such a fancy of the affectionate girl's that I am almost ashamed to mention it, still it might have all the force of a fact when she was really ill. Therefore I set off to Caddy, with my guardian's consent, post-haste; and she and Prince made much of me. Next day I went again to sit with her, and next day I went again. It was a very easy journey, for I had only to rise a little earlier in the morning, and keep my accounts, and attend to housekeeping matters before leaving home. But when I had made these three visits, my guardian said to me, on my return at night:

"Now, little woman, little woman, this will never do. Constant dropping will wear away a stone, and constant coaching will wear out a Dame Durden. We will go to London for a while, and take possession of our old lodgings."

"Not for me, dear Guardian," said I, "for I never feel tired."

"For me then," returned my guardian, "or for Ada, or for both of us. It is somebody's birthday tomorrow, I think."

"Truly I think it is," said I, kissing my darling, who would be twenty-one tomorrow.

"Well," observed my guardian, half pleasantly, half seriously, "that's a great occasion, and will give my fair cousin some necessary business to transact in assertion of her independence, and will make London a more convenient place for all of us. So to London we will go. That being settled, there is another thing—how have you left Caddy?"

"Very unwell, Guardian. I fear it will be some time before she regains her health and strength."

"What do you call some time, now?" asked my guardian, thoughtfully.

"Some weeks, I am afraid."

"Ah!" He began to walk about the room with his hands in his pockets, showing that he had been thinking as much. "Now what do you say about her doctor? Is he a good doctor, my love?"

I felt obliged to confess that I knew nothing to the contrary, but that Prince and I had agreed only that evening that we would like his opinion to be confirmed by some one.

"Well, you know," returned my guardian quickly, "there's Woodcourt."

I had not meant that, and was rather taken by surprise. For a moment, all that I had had in my mind in connexion with Mr. Woodcourt seemed to come back and confuse me.

"You don't object to him, little woman?"

"Object to him, Guardian? Oh no!"

"And you don't think the patient would object to him?"

So far from that, I had no doubt of her being prepared to have a great reliance on him, and to like him very much. I said that he was no stranger to her personally, for she had seen him often in his kind attendance on Miss Flite.

"Very good," said my guardian. "He has been here today, my dear, and I will see him about it tomorrow."

I felt, in this short conversation—though I did not know how, for she was quiet, and we interchanged no look—that my dear girl well remembered how merrily she had clasped me round the waist when no other hands than Caddy's had brought me the little parting token. This caused me to feel that I ought to tell her, and Caddy too, that I was going to be the mistress of Bleak House; and that if I avoided that disclosure any longer, I might become less worthy in my own eyes of its master's love. Therefore when we went upstairs, and had waited listening until the clock struck twelve, in order that only I might be the first to wish my darling all good wishes on her birthday, and to take her to my heart, I set before her, just as I had set before myself, the goodness and honour of her cousin John, and the happy life that was in store for me. If ever my darling were fonder of me at one time than another in all our intercourse, she was surely fondest of me that night. And I was so rejoiced to know it, and so comforted by the sense of having done right in casting this last idle reservation away, that I was ten times happier than I had been before.

Next day we went to London. We found our old lodging vacant, and in half an hour were quietly established there as if we had never gone away. Mr. Woodcourt dined with us, to celebrate my darling's birthday, and we were as pleasant as we could be with the great blank among us that Richard's absence naturally made on such an occasion. After that day I was for some weeks—eight or nine as I remember—very much with Caddy, and thus it fell out that I saw less of Ada at this time than any other since we had first come together, except the time of my own illness. She often came to Caddy's, but our function there was to amuse and cheer her, and we did not talk in our usual confidential manner.

With her husband and her poor little mite of a baby to love, and their home to strive for, what a good creature Caddy was! So self-denying, so uncomplaining, so anxious to get well on their account, so afraid of giving trouble, and so thoughtful of the unassisted labours of her husband and the comforts of old Mr. Turveydrop! I had never known the best of her until now. And it seemed so curious that her pale face and helpless figure should be lying there day after day, where dancing was the business of life.

At Caddy's request, I took the supreme direction of her apartment, trimmed it up, and pushed her, couch and all, into a lighter and more airy and more cheerful corner than she had yet occupied; then, every day, when we were in our neatest array, I used to lay my small small namesake in her arms and sit down to chat or work or read to her. It was at one of the first of these quiet times that I told Caddy about Bleak House.

We had other visitors besides Ada. First of all, we had Prince, who in his hurried intervals of teaching used to come softly in and sit softly down, with a face of loving anxiety for Caddy and the very little child. Whatever Caddy's condition really was, she never failed to declare to Prince that she was all but well—which I, Heaven forgive me, never failed to confirm. This would put Prince in such good spirits that he would sometimes take the kit from his pocket and play a chord or two to astonish the baby—which I never knew it to do in the least degree, for my tiny namesake never noticed it at all.

Then there was Mrs. Jellyby. She would come occasionally with her usual distraught manner, and sit calmly looking miles beyond her grand-

child, as if her attention were absorbed by a young Borrioboolan on its native shores. As bright-eyed as ever, as serene, and as untidy, she would say, "Well, Caddy, child, and how do you do today?" And then would sit amiably smiling, and taking no notice of the reply, or would sweetly glide off into a calculation of the number of letters she had lately received and answered, or of the coffee-bearing power of Borrioboola-Gha.

Then there was old Mr. Turveydrop, who was from morning to night and from night to morning the subject of innumerable precautions. If the baby cried, it was nearly stifled lest the noise should make him uncomfortable. If the fire wanted stirring in the night, it was surreptitiously done lest his rest should be broken. If Caddy required any little comfort that the house contained, she first carefully discussed whether he was likely to require it too. In return for this consideration, he would come into the room once a day, all but blessing it—showing a condescension, and a patronage, and a grace of manner, in dispensing the light of his high-shouldered presence, from which I might have supposed him (if I had not known better) to have been the benefactor of Caddy's life.

"My Caroline," he would say, making the nearest approach that he could to bending over her. "Tell me that you are better today."

"Oh much better, thank you, Mr. Turveydrop," Caddy would reply.

"Delighted! Enchanted! And our dear Miss Summerson. She is not quite prostrated by fatigue?" Here he would kiss his fingers to me, though I am happy to say he had ceased to be particular in his attentions since I had been so altered.

"Not at all," I would assure him.

"Charming! We must take care of our dear Caroline, Miss Summerson. We must spare nothing that will restore her. We must nourish her. My dear Caroline, want for nothing, my love. Frame a wish and gratify it, my daughter. Everything this house contains, everything my room contains, is at your service, my dear. Do not," he would sometimes add, in a burst of Deportment, "even allow my simple requirements to be considered, if they should at any time interfere with your own, my Caroline. Your necessities are greater than mine."

He had established such a long prescriptive right to this Deportment that I several times knew both Caddy and her husband to be melted to tears by these affectionate self-sacrifices.

"Nay, my dears," he would remonstrate, and when I saw Caddy's thin arm about his fat neck as he said it, I would be melted too, though not by the same process. "Nay, nay! I have promised never to leave ye. Be dutiful and affectionate towards me, and I ask no other return. Now, bless ye! I am going to the Park."

He would take the air there, presently, and get an appetite for his hotel dinner. I hope I do old Mr. Turveydrop no wrong, but I never saw any better traits in him than these I faithfully record.

Last of our visitors, there was Mr. Jellyby. Really when he used to come in of an evening and ask Caddy in his meek voice how she was, and then sit down with his head against the wall and make no attempt to say anything more, I liked him very much. If he found me bustling about doing any little thing, he sometimes half took his coat off, as if with an intention of helping by a great exertion; but he never got any further. His sole occupation was to sit with his head against the wall looking hard at the thoughtful baby, and I could not quite divest my mind of a fancy that they understood one another.

I have not counted Mr. Woodcourt among our visitors, because he was now Caddy's regular attendant. She soon began to improve under his care; but he was so gentle, so skilful, so unwearying in the pains he took, that it is not to be wondered at, I am sure. I saw a good deal of Mr. Woodcourt during this time, though not so much as might be supposed, for, knowing Caddy to be safe in his hands, I often slipped home at about the hours when he was expected. We frequently met, notwithstanding. I was quite reconciled to myself now, but I still felt glad to think that he was sorry for me, and he still *was* sorry for me, I believed. He helped Mr. Badger in his professional engagements, which were numerous, and had as yet no settled projects for the future.

It was when Caddy began to recover that I began to notice a change in my dear girl. I cannot say how it first presented itself to me, because I observed it in many slight particulars which were nothing in themselves and only became something when they were pieced together. But I made it out, by putting them together, that Ada was not so frankly cheerful with me as she used to be. Her tenderness for me was as loving and true as ever, I did not for a moment doubt that; but there was a quiet sorrow about her which she did not confide to me, and in which I traced some hidden regret.

Now I could not understand this, and I was so anxious for the happiness of my own pet that it caused me some uneasiness, and set me thinking often. At length, feeling sure that Ada suppressed this something from me lest it should make me unhappy too, it came into my head that she was a little grieved—for me—by what I had told her about Bleak House.

How I persuaded myself that this was likely, I don't know. I had no idea that there was any selfish reference in my doing so. I was not grieved for myself, I was quite contented and quite happy. Still, that Ada might be thinking—for me, though I had abandoned all such thoughts—of what once was, but was now all changed, seemed so easy to believe that I believed it.

What could I do to reassure my darling (I considered then) and show her that I had no such feelings? Well! I could only be as brisk and busy as possible, and that I had tried to be all along. However, as Caddy's illness had certainly interfered, more or less, with my home duties—though I had always been there in the morning to make my guardian's breakfast, and he had a hundred times laughed and said there must be two little women, for this little woman was never missing —I resolved to be doubly diligent and gay. So I went about the house humming all the tunes I knew; and I sat working and working in a desperate manner, and I talked and talked, morning, noon, and night.

And still there was the same shade between me and my darling.

"So, Dame Trot," observed my guardian, shutting up his book one night when we were all three together, "so Woodcourt has restored Caddy Jellyby to the full enjoyment of life again?"

"Yes," I said, "and to be repaid by such gratitude as hers is to be made rich, Guardian."

468 · BLEAK HOUSE

"I wish it was," he returned, "with all my heart."

So did I too, for that matter. I said so.

"Ay! We would make him as rich as a Jew if we knew how. Would we not, little woman?"

I laughed as I worked, and replied that I was not sure about that, for it might spoil him, and he might not be so useful, and there might be many who could ill spare him.

"True," said my guardian. "I had forgotten that. But we would agree to make him rich enough to live, I suppose? Rich enough to work with tolerable peace of mind? Rich enough to have his own happy home, and his own household gods—and household goddess, too, perhaps?"

That was quite another thing, I said. We must all agree in that.

"To be sure," said my guardian. "All of us. I have a great regard for Woodcourt, a high esteem for him, and I have been sounding him delicately about his plans. It is difficult to offer aid to an independent man with that just kind of pride which he possesses. And yet I would be glad to do it if I might, or if I knew how. He seems half inclined for another voyage. But that appears like casting such a man away."

"It might open a new world to him," said I.

"So it might, little woman," my guardian assented. "I doubt if he expects much of the old world. Do you know I have fancied that he sometimes feels some particular disappointment, or misfortune, encountered in it. You never heard of anything of that sort?"

I shook my head.

"Humph," said my guardian. "I am mistaken, I dare say."

As there was a little pause here, which I thought, for my dear girl's satisfaction, had better be filled up, I hummed an air as I worked which was a favourite with my guardian.

"And do you think Mr. Woodcourt will make another voyage?" I asked him, when I had hummed it quietly all through.

"I don't quite know what to think, my dear, but I should say it was likely at present that he will give a long trial to another country."

"I am sure he will take the best wishes of all our hearts with him wherever he goes," said I, "and though they are not riches, he will never be the poorer for them, Guardian, at least."

"Never, little woman," he replied.

I was sitting in my usual place, which was now beside my guardian's chair. That had not been my usual place before the letter, but it was now. I looked up to Ada, who was sitting opposite, and I saw as she looked at me that her eyes were filled with tears, and that tears were falling down her face. I felt that I had only to be placid and merry once for all to undeceive my dear, and set her loving heart at rest. I really was so, and I had nothing to do but to be myself.

So I made my sweet girl lean upon my shoulder—how little thinking what was heavy on her mind!—and I said she was not quite well, and put my arm about her, and took her upstairs. When we were in our own room, and when she might perhaps have told me what I was so unprepared to hear, I gave her no encouragement to confide in me. I never thought she stood in need of it.

"O my dear good Esther," said Ada, "if I could only make up my mind to speak to you and my cousin John, when you are together!"

"Why, my love!" I remonstrated. "Ada? Why should you not speak to us! You surely don't forget, my beauty," said I, smiling, "what quiet, old-fashioned people we are, and how I have settled down to be the discreetest of dames? You don't forget how happily and peacefully my life is all marked out for me, and by whom?"

"No, never, Esther."

"Why then, my dear," said I, "there can be nothing amiss—and why should you not speak to us?"

"Nothing amiss, Esther?" returned Ada. "Oh, when I think of all these years, and of his fatherly care and kindness, and of the old relations among us, and of you, what shall I do, what shall I do!"

I looked at my child in some wonder, but I thought it better not to answer, otherwise than by cheering her, and so I turned off into many little recollections of our life together, and prevented her from saying more. When she lay down to sleep, and not before, I returned to my guardian to say good-night, and then I came back to Ada, and sat near her for a little while.

She was asleep, and I thought as I looked at her that she was a little changed. I had thought so more than once lately. I could not decide, even looking at her while she was unconscious, how she was changed, but something in the familiar beauty of her face looked different to me. My guardian's old hopes of her and Richard arose sorrowfully in my mind, and I said to myself, "She has been anxious about him," and I wondered how that love would end.

When I had come home from Caddy's while she was ill, I had often found Ada at work, and she had always put her work away, and I had never known what it was. Some of it now lay in a drawer near her, which was not quite closed. I did not open the drawer, but I still rather wondered what the work could be, for it was evidently nothing for herself. And I noticed as I kissed my dear, that she lay with one hand under her pillow so that it was hidden.

How much less amiable I must have been than they thought me, how much less amiable than I thought myself, to be so preoccupied with my own cheerfulness and contentment as to think that it only rested with me to put my dear girl right, and set her mind at peace! But I lay down, self-deceived, in that belief. And I awoke in it next day to find that there was still the same shade between me and my darling.

# CHAPTER 51

~~~~~~~~~~~~~~~~~~~~~~~~~~~~~~~~~~~~~~~~~~~~~~~~~~~~~~

*Enlightened*

WHEN Mr. Woodcourt arrived in London, he went, that very same day, to Mr. Vholes's in Symond's Inn. For he never once, from the moment when I entreated him to be a friend to Richard, neglected or forgot his promise. He had told me that he accepted the charge as a sacred trust, and he was ever true to it in that spirit.

He found Mr. Vholes in his office, and informed Mr. Vholes of his agreement with Richard, that he should call there to learn his address.

"Just so, sir," said Mr. Vholes. "Mr. C.'s address is not a hundred miles from here, sir. Would you take a seat, sir?"

Mr. Woodcourt thanked Mr. Vholes, but he had no business with him beyond what he had mentioned.

"Just so, sir. I believe, sir," said Mr. Vholes, still quietly insisting on the seat by not giving the address, "that you have influence with Mr. C. Indeed I am aware that you have."

"I was not aware of it myself," returned Mr. Woodcourt, "but I suppose you know best."

"Sir," rejoined Mr. Vholes, self-contained, as usual, voice and all, "it is a part of my professional duty to know best. It is a part of my professional duty to study and to understand a gentleman who confides his interests to me. In my professional duty I shall not be wanting, sir, if I know it."

Mr. Woodcourt again mentioned the address.

"Give me leave, sir," said Mr. Vholes. "Bear with me for a moment. Sir, Mr. C. is playing for a considerable stake, and cannot play without —need I say what?"

"Money, I presume?"

"Sir," said Mr. Vholes, "to be honest with you, money is the word. Now, sir, upon the chances of Mr. C.'s game I express to you no opinion, *no* opinion. It might be highly impolitic in Mr. C., after playing so long and so high, to leave off; it might be the reverse, I say nothing."

"You seem to forget," returned Mr. Woodcourt, "that I ask you to say nothing, and have no interest in anything you say."

"Pardon me, sir," retorted Mr. Vholes, "you do yourself an injustice! No, sir! Pardon me! You shall not do yourself an injustice. You are interested in anything, and in everything, that relates to your friend. I know human nature much better, sir, than to admit for an instant that a gentleman of your appearance is not interested in whatever concerns his friend."

"Well," replied Mr. Woodcourt, "that may be. I am particularly interested in his address."

"If Mr. C. is to continue to play for this considerable stake, sir, he must have funds. Understand me! There are funds in hand at present. I ask for nothing; there are funds in hand. But for the onward play, more funds must be provided; unless Mr. C. is to throw away what he has already ventured—which is wholly and solely a point for his consideration. This, sir, I take the opportunity of stating openly to you, as the friend of Mr. C. Without funds, I shall always be happy to appear and act for Mr. C., to the extent of all such costs as are safe to be allowed out of the estate: not beyond that. I could not go beyond that, sir, without wronging my three dear girls, or my venerable father in the Vale of Taunton. Whereas, sir, my resolution is (call it weakness or folly if you please) to wrong no one."

Mr. Woodcourt rather sternly rejoined that he was glad to hear it.

"I wish, sir," said Mr. Vholes, "to leave a good name behind me. Therefore I take every opportunity of openly stating to a friend of Mr. C. how Mr. C. is situated. As to myself, sir, the labourer is worthy of his hire. If I undertake to put my shoulder to the wheel, I do it, and I earn what I get. I am here for that purpose."

"And Mr. Carstone's address, Mr. Vholes?"

"Sir," returned Mr. Vholes, "it is next door. On the second story you will find Mr. C.'s apartments. Mr. C. desires to be near his professional adviser, and I am far from objecting, for I court inquiry."

Upon this, Mr. Woodcourt wished Mr. Vholes good-day, and went in search of Richard, the change in whose appearance he began to understand now but too well.

He found him in a dull room, fadedly furnished—much as I had found him in his barrack-room but a little while before, except that he was not writing, but was sitting with a book before him from which his eyes and thoughts were far astray. As the door chanced to be standing open, Mr. Woodcourt was in his presence for some moments without being perceived, and he told me that he never could forget the haggardness of his face, and the dejection of his manner, before he was aroused from his dream.

"Woodcourt, my dear fellow!" cried Richard, starting up with extended hands, "you come upon my vision like a ghost."

"A friendly one," he replied, "and only waiting, as they say ghosts do, to be addressed. How does the mortal world go?" They were seated now, near together.

"Badly enough, and slowly enough," said Richard, "speaking at least for my part of it."

"What part is that?"

"The Chancery part."

"I never heard," returned Mr. Woodcourt, shaking his head, "of its going well yet."

"Nor I," said Richard, moodily. "Who ever did?" He brightened again in a moment, and said, with his natural openness: "Woodcourt, I should be sorry to be misunderstood by you, even if I gained by it in your estimation. You must know that I have done no good this long time. I have not intended to do much harm, but I seem to have been capable of nothing else. It may be that I should have done better by keeping out of the net into which my destiny has worked me; but I think not, though I dare say you will soon hear, if you have not already heard, a very different opinion. To make short of a long story, I am afraid I have wanted an object; but I have an object now—or it has me—and it is too late to discuss it. Take me as I am, and make the best of me."

"A bargain," said Mr. Woodcourt. "Do as much by me in return."

"Oh! You," returned Richard, "you can pursue your art for its own sake, and can put your hand upon the plough and never turn. You and I are very different creatures." He spoke regretfully, and lapsed for a moment into his weary condition. "Well, well!" he cried, shaking it off, "everything has an end. We shall see! So you will take me as I am, and make the best of me?"

"Ay, indeed I will." They shook hands upon it laughingly, but in deep earnestness. I can answer for one of them with my heart of hearts.

"You come as a godsend," said Richard, "for I have seen nobody here yet but Vholes. Woodcourt, there is one subject I should like to mention, for once and for all, in the beginning of our treaty. You can hardly make the best of me if I don't. You know, I dare say, that I have an attachment to my cousin Ada?"

Mr. Woodcourt replied that I had hinted as much to him.

"Now pray," returned Richard, "don't think me a heap of selfishness. Don't suppose that I am splitting my head and half breaking my heart over this miserable Chancery suit for my own rights and interests alone. Ada's are bound up with mine, they can't se separated, Vholes works for both of us. Do think of that!"

He was so very solicitous on this head that Mr. Woodcourt gave him the strongest assurances that he did him no injustice.

"You see," said Richard, with something pathetic in his manner of lingering on the point, "to an upright fellow like you, bringing a friendly face like yours here, I cannot bear the thought of appearing selfish and mean. I want to see Ada righted, Woodcourt, as well as myself; I want to do my utmost to right her as well as myself; I venture what I can scrape together to extricate her as well as myself. Do, I beseech you, think of that!"

Afterwards, when Mr. Woodcourt came to reflect on what had passed, he was so very much impressed by the strength of Richard's anxiety on this point that in telling me generally of his first visit to Symond's Inn, he particularly dwelt upon it. It revived a fear I had had before, that my dear girl's little property would be absorbed by Mr. Vholes, and that Richard's justification to himself would be sincerely this. It was just as I began to take care of Caddy that the interview took place, and I now return to the time when Caddy had recovered, and the shade was still between me and my darling.

I proposed to Ada that morning that we should go and see Richard. It a little surprised me to find that she hesitated, and was not so radiantly willing as I had expected.

"My dear," said I, "you have not had any difference with Richard since I have been so much away?"

"No, Esther."

"Not heard of him, perhaps?" said I.

"Yes, I have heard of him," said Ada.

Such tears in her eyes, and such love in her face. I could not make my darling out. Should I go to Richard's by myself? I said. No, Ada thought I had better not go by myself. Would she go with me? Yes, Ada thought she had better go with me. Should we go now? Yes, let us go now. Well, I could not understand my darling, with the tears in her eyes and the love in her face!

We were soon equipped, and went out. It was a sombre day, and drops of chill rain fell at intervals. It was one of those colourless days when everything looks heavy and harsh. We had first to find out Symond's Inn. We were going to inquire in a shop when Ada said she thought it was near Chancery Lane. "We are not likely to be far out, my love, if we go in that direction," said I. So to Chancery Lane we went, and there, sure enough, we saw it written up: Symond's Inn.

We had next to find out the number. "Or Mr. Vholes's office will do," I recollected, "for Mr. Vholes's office is next door." Upon which Ada said perhaps that was Mr. Vholes's office in the corner there. And it really was.

Then came the question, which of the two next doors? I was going for the one, and my darling was going for the other, and my darling was right again. So up we went to the second story, when we came to Richard's name in great white letters on a hearse-like panel. I should have knocked, but Ada said perhaps we had better turn the handle and go in. Thus we came to Richard, poring over a table covered with dusty bundles of papers which seemed to me like dusty mirrors reflecting his own mind. Wherever I looked I saw the ominous words that ran in it repeated. Jarndyce and Jarndyce.

He received us very affectionately, and we sat down. "If you had

come a little earlier," he said, "you would have found Woodcourt here. There never was such a good fellow as Woodcourt is. He finds time to look in between whiles, when anybody else with half his work to do would be thinking about not being able to come. And he is so cherry, so fresh, so sensible, so earnest, so—everything that I am not, that the place brightens whenever he comes, and darkens whenever he goes again."

"God bless him," I thought, "for his truth to me!"

"He is not so sanguine, Ada," continued Richard, casting his dejected look over the bundles of papers, "as Vholes and I are usually; but he is only an outsider, and is not in the mysteries. We have gone into them, and he has not."

As his look wandered over the papers again, and he passed his two hands over his head, I noticed how sunken and how large his eyes appeared, how dry his lips were, and how his finger-nails were all bitten away.

"Is this a healthy place to live in, Richard, do you think?" said I.

"Why, my dear Minerva," answered Richard, with his old gay laugh, "it is neither a rural nor a cheerful place, and when the sun shines here, you may lay a pretty heavy wager that it is shining brightly in an open spot. But it's well enough for the time. It's near the offices, and near Vholes."

"Perhaps," I hinted, "a change from both—"

"—might do me good?" said Richard, forcing a laugh as he finished the sentence. "I shouldn't wonder! But it can only come in one way now —in one of two ways, I should rather say. Either the suit must be ended, Esther, or the suitor. But it shall be the suit, my dear girl, the suit, my dear girl!"

These latter words were addressed to Ada, who was sitting nearest to him. Her face being turned away from me and towards him, I could not see it.

"We are doing very well," pursued Richard. "Vholes will tell you so. We are really spinning along. Ask Vholes. We are giving them no rest. Vholes knows all their windings and turnings, and we are upon them everywhere. We have astonished them already. We shall rouse up that nest of sleepers, mark my words!"

His hopefulness had long been more painful to me than his despond- ency; it was so unlike hopefulness, had something so fierce in its de- termination to be it, was so hungry and eager, and yet so conscious of being forced and unsustainable, that it had long touched me to the heart. But the commentary upon it now indelibly written in his hand- some face made it far more distressing than it used to be.

"The sight of our dear little woman," said Richard, Ada still remain- ing silent and quiet, "is so natural to me, and her compassionate face is so like the face of old days, that I can't make pretences with her. I fluctuate a little, that's the truth. Sometimes I hope, my dear, and some- times I—don't quite despair, but nearly. I get," said Richard, walking across the room, "so tired!" He took a few turns up and down, and sank upon the sofa. "I get," he repeated gloomily, "so tired. It is such weary weary work!"

He was leaning on his arm, saying these words in a meditative voice and looking at the ground, when my darling rose, put off her bonnet, kneeled down beside him with her golden hair falling like sunlight on his head, clasped her two arms round his neck, and turned her face to me. Oh, what a loving and devoted face I saw!

"Esther, dear," she said very quietly, "I am not going home again." A light shone in upon me all at once. "Never any more. I am going to stay with my dear husband. We have been married above two months. Go home without me, my own Esther, I shall never go home any more!" With those words my darling drew his head down on her breast, and held it there. And if ever in my life I saw a love that nothing but death could change, I saw it then before me.

"Speak to Esther, my dearest," said Richard, breaking the silence presently. "Tell her how it was."

I met her before she could come to me, and folded her in my arms. We neither of us spoke, but with her cheek against my own, I wanted to hear nothing. "My pet," said I. "My love. My poor, poor girl!" I pitied her so much. I was very fond of Richard, but the impulse that I had upon me was to pity her so much.

"Esther, will you forgive me? Will my cousin John forgive me?"

"My dear," said I, "to doubt it for a moment, is to do him a great wrong. And as to me!"—Why, as to me, what had I to forgive!

"All I had was Richard's," Ada said, "and Richard would not take it, Esther, and what could I do but be his wife when I loved him dearly!"

"And you were so fully and so kindly occupied, excellent Dame Durden," said Richard, "that how could we speak to you at such a time! And besides, it was not a long-considered step. We went out one morning and were married."

"And when it was done, Esther," said my darling, "I was always thinking how to tell you, and what to do for the best. And sometimes I thought you ought to know it directly, and sometimes I thought you ought not to know it and to keep it from my cousin John, and I could not tell what to do, and I fretted very much."

How selfish I must have been, not to have thought of this before! I don't know what I said now. I was so sorry, and yet I was so fond of them, and so glad that they were fond of me; I pitied them so much, and yet I felt a kind of pride in their loving one another. I never had experienced such painful and pleasurable emotion at one time, and in my own heart I did not know which predominated. But I was not there to darken their way, I did not do that.

When I was less foolish and more composed, my darling took her wedding-ring from her bosom, and kissed it, and put it on. Then I remembered last night, and I told Richard that ever since her marriage she had worn it at night when there was no one to see. Then Ada blushingly asked me how did I know that, my dear? Then I told Ada how I had seen her hand concealed under her pillow, and had little thought why, my dear. Then they began telling me how it was, all over again.

Thus the time went on, until it became necessary for me to think of returning. When that time arrived it was the worst of all, for then my darling completely broke down. She clung round my neck, calling me by every dear name she could think of, and saying what should she do without me! Nor was Richard much better.

"Why, I declare," said I, "I never saw such a wife. I don't think she loves her husband at all. Here, Richard, take my child, for goodness' sake." But I held her tight all the while, and could have wept over her I don't know how long. "I give this dear young couple notice," said I, "that I am only going away to come back tomorrow, and that I shall be always coming backwards and forwards, until Symond's Inn is tired of the sight of me. So I shall not say good-bye, Richard. For what would be the use of that, you know, when I am coming back so soon!"

I had given my darling to him now, and I meant to go, but I lingered for one more look of the precious face, which it seemed to rive my heart to turn from.

So I said (in a merry bustling manner) that unless they gave me some encouragement to come back, I was not sure that I could take that liberty; upon which my dear girl looked up, faintly smiling through her tears, and I folded her lovely face between my hands, and gave it one last kiss, and laughed, and ran away.

And when I got downstairs, oh, how I cried! It almost seemed to me that I had lost my Ada for ever. I was so lonely, and so blank without her, and it was so desolate to be going home with no hope of seeing her there, that I could get no comfort for a little while.

I came to myself by and by, after a little scolding, and took a coach home. The poor boy whom I had found at Saint Albans had reappeared a short time before, and was lying at the point of death—indeed was then dead, though I did not know it. My guardian had gone out to inquire about him, and did not return to dinner. Being quite alone, I cried a little again, though on the whole, I don't think I behaved so very, very ill.

It was only natural that I should not be quite accustomed to the loss of my darling yet. Three or four hours were not a long time, after years. But my mind dwelt so much upon the uncongenial scene in which I had left her, and I pictured it as such an overshadowed stony-hearted one, and I so longed to be near her, and taking some sort of care of her, that I determined to go back in the evening, only to look up at her windows.

It was foolish, I dare say, but it did not then seem at all so to me, and it does not seem quite so even now. I took Charley into my confidence, and we went out at dusk. It was dark when we came to the new strange home of my dear girl, and there was a light behind the yellow blinds. We walked past cautiously three or four times, looking up, and narrowly missed encountering Mr. Vholes, who came out of his office while we were there and turned his head to look up too before going home. The sight of his lank black figure, and the lonesome air of that nook in the dark, were favourable to the state of my mind. I thought of the youth and love and beauty of my dear girl, shut up in such an ill-assorted refuge, almost as if it were a cruel place. I went back, not quite accustomed yet to the change, but all the better for that hovering about my darling.

My guardian had come home, and was standing thoughtfully by the dark window. When I went in, his face cleared and he came to his seat, but he caught the light upon my face, as I took mine.

"Little woman," said he, "you have been crying."

"Why, yes, Guardian," said I, "I am afraid I have been, a little. Ada has been in such distress, and is so very sorry, Guardian."

I saw in his glance that my words, and my look at her empty place, had prepared him.

"Is she married, my dear?"

I told him all about it, and how her first entreaties had referred to his forgiveness.

"She has no need of it," said he. "Heaven bless her, and her husband!" But just as my first impulse had been to pity her, so was his. "Poor girl, poor girl! Poor Rick! Poor Ada!"

Neither of us spoke after that, until he said with a sigh, "Well, well, my dear! Bleak House is thinning fast."

"But its mistress remains, Guardian." Though I was timid about saying it, I ventured because of the sorrowful tone in which he had spoken. "She will do all she can to make it happy," said I.

"She will succeed, my love!"

The letter had made no difference between us, except that the seat by his side had come to be mine; it made none now. He turned his old bright fatherly look upon me, laid his hand on my hand in his old way, and said again, "She will succeed, my dear. Nevertheless, Bleak House is thinning fast, O little woman!"

# CHAPTER 52

## Obstinacy

But one other day had intervened when, early in the morning as we were going to breakfast, Mr. Woodcourt came in haste with the astounding news that a terrible murder had been committed, for which Mr. George had been apprehended and was in custody. When he told us that a large reward was offered by Sir Leicester Dedlock for the murderer's apprehension, I did not in my first consternation understand why; but a few more words explained to me that the murdered person was Sir Leicester's lawyer, and immediately my mother's dread of him rushed into my remembrance.

This unforseen and violent removal of one whom she had long watched and distrusted, and who had long watched and distrusted her—one for whom she could have had few intervals of kindness, always dreading in him a dangerous and secret enemy—appeared so awful that my first thoughts were of her. How appalling to hear of such a death and be able to feel no pity!

Such crowding reflections, increasing the distress and fear I always felt when the name was mentioned, made me so agitated that I could scarcely hold my place at the table. I was quite unable to follow the conversation until I had had a little time to recover. But when I came to myself, and saw how shocked my guardian was, and found that they were speaking of the suspected man and recalling every favourable impression we had formed of him, out of the good we had known of him, my interest and my fears were so strongly aroused in his behalf that I was quite set up again.

"Guardian, you don't think it possible that he is justly accused?"

"My dear, I *can't* think so. This man whom we have seen so openhearted and compassionate; who, with the might of a giant, has the gentleness of a child; who looks as brave a fellow as ever lived, and is so simple and quiet with it—this man justly accused of such a crime? I can't believe it. It's not that I don't or I won't. I can't!"

"And I can't," said Mr. Woodcourt. "Still, whatever we believe or know of him, we had better not forget that some appearances are against him. He bore an animosity towards the deceased gentleman. He has openly mentioned it in many places. He is said to have expressed himself violently towards him, and he certainly did about him, to my knowledge. He admits that he was alone on the scene of the murder within a few minutes of its commission. I sincerely believe him to be as innocent of any participation in it as I am, but these are all reasons for suspicion falling upon him."

"True," said my guardian, and he added, turning to me, "It would be doing him a very bad service, my dear, to shut our eyes to the truth in any of these respects."

I felt, of course, that we must admit, not only to ourselves but to others, the full force of the circumstances against him. Yet I knew withal (I could not help saying) that their weight would not induce us to desert him in his need.

"Heaven forbid!" returned my guardian. "We will stand by him, as he himself stood by the two poor creatures who are gone." He meant Mr. Gridley and the boy, to both of whom Mr. George had given shelter.

Mr. Woodcourt then told us that the trooper's man had been with him before day, after wandering about the streets all night like a distracted creature. That one of the trooper's first anxieties was that we should not suppose him guilty. That he had charged his messenger to represent his perfect innocence with every solemn assurance he could send us. That Mr. Woodcourt had only quieted the man by undertaking to come to our house very early in the morning with these representations. He added that he was now upon his way to see the prisoner himself.

My guardian said he would go too. Now, besides that I liked the retired soldier very much, and that he liked me, I had that secret interest in what had happened which was only known to my guardian. It seemed to become personally important to myself that the truth should be discovered, and that no innocent people should be suspected; for suspicion, once run wild, might run wilder.

In a word, I felt as if it were my duty and obligation to go with them. My guardian did not seek to dissuade me, and I went.

It was a large prison, with many courts and passages. In an arched room by himself, like a cellar upstairs, with walls so glaringly white that they made the massive iron window-bars and iron-bound door even more profoundly black than they were, we found the trooper standing in a corner. He had been sitting on a bench there, and had risen when he heard the locks and bolts turn.

When he saw us, he came forward a step with his usual heavy tread, and there stopped and made a slight bow. But as I still advanced, putting out my hand to him, he understood us in a moment.

"This is a load off my mind, I do assure you, miss and gentlemen," said he, saluting us with great heartiness and drawing a long breath. "And now I don't so much care how it ends."

He scarcely seemed to be the prisoner. What with his coolness and his soldierly bearing, he looked far more like the prison-guard.

"This is even a rougher place than my gallery to receive a lady in," said Mr. George, "but I know Miss Summerson will make the best of it." As he handed me to the bench on which he had been sitting, I sat down, which seemed to give him great satisfaction.

"I thank you, miss," said he.

"Now, George," observed my guardian, "as we require no new assurances on your part, so I believe we need give you none on ours."

"Not at all, sir. I thank you with all my heart. If I was not innocent of this crime, I couldn't look at you and keep my secret to myself, under the condescension of the present visit. I feel the present visit very much. I am not one of the eloquent sort, but I feel it, Miss Summerson and gentlemen, deeply."

"First," said my guardian, "can we do anything for your personal comfort, George? Is there anything you want that would lessen the hardship of this confinement?"

"Well, sir," replied Mr. George, after a little cogitation, "I am equally obliged to you, but tobacco being against the rules, I can't say that there is."

"You will think of many little things perhaps, by and by. Whenever you do, George, let us know."

"Thank you, sir. Howsoever," observed Mr. George, with one of his sunburnt smiles, "a man who has been knocking about the world in a vagabond kind of a way as long as I have gets on well enough in a place like the present, so far as that goes."

"Next, as to your case," observed my guardian.

"Exactly so, sir," returned Mr. George, folding his arms upon his breast with perfect self-possession and a little curiosity.

"How does it stand now?"

"Why, sir, it is under remand at present. Bucket gives me to understand that he will probably apply for a series of remands from time to time, until the case is more complete. How it is to be made more complete I don't myself see, but I dare say Bucket will manage it somehow."

"Why, Heaven save us, man!" exclaimed my guardian, "you talk of yourself as if you were somebody else!"

"No offence, sir," said Mr. George. "I am very sensible of your kindness. But I don't see how an innocent man is to make up his mind to this kind of thing without knocking his head against the walls unless he takes it in that point of view."

"That is true enough, to a certain extent," returned my guardian, softened. "But my good fellow, even an innocent man must take ordinary precautions to defend himself."

"Certainly, sir. And I have done so. I have stated to the magistrates, 'Gentlemen, I am as innocent of this charge as yourselves; what has been stated against me in the way of facts is perfectly true; I know no more about it.' I intend to continue stating that, sir. What more can I do? It's the truth."

"But the mere truth won't do," rejoined my guardian.

"Won't it indeed, sir? Rather a bad look-out for me!" Mr. George good-humouredly observed.

"You must have a lawyer," pursued my guardian. "We must engage a good one for you."

"I ask your pardon, sir," said Mr. George, with a step backward. "I am equally obliged. But I must decidedly beg to be excused from anything of that sort."

"You won't have a lawyer?"

"No, sir." Mr. George shook his head in the most emphatic manner. "I thank you all the same, sir, but—no lawyer! I don't take kindly to the breed," said Mr. George. "Gridley didn't. And—if you'll excuse my saying so much—I should hardly have thought you did yourself, sir."

"That's Equity," my guardian explained, a little at a loss; "that's Equity, George."

"Is it, indeed, sir?" returned the trooper, in his offhand manner. "I am not acquainted with those shades of names myself, but in a general way I object to the breed."

Unfolding his arms, and changing his position, he stood with one massive hand upon the table and the other on his hip, as complete a picture of a man who was not to be moved from a fixed purpose as ever I saw. It was in vain that we all three talked to him, and endeavoured to persuade him; he listened with that gentleness which went so well with his bluff bearing, but was evidently no more shaken by our representations than his place of confinement was.

"Pray think once more, Mr. George," said I. "Have you no wish in reference to your case?"

"I certainly could wish it to be tried, miss," he returned, "by court-martial; but that is out of the question, as I am well aware. If you will be so good as to favour me with your attention for a couple of minutes, miss, not more, I'll endeavour to explain myself as clearly as I can."

He looked at us all three in turn, shook his head a little as if he were adjusting it in the stock and collar of a tight uniform, and after a moment's reflection went on.

"You see, miss, I have been handcuffed and taken into custody, and brought here. I am a marked and disgraced man, and here I am. My shooting-gallery is rummaged, high and low, by Bucket, such property as I have—'tis small—is turned this way and that till it don't know itself, and (as aforesaid) here I am! I don't particular complain of that. Though I am in these present quarters through no immediately preceding fault of mine, I can very well understand that if I hadn't gone into the vagabond way in my youth, this wouldn't have happened. It *has* happened. Then comes the question, how to meet it.

"Now, the unfortunate deceased was himself a lawyer, and had a pretty tight hold of me. I don't wish to rake up his ashes, but he had what I should call if he was living a devil of a tight hold of me. I don't like his trade the better for that. If I had kept clear of his trade, I should have kept outside this place. But that's not what I mean. Now suppose I had killed him. Suppose I really had discharged into his body any one of those pistols recently fired off that Bucket has found at my place and —might have found there any day since it has been my place. What should I have done as soon as I was hard and fast here? Got a lawyer."

He stopped on hearing some one at the locks and bolts, and did not resume until the door had been opened and was shut again. For what purpose opened, I will mention presently.

"I should have got a lawyer, and he would have said (as I have often read in the newspapers), 'My client says nothing, my client reserves his defence—my client this, that, and t'other.' Well, 'tis not the custom of that breed to go straight, according to my opinion, or to think that other men do. Say I am innocent, and I get a lawyer. He would be as likely to believe me guilty as not, perhaps more. What would he do, whether or not? Act as if I was—shut my mouth up, tell me not to commit myself, keep circumstances back, chop the evidence small, quibble, and get me off perhaps! But Miss Summerson, do I care for getting off in that way or would I rather be hanged in my own way—if you'll excuse my mentioning anything so disagreeable to a lady?

"I would rather be hanged in my own way. And I mean to be! I don't intend to say"—looking round upon us—"that I am more partial to being hanged than another man. What I say is, I must come off clear and full or not at all. Therefore when I hear stated against me what is true, I say it's true, and when they tell me, 'Whatever you say will be used,' I tell them I don't mind that—I mean it to be used. If they can't make me innocent out of the whole truth, they are not likely to do it out of anything less, or anything else. And if they are, it's worth nothing to me."

Taking a pace or two over the stone floor, he came back to the table and finished what he had to say.

"I thank you, miss, and gentlemen both, many times for your attention, and many times more for your interest. That's the plain state of the matter, as it points itself out to a mere trooper with a blunt broadsword kind of a mind. I have never done well in life, beyond my duty as a soldier, and if the worst comes after all, I shall reap pretty much as I have sown. When I got over the first crash of being seized as a murderer, I worked my way round to what you find me now. As such, I shall remain. No relations will be disgraced by me, or made unhappy for me, and—and that's all I've got to say."

The door had been opened to admit another soldier-looking man of less prepossessing appearance at first sight, and a weather-tanned, bright-eyed wholesome woman with a basket, who, from her entrance, had been exceedingly attentive to all Mr. George had said. Mr. George had received them with a familiar nod and a friendly look, but without any more particular greeting in the midst of his address. He now shook them cordially by the hand, and said, "Miss Summerson and gentlemen, this is an old comrade of mine, Matthew Bagnet. And this is his wife, Mrs. Bagnet."

Mr. Bagnet made us a stiff military bow, and Mrs. Bagnet dropped us a curtsey.

"Real good friends of mine they are," said Mr. George. "It was at their house I was taken."

"With a second-hand wiolinceller," Mr. Bagnet put in, twitching his head angrily. "Of a good tone. For a friend. That money was no object to."

"Mat," said Mr. George, "you have heard pretty well all I have been saying to this lady and these two gentlemen. I know it meets your approval?"

Mr. Bagnet, after considering, referred the point to his wife. "Old girl," said he. "Tell him. Whether or not. It meets my approval."

"Why, George," exclaimed Mrs. Bagnet, who had been unpacking her basket, in which there was a piece of cold pickled pork, a little tea and sugar, and a brown loaf, "you ought to know it don't. You ought to know it's enough to drive a person wild to hear you. You won't be got off this way, and you won't be got off that way—what do you mean by such picking and choosing? It's stuff and nonsense, George."

"Don't be severe upon me in my misfortunes, Mrs. Bagnet," said the trooper lightly.

"Oh, bother your misfortunes," cried Mrs. Bagnet, "if they don't make you more reasonable than that comes to. I never was so ashamed in my life to hear a man talk folly as I have been to hear you talk this day to the present company. Lawyers? Why, what but too many cooks should hinder you from having a dozen lawyers, if the gentleman recommended them to you?"

"This is a very sensible woman," said my guardian. "I hope you will persuade him, Mrs. Bagnet."

"Persuade him, sir?" she returned. "Lord bless you, no. You don't know George. Now there!" Mrs. Bagnet left her basket to point him out with both her bare brown hands. "There he stands! As self-willed and as determined a man, in the wrong way, as ever put a human creature under Heaven out of patience! Why, don't I know him!" cried Mrs. Bagnet. "Don't I know you, George! You don't mean to set up for a new character with *me* after all these years, I hope?"

Her friendly indignation had an exemplary effect upon her husband, who shook his head at the trooper several times as a silent recommendation to him to yield. Between whiles, Mrs. Bagnet looked at me, and I understood, from the play of her eyes, that she wished me to do something, though I did not comprehend what.

"But I have given up talking to you, old fellow, years and years," said Mrs. Bagnet as she blew a little dust off the pickled pork, looking at me again, "and when ladies and gentlemen know you as well as I do, they'll give up talking to you too. If you are not too headstrong to accept of a bit of dinner, here it is."

"I accept it with many thanks," returned the trooper.

"Do you though, indeed?" said Mrs. Bagnet, continuing to grumble on good-humouredly. "I'm sure I'm surprised at that. I wonder you don't starve in your own way also. It would only be like you. Perhaps you'll set your mind upon *that*, next." Here she again looked at me, and I now perceived, from her glances at the door and at me, by turns, that she wished us to retire, and to await her outside the prison. Communicating this by similar means to my guardian and Mr. Woodcourt, I rose.

"We hope you will think better of it, Mr. George," said I, "and we shall come to see you again, trusting to find you more reasonable."

"More grateful, Miss Summerson, you can't find me," he returned.

"But more persuadable we can, I hope," said I. "And let me entreat you to consider that the clearing-up of this mystery, and the discovery of the real perpetrator of this deed, may be of the last importance to others besides yourself."

He heard me respectfully, but without much heeding these words, which I spoke, a little turned from him, already on my way to the door; he was observing (this they afterwards told me) my height and figure, which seemed to catch his attention all at once.

" 'Tis curious," said he. "And yet I thought so at the time!"

My guardian asked him what he meant.

"Why, sir," he answered, "when my ill-fortune took me to the dead man's staircase on the night of his murder, I saw a shape so like Miss Summerson's go by me in the dark that I had half a mind to speak to it."

For an instant I felt such a shudder as I never felt before or since, and hope I shall never feel again.

"It came downstairs as I went up," said the trooper, "and crossed the moon-lighted window with a loose black mantle on; I noticed a deep fringe to it. However, it has nothing to do with the present subject, excepting that Miss Summerson looked so like it at the moment that it came into my head."

I cannot separate and define the feelings that arose in me after this; it is enough that the vague duty and obligation I had felt upon me from the first of following the investigation was, without my distinctly daring to ask myself any question, increased, and that I was indignantly sure of there being no possibility of a reason for my being afraid.

We three went out of the prison, and walked up and down at some short distance from the gate. We had not waited long when Mr. and Mrs. Bagnet came out too, and quickly joined us. There was a tear in each of Mrs. Bagnet's eyes, and her face was flushed and hurried. "I didn't let George see what I thought about it, you know, miss," was her first remark when she came up, "but he's in a bad way, poor old fellow!"

"Not with care and prudence, and good help," said my guardian.

"A gentleman like you ought to know best, sir," returned Mrs. Bagnet, hurriedly drying her eyes on the hem of her grey cloak, "but I am uneasy for him. He has been so careless, and said so much that he never meant. The gentlemen of the juries might not understand him as Lignum and me do. And then such a number of circumstances have happened bad for him, and such a number of people will be brought forward to speak against him, and Bucket is so deep. Now I tell you, miss, and when I say miss, I mean all! Just come into the corner of the wall, and I'll tell you!"

Mrs. Bagnet hurried us into a more secluded place, and was at first too breathless to proceed, occasioning Mr. Bagnet to say, "Old girl! Tell 'em!"

"Why then, miss," the old girl proceeded, untying the strings of her bonnet for more air, "you could as soon move Dover Castle as move George on this point, unless you had got a new power to move him with. And I have got it!"

"You are a jewel of a woman," said my guardian. "Go on!"

"Now I tell you, miss," she proceeded, clapping her hands in her hurry and agitation a dozen times in every sentence, "that what he says concerning no relations is all bosh. They don't know of him, but he does know of them. He has said more to me at odd times than to anybody else, and it warn't for nothing that he once spoke to my Woolwich about whitening and wrinkling mothers' heads. For fifty pounds he had seen his mother that day. She's alive, and must be brought here straight!" Instantly Mrs. Bagnet put some pins into her mouth, and began pinning up her skirts all round, a little higher than the level of her grey cloak, which she accomplished with surpassing dispatch and dexterity. "Lignum," said Mrs. Bagnet, "you take care of the children, old man, and give me the umbrella! I'm away to Lincolnshire, to bring that old lady here."

"But bless the woman," cried my guardian with his hand in his pocket, "how is she going? What money has she got?"

Mrs. Bagnet made another application to her skirts, and brought forth a leather purse in which she hastily counted over a few shillings, and which she then shut up with perfect satisfaction.

"Never you mind for me, miss. I'm a soldier's wife, and accustomed to travel my own way. Lignum, old boy"—kissing him—"one for yourself, three for the children. Now I'm away into Lincolnshire after George's mother."

And she actually set off while we three stood looking at one another lost in amazement. She actually trudged away in her grey cloak at a sturdy pace, and turned the corner, and was gone.

"Mr. Bagnet," said my guardian, "do you mean to let her go in that way?"

"Can't help it," he returned. "Made her way home once. From another quarter of the world. With the same grey cloak. And same umbrella. Whatever the old girl says, do. Do it! Whenever the old girl says, *I'll* do it. She does it."

"Then she is as honest and genuine as she looks," rejoined my guardian, "and it is impossible to say more for her."

"She's Colour-Sergeant of the Nonpareil battalion," said Mr. Bagnet, looking at us over his shoulder as he went his way also. "And there's not such another. But I never own to it before her. Discipline must be maintained."

CHAPTER 53

*The Track*

MR. BUCKET and his fat forefinger are much in consultation together under existing circumstances. When Mr. Bucket has a matter of this pressing interest under his consideration, the fat forefinger seems to rise to the dignity of a familiar demon. He puts it to his ears and it whispers information; he puts it to his lips and it enjoins him to secrecy; he rubs it over his nose and it sharpens his scent; he shakes it before a guilty man and it charms him to his destruction.

Otherwise mildly studious in his observation of human nature, on the whole a benignant philosopher not disposed to be severe upon the follies of mankind, Mr. Bucket pervades a vast number of houses, and strolls about an infinity of streets, to outward appearance rather languishing for want of an object. He is in the friendliest condition towards his species, and will drink with most of them. He is free with his money, affable in his manners, innocent in his conversation—but through the placid stream of his life there glides an undercurrent of forefinger.

Time and place cannot bind Mr. Bucket. Like man in the abstract, he is here today and gone tomorrow—but, very unlike man indeed, he is here again the next day. This evening he will be casually looking into the iron extinguishers at the door of Sir Leicester Dedlock's house in town, and tomorrow morning he will be walking on the leads at Chesney Wold, where erst the old man walked whose ghost is propitiated with a hundred guineas. Drawers, desks, pockets, all things belonging to him, Mr. Bucket examines. A few hours afterwards, he and the Roman will be alone together, comparing forefingers.

It is likely that these occupations are irreconcilable with home enjoyment, but it is certain that Mr. Bucket at present does not go home. Though in general he highly appreciates the society of Mrs. Bucket, he holds himself aloof from that dear solace. Mrs. Bucket is dependent on their lodger (fortunately an amiable lady in whom she takes an interest) for companionship and conversation.

A great crowd assembles in Lincoln's Inn Fields on the day of the funeral. Sir Leicester Dedlock attends the ceremony in person. The amount of inconsolable carriages is immense. The Peerage contributes

more four-wheeled affliction than has ever been seen in that neighbourhood.

Quiet among the undertakers and the equipages, and the calves of
so many legs all steeped in grief, Mr. Bucket sits concealed in one of
the inconsolable carriages, and at his ease surveys the crowd through
the lattice blinds. He has a keen eye, and nothing escapes him. "And
there you are, my partner, eh?"—apostrophizing Mrs. Bucket, stationed
on the steps of the deceased's house.

The procession has not started yet, but is waiting for the cause of its
assemblage to be brought out. Mr. Bucket, in the foremost emblazoned
carriage, uses his two fat forefingers to hold the lattice a hair's breadth
open while he looks. And it says a great deal for his attachment, as a
husband, that he is still occupied with Mrs. B. "There you are, my
partner, eh?" he murmuringly repeats. "And our lodger with you. I'm
taking notice of you, Mrs. Bucket."

Mr. Bucket sits with most attentive eyes until the sacked depository
of noble secrets is brought down—Where are all those secrets now?
Does he keep them yet? Did they fly with him on that sudden journey?
—and until the procession moves, and Mr. Bucket's view is changed.
After which he composes himself for an easy ride, and takes note of the
fittings of the carriage, in case he should ever find such knowledge useful.

Mr. Bucket sits out the procession in his own easy manner, and glides
from the carriage when the opportunity he has settled with himself
arrives. He makes for Sir Leicester Dedlock's, which is at present a
sort of home to him, where he comes and goes as he likes at all hours,
where he is always welcome and made much of, and walks in an atmosphere of mysterious greatness.

No knocking or ringing for Mr. Bucket. He has caused himself to be
provided with a key, and can pass in at his pleasure. As he is crossing
the hall, Mercury informs him, "Here's another letter for you, Mr.
Bucket, come by post," and gives it him.

Now although Mr. Bucket walks upstairs to the little library within
the larger one with the face of a man who receives some scores of letters every day, it happens that much correspondence is not incidental
to his life. He is no great scribe, and discourages correspondence with
himself in others, as being too artless and direct a way of doing delicate
business. Further, he often sees damaging letters produced in evidence,
and has occasion to reflect that it was a green thing to write them.
For these reasons he has very little to do with letters, either as sender
or receiver. And yet he has received a round half-dozen within the last
twenty-four hours.

"And this," says Mr. Bucket, spreading it out on the table, "is in the
same hand, and consists of the same two words."

What two words?

He turns the key in the door, ungirdles his black pocket-book (Book of Fate to many), lays another letter by it, and reads, boldly written in each, "Lady Dedlock."

"Yes, yes," says Mr. Bucket. "But I could have made the money without this anonymous information."

Having put the letters in his Book of Fate and girdled it up again, he unlocks the door just in time to admit his dinner, which is brought upon a goodly tray, with a decanter of sherry. Mr. Bucket frequently observes, in friendly circles where there is no restraint, that he likes a toothful of your fine old brown East-Inder sherry better than anything you can offer him. Consequently he fills and empties his glass with a smack of his lips, and is proceeding with his refreshment when an idea enters his mind.

Mr. Bucket softly opens the door of communication between that room and the next, and looks in. The library is deserted, and the fire is sinking low. Mr. Bucket's eye, after taking a pigeon-flight round the room, alights upon a table where letters are usually put as they arrive. Several letters for Sir Leicester are upon it. Mr. Bucket draws near, and examines the directions. "No," he says "there's none in that hand. It's only me as is written to. I can break it to Sir Leicester Dedlock, Baronet, tomorrow."

With that he returns to finish his dinner with a good appetite; and after a light nap, is summoned into the drawing-room. Sir Leicester has received him there these several evenings past.

"Have you anything new to communicate, Officer?" inquires Sir Leicester. "My time is wholly at your disposal, with a view to the vindication of the outraged majesty of the law. If I have not," pursues Sir Leicester, "in the most emphatic manner adjured you, Officer, to exercise your utmost skill in this atrocious case, I particularly desire to take the present opportunity of rectifying any omission I may have made. Let no expense be a consideration. I am prepared to defray all charges. You can incur none, in pursuit of the object you have undertaken, that I shall hesitate for a moment to bear. My mind," Sir Leicester adds, with generous warmth, "has not, as may be easily supposed, recovered its tone since the late diabolical occurrence. It is not likely ever to recover its tone. But it is full of indignation tonight, after undergoing the ordeal of consigning to the tomb the remains of a faithful, a zealous, a devoted adherent." Sir Leicester's voice trembles, and his grey hair stirs upon his head. Tears are in his eyes; the best part of his nature is aroused.

"I declare," he says, "I solemnly declare, that until this crime is discovered and, in the course of justice, punished, I almost feel as if there were a stain upon my name. A gentleman who has devoted a large portion of his life to me, a gentleman who has devoted the last day of his life to me, a gentleman who has constantly sat at my table and slept under my roof, goes from my house to his own and is struck down within an hour of his leaving my house. I cannot say but that he may have been followed from my house, watched at my house, even first marked because of his association with my house—which may have suggested his possessing greater wealth, and being altogether of greater importance than his own retiring demeanour would have indicated. If I cannot, with my means and influence, and my position, bring all the perpetrators of such a crime to light, I fail in the assertion of my respect for that gentleman's memory, and of my fidelity towards one who was ever faithful to me."

While he makes this protestation with great emotion and earnestness, looking round the room as if he were addressing an assembly, Mr. Bucket glances at him with an observant gravity in which there might be, but for the audacity of the thought, a touch of compassion.

"The ceremony of today," continues Sir Leicester, "strikingly illustrative of the respect in which my deceased friend"—he lays a stress upon the word, for death levels all distinctions—"was held by the flower of the land, has, I say, aggravated the shock I have received from this most horrible and audacious crime. If it were my brother who had committed it, I would not spare him."

Mr. Bucket says, "Sir Leicester Dedlock, Baronet, I look upon the case as pretty well complete. It is a beautiful case—a beautiful case—and what little is wanting to complete it I expect to be able to supply in a few hours."

"I am very glad indeed to hear it," says Sir Leicester. "Highly creditable to you."

"Sir Leicester Dedlock, Baronet," returns Mr. Bucket, very seriously, "I hope it may at one and the same time do me credit and prove satisfactory to all. When I depict it as a beautiful case, I mean from my point of view. As considered from other points of view such cases will always involve more or less unpleasantness. Very strange things comes to our knowledge in families. Ay, and even in gen-teel families, in high families, in great families," says Mr. Bucket. "I have had the honour of being employed in high families before; and you have no idea—"

Sir Leicester, deeming it time to dismiss the officer, here majestically interposes. "Very good. Thank you!" and also with a wave of his hand implying not only that there is an end of the discourse, but that if high families fall into low habits they must take the consequences. "You will not forget, Officer," he adds, with condescension, "that I am at your disposal when you please."

Mr. Bucket inquires if tomorrow morning, now, would suit, in case he should be as for'ard as he expects to be. Sir Leicester replies, "All times are alike to me." Mr. Bucket bows.

In his fondness for society, and his adaptability to all grades, Mr. Bucket is presently standing before the hall-fire—bright and warm on the early winter night—admiring Mercury.

"Why, you're six foot two, I suppose?" says Mr. Bucket.

"Three," says Mercury.

"Are you so much? But then, you see, you're broad in proportion, and don't look it. You're not one of the weak-legged ones, you ain't. Was you ever modelled now?" Mr. Bucket asks. Mercury never was modelled. "Then you ought to be, you know," says Mr. Bucket, "and a friend of mine that you'll hear of one day as a Royal Academy Sculptor would stand something handsome to make a drawing of your proportions for the marble. My lady's out, ain't she?"

"Out to dinner."

"Goes out pretty well every day, don't she?"

"Yes."

"Not to be wondered at!" says Mr. Bucket. "Such a fine woman as her, so handsome and so graceful and so elegant, is like a fresh lemon on a dinner-table, ornamental wherever she goes. Was your father in the same way of life as yourself?" Answer in the negative. "Mine was," says Mr. Bucket. "My father was first a page, then a footman, then a butler, then a steward, then an innkeeper. Lived universally respected, and died lamented. Said with his last breath that he considered service the most honourable part of his career, and so it was. I've a brother in service, *and* a brother-in-law. My lady a good temper?"

Mercury replies, "As good as you can expect."

"Ah!" says Mr. Bucket, "A little spoilt? A little capricious? Lord, what can you anticipate when they're so handsome as that? And we like 'em all the better for it, don't we?"

Mercury, with his hands in the pockets of his bright peach-blossom small-clothes, stretches his symmetrical silk legs with the air of a man of gallantry, and can't deny it. Come the roll of wheels and a violent ringing at the bell. "Talk of the angels," says Mr. Bucket. "Here she is!"

The doors are thrown open, and she passes through the hall. Still very pale, she is dressed in slight mourning, and wears two beautiful bracelets. Either their beauty or the beauty of her arms is particularly attractive to Mr. Bucket. He looks at them with an eager eye, and rattles something in his pocket—halfpence perhaps.

Noticing him at his distance, she turns an inquiring look on the other Mercury who has brought her home.

"Mr. Bucket, my lady."

Mr. Bucket makes a leg and comes forward, passing his familiar demon over the region of his mouth.

"Are you waiting to see Sir Leicester?"

"No, my lady, I've seen him!"

"Have you made any new discoveries?"

"A few, my lady."

This is merely in passing. She scarcely makes a stop, and sweeps upstairs alone. Mr. Bucket, moving towards the staircase-foot, watches

her as she goes up the steps the old man came down to his grave, past murderous groups of statuary, repeated with their shadowy weapons on the wall, out of view.

"She's a lovely woman, too, she really is," says Mr. Bucket, coming back to Mercury. "Don't look quite healthy, though."

Is not quite healthy, Mercury informs him. Suffers much from head-aches.

Really? That's a pity! Walking, Mr. Bucket would recommend for that. Well, she tries walking, Mercury rejoins. Walks sometimes for two hours, when she has them bad. By night, too.

"Are you sure you're quite so much as six foot three?" asks Mr. Bucket, "begging your pardon for interrupting you a moment?"

Not a doubt about it.

"You're so well put together that I shouldn't have thought it.— Walks by night, does she? When it's moonlight, though?"

Oh yes. When it's moonlight! Of course. Oh, of course! Conversational and acquiescent on both sides.

"I suppose you ain't in the habit of walking yourself?" says Mr. Bucket. "Not much time for it, I should say?" Besides which, Mercury don't like it. Prefers carriage exercise. "To be sure," says Mr. Bucket. "That makes a difference. Now I think of it," says Mr. Bucket, warming his hands, and looking pleasantly at the blaze, "she went out walking the very night of this business."

"To be sure she did! I let her into the garden over the way."

"And left her there. Certainly you did. I saw you doing it."

"I didn't see *you*," says Mercury.

"I was rather in a hurry," returns Mr. Bucket, "for I was going to visit a aunt of mine that lives at Chelsea. Yes, I chanced to be passing at the time. Let's see. What time might it be? It wasn't ten."

"Half-past nine."

"You're right. So it was. And if I don't deceive myself, my lady was muffled in a loose black mantle with a deep fringe to it?"

"Of course she was."

Of course she was. Mr. Bucket must return to a little work he has to get on with upstairs, but he must shake hands with Mercury in acknowledgment of his agreeable conversation.

## CHAPTER 54

*Springing a Mine*

REFRESHED by sleep, Mr. Bucket rises betimes in the morning, and prepares for a field-day. Smartened up by the aid of a clean shirt and a wet hairbrush, with which instrument, on occasions of ceremony, he lubricates such thin locks as remain to him after his life of severe study, Mr. Bucket lays in a breakfast of two mutton chops as a foundation to work upon, together with tea, eggs, toast, and marmalade on a corresponding scale. Having much enjoyed these strengthening matters, and having held subtle conference with his familiar demon, he confidently instructs Mercury "just to mention quietly to Sir Leicester Dedlock, Baronet, that whenever he's ready for me, I'm ready for him." A gracious message being returned that Sir Leicester will expedite his dressing and join Mr. Bucket in the library within ten minutes, Mr. Bucket repairs to that apartment, and stands before the fire, with his finger on his chin, looking at the blazing coals.

Thoughtful Mr. Bucket is, as a man may be with weighty work to do, but composed, sure, confident. From the expression of his face, he might be a famous whist-player for a large stake—say a hundred guineas certain—with the game in his hand, but with a high reputation involved in his playing his hand out to the last card in a masterly way. Not in the least anxious or disturbed is Mr. Bucket, when Sir Leicester appears, but he eyes the baronet aside as he comes slowly to his easy-chair, with that observant gravity of yesterday in which there might have been yesterday, but for the audacity of the idea, a touch of compassion.

"I am sorry to have kept you waiting, Officer, but I am rather later than my usual hour this morning. I am not well. The agitation, and the indignation from which I have recently suffered have been too much for me. I am subject to—gout," Sir Leicester was going to say "indisposition," and would have said it to anybody else, but Mr. Bucket palpably knows all about it,—"and recent circumstances have brought it on."

As he takes his seat with some difficulty, and with an air of pain, Mr. Bucket draws a little nearer, standing with one of his large hands on the library-table.

"I am not aware, Officer," Sir Leicester observes, raising his eyes to his face, "whether you wish us to be alone, but that is entirely as you please. If you do, well and good. If not, Miss Dedlock would be interested—"

"Why, Sir Leicester Dedlock, Baronet," returns Mr. Bucket, with his head persuasively on one side, and his forefinger pendant at one ear like an earring, "we can't be too private, just at present. You will presently see that we can't be too private. A lady, under the circumstances, and especially in Miss Dedlock's elevated station of society, can't but be agreeable to me, but speaking without a view to myself, I will take the liberty of assuring you that I know we can't be too private."

"That is enough."

"So much so, Sir Leicester Dedlock, Baronet," Mr. Bucket resumes, "that I was on the point of asking your permission to turn the key in the door."

"By all means." Mr. Bucket skilfully and softly takes the precaution.

"Sir Leicester Dedlock, Baronet, I mentioned yesterday evening that I wanted but a very little to complete this case. I have now completed it, and collected proof against the person who did this crime."

"Against the soldier?"

"No, Sir Leicester Dedlock, not the soldier."

Sir Leicester looks astounded, and inquires, "Is the man in custody?" Mr. Bucket tells him, after a pause, "It was a woman."

Sir Leicester leans back in his chair, and breathlessly ejaculates, "Good heaven!"

"Now, Sir Leicester Dedlock, Baronet," Mr. Bucket begins, standing over him with one hand spread out on the library-table and the forefinger of the other in impressive use, "it's my duty to prepare you for a train of circumstances that may, and I go so far as to say that will, give you a shock. But Sir Leicester Dedlock, Baronet, you are a gentleman, and I know what a gentleman is, and what a gentleman is capable of. A gentleman can bear a shock, when it must come, boldly and steadily. A gentleman can make up his mind to stand up against almost any blow. Why, take yourself, Sir Leicester Dedlock, Baronet. If there's a blow to be inflicted on you, you naturally think of your family. You ask yourself, how would all them ancestors of yours have borne that blow, you remember scores of them that would have borne it well, and you bear it well on their accounts, and to maintain the family credit. That's the way you argue, and that's the way you act, Sir Leicester Dedlock, Baronet."

Sir Leicester, leaning back in his chair and grasping the elbows, sits looking at him with a stony face.

"Now, Sir Leicester Dedlock," proceeds Mr. Bucket, "thus preparing you, let me beg of you not to trouble your mind, for a moment, as to anything having come to *my* knowledge. I know so much about so many characters, high and low, that a piece of information more or less don't signify a straw. I don't suppose there's a move on the board that would surprise *me;* and as to this or that move having taken place, why my knowing it is no odds at all, any possible move whatever (provided it's in a wrong direction) being a probable move according to my experience. Therefore what I say to you, Sir Leicester Dedlock, Baronet, is, don't you go and let yourself be put out of the way because of my knowing anything of your family affairs."

"I thank you for your preparation," returns Sir Leicester, after a silence, without moving hand, foot, or feature, "which I hope is not necessary, though I give it credit for being well intended. Be so good as to go on. Also to take a seat, if you have no objection."

None at all. Mr. Bucket brings a chair, "Now, Sir Leicester Dedlock, Baronet, with this short preface I come to the point, Lady Dedlock—" Sir Leicester raises himself in his seat, and stares at him fiercely. Mr. Bucket brings his finger into play as an emollient. "Lady Dedlock, you see she's universally admired. That's what her ladyship is, she's universally admired," says Mr. Bucket.

"I would greatly prefer, officer," Sir Leicester returns stiffly, "my lady's name being entirely omitted from this discussion."

"So would I, Sir Leicester Dedlock, Baronet, but—it's impossible."

"Impossible?"

Mr. Bucket shakes his relentless head. "Sir Leicester Dedlock, Baronet, it's altogether impossible. What I have got to say is about her ladyship. She is the pivot it all turns on."

"Officer," retorts Sir Leicester, with a fiery eye and a quivering lip, "you know your duty. Do your duty, but be careful not to overstep it. I would not suffer it. I would not endure it. You bring my lady's name into this communication, upon your responsibility—upon your responsibility. My lady's name is not a name for common persons to trifle with!"

"Sir Leicester Dedlock, Baronet, I say what I must say, and no more."

"I hope it may prove so. Very well. Go on. Go on, sir!"

Glancing at the angry eyes which now avoid him, and at the angry figure trembling from head to foot yet striving to be still, Mr. Bucket feels his way with his forefinger, and in a low voice proceeds:

"Sir Leicester Dedlock, Baronet, it becomes my duty to tell you that the deceased Mr. Tulkinghorn long entertained mistrusts and suspicions of Lady Dedlock."

"If he had dared to breathe them to me, sir—which he never did— I would have killed him myself!" exclaims Sir Leicester, striking his hand upon the table. But in the very heat and fury of the act he stops, fixed by the knowing eyes of Mr. Bucket, who, with mingled confidence and patience, shakes his head.

"Sir Leicester Dedlock, the deceased Mr. Tulkinghorn was deep and close, and what he fully had in his mind in the very beginning I can't quite take upon myself to say. But I know from his lips that he long ago suspected Lady Dedlock of having discovered, through the sight of some handwriting—in this very house, and when you yourself, Sir Leicester Dedlock, were present—the existence, in great poverty, of a certain person who had been her lover before you courted her, and who ought to have been her husband." Mr. Bucket stops, and deliberately repeats, "ought to have been her husband, not a doubt about it. I know from his lips that when that person soon afterwards died, he suspected Lady Dedlock of visiting his wretched lodging, and his wretched grave, alone and in secret. I know from my own inquiries, and through my eyes and ears, that Lady Dedlock did make such visit, in the dress of her own maid, for the deceased Mr. Tulkinghorn employed me to reckon up her ladyship—if you'll excuse my making use of the term we commonly employ—and I reckoned her up, so far, completely. I confronted the maid, in the chambers in Lincoln's Inn Fields, with a witness who had been Lady Dedlock's guide, and there couldn't be the shadow of a doubt that she had worn the young woman's dress, unknown to her. Sir Leicester Dedlock, Baronet, I did endeavour to pave the way a little towards these unpleasant disclosures yesterday by saying that very strange things happened even in high families sometimes. All this, and more, has happened in your own family, and to and through your own lady. It's my belief that the deceased Mr. Tulkinghorn followed up these inquiries to the hour of his death, and that he and Lady Dedlock even had bad blood between them upon the matter, that very night. Now only you put that to Lady Dedlock, Sir Leicester Dedlock, Baronet, and ask her ladyship whether, even after he had left here, she didn't go down to his chambers with the intention of saying something further to him, dressed in a loose black mantle with a deep fringe to it."

Sir Leicester sits like a statue, gazing at the cruel finger that is probing the life-blood of his heart.

"You put that to her ladyship, Sir Leicester Dedlock, Baronet, from me, Inspector Bucket of the Detective. And if her ladyship makes any difficulty about admitting of it, you tell her that it's no use, that Inspector Bucket knows it, and knows that she passed the soldier as you call him (though he's not in the Army now), and knows that she knows she passed him, on the staircase. Now, Sir Leicester Dedlock, Baronet, why do I relate all this?"

Sir Leicester, who has covered his face with his hands, uttering a single groan, requests him to pause for a moment. By and by he takes his hands away, and so preserves his dignity and outward calmness, though there is no more colour in his face than in his white hair, that Mr. Bucket is a little awed by him. Something frozen and fixed is upon his manner, over and above its usual shell of haughtiness, and Mr. Bucket soon detects an unusual slowness in his speech, with now and then a curious trouble in beginning, which occasions him to utter inarticulate sounds. With such sounds he now breaks silence, soon, however, controlling himself to say, that he does not comprehend why a gentleman so faithful and zealous as the late Mr. Tulkinghorn should have communicated to him nothing of this painful, this distressing, this unlooked-for, this overwhelming, this incredible intelligence.

"Again, Sir Leicester Dedlock, Baronet," returns Mr. Bucket, "put it to her ladyship to clear that up. Put it to her ladyship, if you think it right, from Inspector Bucket of the Detective. You'll find, or I'm much mistaken, that the deceased Mr. Tulkinghorn had the intention of communicating the whole to you as soon as he considered it ripe, and further, that he had given her ladyship so to understand. Why, he might have been going to reveal it the very morning when I examined the body!"

At this juncture, a considerable noise of voices is heard in the hall. Mr. Bucket, after listening, goes to the library-door, softly unlocks and opens it, and listens again. Then he draws in his head, and whispers, hurriedly, but composedly:

"Sir Leicester Dedlock, Baronet, this unfortunate family affair has taken air, as I expected it might, the deceased Mr. Tulkinghorn being cut down so sudden. The chance to hush it is to let in these people now in a wrangle with your footmen. Would you mind sitting quiet— on the family account—while I reckon 'em up? And would you just throw in a nod when I seem to ask you for it?"

Sir Leicester indistinctly answers, "Officer. The best you can, the best you can!" and Mr. Bucket, with a nod and a sagacious crook of the forefinger, slips down into the hall, where the voices quickly die away. He is not long in returning a few paces ahead of Mercury and a brother deity, who bear between them a chair in which is an incapable old man. Another man and two women come behind. Directing the pitching of the chair in an affable and easy manner, Mr. Bucket dismisses the Mercuries, and locks the door again. Sir Leicester looks on at this invasion of the sacred precincts with an icy stare.

"Now perhaps you may know me, ladies and gentlemen," says Mr. Bucket, in a confidential voice. "I am Inspector Bucket of the Detective, I am, and this," producing the tip of his convenient little staff from his breast-pocket, "is my authority. Now you wanted to see Sir Leicester Dedlock, Baronet. Well! You do see him, and, mind you, it ain't every one as is admitted to that honour. Your name, old gentleman, is Smallweed, that's what your name is, I know it well. This other gentleman is in the preaching line, I think?"

"Name of Chadband," Mr. Smallweed puts in.

"Once had a friend and brother sergeant of the same name," says Mr. Bucket, offering his hand, "and consequently feel a liking for it. Mrs. Chadband, no doubt?"

"And Mrs. Snagsby," Mr. Smallweed introduces.

"Husband a law-stationer, and a friend of my own," says Mr. Bucket. "Love him like a brother!—Now, what's up?"

"Do you mean what business have we come upon?" Mr. Smallweed asks, a little dashed by the suddenness of this turn.

"Ah! You know what I mean. Let us hear what it's all about in the presence of Sir Leicester Dedlock, Baronet. Come."

"I was the client and friend of Mr. Tulkinghorn," pipes Grandfather

Smallweed, "I did business with him. I was useful to him, and he was useful to me. Krook, dead and gone, was my brother-in-law. He was own brother to a brimstone magpie—leastways, Mrs. Smallweed. I come into Krook's property. I examined all his papers and all his effects. They was all dug out under my eyes. There was a bundle of letters belonging to a dead and gone lodger, as was hid away at the back of the shelf in the side of Lady Jane's bed—his cat's bed. He hid all manner of things away, everywheres. Mr. Tulkinghorn wanted 'em and got 'em, but I looked 'em over first. I'm a man of business, and I took a squint at 'em. They was letters from the lodger's sweetheart, and she signed Honoria. Dear me, that's not a common name, Honoria, is it? There's no lady in this house that signs Honoria, is there? Oh no, I don't think so! Oh no, I don't think so! And not in the same hand, perhaps? Oh no, I don't think so!"

Here Mr. Smallweed, seized with a fit of coughing in the midst of his triumph, breaks off to ejaculate, "Oh dear me! Oh, Lord! I'm shaken all to pieces!"

"Now when you're ready," says Mr. Bucket, after awaiting his recovery, "to come to anything that concerns Sir Leicester Dedlock, Baronet, here the gentleman sits, you know."

"Haven't I come to it, Mr. Bucket?" cries Grandfather Smallweed. "Isn't the gentleman concerned yet? Not with Captain Hawdon, and his ever affectionate Honoria, and their child into the bargain? Come then, I want to know where those letters are. That concerns me, if it don't concern Sir Leicester Dedlock. I will know where they are. I handed 'em over to my friend and solicitor, Mr. Tulkinghorn, not to anybody else."

"Why, he paid you for them, you know, and handsome, too," says Mr. Bucket.

"I don't care for that. I want to know who's got 'em. And I tell you what we want—what we all here want, Mr. Bucket. We want more painstaking and search-making into this murder. We know where the interest and the motive was, and you have not done enough. If George the vagabond dragoon had any hand in it, he was only an accomplice, and was set on. You know what I mean as well as any man."

"Now I tell you what," says Mr. Bucket, instantaneously altering his manner, coming close to him, "I am damned if I am a-going to have my case spoilt, or interfered with, or anticipated by so much as half a second of time, by any human being in creation. You want more painstaking and search-making? You do? Do you see this hand, and do you think that I don't know the right time to stretch it out and put it on the arm that fired that shot?"

Such is the dread power of the man, and so terribly evident it is

that he makes no idle boast, that Mr. Smallweed begins to apologize.
Mr. Bucket, dismissing his sudden anger, checks him.

"The advice I give you is, Don't you trouble your head about the
murder. That's my affair. You keep half an eye on the newspapers,
and I shouldn't wonder if you was to read something about it before
long, if you look sharp. I know my business, and that's all I've got to
say to you on that subject. Now about those letters. You want to know
who's got 'em. I don't mind telling you. *I* have got 'em. Is that the
packet?" Mr. Smallweed looks, with greedy eyes, at the little bundle
Mr. Bucket produces from a mysterious part of his coat, and identifies
it as the same. "What have you got to say next?" asks Mr. Bucket. "Now
don't open your mouth too wide, because you don't look handsome
when you do it."

"I want five hundred pound."

"No you don't, you mean fifty," says Mr. Bucket, humorously.

It appears, however, that Mr. Smallweed means five hundred.

"I am deputed by Sir Leicester Dedlock, Baronet, to consider (without admitting or promising anything) this bit of business," says Mr.
Bucket,—Sir Leicester mechanically bows his head,—"and you ask me
to consider a proposal of five hundred pounds. Why, it's an unreasonable proposal! Two-fifty would be bad enough, but better than that.
Hadn't you better say two fifty?" Mr. Smallweed is quite clear that he
had better not. "Then," says Mr. Bucket, "let's hear Mr. Chadband.
Lord! Many a time I've heard my old fellow-sergeant of that name,
and a moderate man he was in all respects as ever I come across!"

Thus invited, Mr. Chadband steps forth, and after a little sleek
smiling and a little oil-grinding with the palms of his hands, delivers
himself as follows:

"My friends, we are now—Rachael my wife, and I—in the mansions
of the rich and great. Why are we now in the mansions of the rich and
great, my friends? Is it because we are invited? Because we are bidden
to feast with them, because we are bidden to rejoice with them, because we are bidden to play the lute with them, because we are bidden
to dance with them? No. Then why are we here, my friends? Air we
in possession of a sinful secret, and doe we require corn, and wine,
and oil—or, what is much the same thing, money—for the keeping
thereof? Probably so, my friends."

"You're a man of business, you are," returns Mr. Bucket, very
attentive, "and consequently you're going on to mention what the
nature of your secret is. You are right. You couldn't do better."

"Let us then, my brother, in a spirit of love," says Mr. Chadband,
with a cunning eye, "proceed untoe it. Rachael my wife, advance!"

Mrs. Chadband, more than ready, so advances as to jostle her husband into the background, and confronts Mr. Bucket with a hard frowning smile.

"Since you want to know what we know," says she, "I'll tell you. I helped to bring up Miss Hawdon, her ladyship's daughter. I was in the service of her ladyship's sister, who was very sensitive to the disgrace her ladyship brought upon her, and gave out, even to her ladyship, that the child was dead—she *was* very nearly so—when she was born. But she's alive, and I know her." With these words, and a laugh, and laying a bitter stress on the word "ladyship," Mrs. Chadband folds her arms and looks implacably at Mr. Bucket.

"My friend the law-stationer's good lady, over there," says Mr. Bucket, luring Mrs. Snagsby forward with the finger. "What may *your* game be, ma'am?"

Mrs. Snagsby is at first prevented by tears and lamentations, from stating the nature of her game, but by degrees it confusedly comes to light that she is a woman overwhelmed with injuries and wrongs, whom Mr. Snagsby has habitually deceived, abandoned, and sought to keep in darkness, and whose chief comfort under her afflictions has been the sympathy of the late Mr. Tulkinghorn. She has of late habitually carried to him all her woes. Everybody, it appears, the present company excepted, has plotted against Mrs. Snagsby's peace. There is Mr. Guppy, there is Mr. Weevle, friend of Mr. Guppy, there was Krook, deceased, there was Nimrod, deceased, and there was Jo, deceased; and they were "all in it." In what, Mrs. Snagsby does not with particularity express, but she knows that Jo was Mr. Snagsby's son "as well as if a trumpet had spoken it," and she followed Mr. Snagsby when he went on his last visit to the boy, and if he was not his son, why did he go? Thus did it come to pass that she brought the Chadbands and Mr. Tulkinghorn together, and conferred with Mr. Tulkinghorn on the change in Mr. Guppy, and helped to turn up the circumstances in which the present company are interested, being still, and ever, on the great high road that is to terminate in Mr. Snagsby's full exposure and a matrimonial separation. All this Mrs. Snagsby, as an injured woman, and the friend of Mrs. Chadband, and the follower of Mr. Chadband, and the mourner of the late Mr. Tulkinghorn, is here to certify under the seal of confidence, with every possible confusion and involvement possible and impossible—having no pecuniary motive whatever, no scheme or project but the one mentioned, and bringing here, and taking everywhere, her own atmosphere of jealousy.

"Very good," says Mr. Bucket. "Now I understand you, you know, and, being deputed by Sir Leicester Dedlock, Baronet, to look into this little matter"—again Sir Leicester mechanically bows in confirmation of the statement—"can give it my fair and full attention. Now I won't allude to conspiring to extort money, or anything of that sort, because we are men and women of the world here, and our object is to make things pleasant. But I tell you what I *do* wonder at—I am surprised that you should think of making a noise below in the hall. It was so opposed to your interests. That's what I look at."

"We wanted to get in," pleads Mr. Smallweed.

"Why of course you wanted to get in," Mr. Bucket asserts with cheerfulness, "but for a old gentleman at your time of life—what I call truly venerable, mind you!—with his wits sharpened, as I have no doubt they are, by the loss of the use of his limbs—not to consider that if he don't keep such a business as the present as close as possible it can't be worth a mag to him is so curious! You see your temper got the better of you, that's where you lost ground," says Mr. Bucket in an argumentative and friendly way.

"I only said I wouldn't go without one of the servants came up to Sir Leicester Dedlock," returns Mr. Smallweed.

"That's it! That's where your temper got the better of you. Now you keep it under another time, and you'll make money by it. Shall I ring for them to carry you down?"

"When are we to hear more of this?" Mrs. Chadband sternly demands.

"Bless your heart for a true woman! Always curious, your delightful sex is!" replies Mr. Bucket, with gallantry. "I shall have the pleasure of giving you a call tomorrow or next day—not forgetting Mr. Smallweed and his proposal of two-fifty."

"Five hundred!" exclaims Mr. Smallweed.

"All right! Nominally five hundred." Mr. Bucket has his hand on the bell-rope. "*Shall* I wish you good-day for the present, on the part of myself and the gentleman of the house?" he asks in an insinuating tone.

Nobody having the hardihood to object to his doing so, he does it, and the party retire as they came up. Mr. Bucket follows them to the door, and returning, says with an air of serious business:

"Sir Leicester Dedlock, Baronet, it's for you to consider whether or not to buy this up. I should recommend, on the whole, it's being bought up myself, and I think it may be bought pretty cheap. You see, that little pickled cowcumber of a Mrs. Snagsby has been used by all sides of the speculation, and has done a deal more harm in bringing odds and ends together than if she had meant it. Mr. Tulkinghorn, deceased, he held all these horses in his hand, and could have drove 'em his own way, I haven't a doubt; but he was fetched off the box headforemost, and now they have got their legs over the traces, and are all dragging and pulling their own ways. So it is, and such is life. The cat's away, and the mice they play. Now with regard to the party to be apprehended."

Sir Leicester seems to wake, though his eyes have been wide open, and he looks intently at Mr. Bucket as Mr. Bucket refers to his watch.

"The party to be apprehended is now in this house," proceeds Mr. Bucket, putting up his watch with a steady hand, and with rising spirits, "and I'm about to take her into custody in your presence. Sir Leicester Dedlock, Baronet, don't say a word, nor yet stir. There'll be no noise, and no disturbance at all. I'll come back in the course of the evening, if agreeable to you, and endeavour to meet your wishes respecting this unfortunate family matter, and the nobbiest way of keeping it quiet. Now, Sir Leicester Dedlock, Baronet, don't you be nervous on account of the apprehension at present coming off. You shall see the whole case clear, from first to last."

Mr. Bucket rings, goes to the door, briefly whispers Mercury, shuts the door, and stands behind it with his arms folded. After a suspense of a minute or two, the door slowly opens, and a Frenchwoman enters. Mademoiselle Hortense. The moment she is in the room, Mr. Bucket claps the door to, and puts his back against it. The suddenness of the noise occasions her to turn, and then for the first time she sees Sir Leicester Dedlock in his chair.

"I ask you pardon," she mutters hurriedly. "They tell me there was no one here."

Her step towards the door brings her front to front with Mr. Bucket. Suddenly a spasm shoots across her face, and she turns deadly pale.

"This is my lodger, Sir Leicester Dedlock," says Mr. Bucket, nodding at her. "This foreign young woman has been my lodger for some weeks back."

"What do Sir Leicester care for that, you think, my angel?" returns Mademoiselle, in a jocular strain.

"Why, my angel," returns Mr. Bucket, "we shall see."

Mademoiselle Hortense eyes him with a scowl upon her tight face, which gradually changes into a smile of scorn. "You are very mysterieuse. Are you drunk?"

"Tolerable sober, my angel," returns Mr. Bucket.

"I come from arriving at this so detestable house with your wife. Your wife have left me, since some minutes. They tell me downstairs that your wife is here. I come here, and your wife is not here. What is the intention of this fool's play, say, then?" Mademoiselle demands, with her arms composedly crossed, but with something in her dark cheek beating like a clock. Mr. Bucket merely shakes the finger at her. "Ah my God, you are an unhappy idiot!" cries Mademoiselle, "Leave me to pass downstairs, great pig." With a stamp of her foot, and a menace.

"Now, mademoiselle," says Mr. Bucket, in a cool, determined way, "you go and sit down upon that sofy."

"I will not sit down upon nothing," she replies.

"Now, mademoiselle," repeats Mr. Bucket, making no demonstration, except with the finger; "you sit down upon that sofy."

"Why?"

"Because I take you into custody on a charge of murder. Now I want to be polite to one of your sex and a foreigner, if I can. If I can't, I must be rough, and there's rougher ones outside. What I am to be depends on you. So I recommend you, as a friend, afore another half a blessed moment has passed over your head, to go and sit down upon that sofy."

Mademoiselle complies, saying in a concentrated voice, while that something in her cheek beats fast and hard, "You are a devil."

"Now, you see," Mr. Bucket proceeds approvingly, "you're comfortable, and conducting yourself as I should expect a foreign young woman of your sense to do. So I'll give you a piece of advice, and it's this, Don't you talk too much. You're not expected to say anything here, and you can't keep too quiet a tongue in your head. In short, the less you parlay, the better, you know." Mr. Bucket is very complacent over this French explanation.

Mademoiselle, with that tigerish expansion of the mouth, and her black eyes darting fire upon him, sits upright on the sofa in a rigid state, muttering, "O you Bucket, you are a devil!"

"Now, Sir Leicester Dedlock, Baronet," says Mr. Bucket, and from this time forth the finger never rests, "this young woman, my lodger, was her ladyship's maid at the time I have mentioned to you, and this young woman, besides being extraordinary vehement and passionate against her ladyship after being discharged—"

"Lie!" cries Mademoiselle. "I discharge myself!"

"Now why don't you take my advice?" returns Mr. Bucket in an impressive, almost in an imploring tone. "I'm surprised at the indiscreetness you commit. You'll say something that'll be used against you, you know. Never you mind what I say till it's given in evidence. It is not addressed to you."

"Discharge, too," cries Mademoiselle, furiously, "by her ladyship! Eh, my faith, a pretty ladyship! Why, I r-r-r-ruin my character by remaining with a ladyship so infame!"

"Upon my soul, I wonder at you!" Mr. Bucket remonstrates. "I thought the French were a polite nation, I did, really. Yet to hear a female going on like that before Sir Leicester Dedlock, Baronet!"

"He is a poor abused!" cries Mademoiselle. "I spit upon his house, upon his name, upon his imbecility," all of which she makes the carpet represent. "Oh, that he is a great man! Oh yes, superb! Oh heaven! Bah!"

"Well, Sir Leicester Dedlock," proceeds Mr. Bucket, "this intemperate foreigner also angrily took it into her head that she had established a claim upon Mr. Tulkinghorn, deceased, by attending, on the occasion I told you of, at his chambers, though she was liberally paid for her time and trouble."

"Lie!" cries Mademoiselle. "I ref-use his money altogezzer."

("If you *will* parlay, you know," says Mr. Bucket, parenthetically, "you must take the consequences.") "Now whether she became my lodger, Sir Leicester Dedlock, with any deliberate intention then of doing this deed and blinding me, I give no opinion on; but she lived in my house in that capacity at the time that she was hovering about the chambers of the deceased Mr. Tulkinghorn with a view to wrangle, and likewise persecuting and half frightening the life out of an unfortunate stationer."

"Lie!" cries Mademoiselle. "All lie!"

"The murder was committed, Sir Leicester Dedlock, Baronet, and you know under what circumstances. Now I beg of you to follow me close with your attention for a minute or two. I was sent for, and the case was entrusted to me. I examined the place, and the body, and the papers, and everything. From information I received (from a clerk in the same house) I took George into custody, as having been seen hanging about there on the night and at very nigh the time of the murder; also, as having been overheard in high words with the deceased on former occasions—even threatening him, as the witness made out. If you ask me, Sir Leicester Dedlock, whether from the first I believed George to be the murderer, I tell you candidly no, but he might be, notwithstanding, and there was enough against him to make it my duty to take him, and get him kept under remand. Now, observe!"

As Mr. Bucket bends forward in some excitement—for him—and inaugurates what he is going to say with one ghostly beat of his forefinger in the air, Mademoiselle Hortense fixes her black eyes upon him with a dark frown.

"I went home, Sir Leicester Dedlock, Baronet, at night, and found this young woman having supper with my wife, Mrs. Bucket. She had made a mighty show of being fond of Mrs. Bucket from her first offering herself as our lodger, but that night she made more than ever—in fact, overdid it. Likewise she overdid her respect, and all that, for the lamented memory of the deceased Mr. Tulkinghorn. By the living Lord it flashed upon me, as I sat opposite to her at the table and saw her with a knife in her hand, that she had done it!"

Mademoiselle is hardly audible in straining through her teeth and lips the words "You are a devil."

"Now where," pursues Mr. Bucket, "had she been on the night of the murder? She had been to the theayter. (She really was there, I have since found, both before the deed and after it.) I knew I had an artful customer to deal with, and that proof would be very difficult; and I laid a trap for her—such a trap as I never laid yet, and such a venture as I never made yet. I worked it out in my mind while I was talking to her at supper. When I went upstairs to bed, our house being small and this young woman's ears sharp, I stuffed the sheet into Mrs. Bucket's mouth that she shouldn't say a word of surprise, and told her all about it.—My dear, don't you give your mind to that again, or I shall link your feet together at the ankles." Mr. Bucket, breaking off, has made a noiseless descent upon Mademoiselle.

"What is the matter with you now?" she asks him.

"Don't you think any more," returns Mr. Bucket, with admonitory finger, "of throwing yourself out of window. That's what's the matter with me. Come! Just take my arm. You needn't get up, I'll sit down by you. Now take my arm, will you? I'm a married man, you know. Just take my arm."

Vainly endeavouring to moisten those dry lips, with a painful sound she struggles with herself and complies.

"Now we're all right again. Sir Leicester Dedlock, Baronet, this case could never have been the case it is but for Mrs. Bucket, who is a woman in fifty thousand—in a hundred and fifty thousand! To throw this young woman off her guard, I have never set foot in our house since, though I've communicated with Mrs. Bucket, in the baker's loaves and in the milk, as often as required. My whispered words to Mrs. Bucket, when she had the sheet in her mouth, were, 'My dear, can you throw her off continually with natural accounts of my suspicions against George, and this, and that, and t'other? Can you do without rest, and keep watch upon her, night and day? Can you undertake to say, 'She shall do nothing without my knowledge, she shall be my prisoner without suspecting it, she shall no more escape from me than from death, and her life shall be my life till I have got her, if she did this murder?' Mrs. Bucket says to me, as well as she could speak, on account of the sheet, 'Bucket, I can!' And she has acted up to it glorious!"

"Lies!" Mademoiselle interposes. "All lies, my friend!"

"Sir Leicester Dedlock, Baronet, how did my calculations come out under these circumstances? I was right. What does she try to do? Don't let it give you a turn. To throw the murder on her ladyship."

Sir Leicester rises from his chair, and staggers down again.

"And she got encouragement in it from hearing that I was always here, which was done a-purpose. Now, open that pocket-book of mine, Sir Leicester Dedlock, if I may take the liberty of throwing it towards you, and look at the letters sent to me, each with the two words 'Lady Dedlock,' in it. Open the one directed to yourself, which I stopped this very morning, and read the three words 'Lady Dedlock, Murderess,' in it. These letters have been falling about like a shower of lady-birds. What do you say now to Mrs. Bucket, from her spy-place, having seen them all written by this young woman? What do you say to Mrs. Bucket having watched the posting of 'em every one by this young woman, Sir Leicester Dedlock, Baronet?"

Two things are especially observable as Mr. Bucket proceeds to a conclusion. First, that he seems imperceptibly to establish a dreadful right of property in Mademoiselle. Secondly, that the very atmosphere she breathes seems to narrow and contract about her, as if a close net, or a pall, were being drawn nearer and yet nearer around her breathless figure.

"There is no doubt that her ladyship was on the spot at the eventful period," says Mr. Bucket, "and my foreign friend here saw her, I believe. Her ladyship and George and my foreign friend were all pretty close on one another's heels. But that don't signify any more, so I'll not go into it. I found the wadding of the pistol with which the deceased Mr. Tulkinghorn was shot. It was a bit of the printed description of your house at Chesney Wold. Not much in that, you'll say, Sir Leicester Dedlock, Baronet. No. But when my foreign friend here is so thoroughly off her guard as to think it a safe time to tear up the rest of that leaf, and when Mrs. Bucket puts the pieces together and finds the wadding wanting, it begins to look like Queer Street."

"These are very long lies," Mademoiselle interposes. "Is it that you have almost all finished, or are you speaking always?"

"Sir Leicester Dedlock, Baronet," proceeds Mr. Bucket, who delights in a full title, and does violence to himself when he dispenses with any fragment of it, "the last point in the case, which I am now going to mention, shows the necessity of patience in our business. I watched this young woman yesterday, without her knowledge, when she was looking at the funeral, in company with my wife, who planned to take her there; and I had so much to convict her, and I saw such an expression in her face, and my mind so rose against her malice towards her ladyship, and the time was altogether such a time for bringing down what you may call retribution upon her, that if I had been a younger hand with less experience, I should have taken her, certain. Equally, last night, when her ladyship come home, looking—why, Lord! a man might almost say like Venus rising from the ocean—it was so unpleasant and inconsistent to think of her being charged with a murder of which she was innocent that I felt quite to want to put an end to the job. What should I have lost? Sir Leicester Dedlock, Baronet, I should have lost the weapon. My prisoner here proposed to Mrs. Bucket, after the departure of the funeral, that they should go, per bus, a little ways into the country, and take tea at a very decent house of entertainment. Now near that house of entertainment there's a piece of water. At tea, my prisoner got up to fetch her pocket-handkercher from the bedroom where the bonnets was; she was rather a long time gone, and came back a little out of wind. As soon as they came home this was reported to me by Mrs. Bucket, along with her observations and suspicions. I had the piece of water dragged by moonlight, in presence of a couple of our men, and the pocket-pistol was brought up before it had been there half a dozen hours. Now, my dear, put your arm a little further through mine, and hold it steady and I shan't hurt you!"

In a trice Mr. Bucket snaps a handcuff on her wrist. "That's one," says Mr. Bucket. "Now the other, darling. Two, and all told!" He rises, she rises too.

"Let me put your shawl tidy. I've been lady's maid to a good many before now. Anything wanting to the bonnet? There's a cab at the door."

Mademoiselle Hortense, casting an indignant eye at the glass, shakes herself perfectly neat in one shake and looks, to do her justice, uncommonly genteel.

"Listen then, my angel," says she, after several sarcastic nods. "You are very spiritual. But can you restore him back to life?"

Mr. Bucket answers "Not exactly."

"That is droll. Listen yet one time. You are very spiritual. Can you make a honourable lady of Her?"

"Don't be so malicious," says Mr. Bucket.

"Or a haughty gentleman of *Him?*" cries Mademoiselle, referring to Sir Leicester with ineffable disdain. "Eh! Oh, then regard him! The poor infant! Ha! ha! ha!"

"Come, come, why this is worse parlaying than the other," says Mr. Bucket. "Come along!"

"You cannot do these things? Then you can do as you please with me. It is but the death, it is all the same. Let us go, my angel. Adieu, you old man, grey. I pity you, and I des-pise you!"

With these last words she snaps her teeth together as if her mouth closed with a spring. It is impossible to describe how Mr. Bucket gets her out, but he accomplishes that feat in a manner so peculiar to himself, enfolding and pervading her like a cloud, and hovering away with her as if he were a homely Jupiter and she the object of his affections.

Sir Leicester, left alone, remains in the same attitude as though he were still listening, and his attention were still occupied. At length he gazes round the empty room, and finding it deserted, rises unsteadily to his feet, pushes back his chair, and walks a few steps, supporting himself by the table. Then he stops, and, with more of those inarticulate sounds, lifts up his eyes and seems to stare at something.

Heaven knows what he sees. The green, green woods of Chesney Wold, the noble house, the pictures of his forefathers, strangers defacing

them, thousands of fingers pointing at him, thousands of faces sneering at him. But if such shadows flit before him to his bewilderment, there is one other shadow which he can name with something like distinctness even yet, and to which alone he addresses his tearing of his white hair, and his extended arms.

It is she in association with whom, saving that she has been for years a main fibre of the root of his dignity and pride, he has never had a selfish thought. It is she whom he has loved, admired, honoured, and set up for the world to respect. It is she who, at the core of all the constrained formalities and conventionalities of his life, has been a stock of living tenderness and love, susceptible as nothing else is of being struck with the agony he feels. He sees her almost to the exclusion of himself, and cannot bear to look upon her cast down from the high place she has graced so well.

And, even to the point of his sinking on the ground, oblivious of his suffering, he can yet pronounce her name with something like distinctness in the midst of those intrusive sounds, and in a tone of mourning and compassion rather than reproach.

## CHAPTER 55

*Flight*

INSPECTOR BUCKET of the Detective has not yet struck his great blow, as just now chronicled, but is yet refreshing himself with sleep preparatory to his field-day, when, through the night and along the freezing wintry roads, a chaise and pair comes out of Lincolnshire, making its way towards London.

Mrs. Rouncewell, so many years housekeeper at Chesney Wold, sits within the chaise, and by her side sits Mrs. Bagnet with her grey cloak and umbrella. The old lady cannot make enough of the old girl. She sits, in her stately manner, holding her hand and, regardless of its roughness, puts it often to her lips. "You are a mother, my dear soul," says she many times, "and you found out my George's mother!"

"Why, George," returns Mrs. Bagnet, "was always free with me, ma'am, and when he said at our house to my Woolwich that of all the things my Woolwich could have to think of when he grew to be a man, the comfortablest would be that he had never brought a sorrowful line into his mother's face, or turned a hair of her head grey, then I felt sure, from his way, that something fresh had brought his own mother into his mind. I had often known him say to me, in past times, that he had behaved bad to her."

"Never, my dear!" returns Mrs. Rouncewell, bursting into tears. "My blessing on him, never! He was always fond of me, and loving to me, was my George! But he had a bold spirit, and he ran a little wild, and went for a soldier. And I know he waited at first in letting us know about himself till he should rise to be an officer, and when he didn't rise, I know he considered himself beneath us, and wouldn't be a disgrace to us. For he had a lion heart, had my George, always from a baby!"

Mrs. Bagnet, with the instinctive skill of a good warm heart, leaves the old housekeeper to her emotions for a little while—not without passing the back of her hand across her own motherly eyes—and presently chirps up in her cheery manner:

"So I says to George when I goes to call him in to tea, 'What ails you this afternoon, George, for gracious sake? I have seen all sorts, and I have seen you pretty often in season and out of season, abroad and at home, and I never see you so melancholy penitent.' 'Why, Mrs. Bagnet,' says George, 'it's because I *am* melancholy and penitent both this afternoon that you see me so.' 'What have you done, old fellow?' I says. 'Why, Mrs. Bagnet,' says George, shaking his head, 'what I have done has been done this many a long year, and is best not tried to be undone now. If I ever get to Heaven, it won't be for being a good son to a widowed mother; I say no more.' Then George tells me that he has seen by chance, at the lawyer's office, a fine old lady that has brought his mother plain before him, and he runs on about that old lady till he quite forgets himself, and paints her picture to me as she used to be, years upon years back. So I says to George when he has done, who is this old lady he has seen? And George tells me it's Mrs. Rouncewell, housekeeper for more than half a century to the Dedlock family down at Chesney Wold in Lincolnshire. George has frequently told me before that he's a Lincolnshire man, and I says to my old Lignum that night, 'Lignum, that's his mother for five and for-ty pound!' "

"Bless you, and thank you," says Mrs. Rouncewell. "Bless you, and thank you, my worthy soul!"

"Dear heart!" cries Mrs. Bagnet, in the most natural manner. "No thanks to me, I am sure. Thanks to yourself, ma'am, for being so ready to pay 'em! And mind once more, ma'am, what you had best do on finding George to be your own son is to make him—for your sake—have every sort of help to put himself in the right, and clear himself of a charge of which he is as innocent as you or me. It won't do to have truth and justice on his side, he must have law and lawyers," exclaims the old girl, apparently persuaded that the latter form a separate establishment, and have dissolved partnership with truth and justice for ever and a day.

"He shall have," says Mrs. Rouncewell, "all the help that can be got for him in the world, my dear. I will spend all I have, and thankfully, to procure it. Sir Leicester will do his best, the whole family will do their best. I—I know something, my dear, and will make my own appeal, as his mother parted from him all these years and finding him in a jail at last." Mrs. Bagnet wonders why Mrs. Rouncewell should murmur so distractedly, "My lady, my lady, my lady!" over and over again.

The frosty night wears away, and the dawn breaks, and the post-chaise comes rolling on through the early mist like the ghost of a chaise departed. London reached, the travellers alight, the old housekeeper in great tribulation and confusion, Mrs. Bagnet quite fresh and collected.

But when they set out for the prison where the trooper is confined, the old lady has managed to draw about her, with her lavender-coloured dress, much of the staid calmness which is its usual accompaniment. A wonderfully grave, precise, and handsome piece of old china she looks, though her heart beats fast.

Approaching the cell, they find the door opening and a warder in the act of coming out. The old girl promptly makes a sign of entreaty to him to say nothing; assenting, with a nod, he suffers them to enter as he shuts the door. So George, who is writing at his table, supposing himself to be alone, does not raise his eyes, but remains absorbed. The old housekeeper looks at him, and those wandering hands of hers are quite enough for Mrs. Bagnet's confirmation, even if she could see the mother and the son together, knowing what she knows, and doubt their relationship.

Not a rustle of the housekeeper's dress, not a gesture, not a word betrays her. She stands looking at him as he writes on, all unconscious, and only her fluttering hands give utterance to her emotions. But they are very eloquent, very, very eloquent. Mrs. Bagnet understands them. They speak of gratitude, of joy, of grief, of hope; of inextinguishable affection, cherished with no return since this stalwart man was a stripling, of a better son loved less, and this son loved so fondly and so proudly.

"George Rouncewell! O my dear child, turn and look at me!"

The trooper starts up, clasps his mother round the neck, and falls down on his knees before her. Whether in a late repentance, whether in the first association that comes back upon him, he puts his hands together as a child does when it says its prayers, and raising them towards her breast, bows down his head, and cries.

"My George, my dearest son! Always my favourite, and my favourite still, where have you been these cruel years and years? Grown such a man too, grown such a fine strong man. Grown so like what I knew he must be if it pleased God he was alive!"

She can ask, and he can answer, nothing connected for a time.

"Mother," says the trooper, when they are more composed; "forgive me first of all, for I know my need of it."

Forgive him! She does it with all her heart and soul. She always has done it. She tells him how she has had it written in her will, these many years, that he was her beloved son George. She has never believed any ill of him, never. If she had died without this happiness—and she is an old woman now, and can't look to live very long—she would have blessed him with her last breath, if she had had her senses, as her beloved son George.

"Mother, I have been an undutiful trouble to you, and I have my reward, but of late years I have had a kind of glimmering of a purpose in me, too. When I left home I didn't care much, Mother—I am afraid not a great deal—for leaving, and went away and 'listed, harum-scarum, making believe to think that I cared for nobody, no not I, and that nobody cared for me. So I wrote a line home, Mother, as you too well know, to say I had 'listed under another name, and I went abroad. Abroad, at one time I thought I would write home next year, when I might be better off; and when that year was out, I thought I would write home next year, when I might be better off; and when that year was out again, perhaps I didn't think much about it. So on, from year to year, through a service of ten years, till I began to get older, and to ask myself why should I ever write."

"I don't find any fault, child—but not to ease my mind, George? Not a word to your loving mother, who was growing older too?"

This almost overturns the trooper afresh, but he sets himself up with a great, rough, sounding clearance of his throat.

"Heaven forgive me, Mother, but I thought there would be small consolation then in hearing anything about me. There were you, respected and esteemed. There was my brother, as I read in chance north-country papers now and then, rising to be prosperous and famous. There was I, a dragoon, roving, unsettled, not self-made like him, but self-unmade—all my earlier advantages thrown away, all my little learning unlearnt, nothing picked up but what unfitted me for most things that I could think of. What business had *I* to make myself known? After letting all that time go by me, what good could come of it? The worst was past with you, Mother. I knew by that time (being a man) how you had mourned for me, and wept for me, and prayed for me; and the pain was over, or was softened down, and I was better in your mind as it was."

The old lady sorrowfully shakes her head, and taking one of his powerful hands, lays it lovingly upon her shoulder.

"No, I don't say that it was so, Mother, but that I made it out to be so. I said just now, what good could come of it? Well, my dear Mother, some good might have come of it to myself—and there was the meanness of it. You would have sought me out, you would have purchased my discharge, you would have taken me down to Chesney Wold, you would have brought me and my brother and my brother's family together, you would all have considered anxiously how to do something for me, and set me up as a respectable civilian. But how could any of you feel sure of me, when I couldn't so much as feel sure of myself? How could I look my brother's children in the face and pretend to set them an example—I, the vagabond boy who had run away from home, and been the grief and unhappiness of my mother's life? 'No, George.'

Such were my words, Mother, when I passed this in review before me: 'You have made your bed. Now lie upon it.'"

Mrs. Rouncewell, drawing up her stately form, shakes her head at the old girl with a swelling pride upon her, as much as to say, "I told you so!"

"This was the way I brought myself to think, Mother, that my best amends was to lie upon that bed I had made, and die upon it. And I should have done it (though I have been to see you more than once down at Chesney Wold, when you little thought of me) but for my old comrade's wife here, who I find has been too many for me. But I thank her for it. I thank you for it, Mrs. Bagnet, with all my heart and might."

And now the old lady impresses upon her son George, her own dear recovered boy, her joy and pride, the light of her eyes, the happy close of her life, and every fond name she can think of, that he must be governed by the best advice obtainable by money and influence; that he must yield up his case to the greatest lawyers that can be got; that he must act, in this serious plight, as he shall be advised to act, and must not be self-willed, however right, but must promise to think only of his poor old mother's anxiety and suffering until he is released, or he will break her heart.

"Mother, 'tis little enough to consent to," returns the trooper. "Tell me what I shall do and I'll make a late beginning, and do it. Mrs. Bagnet, you'll take care of my mother, I know? If you'll bring her acquainted with Mr. Jarndyce and Miss Summerson, she will find them of her way of thinking, and they will give her the best advice and assistance."

"And, George," says the old lady, "we must send with all haste for your brother. He is a sensible sound man as they tell me, and will be of great service."

"Mother," returns the trooper, "is it too soon to ask a favour?"

"Surely not, my dear."

"Then grant me this one great favour. Don't let my brother know."

"Not know what, my dear?"

"Not know of me. In fact, Mother, I can't bear it, I can't make up my mind to it. He has proved himself so different from me, and has done so much to raise himself while I've been soldiering, that I haven't brass enough in my composition to see him in this place and under this charge. How could a man like him be expected to have any pleasure in such a discovery? It's impossible. No, keep my secret from him, Mother, keep my secret from my brother, of all men."

"But not always, dear George?"

"Why, Mother, perhaps not for good and all—though I may come to ask that too—but keep it now, I do entreat you. If it's ever broke to him

516 · BLEAK HOUSE

that his rip of a brother has turned up, I could wish," says the trooper, shaking his head very doubtfully, "to break it myself, and be governed by the way in which he seems to take it."

As he evidently has a rooted feeling on this point, and as the depth of it is recognized in Mrs. Bagnet's face, his mother yields her implicit assent to what he asks. For this he thanks her kindly.

"In all other respects, my dear Mother, I'll be as tractable and obedient as you can wish; on this one alone, I stand out. So now I am ready even for the lawyers. I have been drawing up an exact account of what I knew of the deceased, and how I came to be involved in this unfortunate affair. It's entered plain and regular, like an orderly-book, not a word in it but what's wanted for the facts. I did intend to read it, straight on end, whensoever I was called upon to say anything in my defence. I hope I may be let to do it still, but I have no longer a will of my own in this case, and whatever is said or done, I give my promise not to have any."

Matters being brought to this so far satisfactory pass, and time being on the wane, Mrs. Bagnet proposes a departure. Again and again the old lady hangs upon her son's neck, and again and again the trooper holds her to his broad chest.

"Where are you going to take my mother, Mrs. Bagnet?"

"I am going to the town-house, my dear, the family house. I have some business there that must be looked to directly," Mrs. Rouncewell answers.

"Will you see my mother safe there, in a coach, Mrs. Bagnet? But of course I know you will. Why should I ask it?" Why indeed, Mrs. Bagnet expresses with the umbrella. "Take her, my old friend, and take my gratitude along with you. Kisses to Quebec and Malta, love to my godson, a hearty shake of the hand to Lignum, and this for yourself, and I wish it was ten thousand pound in gold, my dear!" So saying, the trooper puts his lips to the old girl's tanned forehead, and the door shuts upon him in his cell.

No entreaties on the part of the good old housekeeper will induce Mrs. Bagnet to retain the coach for her own conveyance home. Jumping out cheerfully at the door of the Dedlock mansion, and handing Mrs. Rouncewell up the steps, the old girl shakes hands and trudges off, arriving soon afterwards in the bosom of the Bagnet family, and falling to washing the greens as if nothing had happened.

My Lady is in that room in which she held her last conference with the murdered man, and is sitting where she sat that night, and is looking at the spot where he stood upon the hearth, studying her so leisurely, when a tap comes at the door. Who is it? Mrs. Rouncewell. What has brought Mrs. Rouncewell to town so unexpectedly?

"Trouble, my lady. Sad trouble. O my lady, may I beg a word with you?"

What new occurrence is it that makes this tranquil old woman tremble so? Far happier than her lady, as her lady has often thought, why does she falter in this manner, and look at her with such strange mistrust?

"What is the matter? Sit down and take your breath."

"O my lady, my lady. I have found my son—my youngest, who went away for a soldier so long ago. And he is in prison, charged with a murder, my lady, of which he is as innocent as—as I am. Accused of the murder of Mr. Tulkinghorn."

What does she mean by this look and this imploring gesture? Why does she come so close? What is the letter that she holds?

"Lady Dedlock, my dear lady, my good lady, my kind lady! You must have a heart to feel for me, you must have a heart to forgive me. I was in this family before you were born. I am devoted to it. But think of my dear son wrongfully accused."

"*I* do not accuse him."

"No, my lady, no. But others do, and he is in prison and in danger. O Lady Dedlock, if you can say but a word to help to clear him, say it!"

What power does she suppose is in the person she petitions to avert this unjust suspicion, if it be unjust? Her lady's handsome eyes regard her with astonishment, almost with fear.

"My lady, I came away last night from Chesney Wold to find my son in my old age, and the step upon the Ghost's Walk was so constant and so solemn that I never heard the like in all these years. Night after night, as it has fallen dark, the sound has echoed through your rooms, but last night it was awfullest. And as it fell dark last night, my lady, I got this letter."

"What letter is it?"

"Hush! Hush!" The housekeeper looks round, and answers in a frightened whisper: "My lady, I have not breathed a word of it, I don't believe what's written in it, I know it can't be true. But my son is in danger, and you must have a heart to pity me. If you know of anything that is not known to others, if you have any suspicion, if you have any clue at all, and any reason for keeping it in your own breast, O my dear lady, think of me and conquer that reason, and let it be known! I know you are not a hard lady, but you go your own way always without help, and you are not familiar with your friends; and all who admire you—and all do—as a beautiful and elegant lady, know you to be one far away from themselves, who can't be approached close. My lady, you may have some proud or angry reason for disdaining to utter something that you know; if so, pray, oh pray, think of a faithful servant whose whole life has been passed in this family which she dearly loves, and relent, and help to clear my son! My lady, my good lady, I am so humble in my place and you are by nature so high and distant that you may not think what I feel for my child; but I feel so much that I have come here to make so bold as to beg and pray you not to be scornful of us, if you can do us any right or justice at this fearful time!"

Lady Dedlock raises her, without one word until she takes the letter from her hand.

"Am I to read this?"

"When I am gone, my lady, if you please, and then remembering the most that I consider possible."

"I know of nothing I can do. I know of nothing I reserve that can affect your son. I have never accused him."

"My lady, you may pity him the more, under a false accusation, after reading the letter."

The old housekeeper leaves her with the letter in her hand. She opens the letter. Spread out upon the paper is a printed account of the discovery of the body as it lay face downward on the floor, shot through the heart, and underneath is written her own name, with the word "Murderess" attached.

It falls out of her hand. It lies where it fell when a servant stands before her announcing the young man of the name of Guppy. The words have probably been repeated several times, for they are ringing in her head before she begins to understand them.

"Let him come in!"

He comes in. Holding the letter in her hand, which she has taken from the floor, she tries to collect her thoughts. In the eyes of Mr. Guppy she is the same Lady Dedlock, holding the same prepared, proud, chilling state.

"Your ladyship may not be at first disposed to excuse this visit from one who has never been welcome to your ladyship—which he don't complain of, for he is bound to confess that there never has been any particular reason on the face of things why he should be—but I hope when I mention my motives to your ladyship, you will not find fault with me," says Mr. Guppy.

"Do so."

"Thank your ladyship. I ought first to explain to your ladyship"—Mr. Guppy sits on the edge of a chair, and puts his hat on the carpet at his feet—"that Miss Summerson, whose image, as I formerly mentioned to your ladyship, was at one period of my life imprinted on my 'art until erased by circumstances over which I had no control, communicated to me, after I had the pleasure of waiting on your ladyship last, that she particularly wished me to take no steps whatever in any manner at all relating to her. And Miss Summerson's wishes being to me a law, I consequently never expected to have the distinguished honour of waiting on your ladyship again. And yet I am here now, my object being to communicate to your ladyship, under the seal of confidence, why I am here."

He cannot do so, she tells him, too plainly or too briefly.

"Nor can I," Mr. Guppy returns with a sense of injury upon him, "too particularly request your ladyship to take particular notice that I have no interested views of my own to serve in coming here. If it was not for my promise to Miss Summerson, and my keeping of it sacred, I shouldn't have darkened these doors again. Your ladyship will remember, when I mention it, that the last time I was here I run against a party very eminent in our profession, and whose loss we all deplore. That party certainly did from that time apply himself to cutting in against me in a way that I will call sharp practice, and did make it, at every turn and point, extremely difficult for me to be sure that I hadn't inadvertently led up to something contrary to Miss Summerson's wishes."

Lady Dedlock looks at him in stern inquiry. Mr. Guppy immediately withdraws his eyes from her face and looks anywhere else.

"Indeed, it has been made so hard," he goes on, "to have any idea what that party was up to, that until the loss which we all deplore I was gravelled—an expression which your ladyship, moving in the higher circles, will be so good as to consider tantamount to 'knocked over.' However, what with the exertion of my humble abilities, and what with the help of a mutual friend by the name of Mr. Tony Weevle (who is of a high aristocratic turn, and has your ladyship's portrait always hanging up in his room), I have now reasons for an apprehension as to which I come to put your ladyship upon your guard. First, will your ladyship allow me to ask you whether you have had any strange visitors this morning? I don't mean fashionable visitors, but such visitors, for instance, as Miss Barbary's old servant, or as a person without the use of his lower extremities, carried upstairs similarly to a Guy?"

"No!"

"Then I assure your ladyship that such visitors have been here, and have been received here. Because I saw them."

"What have I to do with that, or what have you? I do not understand you. What do you mean?"

"Your ladyship, I come to put you on your guard. There may be no occasion for it. Very well. Then I have only done my best to keep my promise to Miss Summerson. I strongly suspect that those letters I was to have brought to your ladyship were not destroyed when I supposed they were. That if there was anything to be blown upon, it *is* blown upon. That the visitors I have alluded to have been here this morning to make money of it. And that the money is made, or making."

Mr. Guppy picks up his hat and rises.

"Your ladyship, you know best whether there's anything in what I say, or whether there's nothing. Something or nothing, I have acted up to Miss Summerson's wishes in letting things alone, and in undoing what I had begun to do, as far as possible; that's sufficient for me. I now take my farewell of your ladyship, and assure you that there's no danger of your ever being waited on by me again."

She scarcely acknowledges these parting words by any look, but when he has been gone a little while, she rings her bell.

"Where is Sir Leicester?" Mercury reports that he is at present shut up in the library, alone. "Has Sir Leicester had any visitors this morning?" Several, on business. Mercury proceeds to a description of them, which has been anticipated by Mr. Guppy. Enough, he may go.

So! All is broken down. Her name is in these many mouths, her husband knows his wrongs, her shame will be published—may be spreading while she thinks about it—and in addition to the thunderbolt so long foreseen by her, so unforeseen by him, she is denounced by an invisible accuser as the murderess of her enemy.

Her enemy he was, and she has often, often, often, wished him dead. Her enemy he is, even in his grave. This dreadful accusation comes upon her like a new torment at his lifeless hand. And when she recalls how she was secretly at his door that night, and how she may be represented to have sent her favourite girl away, so soon before, merely to release herself from observation, she shudders as if the hangman's hands were at her neck. She has thrown herself upon the floor, and lies with her hair all wildly scattered, and her face buried in the cushions of a couch. She rises up, hurries to and fro, flings herself down again, and rocks and moans. The horror that is upon her is unutterable. If she really were the murderess, it could hardly be more intense.

A terrible impression steals upon and overshadows her, that from this pursuer, living or dead—obdurate and imperturbable before her in his well-remembered shape, or not more obdurate and imperturbable in his coffin-bed—there is no escape but in death. Hunted, she flies. The complication of her shame, her dread, remorse, and misery, overwhelms her at its height, and even her strength of self-reliance is overturned, and whirled away like a leaf before a mighty wind.

She hurriedly addresses these lines to her husband, seals, and leaves them on her table.

> If I am sought for, or accused of, his murder, believe that I am wholly innocent. Believe no other good of me, for I am innocent of nothing else that you have heard, or will hear, laid to my charge. He prepared me, on that fatal night, for his disclosure of my guilt to you. After he had left me, I went out, on pretence of walking in the garden

where I sometimes walk, but really to follow him and make one last petition that he would not protract the dreadful suspense on which I have been racked by him, you do not know how long, but would mercifully strike next morning.

I found his house dark and silent. I rang twice at his door, but there was no reply, and I came home.

I have no home left. I will encumber you no more. May you, in your just resentment, be able to forget the unworthy woman on whom you have wasted a most generous devotion—who avoids you only with a deeper shame than that with which she hurries from herself—and who writes this last adieu.

She dresses quickly, leaves all her jewels and her money, listens, goes downstairs when the hall is empty, opens and shuts the great door, flutters away in the shrill frosty wind.

# CHAPTER 56

*Pursuit*

IMPASSIVE, as behooves its high breeding, the Dedlock town-house stares at the other houses in the street of dismal grandeur, and gives no outward sign of anything going wrong within. Carriages rattle, doors are battered at, the world exchanges calls. The Dedlock town-house changes not externally, and hours pass before its exalted dulness is disturbed within. But Volumnia the fair, being subject to the prevalent complaint of boredom, and finding that disorder attacking her spirits with some virulence, ventures at length to repair to the library for change of scene. Her gentle tapping at the door producing no response, she opens it and peeps in. The sprightly Dedlock is reputed, in that grass-grown city of the ancients, Bath, to be stimulated by an urgent curiosity. Certain it is that she avails herself of the present opportunity of hovering over her kinsman's letters and papers, hopping about from table to table, with her glass at her eye. In the course of these researches, she stumbles over something, and turning her glass in that direction, sees her kinsman lying on the ground like a felled tree.

Volumnia's pet little scream acquires a considerable augmentation of reality from this surprise, and the house is quickly in commotion. Servants tear up and down stairs, bells are violently rung, doctors are sent for, and Lady Dedlock is sought in all directions—but not found. Nobody has seen or heard her since she last rang her bell. Her letter to Sir

Leicester is discovered on her table, but it is doubtful yet whether he has not received another missive from another world, requiring to be personally answered.

They lay him down upon his bed, and chafe, and rub, and fan, and put ice to his head, and try every means of restoration. Howbeit, the day has ebbed away and it is night before his stertorous breathing lulls, or his fixed eyes show any consciousness of the candle that is occasionally passed before them. But when this change begins, it goes on, and by and by he nods, or moves his eyes, or even his hand, in token that he hears and comprehends.

He fell down this morning a handsome stately gentleman, somewhat infirm, but of a fine presence, and with a well-filled face. He lies upon his bed an aged man with sunken cheeks, the decrepit shadow of himself. His voice was rich and mellow, and he had so long been thoroughly persuaded of the weight and import to mankind of any word he said that his words really had come to sound as if there were something in them. But now he can only whisper, and what he whispers sounds like what it is—mere jumble and jargon.

His favourite and faithful housekeeper stands at his bedside. It is the first act he notices, and he clearly derives pleasure from it. After vainly trying to make himself understood in speech, he makes signs for a pencil. It is his old housekeeper who makes out what he wants, and brings in a slate. After pausing for some time, he slowly scrawls upon it in a hand that is not his, "Chesney Wold?"

No, she tells him, he is in London. He was taken ill in the library this morning. Right thankful she is that she happened to come to London, and is able to attend upon him.

"It is not an illness of any serious consequence, Sir Leicester. You will be much better tomorrow, Sir Leicester. All the gentlemen say so." This with the tears coursing down her fair old face.

After making a survey of the room, and looking with particular attention all round the bed where the doctors stand, he writes, "My lady."

"My lady went out, Sir Leicester, before you were taken ill, and don't know of your illness yet."

He points again, in great agitation, at the two words. They all try to quiet him, but he points again with increased agitation. On their looking at one another, not knowing what to say, he takes the slate once more, and writes "My lady. For God's sake, where?" And makes an imploring moan.

It is thought better that his old housekeeper should give him Lady Dedlock's letter, the contents of which no one knows or can surmise. She opens it for him, and puts it out for his perusal. Having read it twice by a great effort, he turns it down so that it shall not be seen, and lies moaning. He passes into a kind of relapse, or into a swoon, and it is an hour before he opens his eyes, reclining on his faithful and attached old servant's arm. The doctors know that he is best with her, and stand aloof.

The slate comes into requisition again, but the word he wants to write he cannot remember. His anxiety, his eagerness, and affliction at this pass are pitiable to behold. It seems as if he must go mad in the necessity he feels for haste, and the inability under which he labours of expressing to do what, or to fetch whom. He has written the letter B, and there stopped. Of a sudden, in the height of his misery, he puts Mr. before it. The old housekeeper suggests "Bucket." Thank Heaven! That's his meaning.

Mr. Bucket is found to be downstairs, by appointment. Shall he come up? There is no possibility of misconstruing Sir Leicester's burning wish to see him, or the desire he signifies to have the room cleared of every one but the housekeeper. It is speedily done, and Mr. Bucket appears. Of all men upon earth, Sir Leicester seems to place his sole trust and reliance upon this man.

"Sir Leicester Dedlock, Baronet, I'm sorry to see you like this. I hope you'll cheer up. I'm sure you will, on account of the family credit."

Sir Leicester puts her letter in his hands, and looks intently in his face while he reads it. A new intelligence comes into Mr. Bucket's eye as he reads on; with one hook of his finger he indicates, "Sir Leicester Dedlock, Baronet, I understand you."

Sir Leicester writes upon the slate. "Full forgiveness. Find—" Mr. Bucket stops his hand.

"Sir Leicester Dedlock, Baronet, I'll find her. But my search after her must be begun out of hand. Not a minute must be lost." With the quickness of thought, he follows Sir Leicester Dedlock's look towards a little box upon a table. "Bring it here, Sir Leicester Dedlock, Baronet? Certainly. Open it with one of these here keys? Certainly. The littlest key? To be sure. Take the notes out? So I will. Count 'em. That's soon done. Twenty and thirty's fifty, and twenty's seventy, and fifty's one twenty, and forty's one sixty. Take 'em for expenses? That I'll do, and render an account, of course. Don't spare money? No I won't."

The velocity and certainty of Mr. Bucket's interpretation on all these heads is little short of miraculous. Mrs. Rouncewell, who holds the light, is giddy with the swiftness of his eyes and hands as he starts up, furnished for his journey.

"You're George's mother, old lady, that's about what you are, I believe?" says Mr. Bucket aside, and buttoning his coat.

"Yes, sir, I am his distressed mother."

"So I thought, according to what he mentioned to me just now. Well then, I'll tell you something. You needn't be distressed no more. Your son's all right. Now don't you begin a-crying, because what you've got to do is to take care of Sir Leicester Dedlock, Baronet, and you won't do that by crying. As to your son, he's all right, I tell you, and he sends his loving duty and hoping you're the same. He's discharged honourable, that's about what *he* is, with no imputation on his character. You may trust me, for I took your son. He conducted himself in a game way, too, on that occasion. Sir Leicester Dedlock, Baronet, what you've trusted to me I'll go through with. Don't you be afraid of my turning out of my way, right or left, or taking a sleep, or a wash, or a shave, till I have found what I go in search of. Say everything as is kind and forgiving on your part? Sir Leicester Dedlock, Baronet, I will. And I wish you better, and these family affairs smoothed over—as, Lord! many other family affairs equally has been, and equally will be, to the end of time."

With this peroration, Mr. Bucket, buttoned-up, goes quietly out, looking steadily before him as if he were already piercing the night, in quest of the fugitive. His first step is to take himself to Lady Dedlock's rooms, and look all over them for any trifling indication that may help him. The rooms are in darkness now, and to see Mr. Bucket with a wax-light in his hand, taking a sharp mental inventory of the many delicate objects so curiously at variance with himself, would be to see a sight—which nobody *does* see, as he is particular to lock himself in.

Ever looking about, he has opened a dainty little chest in an inner drawer. His great hand, turning over some gloves which it can scarcely feel, they are so light and soft within it, comes upon a white handkerchief.

"Hum! Let's have a look at *you*," says Mr. Bucket, putting down the light. "What should *you* be kept by yourself for? What's *your* motive? Are you her ladyship's property, or somebody else's? You've got a mark upon you, I suppose?"

He finds it as he speaks: Esther Summerson.

"Oh!" says Mr. Bucket, pausing with his finger at his ear. "Come, I'll take *you*."

He completes his observations as quietly and carefully as he has carried them on, leaves everything else precisely as he found it, glides away after some five minutes in all, and passes into the street. He sets off, full-swing, to the nearest coach-stand, picks out the horse for his money, and directs to be driven to the Shooting Gallery. He dashes to his destination at such a speed that when he stops, the horse half smothers him in a cloud of steam. He runs up the long wooden entry, and finds the trooper smoking his pipe.

"My lad, I haven't a word to spare. Now, honour! All to save a woman. Miss Summerson that was here when Gridley died—that was the name, I know—all right, where does she live?" The trooper has just come from there, and gives him the address. "You won't repent it, George. Good-night!"

He is off again, and gallops away again. Mr. Jarndyce, the only person up in the house, is just going to bed, rises from his book on hearing the rapid ringing at the bell, and comes down to the door in his dressing-gown.

"Don't be alarmed, sir. I've had the pleasure of seeing you before. In-

spector Bucket. Look at that handkerchief, sir, Miss Esther Summerson's. Found it myself put away in a drawer of Lady Dedlock's, quarter of an hour ago. Not a moment to lose. Matter of life or death. There has been a discovery today. Family affairs have come out. Sir Leicester Dedlock, Baronet, has had a fit—apoplexy or paralysis—and couldn't be brought to, and precious time has been lost. Lady Dedlock disappeared this afternoon, and left a letter for him that looks bad. Run your eye over it. Here it is!"

Mr. Jarndyce, having read it, asks him what he thinks.

"I don't know. It looks like suicide. Anyways, there's more and more danger, every minute, of its drawing to that. I'd give a hundred pound an hour to have got the start of the present time. Now, Mr. Jarndyce, I am employed by Sir Leicester Dedlock, Baronet, to follow her and find her—to save her, and take her his forgiveness. I have money and full power, but I want something else. I want Miss Summerson."

"Now, Mr. Jarndyce,"—Mr. Bucket has read his face with the greatest attention all along—"I speak to you as a gentleman of a humane heart, and under such pressing circumstances as don't often happen. If ever delay was dangerous, it's dangerous now; and if ever you couldn't afterwards forgive yourself for causing it, this is the time. Eight or ten hours, worth, as I tell you, a hundred pound apiece at least, have been lost since Lady Dedlock disappeared. I am charged to find her. I am Inspector Bucket. Besides all the rest that's heavy on her, she has upon her, as she believes, suspicion of murder. If I follow her alone, she, being in ignorance of what Sir Leicester Dedlock, Baronet, has communicated to me, may be driven to desperation. But if I follow her in company with a young lady she has a tenderness for, she will give me credit for being friendly. Let me be able to put that young lady for'ard, and I'll save her and prevail with her, if she is alive. Let me come up with her alone—a hard matter—and I'll do my best, but I don't answer for what the best may be. Time flies; it's getting on for one o'clock. When one strikes, there's another hour gone, and it's worth a thousand pound now instead of a hundred."

This is all true, and the pressing nature of the case cannot be questioned. Mr. Jarndyce begs him to remain there while he speaks to Miss Summerson. Mr. Bucket says he will, but acting on his usual principle, does no such thing—following upstairs instead, and keeping his man in sight. In a very little time Mr. Jarndyce comes down, and tells him that Miss Summerson will join him directly, to accompany him where he pleases. Mr. Bucket, satisfied, expresses high approval, and awaits her coming at the door.

Where is she? Living or dead, where is she? If, as he folds the handkerchief and carefully puts it up, it were able, with an enchanted power, to bring before him the place where she found it, and the night landscape near the cottage where it covered the little child, would he descry her there?

## CHAPTER 57

*Esther's Narrative*

I HAD gone to bed and fallen asleep when my guardian knocked at the door of my room and begged me to get up directly. On my hurrying to speak to him and learn what had happened, he told me, after a word or two of preparation, that there had been a discovery at Sir Leicester Dedlock's. That my mother had fled; that a person was now at our door who was empowered to convey to her the fullest assurances of affectionate protection and forgiveness, if he could possibly find her; and that I was sought for to accompany him, in the hope that my entreaties might prevail upon her if his failed. Something to this general purpose I made out; but I was thrown into such a tumult of alarm and hurry and distress that I did not seem, to myself, fully to recover my right mind until hours had passed.

But I dressed and wrapped up expeditiously without waking Charley, or any one, and went down to Mr. Bucket, who was the person entrusted with the secret. In taking me to him my guardian told me this, and also explained how it was that he had come to think of me. Mr. Bucket, by the light of my guardian's candle, read to me a letter that my mother had left upon her table, and within ten minutes of my having been aroused I was sitting beside him, rolling swifty through the streets.

His manner was very keen, and yet considerate, when he explained to me that a great deal might depend on my being able to answer, without confusion, a few questions that he wished to ask me. These were, chiefly, whether I had had much communication with my mother (to whom he only referred as Lady Dedlock), when and where I had spoken with her last, and how she had become possessed of my handkerchief. When I had satisfied him on these points, he asked me particularly to consider—taking time to think—whether, within my knowledge, there was any one, no matter where, in whom she might be at all likely to confide under circumstances of the last necessity. I could think of no one but my guardian.

My companion said to me, after considering within himself for a few moments, that he had made up his mind how to proceed. He was quite willing to tell me what his plan was, but I did not feel clear enough to understand it.

We had not driven very far from our lodgings when we stopped in a by-street at a public-looking place lighted up with gas. Mr. Bucket took me in and sat me in an arm-chair by a bright fire. It was now past one, as I saw by the clock against the wall. Two police officers, looking in their perfectly neat uniform not at all like people who were up all night, were quietly writing at a desk. A third man in uniform, whom Mr. Bucket called and to whom he whispered his instructions, went out, and then the two others advised together while one wrote from Mr. Bucket's subdued dictation. It was a description of my mother that they were busy with, for Mr. Bucket brought it to me when it was done, and read it in a whisper. It was very accurate indeed.

The second officer then copied it out, and called in another man in uniform, who took it up and went away with it. All this was done with the greatest dispatch, and without the waste of a moment, yet nobody was at all hurried. As soon as the paper was sent out upon its travels, the two officers resumed their former quiet work. Mr. Bucket thoughtfully came and warmed the soles of his boots, first one and then the other, at the fire.

"Are you well wrapped up, Miss Summerson?" he asked me as his eyes met mine. "It's a desperate sharp night for a young lady to be out in." I told him I cared for no weather, and was warmly clothed. "It may be a long job," he observed, "but so that it ends well, never mind, miss."

"I pray to Heaven it may end well!" said I.

He nodded comfortingly. "You see, whatever you do, don't you go and fret yourself. You keep yourself cool, and equal for anything that may happen, and it'll be the better for you, the better for me, the better for Lady Dedlock, and the better for Sir Leicester Dedlock, Baronet."

He was really very kind and gentle, and as he stood before the fire warming his boots, and rubbing his face with his forefinger, I felt a confidence in his sagacity which reassured me. It was not yet a quarter to two when I heard horses' feet and wheels outside. "Now, Miss Summerson," said he, "we are off, if you please!"

He gave me his arm, and we found at the door a phaeton or barouche, with a postilion and post-horses. Mr. Bucket handed me in, and took his own seat on the box. The man in uniform whom he had sent to fetch this equipage then handed him up a dark lantern at his request, and when he had given a few directions to the driver, we rattled away.

I was far from sure that I was not in a dream. We rattled with great rapidity through such a labyrinth of streets that I soon lost all idea where we were, except that we had crossed and recrossed the river, and still seemed to be traversing a low-lying waterside. At length we stopped at the corner of a little slimy turning, and I saw my companion, by the light of his lantern, in conference with several men who looked like a mixture of police and sailors. Against the mouldering wall by which they stood, there was a bill, on which I could discern the words, "FOUND DROWNED"; and this, and an inscription about Drags, possessed me with the awful suspicion shadowed forth in our visit to that place.

I remained quiet, but what I suffered in that dreadful spot I never can forget. And still it was like the horror of a dream. After some further conference, Mr. Bucket (whom everybody seemed to know and defer

to) went in with the others at a door, and left me in the carriage. The tide was coming in, as I judged from the sound it made, and I could hear it break at the end of the alley, with a little rush towards me. The thought shuddered through me that it would cast my mother at the horses' feet.

Mr. Bucket came out again, exhorting the others to be vigilant, darkened his lantern, and once more took his seat. "Don't you be alarmed, Miss Summerson, on account of our coming down here," he said, "I only want to have everything in train, and to know that it is in train by looking after it myself. Get on, my lad!"

We called at another office or station for a minute, and crossed the river again. During the whole of this time, and during the whole search, my companion, wrapped up on the box, never relaxed in his vigilance a single moment; but when we crossed the bridge he seemed, if possible, to be more on the alert than before. The river had a fearful look, so overcast and secret, creeping away so fast between the low flat lines of shore, so heavy with indistinct and awful shapes, both of substance and shadow, so deathlike and mysterious. I have seen it many times since then, by sunlight and by moonlight, but never free from the impressions of that journey.

Clattering through the empty streets, we came at length from the pavement on to dark smooth roads, and began to leave the houses behind us. After a while, I recognised the familiar way to Saint Albans. At Barnet, fresh horses were ready for us, and we changed and went on. It was very cold, and the open country was white with snow, though none was falling then.

"An old acquaintance of yours, this road, Miss Summerson," said Mr. Bucket cheerfully.

"Yes," I returned. "Have you gathered any intelligence?"

"None that can be quite depended on," he answered, "but it's early times as yet."

He had gone into every late or early public-house where there was a light, and had got down to talk to the turnpike-keepers. I had heard him ordering drink, and chinking money, and making himself agreeable and merry everywhere; but whenever he took his seat upon the box again, his face resumed its watchful steady look, and he always said to the driver in the same business tone, "Get on, my lad!"

With all these stoppages, it was between five and six o'clock and we were yet a few miles short of Saint Albans, when he came out of one of these houses.

"She's on ahead. Passed through here on foot this evening, about eight or nine. I heard of her first at the archway toll, over at Highgate, but couldn't make quite sure, but she's before us now, safe. Now, my lad, try a gallop!"

We were soon in Saint Albans, and alighted a little before day, when I was just beginning to arrange and comprehend the occurrences of the night and really to believe that they were not a dream. Leaving the carriage at the posting-house and ordering fresh horses to be ready, my companion gave me his arm and we went towards home.

"As this is your regular abode, Miss Summerson, you see," he observed, "I should like to know whether you've been asked for by any stranger answering the description, or whether Mr. Jarndyce has. I don't much expect it, but it might be."

We turned in at the garden-gate.

"Ah!" said Mr. Bucket. "Here we are, and a nice retired place it is. They're early with the kitchen fire, and that denotes good servants. But what you've always got to be careful of with servants is, who comes to see 'em; you never know what they're up to if you don't know that."

The whole household were amazed to see me, without any notice, at that time in the morning, and so accompanied, and their surprise was not diminished by my inquiries. No one, however, had been there. It could not be doubted that this was the truth.

"Then, Miss Summerson," said my companion, "we can't be too soon at the cottage where those brickmakers are to be found. Most inquiries there I leave to you, if you'll be so good as to make 'em. The naturalest way is the best way, and the naturalest way is your own way."

We set off again immediately. On arriving at the cottage, we found it shut up and apparently deserted, but one of the neighbours informed me that the two women and their husbands now lived together in another house, which stood on the margin of the piece of ground where the kilns were. We lost no time in repairing to this place, which was within a few hundred yards, and as the door stood ajar, I pushed it open.

There were only three of them sitting at breakfast, the child lying asleep on a bed in the corner. It was Jenny, the mother of the dead child, who was absent. The other woman rose on seeing me, and the men, though they were, as usual, sulky and silent, each gave me a morose nod of recognition. A look passed between them when Mr. Bucket followed me in, and I was surprised to see that the woman evidently knew him. I had asked leave to enter, of course. Liz rose to give me her own chair, but I sat down on a stool near the fire, and Mr. Bucket took a corner of the bedstead. Now that I had to speak, and was among people with whom I was not familiar, I could not help bursting into tears.

"Liz," said I, "I have come a long way in the night and through the snow, to inquire after a lady—"

"Who has been here, you know," Mr. Bucket struck in, addressing the whole group; "that's the lady the young lady means. The lady that was here last night, you know."

"And who told *you* as there was anybody here?" inquired Jenny's husband.

"A person of the name of Michael Jackson, with a blue welveteen waistcoat with a double row of mother of pearl buttons," Mr. Bucket immediately answered.

"He had as good mind his own business, whoever he is," growled the man.

The woman had not resumed her chair, but stood faltering with her hand upon its broken back, looking at me. I thought she would have spoken to me privately if she had dared. She was still in this attitude of uncertainty when her husband, who was eating, struck the handle of his knife violently on the table, and told her with an oath to mind *her* own business at any rate, and sit down.

"I should like to have seen Jenny very much," said I, "for I am sure she would have told me all she could about this lady, whom I am very anxious indeed—you cannot think how anxious—to overtake. Will Jenny be here soon? Where is she?"

The woman had a great desire to answer, but the man, with another oath, openly kicked at her foot with his heavy boot. He left it to Jenny's husband to say what he chose, and after a dogged silence the latter turned his shaggy head towards me.

"I'm not partial to gentlefolks coming into my place, as you've heerd

me say afore now, I think, miss. I let their places be, and it's curious they can't let my place be. Howsoever, I don't so much complain of you as of some others, and I'm agreeable to make you a civil answer, though I give notice that I'm not a-going to be drawed like a badger. Will Jenny be here soon? No she won't. Where is she? She's gone up to Lunnun."

"Did she go last night?" I asked.

"Did she go last night? Ah! She went last night," he answered.

"But was she here when the lady came? And what did the lady say to her? And where is the lady gone? I beg and pray you to be so kind as to tell me," said I, "for I am in great distress to know."

"If my master would let me speak, and not say a word of harm—" the woman timidly begun.

"Your master," said her husband, "will break your neck if you meddle with wot don't concern you."

After another silence, the husband of the absent woman, turning to me again, answered me with his usual grumbling unwillingness.

"Wos Jenny here when the lady come? Yes, she wos here when the lady come. Wot did the lady say to her? Well, I'll tell you wot the lady said to her. She said, 'You remember me as come one time to talk to you about the young lady as had been a-wisiting of you? You remember me as give you somethink handsome for a handkerchief wot she had left?' Ah, she remembered. So we all did. Well then, wos that young lady up at the house now? No, she warn't up at the house now. The lady was upon a journey all alone, strange as we might think it, and could she rest herself where you're a settin, for a hour or so. Yes she could, and so she did. Then she went—it might be at twenty minutes past eleven, and it might be at twenty minutes past twelve; we ain't got no watches here to know the time by, nor yet clocks. Where did she go? I don't know where she go'd. She went one way, and Jenny went another; one went right to Lunnun, and t'other went right from it. That's all about it."

"Was the lady crying?" I inquired.

"Devil a bit," returned the first man. "Her shoes was the worse, and her clothes was the worse, but she warn't—not as I see."

The woman sat with her arms crossed and her eyes upon the ground. Her husband had turned his seat a little so as to face her, and kept his hammer-like hand upon the table as if it were in readiness to execute his threat if she disobeyed him.

"I hope you will not object to my asking your wife," said I, "how the lady looked?"

"Come, then!" he gruffly cried to her. "You hear what she says. Cut it short, and tell her."

"Bad," replied the woman. "Pale and exhausted. Very bad."

"Did she speak much?"

"Not much, but her voice was hoarse."

"Was she faint?" said I. "Did she eat or drink here?"

"Go on!" said the husband, in answer to her look. "Tell her and cut it short."

"She had a little water, miss, and Jenny fetched her some bread and tea. But she hardly touched it."

"And when she went from here"—Jenny's husband impatiently took me up.

"When she went from here, she went right away Nor'ard by the high road. Ask on the road if you doubt me, and see if it warn't so. Now, there's the end. That's all about it."

I glanced at my companion, and finding that he had already risen and was ready to depart, thanked them for what they had told me, and took my leave. The woman looked full at Mr. Bucket as he went out, and he looked full at her.

"Now, Miss Summerson," he said to me as we walked quickly away. "They've got her ladyship's watch among 'em. That's a positive fact."

"You saw it?" I exclaimed.

"Just as good as saw it," he returned. "Else why should he talk about his 'twenty minutes past,' and about his having no watch to tell the time by? Twenty minutes! He don't usually cut his time so fine as that. Now you see, either her ladyship gave him that watch, or he took it. I think she gave it him. Now what should she give it him for? What should she give it him for?"

He repeated this question to himself several times as we hurried on, appearing to balance between a variety of answers that arose in his mind.

"If time could be spared," said Mr. Bucket—"which is the only thing that can't be spared in this case—I might get it out of that woman; but it's too doubtful a chance to trust to, under present circumstances. They are up to keeping a close eye upon her, and any fool knows that a poor creetur like her, beaten and kicked and scarred and bruised from head to foot, will stand by the husband that ill-uses her through thick and thin. There's something kept back. It's a pity but what we had seen the other woman."

I regretted it exceedingly, for she was very grateful, and I felt sure would have resisted no entreaty of mine.

"It's possible, Miss Summerson," said Mr. Bucket, pondering on it, "that her ladyship sent her up to London with some word for you, and it's possible that her husband got the watch to let her go. It don't come out altogether so plain as to please me, but it's on the cards. Now I don't take kindly to laying out the money of Sir Leicester Dedlock, Baronet, on these Roughs, and I don't see my way to the usefulness of it at present. No! So far, our road, Miss Summerson, is for'ard—straight ahead—and keeping everything quiet!"

We called at home once more, that I might send a hasty note to my guardian, and then we hurried back to where we had left the carriage. The horses were brought out as soon as we were seen coming, and we were on the road again in a few minutes. It had set in snowing at daybreak, and it now snowed hard. The air was so thick with the darkness of the day, and the density of the fall, that we could see but a very little way in any direction. Although it was extremely cold, the snow was but partially frozen, and it churned under the hoofs of the horses into mire and water. They sometimes slipped and floundered for a mile together, and we were obliged to come to a standstill to rest them.

I could eat nothing, and could not sleep, and I grew so nervous under those delays, and the slow pace at which we travelled, that I had an un-reasonable desire upon me to get out and walk. Yielding to my com-panion's better sense, however, I remained where I was. All this time, kept fresh by a certain enjoyment of the work in which he was engaged, he was up and down at every house we came to—addressing people whom he had never beheld before, as old acquaintances, talking and drinking and shaking hands at every bar and tap, friendly with every waggoner, wheelwright, blacksmith, and toll-taker, yet never seeming to lose time, and always mounting to the box again with his watchful, steady face, and his businesslike "Get on, my lad!"

When we were changing horses the next time, he came from the stable-yard with the wet snow encrusted upon him, and dropping off him, and spoke to me at the carriage-side.

"Keep up your spirits. It's certainly true that she came on here, Miss Summerson. There's not a doubt of the dress by this time, and the dress has been seen here. Still on foot. But don't you worry yourself no more than you can help. Get on, my lad!"

The sleet fell all that day unceasingly, a thick mist came on early, and it never rose or lightened for a moment. Such roads I had never seen. I sometimes feared we had missed the way and got into the ploughed grounds, or the marshes. As we advanced, I began to feel mis-givings that my companion lost confidence. He was the same as before with all the roadside people, but he looked graver when he sat by him-self on the box. I saw his finger uneasily going across and across his mouth during the whole of one long weary stage. I overheard that he began to ask the drivers of coaches and other vehicles coming towards us what passengers they had seen in other coaches and vehicles that were in advance. Their replies did not encourage him. He always gave me a reassuring beck of his finger as he got upon the box again, but he seemed perplexed now when he said, "Get on, my lad!"

At last, when we were changing, he told me that he had lost the track of the dress so long that he began to be surprised. It had disappeared here in an unaccountable manner, and we had not come upon it since. But I was not to be down-hearted, he told me, for it was as likely as not that the next stage might set us right again.

The next stage, however, ended as that one ended; we had no new clue. There was a spacious inn here, solitary but a comfortable sub-stantial building, and as we drove in under a large gateway before I knew it, a landlady and her pretty daughters came to the carriage-door, entreating me to alight and refresh myself while the horses were making ready. I thought it would be uncharitable to refuse. They took me up-stairs to a warm room, and left me there. I was frightened when I found them all about me, but I remembered that before I fainted I tried very hard not to do it, and that was some little comfort. They cushioned me up on a large sofa by the fire, and then the comely landlady told me that I must travel no further tonight, but must go to bed. But this put me into such a tremble lest they should detain me there that she soon recalled her words, and compromised for a rest of half an hour.

Punctual to the time, at the half-hour's end the carriage came rumbling under the gateway and they took me down, warmed, refreshed, comforted by kindness, and safe (I assured them) not to faint any more.

The transparent windows with the fire and light, looking so bright and warm from the cold darkness out of doors, were soon gone, and again we were crushing and churning the loose snow. We went on with toil enough, but the dismal roads were not much worse than they had been, and the stage was only nine miles. My companion, smoking on the box, was as vigilant as ever, and as quickly down and up again, when we came to any human abode or any human creature. He had lighted his little dark lantern—which seemed to be a favourite with him, for we had lamps to the carriage—and every now and then he turned it upon me, to see that I was doing well.

We came to the end of the stage, and still the lost trace was not recovered. I looked at him anxiously when we stopped to change; but I knew by his yet graver face, as he stood watching the ostlers, that he had heard nothing. Almost in an instant afterwards, as I leaned back in my seat, he looked in, with his lighted lantern in his hand, an excited and quite different man.

"What is it?" said I, starting. "Is she here?"

"No, no. Don't deceive yourself, my dear. Nobody's here. But I've got it!" The crystallized snow was in his eyelashes, in his hair, lying in ridges on his dress. He had to shake it from his face and get his breath before he spoke to me. "Now, Miss Summerson," said he, beating his finger on the apron, "don't you be disappointed at what I'm a-going to do. You know me. I'm Inspector Bucket, and you can trust me. We've come a long way—never mind. Four horses out there for the next stage up! Quick!"

There was a commotion in the yard, and a man came running out of the stables to know if he meant "up or down."

"Up, I tell you! Up! Ain't it English? Up!"

"Up?" said I, astonished. "To London! Are we going back?"

"Miss Summerson," he answered, "back. Straight back as a die. You know me. Don't be afraid. I'll follow the other, by G—"

"The other?" I repeated. "Who?"

"You called her Jenny, didn't you? I'll follow her. Bring those two pair out here, for a crown a man. Wake up, some of you!"

"You will not desert this lady we are in search of, you will not abandon her on such a night and in such a state of mind as I know her to be in!" said I in an agony, and grasping his hand.

"You are right, my dear, I won't. But I'll follow the other. Look alive here with them horses! Send a man for'ard in the saddle to the next stage, and let him send another for'ard again, and order four on, up, right through. My darling, don't you be afraid!"

These orders, and the way in which he ran about the yard urging them, caused a general excitement that was scarcely less bewildering to me than the sudden change. But our horses were put to with great speed.

"My dear," said Mr. Bucket, jumping to his seat and looking in again, "you'll excuse me if I'm too familiar—don't you fret and worry yourself no more than you can help. I say nothing else at present; but you know me, my dear, now don't you?"

I endeavoured to say that I knew he was far more capable than I of deciding what we ought to do—but was he sure that this was right? Could I not go forward by myself in search of—I grasped his hand again in my distress, and whispered it to him—of my own mother?

"My dear," he answered, "I know, I know, and would I put you wrong, do you think? Inspector Bucket. Now you know me, don't you?" What could I say but yes! "Then you keep up as good a heart as you can, and you rely upon me for standing by you, no less than by Sir Leicester Dedlock, Baronet. Now, are you right there?"

"All right, sir!"

"Off she goes, then. And get on, my lads!"

We were again upon the melancholy road by which we had come, tearing up the miry sleet and thawing snow as if they were torn up by a water-wheel.

# CHAPTER 58

## A Wintry Day and Night

STILL impassive, as behoves its breeding, the Dedlock town-house carries itself as usual towards the street of dismal grandeur.

It is given out that my Lady has gone down into Lincolnshire, but is expected to return presently. Rumour, busy overmuch, however, will not go down into Lincolnshire. It persists in flitting and chattering about town. It knows that that poor unfortunate man Sir Leicester has been sadly used. It hears, my dear child, all sorts of shocking things. It makes the world of five miles round quite merry. Not to know that there is something wrong at the Dedlocks' is to augur yourself unknown. One of the peachy-cheeked charmers is already apprised of all the principal circumstances that will come out before the Lords on Sir Leicester's application for a bill of divorce.

At feasts and festivals also, in firmaments she has often graced and among constellations she outshone but yesterday, she is still the prevalent subject. What is it? Who is it? When was it? Where was it? How was it? She is discussed by her dear friends with all the genteelest slang in vogue, with the last new word, the last new manner, the last new drawl, and the perfection of polite indifference. And not the least amazing circumstance connected with her being vaguely the town-talk is that people who know nothing and ever did know nothing about her think it essential to their reputation to pretend that she is their topic too, and to retail her at second-hand with the last new word, and the last new manner, and the last new drawl, and the last new polite indifference.

So goes the wintry day outside the Dedlock mansion. How within it? Sir Leicester lying in his bed can speak a little, though with difficulty and indistinctness. He is enjoined to silence and to rest, and they have given him some opiate to lull his pain, for his old enemy is very hard with him. He is never asleep, though sometimes he seems to fall into a dull waking doze. He caused his bedstead to be moved out nearer to the window when he heard it was such inclement weather, and his head to be so adjusted that he could see the driving snow and sleet. He watches it as it falls, throughout the whole wintry day.

Upon the least noise in the house, which is kept hushed, his hand is at the pencil. The old housekeeper, sitting by him, knows what he would write, and whispers "No, he has not come back yet, Sir Leicester. It was late last night when he went. He has been but a little time gone yet."

He withdraws his hand, and falls to looking at the sleet and snow again, until they seem, by being long looked at, to fall so thick and fast that he is obliged to close his eyes for a minute on the giddy whirl of white flakes and icy blots. He began to look at them as soon as it was light. The day is not yet far spent when he conceives it to be necessary that her rooms should be prepared for her. It is very cold and wet. Let there be good fires. Let them know that she is expected. Please see to it yourself. He writes to this purpose on the slate, and Mrs. Rouncewell with a heavy heart obeys.

"For I dread, George," the old lady says to her son, who waits below to keep her company when she has a little leisure, "I dread, my dear, that my lady will never more set foot within these walls. Nor yet within the walls of Chesney Wold, my dear."

"That's worse. But why, Mother?"

"When I saw my lady yesterday, George, she looked to me—and I may say at me too—as if the step on the Ghost's Walk had almost walked her down."

"Come, come! You alarm yourself with old-story fears, Mother."

"No I don't, my dear. No I don't. It's going on for sixty year that I have been in this family, and I never had any fears for it before. But it's breaking up, my dear, the great old Dedlock family is breaking up. I am thankful I have lived long enough to be with Sir Leicester in this illness and trouble, for I know I am not too old, nor too useless, to be a welcomer sight to him than anybody else in my place would be. But the step on the Ghost's Walk will walk my lady down, George; it has been many a day behind her, and now it will pass her, and go on."

"Well, Mother dear, I hope not."

"Ah, so do I, George," the old lady returns, shaking her head, and parting her folded hands. "But if my fears come true, and he has to know it, who will tell him!"

"Are these her rooms?"

"These are my lady's rooms, just as she left them."

The old housekeeper and her son remain until the preparations are complete, and then she returns. Volumnia has taken Mrs. Rouncewell's place in the meantime. Volumnia not being supposed to know (and indeed not knowing) what is the matter, has found it a ticklish task to offer appropriate observations. Yielding, therefore, the chair at the bed-side to the quaint old housekeeper, Volumnia sits at a table a little re-moved, sympathetically sighing. Sir Leicester watches the sleet and snow, and listens for the returning steps that he expects.

He has been under his valet's hands this morning, to be made pre-sentable, and is as well got up as the circumstances will allow. He is propped with pillows, his grey hair is brushed in its usual manner, his linen is arranged to a nicety. His eye-glass and his watch are ready to his hand. It is necessary—less to his own dignity now, perhaps, than for her sake—that he should be seen as little disturbed, and as much him-self, as may be. Women will talk, and Volumnia, though a Dedlock, is no exception. He keeps her here, there is little doubt, to prevent her talking somewhere else. He is very ill, but he makes his present stand against distress of mind and body most courageously.

The fair Volumnia, being one of those sprightly girls who cannot long continue silent, compliments Mrs. Rouncewell on her son, declaring that he positively is one of the finest figures she ever saw. Sir Leicester hears this tribute with so much surprise, and stares about him in such a confused way, that Mrs. Rouncewell feels it necessary to explain.

"Miss Dedlock don't speak of my eldest son, Sir Leicester, but my youngest. I have found him. He has come home."

Sir Leicester breaks silence with a harsh cry. "George? Your son George come home, Mrs. Rouncewell?"

The old housekeeper wipes her eyes. "Thank God. Yes, Sir Leicester."

Does this discovery of some one lost, this return of some one so long gone, come upon him as a strong confirmation of his hopes? Does he think, "Shall I not, with the aid I have, recall her safely after this, there being fewer hours in her case than there are years in his?" It is of no use entreating him; he is determined to speak now, and he does. In a thick crowd of sounds, but still intelligibly enough to be understood.

"Why did you not tell me, Mrs. Rouncewell?"

"It happened only yesterday, Sir Leicester, and I doubted your being well enough to be talked to of such things."

"Where is your son George, Mrs. Rouncewell?" asks Sir Leicester.

Mrs. Rouncewell, not a little alarmed by his disregard of the doctor's injunctions, replies, in London.

"Where in London?" Mrs. Rouncewell is constrained to admit that he is in the house.

"Bring him here to my room. Bring him directly." The old lady can do nothing but go in search of him. Sir Leicester, with such power of movement as he has, arranges himself a little, to receive him. When he has done so, he looks out again at the falling sleet and snow, and listens again for the returning steps. A quantity of straw has been tumbled down in the street to deaden the noises there, and she might be driven to the door perhaps without his hearing wheels.

He is lying thus, apparently forgetful of his newer and minor surprise, when the housekeeper returns, accompanied by her trooper son. Mr. George approaches softly to the bedside, makes his bow, squares his chest, and stands, with his face flushed, very heartily ashamed of himself.

"Good heaven, and it is really George Rouncewell!" exclaims Sir Leicester. "Do you remember me, George?"

"I must have a very bad memory indeed, Sir Leicester, if I failed to remember you."

"When I look at you, George Rouncewell," Sir Leicester observes with difficulty, "I see something of a boy at Chesney Wold—I remember well —very well."

He looks at the trooper until tears come into his eyes, and then he looks at the sleet and snow again.

"I ask your pardon, Sir Leicester," says the trooper, "but would you accept of my arms to raise you up? You would lie easier, Sir Leicester, if you would allow me to move you."

"If you please, George Rouncewell, if you will be so good."

The trooper takes him in his arms like a child, lightly raises him, and turns him with his face more towards the window. "Thank you. You have your mother's gentleness," returns Sir Leicester, "and your own strength. Thank you." He signs to him with his hand not to go away. George quietly remains at the bedside, waiting to be spoken to. "Why did you wish for secrecy?"

"Truly I am not much to boast of, Sir Leicester, and I—I should still, Sir Leicester, if you was not so indisposed—which I hope you will not be long—I should still hope for the favour of being allowed to remain unknown in general. That involves explanations not very creditable to myself. I should think it would be universally agreed, Sir Leicester, that I am not much to boast of."

"You have been a soldier," observes Sir Leicester, "and a faithful one."

George makes his military bow. "As far as that goes, Sir Leicester, I have done my duty under discipline."

"You find me," says Sir Leicester, whose eyes are much attracted towards him, "far from well, George Rouncewell."

"I am very sorry both to hear it and to see it, Sir Leicester."

"I am sure you are. No. In addition to my older malady, I have had a sudden and bad attack. Something that deadens—" making an endeavour to pass one hand down one side—"and confuses"—touching his lips.

George, with a look of assent and sympathy, makes another bow. The different times when they were both young men (the trooper much the younger of the two), and looked at one another down at Chesney Wold, arise before them both, and soften both.

Sir Leicester, evidently with a great determination to say, in his own manner, something that is on his mind before relapsing into silence, tries to raise himself among his pillows a little more. George observant of the action, takes him in his arms again and places him as he desires to be. "Thank you, George. You are another self to me. You have often carried my spare gun at Chesney Wold, George. You are familiar to me in these strange circumstances, very familiar." He has put Sir Leicester's sounder arm over his shoulder in lifting him up, and Sir Leicester is slow in drawing it away again as he says these words.

"I was about to add," he presently goes on, "I was about to add, respecting this attack, that it was unfortunately simultaneous with a slight misunderstanding between my lady and myself. I do not mean that there was any difference between us (for there has been none), but that there was a misunderstanding of certain circumstances important only to ourselves, which deprives me, for a little while, of my lady's society. She has found it necessary to make a journey—I trust will shortly return. Volumnia, do I make myself intelligible? The words are not quite under my command."

Volumnia understands him perfectly; and in truth he delivers himself with far greater plainness than could have been supposed possible a minute ago. The effort by which he does so is written in the anxious and labouring expression of his face. Nothing but the strength of his purpose enables him to make it.

"Therefore, Volumnia, I desire to say in your presence—and in the presence of my old retainer and friend Mrs. Rouncewell, whose truth and fidelity no one can question—and in the presence of her son George, who comes back like a familiar recollection of my youth in the home of my ancestors at Chesney Wold—in case I should relapse, in case I should not recover, in case I should lose both my speech and the power of writing, though I hope for better things—"

The old housekeeper weeping silently: Volumnia in the greatest agitation, with the freshest bloom on her cheeks; the trooper with his arms folded and his head a little bent, respectfully attentive. "Therefore I desire to say, and to call you all to witness—beginning, Volumnia, with yourself, most solemnly—that I am on unaltered terms with Lady Dedlock. That I assert no cause whatever of complaint against her. That I have ever had the strongest affection for her, and that I retain it undiminished. Say this to herself, and to every one. If you ever say less than this, you will be guilty of deliberate falsehood to me."

Volumnia tremblingly protests that she will observe his unjunctions to the letter.

"My lady is too high in position, too handsome, too accomplished, too superior in most respects to the best of those by whom she is surrounded, not to have her enemies and traducers, I dare say. Let it be known to them, as I make it known to you, that being of sound mind, memory, and understanding, I revoke no disposition I have made in her favour. I abridge nothing I have ever bestowed upon her. I am on unaltered terms with her, and I recall—having the full power to do it if I were so disposed, as you see—no act I have done for her advantage and happiness."

His formal array of words might have at any other time, as it has often had, something ludicrous in it, but at this time it is serious and affecting. His noble earnestness, his fidelity, his gallant shielding of her, his generous conquest of his own wrong and his own pride for her sake, are simply honourable, manly, and true.

Overpowered by his exertions, he lays his head back on his pillows and closes his eyes—for not more than a minute, when he again resumes his watching of the weather, and his attention to the muffled sounds. In the rendering of those little services, and in the manner of their acceptance, the trooper has become installed as necessary to him. Nothing has been said, but it is quite understood.

The day is now beginning to decline. The mist, and the sleet into which the snow has all resolved itself, are darker, and the blaze begins to tell more vividly upon the room walls and furniture. The gloom augments; the bright gas springs up in the streets; and the pertinacious oil lamps which yet hold their ground there, twinkle gaspingly, like fiery fish out of water—as they are. The world, which has been rumbling over the straw and pulling at the bell, "to inquire," begins to go home, begins to dress, to dine, to discuss its dear friend, with all the last new modes.

Now does Sir Leicester become worse; restless, uneasy, and in great pain. Volumnia, lighting a candle, is bidden to put it out again, for it is not yet dark enough. Yet it is very dark too, as dark as it will be all night. By and by she tries again. No! Put it out. It is not dark enough yet.

His old housekeeper is the first to understand that he is striving to uphold the fiction with himself that it is not growing late.

"Dear Sir Leicester, my honoured master," she softly whispers, "I must, for your own good, and my duty, take the freedom of begging and praying that you will not lie here in the lone darkness, watching and waiting, and dragging through the time. Let me draw the curtains and light the candles, and make things more comfortable about you. The church-clocks will strike the hours just the same, Sir Leicester, and the night will pass away just the same. My lady will come back just the same."

"I know it, Mrs. Rouncewell, but I am weak—and she has been so long gone."

"Not so very long, Sir Leicester. Not twenty-four hours yet."

"But that is a long time. Oh, it is a long time!"

He says it with a groan that wrings her heart.

She knows that this is not a period for bringing the rough light upon him; she thinks his tears too sacred to be seen, even by her. Therefore she sits in the darkness for a while, without a word; then gently begins to move about. Finally he tells her, with recovered self-command, "As you say, Mrs. Rouncewell, it is no worse for being confessed. It is getting late, and they are not come. Light the room!"

When it is lighted, and the weather shut out, it is only left to him to listen. But they find that, however dejected and ill he is, he brightens when a quiet pretence is made of looking at the fires in her rooms, and being sure that everything is ready to receive her. Poor pretence as it is, these allusions to her being expected keep up hope within him.

Midnight comes, and with it the same blank. The carriages in the streets are few, and other late sounds in that neighbourhood there are none. Upon this wintry night it is so still that listening to the intense silence is like looking at intense darkness. The corporation of servants are dismissed to bed (not unwilling to go, for they were up all last night), and only Mrs. Rouncewell and George keep watch in Sir Leicester's room. As the night lags tardily on—or rather when it seems to stop altogether, at between two and three o'clock—they find a restless craving on him to know more about the weather now he cannot see it. Hence George, patrolling regularly every half-hour to the rooms so carefully looked after, extends his march to the hall-door, looks about him, and brings back the best report he can make of the worst of nights; the sleet still falling, and even the stone footways lying ankle-deep in icy sludge.

There is no improvement in the weather. From the portico, from the eaves, from the parapet, from every ledge and post and pillar, drips the thawed snow. It has crept, as if for shelter, into the lintels of the great door—under it, into the corners of the windows, into every chink and crevice of retreat, and there wastes and dies. It is falling still—upon the roof, upon the skylight, even through the skylight, and drip, drip, drip, with the regularity of the Ghost's Walk, on the stone floor below.

"All is still in readiness, George Rouncewell?"

"Quite orderly and right, Sir Leicester."

"No word of any kind?" The trooper shakes his head. "No letter that can possibly have been overlooked?"

But he knows there is no such hope as that, and lays his head down without looking for an answer.

## CHAPTER 59

~~~~~~~~~~~~~~~~~~~~~~~~~~~~~~~~~~~~~~~~

*Esther's Narrative*

IT was three o'clock in the morning when the houses outside London did at last begin to exclude the country, and to close us in with streets. We had made our way along roads in a far worse condition than when we had traversed them by daylight, both the fall and the thaw having lasted ever since; but the energy of my companion never slackened. It had only been, as I thought, of less assistance than the horses in getting us on. I had never heard any variation in his cool "Get on, my lads!" The steadiness and confidence with which he had directed our journey back, I could not account for. Never wavering, he never even stopped to make an inquiry until we were within a few miles of London. A very few words, here and there, were then enough for him; and thus we came, at between three and four o'clock in the morning, into Islington.

We stopped in a high-street, where there was a coach-stand. My companion paid our two drivers, who were as completely covered with splashes as if they had been dragged along the roads like the carriage itself, and giving them some brief direction where to take it, lifted me out of it, and into a hackney-coach he had chosen from the rest.

"Now, my dear," said Mr. Bucket, with his head in at the window, "we're a-going to mark this person down. It may take a little time, but you don't mind that. You're pretty sure that I've got a motive. Ain't you?"

I little thought what it was—little thought in how short a time I should understand it better—but I assured him that I had confidence in him.

"So you may have, my dear," he returned. "And I tell you what! If you only repose half as much confidence in me as I repose in you after what I've experienced of you, that'll do. Lord, you're no trouble at all! I never see a young woman in any station of society—and I've seen many elevated ones too—conduct herself like you have conducted yourself since you was called out of your bed. You're a pattern, you know, that's what you are."

I told him I was very glad, as indeed I was, to have been no hindrance to him, and that I hoped I should be none now.

"My dear," he returned, "when a young lady is as mild as she's game, and as game as she's mild, that's all I ask, and more than I expect. She then becomes a Queen, and that's about what you are yourself."

With these encouraging words—they really were encouraging to me under those lonely and anxious circumstances—he got upon the box and we once more drove away. We appeared to seek out the narrowest and worst streets in London. Whenever I saw him directing the driver, I was prepared for our descending into a deeper complication of such streets, and we never failed to do so.

Sometimes we emerged upon a wider thoroughfare, or came to a larger building than the generality, well lighted. Then we stopped at offices like those we had visited when we began our journey, and I saw him in consultation with others. Sometimes he would get down by an archway, or at a street-corner, and mysteriously show the light of his little lantern. This would attract similar lights from various dark quarters, like so many insects, and a fresh consultation would be held. By degrees we appeared to contract our search within narrower and easier limits. Single police-officers on duty could now tell Mr. Bucket what he wanted to know. At last we stopped for a rather long conversation between him and one of these men, which I supposed to be satisfactory from his manner of nodding from time to time. When it was finished he came to me, looking very busy and very attentive.

"Now, Miss Summerson," he said to me, "you won't be alarmed whatever comes off, I know. It's not necessary for me to give you any further caution than to tell you that we have marked this person down, and that you may be of use to me before I know it myself. I don't like to ask such a thing, my dear, but would you walk a little way?" Of course I got out directly, and took his arm. "It ain't so easy to keep your feet," said Mr. Bucket; "but take time."

Although I looked about me confusedly and hurriedly, as we crossed the street, I thought I knew the place. "Are we in Holborn?" I asked him.

"Yes," said Mr. Bucket. "Do you know this turning?"

"It looks like Chancery Lane."

"And was christened so, my dear," said Mr. Bucket.

We turned down it, and as we went, shuffling through the sleet, I heard the clocks strike half-past five. We passed on in silence, when some one coming towards us on the narrow pavement, wrapped in a cloak, stopped and stood aside to give me room. In the same moment I heard an exclamation of wonder, and my own name, from Mr. Woodcourt. I knew his voice very well.

It was so unexpected, and so—I don't know what to call it, whether pleasant or painful—to come upon it after my feverish wandering journey, that I could not keep back the tears from my eyes. It was like hearing his voice in a strange country.

"My dear Miss Summerson, that you should be out at this hour, and in such weather!"

He had heard from my guardian of my having been called away on some uncommon business, and said so to dispense with any explanation. I told him that we had but just left a coach, and were going—but then I was obliged to look at my companion.

"Why, you see, Mr. Woodcourt"—he had caught the name from me —"we are a-going at present into the next street.—Inspector Bucket."

"May I go with you?" said Mr. Woodcourt.

"Why, Lord!" exclaimed Mr. Bucket, "of course you may."

It was all said in a moment, and they took me between them.

"I have just left Richard," said Mr. Woodcourt. "I have been sitting with him since ten o'clock last night."

"Oh dear me, he is ill!"

"No, no, believe me, not ill, but not quite well. He was depressed and faint—you know he gets so worried and so worn sometimes—and Ada sent to me of course. Well! Richard revived so much after a little while, and Ada was so happy, and so convinced of its being my doing, though God knows I had little enough to do with it, that I remained with him until he had been fast asleep some hours. As fast asleep as she is now, I hope!"

His friendly and familiar way of speaking of them, his unaffected devotion to them, the grateful confidence with which I knew he had inspired my darling, and the comfort he was to her—could I separate all this from his promise to me? How thankless I must have been if it had not recalled the words he said to me when he was so moved by the change in my appearance: "I will accept him as a trust, and it shall be a sacred one!"

We now turned into another narrow street. "Mr. Woodcourt," said Mr. Bucket, who had eyed him closely as we came along, "our business takes us to a law-stationer's here, a certain Mr. Snagsby's. What, you know him, do you?" He was so quick that he saw it in an instant.

"Yes, I know a little of him, and have called upon him at this place."

"Indeed, sir?" said Mr. Bucket. "Then you will be so good as to let me leave Miss Summerson with you for a moment while I go and have half a word with him?"

The last police-officer with whom he had conferred was standing silently behind us. I was not aware of it until he struck in on my saying I heard some one crying.

"Don't be alarmed, miss," he returned. "It's Snagsby's servant."

"Why, you see," said Mr. Bucket, "the girl's subject to fits, and has 'em bad upon her tonight. A most contrary circumstance it is, for I want certain information out of that girl, and she must be brought to reason somehow."

All this passed in a whisper, a door or two from the house in which I could faintly hear crying and moaning. Mr. Bucket went up to the door and knocked. The door was opened, after he had knocked twice, and he went in, leaving us in the street.

"Miss Summerson," said Mr. Woodcourt, "if, without obtruding myself on your confidence, I may remain near you, pray let me do so."

"You are truly kind," I answered. "I need wish to keep no secret of my own from you; if I keep any, it is another's."

"I quite understand. Trust me, I will remain near you only so long as I can fully respect it."

"I trust implicitly to you," I said. "I know and deeply feel how sacredly you keep your promises."

After a short time the little round of light shone out again, and Mr. Bucket advanced towards us in it with his earnest face. "Please to come in, Miss Summerson," he said, "and sit down by the fire. Mr. Woodcourt, from information I have received I understand you are a medical man. Would you look to this girl and see if anything can be done to bring her round? She has a letter somewhere that I particularly want. It's not in her box, and I think it must be about her, but she is so twisted and clenched up that she is difficult to handle without hurting."

We all three went into the house together. In the passage behind the door, stood a scared, sorrowful-looking little man in a grey coat, who seemed to have a naturally polite manner, and spoke meekly.

"Downstairs, if you please, Mr. Bucket," said he. "The lady will excuse the front kitchen; we use it as our workaday sitting-room. The back is Guster's bedroom, and in it she's a-carrying on, poor thing, to a frightful extent!"

We went downstairs, followed by Mr. Snagsby, as I soon found the little man to be. In the front kitchen, sitting by the fire, was Mrs. Snagsby, with very red eyes and a very severe expression of face.

"My little woman," said Mr. Snagsby, entering behind us, "to waive hostilities, for one single moment in the course of this prolonged night, here is Inspector Bucket, Mr. Woodcourt, and a lady." She looked very much astonished. "My little woman," said Mr. Snagsby, sitting down in the remotest corner by the door, "it is not unlikely that you may inquire of me why Inspector Bucket, Mr. Woodcourt, and a lady call upon us in Cook's Court, Cursitor Street, at the present hour. I don't know. I have not the least idea. If I was to be informed, I should despair of understanding, and I'd rather not be told."

He appeared so miserable, sitting with his head upon his hand, and I appeared so unwelcome, that I was going to offer an apology when Mr. Bucket took the matter on himself.

"Now, Mr. Snagsby," said he, "the best thing you can do is to go along with Mr. Woodcourt to look after your Guster."

"My Guster, Mr. Bucket!" said Mr. Snagsby. "Go on, sir, go on. I shall be charged with that next."

"And to hold the candle," pursued Mr. Bucket without correcting himself, "or hold her, or make yourself useful in any way you're asked. Which there's not a man alive more ready to do, for you're a man of urbanity and suavity, you know, and you've got the sort of heart that can feel for another.—Mr. Woodcourt, would you be so good as to see to her, and if you can get that letter from her, to let me have it as soon as ever you can?"

As they went out Mr. Bucket made me sit down in a corner by the fire and take off my wet shoes, which he turned up to dry upon the fender, talking all the time.

"Don't you be at all put out, miss, by the want of a hospitable look from Mrs. Snagsby there, because she's under a mistake altogether. She'll find that out, sooner than will be agreeable to a lady of her generally correct manner of forming her thoughts, because I'm a-going to explain it to her." Here, standing on the hearth with his wet hat and shawls in his hand, himself a pile of wet, he turned to Mrs. Snagsby. "Now the first thing that I say to you, as a married woman, possessing charms that ought to give you confidence in yourself—is, that you've done it."

Mrs. Snagsby looked rather alarmed, relented a little, and faltered what did Mr. Bucket mean?

"What does Mr. Bucket mean?" he repeated. "I'll tell you what he means, ma'am. Go and see Othello acted. That's the tragedy for you." Mrs. Snagsby consciously asked why. "Why?" said Mr. Bucket. "Because you'll come to that, if you don't look out. Why, at the very moment while I speak, I know what your mind's not wholly free from respecting this young lady. But shall I tell you who this young lady is? Now come, you're what I call an intellectual woman, and you know me, and you recollect where you saw me last, and what was talked of in that circle. Don't you? Yes! Very well. This young lady is that young lady."

Mrs. Snagsby appeared to understand the reference better than I did at the time.

"And Toughy—him as you call Jo—was mixed up in the same business, and no other; and the law-writer that you know of was mixed up in the same business, and no other; and your husband, with no more knowledge of it than your great-grandfather, was mixed up (by Mr. Tulkinghorn, deceased, his best customer) in the same business, and no other; and the whole biling of people was mixed up in the same business, and no other. And yet a married woman possessing your attractions shuts her eyes (and sparklers, too), and goes and runs her delicate-formed head against a wall. Why, I am ashamed of you!"

Mrs. Snagsby shook her head, and put her handkerchief to her eyes. "Is that all?" said Mr. Bucket, excitedly. "No. See what happens. Another person mixed up in that business and no other, a person in a wretched state, comes here tonight and is seen a-speaking to your maidservant, and between her and your maidservant there passes a paper that I would give a hundred pound for, down. What do you do? You hide and you watch 'em, and you pounce upon that maidservant—knowing what she's subject to, and what a little thing will bring 'em on—in that surprising manner, and with that severity, that, by the Lord, she goes off and keeps off, when a Life may be hanging upon that girl's words!"

He so thoroughly meant what he said now that I involuntarily clasped my hands. Mr. Woodcourt came in, put a paper into his hand, and went away again.

"Now, Mrs. Snagsby, the only amends you can make," said Mr. Bucket, rapidly glancing at it, "is to let me speak a word to this young lady in private here. And if you know of any help that you can give to that gentleman in the next kitchen there, or can think of any one thing that's likelier than another to bring the girl round, do your swiftest and best!" In an instant she was gone and he had shut the door. "Now, my dear, you're steady, and quite sure of yourself?"

"Quite," said I.

"Whose writing is that?"

It was my mother's. A pencil-writing on a crushed and torn piece of paper blotted with wet. Folded roughly like a letter, and directed to me at my guardian's.

"You know the hand," he said, "and if you are firm enough to read it to me, do! But be particular to a word."

It had been written in portions, at different times. I read what follows:

> I came to the cottage with two objects. First, to see the dear one, if I could, once more—but only to see her—not to speak to her, or let her know that I was near. The other object, to elude pursuit, and to be lost. Do not blame the mother for her share. The assistance that she rendered me, she rendered on my strongest assurance that it was for the dear one's good. You remember her dead child. The men's consent I bought, but her help was freely given.

" 'I came.' That was written," said my companion, "when she rested there. It bears out what I made of it. I was right."

The next was written at another time.

> I have wandered a long distance, and for many hours, and I know that I must soon die. These streets! I have no purpose but to die. When I left, I had a worse, but I am saved from adding that guilt to the rest. Cold, wet, and fatigue are sufficient causes for my being found dead; but I shall die of others, though I suffer from these. It was right that all that had sustained me should give way at once, and that I should die of terror and my conscience.

"Courage," said Mr. Bucket. "There's only a few words more."

Those, too, were written at another time. To all appearance, almost in the dark.

> I have done all I could to be lost. I shall be soon forgotten so, and shall disgrace him least. I have nothing about me by which I can be recognized. This paper I part with now. The place where I shall lie down, if I can get so far, has been often in my mind. Farewell. Forgive.

Mr. Bucket, supporting me with his arm, lowered me gently into my chair. "Cheer up! Don't think me hard with you, my dear, but as soon as ever you feel equal to it, get your shoes on and be ready."

I did as he required, but I was left there a long time, praying for my unhappy mother. They were all occupied with the poor girl, and I heard Mr. Woodcourt directing them, and speaking to her often. At length he came in with Mr. Bucket and said that as it was important to address her gently, he thought it best that I should ask her for whatever information we desired to obtain. There was no doubt that she could now reply to questions, if she were soothed, and not alarmed. The questions, Mr. Bucket said, were how she came by the letter, what passed between her and the person who gave her the letter, and where the person went. Holding my mind as steadily as I could to these points, I went into the next room with them. Mr. Woodcourt at my solicitation went in with us.

The poor girl was sitting on the floor where they had laid her down. They stood around her, though at a little distance, that she might have air. She was not pretty, but she had a plaintive and a good face, though it was still a little wild. I kneeled on the ground beside her, and put her poor head upon my shoulder, whereupon she drew her arm round my neck, and burst into tears.

"My poor girl," said I, laying my face against her forehead, "it seems cruel to trouble you now, but more depends on our knowing something about this letter than I could tell you in an hour."

She began piteously declaring that she didn't mean any harm, she didn't mean any harm, Mrs. Snagsby!

"We are all sure of that," said I. "But pray tell me how you got it."

"Yes, dear lady, I will, and tell you true. I had been out on an errand, dear lady—long after it was dark—quite late; and when I came home, I found a common-looking person, all wet and muddy, looking up at our house. When she saw me coming in at the door, she called me back, and said did I live here, and I said yes, and she said she knew only one or two places about here, but had lost her way and couldn't find them. Oh what shall I do! They won't believe me! She didn't say any harm to me, and I didn't say any harm to her, indeed, Mrs. Snagsby!"

It was necessary for her mistress to comfort her—which she did, I must say, with a good deal of contrition—before she could be got beyond this.

"She could not find those places," said I.

"No!" cried the girl, shaking her head. "No! Couldn't find them. And she was so faint, and lame, and miserable, Oh so wretched! that if you had seen her, Mr. Snagsby, you'd have given her half a crown, I know!"

"Well, Guster my girl," said he, "I hope I should."

"And yet she was so well-spoken," said the girl, looking at me with wide-open eyes, "that it made a person's heart bleed. And so she said to me, did I know the way to the burying-ground? And I asked her which burying-ground. And she said the poor burying-ground not very far from here, where there was an archway, and a step, and an iron gate."

As I watched her face, and soothed her to go on, I saw that Mr. Bucket received this with a look which I could not separate from one of alarm.

"Oh dear, dear!" cried the girl, pressing her hair back with her hands, "what shall I do, what shall I do! She meant the burying-ground where the man was buried that took the sleeping-stuff—that you came home and told us of, Mr. Snagsby—that frightened me so, Mrs. Snagsby. Oh, I am frightened again. Hold me!"

"You are so much better now," said I. "Pray, pray tell me more."

"Yes, I will, yes, I will! But don't be angry with me, that's a dear lady, because I have been so ill. So she said, could I tell her how to find it, and I said yes, and I told her; and she looked at me with eyes like almost as if she was blind, and herself all waving back. And so she took out the letter and showed it me, and said if she was to put that in the post-office, it would be rubbed out and not minded and never sent, and would I take it from her, and send it, and the messenger would be paid at the house? And so I said yes, if it was no harm, and she said no—no harm. And so I took it from her, and she said she had nothing to give me, and I said I was poor myself and consequently wanted nothing. And so she said God bless you! and went the way I had shown her.

Then I came in, and Mrs. Snagsby came behind me from somewhere, and laid hold of me, and I was frightened."

Mr. Woodcourt took her kindly from me. Mr. Bucket wrapped me up, and immediately we were in the street. Mr. Woodcourt hesitated, but I said, "Don't leave me now!" and Mr. Bucket added, "You'll be better with us, we may want you; don't lose time!"

I have the most confused impressions of that walk. I recollect that it was neither night nor day; that morning was dawning, but the street-lamps were not yet put out; that the sleet was still falling, and that all the ways were deep with it. I recollect a few chilled people passing in the streets. I recollect that the stained house fronts put on human shapes and looked at me; that great water-gates seemed to be opening and closing in my head, or in the air; and that the unreal things were more substantial than the real.

At last we stood under a dark and miserable covered way, where one lamp was burning over an iron gate, and where the morning faintly struggled in. The gate was closed. Beyond it was a burial-ground—a dreadful spot where I could dimly see heaps of dishonoured graves and stones, hemmed in by filthy houses. On the step at the gate, drenched in the fearful wet of such a place, which oozed and splashed down everywhere, I saw, with a cry of pity and horror, a woman lying—Jenny, the mother of the dead child.

I ran forward, but they stopped me, and Mr. Woodcourt entreated me, with the greatest earnestness, even with tears, before I went up to the figure to listen for an instant to what Mr. Bucket said. I did so, as I thought. I did so, as I am sure.

"Miss Summerson, you'll understand me, if you think a moment. They changed clothes at the cottage."

They changed clothes at the cottage. I could repeat the words in my mind, and I knew what they meant of themselves, but I attached no meaning to them in any other connexion.

"And one returned," said Mr. Bucket, "and one went on. And the one that went on only went on a certain way agreed upon to deceive, and then turned across-country, and went home. Think a moment!"

I could repeat this in my mind too, but I had not the least idea what it meant. I saw before me, lying on the step, the mother of the dead child. She lay there with one arm creeping round the bar of the iron gate, and seeming to embrace it. She lay there, a distressed, unsheltered, senseless creature. She who had brought my mother's letter, who could give me the only clue to where my mother was, she who was to guide us to rescue and save her whom we had sought so far, who had come to this condition by some means connected with my mother that I could not follow, and might be passing beyond our reach

and help at that moment; she lay there, and they stopped me! I saw,
but did not comprehend, the solemn and compassionate look in Mr.
Woodcourt's face. I saw, but did not comprehend, his touching the
other on the breast to keep him back. I saw him stand uncovered in
the bitter air, with a reverence for something. But my understanding
for all this was gone.

I even heard it said between them:

"Shall she go?"

"She had better go. Her hands should be the first to touch her. They
have a higher right than ours."

I passed on to the gate, and stooped down. I lifted the heavy head,
put the long dank hair aside, and turned the face. It was my mother,
cold and dead.

CHAPTER 60

~~~~~~~~~~~~~~~~~~~~~~~~~~~~~~~~~~~~~~~~~~~~~~~~~~~~

*Perspective*

I PROCEED to other passages of my narrative. From the goodness of all about me, I derived such consolation as I can never think of unmoved. I have already said so much of myself, and so much still remains, that I will not dwell upon my sorrow. I had an illness, but it was not a long one.

During the time of my illness we were still in London, where Mrs. Woodcourt had come, on my guardian's invitation, to stay with us. When my guardian thought me well and cheerful enough to talk with him in our old way, I resumed my work, and my chair beside his. He had appointed the time himself, and we were alone.

"Dame Trot," said he, receiving me with a kiss, "welcome to the Growlery again, my dear. I have a scheme to develop, little woman. I propose to remain here, perhaps for six months, perhaps for a longer time. Quite to settle here for a while, in short."

"And in the meanwhile leave Bleak House?" said I.

"Ay, my dear. Bleak House," he returned, "must learn to take care of itself." I thought his tone sounded sorrowful, but looking at him, I saw his kind face lighted up by its pleasantest smile. "Bleak House," he repeated, and his tone did *not* sound sorrowful, I found, "must learn to take care of itself. It is a long way from Ada, my dear, and Ada stands much in need of you."

"It's like you, Guardian," said I, "to have been taking that into consideration, for a happy surprise to both of us."

"I wish to hear as much and as often of Ada as I can, in this condition of estrangement from poor Rick. Not of her alone, but of him too, poor fellow."

"Have you seen Mr. Woodcourt this morning, Guardian?"

"I see Mr. Woodcourt every morning, Dame Durden."

"Does he still say the same of Richard?"

"Just the same. He knows of no direct bodily illness that he has; on the contrary, he believes that he has none. Yet he is not easy about him, who *can* be?"

My dear girl had been to see us lately every day—sometimes twice in a day. But we had foreseen, all along, that this would only last until

I was quite myself. We knew full well that her fervent heart was as full of affection and gratitude towards her cousin John as it had ever been, and we acquitted Richard of laying any injunctions upon her to stay away; but we knew on the other hand that she felt it a part of her duty to him to be sparing of her visits at our house.

"Dear, unfortunate, mistaken Richard," said I. "When will he awake from his delusion!"

"He is not in the way to do so now, my dear," replied my guardian. "The more he suffers, the more averse he will be to me—having made me the principal representative of the great occasion of his suffering."

I could not help adding, "So unreasonably!"

"Ah, Dame Trot, Dame Trot," returned my guardian, "what shall we find reasonable in Jarndyce and Jarndyce! Unreason and injustice at the top, unreason and injustice at the heart and at the bottom, un- reason and injustice from beginning to end—if it ever has an end—how should poor Rick, always hovering near it, pluck reason out of it? He no more gathers grapes from thorns, or figs from thistles, than older men did in old times."

His gentleness and consideration for Richard whenever we spoke of him touched me so that I was always silent on this subject very soon.

"I suppose the Lord Chancellor, and the Vice-Chancellors, and the whole Chancery battery of great guns would be infinitely astonished by such unreason and injustice in one of their suitors," pursued my guardian. "When those learned gentlemen begin to raise moss-roses from the powder they sow in their wigs, I shall begin to be astonished too!" He checked himself in glancing towards the window to look where the wind was, and leaned on the back of my chair instead. "Well, well, little woman! To go on, my dear. This rock we must leave to time, chance, and hopeful circumstance. We must not shipwreck Ada upon it. She cannot afford, and he cannot afford, the remotest chance of another separation from a friend. Therefore I have particularly begged of Wood- court, and I now particularly beg of you, my dear, not to move this subject with Rick. Let it rest. Next week, next month, next year, sooner or later, he will see me with clearer eyes. I can wait."

But I had already discussed it with him, I confessed, and so, I thought, had Mr. Woodcourt.

"So he tells me," returned my guardian. "Very good. He has made his protest, and Dame Durden has made hers, and there is nothing more to be said about it. Now I come to Mrs. Woodcourt. How do you like her, my dear?"

In answer to this question, which was oddly abrupt, I said I liked her very much, and thought she was more agreeable than she used to be.

"I think so too," said my guardian. "Less pedigree? Not so much of Morgan ap—what's his name?"

That was what I meant, I acknowledged, though he was a very harmless person, even when we had had more of him.

"Still, upon the whole he is as well in his native mountains," said my guardian. "I agree with you. Then, little woman, can I do better for a time than retain Mrs. Woodcourt here?"

No. And yet—

My guardian looked at me, waiting for what I had to say. I had nothing to say. At least I had nothing in my mind that I could say. I had an undefined impression that it might have been better if we had had some other inmate, but I could hardly have explained why, even to myself.

"You see," said my guardian, "our neighbourhood is in Woodcourt's way, and he can come here to see her as often as he likes, and she is familiar to us, and fond of you."

Yes. That was undeniable. I had nothing to say against it. I could not have suggested a better arrangement; but I was not quite easy in my mind. Esther, Esther, why not? Esther, think!

"It is a very good plan indeed, dear Guardian, and we could not do better."

"Good," said my guardian. "It shall be done. Carried unanimously."

"You said, dear Guardian, when we spoke of Mr. Woodcourt before Ada left us, that you thought he would give a long trial to another country. Have you been advising him since?"

"Yes, little woman, pretty often."

"Has he decided to do so?"

"I rather think not."

"Some other prospect has opened to him, perhaps?" said I.

"Why—yes—perhaps," returned my guardian, beginning his answer in a very deliberate manner. "About half a year hence or so, there is a medical attendant for the poor to be appointed at a certain place in Yorkshire. It is a thriving place, pleasantly situated, and seems to present an opening for such a man. I mean a man whose hopes and aims may sometimes lie (as most men's sometimes do, I dare say) above the ordinary level, but to whom the ordinary level will be high enough after all if it should prove to be a way of usefulness and good service leading to no other. All generous spirits are ambitious, I suppose; but the ambition that calmly trusts itself to such a road, instead of spasmodically trying to fly over it, is of the kind I care for. It is Woodcourt's kind."

"And will he get this appointment?" I asked.

"Why, little woman," returned my guardian, smiling, "not being an oracle, I cannot confidently say, but I think so. His reputation stands very high; there were people from that part of the country in the ship-wreck; and, strange to say, I believe the best man has the best chance. You must not suppose it to be a fine endowment. It is a very, very, commonplace affair, my dear, an appointment to a great amount of work and a small amount of pay, but better things will gather about it, it may be fairly hoped."

"The poor of that place will have reason to bless the choice, if it falls on Mr. Woodcourt, Guardian."

"You are right, little woman, that I am sure they will."

We said no more about it, nor did he say a word about the future of Bleak House. But it was the first time I had taken my seat at his side in my mourning dress, and that accounted for it, I considered.

I now began to visit my dear girl every day, in the dark corner where she lived. The morning was my usual time, but whenever I found I had an hour or so to spare, I put on my bonnet and bustled off to Chancery Lane. They were both so glad to see me at all hours, and used to brighten up so when they heard me opening the door and com-ing in (being quite at home, I never knocked), that I had no fear of becoming troublesome just yet.

On these occasions I frequently found Richard absent. At other times he would be writing, or reading papers in the Cause, at that table of his, so covered with papers. Sometimes I would come upon him lingering at the door of Mr. Vholes's office. Sometimes I would meet him in the neighbourhood, lounging about, and biting his nails. I often met him wandering in Lincoln's Inn, near the place where I had first seen him, oh how different, how different!

That the money Ada brought him was melting away, I knew very well. It was not a large amount in the beginning; he had married in debt, and I could not fail to understand, by this time, what was meant by Mr. Vholes's shoulder being at the wheel—as I still heard it was. My dear made the best of housekeepers, and tried hard to save, but I knew that they were getting poorer and poorer every day. She shone in the miserable corner like a beautiful star. She adorned and graced it so that it became another place. Paler than she had been at home, and a little quieter than I had thought natural when she was yet so cheerful and hopeful, her face was so unshadowed that I half believed she was blinded by her love for Richard to his ruinous career.

I went one day to dine with them while I was under this impression. As I turned into Symond's Inn, I met little Miss Flite coming out. She had been to make a stately call upon the wards in Jarndyce, as she still called them, and had derived the highest gratification from that ceremony. Ada had already told me that she called every Monday at five o'clock, with her largest reticule of documents on her arm.

"My dear!" she began. "So delighted! How do you do! So glad to see you. And you are going to visit our interesting Jarndyce wards? *To* be sure? Our beauty is at home, my dear, and will be charmed to see you."

"Then Richard is not come in yet?" said I. "I am glad of that, for I was afraid of being a little late."

"No, he is not come in," returned Miss Flite. "He has had a long day in Court. I left him there, with Vholes. You don't like Vholes, I hope? *Don't* like Vholes. Dan-gerous man!"

"I am afraid you see Richard oftener than ever now?" said I.

"My dearest," returned Miss Flite, "daily and hourly. You know what I told you of the attraction on the Chancellor's table? My dear, next to myself he is the most constant suitor in Court. He begins quite to amuse our little party. Ve-ry friendly little party, are we not?" It was miserable to hear this from her poor mad lips, though it was no surprise. "In short, my valued friend," pursued Miss Flite, advancing her lips to my ear, "I must tell you a secret. I have made him my executor. Nominated, constituted, and appointed him. In my will. Ye-es."

"Indeed?" said I.

"Ye-es," repeated Miss Flite, in her most genteel accents, "my excutor, administrator, and assign. (Our Chancellor phrases, my love.) I have reflected that if I should wear out, he will be able to watch that judgment. Being so very regular in his attendance." It made me sigh to think of him. "I did at one time mean," said Miss Flite, echoing the sigh, "to nominate, constitute, and appoint poor Gridley. Also very regular, my charming girl. I assure you, most exemplary! But he wore out, poor man, so I have appointed his successor. Don't mention it. This is in confidence."

She carefully opened her reticule a little way, and showed me a folded piece of paper inside, as the appointment of which she spoke.

"Another secret, my dear. I have added to my collection of birds."

"Really, Miss Flite?" said I, knowing how it pleased her to have her confidence received with an appearance of interest.

She nodded several times, and her face became overcast and gloomy. "Two more. I call them the Wards in Jarndyce. They are caged up with all the others. With Hope, Joy, Youth, Peace, Rest, Life, Dust, Ashes, Waste, Want, Ruin, Despair, Madness, Death, Cunning, Folly, Words, Wigs, Rags, Sheepskin, Plunder, Precedent, Jargon, Gammon, and Spinach!"

The poor soul kissed me, with the most troubled look I had ever seen in her, and went her way. Her manner of running over the names of her birds, as if she were afraid of hearing them even from her own lips, quite chilled me.

This was not a cheering preparation for my visit, and I could have dispensed with the company of Mr. Vholes when Richard (who arrived within a minute or two after me) brought him to share our dinner. Although it was a very plain one, Ada and Richard were for some minutes both out of the room together, helping to get ready what we were to eat and drink. Mr. Vholes took that opportunity of holding a little conversation in a low voice with me. He came to the window where I was sitting, and began upon Symond's Inn.

"A dull place, Miss Summerson, for a life that is not an official one," said Mr. Vholes. "I hope Mr. Jarndyce is as well as his friends could wish him?"

I thanked Mr. Vholes, and said he was quite well.

"I have not the pleasure to be admitted among the number of his friends myself," said Mr. Vholes, "and I am aware that the gentlemen of our profession are sometimes regarded in such quarters with an unfavourable eye. How do you find Mr. C. looking, Miss Summerson?"

"He looks very ill. Dreadfully anxious."

"Just so," said Mr. Vholes. He stood behind me, feeling the pimples on his face as if they were ornaments, and speaking inwardly and evenly as though there were not a human passion or emotion in his nature.

"Mr. Woodcourt is in attendance upon Mr. C., I believe?" he resumed.

"Mr. Woodcourt is his disinterested friend," I answered.

"But I mean in professional attendance, medical attendance."

"That can do little for an unhappy mind," said I.

"Just so," said Mr. Vholes. So slow, so eager, so bloodless and gaunt, I felt as if Richard were wasting away beneath the eyes of this adviser, and there were something of the Vampire in him. "Miss Summerson," said Mr. Vholes, very slowly, rubbing his gloved hands, "this was an ill-advised marriage of Mr. C.'s."

I begged he would excuse me for discussing it. They had been engaged when they were both very young I told him (a little indignantly), and when the prospect before them was much fairer and brighter. When Richard had not yielded himself to the unhappy influence which now darkened his life.

"Just so," assented Mr. Vholes again. "Still, with a view to everything being openly carried on, I will, with your permission, Miss Summerson, observe to you that I consider this a very ill-advised marriage indeed. I owe the opinion not only to Mr. C.'s connexions, against whom I should naturally wish to protect myself, but also to my own reputation."

"It would become a very different marriage, a much happier and better marriage, another marriage altogether, Mr. Vholes," said I, "if Richard were persuaded to turn his back on the fatal pursuit in which you are engaged with him."

Mr. Vholes, with a noiseless cough into one of his black gloves, inclined his head as if he did not wholly dispute even that.

"Miss Summerson," he said, "it may be so, and I freely admit that the young lady who has taken Mr. C.'s name upon herself in so ill-advised a manner is a highly genteel young lady. As to beauty, I am not a judge of that myself, and I never did give much attention to it from a boy, but I dare say the young lady is equally eligible in that point of view. In reference to Mr. C.'s pursuit of his interests—"

"Oh! His interests, Mr. Vholes!"

"Pardon me," returned Mr. Vholes, going on in exactly the same inward and dispassionate manner. "Mr. C. takes certain interests under certain wills disputed in the suit. It is a term we use. In reference to Mr. C.'s pursuit of his interests, I mentioned to you, Miss Summerson, the first time I had the pleasure of seeing you, in my desire that everything should be openly carried on, that Mr. C. had laid down the principle of watching his own interests, and that when a client of mine laid down a principle which was not of an immoral (that is to say, unlawful) nature, it devolved upon me to carry it out. I *have* carried it out, I *do* carry it out. But I will not smooth things over to any connexion of Mr. C.'s on any account. As open as I was to Mr. Jarndyce, I am to you. I openly say, unpalatable as it may be, that I consider Mr. C.'s affairs in a very bad way, that I consider Mr. C. himself in a very bad way, and that I regard this as an exceedingly ill-advised marriage.—Am I here, sir? Yes, I thank you, I am here, Mr. C., and enjoying the pleasure of some agreeable conversation with Miss Summerson."

He broke off thus in answer to Richard, who addressed him as he came into the room. By this time, I too well understood Mr. Vholes's scrupulous way of saving himself and his respectability not to feel that our worst fears did but keep pace with his client's progress.

We sat down to dinner, and I had an opportunity of observing Richard, anxiously. I found Richard thin and languid, slovenly in his dress, abstracted in his manner, forcing his spirits now and then, and at other intervals relapsing into a dull thoughtfulness. About his large bright eyes that used to be so merry there was a wanness and a restlessness that changed them altogether. I cannot use the expression that he looked old. There is a ruin of youth which is not like age, and into such a ruin Richard's youth and youthful beauty had all fallen away.

He ate little and seemed indifferent what it was, showed himself to be much more impatient than he used to be, and was quick, even with Ada. I thought at first that his old light-hearted manner was all gone, but it shone out of him sometimes, as I had occasionally known little momentary glimpses of my own old face to look out upon me from the glass. His laugh had not quite left him either, but it was like the echo of a joyful sound, and that is always sorrowful. Yet he was as glad as ever, in his old affectionate way, to have me there, and we talked of the old times pleasantly. These did not appear to be interesting to Mr. Vholes, though he occasionally made a gasp which I believe was his smile. He rose shortly after dinner and said that with the permission of the ladies he would retire to his office.

"Always devoted to business, Vholes!" cried Richard.

"Yes, Mr. C.," he returned, "the interests of clients are never to be neglected, sir. They are paramount in the thoughts of a professional man like myself, who wishes to preserve a good name among his fellow-practitioners and society at large. My denying myself the pleasure of the present agreeable conversation may not be wholly irrespective of your own interests, Mr. C."

Richard expressed himself quite sure of that, and lighted Mr. Vholes out. On his return he told us, more than once, that Vholes was a good fellow, a safe fellow, a man who did what he pretended to do, a very good fellow indeed! He was so defiant about it that it struck me he had begun to doubt Mr. Vholes.

Then he threw himself on the sofa, tired out, and Ada and I put things to rights, for they had no other servant than the woman who attended to the chambers. My dear girl had a cottage piano there, and quietly sat down to sing some of Richard's favourites, the lamp being first removed into the next room, as he complained of its hurting his eyes.

I sat between them, at my dear girl's side, and felt very melancholy listening to her sweet voice. I think Richard did too; I think he darkened the room for that reason. She had been singing some time when Mr. Woodcourt came in. Then he sat down by Richard; and half playfully, half earnestly, quite naturally and easily, found out how he felt, and where he had been all day. Presently he proposed to accompany him in a short walk on one of the bridges, as it was a moonlight airy night, and Richard readily consenting, they went out together. They left my dear girl still sitting at the piano, and me still sitting beside her. When they were gone out, I drew my arm round her waist. She put her left hand in mine (I was sitting on that side), but kept her right upon the keys—going over and over them, without striking any note.

"Esther, my dearest," she said, breaking silence, "Richard is never so well, and I am never so easy about him, as when he is with Allan Woodcourt. We have to thank you for that."

I pointed out to my darling how this could scarcely be, because Mr. Woodcourt had come to her cousin John's house, and had known us all there, and because he had always liked Richard and Richard had always liked him, and—and so forth.

"All true," said Ada, "but that he is such a devoted friend to us, we owe to you."

I thought it best to let my dear girl have her way, and to say no more about it. So I said as much.

"Esther, my dearest, I want to be a good wife, a very, very good wife indeed. You shall teach me."

I teach! I said no more, for I noticed the hand that was fluttering over the keys, and I knew that it was not I who ought to speak, that it was she who had something to say to me.

"When I married Richard, I was not insensible to what was before him. I had been perfectly happy for a long time with you, and I had never known any trouble or anxiety, so loved and cared for; but I understood the danger he was in, dear Esther."

"I know, I know, my darling."

"When we were married, I had some little hope that I might be able to convince him of his mistake, that he might come to regard it in a new way as my husband, and not pursue it all the more desperately for my sake—as he does. But if I had not had that hope, I would have married him just the same, Esther. Just the same!" In the momentary firmness of the hand that was never still—a firmness inspired by the utterance of these last words, and dying away with them—I saw the confirmation of her earnest tones. "You are not to think, my dearest Esther, that I fail to see what you see, and fear what you fear. No one can understand him better than I do. The greatest wisdom that ever lived in the world could scarcely know Richard better than my love does."

She spoke so modestly and softly, and her trembling hand expressed such agitation as it moved to and fro upon the silent notes! My dear, dear girl!

"I see him at his worst, every day. I watch him in his sleep. I know every change of his face. But when I married Richard, I was quite determined, Esther, if Heaven would help me, never to show him that I grieved for what he did, and so to make him more unhappy. I want him, when he comes home, to find no trouble in my face. I want him, when he looks at me, to see what he loved in me. I married him to do this, and this supports me."

I felt her trembling more. I waited for what was yet to come, and I now thought I began to know what it was.

"And something else supports me, Esther." She stopped a minute. Stopped speaking only; her hand was still in motion. "I look forward a little while, and I don't know what great aid may come to me. When Richard turns his eyes upon me then, there may be something lying on my breast more eloquent than I have been, with greater power than mine to show him his true course, and win him back." Her hand stopped now. She clasped me in her arms, and I clasped her in mine.

"If that little creature should fail too, Esther, I still look forward. I look forward a long while, through years and years, and think that then, when I am growing old, or when I am dead perhaps, a beautiful woman, his daughter, happily married, may be proud of him and a blessing to him. Or that a generous brave man, as handsome as he used to be, as hopeful, and far more happy, may walk in the sunshine with him, honouring his grey head, and saying to himself, 'I thank God this is my father, ruined by a fatal inheritance, and restored through me!' These hopes uphold me, my dear Esther, and I know they will. Though sometimes even they depart from me, before a dread that arises when I look at Richard."

I tried to cheer my darling, and asked her what it was. Sobbing and weeping, she replied:

"That he may not live to see his child."

CHAPTER 61

*A Discovery*

THE months were gliding away, and my dear girl, sustained by the hopes she had confided in me, was the same beautiful star in the miserable corner. Richard, more worn and haggard, haunted the Court day after day, listlessly sat there the whole day long, when he knew there was no remote chance of the suit being mentioned; and became one of the stock sights of the place. I wonder whether any of the gentlemen remembered him as he was when he first went there.

So completely was he absorbed in his fixed idea, that he used to avow in his cheerful moments that he should never have breathed the fresh air now "but for Woodcourt." It was only Mr. Woodcourt who could occasionally divert his attention, for a few hours at a time, and rouse him, even when he sank into a lethargy of mind and body that alarmed us greatly, and the returns of which became more frequent as the months went on. My dear girl was right in saying that he only pursued his errors the more desperately for her sake. I have no doubt that his desire to retrieve what he had lost was rendered the more intense by his grief for his young wife, and became like the madness of a gamester.

I was there at all hours. When I was there at night, I generally went home with Charley in a coach; sometimes my guardian would meet me in the neighbourhood, and we would walk home together. One evening he had arranged to meet me at eight o'clock. I could not leave, as I usually did, quite punctually at the time, for I was working for my dear girl, and had a few stitches more to do to finish what I was about; but it was within a few minutes of the hour when I gave my darling my last kiss for the night, and hurried downstairs. Mr. Woodcourt went with me, as it was dusk.

When we came to the usual place of meeting—it was close by, and Mr. Woodcourt had often accompanied me before—my guardian was not there. We waited half an hour, walking up and down, but there were no signs of him. We agreed that he was either prevented from coming, or that he had come and gone away, and Mr. Woodcourt proposed to walk home with me. It was the first walk we had ever taken together, except that very short one to the usual place of meeting. We spoke of Richard and Ada the whole way. I did not thank him, in words, for what he had done—my appreciation of it had risen above all words then—but I hoped he might not be without some understanding of what I felt so strongly.

Arriving at home and going upstairs, we found that my guardian was out, and that Mrs. Woodcourt was out too. We were in the very same room into which I had brought my blushing girl when her youthful lover, now her so altered husband, was the choice of her young heart. We were standing by the opened window, looking down into the street, when Mr. Woodcourt spoke to me. I learned in a moment that he loved me. I learned in a moment that my scarred face was all unchanged to him. I learned in a moment that what I had thought was pity and compassion was devoted, generous, faithful love. Oh, too late to know it now, too late, too late. That was the first ungrateful thought I had. Too late.

"When I returned," he told me, "no richer than when I went away, and found you newly risen from a sick-bed, yet so inspired by sweet consideration for others, and so free from a selfish thought—"

"Oh Mr. Woodcourt, forbear, forbear!" I entreated him. "I do not deserve your high praise. I had many selfish thoughts at that time, many!"

"Heaven knows, beloved of my life," said he, "that my praise is not a lover's praise, but the truth. You do not know what all around you see in Esther Summerson, how many hearts she touches and awakens, what sacred admiration and what love she wins."

"Oh Mr. Woodcourt," cried I, "it is a great thing to win love, it is a great thing to win love! I am proud of it, and honoured by it, and the hearing of it causes me to shed these tears of mingled joy and sorrow—joy that I have won it, sorrow that I have not deserved it better—but I am not free to think of yours."

I said it with a stronger heart, for when he praised me thus I aspired to be more worthy of it. It was not too late for that. Although I closed this unforeseen page in my life tonight, I could be worthier of it all through my life. And it was a comfort to me, and an impulse to me, and I felt a dignity rise up within me that was derived from him, when I thought so.

He broke the silence.

"I should poorly show the trust that I have in the dear one who will evermore be as dear to me as now"—and the deep earnestness with which he said it at once strengthened me and made me weep—"if after her assurance that she is not free to think of my love, I urged it. Dear Esther, let me only tell you that the fond idea of you which I took abroad was exalted to the heavens when I came home. I have always hoped, in the first hour when I seemed to stand in any ray of good fortune, to tell you this. I have always feared that I should tell it you in vain. My hopes and fears are both fulfilled tonight. I distress you. I have said enough."

Something seemed to pass into my place that was like the Angel he thought me, and I felt so sorrowful for the loss he had sustained! I wished to help him in his trouble, as I had wished to do when he showed that first commiseration for me.

"Dear Mr. Woodcourt," said I, "before we part tonight, something is left for me to say. I never could say it as I wish—I never shall—but—" I had to think again of being more deserving of his love, and his affliction, before I could go on "—I am deeply sensible of your generosity, and I shall treasure its remembrance to my dying hour. I know full well how changed I am, I know you are not unacquainted with my history, and I know what a noble love that is which is so faithful. What you have said to me could have affected me so much from no other lips, for there are none that could give it such a value to me. It shall not be lost. It shall make me better."

He covered his eyes with his hand, and turned away his head. How could I ever be worthy of those tears?

"If, in the unchanged intercourse we shall have together—in tending

Richard and Ada, and I hope in many happier scenes of life—you ever find anything in me which you can honestly think is better than it used to be, believe that it will have sprung up from tonight, and that I shall owe it to you. And never believe, dear dear Mr. Woodcourt, never believe that I forget this night, or that while my heart beats it can be insensible to the pride and joy of having been beloved by you."

He took my hand, and kissed it. He was like himself again, and I felt still more encouraged.

"I am induced by what you said just now," said I, "to hope that you have succeeded in your endeavour?"

"I have," he answered. "With such help from Mr. Jarndyce as you who know him so well can imagine him to have rendered me, I have succeeded."

"Heaven bless him for it," said I, giving him my hand, "and Heaven bless you in all you do!"

"I shall do it better for the wish," he answered, "it will make me enter on these new duties as on another sacred trust from you."

"Ah! Richard!" I exclaimed involuntarily. "What will he do when you are gone!"

"I am not required to go yet; I would not desert him, dear Miss Summerson, even if I were."

One other thing I felt it needful to touch upon before he left me. I knew that I should not be worthier of the love I could not take if I reserved it.

"Mr. Woodcourt," said I, "you will be glad to know from my lips before I say good-night that in the future, which is clear and bright before me, I am most happy, most fortunate, have nothing to regret or desire." It was indeed a glad hearing to him, he replied. "From my childhood I have been," said I, "the object of the untiring goodness of the best of human beings, to whom I am so bound by every tie and attachment, gratitude, and love that nothing I could do in the compass of a life could express the feelings of a single day."

"I share those feelings," he returned. "You speak of Mr. Jarndyce."

"You know his virtues well," said I, "but few can know the greatness of his character as I know it. All its highest and best qualities have been revealed to me in nothing more brightly than in the shaping out of that future in which I am so happy. And if your highest homage and respect had not been his already—which I know they are—they would have been his, I think, on this assurance, and in the feeling it would have awakened in you towards him for my sake."

He fervently replied that indeed indeed they would have been. I gave him my hand again.

"Good-night," I said. "Good-bye."

"The first until we meet tomorrow, the second as a farewell to this theme between us for ever?"

"Yes."

"Good-night. Good-bye!"

He left me, and I stood at the dark window watching the street. His love, in all its constancy and generosity, had come so suddenly upon me that he had not left me a minute when my fortitude gave way again and the street was blotted out by my rushing tears.

But they were not tears of regret and sorrow. No. He had called me the beloved of his life, and had said I would be evermore as dear to him as I was then, and I felt as if my heart would not hold the triumph of having heard those words. My first wild thought had died away. It was not too late to hear them, for it was not too late to be animated by them to be good, true, grateful, and contented. How easy my path, how much easier than his!

## CHAPTER 62

*Another Discovery*

I HAD not the courage to see any one that night. I had not even the courage to see myself, for I was afraid that my tears might a little reproach me. I went up to my room in the dark, and prayed in the dark, and lay down in the dark to sleep. I had no need of any light to read my guardian's letter by, for I knew it by heart. I took it from the place where I kept it and repeated its contents, and went to sleep with it on my pillow.

I was up very early in the morning, and called Charley to come for a walk. We bought flowers for the breakfast-table, and came back and arranged them, and were as busy as possible. We were so early that I had good time still for Charley's lesson before breakfast. Charley (who was not in the least improved in the old defective article of grammar) came through it with great applause, and we were altogether very notable. When my guardian appeared, he said, "Why, little woman, you look fresher than your flowers!" And Mrs. Woodcourt repeated and translated a passage from the Mewlinnwillinwodd, expressive of my being like a mountain with the sun upon it. This was all so pleasant, that I hope it made me still more like the mountain than I had been before. After breakfast, I waited my opportunity, and peeped about a little, until I saw my guardian in his own room—the room of last night —by himself. Then I made an excuse to go in with my housekeeping keys, shutting the door after me.

"Well, Dame Durden?" said my guardian. The post had brought him several letters, and he was writing. "You want money?"

"No indeed, I have plenty in hand."

"There never was such a Dame Durden," said my guardian, "for making money last."

He had laid down his pen and leaned back in his chair looking at me. I have often spoken of his bright face, but I had never seen it look so bright and good. There was a high happiness upon it, which made me think, "He has been doing some great kindness this morning."

I went up to him and took my usual chair, which was always put at his side.

"Dear Guardian," said I, "I want to speak to you. Have I been remiss in anything?"

"Remiss in anything, my dear!"

"Have I not been what I have meant to be, since—I brought the answer to your letter, Guardian?"

"You have been everything I could desire, my love."

"I am very glad indeed to hear that," I returned. "You know you said to me was this the mistress of Bleak House? And I said yes."

"Yes," said my guardian, nodding his head. He had put his arm about me, as if there were something to protect me from, and looked in my face, smiling.

"Since then," said I, "we have never spoken on the subject except once."

"And then I said Bleak House was thinning fast, and so it was, my dear." "And *I* said," I timidly reminded him, "but its mistress remained." He still held me in the same protecting manner, and with the same bright goodness in his face. "Dear Guardian," said I, "I know how you have felt all that has happened, and how considerate you have been. As so much time has passed, and as you spoke only this morning of my being so well again, perhaps you expect me to renew the subject. Perhaps I ought to do so. I will be the mistress of Bleak House when you please."

"See," he returned gaily, "what a sympathy there must be between us! I have had nothing else, poor Rick excepted—it's a large exception— in my mind. When you came in, I was full of it. When shall we give Bleak House its mistress, little woman?"

"When you please."

"Next month?"

"Next month, dear Guardian."

"The day on which I take the happiest and best step of my life—the day on which I shall be a man more exulting and more enviable than any other man in the world, the day on which I give Bleak House its little mistress—shall be next month, then," said my guardian.

I put my arms round his neck and kissed him, just as I had done on the day when I brought my answer.

A servant came to the door to announce Mr. Bucket, which was quite unnecessary, for Mr. Bucket was already looking in over the servant's shoulder. "Mr. Jarndyce and Miss Summerson," said he, rather out of breath, "with all apologies for intruding, *will* you allow me to order up a person that's on the stairs, and that objects to being left there in case of becoming the subject of observations in his absence? Thank you. Be so good as chair that there Member in this direction, will you?" said Mr. Bucket, beckoning over the banisters.

This singular request produced an old man in a black skull-cap, un-

able to walk, who was carried up by a couple of bearers, and deposited in the room near the door. Mr. Bucket immediately got rid of the bearers, mysteriously shut the door, and bolted it.

"Now you see, Mr. Jarndyce," he then began, putting down his hat and opening his subject with a flourish of his well-remembered finger, "you know me, and Miss Summerson knows me. This gentleman likewise knows me, and his name is Smallweed. The discounting line is his line principally, and he's what you may call a dealer in bills. That's about what *you* are, you know, ain't you?" said Mr. Bucket, stopping a little to address the gentleman in question, who was exceedingly suspicious of him. He seemed about to dispute this designation of himself, when he was seized with a violent fit of coughing. "Now, Moral, you know!" said Mr. Bucket, improving the accident. "Don't you contradict when there ain't no occasion, and you won't be took in that way. Now, Mr. Jarndyce, I've been negotiating with this gentleman on behalf of Sir Leicester Dedlock, Baronet, and one way and another I've been in and out and about his premises a deal. His premises are the premises formerly occupied by Krook, Marine Store Dealer—a relation of this gentleman's that you saw in his lifetime, if I don't mistake?"

My guardian replied "Yes."

"Well! You are to understand," said Mr. Bucket, "that this gentleman he come into Krook's property, and a good deal of magpie property there was. Vast lots of waste paper among the rest. Lord bless you, of no use to nobody!"

The cunning of Mr. Bucket's eye, and the masterly manner in which he contrived, without a look or a word against which his watchful auditor could protest, to let us know that he stated the case according to previous agreement, and could say much more of Mr. Smallweed if he thought it advisable, deprived us of any merit in quite understanding him.

"Being a prudent man, and accustomed to take care of your own affairs, you begin to rummage among the papers as you have come into, don't you?"

"Of course I do," cried Mr. Smallweed.

"Of course you do," said Mr. Bucket, conversationally, "and much to blame you would be if you didn't. And so you chance to find, you know," Mr. Bucket went on, "a paper, with the signature of Jarndyce to it. Don't you?" Mr. Smallweed glanced with a troubled eye at us, and grudgingly nodded assent. "And coming to look at that paper, at your full leisure and convenience, what do you find it to be but a Will, you see. That's the drollery of it," said Mr. Bucket, "what do you find it to be but a Will?"

"I don't know that it's good as a Will, or as anything else," snarled Mr. Smallweed.

Mr. Bucket eyed the old man for a moment—he had slipped and shrunk down in his chair into a mere bundle—as if he were much disposed to pounce upon him; nevertheless, he continued to bend over him with the same agreeable air.

"Notwithstanding which," said Mr. Bucket, "you get a little doubtful and uncomfortable in your mind about it, having a very tender mind of your own. And as you've heard a good deal mentioned regarding a celebrated Chancery Will case, of the same name, and as you know what a card Krook was for buying all manner of old pieces of furniter, and books, and papers, and what not, and never liking to part with 'em, and always a-going to teach himself to read, you begin to think—and you never was more correct in your born days—'Ecod, if I don't look about me, I may get into trouble regarding this Will.'"

"Now, mind how you put it, Bucket," cried the old man anxiously, with his hand at his ear. "Speak up, none of your brimstone tricks. Pick me up, I want to hear better. Oh, Lord, I am shaken to bits!"

Mr. Bucket had certainly picked him up at a dart. However, as soon as he could be heard through Mr. Smallweed's coughing, and his vicious ejaculations of "Oh my bones! Oh dear! I've no breath in my body! I'm worse than the chattering brimstone pig at home!" Mr. Bucket proceeded in the same convivial manner as before.

"So, as I happen to be in the habit of coming about your premises, you take me into your confidence, don't you?" I think it would be impossible to make an admission with more ill-will and a worse grace than Mr. Smallweed displayed when he admitted this. "And I go into the business with you—very pleasant we are over it—and I confirm you in your well-founded fears that you will-get-yourself-in-to-a-most precious line if you don't come out with that there Will," said Mr. Bucket, emphatically, "and accordingly you arrange with me that it shall be delivered up to this present Mr. Jarndyce, on no conditions. If it should prove to be valuable, you trusting yourself to him for your reward—that's about where it is, ain't it?"

"That's what was agreed," Mr. Smallweed assented, with the same bad grace.

"In consequence of which," said Mr. Bucket, dismissing his agreeable manner all at once, and becoming strictly businesslike, "you've got that Will upon your person at the present time; and the only thing that remains for you to do is just to Out with it!"

Having given us one glance out of the corner of his eye, and having given his nose one triumphant rub with his forefinger, Mr. Bucket stood with his eyes fastened on his confidential friend and his hand stretched forth ready to take the paper and present it to my guardian. It was not produced without much reluctance, and many declarations on the part of Mr. Smallweed that he was a poor industrious man, and that he left it to Mr. Jarndyce's honour not to let him lose by his honesty. Little by little, he very slowly took from a breast-pocket a stained discoloured paper, which was much singed upon the outside and a little burnt at the edges, as if it had long ago been thrown upon a fire. Mr.

Bucket lost no time in transferring this paper from Mr. Smallweed to Mr. Jarndyce. As he gave it to my guardian, he whispered behind his fingers:

"Hadn't settled how to make their market of it. Quarrelled and hinted about it. I laid out twenty pound upon it. First, the avaricious grandchildren split upon him, on account of their objections to his living so unreasonably long, and then they split on one another. Lord! There ain't one of the family that wouldn't sell the other for a pound or two, except the old lady—and she's only out of it because she's too weak in her mind to drive a bargain."

"Mr. Bucket," said my guardian aloud, "whatever the worth of this paper may be to any one, my obligations are great to you, and if it be of any worth, I hold myself bound to see Mr. Smallweed remunerated accordingly."

"Not according to your merits, you know," said Mr. Bucket, in friendly explanation to Mr. Smallweed. "Don't you be afraid of that. According to its value."

"That is what I mean," said my guardian. "You may observe, Mr. Bucket, that I abstain from examining this paper myself. The plain truth is, I have forsworn and abjured the whole business these many years, and my soul is sick of it. But Miss Summerson and I will immediately place the paper in the hands of my solicitor in the Cause, and its existence shall be made known without delay to all other parties interested."

"Mr. Jarndyce can't say fairer than that, you understand," observed Mr. Bucket to his fellow-visitor. "And it being now made clear to you that nobody's a-going to be wronged—which must be a great relief to *your* mind—we may proceed with the ceremony of chairing you home again."

He unbolted the door, called in the bearers, wished us good-morning, and with a look full of meaning, and a crook of his finger at parting, went his way. We went our way too, which was to Lincoln's Inn, as quickly as possible. Mr. Kenge was disengaged, and we found him at his table in his dusty room with the inexpressive-looking books and the piles of papers. Chairs having been placed for us by Mr. Guppy, Mr. Kenge expressed the surprise and gratification he felt at the unusual sight of Mr. Jarndyce in his office. He turned over his double eye-glass as he spoke, and was more Conversation Kenge than ever.

"I hope," said Mr. Kenge, "that the genial influence of Miss Summerson"—he bowed to me—"may have induced Mr. Jarndyce"—he bowed to him—"to forgo some little of his animosity towards a Cause and towards a Court which are—shall I say, which take their place in the stately vista of the pillars of our profession?"

"I am inclined to think," returned my guardian, "that Miss Summerson has seen too much of the effects of the Court and the Cause to exert any influence in their favour. Nevertheless, they are a part of the occasion of my being here. Mr. Kenge, before I lay this paper on your desk and have done with it, let me tell you how it has come into my hands." He did so shortly and distinctly.

"It could not, sir," said Mr. Kenge, "have been stated more plainly and to the purpose if it had been a case at law."

"Did you ever know English law, or equity either, plain and to the purpose?" said my guardian.

"Oh fie!" said Mr. Kenge.

At first he had not seemed to attach much importance to the paper, but when he saw it he appeared more interested, and when he had opened and read a little of it through his eye-glass, he became amazed. "Mr. Jarndyce," he said, "you have perused this?"

"Not I!" returned my guardian.

"But my dear sir," said Mr. Kenge, "it is a Will of later date than any in the suit. It appears to be all in the Testator's handwriting. It is duly executed and attested. And even if intended to be cancelled, as might possibly be supposed to be denoted by these marks of fire, it is *not* cancelled. Here it is, a perfect instrument!"

"Well!" said my guardian. "What is that to me?"

"Mr. Guppy!" cried Mr. Kenge, raising his voice. "Mr. Vholes of Symond's Inn. My compliments. Jarndyce and Jarndyce. Glad to speak with him."

Mr. Guppy disappeared.

"You ask me what is this to you, Mr. Jarndyce. If you had perused this document, you would have seen that it reduces your interest considerably, though still leaving it a very handsome one, still leaving it a very handsome one," said Mr. Kenge, waving his hand persuasively and blandly. "You would further have seen that the interests of Mr. Richard Carstone, and of Miss Ada Clare, now Mrs. Richard Carstone, are very materially advanced by it."

"Kenge," said my guardian, "if all the flourishing wealth that the suit brought into this vile Court of Chancery would fall to my two young cousins, I should be well contented. But do you ask *me* to believe that any good is to come of Jarndyce and Jarndyce?"

"Oh really, Mr. Jarndyce! Prejudice, prejudice. My dear sir, this is a very great country, a very great country. Its system of equity is a very great system, a very great system. Really, really!"

My guardian said no more, and Mr. Vholes arrived. He was modestly impressed by Mr. Kenge's professional eminence.

"How do you do, Mr. Vholes? Will you be so good as to take a chair here by me, and look over this paper?"

Mr. Vholes did as he was asked, and seemed to read it every word. He was not excited by it, but he was not excited by anything. When he had well examined it, he retired with Mr. Kenge into a window, and spoke to him at some length. When they had finished, they came back to Mr. Kenge's table, and spoke aloud.

"Well! But this is a very remarkable document, Mr. Vholes?" said Mr. Kenge.

Mr. Vholes said, "Very much so."

"And a very important document, Mr. Vholes?" said Mr. Kenge.

Again Mr. Vholes said, "Very much so."

"And as you say, Mr. Vholes, when the Cause is in the paper next term, this document will be an unexpected and interesting feature in it," said Mr. Kenge, looking loftily at my guardian.

"And when," asked my guardian, rising after a pause, "when is next term?"

"Next term, Mr. Jarndyce, will be next month," said Mr. Kenge. "Of course we shall at once proceed to do what is necessary with this document, and to collect the necessary evidence concerning it, and of course you will receive our usual notification of the Cause being in the paper."

"To which I shall pay, of course, my usual attention."

"Still bent, my dear sir," said Mr. Kenge, showing us through the outer office to the door, "still bent, even with your enlarged mind, on echoing a popular prejudice? We are a great country, Mr. Jarndyce, we are a very great country. This is a great system, Mr. Jarndyce, and would you wish a great country to have a little system? Now, really, really!"

# CHAPTER 63

*Esther's Narrative*

SOON after I had had that conversation with my guardian, he put a sealed paper in my hand one morning, and said, "This is for next month, my dear." I found in it two hundred pounds.

I now began very quietly to make such preparations as I thought were necessary. Regulating my purchases by my guardian's taste, which I knew very well of course, I arranged my wardrobe to please him, and hoped I should be highly successful. I did it all so quietly because I was not quite free from my old apprehension that Ada would be rather sorry, and because my guardian was so quiet himself. I had no doubt that under all the circumstances we should be married in the most private and simple manner.

The only exception I made was Mrs. Woodcourt. I told her that I was going to be married to my guardian, and that we had been engaged some time. She highly approved. She could never do enough for me, and was remarkably softened now, in comparison with what she had been when we first knew her. There was no trouble she would not have taken to have been of use to me; but I need hardly say that I only allowed her to take as little as gratified her kindness without tasking it.

Of course this was not a time to neglect my guardian, and of course it was not a time for neglecting my darling. So I had plenty of occupation—which I was glad of. Meanwhile, I must say I could not agree with my guardian on the subject of the Will, and I had some sanguine hopes of Jarndyce and Jarndyce. Which of us was right will soon appear, but I certainly did encourage expectations. In Richard, the discovery gave occasion for a burst of business and agitation that buoyed him up for a little time; but he had lost the elasticity even of hope now, and seemed to me to retain only its feverish anxieties. From something my guardian said one day when we were talking about this, I understood that my marriage would not take place until after the term-time we had been told to look forward to, and I thought the more, for that, how rejoiced I should be if I could be married when Richard and Ada were a little more prosperous.

The term was very near indeed when my guardian was called out of town, and went down into Yorkshire on Mr. Woodcourt's business. He had told me beforehand that his presence there would be necessary. I had just come in one night from my dear girl's, when a letter from my guardian was brought to me. It asked me to join him in the country, and mentioned by what stage-coach my place was taken, and at what time in the morning I should have to leave town. It added in a postscript that I would not be many hours from Ada.

I set off as appointed early next morning. I travelled all day, wondering all day what I could be wanted for at such a distance; now I thought it might be for this purpose, and now I thought it might be for that purpose; but I was never, never, never near the truth. It was night when I came to my journey's end and found my guardian waiting for me. This was a great relief, for towards evening I had begun to fear that he might be ill. However, there he was, as well as it was possible to be, and when I saw his genial face again at its brightest and best, I said to myself "He has been doing some other great kindness."

Supper was ready at the hotel, and when we were alone at table he said: "Full of curiosity, no doubt, little woman, to know why I have brought you here?"

"Well, Guardian," said I, "without thinking myself a Fatima, or you a Blue Beard, I am a little curious about it."

"Then to ensure your night's rest, my love," he returned, gaily, "I won't wait until tomorrow to tell you. I have very much wished to express to Woodcourt, somehow, my sense of his humanity to poor unfortunate Jo, his inestimable services to my young cousins, and his value to us all. When it was decided that he should settle here, it came into my head that I might ask his acceptance of some unpretending and suitable little place to lay his own head in. I therefore caused such a place to be looked out for, and such a place was found on very easy terms, and I have been touching it up for him and making it habitable. However, when I walked over it the day before yesterday, and it was reported ready, I found that I was not housekeeper enough to know whether things were all as they ought to be. So I sent off for the best little housekeeper that could possibly be got, to come and give me her advice and opinion. And here she is," said my guardian, "laughing and crying both together!"

Because he was so dear, so good, so admirable. I tried to tell him what I thought of him, but I could not articulate a word.

"Tut, tut!" said my guardian. "You make too much of it, little woman. Why, how you sob, Dame Durden, how you sob!"

"It is with exquisite pleasure, Guardian—with a heart full of thanks."

"Well, well," said he, "I am delighted that you approve. I thought you would. I meant it as a pleasant surprise for the little mistress of Bleak House."

I kissed him, and dried my eyes. "I know now!" said I. "I have seen this in your face a long while."

"No, have you really, my dear?" said he. "What a Dame Durden it is to read a face!"

He was so quaintly cheerful that I could not long be otherwise, and was almost ashamed of having been otherwise at all. When I went to bed, I cried. I am bound to confess that I cried; but I hope it was with pleasure, though I am not quite sure it was with pleasure. I repeated every word of the letter twice over.

A most beautiful summer morning succeeded, and after breakfast we went out arm-in-arm to see the house of which I was to give my mighty housekeeping opinion. We entered a flower-garden by a gate in a side wall of which he had the key, and the first thing I saw was that the beds and flowers were all laid out according to the manner of my beds and flowers at home.

"You see, my dear," observed my guardian, standing still, with a delighted face, to watch my looks, "knowing there could be no better plan, I borrowed yours."

We went on by a pretty little orchard, where the cherries were nestling among the green leaves and the shadows of the apple-trees were sporting on the grass, to the house itself—a cottage, quite a rustic cottage of doll's rooms, but such a lovely place, so tranquil and so beautiful, with such a rich and smiling country spread around it, with water

sparkling away into the distance, here all overhung with summergrowth, there turning a humming mill. And still, as we went through the pretty rooms, out at the little rustic verandah doors, and underneath the tiny wooden colonnades garlanded with woodbine, jasmine, and honeysuckle, I saw, in the papering on the walls, in the colours of the furniture, in the arrangement of all the pretty objects, *my* little tastes and fancies, *my* little methods and inventions which they used to laugh at while they praised them, my odd ways everywhere.

I could not say enough in admiration of what was all so beautiful, but one secret doubt arose in my mind when I saw this. I thought, Oh would he be the happier for it! Would it not have been better for his peace that I should not have been so brought before him? Because, although I was not what he thought me, still he loved me very dearly, and it might remind him mournfully of what he believed he had lost.

"And now, little woman," said my guardian, whom I had never seen so proud and joyful as in showing me these things, and watching my appreciation of them, "now, last of all, for the name of this house."

"What is it called, dear Guardian?"

"My child," said he, "come and see."

He took me to the porch, which he had hitherto avoided, and said, pausing before we went out:

"My dear child, don't you guess the name?"

"No!" said I.

We went out of the porch, and he showed me written over it: BLEAK HOUSE.

He led me to a seat among the leaves close by, and sitting down beside me, and taking my hand in his, spoke to me thus:

"My darling girl, in what there has been between us, I have, I hope, been really solicitous for your happiness. When I wrote you the letter to which you brought the answer, I had my own too much in view, but I had yours too. Whether, under different circumstances, I might ever have renewed the old dream I sometimes dreamed when you were very young, of making you my wife one day, I need not ask myself. I did renew it, and I wrote my letter, and you brought your answer."

I was cold, and I trembled violently, but not a word he uttered was lost. As I sat looking fixedly at him, and the sun's rays descended, softly shining through the leaves, upon his bare head, I felt as if the brightness on him must be like the brightness of the Angels.

"Hear me, my love, but do not speak. It is for me to speak now. When it was that I began to doubt whether what I had done would really make you happy is no matter. Woodcourt came home, and I soon had no doubt at all." I clasped him round the neck, and hung my head upon his breast, and wept. "Lie lightly, confidently, here, my child," said he, pressing me gently to him. "I am your guardian and your father now. Rest confidently here. Understand me, my dear girl. I had no doubt of your being contented and happy with me, being so dutiful and so devoted; but I saw with whom you would be happier. That I penetrated his secret when Dame Durden was blind to it is no wonder, for I knew the good that could never change in her, better far than she did. Well! I have long been in Allan Woodcourt's confidence, although he was not, until yesterday, a few hours before you came here, in mine. But I would not have my Esther's bright example lost, I would not have a jot of my dear girl's virtues unobserved and unhonoured, I would not have her admitted on sufferance into the line of Morgan ap Kerrig—no, not for the weight in gold of all the mountains in Wales!"

He stopped to kiss me on the forehead, and I sobbed and wept afresh. "Hush, little woman! Don't cry, this is to be a day of joy. I have looked forward to it," he said exultingly, "for months and months! A few words more, Dame Trot, and I have said my say. Determined not to throw away one atom of my Esther's worth, I took Mrs. Woodcourt into a separate confidence. 'Now, madam,' said I, 'I clearly perceive—and indeed I know, to boot—that your son loves my ward. I am further very sure that my ward loves your son, but will sacrifice her love to a sense of duty and affection, and will sacrifice it so completely, so entirely, so religiously, that you should never suspect it, though you watched her night and day.' Then I told her all our story—ours—yours and mine. 'Now, madam,' said I, 'come you, knowing this, and live with us. Come you and see my child from hour to hour, set what you see, against her pedigree, which is this, and this'—for I scorned to mince it—'and tell me what is the true legitimacy, when you shall have quite made up your mind on that subject.' Why, honour to her old Welsh blood, my dear!" cried my guardian, with enthusiasm, "I believe the heart it animates beats no less warmly, no less admiringly, no less lovingly, towards Dame Durden than my own!"

He tenderly raised my head, and as I clung to him, kissed me in his old fatherly way again and again.

"One more last word. When Allan Woodcourt spoke to you, my dear, he spoke with my knowledge and consent—but I gave him no encouragement, not I, for these surprises were my great reward, and I was too miserly to part with a scrap of it. He was to come and tell me all that passed, and he did. I have no more to say. My dearest, Allan Woodcourt stood beside your father when he lay dead—stood beside your mother. This is Bleak House. This day I give this house its little mistress, and before God, it is the brightest day in all my life!"

He rose, and raised me with him. We were no longer alone. My husband—I have called him by that name full seven happy years now—stood at my side.

"Allan," said my guardian, "take from me a willing gift, the best wife that ever man had. What more can I say for you than that I know you deserve her! Take with her the little home she brings you. You know what she will make it, Allan, you know what she has made its namesake. Let me share its felicity sometimes, and what do I sacrifice? Nothing, nothing." He kissed me once again, and now the tears were in his eyes as he said more softly:

"Esther, my dearest, after so many years there is a kind of parting in this too. I know that my mistake has caused you some distress. Forgive your old guardian, in restoring him to his old place in your affections, and blot it out of your memory. Allan, take my dear."

He moved away from under the green roof of leaves, and stopping in the sunlight outside, and turning cheerfully towards us, said: "I shall be found about here somewhere. It's a west wind, little woman, due west! Let no one thank me any more, for I am going to revert to my bachelor habits, and if anybody disregards this warning, I'll run away, and never come back!"

What happiness was ours that day, what joy, what rest, what hope, what gratitude, what bliss! We were to be married before the month was out, but when we were to come and take possession of our own house was to depend on Richard and Ada.

We all three went home together next day. As soon as we arrived in town, Allan went straight to see Richard, and to carry our joyful news to him and my darling. Late as it was, I meant to go to her for a few minutes before lying down to sleep, but I went home with my guardian first, to make his tea for him, and to occupy the old chair by his side; for I did not like to think of its being empty so soon.

# CHAPTER 64

## Beginning the World

THE term had commenced, and my guardian found an intimation from Mr. Kenge that the Cause would come on in two days. As I had sufficient hopes of the Will to be in a flutter about it, Allan and I agreed to go down to the Court that morning. Richard was extremely agitated, and was so weak and low, though his illness was still of the mind, that my dear girl indeed had sore occasion to be supported. But she looked forward—a very little way now—to the help that was to come to her, and never drooped.

It was at Westminster that the Cause was to come on. It had come on there, I dare say, a hundred times before, but I could not divest myself of an idea that it *might* lead to some result now. We left home directly after breakfast, to be at Westminster Hall in good time, and walked down there through the lively streets—so happily and strangely it seemed!—together.

When we came to Westminster Hall, we found that the day's business was begun. Worse than that, we found such an unusual crowd in the Court of Chancery that it was full to the door, and we could neither see nor hear what was passing within. It appeared to be something droll, for occasionally there was a laugh, and a cry of "Silence!" It appeared to be something that made the professional gentlemen very merry, for there were several young counsellors in wigs and whiskers on the outside of the crowd, and when one of them told the others about it, they put their hands in their pockets and quite doubled themselves up with laughter.

We asked a gentleman by us if he knew what cause was on. He told us Jarndyce and Jarndyce. We asked him if he knew what was doing in it. He said, really, no he did not, nobody ever did, but as well as he could make out, it was over. Over for the day? we asked him. No, he said, over for good. Over for good!

When we heard this unaccountable answer, we looked at one another quite lost in amazement. Could it be possible that the Will had set things right at last, and that Richard and Ada were going to be rich? It seemed too good to be true. Alas, it was!

Our suspense was short, for a break-up soon took place in the crowd, and the people came streaming out looking flushed and hot. Still they were all exceedingly amused, and were more like people coming out from a Farce or a Juggler than from a Court of Justice. We stood aside, watching for any countenance we knew, and presently great bundles of paper began to be carried out—bundles in bags, bundles too large to be got into any bags, immense masses of papers of all shapes and no shapes, which the bearers staggered under, and threw down for the time being, anyhow, on the Hall pavement while they went back to bring out more. Even these clerks were laughing. We glanced at the papers, and seeing Jarndyce and Jarndyce everywhere, asked an official-looking person who was standing in the midst of them whether the Cause was over. Yes, he said, it was all up with it at last! and burst out laughing too.

At this juncture we perceived Mr. Kenge coming out of Court with an affable dignity upon him, listening to Mr. Vholes, who was deferential. Mr. Vholes was the first to see us. "Here is Miss Summerson, sir," he said. "And Mr. Woodcourt."

"Oh indeed! Yes. Truly!" said Mr. Kenge, raising his hat to me with polished politeness. "How do you do? Glad to see you. Mr. Jarndyce is not here?" No. He never came there, I reminded him. "Really," returned Mr. Kenge, "it is as well that he is *not* here today, for his—shall I say, in my good friend's absence, his indomitable singularity of opinion —might have been strengthened, perhaps—not reasonably, but might have been strengthened."

"Pray what has been done today?" asked Allan.

"What has been done?" repeated Mr. Kenge. "Quite so. Yes. Why, not much has been done, not much. We have been checked—brought up suddenly, I would say—upon the—shall I term it threshold?"

"Is this Will considered a genuine document, sir?" said Allan. "Will you tell us that?"

"Most certainly, if I could," said Mr. Kenge, "but we have not gone into that, we have not gone into that. You are to reflect, Mr. Woodcourt," observed Mr. Kenge, "that this has been a great Cause, that this has been a protracted Cause, that this has been a complex Cause. Jarndyce and Jarndyce has been termed, not inaptly, a Monument of Chancery practice."

"And Patience has sat upon it a long time," said Allan.

"Very well indeed, sir," returned Mr. Kenge, with a certain condescending laugh he had. "Very well! You are further to reflect, Mr. Woodcourt, that on the numerous difficulties, contingencies, masterly fictions, and forms of procedure in this great Cause, there has been expended study, ability, eloquence, knowledge, intellect, Mr. Woodcourt, high intellect. For many years, the—a—I would say the flower of the Bar, and the—a—I would presume to add, the matured autumnal fruits of the Woolsack—have been lavished upon Jarndyce and Jarndyce. If the public have the benefit, and if the country have the adornment, of this great Grasp, it must be paid for in money, or money's worth, sir."

"Mr. Kenge," said Allan, appearing enlightened all in a moment, "excuse me, our time presses. Do I understand that the whole estate is found to have been absorbed in costs?"

"Hem! I believe so," returned Mr. Kenge.

"And that thus the suit lapses and melts away?"

"Probably," returned Mr. Kenge.

"My dearest life," whispered Allan, "this will break Richard's heart!"

There was such a shock of apprehension in his face, and he knew Richard so perfectly, and I too had seen so much of his gradual decay, that what my dear girl had said to me in the fulness of her foreboding love sounded like a knell in my ears.

"In case you should be wanting Mr. C., sir," said Mr. Vholes, coming after us, "you'll find him in Court. I left him there resting himself a little. Good-day, sir, good-day, Miss Summerson," and his black buttoned-up unwholesome figure glided away to the low door at the end of the Hall.

"My dear love," said Allan, "leave to me, for a little while, the charge you gave me. Go home with this intelligence, and come to Ada's by and by!"

I would not let him take me to a coach, but entreated him to go to Richard without a moment's delay. Hurrying home, I found my guardian, and told him gradually with what news I had returned. "Little woman," said he, quite unmoved for himself, "to have done with the suit on any terms is a greater blessing than I had looked for. But my poor young cousins!"

We talked about them all the morning, and discussed what it was possible to do. In the afternoon my guardian walked with me to Symond's Inn, and left me at the door. I went upstairs. When my darling heard my footsteps, she came out into the small passage and threw her arms round my neck; but she composed herself directly, and said that Richard had asked for me several times. Allan had found him sitting in the corner of the Court, she told me, like a stone figure. On being roused, he had broken away, and made as if he would have spoken in a fierce voice to the Judge. He was stopped by his mouth being full of blood, and Allan had brought him home.

He was lying on a sofa with his eyes closed when I went in. There were restoratives on the table; the room was made as airy as possible, and was darkened, and was very orderly and quiet. Allan stood behind him, watching him gravely. His face appeared to me to be quite destitute of colour, and now that I saw him without his seeing me I fully saw, for the first time, how worn away he was. But he looked handsomer than I had seen him look for many a day. I sat down by his side in silence. Opening his eyes by and by, he said, in a weak voice, but with his old smile, "Dame Durden, kiss me, my dear!"

It was a great comfort and surprise to me to find him in his low state cheerful and looking forward. He was happier, he said, in our intended marriage than he could find words to tell me. My husband had been a guardian angel to him and Ada, and he blessed us both, and wished us all the joy that life could yield us. I almost felt as if my own heart would have broken when I saw him take my husband's hand and hold it to his breast. He said several times that he must be present at our marriage if he could stand upon his feet. Ada would contrive to take him, somehow, he said. "Yes, surely, dearest Richard!" But as my darling answered him thus hopefully, so serene and beautiful, with the help that was to come to her so near—I knew—I knew!

It was not good for him to talk too much, and when he was silent, we were silent too. Ada leaned upon his pillow, holding his head upon her arm. He dozed often, and whenever he awoke without seeing him, said, first of all, "Where is Woodcourt?"

Evening had come on when I lifted up my eyes and saw my guardian standing in the little hall. "Who is that, Dame Durden?" Richard asked me. The door was behind him, but he had observed in my face that some one was there.

I looked to Allan for advice, and as he nodded "Yes," bent over Richard and told him. My guardian saw what passed, came softly by me in a moment, and laid his hand on Richard's. "O sir," said Richard, "you are a good man, you are a good man!" and burst into tears for the first time.

My guardian, the picture of a good man, sat down in my place, keeping his hand on Richard's.

"My dear Rick," said he, "the clouds have cleared away, and it is bright now. We can see now. We were all bewildered, Rick, more or less. What matters! And how are you, my dear boy?"

"I am very weak, sir, but I hope I shall be stronger. I have to begin the world."

"Ay, truly, well said!" cried my guardian.

"I will not begin it in the old way now," said Richard with a sad smile. "I have learned a lesson now, sir. It was a hard one, but you shall be assured indeed that I have learned it."

"Well, well," said my guardian, comforting him, "well, well, well, dear boy!"

"I was thinking, sir," resumed Richard, "that there is nothing on earth I should so much like to see as their house—Dame Durden's and Woodcourt's house. If I could be removed there when I begin to recover my strength, I feel as if I should get well there sooner than anywhere."

"Why, so have I been thinking too, Rick," said my guardian, "and our little woman likewise; she and I have been talking of it this very day. I dare say her husband won't object. What do you think?"

Richard smiled, and lifted up his arm to touch him as he stood behind the head of the couch.

"I say nothing of Ada," said Richard, "but I think of her, and have thought of her very much. Look at her! See her here, sir, bending over this pillow when she has so much need to rest upon it herself, my dear love, my poor girl!" He clasped her in his arms, and none of us spoke. He gradually released her, and she looked upon us, and looked up to Heaven, and moved her lips. "When I get down to Bleak House," said Richard, "I shall have much to tell you, sir, and you will have much to show me. You will go, won't you?"

"Undoubtedly, dear Rick."

"Thank you—like you, like you," said Richard. "But it's all like you. They have been telling me how you planned it, and how you remembered all Esther's familiar tastes and ways. It will be like coming to the old Bleak House again."

"And you will come there too, I hope, Rick. I am a solitary man now, you know, and it will be a charity to come to me. A charity to come to me, my love!" he repeated to Ada as he gently passed his hand over her golden hair, and put a lock of it to his lips.

"It was a troubled dream?" said Richard clasping both my guardian's hands eagerly.

"Nothing more, Rick, nothing more."

"And you, being a good man, can pass it as such, and forgive and pity the dreamer, and be lenient and encouraging when he wakes?"

"Indeed I can. What am I but another dreamer, Rick?"

"I will begin the world!" said Richard, with a light in his eyes. My husband drew a little nearer towards Ada, and I saw him solemnly lift up his hand to warn my guardian. "When shall I go from this place, to that pleasant country where the old times are, where I shall have strength to tell what Ada has been to me, where I shall be able to recall my many faults and blindnesses, where I shall prepare myself to be a guide to my unborn child?" said Richard. "When shall I go?"

"Dear Rick, when you are strong enough," returned my guardian. "Ada my darling!"

He sought to raise himself a little. Allan raised him so that she could hold him on her bosom, which was what he wanted.

"I have done you many wrongs, my own. I have fallen like a poor stray shadow on your way, I have married you to poverty and trouble, I have scattered your means to the winds. You will forgive me all this, my Ada, before I begin the world?"

A smile irradiated his face as she bent to kiss him. He slowly laid his face down upon her bosom, drew his arms closer round her neck, and with one parting sob began the world. Not this world, Oh not this! The world that sets this right.

When all was still, at a late hour poor crazed Miss Flite came weeping to me and told me she had given her birds their liberty.

## CHAPTER 65

*Down in Lincolnshire*

THERE is a hush upon Chesney Wold in these altered days, as there is upon a portion of the family history. The story goes that Sir Leicester paid some who could have spoken out, to hold their peace; but it is a lame story, feebly whispering and creeping about, and any brighter spark of life it shows soon dies away. It is known for certain that the handsome Lady Dedlock lies in the mausoleum in the park, where the trees arch darkly overhead and the owl is heard at night making the woods ring; but whence she was brought home to be laid among the echoes of that solitary place, or how she died, is all mystery. Some of her old friends, principally to be found among the peachy-cheeked charmers, did once occasionally say, as they toyed in a ghastly manner with large fans when the World assembled together, that they wondered the ashes of the Dedlocks entombed in the mausoleum never rose against the profanation of her company. But the dead-and-gone Dedlocks take it very calmly, and have never been known to object.

Up from among the fern in the hollow, and winding by the bridle-road among the trees, comes sometimes to this lonely spot the sound of horses' hoofs. Then may be seen Sir Leicester—invalided, bent, and almost blind, but of worthy presence yet—riding with a stalwart man beside him, constant to his bridle-rein. When they come to a certain spot before the mausoleum door, Sir Leicester's accustomed horse stops of his own accord, and Sir Leicester, pulling off his hat, is still for a few moments before they ride away.

In one of the lodges of the park, that lodge within sight of the house where, once upon a time, when the waters were out down in Lincolnshire, my Lady used to see the keeper's child, the stalwart man, the trooper formerly, is housed. Some relics of his old calling hang upon the walls, and these it is the chosen recreation of a little lame man about the stable-yard to keep gleaming bright. A busy little man he always is, in the polishing at harness-house doors of anything in the way of a stable-yard that will take a polish. He answers to the name of Phil.

A goodly sight it is to see the grand old housekeeper (harder of hearing now) going to church on the arm of her son, and to observe the relations of both towards Sir Leicester, and his towards them. They have visitors in the high summer weather, when a grey cloak and umbrella, unknown to Chesney Wold at other periods, are seen among the leaves; when two young ladies are occasionally found gambolling in nooks of the park; and when the smoke of two pipes wreathes away into the fragrant evening air from the trooper's door. Then as the evening closes

in, a gruff inflexible voice is heard to say, while two men pace together up and down, "But I never own to it before the old girl. Discipline must be maintained."

The greater part of the house is shut up, and it is a show-house no longer; yet Sir Leicester holds his shrunken state in the long drawing-room for all that, and reposes in his old place before my Lady's picture. Closed in by night with broad screens, and illumined only in that part, the light of the drawing-room seems gradually contracting and dwindling until it shall be no more. A little more, in truth, and it will be all extinguished for Sir Leicester; and the damp door in the mausoleum which shuts so tight, and looks so obdurate, will have opened and received him.

Volumnia, growing with the flight of time pinker as to the red in her face, and yellower as to the white, reads to Sir Leicester in the long evenings, and is driven to various artifices to conceal her yawns, of which the chief and most efficacious is the insertion of the pearl necklace between her rosy lips. The cousins generally are rather shy of Chesney Wold in its dulness, but take to it a little in the shooting-season, when guns are heard in the plantations, and a few scattered beaters and keepers wait at the old places of appointment, for low-spirited twos and threes of cousins.

Thus Chesney Wold. With so much of itself abandoned to darkness and vacancy, with so little change under the summer shining or the wintry lowering, so sombre and motionless always—no flag flying now by day, no rows of lights sparkling by night, with no family to come and go, no visitors to be the souls of pale cold shapes of rooms, no stir of life about it—passion and pride, even to the stranger's eye, have died away from the place in Lincolnshire, and yielded it to dull repose.

## CHAPTER 66

*The Close of Esther's Narrative*

FULL seven happy years I have been the mistress of Bleak House. The few words that I have to add to what I have written are soon penned, then I and the unknown friend to whom I write will part for ever. Not without much dear remembrance on my side. Not without some, I hope, on his or hers.

They gave my darling into my arms, and through many weeks I never left her. The little child who was to have done so much was born before the turf was planted on its father's grave. It was a boy, and I, my husband, and my guardian gave him his father's name. The help that my dear counted on did come to her; though it came, in the Eternal wisdom, for another purpose. Though to bless and restore his mother, not his father, was the errand of this baby, its power was mighty to do it. When I saw the strength of the weak little hand, and how its touch could heal my darling's heart, and raise up hope within her, I felt a new sense of the goodness and the tenderness of God. They throve, and by degrees I saw my dear girl pass into my country garden and walk there with her infant in her arms. I was married then. I was the happiest of the happy.

It was at this time that my guardian joined us, and asked Ada when she would come home.

"Both houses are your home, my dear," said he, "but the older Bleak House claims priority. When you and my boy are strong enough to do it, come and take possession of your home."

Ada called him "her dearest cousin John." But he said, No, it must be Guardian now. He was her guardian henceforth, and the boy's, and he had an old association with the name. So she called him Guardian, and has called him Guardian ever since. The children know him by no other name.—I say the children, I have two little daughters.

It is difficult to believe that Charley (round-eyed still, and not at all grammatical) is married to a miller in our neighbourhood; yet so it is; and even now, looking up from my desk as I write early in the morning at my summer window, I see the very mill beginning to go round. I hope the miller will not spoil Charley; but he is very fond of her, and Charley is rather vain of such a match—for he is well-to-do, and was in great request. So far as my small maid is concerned, I might suppose Time to have stood for seven years as still as the mill did half an hour ago, since little Emma, Charley's sister, is exactly what Charley used to be. Tom, Charley's brother, is apprenticed to the miller, and is a good bashful fellow, always falling in love with somebody, and being ashamed of it.

Caddy Jellyby passed her very last holidays with us, and was a dearer creature than ever, perpetually dancing in and out of the house with the children as if she had never given a dancing-lesson in her life. Caddy keeps her own little carriage now, instead of hiring one, and lives full two miles further westward than Newman Street. She works very hard, her husband (an excellent one) being lame, and able to do very little. Still, she is more than contented, and does all she has to do with all her heart. Mr. Jellyby spends his evenings at her new house with his head against the wall, as he used to do in her old one. I have heard that Mrs. Jellyby was understood to suffer great mortification, from her daughter's ignoble marriage and pursuits, but I hope she got over it in time. She has been disappointed in Borrioboola-Gha, which turned out a failure in consequence of the King of Borrioboola wanting to sell everybody—who survived the climate—for rum; but she has taken up with the rights of women to sit in Parliament, and Caddy tells me it is a Mission involving more correspondence than the old one. I had almost forgotten Caddy's poor little girl. She is not such a mite now, but she is deaf and dumb. I believe there never was a better mother than

Caddy, who learns, in her scanty intervals of leisure, innumerable deaf-and-dumb arts to soften the affliction of her child.

As if I were never to have done with Caddy, I am reminded here of Peepy and old Mr. Turveydrop. Peepy is in the Custom House, and doing extremely well. Old Mr. Turveydrop, very apoplectic, still exhibits his Deportment about town, still enjoys himself in the old manner, is still believed in, in the old way. He is constant in his patronage of Peepy, and is understood to have bequeathed him a favourite French clock in his dressing-room—which is not his property.

With the first money we saved at home, we added to our pretty house

by throwing out a little Growlery expressly for my guardian, which he inaugurated with great splendour the next time he came down to see us. I try to write all this lightly, because my heart is full in drawing to an end, but when I write of him, my tears will have their way. I never look at him but I hear our poor dear Richard calling him a good man. To Ada and her pretty boy, he is the fondest father; to me, he is what he has ever been, and what name can I give to that? He is my husband's best and dearest friend, he is our children's darling, he is the object of our deepest love and veneration. Yet while I feel towards him as if he were a superior being, I am so familiar with him, and so easy with him, that I almost wonder at myself. I have never lost my old names, nor has he lost his; nor do I ever, when he is with us, sit in any other place than in my old chair at his side. Dame Trot, Dame Durden, Little Woman!— all just the same as ever; and I answer, Yes, dear Guardian! just the same.

I have never known the wind to be in the east for a single moment since the day when he took me to the porch to read the name. I remarked to him once that the wind seemed never in the east now, and he said, No, truly, it had finally departed from that quarter on that very day.

I think my darling girl is more beautiful than ever. The sorrow that has been in her face—for it is not there now—seems to have purified even its innocent expression, and to have given it a diviner quality. Sometimes, when I raise my eyes and see her in the black dress that she still wears teaching my Richard, I feel—it is difficult to express—as if it were so good to know that she remembers her dear Esther in her prayers. I call him my Richard! But he says that he has two mamas, and I am one.

We are not rich in the bank, but we have always prospered, and we have quite enough. I never walk out with my husband but I hear the people bless him. I never go into a house of any degree but I hear his praises, or see them in grateful eyes. I never lie down at night but I know that in the course of that day he has alleviated pain, and soothed some fellow-creature in the time of need. I know that from the beds of those who were past recovery thanks have often, often gone up in the last hour for his patient ministration. Is not this to be rich?

The people even praise Me as the doctor's wife. The people even like Me as I go about, and make so much of me that I am quite abashed. I owe it all to him, my love, my pride! They like me for his sake, as I do everything I do in life for his sake.

A night or two ago, after bustling about preparing for my darling and my guardian and little Richard, who are coming tomorrow, I was sitting out in the porch of all places, that dearly memorable porch, when Allan came home. So he said, "My precious little woman, what are you doing here?" And I said, "The moon is shining so brightly, Allan, and the night is so delicious, that I have been sitting here, thinking."

"What have you been thinking about, my dear?" said Allan then.

"How curious you are!" said I. "I am almost ashamed to tell you, but I will. I have been thinking about my old looks—such as they were."

"And what have you been thinking about *them*, my busy bee?" said Allan.

"I have been thinking that I thought it was impossible that you *could* have loved me any better, even if I had retained them."

"—Such as they were?" said Allan, laughing.

"Such as they were, of course."

"My dear Dame Durden," said Allan, drawing my arm through his, "do you ever look in the glass?"

"You know I do, you see me do it."

"And don't you know that you are prettier than you ever were?"

I did not know that, I am not certain that I know it now. But I know that my dearest little pets are very pretty, and that my darling is very beautiful, and that my husband is very handsome, and that my guardian has the brightest and most benevolent face that ever was seen, and that they can very well do without much beauty in me—even supposing—